THE
LYLE
OFFICIAL
ANTIQUES
REVIEW 1987

THE
LYLE
OFFICIAL
ANTIQUES
REVIEW 1987

COMPILED & EDITED BY
ANTHONY CURTIS

The Publishers wish to express their sincere thanks to the following for their
involvement and assistance in the production of this volume:

Karen Douglass (Art Editor)
Janice Moncrieff (Assistant Editor)
Annette Curtis
Nichola Fairburn
Margaret Anderson
Tanya Fairbairn
Frank Burrell
Robert Nisbet
Lynn Martin
David Boland
Eileen Burrell
Sally Dalgliesh

ISBN 0-399-51285-3

Library of Congress Catalog Card Number 74-640592

Printed in the United States of America

1 2 3 4 5 6 7 8 9 10

INTRODUCTION

This year over 100,000 Antique Dealers and Collectors will make full and profitable use of their Lyle Official Antiques Review. They know that only in this one volume will they find the widest possible variety of goods — illustrated, described and given a current market value to assist them to BUY RIGHT AND SELL RIGHT throughout the year of issue.

They know, too, that by building a collection of these immensely valuable volumes year by year, they will equip themselves with an unparalleled reference library of facts, figures and illustrations which, properly used, cannot fail to help them keep one step ahead of the market.

In its sixteen years of publication, Lyle has gone from strength to strength and has become without doubt the pre-eminent book of reference for the antique trade throughout the world. Each of its fact filled pages are packed with precisely the kind of profitable information the professional Dealer needs — including descriptions, illustrations and values of thousands and thousands of individual items carefully selected to give a representative picture of the current market in antiques and collectibles — and remember all values are prices actually paid, based on accurate sales records in the twelve months prior to publication from the best established and most highly respected auction houses and retail outlets in Europe and America.

This is THE book for the Professional Antiques Dealer. 'The Lyle Book' — we've even heard it called 'The Dealer's Bible'.

Compiled and published afresh each year, the Lyle Official Antiques Review is the most comprehensive up-to-date antiques price guide available. THIS COULD BE YOUR WISEST INVESTMENT OF THE YEAR!

ANTHONY CURTIS

All prices quoted in this book are obtained from a variety of auctions in various countries during the twelve months prior to publication and are converted to dollars at the rate of exchange prevalent at the time of sale.

CONTENTS

Advertising Signs. 16

Aeronautical. 20

    Aircraft. 22

    Paintings 23

Arms & Armor 24

    Daggers. 28

    Helmets. 32

    Pistols. 38

    Powder Flasks. 44

    Rifles 46

    Swords 52

    Tsubas. 58

    Weapons 62

Automatons. 63

Barometers. 64

Bronze 68

Buckets 83

Caddies & Boxes 84

Cameras. 90

Chandeliers 93

China 94

    American. 94

    Arita. 96

    Belleek 97

    Berlin 98

    Bow 99

    Bristol. 99

British. 100

Caiger-Smith. 105

Canton 105

Cardew, Michael 106

Carltonware 107

Chelsea 108

Chinese 109

Clarice Cliff 113

Coalport 114

Copeland 114

Coper, Hans 115

Delft. 116

Della Robbia 118

De Morgan 118

Derby 118

Doulton. 119

Dresden. 121

Earthenware. 121

European. 122

Famille Rose 124

Famille Verte 125

French 126

German. 128

Goldscheider 131

Goss 132

Grueby 133

Han 133

Imari. 135
Italian 138
Japanese 140
Jones 142
Kangxi 142
Kutani. 143
Kyoto. 143
Leach, Bernard 144
Leach 144
Lenci . . . . : 145
Liverpool. 145
Longton Hall 146
Lowestoft 146
Lustre 146
Martinware. 147
Mason's 148
Meissen 149
Ming. 154
Minton 155
Moorcroft 159
Nantgarw. 160
Oriental. 160
Parian 160
Paris 161
Pilkington 162
Prattware. 162
Redware 162
Lucie Rie. 163
Rookwood. 164
Royal Dux 164
Ruskin 165
Satsuma. 165
Sevres 167
Shelley 171
Song. 172
Spode 173
Staffordshire 174

Stoneware 179
Tang 182
Terracotta 184
Tournai. 184
Vienna 185
Vyse, Charles 185
Wedgwood 186
Whieldon. 190
Wood 190
Worcester. 191
Clocks & Watches 196
  Bracket Clocks 196
  Carriage Clocks 199
  Clock Sets 202
  Longcase Clocks 204
  Mantel Clocks. 212
  Skeleton Clocks 220
  Wall Clocks 221
  Watches. 224
  Wristwatches 230
Cloisonne. 234
Copper & Brass 238
Costume 244
Decoys 249
Dolls. 250
Enamel 256
Fans 260
Furniture. 262
  Beds 262
  Bookcases 264
  Bureau Bookcases 267
  Bureaux. 270
  Cabinets 274
  Canterburys 279
  Chairs, Dining. 280
    Easy 288
    Elbow 296

ANTIQUES REVIEW

Chests of Drawers 304
Chests on Chests 308
Chests on Stands 310
Chiffoniers 312
Clothes Presses 313
Commodes & Pot Cupboards 314
Commode Chests 315
Corner Cupboards 318
Cupboards 320
Davenports 322
Display Cabinets 324
Dressers 328
Dumbwaiters 330
Kneehole Desks 331
Lowboys 334
Screens 335
Secretaires 338
Secretaire Bookcases 340
Settees & Couches 344
Sideboards 350
Stands 354
Stools 359
Suites 362
Tables 364
  Card & Tea Tables 364
  Center Tables 368
  Console Tables 372
  Dining Tables 374
  Dressing Tables 378
  Drop-Leaf Tables 380
  Gateleg Tables 382
  Large Tables 384
  Occasional Tables 386
  Pembroke Tables 392
  Side Tables 394
  Sofa Tables 398
  Workboxes & Games Tables 400
Writing Tables & Desks 404
Trunks & Coffers 409
Wardrobes & Armoires 412
Washstands 414
Whatnots 415
Wine Coolers 416
Glass 418
  Beakers 418
  Bottles 419
  Bowls 420
  Boxes 421
  Candlesticks 422
  Decanters 423
  Dishes 424
  Drinking Sets 425
  Flasks 426
  Goblets 427
  Jugs 430
  Miscellaneous Glass 431
  Paperweights 432
  Scent Bottles 436
  Shades 437
  Tumblers 437
  Vases 438
  Wine Glasses 444
Gold 448
Horn 452
Indian Art 453
Inros 456
Instruments 458
Iron & Steel 468
Ivory 470
Jade 476
Jewelry 478
Lacquer 482
Lamps 483
Marble 488

Mirrors 490
Miscellaneous 496
Model Ships 500
Model Trains 502
Models 504
Motoring Items 506
Musical Boxes & Polyphones 510
Musical Instruments 514
Netsuke 518
Paper Money 524
Pewter 526
Photographs 530
Pianos 536
Portrait Miniatures 538
Posters 544
Prints 548
Quilts 554
Rugs 556
Samplers 564
Silver 566
  Baskets 566
  Beakers 567
  Bowls 568
  Boxes 570
  Candelabra 572
  Candlesticks 574
  Casters 578
  Centerpieces 579
  Chambersticks 580
  Chocolate Pots 581
  Cigarette Boxes 581
  Cigarette Cases 582
  Claret Jugs 583
  Coasters 584
  Coffee Pots 585
  Cream Jugs 588
  Cruets 589

Cups 590
Dishes 591
Ewers 594
Flatware 595
Frames 598
Goblets 599
Inkstands 600
Jugs 601
Miscellaneous Silver 602
Models 604
Mugs 605
Mustards 606
Nutmegs 607
Porringers 507
Salts 608
Sauceboats 609
Snuff Boxes 610
Tankards 612
Tazzas 614
Tea & Coffee Sets 615
Tea Caddies 618
Tea Kettles 619
Teapots 620
Trays & Salvers 621
Tureens 624
Urns 626
Vases 627
Vinaigrettes 628
Wine Coolers 629
Snuff Bottles 630
Stone 632
Tapestries 634
Textiles 637
Toys 640
Transport 648
Weathervanes 654
Wood 656

Acknowledgements

Abridge Auctions, *(Michael Yewman)*, *Market Place, Abridge, Sussex*
Anderson & Garland, *Anderson House, Market Street, Newcastle*
Ball & Percival, *132 Lord Street, Southport*
Banks & Silvers, *66 Foregate Street, Worcester*
Barbers Fine Art Auctioneers, *(Chobham Ltd.), The Mayford Centre,
   Smarts Heath Rd., Mayford, Woking*
Bearnes, *Rainbow, Avenue Road, Torquay*
Bermondsey Antiques Market, *Tower Bridge Road, London*
Biddle & Webb, *Ladywood Middleway, Birmingham*
Bloomsbury Book Auctions, *3 & 4 Hardwick Street, London*
Boardman Fine Art Auctioneers, *Station Road Corner, Haverhill, Suffolk*
Bonham's, *Montpelier Gardens, Montpelier Street, London*
Bracketts, *27-29 High Street, Tunbridge Wells*
J. R. Bridgford & Sons, *1 Heyes Lane, Alderley Edge, Cheshire*
British Antique Exporters, *206 London Road, Burgess Hill, W. Sussex*
Wm. H. Brown, *Westgate Hall, Grantham, Lincs*
Butler & Hatch Waterman, *86 High Street, Hythe, Kent*
Capes, Dunn & Co., *The Auction Galleries, 38 Charles Street, Manchester*
Chancellors Hollingsworths, *31 High Street, Ascot*
Christie's, *8 King Street, St. James's, London*
Christie's, *502 Park Avenue, New York, N.Y. 10022*
Christie's (Monaco) S.A.N., *Park Palace, 98000 Monte Carlo*
Christie's (Hong Kong) Ltd., *3607 Edinburgh Tower, 15 Queen's Rd. Hong Kong*
Christie's, *Cornelis Schuytstraat 57, 1071 JG, Amsterdam*
Christie's East, *219 East 67th Street, New York, N.Y. 10021*
Christie's & Edmiston's, *164/166 Bath Street, Glasgow*
Christie's S. Kensington, *85 Old Brompton Road, London*
Coles, Knapp & Kennedy, *Georgian Rooms, Ross-on-Wye, Herefordshire*
Cooper Hirst, *Goldway House, Parkway, Chelmsford*
Dacre, Son & Hartley, *1-5 The Grove, Ilkley, Yorkshire*
Dee & Atkinson, *The Exchange Saleroom, Driffield, Yorkshire*
Dreweatts, *Donnington Priory, Newbury, Berkshire*
Hy. Duke & Son, *Weymouth Avenue, Dorchester, Dorset*
Elliott & Green, *40 High Street, Lymington, Hants*
R. H. Ellis & Sons, *44-46 High Street, Worthing, Sussex*
Frank H. Fellows & Son, *Bedford House, 88 Hagley Road, Edgbaston, Birmingham*
Fox & Sons, *41 Chapel Road, Worthing*

ANTIQUES REVIEW

Geering & Colyer, *22-24 High Street, Tunbridge Wells*
Goss & Crested China, *(N. J. Pine), 62 Murray Road, Horndean*
Andrew Grant, *59-60 Foregate Street, Worcester*
Graves, Son & Pilcher, *71 Church Road, Hove, Sussex*
Hobbs & Chambers, *'At the Sign of the Bell', Market Place, Cirencester*
John Hogbin & Son, *8 Queen Street, Deal, Kent*
Edgar Horn, *46-50 South Street, Eastbourne, Sussex*
Jacobs & Hunt, *Lavant Street, Petersfield, Hants*
W. H. Lane & Son, *64 Morrab Road, Penzance, Cornwall*
Lawrence Fine Art, *South Street, Crewkerne, Somerset*
Locke & England, *Walton House, 11 The Parade, Leamington Spa*
Lots Road Chelsea Auction Galleries, *71 Lots Road, London*
Thomas Love & Son, *South St. John Street, Perth*
Mallams, *24 St. Michael's Street, Oxford*
May, Whetter & Grose, *Cornubia Hall, Par, Cornwall*
Morphets, *4-6 Albert Street, Harrogate, Yorkshire*
Neales of Nottingham, *192 Mansfield Road, Nottingham*
D. M. Nesbit & Co., *7 Clarendon Road, Southsea, Hants*
Onslows, *123 Hursley, Winchester, Hants*
Outhwaite & Litherland, *Kingsway Galleries, Fontenoy Street, Liverpool*
Parsons, Welch & Cowell, *49 London Road, Sevenoaks, Kent*
Phillips, *Marylebone Auction Rooms, Hayes Place, London*
Phillips, *65 George Street, Edinburgh*
Phillips, *98 Sauchiehall Street, Glasgow*
Phillips, *Blenstock House, 7 Blenheim Street, New Bond St., London*
Phillips, *The Old House, Station Road, Knowle, Solihull, W. Midlands*
Phillips & Jolly's, *The Auction Rooms, 1 Old King Street, Bath*
John H. Raby & Sons, *21 St. Mary's Road, Bradford*
Reeds Rains, *Trinity House, 114 Northenden Road, Sale, Cheshire*
Russell, Baldwin & Bright, *Ryelands Road, Leominster, Herefordshire*
Sandoe, Luce Panes, *Chipping Manor Salerooms, Wotton-under-Edge*
Robt. W. Skinner Inc., *Bolton Gallery, Route 117, Bolton, Mass*
H. Spencer & Sons Ltd., *20 The Square, Retford, Notts.*
Street Jewellery, *10 Summerhill Terrace, Newcastle-upon-Tyne*
Stride & Son, *Southdown House, St. John's Street, Chichester, Sussex*
G. E. Sworder's & Sons, *19 North Street, Bishops Stortford, Herts*
Vidler & Co., *Auction Offices, Cinque Ports St., Rye, Sussex*
Wallis & Wallis, *West Street Auction Galleries, Lewes, Sussex*
Ward & Partners, *16 High Street, Hythe, Kent*
Warner, Sheppard & Wade, *16-18 Halford Street, Leicester*
Peter Wilson & Co., *Market Street, Nantwich, Cheshire*
Woolley & Wallis, *The Castle Auction Mart, Castle Street, Salisbury*
Worsfolds Auction Galleries, *40 Station Road West, Canterbury*

ANTIQUES
REVIEW 1987

THE Lyle Official Antiques Review is compiled and published with completely fresh information annually, enabling you to begin each new year with an up-to-date knowledge of the current trends, together with the verified values of antiques of all descriptions.

We have endeavored to obtain a balance between the more expensive collector's items and those which, although not in their true sense antiques, are handled daily by the antiques trade.

The illustrations and prices in the following sections have been arranged to make it easy for the reader to assess the period and value of all items with speed.

You will find illustrations for almost every category of antique and curio, together with a corresponding price collated during the last twelve months, from the auction rooms and retail outlets of the major trading countries.

When dealing with the more popular trade pieces, in some instances, a calculation of an average price has been estimated from the varying accounts researched.

As regards prices, when 'one of a pair' is given in the description the price quoted is for a pair and so that we can make maximum use of the available space it is generally considered that one illustration is sufficient.

It will be noted that in some descriptions taken directly from sales catalogues originating from many different countries, terms such as bureau, secretary and davenport are used in a broader sense than is customary, but in all cases the term used is self explanatory.

Ovaltine. (Street Jewellery) $120

Jones' Sewing Machines. (Street Jewellery) $150

His Master's Choice, Kenya Beer. (Street Jewellery) $150

Singer Sewing Machines, 11 x 7½in. (Street Jewellery) $127

Late 19th century American apothecary sign, 3ft. high. (Robt. W. Skinner Inc.) $1,200

Patent Steam Carpet Beating Co, Ltd. (Street Jewellery) $375

W. D. & H. O. Wills, 'Westward Ho!' Smoking Mixture. (Street Jewellery) $112

Morris Service. (Street Jewellery) $187

Rowntree's Chocolates and Pastilles. (Street Jewellery) $67

Raleigh, The All-Steel Bicycle. (Street Jewellery) $180

ADVERTISING SIGNS

An advertising plaque bearing Rowland's Macassar Oil, the reverse impressed T. J. & J. Mayer, Longport, 16 x 22cm. (Phillips) $675

Henko, Maker Holzl, Vienna, 1920's, 28 x 18in. (Street Jewellery) $150

Wills's Star Cigarettes. (Street Jewellery) $120

Depot for Norfolk Champion Boots. (Street Jewellery) $112

Wills's Woodbines. (Street Jewellery) $45

United Kingdom Tea Company's Delicious Teas. (Street Jewellery) $300

Player's Please. (Street Jewellery) $75

Chivers' Carpet Soap. (Street Jewellery) $300

Reckitt's Blue. (Street Jewellery) $450

17

Churchman's 'Tortoiseshell' Smoking Mixture. (Street Jewellery) $262

Ruberoid Roofing, made by Willings & Co., 1930's, 36 x 27in. (Street Jewellery) $112

Depot for 'Swan' Ink. (Street Jewellery) $127

An enamel sign, 'Hush!! He's Busy', a political cartoon of Lloyd George, 51 x 71cm. (Osmond Tricks) $244

Union Castle Line to South & East Africa. (Street Jewellery) $450

Player's Navy Mixture. (Street Jewellery) $225

Rowntree's Elect Cocoa. (Street Jewellery) $60

Blue Band Margarine. (Street Jewellery) $67

Puritan Soap, Pure as the Breeze'. (Street Jewellery) $187

Brasso Metal Polish. (Street Jewellery) $75

Mitchells and Butlers' Ales. (Street Jewellery) $300

Persil, made by Ferro Email, 1930's, 23 x 15in. (Street Jewellery) $120

John Sinclair's Rubicon Twist. (Street Jewellery) $60

Dagenite, The Dependable Accumulators Sold Here. (Street Jewellery) $60

Robin Starch. (Street Jewellery) $262

Fresh Palethorpes Today. (Street Jewellery)$150

Stephens Inks. (Street Jewellery) $127

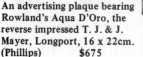

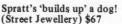

An advertising plaque bearing Rowland's Aqua D'Oro, the reverse impressed T. J. & J. Mayer, Longport, 16 x 22cm. (Phillips) $675

Spratt's 'builds up' a dog! (Street Jewellery) $67

Crow Bar Tobacco, 37 x 24½in., 1920's. (Street Jewellery)$150

AERONAUTICAL

A sheepskin-lined U.S. Army flying jacket, type B-3, size 48. (Christie's) $231

A model of an aeroplane constructed from leaves, matches and other items, made by a Belgian soldier, 1914-16, 5in. long. (Christie's) $42

An openface pocket watch, the white face inscribed 'Shock proof lever, Swiss made' and depicting a monoplane, 2in. diam. (Christie's) $84

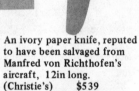

A silk Stevengraph depicting a balloon and entitled 'Many happy returns of the day, made by T. Stevens of Coventry on 28th Feb. 1874', 10in. long. (Christie's) $92

A static display of five stainless steel bi-planes, each plane approx. 2in. long, on a stand, 12in. high. (Christie's) $130

An ivory paper knife, reputed to have been salvaged from Manfred von Richthofen's aircraft, 12in long. (Christie's) $539

A blue enamel oval snuff box, the cover painted with a hot air balloon over the countryside, 2¼in. long. (Christie's) $646

A complimentary Season Pass to the London Aerodrome, Hendon, 1914, issued to John F. Plummer, together with a collection of other related material. (Christie's) $200

A pair of sheepskin-lined flying trousers, type B-1. (Christie's) $115

A commemorative plate depicting Immelmann's Fokker III monoplane, by N. Roe, oil, signed, inscribed and dated 1981, 9in. diam. (Christie's) $241

A silver lapel badge in the form of a gnome engine with propeller, 1¾in. long. (Christie's) $78

One of four silver place-setting holders depicting a Wright flyer, 1½in. high, in presentation case. (Christie's) $589

A color lithograph poster inscribed 'Graceful Parachute Descent', published by H. Miller Junr. & Co., 28 x 18in. (Christie's) $184

A polychrome wax bust of Montgolfier, inscribed 'Discovered Aerostation, 1784', 3¾in. (Christie's) $107

A humorous cartoon by Brookbank, signed, water-color , designer gouache and pastel, 12 x 10in. and a cover from Punch Magazine. (Christie's) $50

A white metal souvenir spoon commemorating the journey of Norwegian airship 'Norge' in 1926, 5in. long. (Christie's) $61

Two of a set of twenty-four colored magic lantern slides depicting early ballooning and flying scenes, in original box. (Christie's) $213

A German glider pilot's zinc badge, 2¼in. high, in presentation case. (Christie's) $75

1939 De Havilland DH94 Moth Minor, Registration G-AFPN, engine de Havilland Gipsy Minor, all up weight 1,550 pounds. (Christie's) $21,560

1943 Auster J/IN, Registration G-AGYD, engine de Havilland Gipsy Major I, all up weight 2,000 pounds. (Christie's) $5,852

1956 Morane Saulnier MS 733 Alcyon, Registration F-BLXU, engine Potez 6D OOA, all up weight 3,680 pounds. (Christie's) $7,700

1942 De Havilland DH 82A Tiger Moth, Registration G-AOGR, engine de Havilland Gipsy Major I, all up weight 1,825 pounds. (Christie's) $21,560

1951 De Havilland DHC 1 Chipmunk, Registration G-BCYE (Military WG350), engine de Havilland Gipsy Major 10 MK2, all up weight 2,100 pounds. (Christie's) $21,560

1941 North American T6G-NT (Harvard), Registration G-BKRA, engine Pratt and Whitney Wasp R-1340-AN-1, all up weight 5,300 pounds. (Christie's) $35,420

1955 Morane Saulnier MS 733 Alcyon, Registration F-GDRO, engine Potez 6D OOA, all up weight 3,680 pounds. (Christie's) $6,468

1935 British Aircraft BA Swallow 2, Registration G-ADPS, engine Pobjoy Cataract II, all up weight 1,500 pounds. (Christie's) $7,700

PAINTINGS

Color lithograph poster published by Masileau & Co., Paris, copyright 1910, Meeting d'Helio-polis, Rougier le Gagnant sur Biplane Voisin, 17¼ x 35in. (Christie's) $198

Short Solent and P.R. Spitfire, by Norman Jones, signed, inscribed and dated 1951, watercolor , 10 x 15¾in. (Christie's)
$170

Fairy Firefly, by Davis, signed, gouache, 10 x 14½in. (Christie's) $142

DH 60 'Gypsy Moth' G-AADS, by Stanley Orton Bradshaw, signed and dated '29, water-color , 9¼ x 13in. (Christie's) $639

Spitfires over Countryside, by Roy Nockolds, signed and dated 1940, watercolor and body-color , 19½ x 16in. (Christie's) $511

Avro trainer, by Stanley Orton Bradshaw, signed and dated '30, gouache heightened with white, 10 x 15in. (Christie's)
$397

Fairy 111D three-seater reconnaissance aeroplane, by Coombe Richards, signed and dated 1927, watercolor , 10 x 14in. (Christie's) $142

DH 60 'Gypsy Moth' G-AADP, by Stanley Orton Bradshaw, signed and dated '29, watercolor , 9 x 13¼in. (Christie's)
$681

23

One of a pair of U.S. Army officer's full dress epaulettes, possibly of Civil War period. (Wallis & Wallis) $138

A decorated Indian steel shield dahl, 14¼in. diam. (Wallis & Wallis) $92

A Nazi period Field Marshal's epaulette with gold and silver embroidery. (Wallis & Wallis) $125

An officer's full dress sporran of The Gordon Highlanders, white goat's hair and five bullion tassels. (Wallis & Wallis) $310

A pair of 17th century iron stirrups decorated in silver and gilt with massed cherry-blossom and meyuimon, signed Kitamura. (Christie's) $1,698

A Prussian officer's full dress sabretache of The 12th Hussars, circa 1890. (Wallis & Wallis) $325

One of a pair of pre 1830 Light Company officer's wings of The 54th (West Norfolk) Regt. (Wallis & Wallis) $296

One of a pair of Indian 18th century gold damascened arm defences, Bazu-Band, 12in. (Wallis & Wallis) $297

A full dress waistbelt and slings for a mounted officer of The Royal Scots. (Wallis & Wallis) $240

ARMS & ARMOR

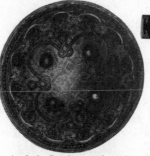

A pair of East India Company
Light Company officer's wings
of The 6th (Bengal?) Regt.
(Wallis & Wallis) $251

An Indo-Persian steel shield
dahl with 4 steel bosses,
gold and silver damascened.
(Wallis & Wallis) $251

A shakudo-nanakoji fuchi-
kashira and kozuka, each
decorated in takabori and
gilt takazogan. (Christie's)
$4,633

An Imperial German Cavalry
officer's full dress sabretache
of The 2nd Hanoverian
Hussars, circa 1850. (Wallis
& Wallis) $458

One of a pair of Georgian
officer's full dress epaulettes of The Royal East India
Vol. (Wallis & Wallis) $58

A breastplate struck with
maker's mark and a musket
ball proof test, circa 1600.
(Wallis & Wallis) $567

Prussian Regt. of Garde du
Corps officer's parade cuir-
ass. (Christie's)
$6,525

A lacquered saddle frame decorated
in gold takamakie on a red ground,
with a pair of stirrups, early 19th
century. (Christie's) $5,287

An officer's silver mounted
shoulder belt and pouch of
The 16th (The Queen's)
Lancers, HM Birmingham
1890. (Wallis & Wallis)
$467

25

A Bandsman's full dress blue tunic of The First Cardigan Vol. Artillery, circa 1905. (Wallis & Wallis) $236

A kebiki-laced kuchiba-iro-odoshi tosei-gusoku. (Christie's) $4,406

A post 1902 Lt. Colonel's part uniform of The Prince of Wales's Own Royal Wiltshire Yeomanry. (Wallis & Wallis) $666

Part of an extensive set of uniforms of The King's Own Regt. of Norfolk (Imperial) Yeomanry. (Christie's) $3,190

The Imperial Russian uniform of Count A. Benckendorff, Ambassador to the Court of St. James's, together with British Court dress cocked hat. (Christie's) $2,465

A suit of armor dated Tenmon gonen (1536). (Christie's) $3,706

A World War II Italian Air Force officer's tunic of Air Rank. (Wallis & Wallis) $458

A complete post 1902 trooper's full dress blue uniform of the City of London Yeomanry (Rough Riders). (Wallis & Wallis) $792

A post 1902 uniform of Lt. Col. C. W. Bowle, Royal Army Medical Corps. (Wallis & Wallis) $666

A South Australia Militia Lancers uniform. (Christie's) $5,510

Part of an officer's 88th Connaught Rangers uniform. (Christie's) $7,250

A uniform of the Gordon Highlanders 3rd (Militia) Bn. (Christie's) $1,160

DAGGERS

ARMS & ARMOR

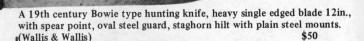

A Malayan kris, wavy laminated blade 15in., foliate chiselled brass cup, wooden garuda, in its two-piece wooden sheath with carved top. (Wallis & Wallis) $85

A 19th century Bowie type hunting knife, heavy single edged blade 12in., with spear point, oval steel guard, staghorn hilt with plain steel mounts. (Wallis & Wallis) $50

A 19th century Indian 'Bowie' style silver mounted hunting knife, broad, single edged, clipped back blade 10¼in., the steel crosspiece secured by sprung catch to sheath, two two-piece staghorn grips, in its tooled leather covered sheath. (Wallis & Wallis) $194

A Bali kris, wavy black and silver coloured pamir blade 15in., with fluted scrolled top, ebonized hilt and sheath carved with a dancing figure. (Wallis & Wallis) $108

An early 19th century Sumbawan executioner's kris, straight, double edged blade 19in., with scrolled fluted top and horn hilt, in its wooden sheath. (Wallis & Wallis) $111

A large 19th century European hunting knife, heavy single edged, broad blade 9½in., with spear point, small oval iron guard, staghorn hilt, in its leather sheath with provision for companion knife. (Wallis & Wallis) $93

A Balkan jambiya, watered double edged blade 10½in., with raised central rib. Black horn hilt, in silver covered wire and filigree ornamented sheath. (Wallis & Wallis) $151

A 1st pattern Field Service Commando fighting knife, blade 6½in., with square shank, by Wilkinson Sword, plated hilt, reversed crossguard, diced hilt and in its leather sheath. (Wallis & Wallis) $458

28

A late Spanish left-hand dagger, shallow diamond section blade 11in.,
with cage-shaped guard with octagonal quillons and wirebound grip.
(Wallis & Wallis) $158

A Bowie knife, straight, single edged blade 7in., with spear point, by
Joseph Rodgers, Sheffield, white metal oval crosspiece and hilt with
diced wood grips, in its leather sheath with belt loop. (Wallis & Wallis)
                                                         $151

A 19th century Tibetan silver mounted dagger, 16¾in., single edged blade
9in., hilt and sheath of embossed and pierced Tibetan silver. (Wallis &
Wallis) $302

A Nazi S.A. dagger by Eickhorn, the sheath with three plated mounts
and covered in brown leather with plated suspension chains of gilt
swastikas and alternating S.A. emblems. (Wallis & Wallis) $208

A George V Scottish officer's dirk set of The Argyll & Sutherland
Highlanders, scallop backed blade 12in., the corded wood hilt with
cast plated mounts and piquet studs, in its leather covered metal
sheath. (Wallis & Wallis) $576

A Nazi N.S.K.K. dagger with plated mounts, in its black painted metal
sheath. (Wallis & Wallis) $93

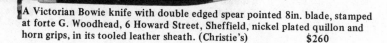

A late 19th century parang, swollen single edged blade 15½in., one-piece
horn hilt carved with a stylized lion's head pommel, inlaid ivory eyes. In
its palmwood scabbard with horn top and belthook. (Wallis & Wallis)
                                                         $122

A Victorian Bowie knife with double edged spear pointed 8in. blade, stamped
at forte G. Woodhead, 6 Howard Street, Sheffield, nickel plated quillon and
horn grips, in its tooled leather sheath. (Christie's) $260

ARMS & ARMOR

A 19th century Malay kris, broad, wavy etched pamir blade 14in., with carved ivory garuda hilt, in its wooden sheath with bone tip. (Wallis & Wallis) $281

A Scottish garter dirk, Skean Dhu, polished blade 4in., with strapwork carved ebony grip set with copper gilt figure of St. Andrew on his cross, in its copper gilt sheath. (Wallis & Wallis) $151

A 19th century Caucasian silver mounted kindjal, double edged watered blade 15in., with deep fullers. Two-piece ivory grips and in its velvet covered sheath. (Wallis & Wallis) $1,188

A Georgian Naval officer's dirk, circa 1812, double edged, tapering blade 6¾in., the turned baluster ivory hilt with turned pommel, in its copper gilt sheath. (Wallis & Wallis) $180

A Naval officer's dirk, by Paul Weyersberg, with brass mounts and wire-bound white grip, in its brass sheath. (Wallis & Wallis) $182

An Indian gold damascened pesh-kabz, blade 9½in., gold damascened with foliage at forte, en-suite with grip strap and back edge. Two-piece ivory grips, in its leather sheath with copper gilt finial. (Wallis & Wallis) $532

A 19th century African Fang tribal knife, 18in., swollen blade 12in. In its wooden sheath covered with monitor skin. (Wallis & Wallis) $43

An Indian dagger, bichwa, curved bi-furcated blade 8in., brass hilt with geometric pattern to guard, baluster inserts to grip. (Wallis & Wallis) $72

A silver mounted mid 17th century English plug bayonet, hollow ground, blade 9¾in., with false edge. Silver crosspiece and ribbed silver ferule. (Wallis & Wallis) $518

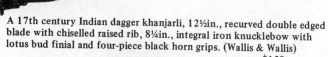

A Nazi Luftwaffe 2nd pattern officer's dagger with grey metal mounts, wirebound white celluloid grip and original bullion dress knot, in its grey metal sheath with original hanging straps and belt clip. (Wallis & Wallis) $115

A 17th century Indian dagger khanjarli, 12½in., recurved double edged blade with chiselled raised rib, 8¼in., integral iron knucklebow with lotus bud finial and four-piece black horn grips. (Wallis & Wallis) $158

A Nazi S.A. dagger by F. Herder, with German silver mounts, in its metal sheath and single leather suspension strap and belt hook. (Wallis & Wallis) $148

HELMETS

An 18-plate oboshi-hoshibachi, the rear plate signed Myochin Munenaga, 17th century. (Christie's) $1,395

An Imperial German Hussar officer's busby of The 17th (Brunswick) Hussars. (Wallis & Wallis) $266

A Nazi Army Desert issue pith helmet with original leather sweat band. (Wallis & Wallis) $96

A Prussian Garde du Corps trooper's helmet, with parade eagle to crown. (Wallis & Wallis) $1,656

A brass helmet much as for officers of the French Carabiniers, 1856-71. (Christie's) $652

The 6th Dragoon Guards (The Carabiniers) officer's gilt helmet with chin-chain. (Christie's) $894

A German burgonet, one-piece skull with tall comb and pierced hinged ear flaps, circa 1600. (Wallis & Wallis) $759

The 17th (Duke of Cambridge's Own) Lancers officer's chapka. (Christie's) $1,639

An officer's Albert pattern helmet of The Bombay Horse Artillery. (Wallis & Wallis) $657

A 62-plate Japanese helmet, kabuto, signed Iye Mushi, with two feather gilt mon and printed doe skin covering. (Wallis & Wallis) $1,859

An Artillery officer's busby by Hawkes & Co., the metal case inscribed Earl of Chester's Rifles. (Christie's) $261

A Czech Army steel helmet, captured by the Nazis, with Nazi oval transfer badge. (Wallis & Wallis) $44

An officer's composite metal eagle-topped helmet of the Prussian Regimental of Garde du Corps. (Christie's) $1,740

A French Dragoons trumpeter's helmet, circa 1870. (Christie's) $696

A British Grenadier's fur mitre cap of 1768 pattern. (Christie's) $2,682

A composite metal helmet generally as for an officer of the Swedish Livregementel till haft but fitted with a painted plate. (Christie's) $377

A 4-plate folding buff, top plate with roped border and pierced sights, circa 1600. (Wallis & Wallis) $825

An embossed and parcel gilt helmet, together with two arm guards, Persia, 19th century. (Robt. W. Skinner Inc.) $700

HELMETS

A Nazi Wehrmacht Russian Front fur-bodied officer's cap. (Wallis & Wallis) $81

A German World War I officer's peaked cap of a Brunswick Infantry Regt., with silk lining. (Wallis & Wallis) $88

A Nazi Panzer round cap with black felt crown and four breather holes. (Wallis & Wallis) $244

An Edward VII helmet of The King's Own Norfolk Imperial Yeomanry. (Wallis & Wallis) $458

An officer's 1855 (French) pattern shako of The Royal Lancashire Militia. (Wallis & Wallis) $370

A blue cloth helmet similar to Royal Artillery but possibly Royal Military Academy, Woolwich. (Christie's) $290

A Bavarian Infantry N.C.O.'s ersatz (pressed felt) pickelhaube with gilt helmet plate and mounts. (Wallis & Wallis) $208

A Nazi Police officer's shako with bullion cockade and silk and leather lining. (Wallis & Wallis) $296

A composite metal helmet generally as for officers of Prussian Line Cuirassier Regts. (Christie's) $696

HELMETS

A Nazi Political Leader's cap. (Wallis & Wallis) $95

A Waffen S.S. fez of The Handschar Division, with cloth eagle and death's head, and black tassel. (Wallis & Wallis) $592

A World War I German officer's peaked cap of Mecklenburg, with scarlet cap band. (Wallis & Wallis) $81

A Victorian officer's Albert pattern helmet of The 4th (Royal Irish) Dragoon Guards. (Wallis & Wallis) $504

A Victorian officer's lance cap of The 17th (Duke of Cambridge's Own) Lancers. (Wallis & Wallis) $1,008

A Victorian officer's helmet of The Royal Horse Guards (The Blues). (Wallis & Wallis) $2,072

A Prussian Staff officer's pickelhaube with silvered 'Line Eagle' helmet plate. (Wallis & Wallis) $414

A composite leather pickelhaube of 1842 pattern, bearing an eagle plate of Prussian Garde-Infanterie pattern. (Christie's) $464

A Prussian Infantryman's ersatz pickelhaube with original leather lining and chinstrap. (Wallis & Wallis) $118

35

HELMETS

An other rank's composite metal helmet of the Prussian Line Cuirassier Regts. (Christie's) $580

A Bavarian Jager Regt. man's ersatz shako with brass helmet plate and cloth cockade. (Wallis & Wallis) $118

A Baden Infantry N.C.O.'s pickelhaube with lacquered brass helmet plate and leather lining. (Wallis & Wallis) $185

The Blandford Yeomanry Cavalry black japanned metal helmet of early 19th century Roman style. (Christie's) $968

The helmet of Captain L. E. G. Oates, 6th (Inniskilling) Dragoons. (Christie's) $3,190

A Victorian officer's shako of The Royal Dockyard Bn., contained in its original japanned tin. (Phillips) $625

A Baden Infantryman's pickelhaube of The 109th Leib Regt., with German silver helmet plate. (Wallis & Wallis) $384

A Nazi Police shako with white metal helmet plate and leather chinstrap. (Wallis & Wallis) $125

A Prussian Artilleryman's ersatz pickelhaube with grey painted helmet plate and mounts. (Wallis & Wallis) $155

A Prussian infantry Reservist officer's pickelhaube with gilt brass helmet plate. (Wallis & Wallis) $224

A Nazi Fire Police steel helmet, black painted finish and aluminium comb. (Wallis & Wallis) $88

An Army Veterinary Dept. officer's helmet (Victorian plate), in metal case. (Christie's) $319

An 18th century Prussian mitre cap, Fusiliermutze, circa 1740-56. (Christie's) $2,831

A post 1902 officer's helmet of The Royal Horse Guards. (Wallis & Wallis) $1,258

The 1st Huntingdonshire Light Horse Volunteers (Duke of Manchester's), black leather helmet. (Christie's) $521

A Hesse Infantryman's pickelhaube, with lacquered brass helmet plate and mounts. (Wallis & Wallis) $266

A Prussian Military 1897 Guard infantryman's pickelhaube with lacquered brass helmet plate, brass spike and mounts. (Wallis & Wallis) $198

A Prussian Artillery officer's pickelhaube, with gilt helmet plate with battle honors 'Peninsula, Waterloo, Gohrde, Colberg 1807'. (Wallis & Wallis) $444

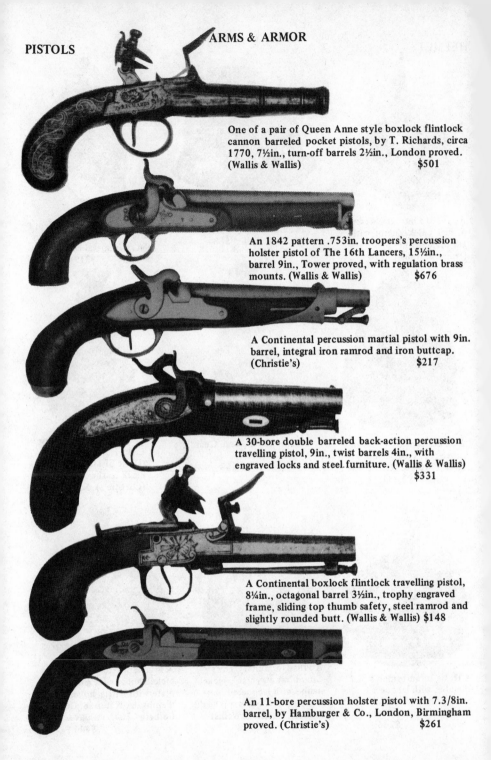

One of a pair of Queen Anne style boxlock flintlock cannon barreled pocket pistols, by T. Richards, circa 1770, 7½in., turn-off barrels 2½in., London proved. (Wallis & Wallis) $501

An 1842 pattern .753in. troopers's percussion holster pistol of The 16th Lancers, 15½in., barrel 9in., Tower proved, with regulation brass mounts. (Wallis & Wallis) $676

A Continental percussion martial pistol with 9in. barrel, integral iron ramrod and iron buttcap. (Christie's) $217

A 30-bore double barreled back-action percussion travelling pistol, 9in., twist barrels 4in., with engraved locks and steel furniture. (Wallis & Wallis) $331

A Continental boxlock flintlock travelling pistol, 8¼in., octagonal barrel 3½in., trophy engraved frame, sliding top thumb safety, steel ramrod and slightly rounded butt. (Wallis & Wallis) $148

An 11-bore percussion holster pistol with 7.3/8in. barrel, by Hamburger & Co., London, Birmingham proved. (Christie's) $261

A 6-shot .44in. Allen & Wheelock single action Army revolver, 13¼in., half octagonal barrel 7½in., trigger guard hinges and acts as rammer lever with two-piece wooden grips. (Wallis & Wallis) $518

A 6-shot bar hammer percussion open frame transitional revolver with 3¾in. octagonal barrel engraved W. H. Edwards, Birmingham proved. (Christie's) $217

A flintlock Dragon pattern flintlock holster pistol with 9in. barrel, iron ramrod and brass furniture, the lockplate stamped Lacy & Co., London, Birmingham proved. (Christie's) $290

A 12-bore Continental military flintlock holster pistol, 15½in., barrel 9in. Fullstocked, regulation lock and steel mounts. (Wallis & Wallis) $296

A 13-bore double barreled French back-action percussion holster pistol, 13in., barrels 7in. Halfstocked, flush fitting steel furniture, ribbed steel throatpipe and steel lanyard ring and ramrod. (Wallis & Wallis) $236

A 26-bore brass barreled flintlock travelling pistol by Farmer, 10½in., barrel 6in., Birmingham proved, engraved Cardiff. Fullstocked, brass furniture and rounded butt. (Wallis & Wallis) $287

39

PISTOLS

A 6-shot .44in. Remington Army single action percussion revolver, 14in., octagonal barrel 8in., stamped Patented Sept. 14 1858, brass trigger guard and two-piece wooden grips. (Wallis & Wallis) $754

A 5-shot 54-bore Beaumont Adams double action percussion revolver 11½in., barrel 5½in., London proved., with side lever rammer and a one-piece chequered walnut grip. (Wallis & Wallis) $460

A 5-shot .38in. bore model 1851 Adam's Patent self-cocking percussion Dragoon revolver, 13½in., barrel 7¾in., London proved, with one-piece chequered wooden grip. (Wallis & Wallis) $290

A 6-shot .44in. Starr Arms Co. single action percussion Army revolver, 13½in., barrel 8in., underlever rammer and one-piece wooden grip. (Wallis & Wallis) $417

A 5-shot 54-bore self-cocking 1851 model Adams percussion revolver, 12in., barrel 6¾in., London proved, with sprung hammer safety and chequered one-piece walnut grip. (Wallis & Wallis) $374

A 6-shot .44in. Magnum Ruger Super Blackhawk single action revolver, 13½in., barrel 7½in., with sidegate loading and ejection. (Wallis & Wallis) $132

A 9mm. Mauser 'Broom Handle' semi auto pistol, 10in., barrel 4in., with two-piece wooden grips. (Wallis & Wallis) $382

A 6-shot .36in. Allen & Wheelock single action Navy percussion revolver, 13¾in., octagonal barrel 8in., with side hammer, trigger guard hinges and acts as rammer lever and two-piece wooden grips. (Wallis & Wallis) $355

A 6-shot Russian Gallard Patent double action revolver, 10in., barrel 5in., top struck with Imperial Eagle. Hinged trigger guard separates barrel from cylinder and cylinder from extractor plate. (Wallis & Wallis) $384

A 6-shot .36in. Colt single action percussion Navy revolver, 13in., barrel 7½in., with brass trigger guard and grip strap stamped '36 Cal'. (Wallis & Wallis) $448

A 5-shot .38in. Tranter's patent double action percussion revolver, 10in., octagonal barrel 4½in., London proved. (Wallis & Wallis) $666

A 5-shot 54-bore model 1851 Adam's Patent self-cocking percussion revolver, 12in., barrel 6in., London proved. Sliding cylinder locking bolt, sprung hammer safety, side lever rammer, chequered walnut butt. (Wallis & Wallis) $740

A 6-shot .31in. self-cocking transitional percussion revolver, 11in., barrel 5½in. Cylinder roll engraved with dogs and deer. Foliate engraved brass backstrap, one-piece chequered walnut grips. (Wallis & Wallis) $503

A 5-shot 54-bore Tranter's Patent double trigger percussion revolver, 12in., barrel 6in., Birmingham proved. Foliate engraved frame, hardened cylinder and buttcap, sprung hammer safety, one-piece chequered walnut butt. (Wallis & Wallis) $592

A 6-shot 54-bore self-cocking transitional percussion revolver, 12¼in., barrel 5¾in., Birmingham proved, plunger type rammer. Fluted cylinder, foliate engraved round steel frame, bar hammer and furniture. (Wallis & Wallis) $488

A 5-shot 38-bore Deane Harding Patent double action percussion revolver, 12in., barrel 6in., London proved, underlever rammer, sliding cylinder locking catch. One-piece chequered grip. (Wallis & Wallis) $547

A 6-shot .45in. enclosed hammer single action percussion revolver by Devisme, No. 43, 13in., barrel 6¼in., swivel catch locks frame to barrel. (Wallis & Wallis) $725

A 6-shot .44in. self-cocking transitional percussion revolver, 11¾in., mirror blued barrel 5¼in., Birmingham proved. Mirror blued cylinder, two-piece polished walnut grip. (Wallis & Wallis) $606

A 6-shot 54-bore Pennell's Patent self-cocking percussion revolver, 13in., octagonal barrel 6½in., Birmingham proved. Hinged catch locking barrel to frame. (Wallis & Wallis)　　　　$1,332

A 5-shot .50in. Beaumont Adams double action percussion revolver No. 1653OR, 14in., barrel 7½in., London proved. Side cylinder locking bolt, sprung hammer safety, side lever rammer, one-piece chequered walnut butt. (Wallis & Wallis)　　　　$925

A 5-shot 54-bore open frame self-cocking percussion revolver by Weston of Brighton, 11½in., barrel 7in., Birmingham proved, underlever rammer. Foliate engraved frame, two-piece chequered walnut grip. (Wallis & Wallis)　$814

A .15in. Continental enclosed action percussion target pistol, 12¾in., tip down smooth bore octagonal barrel 7½in., secured by side lever and opening merely for capping. Steel furniture and fluted walnut butt. (Wallis & Wallis) $340

A 26-bore all steel Scottish flintlock belt pistol by Murdoch of Doune, circa 1770, 12in., barrel 7¾in., foliate engraved, reeded breech, facetted muzzle. Steel fullstock, stock and rounded butt. (Wallis & Wallis)　　　　$1,628

A 6-shot .40in. Wesson's & Leavitt's Patent single action percussion revolver, 15in., barrel 7in., Barrel hinges up when released by catch on cylinder axis pin. (Wallis & Wallis)　　　　$703

A .48in. boxlock sidehammer Continental needle fire holster pistol, 12½in., right octagonal barrel 7in., released by underlever. Scroll engraved frame, side cocking lever and steel furniture, chequered saw handled walnut butt. (Wallis & Wallis)　　　　$340

POWDER FLASKS

A plain copper 3-way powder flask, brass mounts, swivel lid to shot compartment, containing lead shot. (Wallis & Wallis) $13

A brass mounted priming horn, 7½in., charger with fixed nozzle and wrap around spring, twin brass hanging rings and brass end cap. (Wallis & Wallis) $50

A shell embossed copper powder flask, 8in., common white metal top stamped Bartram & Co., with graduated nozzle. (Wallis & Wallis) $103

A gun sized fluted copper powder flask, 7¾in., patent brass top stamped James Dixon & Sons, Sheffield. (Wallis & Wallis) $50

A silver mounted tortoise-shell powder flask, 4in., with silver spout and sprung lever. (Wallis & Wallis) $103

A foliate embossed copper powder flask, 8in., patent top stamped James Dixon & Sons, Sheffield. (Wallis & Wallis) $47

A copper pistol sized powder flask, 4¼in., the common brass top with fixed nozzle. (Wallis & Wallis) $43

A German flattened cowhorn powder flask with Boche charger, 13in., brass mounts and horn nozzle. (Wallis & Wallis) $118

A copper three-way powder flask, 3½in., stamped Sykes, with common brass top with blued spring. (Wallis & Wallis) $88

A bag-shaped copper pistol flask, 5½in., brass top stamped James Dixon & Sons, Sheffield, graduated nozzle from 3/8 to 5/8 drams. (Wallis & Wallis) $110

An Austrian powder flask of lanthorn, 8½in., pear shaped two-piece body with patent brass top. (Wallis & Wallis) $79

An embossed copper powder flask, 8in., with woven design within acanthus borders, common top stamped G. & J. W. Hawksley. (Wallis & Wallis) $81

A pistol sized copper powder flask, 4½in., plain body with lacquered brass top, fixed nozzle and blued spring. (Wallis & Wallis) $37

A brass mounted priming horn, 7½in., wrap around spring to fixed charger, with twin brass hanging rings, brass end cap and green hanging cord. (Wallis & Wallis) $28

A copper powder flask of the type cased with Colts, 4in. (Wallis & Wallis) $100

A gun sized copper powder flask, 7in., of chamfered form, common brass top stamped Sykes Patent. (Wallis & Wallis) $79

A late 17th century turned wooden powder flask of 'doughnut' form, 3in. diam., with steel suspension rings. (Wallis & Wallis) $158

A copper three-way powder flask, 5.1/8in., common brass top with blued spring hinged ball cover to top. (Wallis & Wallis) $74

ARMS & ARMOR

A .44in. rimfire Winchester model 1866 underlever repeating rifle, 44in., octagonal barrel 24in., ladder sight to 800 yards. Brass frame, steel sling swivels, tubular magazine, brass buttcap. (Wallis & Wallis) $2,960

A 28-bore Sharp's Patent breech loading back-action self-priming percussion Cavalry carbine, 39½in., barrel 22in., with Lawrence patent sight to 800 yards. Halfstocked, trigger guard lowers falling block, saddle bar with lanyard ring, steel mounts. (Wallis & Wallis) $814

A double barreled 10-bore x 3in. damascus nitro proved hammer gun by Williams, no. 107744, 48¾in., barrels 32¼in., top lever opening, non-ejector, rebounding hammers, chequered pistol grip and fore-end, 1in. butt extension, together with cleaning kit in wallet. (Wallis & Wallis) $384

A single barreled 8-bore nitro proved back-action underlever hammer sporting gun, 52in., damascus barrel 35½in., engraved E. Cox, foliate engraved action and lock, chequered pistol grip, vacant escutcheon and rubber butt extension. (Wallis & Wallis) $620

A 12-bore Belgian contract Brunswick back-action military percussion rifle, 46½in., barrel 30in., for the belted ball, with tangent rearsight. Regulation brass mounts with large butt trap. (Wallis & Wallis) $295

A .44in. rimfire Winchester model 1866 factory engraved underlever repeating rifle, 44in., barrel 24in. Bronze frame. (Wallis & Wallis) $6,068

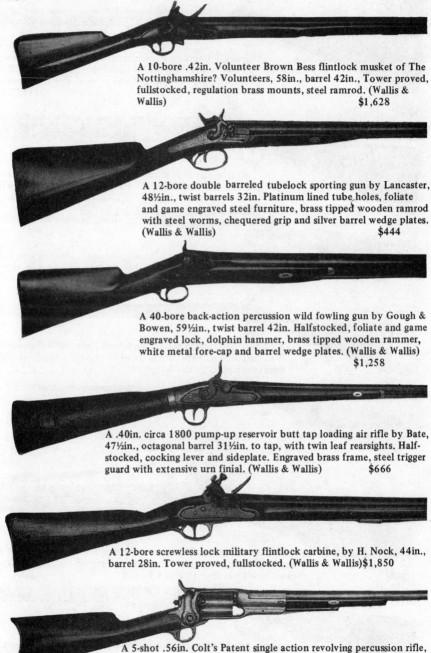

A 10-bore .42in. Volunteer Brown Bess flintlock musket of The Nottinghamshire? Volunteers, 58in., barrel 42in., Tower proved, fullstocked, regulation brass mounts, steel ramrod. (Wallis & Wallis) $1,628

A 12-bore double barreled tubelock sporting gun by Lancaster, 48½in., twist barrels 32in. Platinum lined tube holes, foliate and game engraved steel furniture, brass tipped wooden ramrod with steel worms, chequered grip and silver barrel wedge plates. (Wallis & Wallis) $444

A 40-bore back-action percussion wild fowling gun by Gough & Bowen, 59½in., twist barrel 42in. Halfstocked, foliate and game engraved lock, dolphin hammer, brass tipped wooden rammer, white metal fore-cap and barrel wedge plates. (Wallis & Wallis)
$1,258

A .40in. circa 1800 pump-up reservoir butt tap loading air rifle by Bate, 47½in., octagonal barrel 31½in. to tap, with twin leaf rearsights. Halfstocked, cocking lever and sideplate. Engraved brass frame, steel trigger guard with extensive urn finial. (Wallis & Wallis) $666

A 12-bore screwless lock military flintlock carbine, by H. Nock, 44in., barrel 28in. Tower proved, fullstocked. (Wallis & Wallis)$1,850

A 5-shot .56in. Colt's Patent single action revolving percussion rifle, 43in., barrel 24in., underlever rammer. Fluted cylinder stamped Patented Sept. 10th 1850'. (Wallis & Wallis) $2,516

A single barreled 14-bore percussion sporting gun, 45½in., browned twist barrel 30in., with octagonal gold lined breech engraved J. Blanch & Son, figured walnut stock with chequered wrist. (Wallis & Wallis) $384

An Irish flintlock musketoon, 35in., half octagonal barrel 19in., with flared muzzle. Fullstocked, re-used Brown Bess lock, stamped Pattison. (Wallis & Wallis) $592

A 16-bore double- barreled French percussion sporting gun, breech converted from flintlock, 47in., barrels 31in. Fullstocked, plain steel furniture with French walnut stock. (Wallis & Wallis) $488

A 12-bore back-action percussion sporting gun by Simmons, 46in., twist barrel 30in., with gold breech lines, erased poincon and platinum safety plug. (Wallis & Wallis) $223

A .177in. Militia Patent pre-war round frame air rifle, 39in., barrel 17½in., with octagonal breech. (Wallis & Wallis) $34

A brass barreled flintlock blunderbuss with spring bayonet, circa 1810, 30¼in., half octagonal barrel 14½in., Tower proved with thumb catch released spring bayonet. (Wallis & Wallis) $864

A 16-bore and 6.5mm. snap action drilling combined hammer gun and rifle, 42½in., barrels 26½in., engraved Aug Luneburg Kile with sight mounts, back-action locks, underlever snap action, set right trigger and chequered pistol grip. (Wallis & Wallis) $310

ARMS & ARMOR

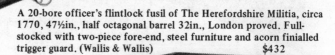

A 20-bore officer's flintlock fusil of The Herefordshire Militia, circa 1770, 47½in., half octagonal barrel 32in., London proved. Full-stocked with two-piece fore-end, steel furniture and acorn finialled trigger guard. (Wallis & Wallis) $432

A 12-bore x 2½in. N.P. side lock ejector 'The Watts Gun' by London Sporting Park Ltd., no. 396, 46in., barrels 28in., top lever opening, gold inlaid auto safe and chequered fore and small, silver escutcheon, 1¾in. butt extension. (Wallis & Wallis) $777

A 16-bore Belgian double barreled flintlock sporting gun made for the Eastern market, 55½in., barrels 39½in., etched with Arabic inscription dated 1880. Halfstocked, foliate engraved locks and white metal furniture. (Wallis & Wallis) $504

A 7mm. (.25in.) Britannia air rifle, no. 1137, 45in., barrel 18½in. to loading port with swivel cover. Hinged catch releases stock and action to cock cylinder. (Wallis & Wallis) $222

A 10-bore E.I.C. New Land pattern sergeant's flintlock musket, 49in., barrel 33¼in., London proved, fixed sights with regulation brass mounts, steel sling swivels and ramrod. (Wallis & Wallis) $674

A Turkish flintlock blunderbuss, 23in., flared barrel 12in. Fullstocked, with engraved steel furniture, the saddle bar with lanyard ring. (Wallis & Wallis) $604

A 12-bore percussion sporting gun by Joseph Manton, No. 6964, 50in., half octagonal barrel 34in., with breech converter's poincon, barrel London proved. (Wallis & Wallis) $460

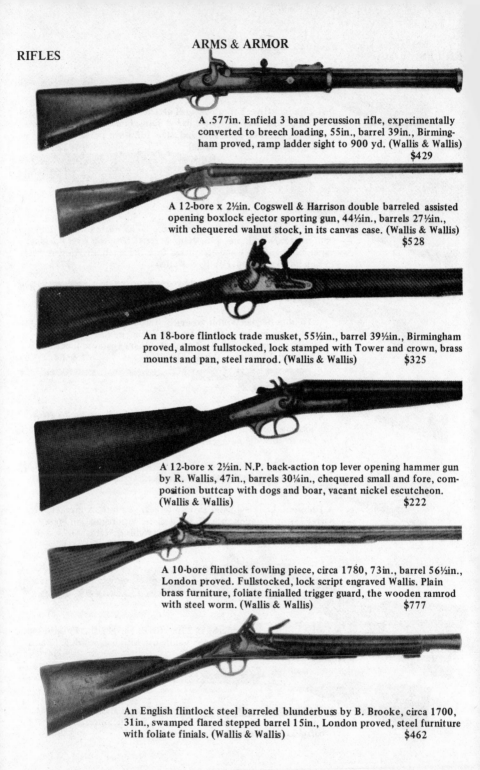

A .577in. Enfield 3 band percussion rifle, experimentally converted to breech loading, 55in., barrel 39in., Birmingham proved, ramp ladder sight to 900 yd. (Wallis & Wallis) $429

A 12-bore x 2½in. Cogswell & Harrison double barreled assisted opening boxlock ejector sporting gun, 44½in., barrels 27½in., with chequered walnut stock, in its canvas case. (Wallis & Wallis) $528

An 18-bore flintlock trade musket, 55½in., barrel 39½in., Birmingham proved, almost fullstocked, lock stamped with Tower and crown, brass mounts and pan, steel ramrod. (Wallis & Wallis) $325

A 12-bore x 2½in. N.P. back-action top lever opening hammer gun by R. Wallis, 47in., barrels 30¼in., chequered small and fore, composition buttcap with dogs and boar, vacant nickel escutcheon. (Wallis & Wallis) $222

A 10-bore flintlock fowling piece, circa 1780, 73in., barrel 56½in., London proved. Fullstocked, lock script engraved Wallis. Plain brass furniture, foliate finialled trigger guard, the wooden ramrod with steel worm. (Wallis & Wallis) $777

An English flintlock steel barreled blunderbuss by B. Brooke, circa 1700, 31in., swamped flared stepped barrel 15in., London proved, steel furniture with foliate finials. (Wallis & Wallis) $462

ARMS & ARMOR

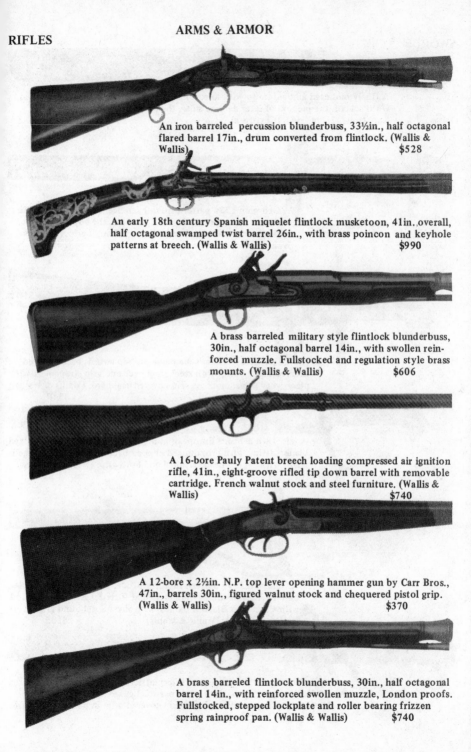

An iron barreled percussion blunderbuss, 33½in., half octagonal flared barrel 17in., drum converted from flintlock. (Wallis & Wallis) $528

An early 18th century Spanish miquelet flintlock musketoon, 41in..overall, half octagonal swamped twist barrel 26in., with brass poincon and keyhole patterns at breech. (Wallis & Wallis) $990

A brass barreled military style flintlock blunderbuss, 30in., half octagonal barrel 14in., with swollen reinforced muzzle. Fullstocked and regulation style brass mounts. (Wallis & Wallis) $606

A 16-bore Pauly Patent breech loading compressed air ignition rifle, 41in., eight-groove rifled tip down barrel with removable cartridge. French walnut stock and steel furniture. (Wallis & Wallis) $740

A 12-bore x 2½in. N.P. top lever opening hammer gun by Carr Bros., 47in., barrels 30in., figured walnut stock and chequered pistol grip. (Wallis & Wallis) $370

A brass barreled flintlock blunderbuss, 30in., half octagonal barrel 14in., with reinforced swollen muzzle, London proofs. Fullstocked, stepped lockplate and roller bearing frizzen spring rainproof pan. (Wallis & Wallis) $740

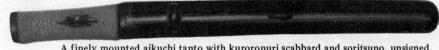

A finely mounted aikuchi tanto with kuroronuri scabbard and soritsuno, unsigned, Goto school, the menuki of later date en suite, the blade in the style of Mino Kanetsune, 28cm. long. (Christie's) $1,615

A Georgian 1796 pattern Infantry officer's sword, blade 31in., etched at forte Craven & Co. Warranted, the copper gilt hilt with double shell guard and silver wirebound grip. (Wallis & Wallis) $145

An Indian Army officer's mameluke hilted sword, broad curved fullered blade 31in., with steel crosspiece and grip strap and two-piece ivory grips, in its ass skin covered scabbard. (Wallis & Wallis) $340

A mid 18th century European hunting sword, curved, single edged blade 18½in., with pronounced clipped back edge, brass half shell guard with eagle's head terminal and horn grip. (Wallis & Wallis) $79

A Georgian 1796 pattern Infantry officer's sword, slim, tapering, double-edged blade 31½in., etched at forte J.J.R. Sohlingen and with the maker Bland & James, with silver wirebound grip, in its leather scabbard. (Wallis & Wallis) $105

A Victorian 1821 pattern Artillery officer's sword, blade 34½in., by Hamburger Rogers, with triple bar steel guard and steel mounts. German silver wirebound fishskin covered grip, in its steel scabbard. (Wallis & Wallis) $93

ARMS & ARMOR

A wakizashi, the red lacquered scabbard simulating cherry bark, fitted with a gilt kogai and shakudo-nanakoji kozuka, the tsuba signed Kazuyoshi, Meiji period, the blade, unsigned, 16th century, 34.2cm. (Christie's)

$5,868

A French smallsword, circa 1750, hollow ground triangular section blade 27in. Steel hilt, foliate chiselled quillon block, woven silver grip wire and iron tape with woven silver Turk's head. (Wallis & Wallis)

$198

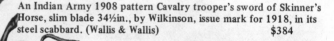

An Indian Army 1908 pattern Cavalry trooper's sword of Skinner's Horse, slim blade 34½in., by Wilkinson, issue mark for 1918, in its steel scabbard. (Wallis & Wallis)

$384

A 19th century hunting sword, plain, single edged blade 13in., steel fluted shell guard, reversed hoof quillons, staghorn hilt with fluted steel pommel, in its leather sheath, with provision for companion knife. (Wallis & Wallis)

$86

A William IV 1831 pattern General officer's mameluke sabre, curved, clipped back blade 30in., by W. Moore, in its leather scabbard with three copper gilt mounts. (Wallis & Wallis)

$396

A George V Coldstream Guards officer's sword, blade 32in., by Johns & Pegg, London, with plated hilt and wirebound fish-skin covered grip, in its plated scabbard. (Wallis & Wallis)

$145

An o-wakizashi, the scabbard covered with Dutch leather, a shibuichi kozuka and a copper kogai, the blade, signed and dated Eiroku ninen, 1559, 51.7cm. long. (Christie's) $1,853

A daisho with mijingai-nuri scabbards decorated with gold hiramakie ho-o and kuro-ronuri kiri, with handashi style sahari-ishimeji fittings decorated with kiri, the blades both honzukuri and torii-zori, unsigned, 66.2cm. long, the wakizashi 47.4cm. long. (Christie's) $2,937

A large katana, the scabbard with brown pine-needle design, the menuki formed as bats in flight, unsigned, the blade signed Kanesada (probably Kanesada III of Mino), 16th century, 76.5cm. long. (Christie's) $3,231

An elaborately mounted tanto, the blade, wide takenokozori with sukashi kurikara horimono, fine mokume hada and komidare hamon of nie, ubu nakago, unsigned, 17th century, 28.8cm. long. (Christie's) $3,672

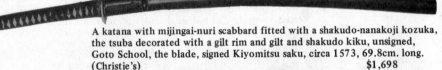

A katana with mijingai-nuri scabbard fitted with a shakudo-nanakoji kozuka, the tsuba decorated with a gilt rim and gilt and shakudo kiku, unsigned, Goto School, the blade, signed Kiyomitsu saku, circa 1573, 69.8cm. long. (Christie's) $1,698

A late Japanese sword tachi, blade 66.4cm., inscribed Tadamitsu, muji hada, chu suguha hamon. Brass aoi tsuba, tsuka, dragon menuki, nashiji lacquered saya. (Wallis & Wallis) $1,702

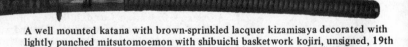

A well mounted katana with brown-sprinkled lacquer kizamisaya decorated with lightly punched mitsutomoemon with shibuichi basketwork kojiri, unsigned, 19th century, 59cm. long. (Christie's) $3,231

A handachi katana, the mura-nashiji scabbard decorated in gold hiramakie, the fuchi signed Nakamura Haruhiro (Hirato school, mid 19th century), the blade signed Noshu Seki, circa 1644, 66.5cm. long. (Christie's) $2,643

A large Shinto katana, broad blade 70.6cm., signed Rikouku Nokami Fujiwara Kanenobu, circa 1764. Bold sanbon sugi hamon, gunome hamon, distinct nie line. Tape bound tsuka, in its black lacquered saya. (Wallis & Wallis) $976

A richly mounted handachi, the nashiji scabbard decorated with kotobuki and other seal characters in gold hiramakie, signed, circa 1800, the blade circa 1661, 69.6cm. long. (Christie's) $4,112

A finely mounted hamidashi tanto with black ishime-nuri scabbard, signed Kitosai Terumitsu, circa 1800, the blade inscribed Yukimune, probably late 15th/early 16th century, Yamashiro School, 24.7cm. long. (Christie's) $1,101

A Japanese World War II Army officer's sword katana, blade 66.5cm., signed Showato with dated Showa 16th year (1943), in shin gunto mounts with leather covered steel saya. (Wallis & Wallis) $171

A late Japanese ito maki-no-tachi, blade 68.7cm., mumei, itame hada, gunome hamon. Tape bound tsuka, black lacquered saya. (Wallis & Wallis) $662

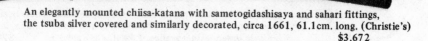

An elegantly mounted chiisa-katana with sametogidashisaya and sahari fittings, the tsuba silver covered and similarly decorated, circa 1661, 61.1cm. long. (Christie's) $3,672

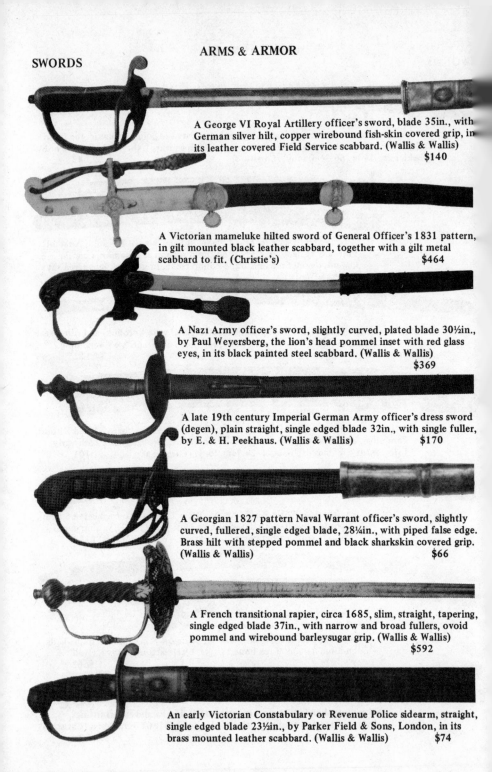

A George VI Royal Artillery officer's sword, blade 35in., with German silver hilt, copper wirebound fish-skin covered grip, in its leather covered Field Service scabbard. (Wallis & Wallis) $140

A Victorian mameluke hilted sword of General Officer's 1831 pattern, in gilt mounted black leather scabbard, together with a gilt metal scabbard to fit. (Christie's) $464

A Nazi Army officer's sword, slightly curved, plated blade 30½in., by Paul Weyersberg, the lion's head pommel inset with red glass eyes, in its black painted steel scabbard. (Wallis & Wallis) $369

A late 19th century Imperial German Army officer's dress sword (degen), plain straight, single edged blade 32in., with single fuller, by E. & H. Peekhaus. (Wallis & Wallis) $170

A Georgian 1827 pattern Naval Warrant officer's sword, slightly curved, fullered, single edged blade, 28¼in., with piped false edge. Brass hilt with stepped pommel and black sharkskin covered grip. (Wallis & Wallis) $66

A French transitional rapier, circa 1685, slim, straight, tapering, single edged blade 37in., with narrow and broad fullers, ovoid pommel and wirebound barleysugar grip. (Wallis & Wallis) $592

An early Victorian Constabulary or Revenue Police sidearm, straight, single edged blade 23½in., by Parker Field & Sons, London, in its brass mounted leather scabbard. (Wallis & Wallis) $74

An Austrian Lorenz Jager carbine sword bayonet, blade 23½in., with broad fuller stamps to socket. (Wallis & Wallis) $66

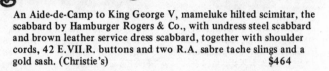

An Aide-de-Camp to King George V, mameluke hilted scimitar, the scabbard by Hamburger Rogers & Co., with undress steel scabbard and brown leather service dress scabbard, together with shoulder cords, 42 E.VII.R. buttons and two R.A. sabre tache slings and a gold sash. (Christie's) $464

A transitional dish hilted rapier, circa 1630, slender blade 41½in., stamped Sebastian Hernantis in the fullers. Foliate chiselled hilt, pierced dish guard and wirebound grip. (Wallis & Wallis) $488

A late Victorian 'Lead Cutter' cutlass, broad, single edged, slightly curved blade 30½in., by Mole, Birmingham, issue stamps for '97, sheet steel guard and ribbed iron grip, in its leather scabbard. (Wallis & Wallis) $129

A French Cavalry officer's sword of 1786 pattern type, straight, broad single fullered, single edged blade 38in., with false edge. Regulation brass guard, fluted brass pommel and leather covered cord wound grip. (Wallis & Wallis) $281

A mid 17th century Cavalry man's half basket hilted broadsword, straight, double edged blade 33in. Brass hilt, stepped bulbous pommel and leather covered grip. (Wallis & Wallis) $488

An 1857 pattern Engineers officer's sword of The 2nd Gloucestershire Engineer Vols., polished fullered single edged blade 33in., with regulation pierced brass gilt hilt and wirebound sharkskin grip. (Wallis & Wallis) $177

TSUBAS

A Japanese iron tsuba, 8.3cm., of mokko form, slightly raised rims with heart-shaped piercings. (Wallis & Wallis) $45

A pierced iron Choshu tsuba, 7.5cm., chiselled with ears of rice in relief. (Wallis & Wallis) $115

A Japanese pierced iron tsuba, 7.8cm., of circular form, pierced with geometric blossom. (Wallis & Wallis) $47

A squared iron tsuba, 6.7cm., chiselled with a prunus and inlaid soft metal flowers. (Wallis & Wallis) $79

A circular iron tsuba, 7.3cm., signed Echizen noju kinai saku, pierced and chiselled with a dragon. (Wallis & Wallis) $100

A Japanese pierced iron tsuba, 9cm., engraved with a stream, lilies, wheel, hexagonal devices and clouds. (Wallis & Wallis) $50

A Sado School tsuba, 7.3cm., signed Sashu no ju Toshioki, chiselled with a flower. (Wallis & Wallis) $79

A Higo pierced iron tsuba, 7.5cm., pierced with a wheel of arrows. (Wallis & Wallis) $92

A Japanese pierced iron tsuba, 8.6cm., of mokko form, pierced with a blossom. (Wallis & Wallis) $47

58

A Japanese iron tsuba, 7cm., of mokko form with shaped lobes. (Wallis & Wallis) $47

A kyo-sukashi tsuba depicting five cranes, unsigned, Edo period, 8.7cm. (Christie's) $263

A heavy Miochi iron mokko tsuba, 8.2cm., of mokume, with udenuki-an and sukashi stylized flower. (Wallis & Wallis) $50

A Japanese pierced iron tsuba, 7.6cm., of eight lobed outline, pierced and chiselled in low relief with part flower heads. (Wallis & Wallis) $47

A circular iron tsuba, 7.1cm., signed Bushu noju kunihiro saku, pierced with waves. (Wallis & Wallis) $62

An oval shibuichi tanto tsuba and associated fuchi-kashira, each signed Hosono Sozaemon Masamori, circa 1700. (Christie's) $440

A Higo iron wakizashi tsuba, 6.8cm., chiselled with basket weave design, gold nunome to edge. (Wallis & Wallis) $158

A Japanese pierced iron tsuba, 7.1cm., thick squared plate with chidori joining various geometric devices. (Wallis & Wallis) $44

A circular iron tsuba, 7.1cm., pierced and chiselled in low relief, two pieces of large flowering foliage. (Wallis & Wallis) $79

One of a pair of circular iron tsuba for a Daisho, 6.9cm. and 7.3cm., signed Choshu-noju-Sakushinao Tomohisa. (Wallis & Wallis) $310

A Higo pierced iron circular tsuba, 7.6cm., thick plate with crane and pine tree. (Wallis & Wallis) $79

A circular iron tsuchimeji tsuba decorated with a gourdvine in copper and brass takazogan in Onin style, 8.2cm., and another. (Christie's) $263

A shallow mokkogata shibuichi tsuba decorated in katakiribori and gilt, inscribed Joi, 6.5cm. (Christie's) $216

A heavy pierced iron Owari tsuba of barbed mokko form, 7.4cm., pierced with bars. (Wallis & Wallis) $72

A Japanese pierced iron tsuba, 7.4cm., of circular form, with a radial pattern of hammers. (Wallis & Wallis) $44

A Japanese pierced iron tsuba, 7.4cm., of circular form, pierced with geometric designs. (Wallis & Wallis) $44

A circular iron tsuba, 7.3cm., signed Bushu noju nagamasa, depicting arrow heads in silhouette with engraved detail. (Wallis & Wallis) $59

A circular iron tsuba, 7cm., inlaid in soft metals with a hanging basket of flowers. (Wallis & Wallis) $79

A circular copper tsuba, 6.7cm. tooled with the trails of snails and applied with five gilt snails, shakudo rim. (Wallis & Wallis) $116

A Japanese pierced iron tsuba, 8cm., of irregular form, finely pierced with geometric devices. (Wallis & Wallis) $50

A shibuichi tsuba in shakudo ishimeji with egrets among rushes in silver and gilt taka-zogan, unsigned, 19th century, 7.2cm. (Christie's) $202

An iron mokko tsuba, 7.8cm., raised swollen rim inlaid with silver tendrils. (Wallis & Wallis) $100

A Japanese pierced iron tsuba, 9.5cm., of mokko form, with geometric piercings and engraved detail. (Wallis & Wallis) $74

A copper tsuba, 6.6cm., signed Hirochika, of rough hammered form. (Wallis & Wallis) $94

A circular iron Soten tsuba, 7.3cm., signed Goshu ju Soheishi sei, details in gold nunome. (Wallis & Wallis) $151

A Japanese pierced iron tsuba, 7.4cm., of irregular form, chiselled as an ear of corn in low relief with leaves. (Wallis & Wallis) $47

A 19th century copper and sentoku hari-ishime hariawase tsuba, Mito Kinko School, 8.4cm. with fitted box. (Christie's) $2,625

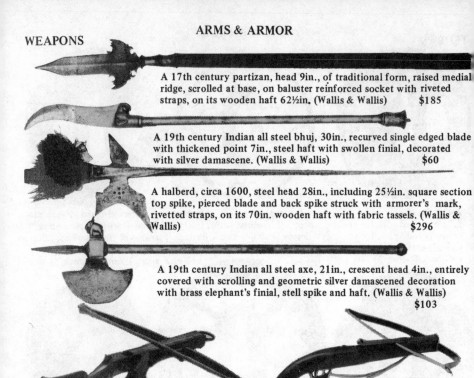

A 17th century partizan, head 9in., of traditional form, raised medial ridge, scrolled at base, on baluster reinforced socket with riveted straps, on its wooden haft 62½in. (Wallis & Wallis) $185

A 19th century Indian all steel bhuj, 30in., recurved single edged blade with thickened point 7in., steel haft with swollen finial, decorated with silver damascene. (Wallis & Wallis) $60

A halberd, circa 1600, steel head 28in., including 25½in. square section top spike, pierced blade and back spike struck with armorer's mark, rivetted straps, on its 70in. wooden haft with fabric tassels. (Wallis & Wallis) $296

A 19th century Indian all steel axe, 21in., crescent head 4in., entirely covered with scrolling and geometric silver damascened decoration with brass elephant's finial, stell spike and haft. (Wallis & Wallis) $103

A late 19th century European target crossbow, 32in., span 31½in. Beech stock, brass lock sides, thumb lever sets action, double set triggers, bridled wheels for cocking lever and original cord and fore-sight. (Wallis & Wallis) $345

An English pistol crossbow for use with darts at a target, 16in., span 15in., walnut stock, foliate engraved steel lock and brass furniture with urn finialled trigger guard. Octagonal brass 'barrel' 8¼in., circa 1800. (Wallis & Wallis) $288

A Continental boar spear, 16th/17th century, diamond section shaped head 15in., with cylindrical socket and integral riveted straps, on its octagonal wooden haft 73½in. (Wallis & Wallis) $138

A 19th century Chinese polearm of glaive form, broad, curved, single edged blade 23 x 5in., with spiked back, on its 50in. hardwood haft. (Wallis & Wallis) $198

A 17th century halberd, head 16in., with broad, shallow diamond section top blade, crescent cutting edge with back spike, on its 70in. wooden haft, silk covered with decorative brass studs. (Wallis & Wallis) $118

AUTOMATONS

An Armand Marseille musical/dancing bisque headed puppet doll, impressed 70·20,5. (Lawrence Fine Art) $777

Late 19th century Continental singing bird automaton in repousse sterling silver gilt casket, 4¼in. wide. (Reeds Rains) $769

A papier mache automaton of a clown, the head inset with fixed blue glass eyes, 18in. high. (Lawrence Fine Art) $843

A German 19th century automaton of an organ grinder with miniature dancers, on a garden stage. (Phillips) $3,750

An automaton mandolin player, with musical movement in base, stamped G. Vichy, Paris, 25½in. high. (Christie's) $2,160

A musical automaton of a bisque headed doll beside a dressing table, marked Simon & Halbig S & H 6, the doll 15in. high. (Christie's) $3,000

A composition headed automaton modelled as a standing Chinese man, 30in. high, French 1880. (Christie's) $9,000

A mid 19th century German portable barrel organ automaton, 52cm. wide. (Phillips) $9,000

A swivel headed clockwork musical walking doll, with a Parisienne type head, 21in. high. (Christie's) $1,500

63

BAROMETERS

A mid 19th century wheel barometer, with 6in. silvered dial, 97cm. high. (Phillips) $387

A 19th century mahogany marine barometer, with twin glazed ivory scales, 94cm. high. (Phillips) $2,235

A mid 19th century mahogany wheel barometer, with level signed Pastorelli, 48¼in. high. (Christie's) $1,323

A 19th century mahogany stick barometer, the plate signed W. Harris & Co., London, 37in. high. (Christie's) $675

A 19th century mahogany stick barometer, the silvered brass plate signed Dollond, London. (Christie's) $1,176

An early 19th century mahogany wheel barometer, the 8in. dial signed J. Watkins, London, 39in. high. (Christie's) $1,617

A 19th century mahogany stick barometer, the silvered brass plate signed Palmer, London, 42¼in. high. (Christie's) $2,205

A George III mahogany clock barometer, 44in. high. (Christie's) $4,116

64

An early 19th century crossbanded mahogany and boxwood strung stick barometer, the scale signed P. Caminada, Fecit, 98cm. high. (Phillips) $596

A Victorian mahogany banjo barometer. (Ball & Percival) $273

A 19th century rosewood stick barometer, signed Trigg, Guildford, 36in. high. (Christie's) $382

A 19th century wheel barometer, the 12in. dial inscribed Zuccani, London, 57in. high. (Parsons, Welch & Cowell) $651

An early 19th century mahogany Sheraton shell wheel barometer, the 8in. dial signed M. Salmone, Oxford, 99cm. high. (Phillips) $521

An early 19th century crossbanded mahogany stick barometer, the scale signed P. Manticha, London, 98cm. high. (Phillips) $521

A late 19th century oak American Forecast or Royal Polytechnic bulb Cistern barometer, 107cm. high. (Phillips) $536

A 19th century mahogany stick barometer, the silvered brass plate signed W., Foyne, 37¾in. high. (Christie's) $705

A late 17th century
walnut stick baro-
meter, the engraved
brass plates for
Summer and Winter,
48in. high.
(Christie's)
$2,499

A 19th century oak
Fisher or Sea Coast
stick barometer,
99cm. high.
(Phillips) $283

A bird's-eye maple
wheel barometer,
the 8in. dial level
signed J. Cetta,
Stroudwater, 39in.
high. (Christie's)
$705

A late 17th century
walnut stick baro-
meter, unsigned,
39½in. high.
(Christie's)
$3,234

An early 18th cen-
tury mahogany
stick barometer, the
brass plate signed
J. Patrick, London,
39in. high.
(Christie's)
$2,646

Early 19th century
aneroid barometer,
thermometer and
hydrometer, by J.
Gricci, Liverpool.
(Capes, Dunn &
Co.) $415

A George III figured
mahogany stick
barometer, the ivory
register signed Gar-
gory, 36in. long.
(Reeds Rains)
$518

An early Georgian
mahogany pillar
barometer signed
A. Grimshaw fecit,
37in. high.
(Christie's)
$1,428

An early 19th century mahogany barometer, marked Pike & Son, 38in. long. (Robt. W. Skinner Inc.) $1,300

A George I walnut signal barometer, the brass plate inscribed Made by John Patrick in the Old Bailey London, 36¼ x 29½in. (Christie's) $9,266

A 19th century mahogany stick barometer, the silvered brass plate signed N: Ortelli & Co: Fecit, 37½in. high. (Christie's) $441

A George III mahogany stick barometer, by J. Somalvico & Son, London, 45in. high. (Christie's) $825

A Georgian mahogany stick barometer, the brass plate signed Wisker York, 36in. high. (Christie's) $632

A 19th century mahogany stick barometer, the silvered brass plate signed J. Hilliard, London, 43in. high. (Christie's) $2,352

A 19th century rosewood wheel barometer, with 6in. dial, level signed Limbach, Hull, 38½in. high. (Christie's) $455

A George III mahogany stick barometer, the brass plate signed J. Bird, London, 37in. high. (Christie's) $1,102

BRONZE

One of a pair of Regency bronze and ormolu tazzas, 8in. diam. (Christie's) $2,192

A bronze model of a pug dog, signed Tsunemitsu, late Meiji/Taisho period, 13cm. high. (Christie's) $1,235

A bronze bust of an Art Nouveau maiden cast after a model by van der Straeton, circa 1900, 31cm. high. (Christie's) $630

A 16th/17th century Ming gilt lacquered bronze seated figure of Buddha, 11in. high. (Christie's) $609

One of a pair of Regency ormolu urns, 10½in. high. (Christie's) $5,950

A 19th century gilt bronze figure of a sporting hound, 'Tom', signed Barye Fils, 8½in. high. (Peter Wilson & Co.) $259

A bronze and silver oviform incense burner and pierced domed cover, 5¼in. high. (Christie's) $3,045

A 19th century bronze rounded rectangular koro and pierced domed cover, 96cm. high. (Christie's) $2,779

One of a pair of bronze rabbits, signed Tsunemitsu saku, late Meiji/Taisho period, one 19cm. high, the other 21cm. long. (Christie's) $2,007

A bronze bowl with swing handle cast after a model by G. Gurschner, signed and stamped with foundry mark K.K.K.F. Wien 1246, circa 1900. 15.5cm. (Christie's) $751

A Japanese bronze figure on stand. (F. H. Fellows & Sons) $2,190

A 19th century bronze model of a seated ape, unsigned, 16cm. high. (Christie's) $2,316

An Austrian cold painted bronze figure of a bearded Arabian warrior sat on a horse, 9¼in. high. (Reeds Rains) $458

A bronze relief of a negro, mounted on velvet in mahogany frame, 10½ x 10in. (Christie's) $469

A 19th century bronze spelter model of a camel with saddle, 10½in. high. (Christie's) $861

Late 19th century bronze sectional model of an eagle perched on rocks, 63cm. high. (Christie's) $1,003

A bronze and marble tazza cast after a model by G. Gurschner, signed, circa 1915, 17.7cm. high. (Christie's) $939

'Fisherman', a bronze vase cast from a model by J. Ofner, inscribed, 17.9cm. high. (Christie's) $783

A bronze equestrian figure of Wellington modelled by Comte D'Orsay, dated 1848, 16in. high. (Christie's) $1,300

An archaic bronze wine beaker, gu, Shang Dynasty, 25.5cm. high. (Christie's) $8,553

A bronze figure of a stag, the oval base inscribed P. J. Mene, circa 1843, 8½in. high. (Anderson & Garland) $864

A directoire bronze bust of a man on marble column, 7¼in. high. (Christie's) $783

A pair of early 19th century bronze reliefs of King George III and Queen Caroline, 8½ x 6½in. (Christie's) $939

One of a pair of early 19th century Italian bronze candlesticks in the style of G. B. Piranesi, 15¾in. high. (Christie's) $1,722

A bronze relief of a Roman Emperor in gilt composition frame, Italian, 17th century, 7½ x 6in. (Christie's) $1,252

A Regency bronze shell ink-stand supported by a dolphin on marble plinth, 5in. high. (Christie's) $2,035

A 19th century bronze conservatory fountain, 35in. high x 26in. wide, standing on an oak table. (Reeds Rains) $6,912

BRONZE

A 19th century bronze figure of a man rowing a boat, signed Jobbagy and stamped F. Dunn & Co., 25¼in. long. (Dacre, Son & Hartley) $691

A Jaeger bronze figure of a young woman on an oval marble base, inscribed, 13½in. high. (Christie's) $513

A Regency bronze, ormolu and amboyna inkstand attributed to Weeks, 12¼in. wide, 7½in. deep. (Christie's) $4,989

A French 19th century classical patinated bronze bust, 25½in. high. (Robt. W. Skinner Inc.) $550

A pair of Regency bronze figures, each with a running figure in classical dress. (Christie's) $707

'Nocturne', a bronze figure of a naked maiden cast after a model by Edward-Louis Collet, 45.7cm. high. (Christie's) $861

A bronze portrait bust of Wellington modelled by H. Weigall, by Elkington Mason & Co., 1853, 16in. high. (Christie's)$416

'Le Forgeron', a gilt bronze and glass lamp, signed Medcat and with foundry plaque, circa 1910, 29.5cm. high. (Christie's) $788

An archaic bronze tripod libation vessel, jue, Western Zhou Dynasty, 18.5cm. high. (Christie's) $2,494

BRONZE

A bronze figure of a recumbent tiger, Han Dynasty, 8cm. wide. (Christie's) $997

A large bronze tripod censer, the shoulders applied with two S-shaped handles, with a Daoguang six-character mark, 54cm. wide. (Christie's) $712

A bronze model of a rat, signed Muroe tancho saku, Meiji period, 14cm. long. (Christie's) $557

A late 19th century bronze figure of Ebisu, unsigned but probably by Miyao, on wood stand, 58.5cm. high. (Christie's) $2,300

A bronze cigarette box in the form of a girl in Middle Eastern dress, 4in. high. (Capes, Dunn & Co.) $504

A mechanical bronze figure cast after a model by C. Kauba, on a square bronze base, circa 1920, 21cm. high. (Christie's) $1,103

A Nepalese gilt bronze figure of Vajradhara seated in vajrasana on a double lotus base, late 15th/16th century, 20.2cm. high. (Christie's) $1,710

A large bronze circular mirror cast with an inscription enclosing three human figures, Han Dynasty, 22.5cm. diam., fitted box. (Christie's) $1,349

A large bronze tripod censer and pierced domed cover, six-character mark, Qing Dynasty, 55cm. high. (Christie's) $427

A bronze dish cast after a model by Gazan Chiparus, circa 1920, 31.5cm. diam. (Christie's) $503

A large bronze model of a hare, signed on the base Hisatoshi, 27cm. long. (Christie's) $2,056

A bronze figure of a flamingo, the base signed Rochard, circa 1925, 47.5cm. high. (Christie's) $1,892

One of a pair of ormolu wall brackets in the Regency style, circa 1740, possibly English, 9in. wide, 11½in. high. (Christie's) $12,830

'Thoughts', a bronze figure cast after a model by M. Giraud Riviere, circa 1930, 17.8cm. high. (Christie's) $709

One of a pair of 19th century bronze baluster vases decorated in iroe hirazogan and takazogan, 30.5cm. high. (Christie's) $2,203

A late Ming gilt bronze figure of an Empress, late 16th/17th century, 32cm. high, with wood stand. (Christie's) $997

A bronze model of a seated rabbit, signed Shosai chu, Meiji period, 17.3cm. long. (Christie's) $1,101

An archaic bronze tripod cauldron, ding, with simple loop handles, Shang Dynasty, 23.6cm. high. (Christie's) $7,840

BRONZE

A bronze group of a mother and two young toads, 7½in. wide. (Christie's) $1,015

A bronze figure, modelled as a discus thrower, mounted on a black marble base, 23cm. high. (Lawrence Fine Art) $96

An early 20th century bronze, cast as a reclining female figure, after Aime Jules Dalou, 7in. long. (Lawrence Fine Art) $944

'Anagke', (Compulsion), a bronze figure cast after a model by Gilbert Bayes, signed and dated 1918, 59cm. high. (Christie's) $15,660

Pair of bronze figures of boy musicians on marble plinths, by Kessler, 9in. high. (Worsfolds) $259

One of a pair of bronze bottle shaped vases decorated in Nikubori and Takubori, 6in. high. (Christie's) $275

A large bronze figure of a girl wearing geta, signed Seiya, Meiji period, 78.5cm. high. (Christie's) $2,162

A Restoration bronze and ormolu encrier on scrolled base cast with foliage, 17in. wide. (Christie's) $3,706

Early 19th century bronze figure of Mercury, 14in. high, on ebonized socle. (Reeds Rains) $13,024

74

A bronze sculpture of Acteon by Emile Henri Laporte, 14in. high. (Worsfolds) $288

One of a pair of Regency bronze and ormolu cassolettes in the form of antique lamps, 8¾in. high. (Christie's)$2,662

One of a set of four gilt metal three-light wall lights of Louis XV style with shaped backplates, 23in. high.(Christie's) $2,423

A bronze figure of a young woman, by S. Kinsburger, 25in. high. (Outhwaite & Litherland) $691

Pair of 19th century Japanese bronze vases of onion shape, 27in. high. (Peter Wilson & Co.) $684

A bronze model of a giraffe, 17in. high. (Christie's) $2,662

A bronze figure cast after a model by Hugo Lederer, modelled as a naked maiden wearing a turban, signed, circa 1925, 43cm. high. (Christie's) $1,096

An equestrian bronze group of Wellington, signed Boyer a Paris and stamped Registered 9, Nov. 1852, 6in. high. (Christie's) $390

A bronze figure of a harlequin, cast after a model by St. Marceaux, signed and dated 1879 and with A. Collas foundry mark, 73cm. high. (Christie's) $1,644

BRONZE

A 19th century French bronze model of a Shetland pony carrying a dead stag, signed I. Bonheur, 22.5 x 25.5cm. (Christie's) $690

A silvered copper and bronze model of a snipe stepping over rocks, Meiji period, 49cm. long. (Christie's) $1,081

Signed French bronze dog, circa 1875. (British Antique Exporters) $271

A gilt bronze figure of Buddha standing, 13th/14th century, 19.2cm. high. (Christie's) $5,417

An early 20th century French bronze statuette of a naked woman, known as 'La Verite Meconnue', after Aime Jules Dalou, 22.5cm. high.(Christie's) $1,456

One of a pair of ormolu three-branch candelabra of Louis XVI design, 16½in. high. (Christie's) $3,888

A late 19th/early 20th century French bronze group of St. Michael on horseback slaying the dragon, signed E. Fremiet, 58.5cm. high. (Christie's) $2,913

A Lorenzl gilt and painted bronze figure of a lady holding the hem of her skirt, on onyx base, 10in. high. (Christie's) $650

French bronze bust, circa 1850. (British Antique Exporters) $198

BRONZE

One of a pair of large 19th century French bronze groups of a setter with a pheasant and a pointer with a hare, signed J. Moigniez, 42cm. high. (Christie's) $10,735

One of a pair of 19th century bronze figural lamps, signed L. V. E. Robert, with milk glass shades, 24in. high without fixture. (Robt. W. Skinner Inc.) $1,100

A 19th century French bronze group of a ten point stag brought down by two Scottish hounds, cast from a model by A. L. Barye, 39 x 57cm. (Christie's) $5,827

One of a pair of 19th century ormolu and bronze nine-light candelabra on hexagonal boulle plinths, the candelabra 46in. high, the pedestals 57in. high.(Christie's) $16,329

A late 19th century English bronze model of a wild cat crouching on a rocky promontory, cast from a model by J. Macallan Swan, 23.5cm. high. (Christie's) $2,453

One of a pair of ormolu candlesticks in the style of the Slodtz brothers, 9½in. high. (Christie's) $2,280

An early 20th century French bronze statuette of a seated nude drying herself, after Aime Jules Dalou, 34.5cm. high. (Christie's) $11,502

An Art Deco bronze figure on a hexagonal base, inscribed Barbara MacDonald, 1936, 27in. high. (Christie's) $1,029

A 19th century French gilt metal model of a seated Chinese fortune teller, 13in. high. (Christie's) $2,488

BRONZE

One of a pair of bronze bears, cast three character mark, 6½in long. (Lawrence Fine Art) $1,116

A gold splashed bronze censer of bucket shape with a flared rim, cast character mark of Hsuan-te, 4½in. diam. (Lawrence Fine Art) $733

A bronze group of toads, 3½in. long. (Lawrence Fine Art) $542

One of a pair of bronze vases cast in high relief with dragons among clouds, 14¾in. high. (Lawrence Fine Art) $446

A bronze square mirror, Tang Dynasty, 10.7cm. square, fitted box. (Christie's) $7,144

A bronze mounted stoneware vase designed by O. Eckmann, 50.5cm. high. (Christie's) $1,409

Bronze figure of 'The Cossack's Adieu', by Eugene Lancere, 1848-86, 16in. high. (Robt. W. Skinner Inc.) $1,800

'Exotic Dancer', a gilt bronze and ivory figure cast and carved from a model by A. Gori, 37.5cm. high. (Christie's) $1,722

A miniature Nepalese gilt bronze figure of a Saviouress seated in lalitasana, 1½in. high. (Lawrence Fine Art) $478

BRONZE

Late 19th century Russian bronze of a wolf, signed Lieberich Fabr. C.F. Woerffel, 5.7/8in. high. (Robt. W. Skinner Inc.) $592

A Friedrich Gornik Viennese bronze casket, the handle modelled as Diana the huntress, circa 1925, 31.5 x 18.5cm. (Christie's) $626

A 19th century bronze of a puppy, Japan, signed on base, 5¼in. high. (Robt. W. Skinner Inc.) $740

A Regency bronze and ormolu inkstand modelled as a dolphin, 3½in. wide. (Christie's) $932

A late Ming gilt lacquered bronze figure of Guandi, 16th/early 17th century, 70cm. high. (Christie's) $3,429

'Dance of the Harlequinade', a gilt bronze and ivory figure, cast and carved after a model by Th. Ullmann, 30cm. high. (Christie's) $1,566

One of a pair of late 19th century bronze incense burners, 14.5/8in. high. (Robt. W. Skinner Inc.) $550

A bronze and champleve enamel duck incense burner, the wings forming the detachable cover, 8in. long. (Lawrence Fine Art) $271

A bronze bell suspended by a dragon loop, ebonized wood frame, 14½in. high. (Lawrence Fine Art) $159

A Godard patinated metal figure, 'Bubble Dance', 35cm. high. (Lawrence Fine Art) $578

A bronze and champleve enamel winged horse incense burner, 12½in. long. (Lawrence Fine Art) $558

A gilt metal figure of a dancing girl, mounted on a cylindrical marble base, 1930's. (Lawrence Fine Art) $146

Late 19th century Japanese bronze vase with elephant head handles, 10½in. high. (Robt. W. Skinner Inc.) $740

An Egyptian bronze cat's head, probably 6th century BC, 1¾in. high.(Lawrence Fine Art) $638

A bronze hu of square baluster section and bracket handles, probably 18th century, 9in. high. (Lawrence Fine Art) $127

'Flower Seller' a gilt bronze and ivory figure cast and carved from a model by A. Gori, 38.5cm. high. (Christie's) $4,071

'The Fan Dancer', a bronze and ivory figure by Chiparus, on marble and onyx base, 15in. high. (Christie's) $6,615

A bronze and champleve enamel group of an elephant and rider, 18in. high. (Lawrence Fine Art) $638

An 18th century archaistic bronze jue, on three splayed triangular legs, 8in. high. (Lawrence Fine Art) $271

A 19th century bronze Foo dog incense burner, China, 9in. high. (Robt. W. Skinner Inc.) $900

A parcel gilt bronze vase cast after a model by Gustav Gurschner, stamped K.K.K.F. Wien 1411, 23cm. high. (Christie's) $500

One of a pair of 19th century Faux bronze planters with gilt lion's head mask handles, 24in. high. (Christie's) $6,600

A pair of 17th century bronze figures of dignitaries, 11in. high. (Lawrence Fine Art) $877

An archaic bronze tripod libation vessel, jue, Western Zhou Dynasty, 20.5cm. high. (Christie's) $3,175

'Dancing Girl', a silvered bronze and ivory figure cast from a model by Lorenzl, decorated by Crejo, 22.3cm. high. (Christie's) $939

'Bat Dancer', a bronze and ivory figure cast and carved after a model by F. Preiss, 23.6cm. high. (Christie's) $5,324

'Sunshade Girl', a gilt bronze and ivory figure cast and carved from a model by F. Preiss, 20.2cm. high. (Christie's) $2,035

BRONZE

A bronze jue with single loop handle headed by an animal mask, 6½in. high. (Lawrence Fine Art) $223

A bronze figure of a naked young lady dancing, by Karl Perl, 24½in. high. (Christie's)$1,584

A Chinese bronze and parcel gilt maroon lacquer buddha, 9½in. high. (Lawrence Fine Art) $350

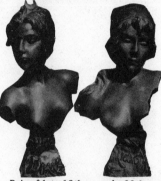

'Priestess', a gilt bronze and ivory figure cast and carved from a model by D. Chiparus, 43cm. high. (Christie's) $4,384

Pair of late 19th or early 20th century French bronze busts of Mignon and Diana, signed on the shoulders E. Villanis, 36.5cm. high. (Christie's) $1,533

A late 19th/early 20th century French parcel gilt bronze statuette of a seated Arab youth, signed E. Peynot, 67.5cm. high. (Christie's) $12,268

A late 19th century French bronze statuette of Diana reclining on a crescent moon, signed Denecheau, revolving on a marble socle, 99cm. high overall. (Christie's) $18,403

A 19th century French bronze statuette of a Turkish warrior, on a naturalistic base, 63cm. high. (Christie's) $9,201

An early 20th century English bronze group of Salome and Herodias, cast from a model by Charles de Sousy Ricketts, 45cm. high. (Christie's) $9,968

A George III mahogany peat bucket of cylindrical tapering form with two brass bands and handle, 15in. diam. (British Antique Exporters)$750

Victorian leather bucket, circa 1860. (British Antique Exporters) $81

A late 18th century brass bound mahogany plate bucket with brass swing handle, 17in. high. (Dacre, Son & Hartley) $979

A George III brass bound mahogany plate bucket with copper liner, 11½in. diam. (Christie's) $1,496

A George III brass bound mahogany plate bucket with later brass liner, 14½in. diam. (Christie's) $3,810

A George III brass bound mahogany plate bucket with later circular liner, 11¼in. diam. (Christie's) $2,661

Early 19th century Dutch brass bound fruitwood and ebonized bucket with carrying handle, 13in. high. (Christie's) $885

A Victorian wooden fire bucket, 1860. (British Antique Exporters) $79

An Irish mid Georgian brass bound mahogany peat bucket with carrying handle, 15in. diam. (Christie's) $3,132

Mahogany tea caddy with ivory key escutcheon, 1850. (British Antique Exporters) $87

Early 19th century Palais Royale casket on four lion's paw feet with serpent handle to the hinged cover, 5in. long. (Christie's) $510

Late 17th/early 18th century Continental tortoiseshell and mother-of-pearl mounted box, 18¼in. wide. (Lawrence Fine Art) $4,395

Early 19th century carved pine watch hutch, 17in. high, 8½in. wide. (Robt. W. Skinner Inc.) $950

A George III satinwood, rosewood and fruitwood tea caddy, the crossbanded lid with a silver plaque with initials J.E.R., 12¾in. wide. (Christie's) $1,676

One of a pair of Regency mahogany knife boxes with turned finials and fitted interiors. (Christie's) $3,680

Late 18th century Anglo-Indian ivory workbox with fitted interior, one drawer and a writing slide, 19in. wide. (Christie's) $1,367

Early 19th century rectangular document box, bunko, 43.1 x 33.9cm. (Christie's) $3,672

A Victorian walnut brass bound letter box, 1850. (British Antique Exporters) $156

Northern Woodlands birch-bark container, Tetes-de-Boule, in the form of a trunk, 10¼in. wide. (Robt. W. Skinner Inc.) $300

An 18th century Anglo-Indian vizagapatam casket with hinged lid and a drawer, 17in. wide. (Christie's) $2,662

Victorian leather box, circa 1880. (British Antique Exporters) $41

Victorian metal bound oak humidor. (British Antique Exporters) $133

A rosewood fitted toilet case with eight glass bottles and boxes, five with Sheffield plated lids, 12½in. wide. (Capes, Dunn & Co.) $79

Late 16th century Momoyama period Christian host box or pyx (seiheibako), 9.1cm. high. (Christie's) $27,993

Victorian mahogany coal box, 1860. (British Antique Exporters) $67

An early 19th century Anglo-Indian vizagapatam ivory and ebony games box, 18in. wide. (Christie's) $1,710

Early 19th century Palais Royale rectangular jewel casket formed as a miniature dressing table, 5½in. long. (Christie's) $766

Late 17th/early 18th century Indo-Portuguese tortoiseshell and mother-of-pearl portable box, 15¾in. wide. (Lawrence Fine Art) $2,035

Victorian rosewood and maple lap desk, 1860. (British Antique Exporters) $251

A Charles X cut steel mounted and maple casket of sarcophagus shape with carrying handles, 19½in. wide. (Christie's) $2,237

One of a pair of George III mahogany cutlery boxes with silver key plates, 8¾in. wide. (Christie's) $1,065

An early 19th century French Palais Royale musical jewel casket in the form of a miniature piano, 8¾in. long. (Christie's) $3,888

A Regency parcel gilt and scarlet lacquer tea cannister, 17½in. high. (Christie's) $1,218

A George III treen pear tea caddy, the lid with a stalk and enclosing a plain interior. (Christie's) $1,522

A George IV rosewood and satinwood writing box, 15½in. wide. (Christie's) $349

One of a pair of William IV black japanned coal boxes with domed oval lids, 20in. wide. (Christie's) $1,508

A wood and lacquer box, the cover inset with a Komai panel decorated in Iroe Hira-zogan, 7¼in. wide. (Christie's) $246

Victorian carved box with fitted interior, 1850. (British Antique Exporters) $164

A black and gold lacquer two handled workbox open-ing to reveal a fitted interior with ivory accessories, 15½in. wide. (Christie's) $290

A Victorian 12in. rectangular coromandel wood and brass bound vanity case, maker's mark J.V. (Parsons Welch & Cowell) $444

A Regency brass inlaid maho-gany writing box with leather lined sloping writing surface, and fitted with a Bramah lock, 20in. wide. (Christie's) $622

One of a pair of George III mahogany cutlery boxes with boxwood stringing, 8¾in. wide. (Christie's) $1,065

A rosewood and Tunbridge-ware tea caddy of waisted form, the domed top depict-ing Battle Abbey, 9in. wide. (Parsons, Welch & Cowell) $490

A Sheraton period cross-banded tea caddy, having two division interior with Bristol blue glass blending bowl, 10¾in. wide. (Geering & Colyer) $431

A Regency black and gilt japanned coal box with rounded rectangular domed lid, and another, 19in. wide. (Christie's) $6,350

A mid 18th century painted pine trinket box, 7½in. wide. (Robt. W. Skinner Inc.) $1,900

A George III mahogany decanter box, the divided interior with six bottles, an oval salver and two glasses, 10½in. wide. (Christie's) $843

Early 19th century Palais Royale musical necessaire formed as a piano, 7½in. long. (Christie's) $2,877

A George III mahogany cutlery box, the shaped top inlaid with the Prince of Wales's feathers, 9in. wide. with another, 9¾in. wide. (Christie's) $1,722

An Anglo-Indian Regency calamander-wood box enclosing a fitted interior, 15½in. wide. (Christie's) $947

One of a pair of Sheraton period knife boxes in inlaid mahogany, original interiors, 13in. high. (Hobbs & Chambers) $1,460

Early 19th century suzuribako decorated in gold, silver and red hiramakie, takamakie, hirame and heidatsu on a nashiji ground, 22.2 x 20.2cm. (Christie's) $2,350

One of a pair of George III mahogany vase-shaped cutlery boxes, 26in. high. (Christie's) $3,888

A 19th century circular kogo decorated in gold hiramakie on a red ground, 7.9cm. diam. (Christie's) $1,101

CADDIES & BOXES

A Momoyama period rectangular black lacquered wood casket with hinged domed cover decorated in gold lacquer and shell inlay, circa 1600. (Christie's) $2,488

Antique cased set of three scent bottles with ormolu mounts and painted porcelain stoppers. (Worsfolds) $230

A brown and gold lacquer box with rounded corners on four winged dragon feet, 8½in. wide. (Christie's) $493

One of a pair of George III mahogany cutlery boxes with fitted interiors and silver key plates, 9in. wide. (Christie's) $3,067

A William and Mary walnut table bureau, the leather-lined fall-flap enclosing a fitted interior, 22¼in. wide. (Christie's) $1,530

A George III shagreen necessaire of shaped upright form, circa 1760, 2¾in. high. (Christie's) $1,555

Late 19th century roironuri two-tiered covered box, unsigned, School of Zeshin, 24.2 x 19.7 x 19.2cm. (Christie's) $2,162

A 17th century Flemish ebony and ivory table cabinet, on later bun feet, 21in. wide. (Christie's) $1,995

A late 19th century rectangular tabako-bon decorated in gold and silver hiramakie, hirame and heidatsu on a yasuriko ground, 20.5cm. wide. (Christie's)$954

A 45 x 107mm. Ernemann Reflex stereoscopic camera of Jumelle-form with Ernemann Doppel Anastigmat 75mm. f 4.5 lenses, in leather case. (Christie's) $256

A Nikkormat FT 2 35mm. single lens reflex camera, with various lenses, in hold-all. (Christie's) $347

A 6 x 9cm. Ontoflex twin-lens reflex camera, No. 8746, with a Tessar lens. (Christie's) $186

A 9 x 12cm. Tropical Goerz Tenax folding plate camera with Xenar lens, in leather case. (Christie's)$270

A 4.5 x 6cm. Ernemann Miniature-Ernoflex folding reflex camera with Ernon 7.5cm. f 3.5 lens in helical mount, in leather case. (Christie's) $675

A quarter-plate Tropical Model Improved Artist Reflex camera manufactured by The London Stereoscopic Co., with Tessar lens. (Christie's) $248

A quarter-plate Gandolfi hand-and-stand camera in mahogany casing, with Aldis Anastigmat lens. (Christie's) $405

A 6 x 9cm. Mentor folding reflex camera with Tessar lens. (Christie's) $198

A 15 x 10cm. Ica Tropical folding plate camera in metal teak casing with Tessar lens in dial-set Compur shutter. (Christie's) $135

An early brass mounted 35mm. hand-cranked cinematograph projector with R.R. lens, 15in. high. (Christie's) $1,755

An Alpa Reflex 35mm. s.l.r. camera, Mod. 6, No. 38996, with Kern Switar, Schneider and Alpa lenses. (Christie's) $337

A wide-angle Rolleiflex twin-lens Reflex camera, No. W 2490454 with Distagon lens, in carrying case. (Christie's) $1,350

A four-lens multiple-exposure camera, probably by J. Lancaster & Sons, taking four 2 x 1½in. exposures on one quarter plate, in mahogany casing. (Christie's) $1,740

A prototype V.P. mono-rail camera in aluminium casing, with Tessar lens. (Christie's) $372

A Stirn's Waistcoat detective camera, No. 5065, in nickel-plated brass casing, taking six circular exposures on circular plate. (Christie's) $696

A Zeiss Contaflex 35mm. twin-lens reflex camera, No. Z 42268 with a Sonnar taking lens and a Sucher-Objectiv lens, and an exposure meter. (Christie's) $558

A 2¼ x 2¼ Redding's Luzo roll-film camera in brass re-inforced mahogany casing, Patent No. 17328. (Christie's) $652

A quarter-plate box-form mahogany survey camera by by J. H. Dallmeyer, London, in mahogany casing with lens, on brass tripod mount. (Christie's) $580

A Leica M2 camera No. 938-006, with 3.5 Elmar 50mm. lens and Leica meter, in leather case. (Onslow's) $372

A Houghton's 45 x 170mm. Royal Mail Stereolette camera in mahogany casing with box-comb joints. (Christie's) $742

A London Stereoscopic Co.'s Stereoscopic changing box camera in mahogany casing, taking paired exposures on 6 x 5.5cm. plates. (Christie's) $551

A tail board folding field camera by Stanley, with Ross 8¾in. wide angle Xpres f4 lens. (Onslow's) $119

A Thornton-Pickard quarter-plate triple extension field camera. (Onslow's) $253

An Ernemann Liliput 4.5 x 6cm. folding bellows vest pocket camera. (Onslow's) $59

A quarter-plate Redding's Luzo box-form roll-film camera in ever-ready case. (Christie's) $797

A Lancaster International field camera, with Busch Rapid Aplanat No. 3 10in. lens, in canvas carrying case. (Onslow's) $149

A Kodak No. 1 Panoram camera Model A. (Onslow's) $111

An ormolu and cut glass six-light chandelier, the boss hung with a profusion of pendant drops, 36in. high. (Christie's) $2,138

A neo-classical giltwood eight-branch chandelier with foliate corona, 28in. high. (Christie's) $2,708

A Regency cut glass and ormolu chandelier with spreading waterfall drops, 38in. high. (Christie's) $6,901

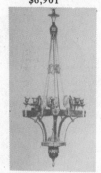

Venetian cut glass triple chandelier hung with cut glass drops, 31in. high. (Worsfolds) $770

Victorian brass three-light chandelier, 1880. (British Antique Exporters) $139

A Charles X ormolu and bronze chandelier, fitted for electricity, 45in. high. (Christie's) $1,140

An Empire ormolu cut glass twelve-light chandelier, the nozzles fitted for electricity, 36in. high. (Christie's) $4,665

A 19th century brass three-tiered chandelier, 47in. diam. (Christie's) $5,500

An Empire ormolu and bronze ten-light lamp, 39in. high. (Christie's) $4,847

AMERICAN

Late 19th century Dedham crackleware vase, incised CPUS, 7in. high. (Robt. W. Skinner Inc.) $1,600

A Walrath pottery pitcher and five mugs, circa 1910, pitcher 6½in. high. (Robt. W. Skinner Inc.) $1,300

A Chelsea Keramic Art pottery vase with blue-green glossy glaze, circa 1885, 11¼in. high. (Robt. W. Skinner Inc.) $550

A 19th century Santa Ana polychrome jar, 12in. diam. (Robt. W. Skinner Inc.) $2,800

An early 20th century Walley Art pottery molded vase, 6¾in. high. (Robt. W. Skinner Inc.) $625

A Santa Clara blackware storage jar, 20½in. high. (Robt. W. Skinner Inc.) $3,000

A Marblehead vase decorated with blue floral trees on slate blue ground, circa 1915, 5¼in. high, 3¼in. diam. (Robt. W. Skinner Inc.) $700

Saturday Evening Girls pottery motto plate, Mass., circa 1914, signed S.G. for Sara Galner, 7½in. diam. (Robt. W. Skinner Inc.) $3,700

A Walrath floral decorated vase, circa 1910, 7in. high. (Robt. W. Skinner Inc.) $1,500

AMERICAN

A majolica handled serving dish, by Griffen, Smith & Hill, Penn., 12.1/8in. long, 1876-90. (Robt. W. Skinner Inc.) $100

A Dedham pottery crackle-ware vase, 8in. high, circa 1900. (Robt. W. Skinner Inc.) $2,100

A majolica serving dish, by Griffen, Smith & Hill, Penn., 1876-90, 12¼in. long. (Robt. W. Skinner Inc.) $175

A decorated Marblehead vase of squat bulbous form with incised leaves and berries, circa 1919, 3½in. high. (Robt. W. Skinner Inc.) $475

A G. E. Ohr pottery vase, the concave-shaped mouth with elongated folded handles, circa 1900, 10in. high. (Robt. W. Skinner Inc.) $3,400

A Marblehead pottery four-colour vase, signed H.T. for Hannah Tutt, circa 1915, 4½in. high, 4.1/8in. diam. (Robt. W. Skinner Inc.) $900

A Weller Dickensware vase, circa 1900, 16in. high. (Robt. W. Skinner Inc.) $325

A finely decorated Hopi Placca pottery bowl. (Robt. W. Skinner Inc.) $504

A Losanti porcelain relief decorated vase by L. McLaughlin, circa 1901-04, 7½in. high. (Robt. W. Skinner Inc.) $10,500

95

Late 17th century Arita blue and white octagonal baluster jar with wood cover, 53cm. high. (Christie's) $4,700

An 18th century Arita blue and white deep bowl decorated with lobed panels, 17.5cm. diam. (Christie's) $1,166

An Arita blue and white broad oviform ewer with loop handle, circa 1670, 24cm. high. (Christie's) $514

Late 17th century Arita blue and white oviform vase, fitted with a silver cover and thumbpiece, probably 18th century, inset with a German thaler of 1660, 19.7cm. high. (Christie's) $699

Late 17th century Arita oviform vase decorated in underglaze blue, 26cm. high. (Christie's) $926

Late 17th century Arita blue and white baluster tankard with loop handle, 19.5cm. high. (Christie's) $1,166

Late 17th century Arita globular apothecary bottle decorated in underglaze blue, 20cm. high. (Christie's) $1,010

Late 19th century Arita model of a seated tiger decorated in iron-red and black enamels and gilt, signed, 15.5cm. high. (Christie's) $926

An Arita apothecary bottle painted in underglaze blue, circa 1665/80, 15½in. high (Christie's) $6,960

BELLEEK

A Belleek 'dolphin' candlestick, modelled as a putto
seated on a dolphin, 19.5cm.
high, no. D343. (Phillips)
$1,078

A pair of Belleek candlestick
figures of a boy and girl
basket bearer, 22cm. high.
(Phillips) $5,328

A Belleek figure of a cooper
standing before two barrels
forming vases, 21cm. high.
(Christie's) $3,080

A Belleek model of a lighthouse, impressed Belleek
and black printed marks,
registration mark for 1873,
23cm. high. (Christie's)
$1,078

A Belleek rectangular plaque
painted by Horatio H. Calder,
black printed Belleek mark,
First Period, 17 x 11.3cm.
(Christie's) $3,850

A Belleek First Period figure
of 'The Crouching Venus',
18¼in. high. (Christie's)
$1,160

A Belleek 'tulip' vase, standing
in a circular basket base encrusted with leaves, 31cm. high,
no. D93. (Phillips)
$3,388

A pair of Belleek figures of
'Meditation' and 'Affection',
35cm. high, nos. D1134 and
D20. (Phillips) $2,772

One of a pair of Belleek
nautilus vases, naturally
modelled and heightened
in pink, 21cm. high.
(Christie's) $1,540

BERLIN

CHINA

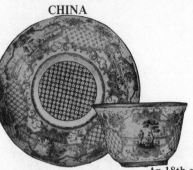

A Berlin two-handled oval ornithological soup tureen and domed cover, blue scepter marks and Pressnummer 35, circa 1760-70, 36cm. wide. (Christie's) $2,478

A Berlin enamel teabowl and matching saucer, workshop of Pierre Fromery, circa 1730, teabowl 2¾in. diam., saucer 4½in. diam. (Christie's) $6,713

An 18th century Berlin faience red lacquered baluster vase and domed cover, mock Chinese seal mark, Funcke's factory, 71cm. high. (Christie's) $2,147

Early 20th century KPM porcelain plaque, 'La Belle Chocolatiere', used as the trade mark for Baker's Cocoa and stamped Dresden, 8¾ x 6in. (Robt. W. Skinner Inc.) $1,400

A Berlin plaque, The Madonna and Child, signed Wagner, 24 x 16cm., impressed scepter and KPM. (Lawrence Fine Art) $638

A 19th century Berlin porcelain KPM plaque, decorated at the Gebruder-Heubach factory, 10 x 7in. (Robt. W. Skinner Inc.) $1,800

A Berlin white three-light candelabrum, blue clove mark and various incised and impressed marks, circa 1770, 28cm. high. (Christie's) $648

A Berlin rectangular plaque painted after F. Sturm, impressed scepter and KPM marks, circa 1880, 31.5 x 25.5cm. (Christie's) $933

A Berlin white group emblematic of medicine from a set of the Sciences modelled by F. E. Meyer, late 18th century, 29cm. high. (Christie's) $729

CHINA

BOW

A Bow square dish painted in a pale Kakiemon palette with the Flaming Tortoise Pattern, circa 1754, about 18.5cm. square. (Christie's) $582

A Bow white figure of an owl with molded overlapping plumage, circa 1758, 19cm. high. (Christie's) $1,840

A pair of Bow figures of a cock and hen, both on scroll molded pad bases, circa 1758, 10cm. high. (Christie's) $5,214

BRISTOL

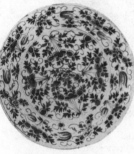

A Bristol delft bowl, the interior painted in iron-red and the exterior in blue, circa 1740, 22.5cm. diam. (Christie's) $3,680

Mid 18th century Bristol delft plate decorated in iron red, blue and green, 13½in. diam. (Woolley & Wallis) $580

A Bristol two-handled cup and trembleuse saucer of ogee outline, marked B6 in blue enamel. (Lawrence Fine Art) $957

A Bristol delft blue-dash Adam and Eve charger, circa 1720, 34cm. diam. (Christie's) $1,005

A Bristol globular teapot and cover with ear-shaped handle, Richard Champion's Factory, circa 1775, 16cm. high. (Christie's) $1,993

A Bristol delft blue-dash tulip charger, the reverse with a tin glaze, circa 1720, 34.5cm. diam. (Christie's) $920

BRITISH

CHINA

Victorian white china foot bath, circa 1880. (British Antique Exporters) $87

A signed Victorian pottery jardiniere, 1875. (British Antique Exporters) $43

Victorian majolica serving plate, 1860. (British Antique Exporters) $21

Victorian blue and white monogrammed slop pail, 1860. (British Antique Exporters) $75

A finely decorated floral bowl and pitcher, circa 1860. (British Antique Exporters) $43

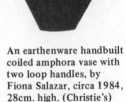

An earthenware handbuilt coiled amphora vase with two loop handles, by Fiona Salazar, circa 1984, 28cm. high. (Christie's) $288

A late 17th century Westerwald blue and gray baluster stoneware jug, the neck and foot within silver mounts, London, probably 1851, 20.5cm. high. (Christie's) $367

Part of a Foley Art china coffee set designed by G. Logan, with printed stylized rose motif and a diamond-shape pattern. (Christie's) $551

Saltglaze water jar, circa 1880. (British Antique Exporters) $74

Victorian floral jug and basin, 1860. (British Antique Exporters) $68

Victorian floral china salad bowl, 1880. (British Antique Exporters) $41

Mid 19th century soup tureen and stand, 'Italian Scenery', by J. Meir & Son, 23in. diam. (Capes, Dunn & Co.) $72

Victorian floral pitcher, circa 1860. (British Antique Exporters) $24

A large Foley Intarsio circular pottery plate painted with sunflowers, 12½in. diam. (Christie's) $224

Early 20th century jug and basin set, 1910. (British Antique Exporters) $29

Victorian biscuit barrel with plated top. (British Antique Exporters) $51

Four historical blue pieces, England, early 19th century, pitcher 6½in. high. (Robt. W. Skinner Inc.)$900

A Yorkshire pearlware portrait bust of an officer, circa 1800, 30cm. high. (Christie's) $1,380

BRITISH

CHINA

An H. & R. Daniel green ground crested dish from the Shrewsbury Service, circa 1827, 48cm. wide. (Christie's) $920

A Parian bust of Wellington wearing military uniform, 14in. high. (Christie's) $234

One of a pair of Caughley quatrefoil sauce tureens and covers, 14.5cm. wide. (Christie's)$1,723

A Brownfield jug modelled as a goose, the handle modelled as a standing monkey pushing open its beak, circa 1860, 35.5cm. high. (Christie's) $393

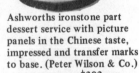

Ashworths ironstone part dessert service with picture panels in the Chinese taste, impressed and transfer marks to base. (Peter Wilson & Co.) $302

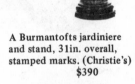

A Burmantofts jardiniere and stand, 31in. overall, stamped marks. (Christie's) $390

An English porcelain oviform jug with angular loop handle, circa 1821, 21.5cm. high. (Christie's) $460

One of a pair of baskets and stands, the baskets with pierced trellis sides and the stands with pierced borders, 8¼in. diam. (Christie's) $1,160

A 14th century English globular jug with grooved strap handle, covered in a greenish ochre iridescent glaze, 28.5cm. high. (Christie's) $613

A Brownfield jug modelled as a cockatoo, standing on logs, his crest forming the spout, 24.6cm. high. (Christie's) $523

A globular green glazed bowl designed by Dr. C. Dresser, 14.5cm. high. (Christie's) $819

A Parian bust of Wellington wearing classical dress, after E. W. Wyon impressed mark, 16in. high. (Christie's) $130

A Morrisware pear-shaped vase painted with mauve flowerheads and green foliage on a blue ground, 11in. high. (Christie's) $290

Part of a set of twenty-five late 18th century English tinglaze tiles. (Woolley & Wallis) $493

An H. J. Wood Bursley Ware vase, slip-trailed and colored 'Seed-Poppy' design, circa 1930-5, 12in. high. (Capes, Dunn & Co.) $100

A Linthorpe teapot, the design attributed to Dr. C. Dresser, 21.3cm. high. (Christie's) $172

A porcelain thrown and laminated triangular spiral vase modelled in pale blue, by D. Feibleman, 14.4cm. high, 1983. (Christie's) $936

A large Louis Wain pottery vase, modelled as a seated cat, 25.4cm. high. (Christie's) $1,734

BRITISH

A porcelain wide bowl, by
Mary Rich, painted in gold
lustre, 1985, 24.3cm. diam.
(Christie's) $281

Floral china chamber pot,
1850. (British Antique
Exporters) $43

Victorian blue and white
tureen by Norman, 1880.
(British Antique Exporters)
$64

A Foley Intarsio tapering
cylindrical vase with bulbous rim, 8½in. high.
(Christie's) $294

A Davenport part dinner service,
decorated with Oriental flowers
in Imari colors , pattern no. 51,
circa 1850-70. (Woolley &
Wallis) $1,238

An R. Philippe white glazed
pottery group, modelled as
a naked lady holding a child,
15¼in. high. (Christie's)
$64

A Lowestoft square inkwell,
the base inscribed in black,
'Eliz,^th. Buckle 1775', 5cm.
high. (Lawrence Fine Art)
$4,306

A Linthorpe flaring organic
form bowl designed by Dr.
C. Dresser, 4in. high.
(Christie's) $617

A majolica tazza, England,
with Art Nouveau poly-
chrome iris decoration,
circa 1900, 9¼in. diam.
(Robt. W. Skinner Inc.)
$125

CAIGER-SMITH

CHINA

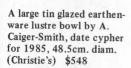

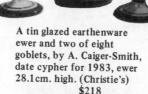

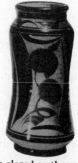

A large tin glazed earthenware lustre bowl by A. Caiger-Smith, date cypher for 1985, 48.5cm. diam. (Christie's) $548

A tin glazed earthenware ewer and two of eight goblets, by A. Caiger-Smith, date cypher for 1983, ewer 28.1cm. high. (Christie's) $218

A tin glazed earthenware albarello by A. Caiger-Smith, date cypher for 1985, 27.3cm. high. (Christie's) $140

CANTON

Late 19th century Oriental footed porcelain fruit bowl, China, 15in. long, 3½in. high. (Robt. W. Skinner Inc.) $850

A 19th century Canton famille rose bowl, painted with birds and butterflies amongst fruit and flower sprays, 37cm. diam. (Christie's) $945

A Canton enamel circular box and cover, painted Qianlong six character mark, 3in. diam. (Christie's) $261

A Canton enamel saucer dish painted with figures standing by a pond, 6¼in. diam. (Christie's) $232

A large Cantonese bowl, 22in. diam. (Edgar Horn) $6,935

A 19th century Canton hexagonal garden seat of barrel shape, decorated in famille rose enamels, 47cm. high. (Lawrence Fine Art) $1,595

MICHAEL CARDEW

CHINA

A stoneware casserole and cover with strap handle, by Michael Cardew, impressed MC and Wenford Bridge seals, circa 1970, 29cm. diam. (Christie's) $374

An earthenware footed bowl by Michael Cardew, impressed MC and Winchcombe Pottery seals, circa 1935, 26cm. diam. (Christie's) $1,440

A large stoneware wide bowl by Michael Cardew, covered in a khaki glaze over white slip, circa 1978, 38cm. diam. (Christie's) $500

An earthenware oviform jug by Michael Cardew, impressed MC and Winchcombe Pottery seal, circa 1930, 22.6cm. high. (Christie's) $359

An earthenware slip-decorated rhyme tankard by Michael Cardew, circa 1926, 13.7cm. high. (Christie's) $489

A stoneware coffee pot and cover by Michael Cardew, impressed MC and Wenford Bridge seals, 25.3cm. high. (Christie's) $288

A stoneware large bowl on shallow foot, attributed to Michael Cardew, Abuja seals obscured by glaze, 27cm. diam. (Christie's)$432

An earthenware tankard, by Michael Cardew, covered in a pale yellow slip with brown base border, circa 1925, 12.8cm. high. (Christie's) $92

An earthenware oval baking dish, decorated by Michael Cardew and molded by E. Comfort, circa 1932, 31.9cm. wide. (Christie's) $939

106

MICHAEL CARDEW

CHINA

A large earthenware bowl on shallow foot by Michael Cardew, dated 1969, 35.4cm. diam. (Christie's) $375

A stoneware dish with flared sides, attributed to Michael Cardew, impressed Wenford Bridge seal, 44cm. wide. (Christie's) $156

A stoneware deep bowl, by Michael Cardew, impressed MC and Wenford Bridge seals, circa 1975, 30.5cm. diam. (Christie's) $548

CARLTONWARE

A Carltonware service decorated in polychrome enamels, coffee pot 20.4cm. high. (Christie's) $1,174

A Carltonware vase with polychrome decoration on a mottled purple and white ground, circa 1930, 26.7cm. high. (Christie's)$315

One of a pair of Carltonware vases, 21cm. high, and a tray, 25cm. wide. (Christie's) $783

A Carltonware rouge royale diamond-shaped dish with two 'fin' handles, 12in.wide. (Capes, Dunn & Co.) $21

A Carltonware oviform ginger jar and cover, painted with clusters of stylized flowerheads and bold geometric bands, 31cm. high. (Christie's) $1,566

A Carltonware plaque painted in gilt, orange, blue, green and white with wisteria and exotic plants, 15½in. diam. (Christie's) $308

CHELSEA

One of a pair of Chelsea leaf dishes, molded as cabbage leaves, red anchor marks, circa 1756, 29cm. and 29.5cm. wide. (Christie's) $2,298

A Chelsea 'Hans Sloane' botanical plate, red anchor and 43 mark, circa 1755, 23.5cm. diam. (Christie's) $6,463

A Chelsea fluted oviform teapot and cover painted in the Kakiemon palette, circa 1752, 12.6cm. high. (Christie's) $5,214

A pair of Chelsea Derby figures of a youth and girl standing before a bocage supporting candle sconces, 29cm. high. (Lawrence Fine Art) $983

A Chelsea lobed teaplant beaker painted in a vivid famille rose palette beneath a chocolate line rim. 1745-49, 7.5cm. high. (Christie's) $7,182

A pair of Chelsea Derby figures, Neptune and Venus and Cupid, on high rocky bases, 24cm. and 25cm. high. (Lawrence Fine Art) $819

A Chelsea silver shaped plate finely painted, circa 1752, 22.5cm. diam. (Christie's) $5,520

A Chelsea apple tureen and cover naturally modelled and colored in green and russet, the base with red 3 mark, circa 1755, 10.5cm. high. (Christie's) $6,134

A Chelsea botanical plate, red anchor mark, circa 1756, 21.5cm. diam. (Christie's) $2,453

One of a pair of biscuit figures of dogs of Fo, K'ang Hsi, 44cm. high. (Lawrence Fine Art) $9,251

A Cizhou brown-glazed oviform jar, Jin/Yuan Dynasty, 32.5cm. diam. (Christie's) $1,140

An ormolu mounted Chinese porcelain vase with husked handles, late Ching, 19½in. high. (Christie's) $2,332

A Cizhou oviform vase with four looped strap handles, Yuan Dynasty, 28cm. high. (Christie's) $784

A pair of Chinese porcelain figures of Immortals, F'u Hsing and possibly Wen Chang, 18¼in. high. (Geering & Colyer) $388

A Yangshao Culture, 3rd/2nd Millennium B.C. Gansu neolithic pottery jar, 30.5cm. high. (Christie's) $2,698

A 1st Millennium B.C. tall red pottery jar, 31.5cm. high. (Christie's) $1,031

One of a pair of green dragon jars and covers, Qianlong six-character seal marks and of the period, 20cm. high. (Christie's) $11,113

Late 18th century pair of Export porcelain covered urns, China, 17½in. high. (Robt. W. Skinner Inc.) $6,250

CHINESE

An 18th century large metallic brown-glazed bottle vase, 58cm. high. (Christie's) $7,128

A Longquan celadon broad globular jarlet under an even grayish green glossy glaze, 13th/14th century, 8cm. diam. (Christie's) $784

A Dehua blanc-de-chine figure of Guanyin seated on rockwork, 17th/18th century, 24cm. high, with fitted box. (Christie's) $2,423

A late 19th century Oriental Export porcelain garden seat, China, 19in. high. (Robt. W. Skinner Inc.) $1,700

A Nankin blue and white porcelain stick stand, painted with prunus blossom, 1ft.11in. high. (Capes, Dunn & Co.) $100

A neolithic pottery two-handled oviform jar, Gansu, Yangshao Culture, 3rd/2nd Millennium B.C., 31.5cm. high. (Christie's) $7,413

A He Chaozong Dehua blanc-de-chine figure of Wen Chang, late 18th/early 19th century, 30.2cm. high. (Christie's) $2,851

A Jun Yao two-handled globular jar with short cylindrical neck, Yuan Dynasty, 20.5cm. diam. (Christie's) $2,708

One of a pair of early 19th century Chinese vases with semi-domed covers, 14¼in. high. (Anderson & Garland) $849

110

CHINESE

CHINA

A neolithic pottery horizontal oil bottle painted in black on a red ground, Gansu, Yangshao Culture, 3rd/2nd Millennium B.C., 12.5cm. long. (Christie's)$712

An 18th century Chinese Export porcelain teapot with silver spout, Chien Lung, circa 1770. (Capes, Dunn & Co.) $54

One of a pair of green and yellow dragon bowls, encircled Yongzheng six-character marks and of the period, 14cm. diam. (Christie's) $9,836

A Transitional Wucai slender pear-shaped vase, circa 1660, 41cm. high. (Christie's) $2,566

A pair of 18th century Chinese porcelain cockerels, 10½in. high. (Dacre, Son & Hartley) $1,440

A green and yellow-glazed buff pottery pear-shaped bottle vase, Liao Dynasty, 23.5cm. high. (Christie's) $5,417

Late 18th century Chinese Export porcelain cider jug with interwoven strap handle, 11½in. high. (Robt. W. Skinner Inc.) $425

A Jizhou bowl decorated in deep chocolate-brown with three quatrefoil motifs on a russet ground, Southern Song Dynasty, 10.8cm. diam. (Christie's) $997

An 18th century He Chaozong Dehua blanc-de-chine figure of a seated lady, impressed three-character seal mark, 13cm. high. (Christie's) $1,995

111

A 19th century trefoil rose medallion porcelain tray, China, 10½in. diam. (Robt. W. Skinner Inc.) $350

Mid 19th century rose Mandarin export porcelain bowl, China, polychrome decorated, 14½in. diam. (Robt. W. Skinner Inc.) $1,100

A 6th century olive glazed oviform jar with four double loop handles, 25.5cm. high. (Christie's) $9,525

A blue, red and white cylindrical vase painted in underglaze blue and copper-red, large Qianlong six-character seal mark and of the period, 47.5cm. high. (Christie's) $15,876

A 3rd/2nd Millennium B.C. Ma Jia Yao neolithic pottery two-handled jar, 26cm. diam. (Christie's) $2,063

One of a pair of K'ang Hsi baluster vases and domed covers, 52cm. and 53cm. high. (Lawrence Fine Art) $1,116

A barrel shaped mug decorated with a panel of figures on a basketwork ground, 5¼in. high. (Christie's) $406

A blue and white dish enamelled in yellow, red, green and aubergine, encircled Xuande six character mark, 9¾in. diam. (Christie's) $1,160

A pear shaped mug painted with figures at various pastimes, 4¾in. high. (Christie's) $65

CHINA

CLARICE CLIFF

A Clarice Cliff Bizarre 'Inspiration' baluster pottery vase, 12½in. high. (Christie's) $650

A Clarice Cliff Bizarre vase, printed marks, molded 370, 15.5cm. high. (Lawrence Fine Art) $321

A Clarice Cliff 'Inspiration' vase of tall baluster shape, circa 1930, 41cm. high. (Christie's) $4,730

A Clarice Cliff Bizarre Fantasque lotus vase, painted with red, orange and yellow leaves, 11¾in. high. (Christie's) $765

A Clarice Cliff Bizarre oviform jug in the 'Snake Tree' pattern, 6¾in. high. (Christie's) $514

A Clarice Cliff 'Fantasque' single-handled 'Isis' vase, printed marks, 24.6cm. high. (Lawrence Fine Art) $449

A Clarice Cliff Fantasque baluster shaped vase, 16¼in. high. (Christie's) $1,617

A Clarice Cliff Bizarre circular wall charger, 45.6cm. diam. (Christie's) $548

A Bizarre Clarice Cliff hand-painted lotus vase with design of trees and houses on blue and white ground, 10½in. high. (Chelsea Auction Galleries) $680

113

CHINA

COALPORT

A Coalport (John Rose) part dessert service painted in the Imari style, circa 1805. (Christie's) $1,686

A Coalport square-shaped dessert dish, painted with a view of Tantallon Castle, by A. Perry, 28.5cm., 1908. (Lawrence Fine Art) $287

A Coalport (John Rose) part dessert service, circa 1810. (Christie's) $383

A Coalport goblet vase, 22.2cm. high, printed mark in green and impressed mark for January 1908. (Lawrence Fine Art) $398

A Coalport blue ground 'Union' part dessert service, circa 1820. (Christie's) $5,367

A Coalport puce ground two handled racing trophy and cover, circa 1853, 28.5cm. high. (Christie's) $920

COPELAND

A Copeland Spode Toby jug, blue printed diaper and floral coat and hat, 8in. high. (Capes, Dunn & Co.) $77

Part of a Copeland & Garrett topographical dessert service, printed blue-green mark and pattern no. 6903, circa 1842. (Christie's) $3,725

A Copeland Parian group, entitled 'Go To Sleep', impressed Art Union of London, J. Durham Sc 1862, 26in. high overall. (Anderson & Garland) $525

HANS COPER

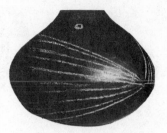

An early stoneware bowl, by Hans Coper, circa 1955, 27.8cm. diam. (Christie's) $10,179

A black stoneware stemmed cup form, by Hans Coper, circa 1965, 16.7cm. high. (Christie's) $5,184

An early stoneware vase, by Hans Coper, the onion-shaped form with white sgraffito linear decoration, circa 1952, 33.2cm. diam. (Christie's) $17,280

A stoneware bulbous bottle, by Hans Coper, circa 1965, 16.9cm. high. (Christie's) $3,758

A stoneware 'Tripot', by Hans Coper, circa 1956, 27.5cm. high. (Christie's) $7,203

A stoneware buff spade-form vase, by Hans Coper, impressed HC seal, 1973, 28.3cm. high. (Christie's) $6,336

A stoneware 'thistle' vase, by Hans Coper, circa 1962, 24cm. high. (Christie's) $7,830

A stoneware shaped cylindrical bottle, by Hans Coper, circa 1966, 20.4cm. high. (Christie's) $2,975

A monumental stoneware shouldered bottle, by Hans Coper, circa 1970, 43cm. high. (Christie's) $12,528

DELFT

A Bristol delft blue and white fluted hexagonal spoon tray, circa 1750, 15cm. wide. (Christie's) $315

One of a pair of 18th century Dutch Delft polychrome chicken tureens and covers, 14cm. long. (Christie's) $11,502

A Bristol delft blue and white documentary deep bowl, circa 1735, 35cm. diam. (Christie's)
$11,491

A Lambeth delft blue and white wet drug jar with scrolling strap handle, circa 1680, 18cm. high. (Christie's) $718

A mid 17th century English delft charger, probably Southwark, 37cm. diam. (Christie's) $920

A Lambeth delft blue and white drug jar for U:Sambuc, circa 1740, 17.5cm. high. (Christie's) $287

A Lambeth delft blue-dash Royalist portrait charger, circa 1705, 35cm. diam. (Christie's) $3,734

A London delft dated blue and white wet drug jar for S. Cichorei.Sympi with date 1659, 20cm. high. (Christie's) $1,226

A London delft Royalist blue and white plate, circa 1715, 22.2cm. diam. (Christie's) $1,380

DELFT

Mid 17th century Southwark delft polychrome armorial salt of rectangular form, 13cm. wide. (Christie's)$6,441

One of a pair of 18th century Dutch Delft poly-chrome cows with yellow horns, 21cm. long. (Christie's) $2,453

One of a pair of Dutch Delft circular polychrome dishes, 14in. diam. (Anderson & Garland) $576

A Dublin delft blue and white baluster vase, circa 1750, 32cm. high. (Christie's) $1,456

A London delft blue-dash tulip charger, circa 1700, 35cm. diam. (Christie's) $1,993   40⁴

A massive London delft dated polychrome armorial drug jar of swelling form, circa 1656, 36cm. high. (Christie's) $25,855

A Bristol delft blue and white barber's bowl, circa 1740, 25.5cm. diam. (Christie's) $1,292

One of a pair of Dutch Delft blue and white gourd shaped vases, circa 1670, with metal covers. (Christie's) $729

A Lambeth delft ballooning plate painted in blue, green, yellow and manganese, circa 1785, 30cm. diam. (Christie's) $1,867

DELLA ROBBIA

A Della Robbia pottery vase by Roseville Pottery, signed with Rozane Ware seal, circa 1906, 8¼in. high. (Robt. W. Skinner Inc.) $850

A Della Robbia wall charger, the base incised DR with a sailing ship and artist's monogram, 47.5cm. diam. (Christie's) $532

A Della Robbia pottery vase, with marks of Chas. Collis, potter and sgraffito artist and G. Russell, Paintress, circa 1903/06, 11in. high. (Capes, Dunn & Co.) $100

DE MORGAN

A William de Morgan ruby lustre charger, decorated with a peacock, circa 1900, 36cm. diam. (Christie's) $803

A small William de Morgan lustre bowl, 5½in. diam. (Christie's) $297

A William de Morgan wall plate designed by Chas. Passenger, 47cm. diam. (Christie's) $1,879

DERBY

A Derby shepherdess in yellow-lined pink jacket, Wm. Duesbury & Co., circa 1765, 24.5cm. high. (Christie's) $582

A pair of Derby figures emblematic of Summer painted in the London studio of Wm. Duesbury, Andrew Planche's period, circa 1753, 16.5cm. high. (Christie's) $3,987

A Derby white figure of John Wilkes, Wm. Duesbury & Co., circa 1765, 29.5cm. high. (Christie's) $489

118

A Royal Doulton figure, 'Dinky Doo', designed by L. Harradine, HN1678, introduced 1934, 12cm. high. (Lawrence Fine Art) $59

A Royal Doulton pottery character jug modelled as Santa Clause, D6690, 7½in. high. (Christie's) $60

'The Mendicant', a Royal Doulton figure designed by L. Harradine, HN1365, introduced 1929, withdrawn 1969, 20.9cm. high. (Lawrence Fine Art) $208

A Doulton Lambeth stoneware golfing jug, circa 1900, 8¾in. high. (Lawrence Fine Art) $947

A Doulton Lambeth faience coffee service, P.O.D.R. mark for 29th May, 1879, coffee pot 26.9cm. high. (Lawrence Fine Art) $321

A Faience oviform vase, by Emily Gillman, impressed Doulton, Lambeth Faience mark, 9¼in. high. (Christie's) $124

'The Old Balloon Seller', Royal Doulton figure, designed by L. Harradine, HN 1315, introduced 1929, impressed date code for 1936, 19cm. high. (Lawrence Fine Art) $77

A Royal Doulton two-handled loving cup commemorating King George V silver jubilee, 10in. high, No. 584 of a limited edition of 1,000. (Christie's) $338

The 'Lily Maid', a Royal Doulton polychrome glazed stoneware fountain figure, designed by Gilbert Bayes, 61.5cm. high. (Christie's) $13,311

DOULTON

A pottery character jug modelled as 'The Hatless Drake', with printed Royal Doulton marks, 6in. high. (Christie's) $3,105

A Royal Doulton figure of 'Lucy Anne', HN 1502, 5½in. high. (Christie's) $91

A Royal Doulton pottery character jug modelled as The Fortune Teller, D 6497, 6¾in. high. (Christie's) $390

A slender oviform vase, by Hannah Barlow, impressed Doulton Lambeth, 1881, 10½in. high. (Christie's) $501

Pair of Doulton saltglazed stoneware baluster vases, circa 1906/7, 12½in. high. (Capes, Dunn & Co.) $288

One of a pair of Royal Doulton baluster shaped vases, by Francis C. Pope, 8¾in. high. (Christie's) $201

A Royal Doulton character jug, St. George, 7½in. high. (Hobbs & Chambers) $73

A Doulton Burslem figure designed by Chas. J. Noke, 33cm. high. (Lawrence Fine Art) $658

A stoneware group modelled as two frogs attacking two mice, 'The Combat', by G. Tinworth, 4in. high. (Christie's) $864

DRESDEN

One of a pair of 'Dresden' schneeballen vases and covers, 58cm. high, crossed swords mark in underglaze blue. (Lawrence Fine Art) $1,116

A Dresden standing figure of a polar bear, 55cm. long, crossed swords mark in underglaze blue. (Lawrence Fine Art) $1,196

One of a pair of Dresden yellow ground oviform vases and covers, 12½in. high. (Christie's) $325

A pair of Dresden candelabra for five lights, on square bases with four scroll feet, 14cm., crossed swords mark in underglaze blue. (Lawrence Fine Art) $1,229

A mantel clock in porcelain drum shaped case in Dresden style, 39cm. high, marked with monogram J.R. (Lawrence Fine Art) $655

Pair of Dresden bulbous vases with covers and painted panels on yellow ground. (Worsfolds) $604

EARTHENWARE

An earthenware circular charger by Ljerka Njers, 1985, 38.5cm. diam. (Christie's) $343

One of a pair of earthenware boxes and covers of square shape, one with incised signature, 4¼in. high. (Lawrence Fine Art) $255

A handbuilt, burnished and polished red clay vase by Magdalene A. N. Odundo, 1985, 34.7cm. high. (Christie's) $1,566

121

EUROPEAN

CHINA

A Northern European faience asparagus tureen and cover naturally modelled, circa 1775, 34.5cm. long. (Christie's) $1,533

A Continental faience figure of King Wenceslaus, mid 18th century, 18.5cm. high. (Christie's) $306

European porcelain serving plate, 1810. (British Antique Exporters) $78

Late 15th century Hispano Moresque albarello in blue and gold lustre, Valencia, 29cm. high. (Christie's) $8,748

A School of Koloman Moser seven-piece porcelain tea service, designed by Jutta Sika, teapot 16.7cm. high. (Christie's) $2,818

An early 20th century Art Nouveau porcelain vase, by Riessner, Stetmacher & Kessel, 13in. high. (Robt. W. Skinner Inc.)$370

A Rozenburg egg-shell square-shaped vase painted with blue and green stylised foliage on a white ground, 11in. high. (Christie's) $950

An ancient pottery hand grenade for 'Greek Fire', 3½in., wheel turned with red glaze. (Wallis & Wallis) $64

A Georges de Feure porcelain figure of a woman in evening dress, inscribed, 30.2cm. high. (Christie's) $626

CHINA

A Strasbourg oval dish with pierced border, blue H/860 mark, circa 1770, 30cm. wide. (Christie's) $324

An Orchies pottery figure, designed by Dax, 13¼in. high, printed and painted marks. (Christie's) $139

Late 18th century Spanish pottery, Alcora cockerel tureen, 23cm. high. (Christie's) $367

An amphora vase of ovoid shape, impressed Amphora and printed Turn Teplitz R. St. K. with maker's device and D. 464, circa 1930, 18.5cm. high.(Christie's) $1,487

A mid 18th century Brussels faience boar's head tureen, cover and stand, the stand 40cm. long. (Christie's) $7,668

An ancient pottery hand grenade for 'Greek Fire', 4½in., of dense black stoneware. (Wallis & Wallis) $64

An ancient pottery hand grenade for 'Greek Fire', 3¾in., wheel turned with green glaze. (Wallis & Wallis) $64

A G. Riviere crackled white pottery figure of a kneeling naked woman, 22in. high. (Christie's) $514

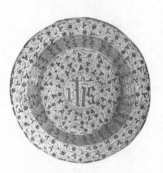

Mid 15th century Hispano Moresque blue and copper lustre deep dish, Valencia, 48cm. diam. (Christie's) $61,236

FAMILLE ROSE

An 18th century famille rose bottle shaped vase, 9in. high. (Christie's) $159

A large famille rose punch bowl painted with panels of figures at play, alternating with panels of flowers on a gilt scrolled ground, 15in. diam. (Christie's) $2,755

A Canton famille rose oviform vase with buddhistic lion handles below a waved rim, 24½in. high. (Christie's) $348

A famille rose cylindrical mug painted with figures in a fenced garden, with dragon handle, 5½in. high. (Christie's) $188

One of a pair of Canton famille rose baluster vases, 15¼in. high. (Christie's) $1,740

A famille rose cylindrical mug painted with a panel of figures in a garden by a pagoda, 5¼in. high. (Christie's) $275

A famille rose oviform armorial tea caddy and odd cover painted with a coat-of-arms, 6in. high. (Christie's) $580

A large famille rose fish bowl extensively decorated, 18in. high. (Edgar Horn) $2,409

A famille rose turquoise-ground baluster vase, gilt incised Qianlong six-character mark and late in the period, 35cm. high. (Christie's) $4,276

124

FAMILLE ROSE

One of a pair of famille rose recumbent buddhistic lion joss stick holders, 4¼in. wide. (Christie's) $1,812

A Canton famille rose oviform vase with buddhistic lion handles, 35in. high. (Christie's) $1,595

One of a pair of Qianlong famille rose two-handled classical urn shaped vases and covers, 26½in. high. (Christie's) $20,300

A famille rose oviform vase, figure painted diaper borders with bird vignettes in reserve, 17½in. high. (Capes, Dunn & Co.) $387

Part of a garniture of five famille rose armorial vases, comprising three baluster vases and two covers, 11¼in. high and two beaker vases, 9¼in. high. (Christie's) $1,421

A Canton famille rose oviform vase with buddhistic lion handles, 24½in. high. (Christie's) $406

FAMILLE VERTE

A famille verte ginger jar and cover on hardwood stand, 9in. high. (Capes, Dunn & Co.) $91

A famille verte fish bowl, the exterior painted with a scene of warriors proceeding to battle, 25in. diam. (Christie's) $5,510

One of a pair of famille verte porcelain vases of square section, 10in. high. (Capes, Dunn & Co.) $119

125

Late 17th century Nevers bleu persan double gourd vase, 34.5cm. high. (Christie's) $407

A late 19th century French rectangular plaque by Lucien Levy, 32 x 22cm. (Christie's) $714

One of a pair of early 19th century ormolu mounted cobalt blue glazed porcelain urns, France, 16in. high. (Robt. W. Skinner Inc.) $2,500

A large Strasbourg surtout-de-table, circa 1750, 52cm. high, the plateau 64cm. wide. (Christie's) $6,134

A porcelain snuff box mounted in England en cage in gold, possibly Tournai, circa 1765, 7.5cm. wide. (Christie's) $8,434

A Vincennes partly glazed white biscuit figure of a sleeping putto resting on a bale of hay, circa 1753, 11cm. high. (Christie's) $1,458

A Rouen bleu persan shaped circular dish, decorated in the 'Gillibaud' style, circa 1700, 36cm. diam. (Christie's) $465

A late 19th century Samson figure of a partridge, blue cross mark, 15cm. high. (Christie's) $123

A French earthenware ornamental circular plaque, signed Belet, circa 1880-1900. (Capes, Dunn & Co.) $180

Late 19th century French porcelain figure group, 'L'Accordec du Village', after Greuze, 16in. long. (Capes, Dunn & Co.) $244

One of a pair of mid 18th century Tournai faience pug dogs, after the original Meissen models by J. J. Kandler, 15.5cm. high. (Christie's)$10,735

A Samson figure of a white rhinoceros after the original by J. J. Kandler, blue cross mark, circa 1880, 22cm. wide. (Christie's)$714

A Louis XVI travelling set, contained in a tulipwood and parquetry case lined with pink watered silk, 35.5cm. wide. (Christie's) $3,240

A large pair of Continental biscuit figures of a man and a woman in 18th century dress, impressed initial marks, probably France, circa 1900, 68cm. high. (Christie's) $1,866

An Aprey faience group, black AP p mark, circa 1770, 24cm. high. (Christie's) $735

Late 17th century Nevers bleu persan shallow bowl with everted rim, 23.5cm. diam. (Christie's) $407

A Limoges model of a leaping fish in pink, green and white glazes, designed by Sandoz, 7½in. high. (Christie's) $294

One of a pair of Marseilles circular dishes painted en camaieu vert, Savy's factory, circa 1770, 28.5cm. diam. (Christie's) $2,430

GERMAN

CHINA

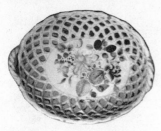

A mid 18th century Bayreuth two-handled oval basket, the pierced basket work sides with yellow lined lattice work, 25cm. wide. (Christie's) $2,300

A Kloster Veilsdorf figure of Capitano Spavento modelled by Wenzel Neu, 1764-65, 16cm. high. (Christie's) $1,533

A mid 18th century German faience asparagus tureen and cover, 17cm. long. (Christie's) $1,840

A mid 18th century Fulda faience frog, 8cm. long. (Christie's) $4,294

A Kloster Veilsdorf figure of Pierrot modelled by Wenzel Neu, 1764-65, 15.5cm. high. (Christie's) $7,668

A Ludwigsburg miniature group of three figures rolling dice, blue interlaced C mark, circa 1775, 8cm. wide. (Christie's) $2,147

A pair of Nymphenburg figures designed by Prof. J. Wackerle of stylized 18th century fops. (Christie's) $3,468

A Thuringian figure of Provender for the Monastery, circa 1775, 11.5cm. high. (Christie's) $874

A Volkstedt circular jagddose of compressed baluster form, the hinged silver gilt mount with waved decoration, blue hayfork and M mark, circa 1760, 9cm. diam. (Christie's) $8,748

128

GERMAN

CHINA

A Kloster Veilsdorf figure of a crouching leopard, probably modelled by Pfranger snr., circa 1775, 12cm. long. (Christie's) $611

A Potschappel two-handled vase and an armorial cover, the vase with crossed T mark, the stand with blue beehive mark, circa 1900, 84cm. high. (Christie's) $1,321

A mid 18th century Erfurt faience cow tureen and cover, 20.5cm. long. (Christie's) $1,150

A Stralsund baluster vase with reticulated sides, circa 1770, 36.5cm. high. (Christie's) $1,226

A German lacquered earthenware baluster vase decorated with chinoiserie landscapes in black and red, 44½in. high. (Christie's) $1,409

A Rosenthal ceramic sculpture by Gerhard Schliepstein, circa 1930, 50.8cm. high. (Christie's) $2,035

A Kloster Veilsdorf figure of Pantalone modelled by Wenzel Neu, 1764-65, 14.5cm. high. (Christie's) $3,067

A stoneware tureen and cover attributed to Reinhold Merkelbach and the design to R. Riemerschmid, 33.5cm. high. (Christie's) $861

Mid 18th century Hannoversch-Munden faience cylindrical tankard with pewter cover, 21.5cm. high. (Christie's) $336

GERMAN

A Limbach figure of St. Johannes Nepomuk, circa 1775, 21cm. high. (Christie's) $1,134

One of a set of five Furstenberg shaped rectangular plaques painted by J. H. Eisentrager, with pastoral scenes after Nilson in landscape vignettes, circa 1765, 12 x 16cm. (Christie's) $29,160

A Kloster Veilsdorf cane handle, formed as a bearded old man, circa 1770, 7.5cm. high. (Christie's) $810

An 18th century German cylindrical pewter mounted tankard, perhaps Altenberg, 27cm. high. (Christie's) $210

A Furstenberg figure of a young girl modelled by Carl G. Schubert, circa 1785, 19cm. high. (Christie's) $486

A Furstenberg white biscuit oval plaque modelled with a portrait bust of J. H. C. v. Selchow, circa 1782, 7.5cm. high. (Christie's) $86

'Winter', a Rosenthal white glazed porcelain figure designed by G. Schliepstein, 18.5cm. high. (Christie's) $343

A German faience Hausmalerei circular dish painted en camaieu rose, early 18th century, 25cm. diam. (Christie's) $2,268

A German blue and white cylindrical tankard, circa 1700, 25cm. high. (Christie's) $891

GOLDSCHEIDER

A Goldscheider pottery figure modelled as a naked young lady holding a fan, and trailing a shawl behind, 13¾in. high. (Christie's) $514

A Goldscheider Art Deco globular lamp base, decorated in white, orange, black and blue with banding, 25cm. high. (Phillips) $243

A china Art Deco figure of a woman, by Goldscheider, Vienna, 15¼in. high. (Robt. W. Skinner Inc.) $222

A china Art Deco figure of a woman by Goldscheider, Vienna, 12½in. high. (Robt. W. Skinner Inc.) $222

A pair of Goldscheider pottery figures of a young girl and a young man, made in Austria, 15in. high. (Christie's) $528

A Goldscheider pottery figure of a woman wearing a beaded costume, on a black oval base, 18in. high. (Christie's) $2,108

A Goldscheider pottery figure modelled as naked young girl with her arms crossed in front of her, 14¼in. high. (Christie's) $617

A Goldscheider pottery mask of a girl looking down, Made in Austria, circa 1925, 23cm. high. (Christie's) $473

A Goldscheider pottery bust of a young woman in the Art Deco style, signed F. Donatello, 23½in. high. (Outhwaite & Litherland) $504

GOSS

A Goss Parian bust of Queen Victoria, for Mortlock's of Oxford Street, 236mm. high. (Phillips) $235

The Feathers Hotel, Ledbury, 114mm. long. (Goss & Crested China) $1,050

Hastings kettle. (Goss & Crested China) $12

Dr Samuel Johnson's House at Lichfield, 75mm. high. (Goss & Crested China) $210

Little girl Goss doll with real hair, porcelain arms, head and legs. (Goss & Crested China) $600

Shakespeare's Cottage, Stratford-on-Avon, 65mm. long. (Goss & Crested China) $97

Flame color pear-shaped vase with grapevine decoration. (Goss & Crested China) $262

Hereford terracotta kettle and lid. (Goss & Crested China) $37

1930's flower girl, 'Daisy', in yellow and green flapper dress. (Goss & Crested China) $270

GRUEBY

A Grueby pottery two-color vase, stamped and paper label, circa 1905, 7in. high. (Robt. W. Skinner Inc.) $550

A Grueby two-color pottery vase, circa 1905, 13in. high. (Robt. W. Skinner Inc.) $5,200

A Grueby pottery vase, stamped and artist signed, circa 1905, 7.7/8in. high. (Robt. W. Skinner Inc.) $1,000

HAN

A green-glazed red pottery table, 43.5cm. wide, and five related eared cups, Han Dynasty. (Christie's) $2,566

A green glazed red pottery model of a house, areas of iridescence and earth encrustation, Han Dynasty, 41cm. wide. (Christie's) $5,397

A green-glazed pottery model of a sheep and pig farm, Han Dynasty, 37cm. wide. (Christie's) $14,256

A red painted pottery horse head, Han Dynasty, 15.5cm. high. (Christie's) $1,425

A green glazed pottery model of a farm house tower in three sections, Han Dynasty, 58.5cm. high. (Christie's) $28,576

A large proto-porcelain jar, the upper part under a semi-opaque olive-green glaze, Han Dynasty, 36.5cm. diam. (Christie's) $1,069

A painted gray pottery figure of a standing stallion, Han Dynasty, 50cm. high. (Christie's) $20,638

A green glazed red pottery model of a tower, Han Dynasty, 61.5cm. high. (Christie's) $53,978

One of a pair of gray pottery horse heads with bulbous eyes, Han Dynasty, 15cm. high. (Christie's) $1,587

A green glazed red pottery bird lamp, Han Dynasty, 64cm. high. (Christie's) $11,907

A green glazed red pottery kidney shaped farm, Han Dynasty, 28cm. wide. (Christie's) $1,746

A green glazed pottery granary jar and related cover, Han Dynasty, 33cm. high. (Christie's) $855

A green glazed pottery hill jar and cover on three feet, Han Dynasty, 21cm. high. (Christie's) $2,423

A green glazed pottery pear-shaped vase, Han Dynasty, 31cm. high. (Christie's) $2,423

red painted gray pottery horse's head, Han Dynasty, 6in. high. (Lawrence Fine Art) $1,595

IMARI

CHINA

An Imari model of a smiling courtesan decorated in underglaze blue, iron-red and gilt, Genroku period, 37.8cm. high. (Christie's) $1,544

A 19th century Imari circular bowl decorated in underglaze blue, iron-red, green, yellow enamels and gilt, 40cm. diam. (Christie's) $1,698

An 18th century Imari model of a roistering Dutchman seated astride a Dutch gin cask, 35.8cm. high. (Christie's) $18,662

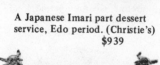

One of a pair of late 17th century Imari baluster vases and covers, 90cm. high. (Christie's) $18,532

A Japanese Imari part dessert service, Edo period. (Christie's) $939

One of a pair of early 19th century Imari porcelain and brass Temple jars, Japan, 16½in. high. (Robt. W. Skinner Inc.) $3,600

One of a pair of late 19th century Imari slender oviform vases, 106cm. high. (Christie's) $19,305

Late 19th century brass mounted Imari tureen, Japan, 16in. wide. (Robt. W. Skinner Inc.) $550

Late 17th century Imari octagonal baluster vase and cover decorated in iron-red and gilt, 85cm. high. (Christie's) $8,494

IMARI

An Imari shaving bowl decorated in iron-red, black enamels and gilt on underglaze blue, Genroku period, 27.5cm. diam. (Christie's) $734

One of a set of five late 17th/early 18th century Imari dishes, 9¼in. diam. (Lawrence Fine Art) $2,048

An Imari shaving bowl decorated in iron-red, dark green and light green, aubergine and black enamels and gilt on a blue ground, Genroku period, 26cm. diam. (Christie's) $617

An octagonal Imari vase decorated in iron-red and black enamels and gilt, Genroku period, 59cm. high. (Christie's) $2,780

An Imari deep bowl and cover decorated in iron-red, enamel and gilt on an underglaze blue ground, Genroku period, 21.5cm. diam. (Christie's) $1,081

Early 19th century Chinese Imari design baluster shaped vase with cover, 33in. high. (Peter Wilson & Co.) $1,728

Late 17th century Imari deep bowl and domed cover, the brass acorn finial of later date, 48.4cm. high. (Christie's) $2,316

An Imari circular plaque painted with flowers, birds and medallions, 18¾in. diam. (Anderson & Garland) $460

A Ko-Imari baluster jar decorated in iron-red, green, yellow and pale aubergine enamels in Kakiemon style, circa 1660-80, 32.8cm. high. (Christie's) $14,688

IMARI

CHINA

Late 19th century large Imari globular jardiniere painted in underglaze blue, iron-red, colors and gilt, 53cm. diam. (Christie's) $2,642

An Imari ship's plate and cover decorated in iron-red, green and aubergine enamels and gilt on underglaze blue, Genroku period, 25.5cm. diam. (Christie's) $1,477

A large Imari dish decorated in iron-red and black enamels and gilt on underglaze blue, Genroku period, 55cm. diam. (Christie's) $3,231

A 19th century Imari porcelain vase decorated in underglaze blue, orange and ochre, 18½in. high. (Robt. W. Skinner Inc.) $600

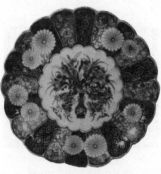

An Imari porcelain circular plaque, the border diaper panelled, 9¾in. diam. (Capes, Dunn & Co.) $60

A Ko-Imari baluster jar decorated with three kirin among peony, circa 1660-80, 33.5cm. high. (Christie's) $13,219

A large Imari dish painted in typical colors, circa 1700, 53.8cm. diam. (Christie's) $1,615

Late 17th/early 18th century Imari oviform vase and cover, decorated in iron-red, enamel and gilt, 50cm. high. (Christie's) $2,316

An Imari shaving dish decorated in underglaze blue, iron-red and gilt, Genroku period, 28cm. wide. (Christie's) $440

137

ITALIAN

A Savona blue and white tankard with entwined handle, mid 18th century, 15.5cm. wide. (Christie's) $675

Early 20th century majolica ewer with swan handle, 17½in. high. (Robt. W. Skinner Inc.) $375

A Cantagalli majolica dish, ogival edged, bold floral design in blue, green and manganese, 15½in. diam. (Capes, Dunn & Co.) $119

A Faenza wet drug jar of ovoid shape with an angled strap handle and straight spout, 22.5cm. high. (Phillips)$562

A Castelli rectangular plaque painted with God appearing to Adam in the Garden of Eden, circa 1725, 21 x 28cm. (Christie's) $1,134

A figure of Winter standing with his arms clasped around his chest, dated on the base 1779, 33.5cm. high. (Christie's) $2,478

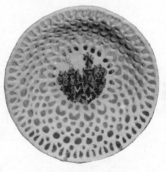

An early 18th century North Italian wet drug jar for Sy. Farfara, probably Savona, 19.5cm. high. (Christie's) $405

A Faenza Compendiario armorial pierced circular tazza, circa 1570, 37.5cm. diam. (Christie's) $648

A Faenza drug vase of compressed baluster form, the contents a. api, circa 1550, 21.5cm. high. (Christie's) $648

ITALIAN

CHINA

A Turin (Rossetti) shaped circular dish, circa 1760, 36cm. diam. (Christie's) $1,944

An armorial wet drug jar painted in blue, the contents Mel.Ros. Solvtivo, circa 1600, possibly Faenza, 24cm. high. (Christie's) $648

An Urbino Istoriato dish painted with the Rape of Proserpine, the reverse inscribed in blue Diplutto et Proserpina, circa 1555, 26cm. diam. (Christie's) $4,374

An Orvieto ewer (brocca) of conventional form, circa 1470, 28cm. high. (Christie's) $17,496

A Castelli rectangular plaque painted with Pan being comforted after the musical contest with Apollo seated, circa 1725, 28cm. square. (Christie's) $1,458

A Castelli large vase of campana form painted in colors and gilt, circa 1720, 41cm. high. (Christie's) $2,250

One of a pair of Faenza polychrome plates, Ferniani's factory, circa 1770, 24cm. diam. (Christie's) $420

A Lenci figure of a rooster, painted marks Lenci 1936 S.P., 29cm. high.(Christie's) $1,566

A Turin (Rossetti) shaped circular dish, blue cross mark, 1735-40, 32.5cm. diam. (Christie's) $486

JAPANESE

A 17th century Kakiemon model of a dragon decorated in iron-red, blue, green and yellow enamels on a white glazed body, 19cm. high. (Christie's)
$13,899

An 18th/19th century Kakiemon type mokkogata teapot with shallow domed cover and arch-shaped handle, 19cm. long. (Christie's)
$1,248

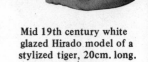

Mid 19th century white glazed Hirado model of a stylized tiger, 20cm. long. (Christie's) $694

A 19th century hexagonal Kyoto Satsuma vase, signed Kinkozan, 31cm. high. (Christie's) $1,081

One of a pair of Kakiemon hexagonal jars and domed covers, Empo/Jokyo period (1673-87), 29.2cm. high. (Christie's)
$14,688

An 18th/early 19th century Kakiemon type cylindrical sake bottle, tokkuri, fitted with a European gilt metal finial, 23cm. high.(Christie's)
$4,700

Late 19th century shaped and pierced baluster Kyoto vase decorated in colored enamels and gilt, signed Donzan seizo, 17cm. high. (Christie's) $1,930

Late 17th century Kakiemon figure of a standing bijin, 36.5cm. high. (Christie's)
$3,672

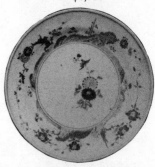

Late 17th century Kakiemon shallow dish decorated in iron-red, blue, green, black and yellow enamels, 21cm. diam. (Christie's)
$2,779

JAPANESE

CHINA

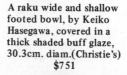

Mid 19th century white glazed Hirado model of a recumbent goat, signed, 19cm. long. (Christie's) $586

A raku wide and shallow footed bowl, by Keiko Hasegawa, covered in a thick shaded buff glaze, 30.3cm. diam.(Christie's) $751

A Kakiemon hanging flower vase, kakehanaike, modelled as a dragon, circa 1660-80, 22cm. long. (Christie's) $6,609

Late 19th century Kyoto vase decorated in colored enamels and gilt, signed Ryozan, 21.5cm. high (Christie's) $2,007

A flattened rectangular press molded bottle by Shoji Hamada covered in a rich khaki glaze, circa 1965, 22cm. high. (Christie's) $2,975

A Kakiemon oviform vase decorated in blue, iron-red, green, yellow and black enamels, circa 1665, 26.5cm. high. (Christie's) $6,949

A Kyoto type circular bowl with foliate rim, signed, Meiji period, 24.2cm. diam. (Christie's) $1,853

A stoneware ewer with loop handle, overglazed in grayish white and blue enamels, Edo period, 20cm. high. (Christie's) $933

A koro and cover on three bud feet, the cover signed in underglaze blue, 7in. high. (Lawrence Fine Art) $2,153

JONES

A George Jones punch bowl
with Mr. Punch lying on his
back supporting the holly-
decorated bowl in his arms,
circa 1875, 36cm. diam.
(Christie's) $4,228

A George Jones tea-set, comprising a tea-pot, coffee-pot,
milk-jug, sugar-basin with lid
and a tray, circa 1873.
(Christie's) $1,458

A George Jones jardiniere,
cobalt blue with turquoise
interior and naturalistic
coloring , 33cm. high.
(Christie's) $874

KANGXI

A Brinjal bowl with everted
rim, 19cm. diam., Kangxi.
(Christie's) $302

A famille verte teapot and
cover formed as a bunch
of bamboo, 18cm. wide,
Kangxi. (Christie's)
$453

A famille verte tazza, 22.5cm.
diam., Kangxi. (Christie's)
$453

One of a pair of famille
verte dishes with wide seeded
green-ground border, 28.5cm.
diam., Kangxi. (Christie's)
$978

A Kangxi blue and white
cylindrical brush holder
with slightly everted rim,
5in. high. (Christie's)
$304

A famille verte dish incised
under the glaze with five-
clawed dragons, encircled
Kangxi six-character mark
and of the period, 25cm.
diam. (Christie's)
$7,128

KUTANI

CHINA

A 19th century Japanese Kutani porcelain punch bowl on teakwood stand, 14¾in. diam. (Robt. W. Skinner Inc.)$1,400

One of a pair of 19th century Ao-Kutani baluster vases, signed Kyusekirin, 52cm. high. (Christie's) $1,762

A 19th century Ao-Kutani saucer dish, signed Dai Nihon Kutani sei, Fukuriken, 59.3cm. diam. (Christie's) $881

KYOTO

A Kyoto compressed globular koro, signed Kinzan, Meiji period, 8.2cm. diam. (Christie's) $1,175

A Kyoto cylindrical vase decorated in colors and gilt on a royal blue ground, signed Kinkozan zo and Senzan, Meiji period, 11.8cm. high. (Christie's) $851

Late 19th century Kyoto chrysanthemum-shaped deep bowl decorated in colors and gilt, signed Kizan kore o tsukuru, 29.8cm. diam. (Christie's) $1,248

A Kyoto tapering rectangular vase painted with panels of a daimyo and his retainers, signed Nihon Yozan, Meiji period, 12.7cm. high. (Christie's) $909

A Kyoto trumpet-shaped beaker vase decorated in colored enamels and gilt, signed Kinkozan, Meiji period, 17.8cm. high. (Christie's) $1,395

Late 19th century Kyoto hexagonal vase decorated in colors and gilt on a royal blue ground, signed Kinkozan zo, 43.6cm. high. (Christie's) $2,937

143

LEACH, BERNARD

CHINA

A stoneware rectangular slab bottle by Bernard Leach, covered in a rich iron-red glaze, circa 1955, 18.5cm. high. (Christie's) $432

A stoneware teapot with cane handle by Bernard Leach, circa 1920, 17.2cm. high. (Christie's) $1,080

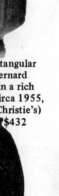

A stoneware large oviform vase by Bernard Leach, impressed BL and St. Ives seals, circa 1958, 34.3cm. high. (Christie's) $1,008

A slip-trailed soft raku bowl by Bernard Leach, impressed BL and St. Ives seals, circa 1920, 23.2cm. diam. (Christie's) $1,152

A stoneware flattened rectangular slab bottle by B. Leach, impressed BL and St. Ives seals, circa 1960, 20.2cm. high.(Christie's) $1,879

A stoneware barrel shaped bottle by Bernard Leach, impressed BL and St. Ives seals, circa 1970, 23.1cm. high. (Christie's) $343

LEACH

A stoneware cut decorated bottle by Janet Leach, impressed JL and St. Ives seals, circa 1958, 25.4cm. high. (Christie's) $288

A stoneware tall pear shaped vase with two lugged handles, by John Leach, impressed JL seal and Muchelney, 1985, 29.8cm. high. (Christie's) $218

A black stoneware vase by Janet Leach, 1984, 27.3cm. high. (Christie's)$281

144

LENCI

CHINA

A Lenci pottery wall mask modelled as a head of a young woman wearing a scarf, 12in. wide. (Christie's) $205

A Lenci pottery figure modelled as a young girl standing beside a sledge, 13¼in. high. (Christie's) $661

A Lenci pottery wall mask modelled as a young girl wearing a head scarf, 11½in. wide. (Christie's)$288

LIVERPOOL

One of a pair of Liverpool delft plates, circa 1760-75, 13¼in. diam. (Woolley & Wallis) $435

A Liverpool milk jug of spirally molded helmet form with scroll handle, Philip Christian's Factory, circa 1770, 9cm. high. (Christie's) $428

A Liverpool delft bowl decorated in blue and manganese purple, 18th century, 10½in. diam. (Woolley & Wallis) $609

An early Chaffers Liverpool bell shape mug, with spurred handle, painted in blue, iron-red and gilt, 9cm. high. (Phillips) $858

A Liverpool blue and white shell molded pickle dish, perhaps Richard Chaffer's Factory, circa 1755, 9.5cm. wide. (Christie's) $214

A Liverpool creamware inscribed and dated armorial oviform jug with loop handle, 1792, 14.5cm. high. (Christie's) $766

CHINA

LONGTON HALL

A Longton Hall blue and white coffee cup of flared form with split twig handle, circa 1755. (Christie's) $1,226

A Longton Hall grape box and cover, circa 1755, 12cm. wide. (Christie's) $11,491

A Longton Hall mug of flattened bell shape, with pointed 'broken' handle, 16cm. high. (Phillips) $592

LOWESTOFT

A Lowestoft blue and white arched rectangular tea caddy, blue crescent mark, circa 1775, 10cm. high. (Christie's) $243

A Lowestoft blue and white patty pan, blue crescent mark, circa 1768, 10.5cm. diam. (Christie's) $228

A Lowestoft blue and white rectangular octagonal tea caddy, circa 1765, 13cm. high. (Christie's) $1,686

LUSTRE

19th century Sunderland lustre ovoid jug, decorated with sailing ship, 5½in. high. (W. H. Lane & Son) $127

A Maws red lustre circular plate outlined in gilt, 13in. diam. (Christie's) $108

A large Bernard Moore lustre pottery jardiniere, 11½in. high. (Christie's) $892

MARTINWARE

A Martin Bros. oviform single-handled pottery jug, in an uneven gray glaze with deeper brown patches, 9¼in. high. (Christie's) $250

A Martin Bros. stoneware jug, the bulbous body suggesting a sea-creature, 21.8cm. high. (Christie's) $626

A Martin Bros. stoneware 'judge' bird tobacco jar and cover, London & Southall 4-1889, 25.8cm. high. (Christie's) $3,445

A Martin Bros. stoneware grotesque double-face jug, London and Southall G 1897, 17.3cm. high. (Christie's) $594

A Martin Bros. stoneware slender oviform vase, London Southall, 1889, 13in. high. (Christie's) $405

A Martinware gourd single-handled lobed pottery jug, London Southall, circa 1900, 10in. high. (Christie's) $513

A Martin Brothers stoneware vase with incised decoration of flowering lilies and a dragon-fly, London & Southall 18.7.84, 20.5cm. high. (Christie's) $551

A Martin Bros. face flask with two handles, incised marks dated 1901, 8in. high. (Christie's) $1,102

A Martin Bros. stoneware tobacco jar and cover, modelled as a grotesque grinning cat, 1885, 22cm. high. (Christie's) $10,962

147

MARTINWARE

CHINA

A Martin Bros stoneware
spherical vase, London
Southall, 1892, 9in. high.
(Christie's) $472

A Martinware flattened
oviform pottery vase,
London Southall, 1899,
12in. high. (Christie's)
$229

A Martin Bros. stoneware
grotesque, double face jug
with strap handle, 1897,
22.8cm. high. (Christie's)
$1,879

MASON'S

A Mason's ironstone part dinner service transfer-printed and painted in
iron-red, blue, green and ochre in the Oriental style, pattern no. 1841,
circa 1835. (Christie's) $2,115

One of a pair of Mason's
blue and gilt two handled
vases and covers, 20in. high.
(F. H. Fellows & Sons)
$1,460

Part of a Mason's patent
ironstone china dessert
service with a blue glaze,
gilt and enamelled, circa
1820. (Lawrence Fine Art)
$239

A massive Mason's ironstone
ewer of vase shape with
double scroll handle, circa
1820, 67cm. high.
(Christie's) $994

A Meissen tau-shaped cane handle painted by Bonaventura G. Hauer, circa 1740, 12cm. long. (Christie's) $1,944

A Meissen pipe bowl modelled as a recumbent sheep-dog with hinged neck, circa 1745, 8cm. long. (Christie's) $1,303

A Meissen figure of a mallard duck, blue crossed swords mark at back, circa 1740, 28cm. high. (Christie's) $3,834

A late Meissen pate-sur-pate baluster vase with cylindrical cover, 9¼in. high.(Christie's) $882

Pair of 19th century Meissen vases and covers. (F. H. Fellows & Sons) $876

A Meissen figure of Mezzetin, blue crossed swords mark under the base, circa 1742, 15.5cm. high. (Christie's) $5,367

A Meissen shaped circular plate after the Chelsea original, circa 1770, 22cm. diam., blue crossed swords and dot mark. (Christie's) $611

One of a pair of Meissen candlesticks, blue crossed swords marks, circa 1745, 23.5cm. high. (Christie's) $766

A Meissen plate from the Swan service modelled by J. F. Eberlein & J. J. Kandler for Count Bruhl, circa 1738, 23.5cm. diam. (Christie's) $13,770

MEISSEN

CHINA

A Meissen baluster chinoiserie cream-pot and cover painted in the Horoldt workshop, gilt 10 mark, circa 1725, 12.5cm. wide. (Christie's) $2,106

A Meissen miniature figure of a rabbit, circa 1750, on gilt metal base, the rabbit 3.5cm. long. (Christie's) $486

One of a pair of Meissen coffee cups and saucers, blue crossed swords marks, Pressnummer 2 and 24, circa 1745. (Christie's) $1,749

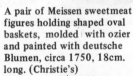

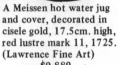

A Meissen figure of a cat, incised mark on base, circa 1740, 18.5cm. high. (Christie's) $3,373

A pair of Meissen sweetmeat figures holding shaped oval baskets, molded with ozier and painted with deutsche Blumen, circa 1750, 18cm. long. (Christie's) $1,020

A Meissen hot water jug and cover, decorated in cisele gold, 17.5cm. high, red lustre mark 11, 1725. (Lawrence Fine Art) $9,889

A Meissen figure of a shepherdess modelled by Meyer & Kandler, circa 1750, 23.5cm. high. (Christie's) $1,296

A Meissen rectangular snuff box, the porcelain circa 1745, the silver London 1818, maker's mark of Chas. Rawlings, 9cm. wide. (Christie's) $1,166 f

A Meissen rectangular tea caddy and cover, traces of blue crossed swords mark on base, circa 1770, 12.5cm. high. (Christie's) $1,539

A Meissen pale turquoise ground circular bowl, blue crossed swords mark and gilder's mark 10, circa 1740, 15.5cm. diam. (Christie's) $1,296

A Meissen inverted baluster teapot and cover, blue crossed swords mark and painter's mark 56 in puce, circa 1750, 14.5cm. wide. (Christie's) $810

A Meissen compressed oviform cream-pot and shallow domed cover, gilder's mark 2 to each piece, circa 1730, 12.5cm. wide. (Christie's) $1,782

A Meissen centerpiece, incised 1931, 42in. high. (F. H. Fellows & Sons) $2,336

Pair of Louis XV ormolu mounted Meissen figures of a cockerel and hen, naturally modelled by J. J. Kandler, circa 1745. (Christie's) $10,735

A Meissen figure of a pilgrim modelled by J. J. Kandler, blue crossed swords mark at back, circa 1745, 29cm. high. (Christie's) $1,150

A Meissen figure of a Malabar musician modelled by F. E. Meyer, circa 1770, 17.5cm. high. (Christie's) $567

A Meissen teapot and cover, decorated in cisele gold, 12cm. high, red lustre workman's cross mark, 1725. (Lawrence Fine Art) $8,772

A Meissen Bergleute-shaped baluster jug and domed cover, blue crossed swords and dot mark, circa 1765, 28cm. high. (Christie's) $5,670

MEISSEN

A Meissen bombe-shaped snuff box with contemporary silver mounts, scroll thumbpiece, circa 1745, 7cm. wide. (Christie's) $2,187

A Meissen figure of a rhinoceros modelled by J. J. Kandler after Albrecht Durer, 1735-40, 17cm. long. (Christie's) $2,300

A Meissen chinoiserie dish, the center painted by C. F. Herold, blue crossed swords mark, circa 1734. (Christie's) $18,403

A Meissen circular snuff box and cover painted by B. G. Hauer, the interior of the base solid gilt, 1725-30, 7.5cm. diam. (Christie's) $27,604

A Meissen two-handled quatrefoil tray and four cups, blue crossed swords marks and Pressnummer 24 and 26, circa 1740. (Christie's) $9,968

A Meissen figure of a jay modelled by J. J. Kandler, circa 1745, 39cm. high. (Christie's) $16,869

A Meissen bullet-shaped vase and cover in blue with decorated panels, on stand. (F. H. Fellows & Sons) $613

One of two Meissen figures of seated cats modelled by J. J. Kandler, circa 1740, 17.5cm. high. (Christie's) $9,201

A Meissen oval bombe-shaped snuff box and cover, 1725-28, 7cm. wide. (Christie's) $13,802

MEISSEN

A Meissen oval bombe-shaped snuff box and cover painted en camaieu rose, 1730-40, 7.5cm. wide. (Christie's) $6,441

A Meissen dolphin tureen and cover, blue crossed swords mark, circa 1750, 24cm. long. (Christie's) $2,147

A Meissen KPM oblong sugar box and cover painted in the Horoldt workshop, 1723-25, 10.5cm. long. (Christie's) $13,035

A Meissen rectangular snuff box and cover with contemporary two-colour gold mounts, circa 1750, 8.5cm. wide. (Christie's) $9,968

A Meissen group of a scantily draped woman at her toilet, blue crossed swords marks and incised numerals, circa 1880, 15.5cm. high. (Christie's) $496

A Meissen rectangular yellow-ground tea caddy painted in a Kakiemon palette, blue crossed swords mark and former's mark of Seidel, circa 1730, 10cm. high. (Christie's)$1,239

A Meissen group of Die Polnische Verlobung modelled as a sultan with his Polish bride and Polish soldier servant, circa 1745, 15cm. high. (Christie's) $9,201

One of a pair of Meissen pug dogs modelled by J. J. Kandler and P. Reinicke, one with blue crossed swords mark on base, circa 1745, 15cm. high. (Christie's) $4,600

A Meissen model of a cottage modelled by J. J. Kandler for Count Bruhl, 1745-8, 15cm. wide. (Christie's) $9,201

A blue and white dragon bowl, encircled Kangxi six-character mark and of the period, 15.5cm. diam. (Christie's) $5,702

A 16th century Ming green and black enamelled brush rest, 20cm. high. (Christie's) $1,905

A blue and white saucer dish, encircled Yongzheng six-character mark and of the period, 17.4cm. diam. (Christie's) $2,138

Late 17th/early 18th century shield-shaped Arita dish, the base with three spur marks and a Ming Chenghua mark, 12.4cm. (Christie's) $933

One of a pair of blue and white late 18th century hexagonal barrel-shaped garden seats, 49cm. high. (Christie's) $4,847

A Ming green dragon dish encircled Zhengde six-character mark and of the period, 23cm. diam., with fitted box. (Christie's) $5,987

An early Ming blue and white saucer dish, Xuande, 27.4cm. diam. (Christie's) $23,814

An early Ming blue and white vase, meiping, painted in a deep blue, Yongle, 28.5cm. high. (Christie's) $23,814

A Ming blue and white broad oviform jar, encircled Jiajing six-character mark and of the period, 17.2cm. high. (Christie's) $2,280

154

MING

A late Ming Wucai saucer dish, encircled Wanli six-character mark and of the period, 19cm. diam. (Christie's) $7,128

A Ming Wucai square dish, unenclosed Jiajing six-character mark and of the period, 17cm. square. (Christie's) $2,423

A late Ming Wucai barrel-shaped jar and cover, the base with Wanli six-character mark and of the period, 15cm. diam., fitted box. (Christie's) $50,803

MINTON

A Minton turquoise ground pate-sur-pate part dessert service decorated by Desire Leroy, pattern no. G1859, circa 1878. (Christie's) $2,760

A Minton vase and cover, painted by H. Boullemier, the reverse by W. Payne, 18cm. high, mark in gold. (Lawrence Fine Art) $95

A Minton aquarium hexagonal plate, decorated in polychrome colors with three frogs resting, impressed date marks for 1882, 37.6cm. diam. (Christie's) $500

One of a pair of Minton 'moon' vases with gilt loop handles, 26.5cm. high. (Lawrence Fine Art) $669

MINTON

A Minton vase of classical shape on square pedestal base, impressed Minton 980 and with date code for 1864, 96.5cm. high. (Christie's) $26,244

A Minton double candle-snuffer, modelled as busts of a Medieval pair, the tray impressed Minton mark 427 and date code for 1865, 11cm. high. (Christie's) $801

A large Minton two-handled vase, amphora shape, impressed IA and with date code for 1859, 70cm. high. (Christie's)$11,664

A Minton 'Amorini' fountain modelled as a pair of cherubs, impressed Minton 911 and with date code for 1868, 65cm. high. (Christie's) $5,832

A Minton jardiniere and underdish with molded decoration overall of rambling flowers, date code for 1858 on jardiniere, 37cm. high. (Christie's) $2,478

A Minton figure, 'Vintager with basket in each hand', impressed Minton. (Christie's) $874

A Minton honeycomb dish modelled as a beehive, impressed Minton 1499 and date code for 1877, 18cm. high. (Christie's) $2,916

A Minton figural lamp stand, impressed Minton 1517 and with date code for 1881, 35.6cm. high. (Christie's) $2,478

A monkey 'match pot', impressed Minton 1692 and date code for 1873, 19.6cm. high. (Christie's) $2,332

MINTON

One of a pair of large Minton vases, the handles modelled as two writhing snakes, circa 1870, 62cm. high. (Christie's) $5,103

One of a pair of Minton flared rectangular spill vases with gilt fixed ring handles, circa 1880, 29cm. wide. (Christie's) $2,021

A large amphora-shaped Minton vase on stand, impressed Minton and date code for 1866, 91cm. high. (Christie's) $1,749

A Minton jardiniere and stand, designed by Albert Carrier de Belleuse, impressed Minton 990 and date code for 1882, 168cm. high. (Christie's) $34,992

A Minton 'Christmas Jug', the handle modelled as entwined holly branches, impressed Minton 580 (circa 1870), 22.5cm. high. (Christie's) $1,166

A Minton 'Perforated Garden Pedestal', impressed Minton 451 and date code for 1865, 80.5cm. high. (Christie's) $729

A Minton lidded 'Tower Jug', impressed Minton 1231 and date code for 1869, 34.5cm. high. (Christie's) $232

A Minton figural group, 'Shell Carriers', impressed Minton 1296 and date code for 1862, 28cm. high. (Christie's) $947

A Minton 'Palissy' vase formed as a ewer, impressed Minton 900 and date code for 1872, 37cm. high. (Christie's) $437

A Minton teapot modelled as a Chinaman holding a mask from which the spout projects, circa 1875, 14.4cm. high. (Christie's) $729

A Minton majolica jardiniere embossed with foxgloves and ferns, 1ft.7in. wide over the handles, 13in. high, date marked for 1871. (Hobbs & Chambers) $876

A Minton majolica game tureen, cover and liner, year cypher for 1860. (Woolley & Wallis) $892

A large Minton 'moon flask' vase with two lug handles, circa 1890, 43.2cm. high. (Christie's) $551

A pair of Minton full figure Toby jugs, impressed Minton 1104 and 1140 and with date stamps for 1867, restored, 28cm. and 28.4cm. high. (Christie's) $947

A Minton figure, 'Seahorse with Shell', after Carrier-Belleuse, impressed Minton 326 and with date code for 1872, 41.5cm. high. (Christie's) $1,895

A Minton blue-ground Wellington vase with gilt rams' mask handles, painted in the manner of Steel, circa 1835, 38cm. high. (Christie's) $616

A Minton Parian group of a nude female figure seated on the back of a lion, circa 1847-48, 1ft.3½in. high. (Hobbs & Chambers) $73

One of a pair of Minton 'Persian' pattern pottery vases decorated in the style of C. Dresser, 11in. high. (Christie's) $567

A Moorcroft bowl with plated mount of squat bulbous form, 18.5cm. diam. (Lawrence Fine Art) $176

A Moorcroft broad baluster pottery vase made for Liberty & Co., 8in. high. (Christie's) $594

A Moorcroft squat shaped vase in the toadstool pattern, 7¾in. wide. (Christie's) $588

A William Moorcroft grape pattern vase of ovoid form, 16in. high. (Capes, Dunn & Co.) $316

A Moorcroft circular pottery dish painted in the Leaf and Berry pattern, 11½in. diam. (Christie's) $114

One of a pair of Moorcroft Dawn pattern vases of ovoid form, 18.5cm. high. (Lawrence Fine Art) $610

A Moorcroft globular pottery vase modelled with a swimming fish, outlined in blue on a pale green ground, 6½in. high. (Christie's) $189

A Moorcroft Macintyre two-handled vase, design no. 360574, signed in green W. Moorcroft, 19cm. high. (Lawrence Fine Art) $449

A Moorcroft pottery oviform vase made for Liberty & Co., in the Toadstool pattern, 10in. high, signed in green. (Christie's) $1,029

NANTGARW

CHINA

A Nantgarw plate, London decorated with a branch and loose mulberries, 24.2cm. diam. (Lawrence Fine Art) $491

A Nantgarw topographical plate, named in red script on the reverse, circa 1820, 21.5cm. diam. (Christie's) $1,686

A Nantgarw plate, London decorated with a bouquet of flowers, 23.4cm. diam. (Lawrence Fine Art) $753

ORIENTAL

Mid 19th century Oriental plate. (British Antique Exporters) $17

A Safavid tile panel with a figure of Sagittarius surrounded by palmettes, 4ft. 1in. x 2ft.10in. (Christie's) $14,877

One of a pair of earthenware bowls and covers of compressed circular shape, 7in. diam. (Lawrence Fine Art) $382

PARIAN

A colored Parian group modelled as a young girl on rockwork, entitled 'You can't read', 12¼in. high, possibly by Robinson & Leadbetter. (Christie's) $222

A Parian standing female figure, probably Belleek but unmarked, 36.5cm. high. (Lawrence Fine Art) $159

One of a pair of glazed Parian figure brackets, allegorical figures in rock-like niches, 9½in. high. (Capes, Dunn & Co.) $163

A Paris (Nast) ornithological part tea and coffee service, circa 1810.
(Christie's) $9,968

A Paris matt blue ground part coffee service, circa 1815. (Christie's)
$766

A Paris (Nast) ornithological part dessert service, circa 1810. (Christie's)
$10,735

CHINA

PILKINGTON

A Pilkington Lancastrian tall baluster vase with molded strapwork at the neck decorated by Richard Joyce in bronze and ruby lustre, date code for 1908, 41.9cm. high. (Christie's) $315

A Pilkington Lancastrian deep bowl designed by Walter Crane and decorated by Wm. S. Mycock, date code for 1913, 21.6cm. high.(Christie's) $1,261

A Pilkington Lancastrian baluster vase decorated by Wm. S. Mycock in golden lustre, date code for 1910, 21.8cm. high. (Christie's) $598

PRATTWARE

A Prattware pot lid depicting Strathfieldsay, 5in. diam. (Christie's) $71

A large Prattware two-handled loving cup, bearing the Jolly Topers, malachite ground, gold line decoration. (Phillips) $661

A Prattware pot lid depicting Wellington seated, 5in. diam. (Christie's) $117

REDWARE

A 19th century Redware deep platter, with squiggle decoration, 17½in. long. (Robt. W. Skinner Inc.) $1,100

A 19th century Redware covered jar, Gonic pottery, New Hampshire, 11½in. high. (Robt. W. Skinner Inc.) $550

One of two 19th century Redware shallow circular dishes with crimped rims, 12¼in. diam. (Robt. W. Skinner Inc.)$350

LUCIE RIE

CHINA

A stoneware 'knitted' bowl, by Lucie Rie, inlaid and speckled with copper manganese, circa 1981, 25.2cm. diam. (Christie's) $1,879

A porcelain sgraffito and inlaid bottle by Lucie Rie, circa 1980, 21.4cm. high. (Christie's) $1,008

A stoneware bowl by Lucie Rie, covered in a shiny white glaze peppered with russet, circa 1956, 30.1cm. diam. (Christie's) $1,331

A porcelain sgraffito bottle covered in a bronze manganese glaze with sgraffito lines, by Lucie Rie, circa 1980, 25.3cm. high. (Christie's) $1,324

A stoneware teapot and cover by Lucie Rie, covered in a matt manganese glaze, circa 1958, 15cm. high. (Christie's) $469

A stoneware oviform bottle with wide scooped rim, by Lucie Rie, circa 1975, 27.9cm. high. (Christie's) $1,368

A stoneware bowl covered in a white glaze thickening to droplets, by Lucie Rie, circa 1960, 16.8cm. wide. (Christie's) $359

A porcelain mallet shaped bottle, covered in a mottled pastel green glaze with pale coral spiral, by Lucie Rie, circa 1967, 29.8cm. high. (Christie's) $4,698

A porcelain wide bowl covered in pastel green glaze. heightened with amber and coral, by Lucie Rie, circa 1967, 32.9cm. diam. (Christie's) $6,890

163

ROOKWOOD

CHINA

A Rookwood pottery iris glaze vase, signed by F. D.H. Rothenbush, circa 1904, 9in. high. (Robt. W. Skinner Inc.) $300

A Rookwood pottery vase with sterling silver overlay, circa 1899, signed by J. Zettel, 8½in. high. (Robt. W. Skinner Inc.) $2,300

A Rookwood pottery iris glaze vase, initialled by Olga G. Reed, circa 1902, 7¼in. high. (Robt. W. Skinner Inc.) $381

A Rookwood pottery Indian squaw portrait vase, circa 1899, 11in. high. (Robt. W. Skinner Inc.) $650

A Rookwood pottery standard glaze vase, initialled by Clara C. Linderman, 1904, 8¾in. high. (Robt. W. Skinner Inc.) $324

A Rookwood standard glaze pottery Indian portrait vase, decorated by Grace Young, date cypher for 1905, 30.5cm. high. (Christie's) $4,620

ROYAL DUX

Large Royal Dux group with camel and Bedouin seated on its back, 19¾in. high. (Reeds Rains) $835

An Art Nouveau Royal Dux figural vase modelled as a tree trunk with a maiden climbing around the side, 46cm. high. (Phillips) $364

A Royal Dux Art Nouveau conch shell group with three water nymphs in relief, 17½in. high. (Reeds Rains) $676

RUSKIN

CHINA

A Ruskin high-fired trans-mutation glazed vase, 1911, 38cm. high. (Christie's) $594

A Ruskin flambe vase, mallet-shaped with blue and red speckled glaze, 1909, 17.4cm. high. (Christie's) $236

A large Ruskin high fired transmutation glaze vase and matching circular step-ped stand, England, circa 1930, 36cm. high includ-ing stand. (Christie's) $346

A Ruskin high fired shaped cylindrical vase, 1925, 23.6cm. high. (Christie's) $600

A large Ruskin low-fired crystalline glaze vase of swollen cylindrical shape, England, 1926, 41.5cm. high. (Christie's) $283

A Ruskin high fired transmu-tation glaze vase, England, 1933, 21cm. high. (Christie's) $283

SATSUMA

A 19th century Satsuma broad oviform jar and domed cover with knob finial, signed Kintozan, 48cm. high. (Christie's) $660

Pair of Japanese Satsuma pottery vases, 5in. high. (Hobbs & Chambers) $67

A 19th century large Sat-suma vase, Japan, signed on base, 15¼in. high. (Robt. W. Skinner Inc.) $1,000

SATSUMA

A Satsuma pottery cylindrical box, the cover painted and gilded with geishas, 3in. diam. (Reeds Rains) $288

Late 19th century Satsuma model of a recumbent caparisoned elephant, signed, 25cm. long. (Christie's) $1,389

A Satsuma pottery pot pourri bowl on three feet in the form of grotesque heads, 8½in. diam. (Capes, Dunn & Co.) $136

A Satsuma oviform vase enamelled in black, red and green and gilt, 12in. high. (Christie's) $2,175

A pair of Satsuma pottery vases, 9¼in. high, on carved wood bases. (Reeds Rains) $460

Late 19th century Satsuma oviform vase decorated in colors and gilt, 62cm. high. (Christie's) $1,853

A Satsuma miniature teapot, signed on base, 4in. high. (Reeds Rains) $460

A 19th century Satsuma broad oviform jar on shallow tripod feet, 25cm. high. (Christie's) $2,496

A 19th century large Satsuma oviform vase, signed Satsuma Tansai above an iron-red Shimazu mon, 50.2cm. high. (Christie's) $1,175

SEVRES

A Sevres pattern gilt bronze oval two-handled jardiniere, circa 1860, 44.5cm. wide. (Christie's) $1,380

A Sevres teacup and saucer, blue interlaced L marks, enclosing the date letters ii for 1786 and painter's mark of J. Fontaine. (Christie's) $355

A Sevres green ground deep bowl, blue interlaced L marks enclosing the date letter q for 1769, and painter's mark of Nicquet, 23,5cm. diam. (Christie's) $1,533

A large Sevres pattern royal-blue ground gilt bronze mounted two-handled vase, circa 1880, 90cm. high. (Christie's) $3,220

A Sevres tete-a-tete service with Wittelsbach borders, blue interlaced L marks and HY, circa 1763, the tray 30cm. wide. (Christie's) $5,670

A Sevres biscuit figure of Bossuet, modelled by A. Pajou from the Serie des Grands Hommes, circa 1783, 47cm. high. (Christie's) $4,050

A Sevres Art Deco porcelain figure of a lady in evening dress designed by Odart-chenko, 28cm. high. (Christie's) $548

A Sevres ornithological cushion-shaped dish, blue interlaced L marks enclosing the date letter q for 1769 and painter's mark of Castel, 22cm. wide. (Christie's) $891

A Sevres pattern pink ground gilt metal mounted tapering oviform two-handled vase and cover, late 19th century, 43.5cm. high. (Christie's) $460

SEVRES

A Sevres porcelain shallow dish, 8½in. diam., the reverse with date mark for 1772, initials for Nicquet. (Hobbs & Chambers) $248

A Sevres white biscuit group of Le Valet de Chien modelled by Blondeau after Oudry, circa 1776, 30.5cm. long.(Christie's) $1,749

A Sevres bleu nouveau baluster milk jug, blue interlaced L mark enclosing the date letter q for 1769, and painter's mark B, 12cm. high. (Christie's)$613

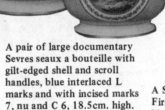

A Sevres-pattern porcelain and ormolu mounted mantel clock, imitation interlaced L and initial marks, circa 1880, 61.5cm. high. (Christie's) $3,732

A pair of large documentary Sevres seaux a bouteille with gilt-edged shell and scroll handles, blue interlaced L marks and with incised marks 7, nu and C 6, 18.5cm. high. (Christie's) $20,412

A Sevres bust of Napoleon as First Consul, dated 1802, 29cm. high. (Christie's) $1,093

A Sevres ornithological circular sugar bowl and cover, blue interlaced L marks enclosing the date letter U for 1773 and painter's mark of Evans, 11.5cm. high. (Christie's) $766

A pair of Sevres-pattern bleuceleste ground ormolu mounted baluster vases, circa 1860, 60cm. high. (Christie's) $3,110

A Sevres ecuelle cover and stand, the stand with date letter K for 1763 and the ecuelle with small q for 1769, 20cm. diam. (Christie's) $2,624

SEVRES

CHINA

A Sevres bleu lapis two-handled seau a bouteille, blue interlaced L mark enclosing the date letter F for 1758 and with painter's mark of Jean Pierre Le Doux, 19cm. high. (Christie's) $13,122

A Sevres biscuit group of The Judgement of Paris, circa 1781, 41cm. high. (Christie's) $1,895

One of a pair of Sevres two-handled tureens and covers, incised marks, circa 1765. (Christie's) $1,993

A Sevres bleu nouveau cylindrical cup and saucer, blue interlaced L marks, and painter's mark C.D. and incised 40, circa 1780. (Christie's) $613

A pair of Sevres-pattern square bottles and stoppers decorated with portraits of Louis XIV and Me. de Lamballe, circa 1880, 15.5cm. high. (Christie's) $1,555

A Sevres bleu nouveau cylindrical coffee cup and saucer, blue interlaced L marks enclosing the date letters EE for 1782. (Christie's) $766

A Sevres soup plate from the Madame du Barry Service, blue interlaced L marks enclosing the date letter S for 1771, and painter's mark of Bulidon, 24cm. diam. (Christie's) $1,993

A pair of Sevres-pattern turquoise ground gilt metal mounted vases and covers, circa 1860, 55cm. high. (Christie's) $3,732

One of forty-four 18th century Sevres shaped circular plates, 25cm. diam. (Christie's) $3,207

SEVRES

A Sevres circular sugar bowl and a cover painted en camaieu rose, circa 1765, 10cm. high. (Christie's) $420

A Sevres bleu celeste cylindrical cup and saucer, blue interlaced L marks, the saucer with the date letter F for 1758. (Christie's) $324

A Sevres bleu nouveau circular sugar bowl and cover, circa 1795, 12.5cm. high. (Christie's) $324

One of a pair of late 19th century Sevres pattern metal mounted turquoise gound oviform vases, 84cm. high. (Christie's) $8,434

A Sevres apple-green cup and saucer, blue interlaced L marks enclosing the date letter F for 1758, and painter's mark of Buteux aine. (Christie's) $1,686

A Sevres biscuit standing figure of Marechal de Turenne modelled by A. Pajou from the Serie des Grands Hommes, circa 1783, 48cm. high. (Christie's) $4,860

One of a pair of Sevres plates, blue interlaced L marks enclosing the date letters CC for 1780, 24cm. diam. (Christie's) $324

A Sevres circular sugar bowl and cover, blue interlaced L marks enclosing the date letter S for 1771, 12cm. high. (Christie's) $517

A jewelled Sevres cylindrical cup and saucer, gilt interlaced L marks and painter's marks LG of Le Guay, circa 1783. (Christie's) $12,150

A Shelley bone china 'Tea for Two' service of eight pieces, Eric Slater's 'Mode' shape in orange and black enamels. (Capes, Dunn & Co.) $172

A Shelley part tea service, comprising an octagonal milk jug, sugar bowl, sandwich plate, six side plates and six cups and saucers, registered no. 723404. (Lawrence Fine Art) $146

A Shelley 'Mode' shape part teaset, comprising a milk jug, sugar bowl, six cups and saucers, six side plates and one sandwich plate, registered no. 756533. (Lawrence Fine Art) $321

SONG

A Northern Celadon conical bowl molded with two ladies reclining amongst clouds, Song Dynasty, 16.5cm. diam., fitted box. (Christie's) $9,525

A Jun Yao globular jar with two looped straight handles, Song Dynasty, 15cm. diam. (Christie's) $2,381

A Ding Yao lobed hexafoil dish, clear ivory glaze thinning towards the unglazed rim, Song Dynasty, 17.8cm. diam. (Christie's) $1,587

A Cizhou painted pillow molded from two parts as a lady recumbent, Song Dynasty, 33cm. wide. (Christie's) $12,117

A Northern Celadon bowl carved and combed with a continuous leaf scroll, Song Dynasty, 22cm. diam., fitted box. (Christie's) $2,540

A Ding type stem bowl, ivory white glaze, Northern Song Dynasty, 8.9cm. diam. (Christie's) $1,031

A Northern Celadon conical bowl, Song Dynasty, 11.4cm. diam. (Christie's) $2,381

A Jun Yao tripod censer under a rich lavender glaze thinning to an olive translucency at the rim, Song Dynasty, 6.5cm. diam. (Christie's) $1,428

A large Northern Celadon bowl freely carved with a deer amongst scrolling foliage, Song Dynasty, 21cm. diam., fitted box. (Christie's) $5,556

Part of a twenty-eight piece Spode tea service, painted with the 'Brocade' pattern, after Worcester. (Phillips) $1,361

One of a pair of Spode urn-shaped pot pourri vases, pierced weights and covers, circa 1820, 13.5cm. high. (Christie's) $1,220

Part of a thirty-four piece Spode tea service, painted with a Japan pattern of flowers and foliage, no. 2213. (Phillips) $1,036

Part of a twenty piece Spode pottery dessert service, printed in brown with vases decorated with groups of classical figures on a marbled ground with fruiting vine, with yellow rims. (Lawrence Fine Art) $1,606

A Spode pot pourri jar, cover and inner lid, with gilt loop handles, 23cm. high, marked Spode 2063 in red. (Lawrence Fine Art) $255

Six Spode 'Old Concord' design coffee cups and saucers, date impressed for 1952. (Capes, Dunn & Co.) $72

A Spode tulip cup with green stalk handle, script mark in red, circa 1820, 7cm. high. (Christie's) $766

STAFFORDSHIRE

A Staffordshire soup tureen and undertray, by R. Hall, circa 1825, 12in. high. (Robt. W. Skinner Inc.) $950

A Staffordshire saltglaze sauceboat with strap handle on three mask and paw feet, circa 1750, 20cm. wide. (Christie's) $1,292

A Staffordshire jug depicting Wellington at Salamanca, 5½in. high. (Christie's) $117

A Staffordshire pearlware box and cover modelled as a dog, the screw cover with the initials ET, circa 1815, 5cm. wide. (Christie's) $1,840

A pair of Staffordshire pugilist figures modelled as the boxers Mollineux and Cribb, circa 1810, 22cm. high. (Christie's) $2,729

An Obadiah Sherratt group of Polito's menagerie, circa 1830, 29.5cm. high. (Christie's) $21,546

A Staffordshire salt-glazed stoneware cylindrical mug, circa 1750, 6in. high. (Capes, Dunn & Co.) $136

One of a pair of late 18th century Staffordshire pottery cow creamers, 6¼in. long. (Dacre, Son & Hartley) $2,304

A Staffordshire Toby jug of conventional type, seated holding a frothing jug of ale, circa 1780, 24.5cm. high. (Christie's) $613

STAFFORDSHIRE

A Staffordshire slipware inscribed and dated two-handled loving cup, circa 1763, 17.5cm. high. (Christie's)$2,298

A Staffordshire saltglaze tartan ground Royalist teapot and cover with loop handle, circa 1750, 14cm. high. (Christie's) $15,336

A Staffordshire blue and white mug with molded decoration depicting soldiers with trophies from Vittoria greeting Wellington, 5in. high. (Christie's) $78

A Staffordshire full length standing figure of Wellington, 13in. high.(Christie's) $91

A Staffordshire part tea-service printed in gray mono-chrome with bust and other portraits of Wellington. (Christie's) $364

A 19th century Stafford-shire figure of Benjamin Franklin, 14in. high. (Robt. W. Skinner Inc.)$300

A Staffordshire blue and white cylindrical mug prin-ted with equestrian figures of The Duke of Wellington and Lord Hill, 4¾in. high. (Christie's) $260

A Staffordshire brown and white part glazed Parian jug with portraits of Wel-lington and Blucher, inscribed Jane Roberte, 7½in. high. (Christie's) $247

A Staffordshire jug printed and colored with an eques-trian portrait of the Duke of Wellington. (Christie's) $221

175

STAFFORDSHIRE

A creamware model of a recumbent sheep, with brown markings, on oval shaped base, circa 1780, 3¼in. high. (Christie's) $193

A pottery sauceboat in the form of a duck, circa 1785, 6½in. wide, perhaps York-shire. (Christie's) $819

An early 19th century Staffordshire soup tureen with high domed cover, 12in. high. (Robt. W. Skinner Inc.) $900

Part of a Staffordshire dinner service of ninety-two pieces, decorated in red, blue and yellow in Chinese style with vases and utensils in octagonal panels. (Lawrence Fine Art) $2,552

A money box modelled as a chapel, inscribed Salley Harper Hougate March 16th 1845, 6¾in. high. (Christie's) $652

A figure of George Parr, holding a cricket ball in his right hand, circa 1865, 14in. high. (Christie's) $819

A pastille burner modelled as a cottage, on oval gilt lined base, 6in. high. (Christie's) $261

A creamware model of a recumbent sheep, facing to the right, 3¼in. high. (Christie's) $283

A pair of rabbits with black markings, recumbent facing right and left, eating lettuce leaves, 5in. high. (Christie's) $2,900

A blue Staffordshire sauce-boat, ladle and tray, by J. Stubbs, 1822-35, 6½in. high. (Christie's) $1,320

A figure of a huntsman, holding a hunting horn in his right hand, circa 1795, 9¼in. high. (Christie's) $253

A pair of well modelled spaniels with brown markings, wearing gilt collars, 10¼in. high. (Christie's) $1,740

A figure of The Tichborne Claimant, holding a bird on his left hand, a rifle at his side, 14in. high. (Christie's) $406

A figure of Peace, modelled as a woman wearing loose robes, the emblems of War at her side, circa 1810, 8¼in. high. (Christie's) $126

A pair of spill vases modelled as horses with foals recumbent at their feet, 12½in. high. (Christie's) $348

A white and gilt figure of Henry Joy McCracken, wearing a short coat, breeches and stockings, 13in. high. (Christie's) $232

STAFFORDSHIRE

CHINA

A group modelled as Hercules wrestling with a bull, circa 1810, 5½in. high. (Christie's) $1,266

A well modelled group of a lion with a recumbent lamb at it's feet, circa 1850, 7in. high. (Christie's) $417

A pastille burner modelled as a cottage with an iron-red doorway flanked by flowers and trees, on an oval shaped base, 6in. high. (Christie's) $377

A figure of Theobald Wolfe Tone holding two flags across his chest, the oval base named in gilt script, 13½in. high. (Christie's) $435

A pair of figures of the Prince of Wales and Prince Alfred, circa 1858, 10¾in. high. (Christie's) $387

A figure of Wellington standing, wearing full military uniform and full length cloak, on raised pink lustre marbled base, 13in. high. (Christie's) $261

A group of Napoleon III and Empress Eugenie, the oval base named in gilt molded capitals, circa 1854, 12in. high. (Christie's) $238

An Obadiah Sherratt group, entitled 'Grecian and Daughter', 9in. high. (Christie's) $942

A group of Victoria standing with her arm around The Princess Royal, circa 1842, 10in. high. (Christie's) $141

STONEWARE

A salt-glazed stoneware two-gallon butter churn. circa 1840, probably New York, 13½in. high. (Christie's) $572

A handbuilt stoneware bird bowl by Albert Diato, circa 1955, 36.3cm. wide. (Christie's) $500

A handbuilt stoneware spout pot by Elizabeth Fritsch, circa 1974, 30.4cm. high. (Christie's) $5,324

A stoneware press molded rectangular bottle, by Kanjiro Kawai, covered in grayish-white glaze with khaki rims, circa 1952, 21.9cm. high. (Christie's) $1,096

A slab built stoneware platter by Jacqueline Poncelet with cut rim, circa 1981, 47.9cm. wide. (Christie's) $469

An early handbuilt vase by Elizabeth Fritsch, circa 1970, 12.6cm. high. (Christie's) $1,879

A stoneware cylindrical vase by John Ward, circa 1983, 16.6cm. high. (Christie's) $171

A stoneware tall flattened bottle by Joanna Constantinidis, covered in a semi-matt dark iron brown glaze, 1969, 43cm. high. (Christie's) $562

A Nottingham type glazed red stoneware posset pot, dated 1791, 9½in. high. (Christie's) $1,650

179

STONEWARE

A Westerwald gray stoneware spirit barrel, 33.5cm. high. (Christie's) $1,093

A porcelain landscape plate textured and decorated with muslin and leaf indentation, by Ljerka Njers, 27.5cm. diam. (Christie's)$316

A stoneware bowl with rounded sides, by Katharine Pleydell-Bouverie, circa 1930, 18.5cm. diam. (Christie's) $1,008

A Bottger polished brown stoneware baluster coffee pot and domed cover, circa 1715, 17.5cm. high. (Christie's)$13,851

Pair of tall salt-glazed stoneware vases, colored gray-green with blue and ochre details, initials of Bessie Newbury, circa 1912-18, 12in. high. (Capes, Dunn & Co.) $79

A 17th century Westerwald large oviform jug, 36cm. high. (Christie's) $874

A large stoneware oviform vase by Margaret Rey, impressed seal, circa 1930, 30.2cm. high. (Christie's) $160

A stoneware tall vase of oval rectangular section, by Joanna Constantinidis, 1971, 66.5cm. high. (Christie's) $547

A Nottingham stoneware carved mug with grooved loop handle, circa 1700, 10.5cm. high. (Christie's) $1,220

STONEWARE

A porcelain flask form vase by Wm. Marshall, circa 1983, 26.2cm. high. (Christie's) $403

A large stoneware footed circular dish, incised James Tower 84 and with paper label inscribed James Tower No. 167 Reflections, 54.4cm. diam. (Christie's) $576

A stoneware large grain jar and cover with two crescent shaped handles, by Audu Mugu Sokoto, circa 1960, 60.3cm. high. (Christie's) $403

A large molded stoneware vase of swelling rectangular section, incised James Tower 84, 54.3cm. high. (Christie's) $720

Pair of inverted baluster form salt-glazed stoneware vases, initials of Florence E. Barlow, circa 1902-5, 10½in. high. (Capes, Dunn & Co.) $302

An English brown glazed stoneware wall mask, modelled as Comedy, 24in. high. (Christie's) $172

A stoneware press molded rectangular dish by Wm. Marshall, impressed and incised WM, incised date 83, 31cm. wide. (Christie's) $72

A Tapio Wirkkala stoneware vase of speckled stone color, circa 1955, 15cm. high. (Christie's) $315

A stoneware water pot by Ladi Kwali, made at Abuja, circa 1960, 29cm. high. (Christie's) $288

TANG

A red pottery figure of a
mounted attendant, Tang
Dynasty, 31.5cm. high.
(Christie's) $1,746

A blue splashed straw glazed
buff pottery bowl, Tang
Dynasty, 9.8cm. diam.
(Christie's) $1,349

A painted red pottery figure
of a court lady, Tang Dynasty, 44.5cm. high.
(Christie's) $92,080

A Sancai buff pottery figure
of a court attendant, Tang
Dynasty, 100.5cm. high.
(Christie's)
$38,102

A phosphatic splashed brown
glazed oviform jar with two
strap handles, Tang Dynasty,
18cm. high. (Christie's)
$2,540

An unglazed buff pottery
figure of a Western Asiatic
with curly hair, Tang
Dynasty, 26cm. high.
(Christie's) $2,063

A red pottery figure of a
mounted lady attendant,
Tang Dynasty, 29.5cm. high.
(Christie's) $1,190

A red pottery figure of a
standing camel, Tang Dynasty,
38cm. high. (Christie's)
$1,746

An unglazed buff pottery
figure of a seated lady
musician, Tang Dynasty,
19.5cm. high.(Christie's)
$1,905

TANG

An unglazed buff pottery
figure of a court lady,
Tang Dynasty, 10in. high.
(Lawrence Fine Art)
$877

A straw-glazed buff pottery
figure of a standing ox,
Tang Dynasty, 22cm. wide.
(Christie's) $7,128

An unglazed buff pottery
figure of a court attendant,
Tang Dynasty, 70cm. high.
(Christie's) $1,568

A Sancai pottery figure of
a caparisoned horse, Tang
Dynasty, 77cm. high.
(Christie's)
$349,272

A blue glazed tripod cylindrical jar standing on lion's
paw feet, Tang Dynasty,
18cm. diam., with fitted
box. (Christie's)
$20,638

A red pottery figure of a
tall standing horse, Tang
Dynasty, 43.5cm. high.
(Christie's)$4,127

A large Sancai pottery figure
of a standing Bactrian camel,
Tang Dynasty, 65cm. high.
(Christie's) $28,512

A straw and ochre glazed
standing pottery figure of
a groom, Tang Dynasty,
29cm. high. (Christie's)
$1,587

A straw-glazed buff pottery
figure of a standing horse,
Sui/early Tang Dynasty,
31.5cm. high. (Christie's)
$5,132

TERRACOTTA

CHINA

A French terracotta bust of an 18th century lady with dressed hair, 16in. high. (Christie's) $2,505

A pair of Regency painted terracotta figures modelled as Chinese ladies, 8½in. and 8in. high. (Christie's) $366

A French terracotta bust of an 18th century boy, 18in. high. (Christie's) $3,288

TOURNAI

A Tournai spirally molded, blue and white part coffee service, circa 1770. (Christie's) $567

Part of a one hundred and sixty-two piece Tournai white and gold dinner service, gilt crossed swords and star marks, and tower marks, circa 1770. (Christie's) $6,480

A Tournai ornithological oviform jar and cover from the Duc d'Orleans service, circa 1787, 18.5cm. high. (Christie's) $1,539

One of seven Tournai shaped circular plates painted with sprays of fruit and flowers, circa 1770, 24cm. diam. (Christie's) $972

One of a pair of Tournai two-handled seaux a glace covers and liners with molded Ozier borders, circa 1770, 25cm. wide. (Christie's) $355

184

VIENNA

A Vienna Du Paquier candle sconce or girandole, circa 1730, 39.5cm. high. (Christie's) $6,000

A 19th century pair of Vienna vases and covers, 31.5cm. high, shield mark in underglaze blue. (Lawrence Fine Art) $797

A Du Paquier Vienna 'Schwarzlot' plate from the service made for Count Trivulzio of Milan, 21cm. diam. (Phillips) $1,184

A Vienna white figure of St. Paul, blue beehive mark, circa 1760, 47cm. high. (Christie's) $1,321

A 'Vienna' gold-ground tete-a-tete, decorated with scénes from classical mythology, circa 1880, the tray 32.5cm. wide. (Christie's) $1,710

One of a pair of Vienna tea-cups and saucers painted in purple monochrome, blue beehive marks Pressnummer 5, circa 1750. (Christie's) $590

CHARLES VYSE

A Charles Vyse figure of a Shire horse, on rectangular base, 28.5cm. high. (Christie's) $423

A Charles Vyse figure of a ribbon seller on a square plinth, circa 1925, 30.5cm. high, including plinth. (Christie's) $946

A Charles Vyse pottery figure of The Piccadilly Rose Woman, modelled as a plump lady, 10in. high. (Christie's) $742

CHINA

A Wedgwood blue jasper dip cylindrical coffee cup and deep saucer, impressed mark. (Christie's) $444

A Wedgwood Fairyland lustre circular footed bowl, printed Portland Vase mark and pattern no. Z5360/2, circa 1925, 23.5cm. diam. (Christie's) $718

A Wedgwood 'Chintz' cream-ware teapot and cover of globular shape with baluster finial, 13cm. high. (Phillips) $1,386

A Wedgwood black basalt bust of George II, circa 1790, 22.5cm. high. (Christie's) $1,150

A pair of Wedgwood bronzed black basalt triton candlesticks of conventional type, impressed marks, circa 1880, 27cm. high. (Christie's) $996

A Wedgwood & Bentley black basalt miniature bust of Aristophanes, circa 1775, 11cm. high. (Christie's) $1,993

A 19th century Wedgwood blue and white jasper vase, 12in. high. (Christie's) $735

A Wedgwood blue and white jasper plaque, portrait of Dr. Priestley, attributed to Hack-wood, 10 x 8cm. (Lawrence Fine Art) $111

A Wedgwood terracotta bust of Locke, impressed mark and inscribed on the reverse, circa 1785, 21.5cm. high. (Christie's)$287

CHINA

A Wedgwood Whieldon pine-apple teapot and cover, 10cm. high. (Phillips) $1,386

A Wedgwood Fairyland lustre octagonal bowl, printed Portland Vase mark in gold and pattern no. Z4968T, circa 1925, 16cm. wide. (Christie's) $1,149

A Wedgwood creamware globular teapot and cover, painted in the manner of David Rhodes, circa 1768, 15cm. high. (Christie's) $2,913

A Wedgwood blue and white jasper portrait medallion of William Pitt The Younger, circa 1790, 9.5cm. high. (Christie's) $574

A pair of Wedgwood black basalt griffin candlesticks, circa 1795, 34cm. high. (Christie's) $1,840

A Wedgwood Fairyland lustre circular bowl, the exterior painted with birds in flight on a green ground, 11in. diam. (Christie's) $521

A black basalt tea kettle and cover, circa 1800, 23.5cm. high, (base cracked, rim to cover repaired). (Christie's) $359

A Wedgwood blue and white jasper oval plaque, portrait of J. Philip Elers, the potter, modelled by Wm. Hackwood, 10.7 x 7.4cm. (Lawrence Fine Art) $159

A blue and white jasper two-handled oviform vase on black basalt base, probably Adams, circa 1800, 28cm. high. (Christie's) $430

187

WEDGWOOD

CHINA

Part of a black basalt tea-service, comprising a teapot, milk jug, sugar bowl and slop basin, circa 1800.(Christie's) $344

A Wedgwood Fairyland lustre octagonal bowl, the exterior decorated with panels of river scenes, 10¼in. wide. (Christie's) $1,160

A Wedgwood creamware teapot and cover with flower finial, 11cm. high. (Phillips) $693

One of a pair of Wedgwood & Bentley black basalt ovi-form ewers, circa 1775, 31cm. high. (Christie's) $996

A pair of Wedgwood and Bentley black basalt oval portrait plaques of Vespasian and Nero, circa 1777, 20cm. high. (Christie's) $2,585

One of a pair of Wedgwood three- color jasper urn-shaped vases and covers, circa 1860, 33cm. high. (Christie's) $2,441

A Wedgwood vase designed by Keith Murray, 16.5cm. high. (Christie's) $121

A Wedgwood charger, the cobalt blue ground with raised polychrome decoration, 38.5cm. diam. (Christie's) $1,166

A Wedgwood blue and white jasper bulb pot and cover, impressed mark and V, circa 1785, 24cm. high.(Christie's) $1,840

A Wedgwood black basalt
Egyptian inkstand, impressed
mark, circa 1810, 29.5cm. wide.
(Christie's) $3,160

A Wedgwood Whieldon cauli-
flower teapot and cover,
11.5cm. high. (Phillips)
$924

A Wedgwood three- color
jasper figure of a reclining
child modelled by Wm.
Hackwood after the Della
Robbia original, circa 1785,
14.3cm. long. (Christie's)
$15,336

A Wedgwood pot pourri vase
and pierced cover, the central
area painted by H. Beardmore,
signed, 34.5cm. high.
(Phillips) $462

Part of a Wedgwood coffee
set, designed by Keith
Murray, all with printed
marks. (Christie's)
$184

A Wedgwood comport, oval
base surmounted by a stem
modelled as dolphins sup-
porting a conch shell, date
code for 1884, 42.5cm. high.
(Christie's) $1,166

A Wedgwood & Bentley
black basalt hare's head
stirrup cup, circa 1775,
16cm. high. (Christie's)
$13,035

A Wedgwood blue and white
jasper plaque, portrait of T.
Bentley, 11.5 x 8.5cm.
(Lawrence Fine Art)
$350

A Wedgwood & Bentley
black basalt compressed
globular vase and cover,
circa 1775, 16.5cm. high.
(Christie's) $1,150

A Whieldon cow creamer
and cover, 15cm. long.
(Phillips) $3,108

WOOD

A Whieldon green-ground
cornucopia wall-pocket of
spirally molded form,
circa 1750, 26.5cm. high.
(Christie's) $1,303

A Whieldon globular teapot
and cover with crabstock
spout, handle and finial
mottled in manganese, circa
1760, 11.5cm. high.
(Christie's) $996

A Ralph Wood Bacchus
mask jug, circa 1775,
23.5cm. high.(Christie's)
$545

An Enoch Wood model of
a stag, circa 1800, 29cm.
high. (Christie's)
$2,441

A Ralph Wood group of the
Vicar and Moses of conventional type, circa 1770,
21.5cm. high. (Christie's)
$643

A Ralph Wood model of a
polar bear wearing a collar,
9.5cm. wide. (Christie's)
$1,150

A Ralph Wood Toby jug of
conventional type, circa
1770, 25cm. high. (Chris-
tie's) $888

An Enoch Wood model of
a lion, circa 1790, 29cm.
wide. (Christie's)
$790

WORCESTER

One of a pair of First Period Worcester circular butter tubs, covers and stands, 10.7cm. wide, square seal marks in underglaze blue. (Lawrence Fine Art) $2,552

A pair of Royal Worcester figures modelled as a lady and gentleman, 14in. high, circa 1887. (Christie's) $1,480

An oval Royal Worcester plaque, painted by John Stinton, signed, 16 x 24.5cm., printed mark in puce, 1906. (Lawrence Fine Art) $1,515

One of a pair of First Period Worcester blue scale oviform vases and covers, 16cm. high, square seal marks in underglaze blue. (Lawrence Fine Art) $2,631

A First Period Worcester apple-green teacup and saucer, crossed swords mark and 9 in underglaze blue. (Lawrence Fine Art) $574

A Hadley's Worcester lobed pear shaped jug with lion mask terminal and leaf molded handle, 9in. high. (Christie's) $444

A Royal Worcester pot pourri vase and pierced cover, with angular scroll handles, 24cm. high, printed mark in puce. (Lawrence Fine Art) $701

Pair of Royal Worcester vases and covers in Sevres style, signed J. Rushton, date letter for 1870, 39cm. high. (Lawrence Fine Art) $3,030

A Royal Worcester figure of Karan Singh, the trinket maker, 13cm. high, from the Indian Craftsman Series, shape 1204, 1884. (Lawrence Fine Art) $542

WORCESTER

A Worcester yellow ground honeycomb molded oval dish, circa 1770, 30.5cm. wide. (Christie's) $7,668

One of a pair of Royal Worcester vases painted by Stinton, signed, 6in. high. (Reeds Rains) $503

A Worcester blue and white faceted oval creamboat painted with the Root Pattern, circa 1758, 10cm. wide. (Christie's) $1,456

A Worcester pink scale soup plate painted in the atelier of James Giles, circa 1770, 22.5cm. diam. (Christie's) $2,760

A Worcester blue and white baluster coffee pot and cover painted with an early version of the Plantation Pattern, circa 1754, 17cm. high. (Christie's) $1,456

A Worcester yellow scale saucer dish painted with exotic birds and insects, circa 1765, 18.5cm. diam. (Christie's) $5,520

A Worcester baluster mug with the monogram GG, circa 1770, 9cm. high. (Christie's) $1,380

A Worcester plate painted in the atelier of James Giles in puce camaieu, circa 1770, 22.5cm. diam. (Christie's) $2,607

A Worcester blue scale small jug with exotic birds among shrubs and trees, blue square seal mark, circa 1770, 9cm. high. (Christie's) $1,533

A Worcester blue and white chamber candlestick with scroll handle, blue W mark, circa 1770, 14.5cm. wide. (Christie's) $2,872

A Royal Worcester aesthetic teapot and cover, modelled as the upper part of a body, 15.5cm. high. (Christie's) $1,073

A Worcester oval sauceboat of small size, circa 1754, 16.5cm. wide. (Christie's) $1,364

A Worcester plate painted in the atelier of James Giles, circa 1770, 22.5cm. diam. (Christie's) $843

A Royal Worcester three-light candelabrum, by J. Hadley, 19in. high. (Reeds Rains) $1,302

A Worcester blue scale plate painted in the atelier of James Giles, circa 1770, 21cm. diam. (Christie's) $460

A Worcester Imari pattern armorial mug, blue square seal mark, circa 1770, 9cm. high. (Christie's) $1,150

A Worcester blue and white baluster cream jug painted with the Peony Pattern, circa 1758, 7.5cm. high. (Christie's) $428

A Worcester blue and white small flared mug, painted with the Tambourine Pattern, circa 1756, 6cm. high. (Christie's) $766

WORCESTER

A Chamberlain's Worcester rectangular two-handled tray, painted with Buckingham Palace, circa 1840, 33.5cm. wide. (Christie's) $1,710

A Royal Worcester 'ivory' mermaid and nautilus center-piece, decorated by Callow-hill, circa 1878. (Christie's) $1,399

One of a pair of Royal Worcester 'ivory' two-handled vases, pattern no. 1169, circa 1885, 30.5cm. high. (Christie's) $1,321

A Worcester, Flight & Barr blue ground spill vase, circa 1805, 12cm. high. (Christie's) $544

A Worcester blue and white foliage molded dish, circa 1765, 27cm. wide. (Christie's) $1,149

A Worcester, Flight & Barr, canary-yellow ground flared flower pot with fixed gilt ring handles, circa 1805, 16cm. high. (Christie's) $2,021

A Royal Worcester reticulated globular vase in the manner of George Owen, inscribed January 4th 1895, 11cm. high. (Christie's) $652

A Royal Worcester bone china demi-tasse coffee set, with R.W. mark for 1923, and London import mark for 1908. (Capes, Dunn & Co.) $151

A Chamberlain's Worcester globular vase and cover with gilt shell handles, painted by H. Chamberlain, circa 1810, 25cm. high. (Christie's) $1,088

A Royal Worcester reticulated oviform vase by George Owen, pattern no. 1969, gilt marks and date code for 1912, 17cm. high. (Christie's) $2,799

A Worcester quatrefoil two-handled chestnut basket, pierced cover and stand, circa 1770, the stand 25.5cm. wide. (Christie's)
$5,745

A Worcester quatrefoil baluster vase painted in Kakiemon palette, circa 1758, 16cm. high. (Christie's)
$10,773

A Worcester three-tier centerpiece on a pierced shell and coral encrusted base, circa 1770, 25.5cm. high. (Christie's) $1,867

A pair of Royal Worcester glazed Parian figures of Paul and Virginia, circa 1865, 33cm. high. (Christie's) $684

A Worcester flared wine funnel painted in a famille verte palette with an Oriental holding a fan, circa 1755, 13.5cm. high. (Christie's)
$17,236

A Worcester, Flight & Barr, goblet, script mark and incised B, circa 1805, 12cm. high. (Christie's)
$1,399

A Worcester plate of Grubbe type painted in the atelier of James Giles, circa 1770, 23cm. diam. (Christie's)
$4,021

Part of a Chamberlain's Worcester apricot ground garniture, comprising a vase of urn shape and two beaker vases, circa 1805, 28cm. and 15.5cm. high. (Christie's)
$622

BRACKET CLOCKS

A George III ebonized musical bracket clock, dial signed Robt. Ramsey London, 24in. high. (Christie's) $5,443

A Charles II ebonized striking bracket clock, the square dial signed Hen. Jones London, 16in. high. (Christie's) $4,600

A George I ebonized striking bracket clock, the dial signed Ed. Bayley London, 19in. high. (Christie's) $1,840

An ebony veneered quarter repeating bracket clock, the dials signed Henry Fish, Royal Exchange London, 17½in. high. (Lawrence Fine Art) $4,232

A mahogany veneered bracket clock, signed in the arch Richd. Ward, Winchester, 18½in. high. (Lawrence Fine Art) $2,523

Late 18th century Austrian petite sonnerie bracket clock with carrying handle, 18½in. high. (Christie's) $660

A red walnut quarter repeating bracket clock, signed on the chapter ring Asselin, London, 19in. high. (Lawrence Fine Art) $1,383

A George II ebonized grand sonnerie bracket clock, the dial signed Thos. Hughes, London, 9¾in. high. (Christie's) $7,938

A mid Georgian mahogany or red walnut striking bracket clock with brass handle, 19in. high. (Christie's) $1,686

BRACKET CLOCKS

A Chinese carved hardwood bracket clock on stand, the movement with twin chain fusees, 22½in. high. (Christie's) $1,399

A James II ebonized Roman striking bracket clock of Phase III Type, signed Joseph Knibb, 12in. high. (Christie's) $16,869

A George III mahogany striking bracket clock with brass handle, dial signed John Taylor London, 19½in. high. (Christie's) $1,944

A George III mahogany striking bracket clock with brass handle, signed Benj. Ward London, 18½in. high. (Christie's) $3,987

A George III ebonized bracket clock, the 7in. dial signed Alexdr. Cumming, London, 18½in. high. (Bermondsey) $1,400

A George III ebonized striking bracket clock, the dial signed George Flashman London, 14in. high. (Christie's) $1,226

A George III mahogany or red walnut striking bracket clock, the plaque signed Yeldrae Notron London 1053, 18in. high. (Christie's) $1,840

A George III ebonized bracket clock, signed Eardley Norton, London, 19½in. high. (Christie's) $2,200

A George II brown japanned bracket clock, dial signed Jn. Cotton London, 16¼in. high. (Christie's) $1,399

BRACKET CLOCKS

An early George III ebonized striking bracket clock, the dial signed Robt. & Peter Higgs, London, 17½in. high. (Christie's)
$11,113

A Regency boulle bracket clock, the dial signed Balthazar a Paris, with later movement, 39½in. high. (Christie's) $2,332

A George III scarlet and gold japanned bracket clock, made for the Turkish market, the dial signed Wm. Dunant, London, 22½in. high. (Christie's)
$10,713

A Regency boulle bracket clock, the dial signed Paliand a Besancon, 39½in. high. (Christie's)
$1,866

A Regency period mahogany and brass bracket clock, dial signed Thomas Pace, London, 19in. high. (Reeds Rains) $1,053

A French 18th century gilt brass mounted and inlaid rosewood bracket clock, signed Jean Tolly a Paris, 36in. high. (Lawrence Fine Art) $1,546

A George II ebonized striking bracket clock, plaque signed Willm Morgan London, 21½in. high. (Christie's)
$1,380

A George III satinwood 'balloon' bracket clock, the enamel dial signed Webster London, 24in. high. (Christie's) $6,220

A mid-Georgian ebonized striking bracket clock, the dial signed John Fladgate London, 18½in. high. (Christie's) $2,021

CARRIAGE CLOCKS

A brass grande sonnerie striking carriage clock, gorge case, stamp of Drocourt, 6in. high. (Christie's) $1,933

Victorian carriage clock with cloisonne panels, 1860. (British Antique Exporters) $249

A lacquered brass striking carriage clock, the movement with lever platform, 6½in. high. (Christie's) $714

A brass one-piece striking carriage clock by Paul Garnier Hger. De La Marine A Paris, 6¼in. high. (Christie's) $1,840

A silver gilt and enamel miniature 'carriage clock', 1¾in. high. (Christie's) $1,226

An English chronometer carriage timepiece, by Dent, London, with mahogany carrying case, 8½in. high. (Lawrence Fine Art) $10,582

A gilt brass striking carriage clock, stamp of Henri Jacot, 5½in. high. (Christie's) $920

A satinwood four glass striking carriage clock, the dial signed Arnold & Dent London No 408, 8¾in. high. (Christie's) $4,976

A French carriage clock with morocco travelling case and key, by F. A. Margaine, Paris, 6in. high. (Capes, Dunn & Co.) $568

CARRIAGE CLOCKS

A French brass carriage timepiece with cylinder movement, in a plain pillared case, 6in. high. (Phillips) $352

A 19th century French ormolu carriage clock, the lever movement striking on a gong with push repeat and alarm, 8½in. high. (Phillips) $1,012

A 19th century French brass carriage clock, the lever movement with petite sonnerie, the dial signed for Dent London, 7in. high. (Phillips) $1,215

A 19th century French brass carriage clock, signed on the backplate Bolviller A Paris, 7in. high.(Phillips) $764

A gold mounted tortoiseshell miniature carriage timepiece, maker's mark CD, 1906, 9.5cm. high. (Lawrence Fine Art) $1,307

Lacquered brass petite sonnerie small sized carriage clock with split bimetallic balance to silvered lever platform, 4¼in. high. (Christie's) $1,206

A 19th century French gilt brass carriage clock, the lever movement striking on a bell with alarm, 6¼in. high. (Phillips) $323

A silver and shagreen miniature travelling timepiece, the enamel dial signed W. Thornhill & Co., Paris, 3in. high. (Phillips) $367

A 19th century French brass carriage clock, the lever movement with quarter striking on two gongs, 7in. high. (Phillips) $486

CARRIAGE CLOCKS

A 19th century French gilt brass carriage clock, the backplate bearing the Drocourt trademark, 6½in. high. (Phillips) $1,282

A French brass carriage clock, the lever movement striking on a gong, 4¾in. high. (Phillips) $220

A 19th century French gilt brass carriage clock, bearing the Jacot trademark on the backplate, 6¾in. high. (Phillips) $1,146

A brass quarter striking carriage clock signed 7669 Leroy & Fils Palais Royal 13-15 Paris, 5¼in. high. (Christie's) $1,045

A 19th century French brass carriage clock, the lever movement striking on a gong with alarm and push repeat, 7½in. high. (Phillips) $1,911

A gilt metal early multipiece carriage clock signed Leroy a Paris on backplate, 5in. high. (Christie's) $514

An Austrian brass grande sonnerie carriage clock with calendar, 5½in. high. (Christie's) $2,413

A 19th century French gilt brass carriage clock, signed on the back plate E. Dent, Paris, 944, 5½in. high. (Phillips) $2,719

Late 19th century French brass repeating alarm carriage clock, the dial signed E. Caldwell & Co., Philadelphia, 7½in. high. (Reeds Rains) $1,154

CLOCK SETS

A Sevres pattern pink-ground porcelain and gilt bronze composite garniture-du-cheminee, circa 1880, the clock 34cm. wide, the vases 26.5cm. high. (Christie's) $1,150

A 19th century French ormolu clock garniture, 1ft.1½in. high, together with matching pair of two branch candelabra. (Phillips) $1,470

19th century Meissen blue and white clock set by Lund & Blockley, 39in. high. (Bermondsey) $1,300

A pale Royal rouge marble and ormolu three-piece clock set, the lidded urn holding the clock, with two four-branch, four light candelabra, all 34in. high. (Andrew Grant) $8,928

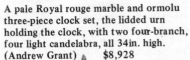

A 19th century French ormolu and porcelain clock garniture, the enamel dial signed Lenoir a Paris, 1ft.8½in. high, together with a matching pair of three branch candelabra. (Phillips) $2,793

A white marble and gilt metal three-piece clock set, by J. Marti & Cie., the clock 23in. high, the urns 17in. high. (Andrew Grant) $1,368

CLOCK SETS

A 19th century French silver plated three-piece clock garniture, the striking movement by S. Marti & Cie, 16in. high, together with two five-light candelabra, 19in. high. (Parsons, Welch & Cowell) $670

A Second Empire ormolu and green marble clock set on the theme of the Oath of the Horatii, the side pieces formed as ewers. (Christie's) $6,434

19th century Sevres porcelain garniture de cheminee, by S. Wartenberg, Paris. (Bermondsey) $2,400

An Empire ormolu mounted bronzed mantel clock with a seated figure of Ceres, and a pair of urn-shaped cassolettes, 41cm. high. (Christie's) $2,619

A 19th century French ormolu clock garniture, the clock contained in a drum, 2ft.9in. high, together with matching pair of seven branch candelabra, 2ft.10in. high. (Phillips) $2,430

A French ormolu and porcelain mounted three-piece clock garniture, the clock 13in. high, the side pieces 13¾in. high. (Parsons, Welch & Cowell) $465

Country Chippendale walnut tall case clock, by A. Hutchins, circa 1800, 86in. high. (Robt. W. Skinner Inc.) $3,200

Federal mahogany inlaid tall case clock, circa 1790, 98in. high. (Robt. W. Skinner Inc.) $3,500

A George II mahogany Yorkshire longcase clock, by Thos. Crofts, Halton, 94in. high. (Reeds Rains) $3,552

A Federal mahogany tall case clock, inscribed O. Hopkins, 1756, 95in. high. (Christie's) $605

A George III mahogany longcase clock, signed G. Forster, Sittingbourne, 7ft. 5in. high. (Phillips) $2,646

A Queen Anne longcase clock movement with five ringed pillars, the dial signed Samuel Stevens London, 6ft. 8in. high. (Christie's) $4,762

A Federal cherrywood tallcase clock, dial signed by Christian Winters, circa 1800, 97in. high. (Christie's) $4,400

A Georgian mahogany longcase clock, signed on a cartouche John Hart, Yarmouth, 7ft.6in. high. (Phillips) $2,700

LONGCASE CLOCKS

A Federal inlaid mahogany tallcase clock, dial signed Alex. J. Willard, early 19th century, 86¾in. high. (Christie's) $3,520

A George II green japanned chiming longcase clock, the dial signed John Taylor London, 8ft. 3in. high.(Christie's) $3,810

A Chippendale mahogany tallcase clock, dial signed by Joseph and John Hollingshead, circa 1780, 98in. high. (Christie's) $12,100

A walnut longcase clock, signed W. Donald, Glasgow, 7ft.1½in. high. (Lawrence Fine Art) $1,302

Late 18th century oak and brown oak banded eight-day longcase clock, the dial signed R. Street. (Peter Wilson & Co.) $936

Federal inlaid mahogany tall clock, by E. Embree, circa 1790, 94½in. high. (Robt. W. Skinner Inc.) $14,000

A mahogany cased three-weight Westminster chime grandfather clock, circa 1900.(British Antique Exporters) $760

A Federal cherrywood tallcase clock, dial signed by Samuel Shourds, circa 1770, 89¼in. high. (Christie's) $2,420

LONGCASE CLOCKS

An oak longcase clock, signed J. Green, Nantwich, 7ft. high. (Lawrence Fine Art) $1,546

A Federal cherry inlaid dwarf time-piece, Mass., circa 1810, 43in. high. (Robt. W. Skinner Inc.) $3,250

A George III mahogany eight-day striking longcase clock, 7ft.10in. high. (Woolley & Wallis) $1,450

A Regency mahogany longcase regulator, the 12in. dial signed Grimalde London, 6ft.1in. high. (Christie's) $9,208

A Federal cherry-wood tall case clock, circa 1810-30. (Christie's) $2,200

A 19th century mahogany longcase clock, the dial signed Brysons, Edinburgh, 6ft.6in. high. (Phillips) $1,176

A Federal inlaid mahogany tallcase clock, dial signed by Aaron Willard, 1805-10, 88½in. high. (Christie's) $24,200

A Queen Anne walnut longcase clock, the dial signed Jn. Motley London, 7ft.1in. high. (Christie's) $2,540

LONGCASE CLOCKS

A week-going walnut longcase clock, the 12in. square dial signed at the base Geo. Graham, London, 7ft. 8½in. high. (Christie's) $43,545

A late 17th century walnut longcase clock, by Daniel Quare, London, 6ft.8in. high. (Phillips) $16,170

An early 18th century walnut quarter chiming longcase clock, by Claude Du Chesne, London, 8ft.1in. high. (Phillips) $12,495

A late 18th century Irish eight-day, striking, mahogany longcase clock, 7ft.3in. high. (Woolley & Wallis) $1,324

A late 17th century longcase clock, by R. Seignior, London, 6ft.8in. high. (Phillips) $5,586

An early 18th century walnut and floral marquetry longcase clock, signed Cartwright, 7ft.2in. high. (Phillips) $7,938 £5,400

A Federal inlaid mahogany tallcase clock, dial signed by Aaron Willard, circa 1805-10, 94½in. high. (Christie's) $15,400

Cherry tall case clock, by Jacob Hosteter, 94½in. high. (Robt. W. Skinner Inc.) $1,700

LONGCASE CLOCKS

An 18th century walnut longcase clock, by Windmills, London, 7ft.7in. high. (Andrew Grant) $1,224

Early 19th century painted pine tall case clock by A. Edwards, Mass., 91in. high. (Robt. W. Skinner Inc.) $850

A mahogany longcase clock by Nathaniel Brown, Manchester, 95½in. high. (Reeds Rains) $3,816

A Queen Anne green japanned longcase clock, dial signed Markwick, London, 7ft.11in. high. (Christie's) $3,810

A Federal cherry inlaid tall case clock, by J. Loring, Mass., circa 1800, 87in. high. (Robt. W. Skinner Inc.) $6,250

A 19th century burr walnut and mahogany longcase clock, maker's name John Elliott, London, 7ft.6in. high. (Andrew Grant) $3,024

A mid Georgian ormolu mounted walnut clock by Jno. Melling, Chester, 88½in. high. (Christie's) $12,117

An 18th century mahogany longcase clock, maker John Berry, London, 7ft. high. (Andrew Grant) $3,168

LONGCASE CLOCKS

A scarlet lacquer longcase clock, signed Micha. Shields, Aldgate, 96in. high. (Christie's) $3,520

A George I green japanned longcase clock, signed Newman Cartwright, 105in. high. (Christie's) $4,687

An ormolu mounted amaranth and tulipwood longcase regulator clock, dial signed Le Roy a Paris, 88in. high. (Christie's) $7,413

A George III eight-day longcase clock by Wm. Carpenier, 7ft.10in. high. (Edgar Horn) $4,307

A Federal cherry-wood inlaid tall-case clock, 1800/10, 93½in. high. (Christie's) $3,300

A William III walnut and marquetry long-case clock, the 11in. dial signed Asselin London, 6ft.11in. high. (Christie's) $7,776

A Federal eagle-inlaid mahogany tallcase clock, works signed by Effingham Embree, N.Y., 1790/95, 101in. high. (Christie's) $27,500

A late Stuart Provincial burr walnut long-case clock, dial signed Tho. Power, 6ft. 6in. high. (Christie's) $4,762

209

LONGCASE CLOCKS

A carved walnut musical clock with ten Symphonion metal discs, 7ft.5in. high. (Andrew Grant)
$6,912

A Federal mahogany inlaid tall case clock, by Lebbeus Bailey, circa 1815, 91in. high. (Robt. W. Skinner Inc.)
$15,000

Late 18th century oak and crossbanded longcase clock, by D. Collier, Gatley, 80in. high. (Reeds Rains)
$1,953

A Dutch burr walnut musical longcase clock, signed N. Wyland, Amsterdam, mid 18th century, 113in. high. (Christie's)
$5,500

A George III figured mahogany longcase clock with eight-day movement, by J. Lomax of Blackburn, 7ft.4in. high.(Capes, Dunn & Co.)
$1,411

A Gustav Stickley oak tall case clock, circa 1902-04, 71in. high. (Robt. W. Skinner Inc.)
$7,750

Federal walnut tall case clock, possibly Penn., circa 1820, 81in. high. (Robt. W. Skinner Inc.)
$1,800

A 19th century style mahogany longcase clock, 8ft.4in. high. (Andrew Grant)
$5,472

LONGCASE CLOCKS

A tallcase clock, dial signed S. Brenneiser, Penn., circa 1810. (Christie's) $5,500

A gilt metal mounted marquetry longcase clock of Louis XV style, 90in. high. (Christie's) $3,421

A Federal cherrywood tallcase clock, works signed by B. Willard, Mass., 87in. high. (Christie's) $7,150

A Victorian mahogany eight-day striking longcase clock, circa 1850. (Peter Wilson & Co.) $828

A Symphonion musical longcase clock with 'sublime harmony' twin comb 11.7/8in. movement, 78in. high.(Christie's) $3,828

A George I Vernis Martin longcase clock, the 12½in. dial signed Wm. Stephens, Godalming, 7ft. high. (Christie's) $3,067

A Victorian mahogany longcase regulator, the dial signed P. G. Dodd & Son, 6ft.3in. high. (Christie's)$2,857

A George III dark green japanned longcase clock, dial signed Thomas A. Deptford, 7ft.6in. high. (Christie's) $2,760

MANTEL CLOCKS

A 19th century French white marble and ormolu mounted lyre clock, 1ft.4in. high. (Phillips) $1,250

An early 19th century ormolu mantel clock, 1ft.9in. high. (Phillips) $999

A Federal inlaid mahogany shelf clock, by David Wood, Mass., circa 1800, 33¾in. high. (Christie's)
$55,000

A Louis XVI white marble and ormolu mantel clock, the enamel dial inscribed A Paris, 1ft.10½in. high. (Phillips) $1,396

A George III mahogany mantel timepiece, the dial signed Absolon, London, 10in. high. (Phillips)
$735

A Germanic Renaissance gilt metal table clock case, the backplate signed Johannes Benner Aug., the case partly 16th/17th century, the movement 17th century, 17in. high. (Christie's) $4,773

A Regency gilt bronze automaton mantel clock, the case in the form of a bird cage, signed Borrell, London, 1ft.7in. high. (Phillips) $8,085

A fin de siecle 'bras en l'air' mantel clock with a gilt metal female figure against an enamel background, 17in. high. (Christie's)
$3,540

A French 19th century ormolu mantel clock, on an oval rosewood plinth under a glass shade, 1ft.3in. high. (Phillips) $1,058

A 19th century French ormolu and porcelain mounted mantel clock, the dial signed E. W. Streeter, 11in. high. (Phillips) $793

A French Louis XV style bronze and ormolu mantel clock, the enamel dial signed Thuillier A Paris, 1ft.3½in. high. (Phillips) $2,058

A 19th century gilt brass mantel timepiece, the enamel dial signed Ecole Horlogerie de Paris, 1ft.6⅝in. high. (Phillips) $955

A French Louis XVI style black marble and ormolu mounted mantel clock, 1ft. 9in. high. (Phillips) $1,396

A Regency mahogany striking mantel clock, the dial signed Bateman, Great Tower Street, London, 13½in. diam. (Christie's) $2,252

A Louis XVI white marble and ormolu mounted mantel clock, the dial signed Hardy A Paris, 1ft.2in. high. (Phillips) $1,250

A Regency rosewood mantel timepiece, the dial signed Arnold & Dent, Strand, London, 10¼in. high. (Phillips) $955

A bronze and ormolu mantel clock of Louis XVI design with horizontal movement contained in an urn. (Christie's) $4,276

A mahogany mantel clock, by Breguet, 11¼in. high. (Phillips) $6,174

MANTEL CLOCKS

Victorian marble and malachite clock, 1880. (British Antique Exporters) $108

An early Victorian gilt metal carriage clock case, in the manner of T. Cole, 11½in. high. $3,373 (Christie's)

Victorian malachite and marble clock, 1860. (British Antique Exporters) $294

A French 'Rheims' cathedral clock, the movement with Brocot type suspension, 21½in. high. (Lawrence Fine Art) $1,953

A Foley 'Intarsio' earthenware clock case in the form of a miniature longcase clock, circa 1900, 33.8cm. high. (Lawrence Fine Art) $706

A French Empire striking clock, the movement with outside count wheel, 21in. high. (Andrew Grant) $792

A miniature enamel and gilt clock, Austria, the urn shape vase houses a Swiss movement, eight-day clock. (Robt. W. Skinner Inc.) $1,776

A Westminster chime Admiral's hat clock, circa 1900. (British Antique Exporters) $24

A lady's boudoir timepiece in the form of an ormolu mounted cut glass scent bottle, signed Jas. Watts, London, 6½in. high. (Lawrence Fine Art) $1,139

214

MANTEL CLOCKS

An ormolu mounted porphyry tripod vase clock of Athenienne form, 20in. high. (Christie's) $8,268

Victorian black marble mantel clock, 1880. (British Antique Exporters) $128

A 19th century ormolu mantel clock, marketed by Bigelow Kennard & Co., Boston, 24in. high. (Robt. W. Skinner Inc.)$850

Orrery clock under glass dome, Limited Edition numbered 259. (Worsfolds) $352

An Art Deco green onyx mantel clock with ivory figures carved after a model by F. Preiss, 25.2cm. high. (Christie's) $2,349

An ebonized pendule religieuse, signed Nicolas Brodon, Paris, circa 1680, 18in. high. (Christie's) $4,400

A French brass and enamel four glass clock with singing bird automaton, 30½in. high. (Christie's) $4,199

A gilt bronze mantel clock in the form of a pump with white enamel face, 7¼in. high. (Andrew Grant) $1,160

An American walnut framed mantel clock, circa 1890. (British Antique Exporters) $83

MANTEL CLOCKS

A mid 19th century gilt metal mantel clock in the form of a Gothic tower, 28in. high. (Andrew Grant) $936

A bronze and ormolu clock, the dial signed Raingo Fres, Paris, 25in. wide.(Christie's) $2,423

An Empire gilt metal and bronze mantel clock, the base shaped as an orange tub, 17in. high.(Christie's) $4,354

A gilt metal calendar strut clock, the backplate stamped Thos. Cole, London, 5½in. high. (Christie's) $2,693

A German gilt brass octagonal quarter striking table clock, the verge movement signed Christoph Forcker, Breslau, 3¾in. high. (Christie's)$3,175

An Empire carved mahogany and veneer shelf clock, by Hotchkiss & Benedict, N.Y., circa 1825, 39in. high. (Robt. W. Skinner Inc.) $500

A mid 19th century gilt metal striking mantel clock, 20½in. high. (Andrew Grant) $1,036

A French red marble perpetual calendar mantel clock and barometer, 18½in. high. (Lawrence Fine Art) $1,139

A Regency mahogany mantel timepiece signed Weeks Museum, Coventry St., on the enamel dial, 12in. high. (Christie's) $1,508

MANTEL CLOCKS

A late Empire bronze ormolu and griotte marble mantel clock, 17½in. wide. (Christie's) $1,477

An Empire ormolu mantel clock, the silk-suspended countwheel striking movement with enamel dial, 19in. wide. (Christie's) $2,332

Early 17th century South German gilt metal tabernacle clock or turmuhr, 19¼in. high. (Christie's) $15,876

A 19th century French porcelain mantel clock with eight-day striking movement, inscribed Raingo Freres, Paris, 15in. high. (Capes, Dunn & Co.) $302

An ornate metal elephant clock with eight-day chiming movement, outside count wheel, 21in. high. (Andrew Grant) $864

An Italian ormolu and cut glass portico mantel clock with chased dial, signed Ld Lacroix a Turin, 16½in. high. (Christie's) $1,568

An early 19th century rosewood bracket clock by B. Lautier of Bath, 43cm. high. (Andrew Grant) $2,736

A Louis XVI ormolu mantel clock, the dial signed Le Nepveu a Paris, 12in. wide. (Christie's) $997

A Royal Presentation ormolu mounted ebony grande sonnerie spring clock by Thos. Tompion, London, No. 278, circa 1700, 28in. high. (Christie's) $365,148

A Viennese silver, enamel and gemset desk clock on oval base with two dolphin supports, 4¼in. high. (Christie's) $777

Early 18th century German gilt brass octagonal table clock, the top plate signed L. Petitot, Berlin, 4¼in. diam. (Christie's) $4,445

A mid 17th century South German negro automaton clock, 11½in. high. (Christie's) $5,715

An Edwardian inlaid mahogany mantel or bracket clock, with silvered dial, 16¾in. high. (Capes, Dunn & Co.) $230

A Victorian satinwood four glass mantel timepiece, dial signed Webster, Queen Victoria Street, London, 17273, 7¾in. high. (Christie's) $2,566

A Liberty & Co. Tudric pewter 'Architectural' mantel clock, circa 1920, 7¼in. high. (Robt. W. Skinner Inc.) $750

A Liberty pewter and enamel table clock designed by Archibald Knox, circa 1900, 14.2cm. high. (Christie's) $1,879

A three-dimensional wood model picture clock showing a French Chateau, under glass dome, 21½in. high. (Andrew Grant) $1,728

An Empire carved mahogany shelf clock, by Riley Whiting, Conn., circa 1825, 29½in. high. (Robt. W. Skinner Inc.) $250

Late 19th century French champleve and ormolu desk timepiece, 8in. high. (Robt. W. Skinner Inc.)$475

A mid 16th century South German gilt brass drum clock case, 2¾in. diam. (Christie's) $1,270

A Meissen (Teichert) clock-case, blue Meissen mark, the movement by Lenzkirch, circa 1900, 51cm. high. (Christie's) $933

A French gilt metal striking mantel clock with blue porcelain face, 28in. high. (Andrew Grant) $936

A chiming and repeating dome top bracket clock, nine bells and one gong, 19½in. high. (Andrew Grant) $1,584

A French rosewood regulateur de table, signed Breguet et Fils on the silvered dial, 25¼in. high. (Christie's)$9,350

A South German silver fronted telleruhr, the circular movement signed Matthias Geill, on ebonized stand, 14in. high. (Christie's) $10,319

A Regency ormolu mantel clock, the dial in drum-shaped case, 9½in. wide. (Christie's) $1,331

A Liberty & Co. pewter, copper and turquoise enamel clock, marked Tudric 0150, circa 1900, 33cm. high. (Christie's) $867

SKELETON CLOCKS

A 19th century English brass skeleton clock with steel chapter ring, on white marble oval base and under a glass dome, 18in. high. (Peter Wilson & Co.)$1,043

A 19th century brass skeleton clock, on an oval rosewood base, under a glass shade, 1ft. 11in. high. (Phillips) $2,295

A Victorian brass chiming skeleton clock on rosewood base with replacement perspex gabled cover, 24in. high. (Christie's) $3,701

15in. brass skeleton timepiece with strike and chain drive, under dome. (Worsfolds) $326

A brass three-train 'Westminster Abbey' skeleton clock, striking on gong and nest of eight bells having mercury pendulum, 24in. high. (Andrew Grant) $6,048

A Victorian brass skeleton chiming clock of York Minster type, 27½in. high overall. (Christie's) $4,827

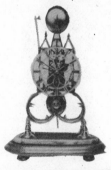

Mid Victorian brass skeleton timepiece with fretted silvered dial, 16in. high. (Bermondsey) $450

A 19th century skeleton timepiece, the glass dial with visible motion work, 7½in. high. (Phillips) $702

An English brass striking skeleton clock of York Minster type, on wood base with glass dome, 59cm. high. (Christie's) $1,930

A Federal mahogany gilt-wood and eglomise banjo clock, by Aaron Willard, 1820/25, 33¾in. high. (Christie's) $2,860

A Louis XVI ormolu cartel clock, the enamel dial signed Charles Le Roy a Paris, 13in. high. (Christie's)
$1,866

A wall clock, by Sewill (maker to the Royal Navy), Liverpool, 40in. high. (Peter Wilson & Co.)
$201

A mid 19th century Bieder-meier mahogany Vienna regulator, 40½in. high. (Christie's)$7,144

A George III eight-day wall clock, the dial inscribed Gray and Reynolds, Wim-borne, 16in. high. (Woolley & Wallis) $1,872

A mahogany Vienna regulator with satin birch line inlay to the glazed case, 19th century, 36½in. high. (Christie's)
$2,853

A Louis XVI cartel clock, the dial signed Charles Le Roy a Paris, 37in. high. (Christie's)$4,665

Federal giltwood mahogany banjo timepiece, by Lemuel Curtis, Mass., circa 1820, 32in. high. (Robt. W. Skinner Inc.) $5,750

A Continental striking cartel clock with white enamel face, overall length 25½in. (Andrew Grant) $892

CLOCKS & WATCHES

A French electrical wall regulator signed Systeme Campiche de Metz and Mees Nancy on the dial. (Christie's) $1,226

A massive walnut and ebonized single train weight-driven Vienna regulator, with 9.5in. enamel face. (Andrew Grant) $2,880

An early 19th century American mahogany cased wall clock, 30in. high. (Robt. W. Skinner Inc.) $775

An early 19th century French ormolu cased wall clock with eight-day movement, 30in. high, overall. (Bermondsey) $1,400

A 19th century rosewood and ormolu mounted wall clock and barometer, the dial signed Aubert & Klaftenberger, London, 4ft.2in. high. (Phillips) $4,704

18th century German Zappler wall clock with brass and iron thirty-hour movement. (Christie's) $1,100

A Continental eight-day mahogany weight driven two-train Vienna regulator, 58in. high. (Andrew Grant) $489

A Japanese gilt brass miniature lantern clock, 5¾in. high. (Christie's) $1,793

A Federal giltwood banjo timepiece with painted dial and eight-day weight driven movement, circa 1820, 41in. high. (Robt. W. Skinner Inc.) $1,200

WALL CLOCKS

A late Biedermeier rosewood Vienna regulator stamped Crot Berlin 302 on the backplate of the weight driven movement, 39½in. high. (Christie's) $1,166

An adapted George III brass mounted mahogany wall clock, the dial signed Mattw. & Willm. Dutton, London, 38in. high. (Christie's) $1,866

A Federal mahogany and giltwood presentation banjo timepiece, Mass., circa 1820, 40in. high. (Robt. W. Skinner Inc.) $1,800

A Federal mahogany and eglomise banjo clock, by Warren, Mass., 1815/30, 30in. high. (Christie's) $3,080

A George III mahogany wall timepiece, the 12in. silvered dial signed Jefferys, London, 1ft.4½in. high. (Phillips) $1,764

A Japanese pillar clock, the hood with glazed lift-up front, 19¾in. high. (Lawrence Fine Art) $846

A Georgian mahogany wall timepiece, the 1ft.7in. diam. painted wood dial signed Field, Bath, 3ft.7in. high. (Phillips) $882

A Federal mahogany and giltwood presentation banjo timepiece, Mass., 37in. long. (Robt. W. Skinner Inc.) $1,800

A mid Georgian black japanned tavern or Act of Parliament clock signed Robert Allam, London, on the shaped 30in. dial, 59in. high. (Christie's) $5,827

WATCHES

A gold quarter repeating duplex watch, the movement signed Rd. Webster, Cornhill, London, 5248, 53mm. diam. (Christie's) $949

A Dutch enamel and silver pair cased verge watch with false pendulum, signed Martineau, London, 52mm. diam. (Christie's) $1,485

A French gold and enamel pocket compass sundial, signed Armand a Paris, 50mm. diam. (Christie's) $690

A chased and enamelled platinum openface watch, signed P. Philippe & Co., no. 200063, 43mm. diam. (Christie's) $1,320

A French gold and enamel verge watch with wound through enamel dial, 57mm. diam. (Christie's) $4,140

A Swiss gold and enamel musical automaton verge watch, circa 1820, 60mm. diam. (Christie's) $19,051

A French quarter repeating cylinder watch, the gold cuvette signed Le Roy et fils Horogers Du Roi A Paris No. 4001, 45mm. diam. (Christie's) $1,270

A gold openface minute repeating chronograph with register, signed Touchon & Co., Geneva, 18ct. gold case, 52mm. diam. (Christie's) $1,980

A gold duplex watch, the full plate movement signed John Newton, London, No. 604, 54mm. diam. (Christie's) $766

WATCHES

A Swiss gold openface split-second chronograph, retailed by Tiffany & Co., N.Y., 18ct. gold case, 51mm. diam. (Christie's) $1,650

A gold and enamel reversible hunter or openface lever watch, the three-quarter plate movement signed Hamilton & Co., London, No. 35103, 41mm. diam. (Christie's) $1,042

A gold pair cased watch, the full plate movement signed David Whitelaw, No. 120, and inscribed Edw Henderson, Edinburgh 1815, 55mm. diam. (Christie's) $489

A French gold and enamel cylinder watch, the movement signed Breguet A Paris, 51mm. diam. (Christie's) $2,300

A Swiss gold openface skeletonized quarter repeating verge watch with erotic automaton, circa 1820, 56mm. diam. (Christie's) $6,600

A repousse gold pair-cased verge watch, signed J. Markham, London, no. 6828, 51mm. diam. (Christie's) $1,840

A Swiss gold openface musical quarter repeating watch, circa 1820, 56mm. diam. (Christie's) $2,970

A gold duplex watch, the movement signed Radford, Leeds, No. 2588, 53mm. diam. (Christie's) $1,380

A multi-color gold filled hunter cased pocket watch, signed Illinois Watch Co., fifteen jewel movement, 53mm. diam. (Christie's) $275

A French gold and enamel verge watch, the bridgecock movement signed Chevalier et Comp^e 1829, 50mm. diam. (Christie's) $1,150

A verge watch, the movement signed Daniel Delander, London, 334, 55mm. diam. (Christie's) $933

A French gold and enamel cylinder watch, the gold cuvette signed J. A. Rossay Palais Royal No 133 Paris, No 2431, 40mm. diam. (Christie's) $1,010

A gold openface chronograph with calendar and moon phases, Swiss, circa 1885, 50mm. diam. (Christie's) $1,540

An enamelled gold cylinder watch, signed F. delynne a Paris, no. 206, 40mm. diam. (Christie's) $3,680

A silver pair cased verge watch with automaton, signed Sylvester, London, no. 6788, 55mm. diam. (Christie's) $880

A small gold openface five-minute repeating watch, signed Fayette S. Giles, 36mm. diam. (Christie's) $1,650

An 18ct. gold open faced keywind watch, the engraved cock signed Margeret Wilson, hallmarked 1845, 44mm. diam. (Lawrence Fine Art) $260

A gold openface quarter repeating watch with automaton, 18ct. gold case, 56mm. diam. (Christie's) $2,640

An 18ct. gold openface five-minute repeating watch, signed P. Philippe & Co., no. 97353, dial signed Tiffany & Co., 45mm. diam. (Christie's) $3,300

A slim gold and enamel open faced keywind watch with Lepine calibre movement. (Lawrence Fine Art) $1,058

A French gold jump hour cylinder watch, the gold cuvette signed Leroy hger Du Roi Palais Royal No. 114 cof, No. 4780, 42mm. diam. (Christie's) $2,332

An 18ct. gold open faced keywind watch, signed Cooper, Colchester, hallmarked 1866, 45mm. diam. (Lawrence Fine Art) $293

An enamelled gold openface watch, signed P. Philippe & Co., nickel eighteen-jewel cal. 17-170 movement, 44mm. diam. (Christie's) $1,430

A gold quarter repeating jump hour ruby cylinder watch, inscribed Breguet No. 2097, 48mm. diam. (Christie's) $4,445

A Swiss gold openface quarter repeating musical watch, signed Breguet, 56mm. diam. (Christie's) $2,640

A gold jump seconds dual time cylinder watch, gold cuvette signed Breguet a Paris No 4275, 55mm. diam. (Christie's) $3,110

A gold openface quarter repeating duplex watch, signed Vulliamy, London, 18ct. gold case, 1835, 45mm. diam. (Christie's) $1,430

WATCHES

A gold hunter cased minute repeating watch, signed J. Jurgensen, Copenhagen, 18ct. gold case, 53mm. diam. (Christie's) $6,050

A gold hunter cased quarter repeating duplex watch, signed Courvoisier Freres, 18ct. gold case, 50mm. diam. (Christie's) $1,100

A Swiss gold hunter cased minute repeating keyless lever perpetual calendar watch, 57mm. diam. (Christie's) $14,152

Mid 19th century Swiss three color gold, pearl, turquoise and pink stone watch. (Robt. W. Skinner Inc.) $814

A 9ct. gold combined cigarette lighter and watch by Dunhill, the base stamped Made in Switzerland, 5.3cm. high. (Lawrence Fine Art) $877

An open faced keyless cylinder fob watch, the movement stamped Savoye Freres & Cie, signed on the cuvette Faucard a Dinard, 30mm. diam. (Lawrence Fine Art) $211

A French gold skeletonized cylinder calendar watch, the dial plate signed Fleury A Nantes, 33mm. diam. (Christie's) $1,477

A gold hunter cased lever watch, signed J. Jurgensen, Copenhagen, 18ct. gold case, 50mm. diam. (Christie's) $1,430

An 18ct. gold lever watch, the gold dial inscribed with twenty-four hour divisions, the case marked London 1860, 50mm. diam. (Phillips) $808

WATCHES

A silver repousse pair cased striking coach clock watch, signed Johan, Georg Brodt, circa 1725, 126mm. diam. (Christie's)
$15,876

A 19th century Austrian silver gilt, enamel and rock crystal verge watch, 68mm. across. (Phillips)
$2,940

An 18ct. gold openface watch minute repeating on three gongs, signed P. Philippe & Co., Geneve, 48mm. diam. (Christie's) $13,200

A 19th century French gold quarter repeating Jaquemart automaton watch, 56mm. diam. (Phillips) $5,585

A gold pocket chronometer, the movement signed John Arnold & Son, 53mm. diam. (Christie's) $7,620

A Swiss open faced keywind watch, stamped Stauffer, Ce. De-Fond, 38mm. diam. (Lawrence Fine Art)
$130

An 18th century verge pocket watch with silver dial and case, by J. Hocker, Reading. (Capes, Dunn & Co.) $273

A gold Karrusel lever watch, the movement signed John Dyson & Sons Leeds, 55mm. diam. (Christie's)
$5,080

A 19th century Swiss three-color gold, turquoise and pink stone watch. (Robt. W. Skinner Inc.) $703

WRISTWATCHES

An 18ct. gold circular wristwatch, the movement signed European Watch and Clock Co. Inc., the dial inscribed Cartier, 30mm. diam. (Phillips) $911

An 18ct. gold self-winding wristwatch with perpetual calendar, signed P. Philippe & Co., Geneve, no. 1119138. (Christie's) $9,350

A gent's gold wristwatch by Vacheron & Constantin, the signed gold dial inscribed Verga, 35mm. diam. (Phillips) $955

A 14ct. gold self-winding wristwatch with center seconds, signed Rolex Oyster Perpetual. (Christie's) $715

A gold wristwatch, signed Patek Philippe & Co., Geneva, no. 1219325, with 18-jewel cal. 23-300 PM movement. (Christie's) $1,650

An 18ct. gold self-winding calendar wristwatch with center seconds, signed Rolex Oyster Perpetual, and a gold filled bracelet. (Christie's) $1,980

A lady's Viennese gold wristwatch with square face, the bracelet formed from articulated rectangular plaques, total length 16.50cm. (Phillips) $710

A 14ct. gold snake bracelet watch, 'Blancpain', 91gr. without movement. (Robt. W. Skinner Inc.) $1,700

A gent's Swiss gold wristwatch by Movado, 34mm. diam. (Phillips) $1,764

WRISTWATCHES

A lady's platinum wristwatch, set with 24 small brilliant-cut diamonds, on black silk cords. (Parsons, Welch & Cowell) $168

A gold center second wristwatch with perpetual calendar, signed Patek Philippe & Co., Geneva, no. 888001. (Christie's) $26,000

A gold coin watch, 'Le Jour' Swiss movement, in a twenty dollar United States gold piece dated 1904. (Robt. W. Skinner Inc.) $1,400

A gold wrist chronograph, signed P. Philippe & Co., Geneve, no. 868978, nickel twenty-three jewel cal. 13-130 movement. (Christie's) $7,920

An 18ct. gold wristwatch, signed P. Philippe & Co., Geneve, nickel eighteen-jewel cal. 9'''-90 movement. (Christie's) $3,080

A gold wristwatch with center seconds, signed P. Philippe & Co., Geneve, nickel eighteen-jewel cal. 27-SC movement. (Christie's) $1,760

A Concorde Watch Co. lady's watch, yellow metal set with peridots, topaz, diamonds and pearls. (Christie's) $3,132

A Cartier gold wristwatch, rectangular face, hexagonal winder set with a sapphire. (Christie's) $8,672

A lady's platinum and diamond wristwatch, signed P. Philippe & Co., Geneve, no. 199809. (Christie's) $1,100

WRISTWATCHES

A lady's platinum wrist-watch, signed P. Philippe & Co., Geneve. (Christie's) $715

A Georg Jensen watch designed by Torun Bulow-Hube, round face with no numerals. (Christie's) $1,641

A gold wristwatch and brace-let, signed P. Philippe & Co., Geneve, no. 851446, 18ct. (Christie's) $1,100

A gold wristwatch, signed P. Philippe & Co., Geneve, nickel eighteen-jewel cal. 23-300PM movement. (Christie's) $1,540

A gold wristwatch, signed Patek Philippe & Co., Geneva, no. 794766, with 18-jewel cal. 23-300 movement. (Christie's) $1,980

A gold World Time wristwatch, signed Patek Philippe & Co., Geneva, no. 929572, the leather strap with 18ct. gold buckle. (Christie's) $20,000

A gentleman's 18ct. gold wristwatch, Patek Philippe, Geneva, with white dial. (Robt. W. Skinner Inc.) $1,100

An 18ct. gold wristwatch, signed P. Philippe & Co., Geneve, nickel eighteen-jewel cal. 23-300 movement. (Christie's) $2,640

A lady's 18ct. yellow gold wristwatch, Patek Philippe, jeweled Swiss movement. (Robt. W. Skinner Inc.) $1,200

WRISTWATCHES

An 18ct. gold wristwatch,
signed Patek Philippe & Co.,
Geneva, no. 743586, with
an 18ct. gold mesh bracelet.
(Christie's) $1,210

A gent's gold rectangular
digital wristwatch, on a
gold bracelet. (Phillips)
$558

An 18ct. gold wristwatch
with fifteen jewel movement,
signed Le Coultre Co., dated
1934. (Christie's)
$1,540

An 18ct. gold wristwatch,
signed P. Philippe & Co.,
Geneve, nickel eighteen-
jewel movement. (Chris-
tie's) $1,540

A 14ct. gold, ruby and
diamond watch, covered
Swiss jeweled movement,
circa 1940. (Robt. W.
Skinner Inc.)
$2,000

An 18ct. gold wristwatch
with 21-jewel movement,
signed Corum. (Christie's)
$380

A lady's rose gold wristwatch,
signed Rolex, gold hands 17-
jewel movement with an 18ct.
gold bracelet. (Christie's)
$990

A gold wristwatch within
an 18ct. gold case, signed
Audemars Piguet, with 14ct.
mesh bracelet. (Christie's)
$1,045

A gentleman's 14ct. gold
wristwatch, 'Le Coultre',
automatic, Master Mariner,
white dial and with a leather
band. (Robt. W. Skinner
Inc.) $150

CLOISONNE

A cloisonne enamelled bowl
with a design of dragons on
black background, 12in.
diam. (Capes, Dunn & Co.)
$141

A cloisonne enamel and gilt
bronze censer and cover,
modelled as a recumbent
elephant, late Qianlong,
19.5cm. wide. (Christie's)
$1,630

A large 17th century cloisonne
enamel two-handled censer,
41cm. wide. (Christie's)
$2,954

A 17th century cloisonne
enamel shallow dish, the
rim with cloud scrolls,
18.2cm. diam. (Christie's)
$750

An Ota Tameshiro slender
pear-shaped cloisonne enamel
vase, Meiji period, 24cm.
high. and another. (Christie's)
$1,184

A 16th century cloisonne
enamel tripod circular dish
decorated on a pale-blue
ground with a meander of
peony and hibiscus, 19.8cm.
diam. (Christie's)
$1,050

One of a pair of late 19th
century cloisonne enamel
oviform vases, with wood
stands, 36cm. high.
(Christie's) $1,028

A cloisonne enamel and
gilt bronze mounted censer
and domed cover with large
lotus finial, 18th century,
53cm. high. (Christie's)
$4,200

A 17th century cloisonne
enamel pear-shaped vase
with taotie and loose ring
handles, 39cm. high.
(Christie's) $855

234

A small late 19th century cloisonne enamel vase and cover with ball finial, 11.5cm. high. (Christie's) $954

A cloisonne enamel hand-warmer and pierced cover with hinged arched handle, Qianlong, 18.5cm. wide. (Christie's) $733

A cloisonne enamel tripod censer and domed cover, circa 1880, 51cm. high. (Christie's) $3,283

A large Ming cloisonne enamel deep dish, integral cloisonne enamel mark at the base centre, 50cm. diam. (Christie's) $25,401

One of a pair of cloisonne enamelled vases, ovoid with waisted necks, 12in. high. (Capes, Dunn & Co.) $187

A 16th century cloisonne enamel shallow dish, 16.3cm. diam. (Christie's) $4,800

A tall tapering cloisonne vase decorated in colored enamels, signed Daihei, Meiji period, 25.1cm. high. (Christie's) $647

A pair of late 19th century cloisonne canted oviform vases in various colored enamels, 31cm. high. (Christie's) $1,776

A cloisonne enamel and gilt copper wig stand, Qianlong, 32cm. high. (Christie's) $952

A cloisonne enamel and gilt bronze circular box and cover, Qianlong, 37.5cm. diam. (Christie's) $8,268

Late 19th century cloisonne cabinet decorated in various colored enamels, 14.5 x 9 x 12cm. (Christie's) $1,110

A Japanese cloisonne shallow dish of octagonal form, 14in. diam. (W. H. Lane & Son) $288

A large cloisonne oviform vase decorated on a royal blue ground, 25½in. high. (Christie's) $1,232

Two 18th century cloisonne enamel and gilt bronze Ruyi sceptres, 31cm. long. (Christie's) $3,000

A cloisonne enamel tapering hexagonal vase, signed Kyoto Namikawa, circa 1900, 24.5cm. high. (Christie's) $3,231

A cloisonne oviform vase decorated in various colored enamels on a royal blue ground, Meiji/Taisho period, 19.5cm. high. (Christie's) $710

A rounded rectangular cloisonne enamel vase with trumpet-shaped neck, Meiji period, 44.6cm. high. (Christie's) $2,368

A late Ming cloisonne enamel Hu-shaped vase, Wanli, 41.5cm. high. (Christie's) $1,149

CLOISONNE

A late Ming cloisonne enamel tripod dish with everted rim, 16th century, 16.2cm. diam. (Christie's) $619

One of a pair of cloisonne enamel vases and covers, 6in. high. (Lawrence Fine Art) $446

A 16th century cloisonne enamel shallow tripod dish on three short feet, 16.5cm. diam. (Christie's) $1,125

Late 19th century cloisonne enamel oviform vase with flaring neck, 61.5cm. high. (Christie's) $4,440

A pair of 19th century cloisonne enamel and gilt bronze cockerels, 17½in. high. (Bermondsey) $2,100

Late 19th century large cloisonne enamel hexagonal vase with flaring neck and spreading foot, 66.4cm. high. (Christie's) $4,440

Late 19th century cloisonne lacquer on porcelain covered jar, Japan, 18in. high. (Robt. W. Skinner Inc.) $875

A cloisonne enamel barrel shaped bowl on three small gilt metal lingzhi feet, 10cm. diam. (Christie's) $820

An early 19th century cloisonne enamel vase with ring handles, 15¼in. high. (Bermondsey) $1,250

Victorian pressed brass magazine rack, 1880. (British Antique Exporters) $32

Victorian brass jardiniere, 1880. (British Antique Exporters) $48

Victorian brass and oak letter rack, 1880. (British Antique Exporters) $67

Victorian brass preserving pan, 1850. (British Antique Exporters) $59

Victorian copper coal bin seat, circa 1880. (British Antique Exporters) $72

Victorian copper kettle, circa 1850. (British Antique Exporters) $66

Victorian copper firescreen with inset mirror, circa 1880. (British Antique Exporters) $43

A Jean Dunand lacquered metal bowl, signed in red lacquer, circa 1925, 10cm. high. (Christie's) $1,252

Late 19th century Art Nouveau style brass coal box. (British Antique Exporters) $82

COPPER & BRASS

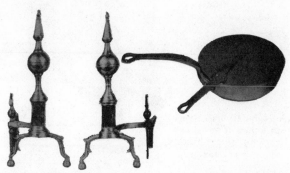

A gilt and inlaid copper cylindrical censer, six-character mark of Yun Wenming, 17th century, 11.7cm. diam. (Christie's) $1,853

A pair of brass andirons, probably by R. Wittingham, N.Y., circa 1810, 25in. high. (Christie's) $1,430

Victorian copper pan and lid, 1860. (British Antique Exporters) $70

Late 19th century brass gong with hammer. (British Antique Exporters) $101

A Victorian brass and wood paper rack, circa 1880. (British Antique Exporters) $24

An early 20th century Arts & Crafts hammered copper umbrella stand, 25in. high. (Robt. W. Skinner Inc.) $400

Mid 19th century copper electrotype model of the Vendome Column, 52in. high, the base 7¾in. square. (Christie's) $14,877

A George III brass and steel fender of Adam style with vase finials, and a bowed fender, 48½in. wide. (Christie's) $12,117

Victorian brass coal bucket 1880. (British Antique Exporters) $72

A George III brass serpentine fender of waved outline, 54in. wide.(Christie's) $1,331

A brass framed ebony ultimatum brace by Robt. Marples, Sheffield, 13in. long. (Dacre, Son & Hartley) $155

A Regency brass and steel fender on bun feet, 55in. wide. (Christie's) $3,057

Pair of Victorian brass and onyx candelabra, 1875. (British Antique Exporters) $205

One of a pair of brass bound mahogany jardinieres of ribbed outline, 10¼in. diam. (Christie's) $4,183

Late 19th century mahogany and brass gong with hammer. (British Antique Exporters) $58

A rosewood box plane with cast brass sole plate and steel blade by Hearnshaw Bros., 7½in. long. (Dacre, Son & Hartley) $96

A Benham & Froud copper and brass kettle on wrought iron stand, designed by Dr. Christopher Dresser, 85cm. high. (Christie's) $459

A pair of Federal brass andirons, 1800-10, 27in. high. (Christie's) $1,430

COPPER & BRASS

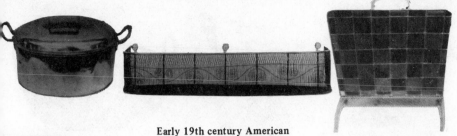

Copper fish kettle and lid, 1880. (British Antique Exporters) $93

Early 19th century American brass and wire mesh fireplace fender, D-shaped, 15½in. wide. (Christie's) $825

Victorian brass and leaded glass firescreen, 1880. (British Antique Exporters) $66

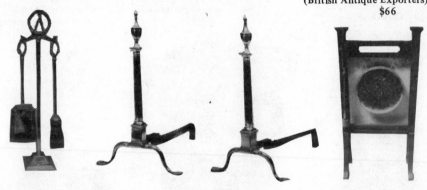

Late Victorian brass companion set, 1880. (British Antique Exporters) $29

Chippendale brass andirons, the urn tops on turned tapering shafts, circa 1780, 22in. high. (Robt. W. Skinner Inc.) $1,600

Victorian brass gong and stand, 1880. (British Antique Exporters) $81

A pair of brass andirons with a shovel and poker, New York, 1800-15, 22in. high. (Christie's) $825

A Siebe, Gorman & Co. brass and copper diver's helmet, English, circa 1920, 19in. high. (Lawrence Fine Art) $976

A pair of Federal late 18th/early 19th century bell metal andirons, 24in. high. (Christie's) $1,320

A seven-branch brass candle-stick, the design attributed to Bernhard Pankok, 29.8cm. high. (Christie's)
$2,035

Victorian brass coal shovel. (British Antique Exporters)
$16

A Georgian copper two-handled pan, circa 1800. (British Antique Exporters)
$74

A Dutch brass octagonal lantern with segmented domed corona, fitted for electricity, 36in. high. (Christie's) $3,110

Late 19th century brass coal bin with upholstered top. (British Antique Exporters) $64

One of a pair of Anglo-Indian brass jardinieres on later stained oak bases, 41in. high. (Christie's)
$2,975

Victorian brass firescreen, 1860. (British Antique Exporters) $43

Large embossed brass jardi-niere on claw feet. (Ball & Percival) $403

Victorian brass jardiniere on paw feet, 1880. (British Antique Exporters) $55

Victorian copper jardiniere, 1860. (British Antique Exporters) $51

Late 19th century embossed brass ashtray. (British Antique Exporters) $16

A Victorian copper kettle, 1860. (British Antique Exporters) $48

Barlow's patent brass candlestick, Birmingham, England, circa 1839, 7.3/8in. high. (Robt. W. Skinner Inc.) $500

A George III brass and steel basket grate, 34¼in. wide, 30½in. high. (Christie's) $7,047

Victorian pressed brass bellows, circa 1880. (British Antique Exporters) $33

A Benham & Froud brass kettle designed by Dr. C. Dresser, on three spiked feet, 24.5cm. high. (Christie's) $473

A circular embossed brass double ended box, 1.7/8in. diam., with bust of Duke of Wellington on one side. (Wallis & Wallis) $29

Copper milk churn with cover. (Ball & Percival) $95

A pair of lady's wedding shoes of ivory satin embroidered with silver thread, belonging to Margaret Gladstone, circa 1784. (Christie's) $589

A child's or young lady's hat of ivory silk quilted with a scale design and trimmed with a rosette of ivory ribbons, circa 1820. (Christie's) $655

A pair of lady's shoes of emerald green damask with low heels, mid 18th century. (Christie's) $327

A black satin bonnet trimmed with pleating, circa 1880. (Christie's) $26

A muslin dress with an under-dress of saxe blue silk taffeta, circa 1880. (Christie's) $432

A pair of white kid gloves with deep cuffs of white satin embroidered in silver thread and sequins, mid 17th century. (Christie's) $3,744

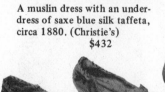

A lady's glove of white kid, the deep cuff of ivory satin lined with pink silk, early 17th century. (Christie's) $366

A pair of lady's high heeled shoes of ivory silk embroidered in silver thread, early 18th century. (Christie's) $628

A straw bonnet with deep brim, trimmed later with satin with chine silk ribbon and artificial flowers, circa 1830. (Christie's) $340

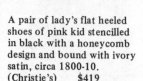

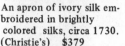

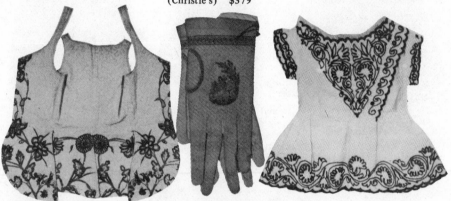

A pair of lady's flat heeled shoes of pink kid stencilled in black with a honeycomb design and bound with ivory satin, circa 1800-10. (Christie's) $419

An apron of ivory silk embroidered in brightly colored silks, circa 1730. (Christie's) $379

A pair of lady's high heeled shoes of black kid bound with black braid, circa 1785. (Christie's) $248

A lady's waistcoat of white cotton quilted in white silk and embroidered in yellow and red wools, English, circa 1730. (Christie's) $4,032

A pair of gloves of pale cream chamois leather, engraved under the thumb, F. Bull & Co., Jan 4th 1791, and a single glove of darker colour. (Christie's) $288

A boy's side fastening tunic of white pique embroidered in red cord with scrolling flowers. (Christie's) $201

A pair of 19th century tin anniversary skates with adjustable strap at ankle and foot, 9in. long. (Robt. W. Skinner Inc.) $550

A bonnet of brown striped plaited straw trimmed with brown figured ribbons, edged with a fringe, circa 1850. (Christie's) $65

A pair of lady's shoes of ivory silk brocaded with sprays of pale green and yellow flowers with kid rands and heels, circa 1750. (Christie's) $786

A suit of rust-colored wool with deep cuffs and wide skirts, circa 1760. (Christie's) $7,200

A mid Victorian orange and purple flowered cream silk dress with boned bodice and slight train. (Dacre, Son & Hartley) $244

An open robe of cotton printed overall with red and blue convolvulus with red stems against a gray ground, circa 1785. (Christie's) $2,882

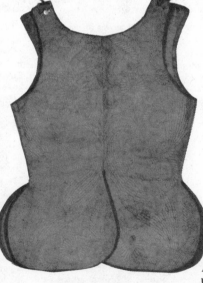

A cotton dress printed with sprigs of brown leaves, with a handkerchief front, circa 1810. (Christie's) $497

A lady's waistcoat of linen finely quilted in yellow silk, English, circa 1730. (Christie's) $3,275

A dress of pale pink silk figured with sprays of flowers, the sleeves, bodice and hem decorated with pink satin rouleaux, circa 1815. (Christie's) $547

A gentleman's suit of deep blue satin, French, Lyons, circa 1770. (Christie's) $3,930

A jacket and skirt of maroon figured silk brocaded with white stripes sprigged in pink and blue, circa 1770. (Christie's) $3,744

A sleeved waistcoat of emerald green figured, voided silk, woven with sprays of flower heads, English, circa 1730. (Christie's) $1,179

An open robe of pale yellow silk lustre, the neckline edged with 18th century Binche lace. (Christie's) $2,592

A chasuble of bottle green velvet, the Flemish orphrey worked in gold thread and colored silks, circa 1480, the velvet second half of the 15th century. (Christie's) $890

A fine full length evening mantle of gray facecloth, by Rouff, 13 Boulevard Hausmann, Paris, 1900. (Christie's) $144

A painted silk purse, inscribed in ink 'Judith N. Peaslee, painted under the care of Miss C. Gage, Bradford Academy, 1812', Mass. (Robt. W. Skinner Inc.) $500

A chasuble of crimson cut velvet woven with trailing stems and sprigs of leaves, 15th century. (Christie's) $1,179

A gentleman's suit of voided velvet woven with pink and black sprigs against a pale blue silk ground, French, circa 1790, together with a waistcoat, circa 1770. (Christie's) $366

A pair of lady's high-heeled shoes of royal blue velvet bound with blue braid, English, circa 1640. (Christie's) $11,520

A dress of ivory silk woven with satin stripes, the bodice trimmed with ivory satin and with blond lace, lined with silk, circa 1830. (Christie's) $1,834

A headdress of blue silk damask heavily embroidered with metal thread, artificial pearls and colored glass, 1895. (Christie's) $37

A dress of ivory satin printed in vertical bands of gray fleck design and a larger pink and gray chine design, circa 1834. (Christie's) $1,572

DECOYS

A painted cedar hen canvas-back decoy, made by L. T. Ward Bros, 1936, 15in. long. (Christie's) $3,850

A painted wooden Maine Flying Scoter decoy, by 'Gus' Aaron Wilson, circa 1880/1920, together with two black-painted wooden duck decoys. (Christie's) $4,620

A Canada Goose decoy, by George Boyd, early 20th century, 29in. long. (Christie's) $1,760

Two late 19th century painted wooden decoys, one 10in. long, the other 11½in. long. (Christie's) $330

A pair of painted wooden American Merganser decoys, a hen and drake, by L. T. Holmes, circa 1855/65 (Christie's) $93,500

Two late 19th century painted wooden decoys, 9½in. long. (Christie's) $300

A painted wooden hollow constructed Canada Goose decoy, by Chas. H. Hart, Mass., circa 1890/1915, 20½in. long. (Christie's) $4,400

A painted wooden Primitive Brant decoy, three-piece laminated construction, 18in. long. (Christie's) $242

A painted wooden oversized Golden Eye decoy, by 'Gus' Aaron Wilson, circa 1880/1920, 20in. long.(Christie's) $1,760

A poured-wax child doll with fixed pale blue eyes, 20in. high, in box. (Christie's) $497

An early 19th century crudely carved wood doll with blue enamel and nail eyes and painted limbs, 15½in. high. (Anderson & Garland) $216

A jointed wooden doll with painted features and real blond hair wig, circa 1845. (Christie's) $314

A bisque headed bebe with jointed wood and composition body, marked BRU Jner 4, 13in. high. (Christie's) $2,358

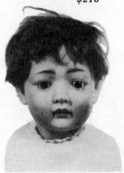

A bisque headed character baby doll, marked K & W 13, Konig and Wernicke, 24in. high. (Christie's) $497

A bisque headed bebe with jointed composition and wood body, by Steiner, 12in. high. (Christie's) $1,441

A bisque headed bebe with papier mache jointed body, marked 12 by Steiner, 29in. high. (Christie's) $3,144

A bisque headed character baby doll with blue intaglio googly eyes, marked C93?52 6/0M, 9in. high. (Christie's) $524

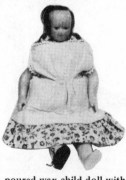

A poured-wax child doll with lace edged underclothes, circa 1851, 13in. high. (Christie's) $419

A wax over composition headed doll with smiling painted face, circa 1878, 7in. high. (Christie's) $98

A bisque headed clockwork walking, talking bebe petit pas, marked BRU Jne R 11, 24in. high. (Christie's) $3,275

An all-bisque googly-eyed doll's house doll with smiling water-melon closed mouth, 4in. high. (Christie's) $288

A poured-wax child doll with blue wired sleeping eyes, the stuffed body with bisque limbs in original nightgown, 21in. high. (Christie's) $419

A bisque headed bebe with composition jointed body, marked FTE C 3/0 by Steiner, 10in. high. (Christie's) $1,572

A bisque headed child doll with auburn wig and jointed composition body, 32in. high. (Christie's)$524

A bisque headed autoperi-patetikos doll with painted blue eyes and brown kid arms, 10in. high. (Christie's) $262

A bisque swivel headed Parisienne, 17½in. high without stand, the head marked 3. (Christie's) $4,716

A bisque two-faced doll with original blonde wig and with jointed composition body, 11in. high. (Christie's) $1,179

A bisque headed character child doll with blue sleeping eyes, marked K*R SH115/A 42, 16½in. high. (Christie's) $3,243

A cloth doll painted in oils with gray eyes and blonde painted short hair, 23in. high. (Christie's) $282

A painted wooden Grodenthal type doll with gray curls, circa 1835, 12½in. high. (Christie's) $792

A painted felt doll modelled as a young girl, marked on the feet Lenci, 25in. high. (Christie's) $239

An early 19th century group of painted wooden headed dolls, 'There was an old woman who lived in a shoe', 5in. long. (Dacre, Son & Hartley) $178

Late 19th century German bisque headed novelty doll, 13in. high. (Bermondsey) $450

A waxed shoulder composition doll with painted closed mouth and fixed blue eyes, 30in. high. (Lawrence Fine Art) $458

A bisque headed character baby doll with open closed mouth, marked 211 J.D.K., 17in. high. (Christie's) $535

A fine German character doll by Kestner, with original clothes, 13in. high, circa 1915. (Bermondsey) $2,100

A bisque shoulder headed doll with brown sleeping eyes, marked 309,5, 17in. high. (Christie's) $294

A Bru Teteur bisque doll, French, circa 1875, 19in. high. (Lawrence Fine Art) $6,468

A bisque shoulder headed doll with fixed blue eyes, marked Goss 18, 17in. high. (Christie's) $576

An early Grodenthal type painted wooden doll with brown eyes, circa 1820, 18in. high. (Christie's) $2,058

A Franz Schmidt bebe doll with sleeping brown eyes, open mouth and composition body, 9in. high. (Hobbs & Chambers) $187

A Scottish boy doll in Highland dress, with bisque head, in original box marked 'Kelly Boy 306', 12in. high. (Lawrence Fine Art) $162

A bisque headed doll with jointed composition body, marked Armand Marseille, Germany A9M, 24in. high. (Dacre, Son & Hartley) $283

A bisque headed bebe, marked J. Steiner Paris, SreA.3, 11in. high. (Christie's) $1,152

A bisque headed doll with glass eyes, open mouth and composition body, marked S.F.B.J. 60 Paris, 18in. high. (Dacre, Son & Hartley) $163

A china doll of an Irish gentleman, with gusseted kid body and china lower limbs, 13in. high. (Lawrence Fine Art)$176

A painted cloth doll with brown painted hair, the stuffed body jointed at hip and shoulder, by Kathe Kruse, 17in. high. (Christie's) $518

A Jumeau bisque doll, French, circa 1880, 15in. high. (Lawrence Fine Art) $1,940

A bisque headed doll with moving eyes, marked on head A.M. 4DEP, Made in Germany, 19in. high. (Dacre, Son & Hartley) $268

A clockwork toy of a bisque headed doll pulling a two-wheeled cart, marked 1079 Halbig S & H 7½, by Toullet Decamps. (Christie's) $792

Early 20th century German character doll by Kathe Kruse, 17in. high. (Bermondsey) $425

A bisque headed doll with composition body, marked Porzellan Fabrik Burggrub Daslachende Baby, 1930/3/ Made in Germany DRGM, 18in. high. (Dacre, Son & Hartley) $640

A Dep Tete Jumeau bisque headed doll, impressed DEP 8, with jointed wood and composition body, 19in. high. (Lawrence Fine Art) $518

A wax over composition shoulder headed doll with short, blonde, curly wool wig, 1810-15, 14in. high. (Christie's) $345

DOLLS

A bisque headed doll with tinted complexion and kid covered body, 21in. high. (Dacre, Son & Hartley) $372

A wax over composition shoulder headed doll, the blue eyes wired from the waist. (Christie's) $432

A bisque headed bebe with five upper teeth, fixed brown eyes and pierced ears, 18½in. high. (Christie's) $1,152

An English mid 19th century vendor doll of wood and cloth, under glass dome with turned walnut base, 16in. high. (Robt. W. Skinner Inc.) $3,000

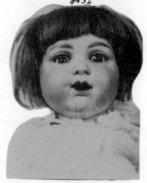

An Armand Marseille '980' bisque headed doll with open and shut eyes, dressed, 22in. high. (Reeds Rains) $266

An American 'Shirley Temple' personality doll, 21in. high, circa 1935. (Bermondsey) $675

A wax composition doll, with sleeping blue eyes, fair wig and stuffed cloth body, 14in. long. (Lawrence Fine Art) $414

A bisque headed child doll, marked SFBJ Paris 14, 32in. high, original box marked Bebe Francais. (Christie's) $1,128

A fine French bisque headed doll by Emile Jumeau, circa 1885, 15in. high. (Bermondsey) $2,100

A Battersea enamel plaque transfer printed and painted after Ravenet with The Gipsy Fortune-Teller, circa 1750, 4.1/8in. long. (Christie's) $1,198

A 19th century Viennese silver gilt and enamel model of three gemset birds perched in a dead tree, 4.3/8in. high. (Christie's) $622

An English enamel plaque transfer printed and painted with Les Amours Pastorale after Boucher, 4.1/8in. long. (Christie's) $1,278

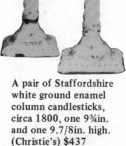

Two Staffordshire white enamel tapersticks with gilt metal mounts, circa 1765, one 6.3/8in. and one 6½in. high. (Christie's) $1,866

A Viennese enamel sweetmeat dish with gilt metal mounts, circa 1900, 6.3/8in. high. (Christie's) $1,174

A pair of Staffordshire white ground enamel column candlesticks, circa 1800, one 9¾in. and one 9.7/8in. high. (Christie's) $437

An enamelled presentation snuff box, the cover with applied diamond set crowned initials for Tsar Nicholas II, 4in. long, 11oz.4dwt. (Christie's) $9,396

A South German double enamel snuff box of waisted form with waved gilt metal mounts, circa 1740, 3in. high. (Christie's) $1,555

A white metal and enamel box with parcel gilt interior, circa 1900, 10.3cm. diam. (Christie's) $861

ENAMEL

One of a pair of Birmingham rectangular white ground enamel caskets, with original gilt metal mounts, circa 1765, each 3½in. long. (Christie's) $5,637

One of a pair of late 19th century Viennese silver mounted enamel cornucopiae, by Hermann Bohm, 8½in. long. (Christie's) $3,036

An English enamel plaque transfer printed and painted after Boucher with La Toilette Pastorale, circa 1755, probably Birmingham, 4.1/8in. long. (Christie's) $2,077

Pair of Staffordshire enamel mustard pots with gilt metal mounts, on three pad feet, circa 1770, probably Birmingham, each 5½in. high. (Christie's) $5,443

Late 19th century Viennese silver and enamel mounted rock crystal tazza, 6½in. high. (Christie's) $2,877

Two Staffordshire white ground enamel candlesticks, with gilt metal mounts, circa 1770, 9.5/8in. high. (Christie's) $656

A Staffordshire enamel etui of upright form, with original gilt metal mounts, circa 1770, 4.1/8in. high. (Christie's) $1,399

Two Staffordshire oval enamel portrait plaques, circa 1765, probably Birmingham, each 3¼in. (Christie's) $2.799

One of three late 19th and 20th century enamel on copper religious plaques, 11¾in. wide. (Robt. W. Skinner Inc.) $425

A Staffordshire enamel bonbonniere formed as a lemon,
with gilt metal mounted
hinged lid, 3in. long. (Christie's) $1,252

Late 19th century Viennese
silver mounted enamel horn,
by Hermann Bohm, 27½in.
long. (Christie's)
$5,594

A Cantonese enamel scal-
loped bowl filled with ivory
balls, 11½in. diam. (Christie's) $4,071

An 18th century Limoges
style enamel on copper
plate, 7.7/8in. diam. (Robt.
W. Skinner Inc.)
$600

A 19th century German
casket, with indented corners,
19cm. long. (Lawrence Fine
Art) $797

A Bilston enamel combined
bonbonniere and patch box,
5cm. high. (Lawrence Fine
Art) $1,116

An early 19th century Swiss
rectangular enamel plaque
painted with a landscape,
2.5/8in. long. (Christie's)
$901

A 19th century champleve
enamel and patinated brass
oil burning floor lamp,
China, 61¾in. high. (Robt.
W. Skinner Inc.)
$1,100

A 19th century Naples casket,
26.5cm. long. (Lawrence Fine
Art) $717

An enamelled shaped hexa-
gonal Freedom casket of
Indian inspiration, Chester,
1888, maker's mark AP,
18ct., 8¼in. long. (Christie's) $9,396

A Staffordshire enamel snuff
box in the form of a court
shoe, circa 1780, 3¼in. long.
(Christie's) $466

A German oblong enamel
snuff box painted on the
cover with a peasant driving
his mules in a landscape, circa
1760, 3.5/8in. long. (Christie's)
$1,477

A South Staffordshire enamel
snuff box with gilt metal
mount, 8cm. long. (Lawrence
Fine Art) $1,499

A Staffordshire white enamel
combined bodkin case, scent
bottle and thimble, circa
1765, 5.3/8in. long.
(Christie's) $855

An unrecorded Battersea
enamel plaque, transfer
printed and painted after
Ravenet, 4.1/8in. long.
(Christie's)$1,758

A large oval snuff box with
deep blue guilloche enamel
panels, the cover with diamond set monogram, 3½in.
long. (Christie's)
$8,613

A Swiss oblong enamel plaque painted with a classical
marriage ceremony, the enamel circa 1820, probably by
Soiron, 2.5/8in. long.
(Christie's) $1,166

A Swiss circular gold and
enamel snuff box, circa
1800, in fitted case, 3in.
diam. (Christie's)
$4,475

An early 18th century Italian fan with carved
ivory sticks decorated with silver pique and
cloute with carved mother-of-pearl, 27cm.
long. (Phillips) $355

A late 19th century French fan with plain
mother-of-pearl sticks, signed B. Bisson de
Recy, 27cm. long. (Phillips) $192

A fan, the leaf trompe l'oeil of water colors
and engravings lying on pink and mauve
silk, strewn with lace, 11½in., Anglo-Italian,
circa 1760. (Christie's) $1,249

An English fan, the serpentine ivory sticks
pique with silver and when closed the handle
forms a serpent, circa 1730, 10in. (Christie's)
$261

A late 18th century fan with wood sticks
and carved guards, 29cm. long. (Phillips)
$592

A French silk leaf fan, the ivory sticks pierced
and silvered, 10½in., 1756. (Christie's)
$725

An early 18th century bone brise fan painted
with pairs of lovers, birds, flowers and
chinoiserie, 20cm. long, probably Dutch.
(Phillips) $236

Mid 18th century fan, the leaf Italian, the
sticks Flemish or English, 12in. (Christie's)
$841

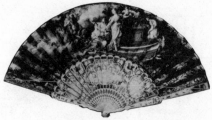

An Oriental ivory fan, gold takamakie lacquer landscape scenes with okibirame accents, with attached ojimi bead. (Robt. W. Skinner Inc.) $259

A mid 18th century French fan with carved and pierced ivory sticks, 26cm. long. (Phillips) $888

A mid 18th century French fan with carved, pierced silver and gilt mother-of-pearl sticks, 29cm. long. (Phillips) $148

A fan, the leaf a hand- colored etching with detailed Almanack for the year 1794, with plain wooden sticks, 11in. (Christie's) $264

A fan, the leaf painted with shepherds and shepherdesses, the handle carved to show a vine when closed, 10in., English or Flemish, circa 1750. (Christie's) $588

A mid 19th century fan with carved, pierced and gilded mother-of-pearl sticks, the printed leaf design by Johann Zoffany, 27cm. long. (Phillips) $140

A fan, the chickenskin leaf painted with classical vignettes of slaves and satyrs, with plain ivory sticks, 10½in., Italian, circa 1780. (Christie's) $588

A late 19th century French fan with gilded ivory sticks, 35cm. long. (Phillips) $444

BEDS

Victorian brass and iron bed, 1875. (British Antique Exporters) $182

An Empire mahogany lit en bateau with box spring, 54in. wide, 73in. long. (Christie's) $4,276

Late 19th century Jacobean style oak bedstead. (British Antique Exporters) $99

A late Federal carved mahogany bedstead, the footposts on brass ball feet, 57in. wide. (Christie's) $8,800

Victorian mahogany bed head, circa 1880. (British Antique Exporters) $82

A Federal carved maple highpost bedstead, Mass., 1790-1810, 57in. wide. (Christie's) $7,150

A mahogany four-poster bed with box spring, 60in. wide. (Christie's) $2,741

A Federal maple and birch tall post tester bed, New England, circa 1820, 57in. wide, 80in. long. (Robt. W. Skinner Inc.) $3,500

A Georgian mahogany fourpost bed, the canopy with breakfront cornice on reeded posts inlaid with satinwood panels, 72in. wide. (Christie's) $6,320

BEDS

Early 19th century Federal painted walnut pencil-post bedstead, North Carolina, 52½in. wide, overall. (Christie's) $4,180

A Portuguese rosewood bed with pierced open headboard and with box spring, 18th century, 42in. wide. (Christie's) $3,078

A late Federal figured maple bedstead, 62in. wide, overall. (Christie's) $1,870

A 17th century oak four-poster bed with panelled headboard, 64in. wide, 93in. high. (Christie's) $3,537

A Federal maple highpost bedstead, New England, 1800-20, 54in. wide. (Christie's) $4,180

A mahogany four-poster bed with molded canopy and floral chintz hangings, George III and later, 60in. wide. (Christie's) $4,344

A mahogany four-poster bed with plain headboard and square pillars, 61in. wide, 84in. high. (Christie's) $2,546

A mahogany four-post bed with waved shaped and molded cornice, 94in. wide. (Christie's) $2,237

A 17th century oak four-poster bed, the tester with molded cornice and carved frieze, 156cm. wide. (Phillips) $3,014

BOOKCASES

A Regency mahogany open bookcase on turned feet, 34½in. wide. (Christie's) $2,263

A Regency burr yew breakfront bookcase supplied by Marsh & Tatham to the Prince of Wales at Carlton House, 73½in. wide. (Christie's) $211,410

Victorian inlaid mahogany revolving bookcase, circa 1860. (British Antique Exporters) $463

A George III mahogany breakfront library bookcase, 64in. wide. (Christie's) $25,056

An oak book press of the Pepys model with glazed cupboard doors on bun feet. (Christie's) $5,376

A George III mahogany breakfront bookcase with four plain glazed doors, 83in. wide. (Lawrence Fine Art) $11,396

A George III mahogany breakfront bookcase with moulded dentilled cornice, 95½in. wide. (Christie's) $5,950

A George III mahogany bookcase with two geometrically glazed doors, 59½in. wide, 98in. high. (Christie's) $2,916

A Regency mahogany breakfront bookcase on plinth base, 93in. wide. (Christie's) $18,792

BOOKCASES

A George III mahogany bookcase of Gothic style, designed for an alcove, 36¾in. wide, 82½in. high. (Christie's) $2,405

A Regency rosewood dwarf bookcase, formerly with a superstructure, 42¼in. wide. (Christie's) $7,830

An early 19th century Regency brass inlaid ebony open bookcase, 54in. wide. (Christie's) $13,311

A 19th century mahogany breakfront library bookcase with four glazed doors, 11ft. wide. (Lawrence Fine Art) $4,785

A Victorian carved mahogany library bookcase on plinth base, 2ft.10in. wide. (Capes, Dunn & Co.) $489

A Regency mahogany breakfront bookcase in the manner of Gillows, with six glazed doors, 143½in. wide. (Christie's) $34,732

A 19th century copy of an Adams' style mahogany bookcase, 5ft.6in. wide. (Butler & Hatch Waterman) $1,800

Large stripped pine bookcase on cupboard, the two glazed doors enclosing three shaped shelves, 7ft. high. (Worsfolds) $864

A mahogany bookcase with six glazed doors over three compartments, circa 1920, 90in. high. (Peter Wilson & Co.) $792

BOOKCASES

A Regency mahogany breakfront bookcase in the manner of Gillows, 196in. wide. (Christie's) $15,660

Six section Globe Wernicke cabinet, 1880. (British Antique Exporters) $394

A Regency rosewood dwarf bookcase, the breakfront with gray marble top, 83in. wide. (Christie's) $17,226

A mahogany breakfront bookcase with two pairs of glazed cupboard doors, 91in. wide. (Christie's) $4,344

A George II mahogany bookcase, the doors opening to a divided interior, circa 1730-50, 58¼in. wide. (Christie's) $7,700

A Charles II oak bookcase with a pair of glazed and panelled cupboard doors, 55in. wide. (Christie's) $10,659

A mahogany breakfront bookcase with molded broken pediment, 80in. wide. (Christie's) $4,344

A Simpoles chapter bookcase of oak and leaded glass, 7ft.9in. wide. (J. R. Bridgford & Sons) $1,296

One of a pair of mahogany breakfront bookcases with two pairs of glazed cupboard doors, 82in. wide.(Christie's) $11,309

BUREAU BOOKCASES

A mid Georgian mahogany bureau cabinet with glazed cupboard doors, 45in. wide. (Christie's) $8,035

A George I walnut bureau cabinet with later-glazed arched cupboard door, 21½in. wide. (Christie's) $22,809

A mid-Georgian mahogany bureau cabinet, the glazed doors enclosing a partially fitted interior, 92in. high. (Christie's)$16,070

A Queen Anne walnut bureau cabinet, the baize lined sloping flap enclosing a fitted interior, 43in. wide. (Christie's) $14,094

Chippendale mahogany secretary desk on four ogee bracket feet, Rhode Island, circa 1780, 42in. wide. (Robt. W. Skinner Inc.) $17,000

A Chippendale mahogany blockfront secretary desk, circa 1780, 42in. wide. (Robt. W. Skinner Inc.) $50,000

A George II rosewood and walnut bureau cabinet with sloping flap enclosing a fitted interior, 38in. wide. (Christie's)$40,176

A George I walnut desk and bookcase, circa 1720, 38in. wide. (Christie's) $4,180

A George III mahogany desk and bookcase, the desk section with slant lid enclosing compartmented interior, 39¼in. wide. (Christie's) $4,400

BUREAU BOOKCASES

A Queen Anne scarlet lacquer bureau cabinet, decorated overall in raised gilt with chinoiserie figures and birds, 37½in. wide. (Christie's) $43,416

An early Georgian walnut bureau cabinet, the sloping flap enclosing a fitted interior, 37½in. wide. (Christie's) $6,436

A George III mahogany bureau bookcase on ogee bracket feet, 44in. wide. (Christie's) $3,353

Late 18th century George III mahogany secretary, 37¼in. wide. (Robt. W. Skinner Inc.) $1,800

A black and gold lacquer bureau cabinet, the mirrored cupboard doors enclosing a fitted interior, 40½in. wide. (Christie's) $28,188

1930's oak bureau bookcase with glazed top. (British Antique Exporters) $159

A George II walnut bureau cabinet, the doors enclosing a fitted interior, 42in. wide. (Christie's) $37,497

A Georgian oak bureau bookcase, the doors with bands of mahogany and original brass handles, 42in. wide. (Lawrence Fine Art) $925

A Chippendale cherrywood secretary bookcase, in two sections, circa 1765-80, 38in. wide. (Christie's) $9,900

BUREAU BOOKCASES

An early George III mahogany bureau bookcase, the bureau with fitted interior, 40in. wide. (Lawrence Fine Art) $4,232

An early George III mahogany bureau cabinet with an arched mirror glazed cupboard door, 33in. wide. (Christie's) $9,396

A George II walnut bureau cabinet, the fall-flap enclosing a fitted interior, 33in. wide. (Christie's) $4,687

A Queen Anne walnut bureau cabinet, the fall-flap enclosing a fitted interior, 43½in. wide. (Christie's) $53,244

A Queen Anne brown and gold lacquer bureau cabinet, the mirror cupboard doors enclosing a fitted interior, 40½in. wide. (Christie's) $52,099

A Chippendale cherrywood desk and bookcase, in two sections, 1760-90, 41½in. wide. (Christie's) $17,600

A Queen Anne walnut and burr walnut bureau cabinet, with two pairs of carrying handles, 41in. wide. (Christie's) $45,532

A Chippendale transitional mahogany secretary, circa 1790, 46in. wide. (Robt. W. Skinner Inc.) $5,750

A Queen Anne walnut bureau cabinet with two candle slides, 39in. wide. (Christie's) $8,046

BUREAUX

An 18th century oak bureau with sloping fall front, fitted interior, 2ft.10in. wide. (Hobbs & Chambers) $828

A Chippendale tiger maple slant lid desk, New England, circa 1770, 35¼in. wide. (Robt. W. Skinner Inc.) $5,750

A Queen Anne scarlet lacquer bureau with fitted interior, on later bracket feet, 37½in. wide. (Christie's) $16,869

A Chippendale walnut slant front desk, 1760/90, 43in. wide. (Christie's) $3,300

A Chippendale mahogany reverse serpentine slant front desk, 1760/80, 44in. wide. (Christie's) $4,950

An early Georgian oak bureau with double half round moldings , 38in. wide. (Lawrence Fine Art) $1,244

Country Chippendale maple slant top desk, circa 1780, 36in. wide. (Robt. W. Skinner Inc.) $2,700

A George III mahogany bureau, the baize lined fall-flap flanked by two hinged flaps enclosing a fitted interior, 57½in. wide. (Christie's) $21,141

A George III oak bureau with narrow mahogany crossbanding, 36in. wide. (Lawrence Fine Art) $1,403

BUREAUX

A Chippendale mahogany
oxbow desk, circa 1780,
41¾in. wide. (Robt. W.
Skinner Inc.)
$7,250

A fine Victorian mahogany
and marquetry cylinder
bureau, 1875. (British
Antique Exporters)
$1,132

A walnut and other woods,
marquetry desk, Holland,
circa 1760, 54in. wide.
(Robt. W. Skinner Inc.)
$10,000

A Chippendale mahogany
slant top desk, Mass., circa
1780, 38in. wide. (Robt. W.
Skinner Inc.) $4,750

A Chippendale tiger maple
and maple slant top desk,
New England, circa 1780,
36in. wide. (Robt. W. Skinner Inc.) $2,700

A William and Mary walnut
bureau, the sloping flap
enclosing a fitted interior,
38in. wide. (Christie's)
$4,228

A Country Federal maple
slant lid desk, New England,
circa 1810, 40¼in. wide.
(Robt. W. Skinner Inc.)
$1,200

An early Georgian walnut
bureau, the fall-flap enclosing a fitted interior, 39in.
wide. (Christie's)
$4,384

Early 20th century oak
bureau. (British Antique
Exporters) $275

BUREAUX

A William and Mary burr walnut bureau, the fall-flap enclosing a fitted interior with a well, 41in. wide. (Christie's)$12,830

A Queen Anne cherry desk on frame, with fall-front, New England, circa 1760, 34in. wide. (Robt. W. Skinner Inc.) $3,500

A William and Mary pollard oak bureau, the fall-flap enclosing a fitted interior, with a glass and marble recess dated 1698, 38in. wide. (Christie's) $18,532

A Gustav Stickley drop-front desk, the doors opening to reveal a fitted interior, circa 1906, 38in. wide. (Robt. W. Skinner Inc.) $2,400

A Country Federal cherry-wood slant front desk, Mass., circa 1800, 40½in. wide. (Robt. W. Skinner Inc.) $1,600

Early 20th century Jacobean-style oak secretary, 30½in. wide. (Robt. W. Skinner Inc.) $750

A Country Federal cherry slant lid desk, New England, circa 1800, 40½in. wide. (Robt. W. Skinner Inc.) $1,800

A William and Mary burr-yew bureau, the sloping flap enclosing a stepped fitted interior, 31½in. wide. (Christie's) $4,561

A Federal birch, cherry and mahogany veneer slant lid desk, probably N. Hampshire, circa 1810, 39½in. wide. (Robt. W. Skinner Inc.) $1,000

FURNITURE

A late 18th century Italian marquetry bureau with crossbanded fall-flap inlaid with a landscape scene, 48in. wide. (Christie's) $2,851

A Louis XV kingwood and marquetry bureau de dame by A. M. Criaerd, 29½in. wide. (Christie's) $3,421

A Dutch walnut and marquetry bureau, the ogee sloping flap enclosing a fitted interior, 52in. wide. (Christie's) $5,702

A George II walnut and burr walnut bureau, the sloping flap enclosing a leather lined interior, 29in. wide. (Christie's) $10,044

A George III satinwood cylinder bureau, the top with leather lined domed tambour shutter, 30½in. wide. (Christie's) $12,700

A George III mahogany and sycamore bureau with leather lined shaped spreading fall-flap enclosing a fitted interior, 30in. wide. (Christie's) $3,790

A William and Mary walnut bureau, the sloping flap enclosing a fitted interior, 36in. wide. (Christie's) $6,415

A George III mahogany and satinwood cylinder bureau, the solid cylinder enclosing a fitted interior, 45in. wide. (Christie's) $8,704

A Chippendale maple and pine slant front desk, New England, circa 1780, 39in. wide. (Robt. W. Skinner Inc.) $2,100

CABINETS

A Regency satinwood side cabinet with an inset gray marble top, the door filled with pleated aquamarine silk, 21½in. wide.(Christie's) $5,659

One of a pair of early George III rosewood cabinets on stands, each with pierced fretwork gallery, 37in. wide. (Christie's) $34,732

An ormolu mounted king-wood cabinet on stand on turned tapering legs, 26½in. wide. (Christie's) $4,276

An 18th century silver mounted Indo-Portuguese ivory inlaid hardwood cabinet on stand, 38in. wide.(Christie's) $14,256

Mid 17th century ormolu mounted kingwood strong-box, possibly Flemish or German, 36in. wide, 48½in. high. (Christie's) $17,409

An Art Deco wrought iron and zebra wood cabinet, carved signature J. Cayette, Nancy, circa 1925, 115cm. high. (Christie's) $2,049

A 17th century Spanish ivory and tortoiseshell inlaid rose-wood and walnut cabinet on stand of papleira type, 43in. wide. (Christie's) $4,561

A 19th century rectangular roironuri cabinet, the base fitted with a drawer below two hinged doors, 45.8 x 44 x 28.4cm. (Christie's) $1,726

A Regency pollard oak and burr-yew dwarf cabinet, the top with ebony bandings, 26in. wide. (Christie's) $4,283

CABINETS

A William and Mary oyster-veneered walnut cabinet on stand, 36½in. wide. (Christie's) $5,356

A Sue et Mare rosewood, ebonized and marquetry music cabinet on elongated ebonized legs, 95.2cm. wide. (Christie's) $4,415

A 17th century Flemish or North German ebony cabinet on stand, the frieze drawer inlaid with a reversible backgammon and chess board, 33½in. wide. (Christie's) $9,979

A William and Mary oyster veneered laburnum cabinet on stand, 37in. wide. (Christie's) $25,660

A late 18th century Anglo-Indian engraved ivory and tortoiseshell veneered table cabinet, 19in. wide. (Christie's) $4,561

A Wm. Watt ebonized side cabinet designed by E. W. Godwin, 197.4cm. high by 128.6cm. wide. (Christie's) $7,884

A 19th century North Italian ivory mounted ebony cabinet on stand with stepped baluster gallery, stamped Pogliani, 32in. wide. (Christie's) $2,708

An oak bedside cabinet with bronze drop handles, by P. Waals assisted by P. Burchett, 1928, 78.9cm. high. (Christie's) $1,892

A 19th century North Italian ivory inlaid ebony cabinet in the Renaissance style, in two parts, 67in. wide. (Christie's) $16,394

CABINETS

An 18th century Portuguese Colonial rosewood table cabinet, the front with various sized drawers, 13in. wide. (Christie's) $777

An 18th century vizigatapam ivory inlaid hardwood table cabinet, with carrying handles, 17½in. wide. (Christie's) $3,421

A Regency gilt metal mounted mahogany breakfront side cabinet, the doors filled with gilt trelliswork and mushroom silk pleats, 56in. wide. (Christie's) $5,214

A mid Victorian walnut and inlaid side cabinet with glazed door, 34½in. wide. (Dacre, Son & Hartley) $720

A Regency lacquer side cabinet, the ebonized top with pierced ormolu gallery, 43¼in. wide. (Christie's) $12,528

A Victorian inlaid walnut and gilt metal mounted side cabinet, 32in. wide. (Reeds Rains) $633

A Dutch walnut and marquetry cabinet on stand, 43in. wide. (Christie's) $3,110

A Regency ebonized and lacquer dwarf cabinet with Carrara marble top and cedar lined interior, 39½in. wide. (Christie's) $10,962

A Charles II black and gold lacquered cabinet on stand, 45in. wide. (Christie's) $15,660

CABINETS

A Regency parcel gilt, ebonized and simulated rosewood breakfront dwarf cabinet with inset molded Carrara marble top, 47½in. wide. (Christie's) $13,311

A Dutch walnut child's bureau cabinet with fall-flap enclosing a fitted interior, 31in. wide. (Christie's) $4,199

A Regency brass inlaid ebony and satinwood breakfront side cabinet, 36½in. wide. (Christie's) $2,607

One of a pair of Empire gilt metal mounted mahogany pedestal cabinets with inset gray marble tops.(Christie's) $9,331

One of a pair of Regency rosewood side cabinets, 51in. wide. (Christie's) $53,244

A Gustav Stickley oak music cabinet, the ten pane single door with amber glass, circa 1912, 47¼in. high. (Robt. W. Skinner Inc.) $2,300

A 17th century Flemish ebony, tortoiseshell and painted cabinet on stand, 38in. wide. (Christie's) $13,996

A William III walnut veneered cabinet on stand, the molded frieze fitted with two drawers. (Woolley & Wallis) $3,915

A Flemish brass bound ebony coffre-port with carrying handles, the coffre 17th century, the stand early Georgian, 28in. wide.(Christie's) $4,976

CABINETS

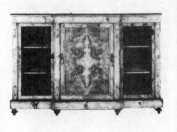

A Regency brass inlaid rosewood side cabinet with
stepped green mottled
scagliola marble top, 48½in.
wide. (Christie's)
$5,632

One of a pair of Biedermeier
satin birch and ebonized
side cabinets, 21in. wide.
(Christie's) $1,944

A Victorian boxwood banded
walnut breakfront credenza
with gilt metal mounts,
165cm. wide. (Phillips)
$1,027

A William and Mary walnut
cabinet on stand, the stand
mid Georgian, 44½in. wide.
(Christie's) $3,758

An Edwardian mahogany
pedestal filing cabinet with
sliding trays, 20in. wide.
(Christie's) $279

A William and Mary burr
walnut cabinet on chest.,
the doors with chased gilt
lockplate and hinges, 44in.
wide. (Christie's)
$19,958

An early Georgian black
and gold lacquer cabinet
on a George III stand, 41in.
wide. (Christie's)
$2,494

A Goanese ivory inlaid ebony
and hardwood cabinet on
stand, the drawers with ivory
studs, 42in. wide. (Christie's)
$15,184

An Italian walnut and burr
walnut 'Bambocci' cabinet
on stand, the cabinet late
16th century, 34¼in. wide.
(Christie's) $7,290

A Regency mahogany canterbury, trade label of 'Andw. Fleming & Co., Kirkaldy', 20in. wide. (Christie's) $3,283

An early Victorian rosewood X-frame canterbury, 20in. wide. (Reeds Rains) $604

A Victorian mahogany canterbury. (John Hogbin & Son) $793

A Regency mahogany three-division canterbury with slatted sides and a drawer in the base, 19in. wide. (Christie's) $929

Victorian walnut music canterbury/whatnot, 1860. (British Antique Exporters) $545

A Victorian burr walnut music canterbury of three divisions with spindle turned columns, 1ft.9in. wide. (Capes, Dunn & Co.) $585

Victorian walnut music canterbury, circa 1880. (British Antique Exporters) $341

A Regency mahogany canterbury with frieze drawer, 20in. wide. (Christie's) $2,954

A Victorian rosewood three division canterbury, 20¼in. wide. (Geering & Colyer) $769

DINING CHAIRS

One of a set of six William IV rosewood dining chairs upholstered in buttoned orange suede. (Christie's) $3,218

One of a set of six late 18th century Queen Anne walnut side chairs, Spain. (Robt. W. Skinner Inc.) $1,500

One of a set of eight Victorian mahogany dining chairs with buttoned red leather upholstered seats. (Lawrence Fine Art) $2,279

One of a set of four Chippendale cherrywood side chairs, 1780-1800. (Christie's) $4,950

One of a set of six grain painted and stencilled fancy chairs, New England, 1820-30. (Christie's) $825

A Chippendale mahogany side chair on cabriole legs ending in claw and ball feet, Mass., circa 1780. (Robt. W. Skinner Inc.) $1,850

A Queen Anne maple side chair, Mass., circa 1770. (Robt. W. Skinner Inc.) $3,500

One of a set of six Queen Anne walnut side chairs, 1740-60. (Christie's) $28,600

One of a set of six mahogany and mahogany veneer Empire classical revival side chairs, Boston, circa 1830. (Robt. W. Skinner Inc.) $4,100

DINING CHAIRS

Victorian mahogany turned leg chair, 1860. (British Antique Exporters) $63

One of a set of eight Federal mahogany side chairs with shield backs, circa 1795. (Robt. W. Skinner Inc.) $7,500

One of a set of four mahogany balloon back chairs, 1860. (British Antique Exporters) $681

One of a set of eight late Georgian mahogany dining chairs, including two with arms. (Lawrence Fine Art) $8,140

One of a set of early 19th century fancy painted side chairs, New England. (Christie's) $3,300

A Chippendale mahogany side chair with slip seat, Phila., circa 1770. (Robt. W. Skinner Inc.) $3,600

A Federal mahogany shield back side chair with upholstered bow front seat, circa 1800. (Robt. W. Skinner Inc.) $500

One of a set of four Federal carved mahogany side chairs, 1790-1800. (Christie's) $3,520

One of a set of six carved oak dining chairs, 1860. (British Antique Exporters) $487

DINING CHAIRS

One of a pair of George III yellow-painted chairs with gothic-arcaded backs. (Christie's) $6,577

A Chippendale mahogany side chair, with a serpentine crest rail, circa 1760/85, 38in. high. (Christie's) $1,650

One of a set of eight ebonized and parcel gilt dining chairs on sabre legs with drop-in seats, upholstered in pale yellow silk. (Christie's) $2,770

A Regency cream and brown painted bamboo pattern chair, the caned seat with squab cushion, and another en suite. (Christie's) $5,637

One of a set of thirteen Regency mahogany dining chairs, including a pair of armchairs. (Christie's) $12,268

A Chippendale walnut side chair on cabriole legs with shell carved knees and claw and ball feet, 1760/80. (Christie's)$16,500

One of a pair of Chippendale mahogany slipper chairs, 1750/80, 36½in. high. (Christie's) $1,100

One of a set of six Regency simulated rosewood and parcel gilt dining chairs. (Christie's) $21,924

A Queen Anne walnut side chair with balloon shaped seat, 1740/60, 41in. high. (Christie's) $13,200

DINING CHAIRS

One of a set of eight George III stained beechwood dining chairs, the backs filled with trelliswork and pilasters, and a set of four en suite of a later date. (Christie's) $10,179

One of a set of six Victorian walnut small chairs with button upholstered seats. (Lawrence Fine Art) $1,196

One of a set of ten painted 'fancy' chairs, with balloon rush seats, New England, circa 1825, 33½in. high. (Robt. W. Skinner Inc.) $2,700

One of a set of twelve Harlequin Dutch marquetry dining chairs. (Christie's) $7,776

A Chippendale mahogany side chair, circa 1780, 37in. high. (Robt. W. Skinner Inc.) $2,300

A Queen Anne walnut side chair with yoked crest, 1740/60, 40½in. high. (Christie's) $9,900

One of a set of four Dutch marquetry inlaid dining chairs with drop-in seats. (Worsfolds) $1,296

One of a set of eight George III mahogany dining chairs, including two armchairs. (Christie's) $8,143

One of a set of four and a similar pair of Federal mahogany side chairs, N.Y., 1800/10, on molded sabre legs. (Christie's) $3,030

DINING CHAIRS

One of four spindle back single chairs with rush seats and loose seat cushions in floral tapestry. (Capes, Dunn & Co.) $936

One of a set of four Swiss oak hall chairs with pierced, shaped molded backs carved with wolves' heads. (Christie's) $777

One of a set of seven Regency mahogany chairs with solid seats, one stamped KL, one H, one S, one KL and H and one KL and S. (Christie's) $8,613

A George II mahogany dining chair with interlaced gothic pattern and figure of eight splat. (Christie's) $1,879

One of a set of eight Regency simulated rosewood dining chairs in beech. (Hobbs & Chambers) $633

One of a set of late 19th century Queen Anne-style mahogany side chairs, England. (Robt. W. Skinner Inc.) $1,900

One of a set of six George III mahogany dining chairs with bowed padded seats. (Christie's) $3,834

One of a set of five Chippendale-style mahogany dining chairs. (Hobbs & Chambers) $1,944

One of a set of six mahogany dining chairs, in the Georgian style with shield shaped backs. (Lawrence Fine Art) $1,435

DINING CHAIRS

One of a set of eight Regency mahogany dining chairs of Gothic style with padded seats and molded square legs. (Christie's) $5,214

Late 18th century Windsor ash and maple fan back side chair, New England, 36in. high. (Robt. W. Skinner Inc.) $900

One of a set of four George III grained hall chairs with solid bowed seats. (Christie's) $1,989

One of a set of five George I red walnut dining chairs, including a pair of armchairs. (Christie's) $7,830

One of a set of eight mahogany dining chairs with drop-in upholstered seats. (Christie's) $3,265

One of a set of four Victorian rosewood dining chairs with pierced balloon backs carved with foliage. (Christie's) $3,834

One of a set of four Macclesfield ladder back chairs with rush seats. (Peter Wilson & Co.) $1,008

A William and Mary carved maple side chair, Mass., circa 1700, 48in. high. (Robt. W. Skinner Inc.) $4,250

One of a set of six Regency ebonized dining chairs with bowed seats, four stamped SG. (Christie's) $2,607

DINING CHAIRS

One of a set of six Regency mahogany dining chairs with tablet toprails. (Christie's) $3,395

One of a pair of early 18th century Italian walnut side chairs with padded backs and seats covered in floral-decorated leather. (Christie's) $926

One of a set of eight early George III mahogany dining chairs with pierced vase-shaped splats. (Christie's) $37,497

One of a set of six George III mahogany side chairs with shield-shaped backs. (Christie's) $6,026

One of a set of four George III mahogany dining chairs, stamped E, together with a pair of armchairs and a pair of side chairs of later date. (Christie's) $7,128

One of a set of eight Regency cream painted simulated bamboo side chairs, the cane filled seats with pink silk cushions. (Christie's) $5,093

One of a set of four George II mahogany chairs with bowed drop-in seats. (Christie's) $18,748

One of a set of twelve George IV oak dining chairs in the manner of Morel & Seddon. (Christie's) $19,958

A George I walnut dining chair, the cartouche-shaped padded back and seat on cabriole legs. (Christie's) $1,968

DINING CHAIRS

One of a set of four George III mahogany side chairs with molded oval pierced 'umbrella' backs. (Christie's) $6,026

One of a set of six mid-Georgian mahogany dining chairs with drop-in needle-work-upholstered seats. (Christie's) $7,840

A George III mahogany chair with oval padded back and serpentine seat covered in cafe-au-lait silk. (Christie's) $729

One of a set of eight late 18th century Dutch neo-classical mahogany dining chairs with bowed uphol-stered seats. (Christie's) $6,415

One of a set of twelve Regency mahogany dining chairs with panelled backs and X-shaped splats. (Christie's) $9,196

A Serrurier-Bovy 'Silex' dismantling mahogany chair, circa 1905. (Christie's) $315

One of a set of four George III cream and green painted dining chairs with shield-shaped backs. (Christie's) $1,607

A George II walnut chair in the manner of Grendey, with drop-in seat.(Christie's) $1,697

One of a pair of Regency mahogany hall chairs, the sabre back legs joined by ring-turned stretchers. (Christie's) $6,026

EASY CHAIRS

A Regency beechwood tub armchair, the back filled with cane and with green leather squab cushion. (Christie's) $1,528

Tecno 'P 45' adjustable reclining wing armchair, designed by O. Borsani. (Christie's) $234

An early George III mahogany library armchair, covered in gros and petit point needlework in wool and silk, 28in. wide. (Christie's)
$15,660

A Federal mahogany easy chair, on square tapering legs joined by a box stretcher, New England, 1790-1800. (Christie's) $2,640

One of a pair of George III stained beechwood bergeres of Louis XV style with buttoned leather backs and bowed seats. (Christie's)
$9,201

A Queen Anne walnut wing armchair upholstered in olive leather. (Christie's)
$7,241

A Queen Anne walnut armchair, upholstered in lime green silk. (Christie's)
$3,915

A Charles II walnut open armchair, the upholstered seat covered in floral gros point needlework. (Christie's) $2,035

A George I walnut wing armchair with out-scrolled arm supports and shell cabriole legs. (Christie's)
$3,218

EASY CHAIRS

One of a pair of painted beech frame armchairs in the French manner, English, circa 1775. (Woolley & Wallis) $5,754

One of a pair of mid 19th century walnut folding armchairs with suede backs and seats, the frames carved to simulate bamboo. (Christie's) $3,862

One of a set of three George III giltwood open armchairs covered in coral silk. (Christie's) $11,745

One of a pair of George II giltwood open armchairs, the backs and seats covered with contemporary tapestry woven in wool and silk, 41½in. high. (Christie's) $133,110

One of a pair of Regency mahogany bergeres, with distressed upholstery in ribbed frames. (Christie's) $5,481

A George I mahogany easy chair on cabriole legs with slipper feet, 1720-30. (Christie's) $3,080

A Federal upholstered mahogany lolling chair, circa 1775-95. (Christie's) $3,300

A William IV mahogany library armchair with cane filled back, arms and seat, with leather squab cushions. (Christie's) $1,609

A 17th century walnut and beechwood armchair, the seat covered in floral gros and petit point needlework. (Christie's) $1,331

289

EASY CHAIRS

A beechwood fauteuil of Louis XV style with seat covered in 18th century gros and petit point needlework. (Christie's) $4,134

A Venetian silver and painted grotto chair, the shaped back pierced with a dolphin, also bearing a paper trade label Frateli Rotali, Venezia. (Christie's) $1,995

A William IV rosewood armchair with button-upholstered tub back and armrests. (Christie's) $2,546

A George III mahogany library armchair, the back and seat upholstered in green floral silk. (Christie's) $4,687

One of a pair of large mid 19th century ormolu mounted bergeres in the Empire style, the backs and seats covered in yellow silk. (Christie's) $12,830

One of a pair of open armchairs, the backs and seats upholstered in gros point foliate needlework, late 17th century. (Christie's) $2,971

One of a pair of mahogany open armchairs with upholstered shield-shaped backs and bowed seats. (Christie's) $5,356

A George III giltwood bergere in the manner of J. Linnell, inscribed 'Roberts 1784' on the frame under the upholstery. (Christie's) $4,631

One of a pair of Louis XV beechwood fauteuils with cartouche-shaped padded backs and serpentine upholstered seats. (Christie's) $3,421

EASY CHAIRS

A 17th century beechwood X-framed open armchair covered in fragments of contemporary associated tapestry. (Christie's) $5,702

One of a pair of mid 19th century ormolu mounted mahogany bergeres in the Empire style. (Christie's) $9,979

A mid 18th century Venetian parcel gilt and aquamarine open armchair, the padded back and seat upholstered in point d'hongerie velvet. (Christie's) $1,425

A Regency mahogany bergere with moulded arm supports and fluted tapering legs, the seat re-caned. (Christie's) $1,131

A William IV mahogany armchair with scrolled shaped leather upholstered back and seat and ring-turned tapering legs. (Christie's) $3,207

A William and Mary walnut open armchair, the back and seat upholstered in yellow damask.(Christie's) $2,280

A Louis XV walnut bergere a oreilles with cushion seat covered in gros and petit point needlework. (Christie's) $6,557

A George III mahogany library armchair with padded back and seat. (Christie's) $5,093

A Louis XV beige-painted bergere, by J. B. Boulard, with shaped back and padded seat. (Christie's) $2,280 £1,

EASY CHAIRS

A Charles II oak sleeping armchair, the hinged back, wings and seat upholstered in raspberry damask. (Christie's) $4,134

One of a pair of George IV giltwood open armchairs in the rococo style, attributed to Gillows of Lancaster. (Christie's) $17,107

One of a pair of George III mahogany library armchairs upholstered in pale gray floral silk. (Christie's) $34,819

One of a pair of early George III mahogany library armchairs with padded backs, arm supports and seats. (Christie's) $8,704

One of a pair of William and Mary scarlet and gold lacquer X-frame open armchairs, 26½in. wide. (Christie's) $40,176

A George III mahogany wing armchair upholstered in green leather. (Christie's) $2,544

A Charles II walnut open armchair, the back and seat upholstered in green velvet damask. (Christie's) $3,421

A Regency mahogany tub armchair, the back and seat upholstered in tan leather. (Christie's) $4,553

A Regency mahogany open armchair with railed simulated bamboo back and padded arm supports and seat with leather cushion. (Christie's) $1,239

EASY CHAIRS

An early George III parcel gilt and cream painted open armchair upholstered in floral needlework. (Christie's) $4,285

A walnut open armchair with arched padded back and seat covered in floral tapestry woven with fables. (Christie's) $6,160

A Regency giltwood throne armchair, attributed to Morel & Hughes. (Christie's) $28,512

A George III mahogany armchair upholstered in blue velvet, partly re-railed. (Christie's) $3,961

A Queen Anne walnut wing armchair with eared padded back, 36½in. wide. (Christie's) $45,532

One of a pair of mid-Georgian mahogany library armchairs with padded backs, armrests and seats.(Christie's) $22,766

A Charles I beech open armchair, the back and seat upholstered in gold and crimson velvet damask. (Christie's) $1,999

A William and Mary walnut wing armchair upholstered in fruiting and floral tapestry. (Christie's) $14,256

A Queen Anne walnut wing armchair upholstered in gros point needlework. (Christie's) $9,266

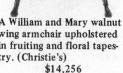

EASY CHAIRS

A Renaissance Revival carved rosewood armchair, attributed to J. Jelliff, N.J., circa 1865, 29in. wide. (Robt. W. Skinner Inc.) $1,900

A Louis XV carved and gilded wood fauteuil upholstered in contemporary tapestry. (Dacre, Son & Hartley) $756

One of a pair of George III giltwood open armchairs with serpentine seats. (Christie's) $5,011

One of a set of six George II giltwood side chairs, the back and seat upholstered in crimson cut velvet, 27in. wide. (Christie's) $166,428

A mid Victorian easy armchair with buttoned back and seat upholstered in floral cut velvet and green velvet. (Christie's) $5,950

A George III mahogany side chair upholstered in gros point floral needlework. (Christie's) $1,566

One of a pair of Victorian ebonized low chairs covered in blue felt applique with foliage and scrolls. (Christie's) $2,349

A child's mahogany rocking chair commode, 2ft. high. (Capes, Dunn & Co.) $79

An early George III design mahogany open armchair upholstered in maroon velvet, 25in. wide. (Christie's) $1,722

EASY CHAIRS

A Regency mahogany correction chair upholstered in floral needlework on a caramel ground. (Christie's) $729

A rococo Revival laminated rosewood upholstered armchair, attributed to J. H. Belter, New York, circa 1865. (Robt. W. Skinner Inc.) $7,500

A mid Victorian mahogany armchair, upholstered in oxblood buttoned leather. (Christie's) $2,975

One of a pair of laminated rosewood chairs, attributed to J. H. Belter, circa 1855, 38in. high. (Robt. W. Skinner Inc.) $2,700

A mid Georgian Cuban mahogany Gainsborough armchair on cabriole legs, upholstered in yellow damask. (Dacre, Son & Hartley) $3,168

A late 17th century beechwood side chair upholstered with sections of floral gros point needlework. (Christie's) $1,644

A giltwood bergere with shaped back and sides ending in dolphin heads, circa 1840. (Christie's) $3,915

A child's miniature mahogany rocking commode with hinged seat, 18th century. (Christie's) $510

A Gustav Stickley willow armchair, circa 1907, 39in. high, 31in. wide. (Robt. W. Skinner Inc.) $400

ELBOW CHAIRS

One of six Regency painted elbow chairs, the beech frames with rectangular and canted openwork backs and cane seats. (Lawrence Fine Art) $5,535

Early 19th century comb-back rocker, New England, 39in. high. (Christie's) $495

A Chippendale walnut arm-chair on Marlborough legs, 1760-90, 42in. high. (Christie's) $2,200

A Chippendale mahogany open armchair, circa 1770-85. (Christie's) $12,100

One of a set of eight Regency mahogany dining chairs with cane filled seats and sabre legs. (Christie's) $5,793

One of a pair of George III green-painted beechwood open armchairs with shaped drop-in seats. (Christie's) $4,183

An 18th century turned and painted bannister back arm-chair, New England. (Robt. W. Skinner Inc.) $1,500

One of a pair of satinwood open armchairs of Regency design, the caned seats with squab cushions. (Christie's) $6,894

One of a pair of early 19th century Gothic open arm-chairs with later solid seats. (Christie's) $8,367

ELBOW CHAIRS

A mid 19th century Windsor writing armchair on rockers, 43½in. high. (Christie's) $1,100

Victorian oak revolving office chair. (British Antique Exporters) $94

Windsor maple, ash and pine bowback armchair, New England, circa 1780. (Robt. W. Skinner Inc.)
$1,600

A Chippendale mahogany open armchair on Marlborough legs, (Christie's) $1,320

A George III mahogany open armchair with padded serpentine seat. (Christie's) $3,175

A Regency mahogany open armchair of gothic style with pierced arcaded back. (Christie's) $1,931

One of a pair of George III mahogany open armchairs, the seats upholstered with yellow floral damask. (Christie's) $2,790

A Queen Anne maple corner chair with stepped horseshoe shaped back, 1735-65. (Christie's) $880

An early Georgian walnut open armchair with drop-in needlework seat. (Christie's) $965

ELBOW CHAIRS

One of a pair of Regency cream painted and gilded open armchairs with caned backs and seats. (Christie's) $1,722

A Charles II walnut open armchair with cane-filled back and seat. (Christie's) $2,818

One of a set of five George III mahogany dining chairs, with bowed padded seats. (Christie's) $2,975

A William and Mary bannister back armchair, circa 1730, Conn., 49¾in. high. (Robt. W. Skinner Inc.) $1,700

One of two late 18th century brace-back continuous arm Windsors, 38in. high. (Christie's) $3,850

A Pilgrim Century turned oak armchair, with a rush seat, circa 1670/1710, 42½in. high. (Christie's) $330

A gilt gesso open armchair of George I design, the drop-in seat covered with gros and petit point needlework. (Christie's) $1,566

A grain painted rocker, circa 1840, 45in. high. (Robt. W. Skinner Inc.) $850

A green painted bowback Windsor armchair, circa 1780. (Robt. W. Skinner Inc.) $3,000

One of a set of six Wallace Nutting ash, pine and maple bowback Windsor chairs, Mass., circa 1920, 41in. high. (Robt. W. Skinner Inc.) $5,000

One of a pair of late George III mahogany shield-back armchairs, circa 1790/1810, 39in. high. (Christie's) $1,870

A Windsor ash and maple writing armchair, America, circa 1800, 43in. high. (Robt. W. Skinner Inc.) $1,900

A George III green painted open armchair, the shaped caned seat with squab cushion. (Christie's) $548

A Queen Anne walnut armchair with arched back and bowed seat, on pad feet. (Christie's) $7,365

Early 19th century mahogany open armchair with leather padded seat. (Christie's) $3,265

One of a pair of George III cream and green painted open armchairs, with bowed cane-filled seats. (Christie's) $1,722

One of a pair of early 19th century yewwood Windsor elbow chairs with bow backs and pierced splats. (Lawrence Fine Art) $1,515

One of a pair of Regency painted open armchairs, the later solid seats with squab cusions. (Christie's) $3,288

ELBOW CHAIRS

One of a pair of George III mahogany open armchairs with tapering beaded railed backs. (Christie's) $1,556

One of a pair of Regency mahogany metamorphic library armchairs, the seat opening to reveal four treads, 23in. wide. (Christie's) $16,070

One of a set of four parcel gilt and green painted side chairs with cane-filled backs and seats, mid 18th century. (Christie's) $3,749

One of a pair of Regency painted satinwood open armchairs with heart-shaped backs. (Christie's) $9,979

One of a pair of mid 18th century Dutch walnut burgomaster's chairs, the pierced tub backs with carved head finials. (Christie's) $9,979

One of a set of nine satin-wood and cream-painted open armchairs with U-shaped cane-filled toprails. (Christie's) $64,152

One of a set of six parcel gilt and simulated rosewood open armchairs of Regency style. (Christie's) $8,488

A Regency metamorphic library armchair attributed to Morgan & Saunders, the seat opening to reveal four treads. (Christie's) $4,989

One of a pair of mahogany, Mason's open armchairs, with hinged foot rests, possibly Irish. (Christie's) $3,537

ELBOW CHAIRS

One of a set of eight walnut and mahogany dining chairs and two open armchairs by J. Henry Sellers. (Christie's) $4,730

One of a pair of Regency parcel gilt and black painted open armchairs, the seats upholstered in aquamarine silk. (Christie's) $5,376

One of a pair of Italian Empire parcel gilt and cream painted fauteuils with padded backs and seats. (Christie's) $4,561

One of a set of three late George III painted open armchairs with caned seats, two with squab cushions, and a chair and triple-backed sofa en suite. (Christie's) $3,214

One of a pair of George II mahogany hall armchairs, and a settee, 49in. wide. (Christie's) $19,958

One of a set of eight George III painted open armchairs with shield-shaped backs, 21½in. wide. (Christie's) $14,256

A late 18th century Italian walnut open armchair with upholstered seat. (Christie's) $997

A George III green and gold lacquer open armchair with pierced oval wheelback. (Christie's) $3,749

A Regency beechwood fauteuil with arched caned back and serpentine seat in molded frame. (Christie's) $1,639

ELBOW CHAIRS

A Windsor open armchair with yewwood hoop back, rails and arms, and elm seat. (Capes, Dunn & Co.) $201

One of a pair of Regency mahogany open armchairs, the later caned seats with leather squab cushions. (Christie's) $7,516

A George I walnut open armchair, with shepherd's crook arms and drop-in padded seat. (Christie's) $18,009

A George IV mahogany reading chair attributed to Morgan & Saunders. (Christie's) $3,445

A George I walnut open armchair with shell and husk cabriole legs and pad feet. (Christie's) $6,264

A George III mahogany folding campaign chair with arched and hinged leather covered back. (Christie's) $1,088

A Windsor comb-back rocking armchair, the saddle seat resting on bamboo turned legs, circa 1800, 48in. high. (Robt. W. Skinner Inc.) $400

One of a pair of Victorian open arm dining chairs with cane seats. (Butler & Hatch Waterman) $2,664

A turned maple and ash ladder back armchair, New England, circa 1720, 47½in. high. (Robt. W. Skinner Inc.) $2,000

ELBOW CHAIRS

A Windsor bowback brace-back armchair, New England, circa 1780, 37½in. high. (Robt. W. Skinner Inc.) $3,200

A 19th century Dutch walnut and marquetry elbow chair with spoon back, needlework upholstered drop-in seat and cabriole legs. (Dacre, Son & Hartley) $432

One of a set of six George III painted open armchairs with later caned seats and ivory damask squab cushions. (Christie's) $26,622

A William and Mary walnut open armchair, with shaped railed splats and padded seat. (Christie's) $1,174

A George III parcel gilt and pale blue painted open arm-chair, upholstered in rose velvet. (Christie's) $2,035

One of a pair of late 18th century black and gold lac-quer open armchairs with upholstered seats. (Christie's) $5,481

A William and Mary maple and ash slat back turned armchair, New England, circa 1710. (Robt. W. Skinner Inc.) $1,400

One of a pair of early George III mahogany open armchairs with drop-in cir-cular seats. (Christie's) $5,950

One of a pair of painted beechwood open armchairs, the shield shaped backs with Prince of Wales plumes. (Christie's) $2,505

CHESTS OF DRAWERS

A mid Georgian mahogany chest with four graduated drawers on bracket feet, 30in. wide. (Christie's) $2,662

A late Federal mahogany veneer bowfront chest of drawers, 1800/20, 43½in. wide. (Christie's) $935

A Chippendale cherrywood chest of drawers, 1760/90, 40in. wide. (Christie's) $1,760

A Queen Anne tiger maple chest of drawers, New England, circa 1750, 36in. wide. (Robt. W. Skinner Inc.) $2,900

A Chippendale maple chest of drawers on bracket feet, New England, circa 1770, 34in. wide. (Robt. W. Skinner Inc.) $3,300

A walnut bachelor's chest with crossbanded folding top, 31½in. wide. (Christie's) $21,924

A Queen Anne walnut bachelor's chest with hinged top, on bracket feet, 29½in. wide. (Christie's) $37,584

A late Federal inlaid mahogany bowfront chest of drawers, Mass., 1800/20, 44¾in. wide. (Christie's) $4,400

A Chippendale mahogany chest of drawers, circa 1780, 40in. long. (Robt. W. Skinner Inc.) $6,100

CHESTS OF DRAWERS

A Louis XV French Provincial walnut chest of serpentine and swelling shape, 49½in. wide. (Lawrence Fine Art) $6,512

A George III mahogany chest with four graduated long drawers, 49in. wide. (Christie's)$13,311

A walnut bachelor's chest with crossbanded hinged top, the sides with carrying handles, 30in. wide. (Christie's) $9,979

A George III satinwood and mahogany serpentine chest, 41¼in. wide. (Christie's) $7,464

A Country Chippendale cherry grain painted tall chest, New England, circa 1800, 37in. wide. (Robt. W. Skinner Inc.) $2,600

A Federal cherry and bird's-eye maple veneered bow-front bureau, Mass., circa 1800, 39in. wide. (Robt. W. Skinner Inc.) $5,000

A George III mahogany chest with crossbanded serpentine top, the fitted top drawer with baize lined slide and easel mirror, 36in. wide. (Christie's) $13,311

A Queen Anne mahogany block-front chest of drawers, Mass., 1750/80, 33½in. wide. (Christie's) $38,500

A George III mahogany chest with four graduated long drawers, mounted with gilt metal rococo handles, 37in. wide. (Christie's) $5,950

CHESTS OF DRAWERS

A Chippendale fruitwood reverse serpentine chest of drawers, Mass., circa 1780, 38in. wide. (Robt. W. Skinner Inc.) $14,000

A George III mahogany chest with molded serpentine top, baize lined writing slide and four graduated long drawers, 48in. wide. (Christie's) $4,071

A George III mahogany chest with molded serpentine top, 42in. wide. (Christie's) $5,481

A Federal inlaid cherrywood chest of drawers, circa 1780/1810, 39in. wide. (Christie's) $2,860

A Queen Anne maple chest of drawers with replaced Queen Anne style brasses, Rhode Island, circa 1750, 35in. wide. (Robt. W. Skinner Inc.) $1,600

A Queen Anne walnut chest with three short and three long drawers, 29½in. wide. (Christie's) $28,188

A Federal mahogany veneer bowfront chest of drawers, 1800-20, 35½in. wide. (Christie's) $1,870

A Chippendale cherrywood reverse serpentine front chest of drawers, 1760-90, 42¼in. wide. (Christie's) $2,860

A Queen Anne painted pine blanket chest, circa 1740, 37¼in. wide. (Robt. W. Skinner Inc.) $850

CHESTS OF DRAWERS

A Chippendale mahogany reverse serpentine chest of drawers, 1760-90, 38in. wide. (Christie's) $8,800

A Chippendale birch chest of drawers on bracket feet, 38½in. wide. (Christie's) $1,870

A Chippendale mahogany and mahogany veneered bowfront chest with ball handles, Mass., circa 1790, 42¼in. wide. (Robt. W. Skinner Inc.) $3,750

A Queen Anne oyster veneered walnut chest, the top with geometric fruitwood stringing, on later bun feet. (Christie's) $7,241

A Chippendale maple tall chest of drawers, New England, circa 1760, 36in. wide. (Robt. W. Skinner Inc.) $2,200

A small George III mahogany chest with a caddy top, the front inset slide with brass knob handles, 31½in. wide. (Woolley & Wallis) $2,055

Victorian mahogany baronial chest of drawers, 1860. (British Antique Exporters) $363

A mahogany bachelor's chest, the hinged rectangular top with writing slide and four graduated long drawers, 31in. wide. (Christie's) $3,057

A Chippendale mahogany chest of drawers, 1765-85, 40in. wide. (Christie's) $3,080

FURNITURE

A Charles II walnut and marquetry cabinet on chest, on later bracket feet, 49½in. wide. (Christie's) $12,528

A James Bartram Chippendale mahogany chest on chest, in two sections, circa 1750/70, 44½in. wide. (Christie's) $110,000

An early Georgian walnut tallboy with moulded concave cornice, 43¼in. wide. (Christie's) $6,706

A Chippendale cherrywood chest on chest, in two sections, 1760/80, 41in. wide. (Christie's) $4,950

A Chippendale tiger maple tall chest with six graduated thumb molded drawers, circa 1770, 36in. wide. (Robt. W. Skinner Inc.) $4,000

A Queen Anne walnut tallboy with chamfered cavetto cornice, 44in. wide. (Christie's) $5,481

A mid Georgian oak tallboy, the base with two long drawers, 46in. wide. (Christie's) $1,566

Georgian mahogany chest on chest, 1780. (British Antique Exporters) $1,080

A George III mahogany tallboy with figured front and original brass handles, 47in. wide. (Lawrence Fine Art) $8,954

CHESTS ON CHESTS

A Queen Anne walnut and burr walnut tallboy, the lower part with a secretaire drawer, 43in. wide. (Christie's) $18,792

A Chippendale walnut chest on chest on ogee bracket feet, 44in. wide, 1760-90. (Christie's)$37,400

A Chippendale cherrywood chest on chest, in two sections, 1765-85, 38½in. wide. (Christie's) $8,250

A Chippendale maple chest on chest, circa 1770-85, 38in. wide. (Christie's) $4,180

A Queen Anne walnut cabinet-on-chest on later bracket feet, 39½in. wide. (Christie's) $7,959

A George III mahogany tallboy with key-patterned cornice, 44½in. wide. (Christie's) $3,207

A George III mahogany tallboy, the base fitted with a secretaire drawer, 44in. wide. (Christie's) $3,758

A Chippendale maple tall chest, Rhode Island, circa 1780, 35.3/8in. wide. (Robt. W. Skinner Inc.) $3,000

A George III mahogany tallboy with three short and six long drawers, 49in. wide. (Christie's) $6,114

CHESTS ON STANDS

A Queen Anne maple high-boy, New Jersey, circa 1730, 37in. wide. (Robt. W. Skinner Inc.)
$8,500

A Queen Anne cherrywood bonnet top high chest, circa 1740-70, 41in. wide. (Christie's)
$26,400

A Chippendale maple highboy with original brasses, circa 1760, 38in. wide. (Robt. W. Skinner Inc.)
$10,000

A William and Mary maple and burl walnut veneer high-boy, Mass., circa 1730, 39½in. wide. (Robt. W. Skinner Inc.)
$3,900

A walnut chest-on-stand, the base with six various sized drawers, 42in. wide. (Christie's) $3,218

A Queen Anne walnut veneer high chest of drawers, 1735-50, 40in. wide. (Christie's) $5,280

A Queen Anne walnut chest-on-stand with two short and three graduated long drawers on the upper chest, 43in. wide. (Christie's) $2,263

A Queen Anne walnut chest on frame, in two sections, Penn., 1750-80, 69in. high. (Christie's) $6,600

A Queen Anne maple high chest of drawers, in two sections, Mass., 1740/60, 36in. wide. (Christie's)
$10,450

CHESTS ON STANDS

A Queen Anne walnut high chest on frame, 1750-70, 40½in. wide. (Christie's) $10,450

A Queen Anne cherrywood highboy, probably Wethersfield, Conn., circa 1740-65, 37½in. wide. (Christie's) $15,400

Queen Anne maple highboy with five graduated drawers, one long drawer and three split drawers, circa 1740, 75¼in. high. (Robt. W. Skinner Inc.) $23,000

A Queen Anne cherrywood high chest of drawers, in two sections, circa 1740-70, 39in. wide. (Christie's) $8,800

A Queen Anne oyster veneered walnut chest-on-stand, 36in. wide. (Christie's) $10,459

A William and Mary walnut and oak chest-on-stand, 40½in. wide. (Christie's) $1,770

A William and Mary birch high chest of drawers, in two sections, 1710-20, 44in. wide. (Christie's) $10,450

A Queen Anne oak grain painted chest on frame, England, circa 1730, 38in. wide. (Robt. W. Skinner Inc.) $3,000

A Queen Anne burl and walnut veneer highboy, Mass., circa 1740, 61¼in. high. (Robt. W. Skinner Inc.) $16,000

311

CHIFFONIERS

An early Victorian rosewood chiffonier, stamped W. Stratford, 50in. wide. (Christie's) **$900**

A William IV rosewood and parcel gilt breakfront chiffonier, the doors filled with lime-green silk pleats, 70in. wide. (Christie's) **$4,183**

A Regency ebonized maple-wood and bois clair chiffonier with two open shelves, 34in. wide. (Christie's) **$4,071**

A William IV figured mahogany chiffonier with scroll carved bracket supports, 3ft. 10in. wide. (Capes, Dunn & Co.) **$950**

A Victorian walnut inlaid chiffonier with triple arched mirror back, 5ft. wide. (Peter Wilson & Co.) **$782**

A Regency rosewood chiffonier with small canopy back and on four bun feet, 36in. wide. (Reeds Rains) **$1,036**

An early Victorian mahogany chiffonier, the top with a three-quarter galleried super-structure, 40in. wide. (Christie's) **$1,192**

A William IV mahogany chiffonier, the base with two recessed mirror panelled doors, 42in. wide. (Christie's) **$1,837**

One of a pair of mid Victorian satinwood, purpleheart and gilt metal mounted chiffoniers applied with blue Wedgwood plaques, 42in. wide. (Christie's) **$9,201**

CLOTHES PRESSES

An early George III sycamore clothes press on re-inforced ogee bracket feet, 45½in. wide. (Christie's) $2,624

A George II mahogany clothes press, the cornice with foliate and egg-and-dart border, 53in. wide. (Christie's) $35,640

A Federal mahogany linen press, in two sections, New York, 1800-15, 46¼in. wide. (Christie's) $4,400

A Chippendale mahogany and mahogany veneer linen press, circa 1780, 48in. wide. (Robt. W. Skinner Inc.) $16,000

A Federal inlaid mahogany linen press, in two sections, probably New York, circa 1785-1805, 45in. wide. (Christie's) $6,050

A Federal mahogany linen press, signed by I. Bailey, New Jersey, 1807, 48in. wide. (Christie's) $8,250

A George III satinwood clothes press, the cupboard doors enclosing five slides, 49½in. wide. (Christie's) $5,637

A George III fiddleback mahogany serpentine clothes press, 54in. wide. (Christie's) $28,576

A small Regency mahogany clothes press on sabre feet with square toes, 36¼in. wide. (Christie's) $7,241

A late 18th century mahogany commode with tambour front and tray top, 20½in. wide. (Bermondsey) $450

Victorian mahogany pot cupboard with marble top. (British Antique Exporters) $148

A fine quality late 18th century mahogany tray top commode, complete with bowl, 20½in. wide. (Bermondsey) $1,000

An early 19th century flame mahogany pot cupboard with a figured marble top. (Bermondsey) $175

Victorian walnut pot cupboard, circa 1860. (British Antique Exporters) $114

One of a pair of Biedermeier mahogany bedside cupboards with hinged tops, 22in. wide. (Christie's) $26,622

A George III mahogany bow front bedside commode, 21in. wide. (Christie's) $1,350

A Georgian mahogany enclosed washstand/commode with fold-over top, rising mirror and fitted compartments and basin, 18in. wide. (Lawrence Fine Art) $877

George III mahogany tray top commode with cupboard above sliding drawer, 20in. wide. (Reeds Rains) $403

314

COMMODE CHESTS

A directoire gilt metal mounted mahogany commode on turned tapering feet, 50in. wide. (Christie's) $3,706

An Italian walnut and marquetry commode in the style of Maggiolini, 45in. wide. (Christie's) $2,799

One of a pair of South German walnut and fruitwood parquetry commodes, late 18th century, 51½in. wide. (Christie's)$22,680

A George III satinwood commode crossbanded with rosewood and inlaid with amaranth bands, 47¼in. wide. (Christie's) $11,421

A Louis XV kingwood and marquetry miniature commode, the serpentine top inlaid with a musical trophy, 19½in. wide. (Christie's) $1,910

A George III cream and black painted commode on parcel gilt square tapering fluted legs, 62in. wide. (Christie's) $23,490

An Edwardian painted satinwood commode with D-shaped top inlaid with a halved bat's wing motif, 51in. wide. (Christie's) $5,149

A George III satinwood and marquetry commode in the French style, 45in. wide. (Christie's) $41,277

One of a pair of satinwood commodes crossbanded in rosewood with serpentine tops, 33½in. wide. (Christie's) $8,648

COMMODE CHESTS

A Louis XV ormolu mounted kingwood and rosewood commode, with molded serpentine breche violette marble top, 52½in. wide. (Christie's) $6,220

An early 19th century German walnut parquetry commode, 50½in. wide. (Robt. W. Skinner Inc.) $2,200

An 18th century Italian walnut serpentine commode, fitted with three long drawers outlined in fruitwood, 51½in. wide. (Christie's)$2,851

A George III satinwood commode with eared oval top, 43in. wide. (Christie's) $14,094

A 19th century Louis XV-style commode with nolded breccia marble top, 40¼in. wide. (Robt. W. Skinner Inc.) $1,200

A mid 18th century French provincial carved, painted and gilded wood commode, 37½in. wide. (Dacre, Son & Hartley) $403

A mid 18th century Venetian parcel gilt and painted commode with serpentine marbleized top, 37in. wide. (Christie's) $2,488

An 18th century French provincial oak commode with waved apron and shaped feet, 47in. wide. (Christie's) $4,665

An ormolu mounted kingwood and tulipwood breakfront commode with molded breccia marble top, 38in. wide. (Christie's) $3,136

A George III mahogany commode with crossbanded hinged rectangular top, 50in. wide. (Christie's) $5,356

A sycamore and marquetry serpentine commode on stepped ormolu feet, 71½in. wide. (Christie's) $4,665

An early George I mahogany commode of concave bombe outline, 39in. wide. (Christie's) $37,497

A George III mahogany commode with serpentine top above a slide, 45in. wide. (Christie's) $12,722

One of a pair of George III satinwood, sycamore and marquetry commodes, 46in. wide. (Christie's) $28,944

An ormolu mounted kingwood and floral marquetry bombe commode of Louis XV style, 51½in. wide. (Christie's) $2,954

A George III mahogany serpentine commode with four graduated long drawers, 46½in. wide. (Christie's) $13,024

Mid 18th century Danish rosewood and parcel gilt commode with white marble top, 28in. wide. (Christie's) $2,954

A George II mahogany dressing commode with lobed serpentine top and a drawer above a central cupboard door, 55½in. wide. (Christie's) $15,919

CORNER CUPBOARDS

A late Georgian oak barrel back corner cupboard, the upper part 89½in. high, the lower part 31in. high, top illustrated. (Lawrence Fine Art) $877

Mid 18th century German ormolu mounted walnut corner cabinet, 33in. wide. (Christie's) $1,866

A carved oak corner cabinet with pentagonal bevelled glass front, Mass., circa 1900, 80¼in. high. (Robt. W. Skinner Inc.)
$2,400

A Federal cherrywood corner cupboard, American, 1790/1810, 50½in. wide. (Christie's) $2,640

A George I black and gold lacquer corner cupboard, 22in. wide. (Christie's)
$1,367

A Federal cherrywood corner cupboard in two sections circa 1820-60, 42in. wide. (Christie's) $2,860

A Chippendale pine corner cupboard, 1760-90, 78½in. high. (Christie's)
$5,280

A Federal pine corner cupboard on straight bracket feet, 50¾in. wide, 1780-1800. (Christie's)
$3,740

A pine corner cupboard with three shaped open shelves, New England, circa 1750, 37in. wide. (Robt. W. Skinner Inc.)
$1,300

CORNER CUPBOARDS

An early 18th century Dutch black japanned corner cupboard with a single panelled door, 21in. wide. (Christie's) $997

A mahogany bow-fronted corner cupboard inlaid with Prince of Wales Feathers. (Ball & Percival) $864

A George I scarlet and gold lacquer corner cupboard with arched bevelled glazed cupboard door, 24in. wide. (Christie's) $7,241

Victorian inlaid mahogany swan neck corner cupboard. (British Antique Exporters) $1,452

A painted cherry and pine hanging corner cupboard, circa 1790, New Jersey, 36½in. wide. (Robt. W. Skinner Inc.) $2,200

A Dutch walnut and marquetry corner cupboard, the top inset with a clock, 30in. wide, 99in. high. (Christie's) $3,732

A cherry corner cupboard with clock, Penn., circa 1815, 83in. high. (Robt. W. Skinner Inc.) $2,500

A late Chippendale cherry-wood corner cupboard, American, circa 1785/1810, 45in. wide. (Christie's) $3,300

A Country Federal cherry corner cupboard, Penn., circa 1820, 56½in. wide. (Robt. W. Skinner Inc.) $1,200

CUPBOARDS

A butternut and pine cupboard on tall bracket feet, New England or Canada, 49in. wide. (Robt. W. Skinner Inc.) $850

A George III mahogany side cabinet of D-shape, the front with two panel doors enclosing four small drawers and two long drawers, 60in. wide. (Lawrence Fine Art) $2,930

A 17th century Flemish oak cupboard, the lower part with a drawer with lion mask corbels, 55in. wide. (Lawrence Fine Art) $3,349

An early George III mahogany cupboard with original brass handles, 44in. wide. (Lawrence Fine Art) $2,442

An early 17th century James I inlaid oak court cupboard, 49in. wide. (Robt. W. Skinner Inc.) $4,750

Mid 18th century French provincial oak cupboard, the doors partly filled with wire, 47in. wide. (Christie's) $3,110

A partly 18th century oak cupboard on bracket feet, 62in. wide. (Lawrence Fine Art) $2,767

A small painted pine cupboard with four interior shelves, circa 1810, 25¼in. wide. (Robt. W. Skinner Inc.) $2,300

A green painted pine blanket chest/cupboard with lift top, probably Long Island, circa 1785/1825, 43½in. wide. (Christie's) $2,970

CUPBOARDS

Late 18th century pine pewter cupboard, America, 41in. wide. (Robt. W. Skinner Inc.) $6,750

An early 17th century oak food cupboard on turned legs and platform stretcher, 50¼in. wide. (Christie's) $5,322

A grain painted walnut cupboard, Penn., circa 1820, 82½in. wide. (Robt. W. Skinner Inc.) $1,200

A Federal tiger maple cupboard with two glazed doors, 1800-10, 54½in. wide. (Christie's) $4,180

A 17th century Flemish rosewood, oak, ebonized and tortoiseshell cupboard, 64½in. wide.(Christie's) $3,888

A Federal pine step back cupboard, New England, circa 1810, 51in. wide. (Robt. W. Skinner Inc.) $1,800

An 18th century oak livery cupboard with brass drop handles, 5ft.6in. x 6ft.9in. high. (Capes, Dunn & Co.) $1,224

An English oak corner buffet, circa 1900, 111cm. wide. (Christie's) $313

A pine step back cupboard, New England, circa 1800, 58½in. wide. (Robt. W. Skinner Inc.) $2,000

FURNITURE

A Victorian walnut daven-
port with ebony inlay and
hinged lid to stationery
compartment, 21 in. wide.
(Butler & Hatch Waterman)
$504

A Victorian figured walnut
davenport with hinged top,
the base with four short
and four dummy drawers,
1ft.9in. wide. (Capes, Dunn
& Co.) $1,008

An early Victorian figured
walnut davenport, the sur-
prise pop-up top with three-
quarter gallery, 22½in. wide.
(Christie's) $2,250

A Victorian walnut davenport,
the rectangular coffered top
fitted with a sprung stationery
compartment. (Christie's)
$2,499

Victorian inlaid walnut
davenport, 1880. (British
Antique Exporters)
$579

An early Victorian oak davenport,
with hinged leather lined writing
panel and four long graduated
drawers, 21½in. wide.
(Christie's) $750

A Victorian rosewood
davenport, the rectangular
top with a three-quarter
gallery, 24in. wide.
(Christie's) $1,162

A George III mahogany
davenport with carrying
handle and leather lined
swivelling sloping flap,
15½in. wide. (Christie's)
$9,201

A Victorian burr walnut
davenport with a sliding
hinged writing slope, 33in.
high. (Anderson & Garland)
$1,065

Victorian walnut davenport with shaped legs, 1860. (British Antique Exporters) $1,264

Victorian mahogany davenport with galleried stationery box, 22in. wide. (Coles, Knapp & Kennedy) $558

A Regency davenport with gilt metal three-quarter pierced gallery, 20½in. wide. (Christie's) $2,954

A mid Victorian gilt and mother-of-pearl, black japanned, papier mache davenport on bun feet, 27in. wide. (Christie's) $2,954

A rosewood davenport with balustrade gallery, 23in. wide. (Outhwaite & Litherland) $1,232

A Killarney arbutus wood davenport inlaid with architectural subject ovals, 31½in. wide. (Christie's) $5,920

An inlaid burr walnut davenport with sycamore interior, late 19th century. (Peter Wilson & Co.) $1,188

A Regency calamander wood davenport, the turned feet with brass castors, 21¼in. wide, circa 1820. (Woolley & Wallis) $1,562

An inlaid burr walnut davenport with three-quarter pierced gallery, 24¾in. wide. (Christie's) $2,760

FURNITURE

DISPLAY CABINETS

An Edwardian satinwood display cabinet, the front with central glazed panel flanked by bowed glazed doors, 42in. wide. (Lawrence Fine Art) $1,435

Art Nouveau style oak display cabinet. (British Antique Exporters) $383

Late 19th century Louis XVI style ormolu mounted marquetry vitrine, America, 38in. wide. (Robt. W. Skinner Inc.) $3,000

An Edwardian mahogany inlaid bow front corner display case with low gallery. (Peter Wilson & Co.) $432

An Edwardian mahogany display cabinet crossbanded in satinwood, 57½in. wide. (Christie's) $1,984

An Edwardian satinwood display cabinet painted with flowers, ribbon-tied foliate scrolls and grisaille panels, 41in. wide. (Christie's) $3,384

Victorian walnut and ormolu display cabinet, 1860. (British Antique Exporters) $1,944

A figured walnut veneered display cabinet with shaped cresting above the glazed doors, 214cm. wide. (Christie's) $8,731

A Dutch walnut and marquetry veneered display cabinet, 46in. wide. (Butler & Hatch Waterman) $3,550

324

DISPLAY CABINETS

Gustav Stickley one door china closet, circa 1907, no. 820, 36in. wide. (Robt. W. Skinner Inc.) $1,300

A Dutch walnut and marquetry display cabinet on later bun feet, 73in. wide. (Christie's) $6,998

A Colonial calamander display cabinet, the drawers with silver plated handles, early 19th century, 57in. wide. (Christie's) $2,430

A Regency mahogany cabinet of small size, 20½in. wide. (Lawrence Fine Art) $3,011

A Victorian ebonized and brass inlaid side cabinet with glazed bow-fronted doors, 4ft.6in. wide. (Capes, Dunn & Co.) $710

Late 19th century mahogany Chinese Chippendale design display cabinet on stand, 49 x 26 x 84in. high. (Peter Wilson & Co.) $4,752

Late Victorian mahogany china display cabinet with carved surmount, 4ft. wide. (Hobbs & Chambers) $1,258

A Dutch walnut and marquetry display cabinet with a pair of glazed doors, 59in. wide. (Christie's) $4,155

An Edwardian satinwood breakfront china cabinet in Sheraton revival style, 4ft.9in. wide. (Woolley & Wallis) $3,456

FURNITURE

An Art Nouveau mahogany breakfront cabinet, probably made by Liberty, circa 1898, 139cm. wide. (Lawrence Fine Art) $803

A Victorian rococo style mahogany side cabinet with arch top oblong mirror panel back, 5ft. wide. (Capes, Dunn & Co.) $1,562

An Edwardian George III style satinwood display cabinet banded in ebony, 48in. wide. (Christie's) $2,205

A shaped Dutch marquetry, domed top, display cabinet with brass handles, 4ft.0½in. wide. (Geering & Colyer) $2,736

A 19th century Dutch walnut veneered showcase cabinet, 225cm. high. (Christie's) $4,595

A walnut showcase cabinet, the single door and sides with glass panels, probably Dutch, 18th/19th century, 218cm. high. (Christie's) $4,136

A 19th century French mahogany and brass cabinet with brass borders and ·mounts, 52in. wide. (Lawrence Fine Art) $1,953

A figured walnut veneered display cabinet, 233cm. high. (Christie's) $4,365

An Edwardian inlaid mahogany display cabinet with center serpentine shaped drawer, 50in. wide. (Reeds Rains) $1,656

DISPLAY CABINETS

Late 19th century Japanese lacquer display cabinet, 70in. high. (Robt. W. Skinner Inc.) $5,700

An Edwardian Art Nouveau mahogany side cabinet with boxwood, satinwood and harewood stylised floral inlay, 4ft. wide. (Capes, Dunn & Co.) $624

Late 18th century Netherlands rococo mahogany marquetry cabinet, 56in. wide. (Robt. W. Skinner Inc.) $7,700

A Georgian style carved mahogany display side cabinet of serpentine outline, 4ft.4in. wide. (Capes, Dunn & Co.) $1,512

Art Nouveau style oak china cabinet, 1920. (British Antique Exporters) $98

A Wylie & Lochhead mahogany display cabinet, designed by E. A. Taylor, 88cm. wide. (Christie's) $2,505

An Edwardian mahogany china display cabinet with Gothic style astragal glazing, 4ft.6in. wide. (Capes, Dunn & Co.) $748

A black and gold lacquer display cabinet with two brass mounted oval panelled glazed doors, 50½in. wide. (Christie's) $4,698

An Edwardian mahogany display cabinet, inlaid with chequered boxwood lines and harewood, 52in. wide. (Christie's) $1,800

DRESSERS

A mid 18th century oak dresser with brass drop handles and escutcheons, 98in. long. (Dacre, Son & Hartley) $3,744

An early Georgian low oak dresser with rectangular top, 65in. wide. Lawrence Fine Art) $797

An early Georgian oak dresser with moulded rectangular top, the frieze with three drawers, 73½in. wide. (Christie's) $3,353

A Georgian oak dresser with plate rack. (F. H. Fellows & Sons) $2,920

An oak dresser on square cabriole legs and pad feet, mid 18th century, 78in. wide. (Christie's) $5,322

A George III oak dresser with mahogany crossbanding throughout, 85½in. wide. (Lawrence Fine Art) $2,930

An 18th century low oak dresser with a moulded top above three frieze drawers, 90 x 32in. high. (Lawrence Fine Art) $2,711

A Georgian oak dresser, the upper part fitted with open shelves flanked by two spice cupboards, 6ft.4in. wide. (Geering & Colyer) $3,150

An early 19th century oak and fruitwood dresser base with three drawers, on cabriole legs, 79in. wide. (Christie's) $4,344

FURNITURE

DRESSERS

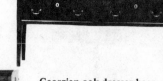

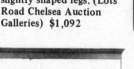

Georgian oak dresser base of two deep drawers on slightly shaped legs. (Lots Road Chelsea Auction Galleries) $1,092

An oak three-drawer dresser with three baluster turned front legs, circa 1700, 6ft. 3in. long. (Peter Wilson & Co.) $5,760

An 18th century oak dresser of fine patina and colour, 86½in. wide. (Christie's) $5,942

An early 18th century Southern Welsh oak enclosed dresser raised on stump feet, 158cm. wide. (Osmond Tricks) $1,859

A George III oak dresser with three drawers to the base and open shelves above, 63in. wide. (Chelsea Auction Galleries) $2,664

A mid 18th century oak dresser, the three drawers with brass knobs, 69in. wide.(Dacre, Son & Hartley) $1,500

A George III low oak dresser with three frieze drawers, 82in. wide. (Lawrence Fine Art) $1,355

Victorian oak Welsh dresser, circa 1880. (British Antique Exporters) $675

A Georgian low oak dresser fitted with three frieze drawers, 80in. wide. (Lawrence Fine Art) $2,392

FURNITURE

A George III mahogany
three-tier dumbwaiter on
vase-shaped shaft, foliate
cabriole legs and pad feet,
42in. wide. (Christie's)
$2,588

A mid Georgian mahogany
two-tier dumb waiter with
circular trays and turned
vase-shaped shaft. (Christie's)
$2,147

A George III mahogany
three-tier dumbwaiter,
46in. high. (Christie's)
$2,192

A late Georgian mahogany
two-tier dumb waiter, each
circular tier with two flaps,
36in. high. (Lawrence Fine
Art) $1,790

A Georgian mahogany three-
tier dumbwaiter, 48in. high.
(Outhwaite & Litherland)
$609

A George III two-tier mahogany dumbwaiter with
molded circular shelves,
37in. high. (Christie's)
$1,218

A Regency mahogany three-
tier dumbwaiter with graduated twin-flap shelves, 23½in.
wide, 45½in. high.(Christie's)
$919

A George III mahogany two-
tier dumbwaiter, 20½in.
wide, 36in. high. (Christie's)
$7,840

A mid Georgian mahogany
dumb waiter with two
turned tiers, 20in. diam.
(Christie's) $2,574

KNEEHOLE DESKS

A George III mahogany partner's desk with leather lined top and nine drawers on both sides. 60¼in. wide. (Christie's) $6,577

A 20th century mahogany partner's desk, Steven Smith, Boston, with brass pulls and escutcheons, 58in. long. (Robt. W. Skinner Inc.) $3,000

A George III mahogany pedestal desk with moulded, scarlet leather lined rectangular top, 54in. wide. (Christie's) $1,496

An early Georgian pollard elm kneehole desk, 37½in. wide. (Christie's) $3,540

A Queen Anne walnut kneehole desk on bracket feet, the sides with gilt metal carrying handles, 27¾in. wide. (Christie's) $17,463

An early George III mahogany serpentine kneehole desk with gadrooned top and a fitted secretaire drawer, 44½in. wide. (Christie's) $12,873

A Queen Anne walnut kneehole desk with folding top, enclosing an oak lined interior, 46in. wide. (Christie's) $10,179

Oak twin pedestal roll-top desk, 1900. (British Antique Exporters) $984

A Regency mahogany partner's desk with leather lined top, four slides and three frieze drawers, 66in. wide. (Christie's) $4,158

331

KNEEHOLE DESKS

A Regency mahogany partner's desk with leather lined top, 77½in. wide. (Christie's) $5,103

A George III mahogany partner's desk with leather lined top, 59½in. wide. (Christie's) $4,527

A mid 18th century Italian walnut and marquetry kneehole desk on cabriole legs and square pad feet. (Christie's) $7,413

An early Georgian walnut kneehole desk with one long and eight short drawers, 32in. wide. (Christie's) $5,443

A Queen Anne walnut kneehole desk of golden color, 32in. wide. (Christie's) $15,919

A Queen Anne pollard elm kneehole desk, the top crossbanded with oak herringbone bands, 33in. wide. (Christie's) $4,553

A Country Federal cherry partner's desk, circa 1820, 53½in. wide. (Robt. W. Skinner Inc.) $3,000

A George III mahogany kneehole secretaire in the manner of Gillows, with leather lined top, 49½in. wide. (Christie's) $3,991

A George III mahogany partner's desk, the kneehole flanked by six graduated drawers, 55in. wide. (Christie's) $10,179

George III mahogany tambour pedestal desk. (Hobbs & Chambers) $2,160

An English Arts & Crafts brass mounted mahogany, sycamore and walnut marquetry partner's desk, 129.6cm. wide. (Christie's) $3,626

Twin pedestal oak rolltop desk, 1880. (British Antique Exporters) $1,588

A mahogany partner's desk with leather lined top and thirteen drawers, 46½in. wide. (Christie's) $3,288

An early Georgian walnut and burr walnut kneehole desk on ogee bracket feet, 34in. wide. (Christie's) $5,950

A late 18th century Italian walnut and marquetry kneehole desk, the top inlaid with a musical trophy, 36in. wide. (Christie's) $1,140

A George III mahogany kneehole desk with seven various sized drawers, 33in. wide. (Christie's) $2,505

An oyster veneered kingwood kneehole desk of Mazarin form, late 17th century, 33½in. wide. (Christie's) $10,179

A Queen Anne walnut kneehole desk on later bun feet, 36½in. wide. (Christie's) $3,395

LOWBOYS

A Chippendale style carved walnut dressing table on acanthus carved cabriole legs, 36in. wide.(Christie's)
$2,090

George I oak lowboy. (Hobbs & Chambers)
$1,123

A George II mahogany rectangular lowboy, the drawers with wooden handles, 32in. wide. (Dreweatts)
$3,750

A Queen Anne maple dressing table on four cabriole legs ending in pad feet, circa 1760, 33in. wide. (Robt. W. Skinner Inc.)
$9,500

A Queen Anne maple dressing table with one long and three short drawers, 31¾in. wide. (Christie's) $1,540

An early Georgian walnut lowboy with three drawers above the waved apron, 32in. wide. (Christie's)
$2,091

A walnut lowboy, the shaped frieze with three drawers on shell and husk cabriole legs, 30½in. wide. (Christie's)
$67,050

A Dutch burr walnut lowboy with molded waved top, early 18th century, 30in. wide. (Christie's)
$4,568

A Queen Anne walnut dressing table on tapering cylindrical legs with disc feet, 33in. wide, 1735-50. (Christie's) $8,800

SCREENS

Victorian mahogany three-fold screen, 1880. (British Antique Exporters) $194

Late 18th century coromandel twelve-fold screen, China, 99½in. high, panel width 19½in. (Robt. W. Skinner Inc.) $18,000

One of a pair of Regency parcel gilt and cream painted firescreens with later glazed adjustable panels, 18in. wide. (Christie's) $578

A mahogany polescreen with rectangular petit point needlework panel worked with the parable of the Prodigal Son, 60in. high. (Christie's) $5,471

A four-leaf screen decorated with 18th century Chinese wallpaper, each leaf 86 x 21½in. (Christie's) $5,065

Regency rosewood pole screen, circa 1830. (British Antique Exporters) $232

Chinese two-fold inlaid screen, 1860. (British Antique Exporters) $344

Victorian bamboo fire-screen, 1880. (British Antique Exporters)$55

A late 19th century black and gold lacquer four-leaf screen, 77 x 26in. (Christie's) $2,413

SCREENS

A Chinese Export black and gold lacquer eight-leaf screen depicting the history of tea-making, 18th century, each leaf 84 x 21½in. (Christie's) $27,496

One of a pair of George III mahogany polescreens, the adjustable panels with later silk floral sprays, 14½in. wide. (Christie's) $466

A late 18th/early 19th century Chinese painted six-leaf screen decorated in colours with an extensive view, each leaf 23½in. wide, 83in. high. (Christie's) $17,409

Late 19th century ivory mounted two-leaf table screen, signed Shizan (for the Shibayama inlay) and Shinko (for the lacquer decoration). (Christie's) $3,231

A Victorian wooden fencing, Maine, circa 1850, 39½in. high, total length 172in. (Robt. W. Skinner Inc.) $475

A six-leaf Japanese screen, sumi and coloi on gold paper, signed, 26 x 80in. each leaf. (Edgar Horn) $3,285

An 18th century Chinese Export black and gold lacquer eight-leaf screen, each leaf 22in. wide, 76½in. high. (Christie's) $9,201

One of a pair of Regency giltwood screens, with glazed Beauvais tapestry panels, 24½in. wide. (Christie's) $1,409

Late 19th century ivory mounted two-leaf lacquer table screen decorated in Shibayama style, signed Masayuki, each panel 30 x 16.5cm. (Christie's) $2,056

FURNITURE

SCREENS

An 18th century Dutch six-leaf canvas screen painted with rustic scenes, each leaf 21¼in. wide, 65¼in. high. (Christie's) $4,600

One of a pair of William IV rosewood polescreens, the brass shafts with faded crimson silk banners, 19in. wide. (Christie's) $939

An 18th century Chinese black and gold lacquer eight-leaf screen, each leaf 81in. high, 21in. wide. (Christie's) $29,462

An 18th century coromandel lacquer eight-leaf screen incised and decorated in colors , each leaf 15¾in. wide, 83in. high. (Christie's) $6,026

A Victorian mahogany polescreen with oval framed adjustable screen, circa 1870. (Peter Wilson & Co.) $374

A Japanese Export lacquer and Shibayama inlaid two-fold screen, decorated in bone, mother-of-pearl, ivory and hardwood, each fold 2ft.5½in. wide, 5ft.7in. high. (Capes, Dunn & Co.) $878

An 18th century Dutch painted and gilded leather six-leaf screen, each leaf 108in. high, 21in. wide. (Christie's) $5,598

A Charles X fruitwood and ebonized firescreen with glazed needlework panel, 53½in. high. (Christie's) $2,192

A late 19th century four-fold low screen in maroon velvet and bands of Berlin woolwork, 41in. high, each fold 18in. (Christie's) $3,445

Late 18th/early 19th century gilt metal mounted mahogany secretaire a abattant, 37½in. wide. (Christie's)$2,332

A George III mahogany secretaire chest, the top with hinged flap, 60in. wide. (Christie's) $5,788

A late George III mahogany secretaire cabinet, the doors enclosing sliding tray shelves, 46in. wide. (Lawrence Fine Art) $1,953

A George III mahogany secretaire cabinet, 30in. wide, 63½in. high. (Christie's) $10,962

A Federal inlaid mahogany bureau desk, possibly by M. Allison, 1790/1810, N.Y., 46½in. wide. (Christie's) $4,400

A Regency rosewood secretaire cabinet, the baize-lined drawer with fitted interior, 23in. wide. (Christie's) $16,443

A pale mahogany Campaign chest with central secretaire drawer. (Worsfolds) $1,440

A late George III mahogany and partridgewood secretaire, 30½in. wide. (Christie's) $2,091

An Empire painted bureau with original brass pulls, New England, circa 1825, 41in. wide. (Robt. W. Skinner Inc.) $3,200

SECRETAIRES

A 19th century German
(Ludwig II) ormolu moun-
ted Japanese black and
gold lacquer cartonnier,
46½in. wide. (Christie's)
$29,548

A George III mahogany
secretaire on ogee bracket
feet, 32½in. wide.
(Christie's)
$43,416

A George III mahogany
secretaire cabinet on fluted
square legs and block feet,
43in. wide. (Christie's)
$100,440

A Louis XV kingwood
semainier of bombe outline,
the seven drawers inlaid a
deux faces, stamped F. C.
Franc JME, 26in. wide.
(Christie's) $4,354

A Chippendale mahogany
bureau with four drawers,
Boston, circa 1790, 36½in.
wide. (Robt. W. Skinner
Inc.) $18,000

A George III satinwood
secretaire, with fitted secretaire drawer above two long
and one deep drawer, 32½in.
wide. (Christie's)
$8,850

An 18th century walnut
secretaire a abattant with
fall front, 36in. wide.
(Worsfolds) $4,320

A Louis XVI kingwood and
tulipwood semainier by J.
J. Kirschenbach, 56in. high.
(Christie's) $4,276

Late 19th century marque-
try secretaire with pull-out
secretary drawer, Holland,
41½in. wide. (Robt. W.
Skinner Inc.)
$1,200

SECRETAIRE BOOKCASES

One of a pair of Regency mahogany secretaire bookcases, 47½in. wide. (Christie's)$11,491

A Regency mahogany secretaire bookcase on plinth base, 37½in. wide. (Christie's) $4,082

A Federal inlaid mahogany secretary, Mass., 1800-20, 36in. wide. (Christie's) $4,620

An Empire stencilled mahogany secretary in two parts, New York, 1820-30, 42¼in. wide. (Christie's) $7,480

A Federal mahogany secretary bookcase, in two parts, circa 1805/25, 39½in. wide. (Christie's) $3,300

An Irish mid-Georgian mahogany kneehole secretaire bookcase, 40in. wide. (Christie's) $9,477

A Regency mahogany secretaire cabinet with two gothic pattern glazed cupboard doors, 43in. wide. (Christie's) $5,211

A Federal inlaid mahogany and bird's-eye maple desk and bookcase, 1790/1810, 41in. wide. (Christie's) $19,800

A George III mahogany secretaire cabinet with later silver lined interior, 36½in. wide. (Christie's) $10,179

SECRETAIRE BOOKCASES

A Federal mahogany ven-
eered secretary, Mass., 1800-
1810, 41¾in. wide.
(Christie's) $7,700

A Regency mahogany secre-
taire bookcase, 48½in. wide.
(Lacy Scott) $4,205

Federal mahogany butler's
secretary, with high French
feet, circa 1810, 41in. wide.
(Robt. W. Skinner Inc.)
$7,750

A 19th century oak twin
pedestal cylinder top desk/
bookcase, 3ft.8in. wide.
(Bridgfords) $803

A George III mahogany
secretaire cabinet with
molded tear-drop cor-
nice, 49in. wide.
(Christie's)$4,957

A Federal mahogany secre-
tary with two glazed panel
doors with crosshatching,
circa 1795, 41in. wide.
(Robt. W. Skinner Inc.)
$4,750

An early 19th century
Regency mahogany secretary
with adjustable shelves,
47in. wide. (Robt. W.
Skinner Inc.)
$2,700

A Victorian Arts & Crafts
carved walnut Masonic
secretaire, 4ft.2in. wide.
(Capes, Dunn & Co.)
$864

An Edwardian mahogany
secretaire bookcase in the
Sheraton revival manner,
240 x 127cm. (Phillips)
$2,192

SECRETAIRE BOOKCASES

A George III mahogany and satinwood secretaire cabinet, 49in. wide. (Christie's) $9,201

A mahogany secretaire bookcase with four glazed doors enclosing adjustable shelves, 55in. wide. (Christie's) $2,384

A Federal mahogany and mahogany veneer inlaid secretary, Mass., circa 1815, 39in. wide. (Robt. W. Skinner Inc.) $4,500

A late George III mahogany secretaire bookcase, the glazed panel doors enclosing adjustable shelves, 43in. wide. (Anderson & Garland) $5,040

A George III mahogany secretaire bookcase, the frieze inlaid with fruitwood foliate ovals, 102in. wide. (Christie's) $8,613

A George III mahogany secretaire cabinet with two glazed doors, 49in. wide. (Christie's) $4,827

A George III satinwood secretaire cabinet with geometrically-glazed doors, 31½in. wide. (Christie's) $27,496

A George III mahogany secretaire bookcase, the interior with adjustable shelves, 3ft.7in. wide. (Woolley & Wallis) $3,425

A George III mahogany secretaire cabinet, the secretaire drawer with fruitwood and maple veneers, 43½in. wide. (Christie's) $4,344

A George III mahogany secretaire cabinet with a pair of glazed cupboard doors, 43½in. wide. (Christie's) $6,436

A Federal mahogany secretary with glazed panel doors above a fold-down writing surface, circa 1795, 40in. wide. (Robt. W. Skinner Inc.) $7,500

A Regency mahogany secretaire cabinet, the doors flanked by ebony moldings, 49in. wide. (Christie's) $6,512

A George III mahogany and satinwood secretaire bookcase with baize lined fitted secretaire drawer, 39½in. wide. (Christie's) $3,680

An English 19th century Chippendale style mahogany secretaire cabinet, 86in. long. (Robt. W. Skinner Inc.) $22,000

A George III satinwood and rosewood secretaire cabinet, the baize-lined fall-flap enclosing a fitted interior, 36in. wide. (Christie's) $12,052

A George III mahogany secretaire cabinet with a pair of glazed cupboard doors, 45½in. wide. (Christie's) $3,395

A Georgian secretaire bookcase with glazed doors enclosing brocade lined shelves. (Worsfolds) $1,820

A satinwood secretaire bookcase, late 18th century, possibly Anglo-Indian, 31½in. wide. (Christie's) $5,786

SETTEES & COUCHES

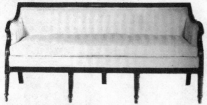

A Federal upholstered mahogany sofa on ring turned and reeded legs, circa 1800-15, 75½in. long. (Christie's) $4,950

A Federal mahogany sofa, the padded back with arched crest, 1790-1810, 80¼in. wide. (Christie's) $4,400

A Regency mahogany hall bench, the scrolled sabre legs with turned baluster carrying handles, stamped James Winter 101 Wardour St., 47in. wide. (Christie's) $7,959

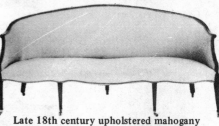

Late 18th century upholstered mahogany Sheraton sofa, 79in. long. (Robt. W. Skinner Inc.) $1,500

A 19th century Netherlands rococo style mahogany and marquetry inlaid settee, overall exotic wood and mother-of-pearl floral and bird inlay, 49in. wide. (Robt. W. Skinner Inc.) $1,200

A 19th century Jacobean-style carved oak hall settle with lift-up seat, 66¾in. wide. (Robt. W. Skinner Inc.) $650

A Federal carved mahogany sofa, Phila., 1805-20, 75¾in. long. (Christie's) $4,950

A classical upholstered mahogany cylinder arm sofa, circa 1810-30, 72in. long. (Christie's) $990

SETTEES & COUCHES

A Federal mahogany carved sofa, the arched crest rail with grape and vine decoration, 75in. wide. (Robt. W. Skinner Inc.) $2,000

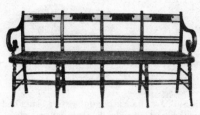

One of a pair of grain painted 'fancy' settees, each with a back of four sections, 74in. wide, 1800-10. (Christie's) $4,950

19th century oak settle, circa 1890. (British Antique Exporters) $162

A Victorian mahogany framed settee, circa 1860. (British Antique Exporters) $453

A Regency simulated bamboo sofa with pierced triple chairback, cane filled seat and squab cushion, 54in. wide. (Christie's) $2,413

Georgian pine settle, circa 1770. (British Antique Exporters) $346

A George III mahogany sofa with serpentine back, Irish, late 18th century, 86in. wide. (Christie's) $3,300

A Federal mahogany sofa, the upholstered back and seat with beaded bow front, probably Mass., circa 1810, 73in. wide. (Robt. W. Skinner Inc.) $3,700

SETTEES & COUCHES

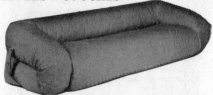

'Anfibio', a white leather upholstered sofa bed designed by Alessandro Becchi, 240cm. wide. (Christie's) $867

A laminated birchwood chaise longue designed by Bruno Mathsson, Made in Sweden, 151cm. long. (Christie's) $709

A George III mahogany humpback sofa with plum-colored floral damask loose cover, squab and four cushions, 85in. wide. (Christie's) $6,696

One of a pair of Regency rosewood sofas with triple cushion backs and cushion seats covered in green velvet, 77in. wide. (Christie's) $16,070

A small, George III, mahogany humpback sofa with upholstered back, scrolled arms and waved seat on square tapering legs, 63in. wide. (Christie's) $8,268

A walnut sofa with padded back and seat, with outscrolled arm supports, on shell and husk cabriole legs and pad feet, 62in. wide. (Christie's) $4,631

One of a pair of George II mahogany hall settles with solid seats, on turned tapering foliate legs and stepped turned feet, 49in. wide. (Christie's) $64,281

A George III mahogany sofa upholstered in apricot silk, 66in. wide. (Christie's) $2,678

FURNITURE

'Djinn series', an upholstered chaise longue designed by Olivier Mourgue, in green nylon stretch jersey, circa 1965, 170cm. long. (Christie's) $1,103

One of a pair of George II carved pine sofas with waved drop-in seats, 144in. wide. (Christie's) $40,176

A Regency mahogany sofa with double-scrolled padded back and squab cushion upholstered in green watered silk stripes, 78in. wide. (Christie's) $2,546

A George III mahogany sofa, the arched padded back, out-scrolled arms and bowed seat on molded square legs, 77in. wide. (Christie's) $5,942

A George I walnut twin-back settee with drop-in bowed seat, the arm supports carved with eagle's heads, on shell and husk cabriole legs, 55½in. wide.   (Christie's) $12,117

One of a set of four parcel gilt and gray painted corner chairs, forming a sociable, with yellow silk backs and seats. (Christie's) $4,385

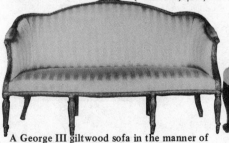

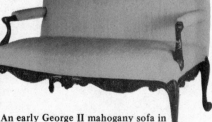

A George III giltwood sofa in the manner of John Linnell, the back and serpentine seat upholstered in striped ivory silk, 69in. wide. (Christie's) $8,393

An early George II mahogany sofa in the French taste, the serpentine seat covered in green silk repp, 61in. wide. (Christie's) $4,341

SETTEES & COUCHES

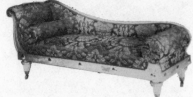

A William IV giltwood chaise longue with scrolled upholstered back, seat and footrest, 92in. wide. (Christie's) $1,456

One of a pair of George II mahogany twin chairback settees, with arms ending in eagles' masks, 64in. wide. (Christie's)
$24,105

Part of a carved mahogany bergere lounge suite of five pieces, the settee with three-panel back and padded seat. (Capes, Dunn & Co.) $2,016

A 'Lip' sofa after a design by Salvador Dali, upholstered in red nylon stretch fabric, 209cm. wide. (Christie's) $2,192

A George III giltwood small sofa in the manner of Thos. Chippendale, the back and seat covered in blue and white floral printed cotton, 58in. wide. (Christie's) $3,132

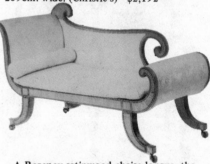

A Regency satinwood chaise longue, the scrolled back crossbanded with rosewood and framed by ebonized and boxwood lines, 67in. wide. (Christie's)
$6,531

An L. & J. G. Stickley slat-back settle, style no. 281, with spring cushion seat, circa 1912, 76in. wide. (Robt. W. Skinner Inc.)
$1,600

A Federal mahogany sofa on ring turned reeded legs and brass castors, 75in. long, circa 1815. (Robt. W. Skinner Inc.)
$5,750

SETTEES & COUCHES

An early Georgian walnut settee, the arched padded back and seat upholstered in blue-gray patterned silk, on cabriole legs and pad feet, 58in. wide. (Christie's) $3,790

Late 19th century rococo Revival rosewood settee, N. Schott, America, 65in. wide. (Robt. W. Skinner Inc.) $250

A Louis XVI giltwood canape with curved and arched padded back and bowed seat covered in floral gros point needlework, 93in. wide. (Christie's) $4,384

A late 19th century rococo Revival rosewood sofa, impressed Gentso?, America, 84in. wide. (Robt. W. Skinner Inc.) $300

A Chippendale upholstered sofa, the serpentine back flanked by outward flaring arms, circa 1780, 80in. long. (Robt. W. Skinner Inc.) $3,400

A George III mahogany humpback sofa upholstered in raspberry floral damask, 82in. wide. (Christie's) $4,384

A 19th century Netherlands rococo style mahogany and marquetry settee, overall inlay of exotic woods, ivory and mother-of-pearl with bird and floral motifs, 71in. long. (Robt. W. Skinner Inc.) $2,000

A rococo Revival laminated rosewood settee, attributed to John Henry Belter, New York, circa 1855, 66in. wide. (Robt. W. Skinner Inc.) $8,000

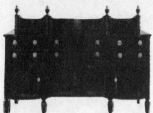

A Federal mahogany sideboard on turned and reeded legs, 1800-10, 96in. long. (Christie's) $3,080

A late Federal mahogany sideboard on tapering leaf carved feet, Mass., 1800-10, 78in. wide. (Christie's) $330

Small Federal cherry inlaid sideboard, New England, circa 1815, 44in. wide. (Robt. W. Skinner Inc.) $1,400

A Federal mahogany sideboard with serpentine top, Maryland, 1790-1810, 72in. wide. (Christie's) $11,000

A Regency mahogany sideboard with ebony stringing and bowed top, 69½in. wide. (Christie's) $5,149

A Louis XVI style ebonized sideboard with bronze and ormolu mountings, America, 1865-70, approx. 69in. wide. (Robt. W. Skinner Inc.) $1,800

A Federal mahogany sideboard with D-shaped top, Rhode Island, 1790-1810, 67in. long. (Christie's) $7,700

A Federal mahogany veneer sideboard with bowed rectangular top, 1790-1815, 70in. wide. (Christie's) $4,400

A Federal mahogany sideboard, the top shaped to fit a curved recess, circa 1790, 73in. wide. (Christie's) $7,150

A classical mahogany sideboard with marble top, New York, 1815-25, 75in. long. (Christie's) $3,300

A Federal mahogany inlaid sideboard, the four square tapering legs with tiger maple banded burl panels, stringing and bellflower inlay, circa 1790, 72in. wide. (Robt. W. Skinner Inc.) $8,500

A George III mahogany sideboard with serpentine top, with one frieze drawer, flanked by two deep drawers, one a cellarette drawer, 79in. wide. (Christie's) $2,896

Late 19th century carved teak sideboard, China, 48in. wide. (Robt. W. Skinner Inc.) $1,200

A Federal mahogany sideboard, the front with a pair of cockbeaded short drawers centered by a bowed long drawer, 69½in. long, circa 1785-1800. (Christie's) $4,950

A Federal mahogany sideboard, the top with broad ovolo corners, circa 1795, 69in. wide. (Robt. W. Skinner Inc.) $7,250

A Federal mahogany inlaid sideboard with bow front, Mass., circa 1815, 70in. wide. (Robt. W. Skinner Inc.) $9,000

SIDEBOARDS

A late Georgian mahogany sweep front sideboard on six turned supports, 54¼in. wide. (Lawrence Fine Art) $2,233

A Federal inlaid mahogany serpentine front sideboard, circa 1780/1800, 74½in. wide. (Christie's) $9,350

A George III mahogany sideboard with bowed concave centered top, the drawer crossbanded with rosewood in the arched centre, 72in. wide. (Christie's)
$14,877

A George III mahogany serpentine sideboard with a central drawer above an arch, flanked by deep drawers, 67in. wide. (Lawrence Fine Art) $11,396

A George III mahogany and satinwood sideboard with crossbanded D-shaped top, 48in. wide. (Christie's) $8,704

A Victorian mahogany mirror back sideboard outlined in simulated malachite, the lower section with six snakewood panels, 198cm. high. (Osmond Tricks) $648

A Victorian rococo style flame mahogany pedestal sideboard with two central serpentine drawers, 7ft. wide. (Capes, Dunn & Co.) $568

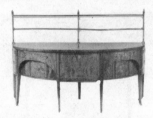

A George III mahogany demi-lune sideboard, the ormolu backrail with vase finials, 90in. wide. (Christie's) $2,916

SIDEBOARDS

A Regency mahogany breakfront sideboard on square tapering legs and spade feet, 76in. wide. (Christie's) $5,214

A George III mahogany and satinwood sideboard with gilt metal and enamel handles, Scottish, 103in. wide. (Christie's) $13,311

Georgian mahogany four-door sideboard, 1840. (British Antique Exporters) $1,286

Victorian oak sideboard with pediment, 1895. (British Antique Exporters) $144

A Federal mahogany sideboard, the top with bowed front edge, circa 1795/1815, 75½in. wide. (Christie's) $3,960

A George III mahogany sideboard with crossbanded serpentine top, 65½in. wide. (Christie's) $8,613

A Sheraton period mahogany sideboard inlaid with satinwood and ebony herringbone stringing, 68in. wide. (Morphets) $1,944

A George III mahogany and satinwood bow fronted sideboard with a cellarette drawer to the right and a cupboard to the left, 72in. wide. (Christie's) $5,093

STANDS

Victorian brass bound oak
jardiniere, circa 1880.
(British Antique Exporters)
$72

Victorian inlaid mahogany
towel rail, circa 1880.
(British Antique Exporters)
$93

An ormolu mounted
amboyna gueridon in the
manner of Weisweiler, the
top with turquoise ground
saucer inscribed Sevres RF
Sc, 30in. high. (Christie's)
$3,288

Victorian oak tiled back
hall stand, 1860. (British
Antique Exporters)
$264

A George III mahogany
library steps table with
molded hinged top, 48in.
high, extended. (Christie's)
$3,132

An 18th century style mahogany urn stand with tray top,
11in. wide. (Capes, Dunn &
Co.) $273

A tripod cherry candlestand
with candle drawer, Mass.,
circa 1760, 25½in. high.
(Robt. W. Skinner Inc.)
$5,000

A Regency brass music stand with
blue painted and gilded rest pierced
with oak leaves and acorns, 60½in.
high. (Christie's) $1,473

Victorian brass banded
oak fern stand, 1880.
(British Antique Exporters)
$105

STANDS

A William and Mary walnut torchere with molded circular top, spirally-turned shaft and scrolled tripartite base, 12in. diam. (Christie's) $801

One of a set of George III mahogany library steps, with carrying handles, 30in. wide. (Christie's) $4,071

Victorian oak barley twist cakestand, 1860. (British Antique Exporters) $52

A Regency rosewood duet music stand, the pierced top filled with lyres. (Christie's) $947

A Regency mahogany reading stand, the sloping writing surface lined with tooled green leather, 23½in. wide. (Christie's)$21,924

A Regency burr walnut and giltwood torchere with concave-sided triangular top, 17in. wide.(Christie's) $4,285

A Regency brass inlaid rosewood teapoy with Bramah lock and carrying handles, 17½in. wide. (Christie's) $3,207

Victorian mahogany butler's tray, 1850. (British Antique Exporters) $180

Victorian oak double-shelf cakestand, 1880. (British Antique Exporters) $112

STANDS

A mid Victorian black, gilt and mother-of-pearl japanned papier mache music stand, 50¼in. high. (Christie's) $820

A Regency mahogany three-tier etagere, the gray marble shelves with ormolu galleries, 24½in. wide. (Christie's) $14,094

A polished chromium hat stand made for Bazzi in Milan, 51.6cm. high. (Christie's) $656

A Federal mahogany candlestand with octagonal top, New England, 1790-1810, 21¼in. wide. (Christie's) $550

A William and Mary walnut stand, Penn., 1700-40, 25¼in. wide. (Christie's) $1,870

A Chippendale mahogany birdcage candlestand with a dished and molded circular tilt top, 1760-90, 23½in. diam. (Christie's) $4,620

A Chippendale mahogany candlestand with tilt top, the legs terminating in padded snake feet, circa 1770, 27in. high. (Robt. W. Skinner Inc.) $3,200

A pair of white painted and gilded tripod torcheres, the tops 13in. diam. (Christie's) $5,080

One of a pair of classical Revival carved and gilt pedestals with marble tops, circa 1835, 36½in. high. (Robt. W. Skinner Inc.) $4,600

A Federal inlaid mahogany candlestand on a vase-turned pedestal, 1790-1810, 29½in. high. (Christie's) $1,760

A pine easel, adjustable, on a trestle base, with castors, 29in. wide. (Christie's) $715

A Country Federal painted candlestand with oval top, circa 1810, 20in. wide. (Robt. W. Skinner Inc.) $1,500

A Chippendale mahogany candlestand with circular tilt top, 1760-80, 22in. diam. (Christie's) $1,045

An early Victorian walnut coal bin of sarcophagus form with coffered top and hinged front with metal liner, 21in. wide.(Christie's) $1,533

Chippendale cherry candle-stand, the square top on vase turned post and tripod cabriole leg base, 26in. high, circa 1780. (Robt. W. Skinner Inc.) $1,200

Victorian oak bookstand, 1880. (British Antique Exporters) $87

A Federal mahogany tilt top candlestand, 1790-1810, 26in. wide. (Christie's) $825

One of a pair of giltwood stands with stepped circular white marble tops, 19in. wide. (Christie's) $4,860

STANDS

An ormolu mounted mahogany gueridon in the manner of Weisweiler, 30½in. high. (Christie's)
$5,637

Victorian pine and cast iron butter maker, 1860. (British Antique Exporters)
$290

A Chippendale mahogany bird cage candlestand, Phila., circa 1760, 27½in. high. (Robt. W. Skinner Inc.)
$4,500

Victorian oak hall stand, 1860. (British Antique Exporters) $186

Victorian oak three-tiered buffet, circa 1870. (British Antique Exporters)
$166

A Japonnaiserie bamboo and porcelain hat and coat stand, 51in. wide, 84in. high. (Christie's)
$1,879

A painted pine candlestand, New England, circa 1780, 27in. high, 20in. diam. (Robt. W. Skinner Inc.)$900

A late Federal pine stand, with single drawer above two cupboard doors, 1810 30, 22½in. wide.(Christie's)
$528

One of a pair of George III giltwood torcheres on cloven hoof feet, 49½in. high. (Christie's)
$16,070

A mahogany fender stool, the seat covered in floral gros and petit point needlework on mid 18th century cabriole legs, 45½in. wide. (Christie's)$20,358

Victorian footstool with beaded cover, 1850. (British Antique Exporters) $75

A George III mahogany stool with button-upholstered crimson velvet seat, 36in. long. (Christie's) $3,132

Victorian mahogany revolving piano stool, 1860. (British Antique Exporters) $110

Late 19th century mahogany piano stool. (British Antique Exporters) $20

A walnut stool, the oval padded seat on splayed club legs and pad feet, 20in. wide. (Christie's) $1,686

An early 17th century oak joint stool on fluted tapering legs joined by plain stretchers, 17in. wide. (Christie's) $926

One of a pair of George III pine window seats with differently upholstered bowed seats and double-scrolled ends, 48½in. wide. (Christie's) £7,840

A Middle Eastern hardwood stool with saddle seat, inlaid with ivory stylized flowerheads, 17in. wide. (Christie's) $626

STOOLS

A Queen Anne walnut stool, the rectangular seat covered in floral tapestry woven with a fable, 18¾in. wide. (Christie's) $5,088

One of a pair of George III simulated rosewood window seats with bowed seats and double scroll ends upholstered in rose velvet, 46in. wide. (Christie's) $14,094

A George I walnut stool with drop-in seat covered with floral petit point needlework, 22in. wide. (Christie's) $17,226

A George II mahogany stool with bowed rectangular needlework upholstered drop-in seat, possibly Irish, 20½in. wide. (Christie's) $2,332

One of a set of six 17th century oak joint stools, 18in. wide. (Christie's) $37,584

One of a pair of George III mahogany stools, one branded VR BP N22224 1866, 23½in. wide. (Christie's) $17,366

A Derby & Co. oak window seat, the cut-out armrests with spindle supports, circa 1910, 28in. high. (Robt. W. Skinner Inc.) $375

An early Victorian mahogany octagonal seat, the hinged lid upholstered in floral needlework, 20¼in. wide. (Christie's) $4,071

A William and Mary walnut stool upholstered with a fragment of early 17th century tapestry, 17in. wide. (Christie's) $2,851

STOOLS

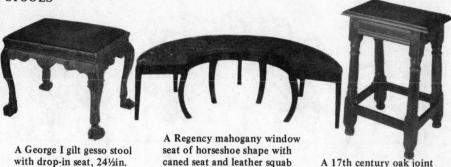

A George I gilt gesso stool with drop-in seat, 24½in. wide. (Christie's) $32,886

A Regency mahogany window seat of horseshoe shape with caned seat and leather squab cushion, 63in. wide. (Christie's) $10,179

A 17th century oak joint stool with ring-turned legs joined by plain stretchers, 17¼in. wide. (Christie's) $1,354

A walnut and parcel gilt stool of George I style, the drop-in seat painted in gilt and scarlet with a coat-of-arms, 26in. wide. (Christie's) $2,678

One of a pair of Regency mahogany music stools with lyre-shaped carved splat backs. (Reeds Rains) $2,592

A George I walnut stool with rectangular needlework drop-in seat, on shell and foliate cabriole legs, 22in. wide. (Christie's) $3,132

A Chinese scarlet and gold lacquer circular panel, now associated with a chinoiserie bamboo pattern parcel gilt stool, 17in. diam. (Christie's) $1,252

Late 19th century pottery garden seat, probably France, whimsically depicting a cushion resting on a basket, 20in. high. (Robt. W. Skinner Inc.) $750

Late 17th/early 18th century oak and elm joint stool, 18½in. wide. (Christie's) $2,280

SUITES

Two of a set of six 18th century German walnut fauteuils and canape, upholstered in gros and petit point needlework, the canape 51in. wide. (Christie's) $7,452

An Edwardian mahogany drawingroom suite of seven pieces, with satinwood panel and boxwood string inlay. (Capes, Dunn & Co.) $648

Part of a suite of early George III mahogany seat furniture, the sofa with serpentine back and seat, 84in. long. (Dreweatts) $54,000

A suite of George III mahogany seat furniture comprising a set of four
library armchairs, upholstered in gros and petit-point needlework, a
window seat and a sofa, the window seat 51in. wide, the sofa 84in.
wide. (Christie's) $46,980

Two of a set of eight open armchairs, one of three window seats and a sofa
all with caned seats with squab cushions, the sofa 72½in. wide.
(Christie's) $63,027

Two of a set of six early George III mahogany dining chairs, the seats covered
in gros point floral needlework and a humpback sofa , 78in. wide. (Christie's)
                                                      $34,133

FURNITURE

CARD & TEA TABLES

A Federal mahogany card table, attributed to Chas. H. Lannvier, circa 1800-15, 36in. wide. (Christie's) $3,080

Victorian walnut card table, 1850. (British Antique Exporters) $1,147

Federal mahogany and mahogany veneer card table, with serpentine shaped folding top, Mass., circa 1790, 37in. wide. (Robt. W. Skinner Inc.) $6,250

Late 18th century George III mahogany demi-lune card table, England, 36in. wide. (Robt. W. Skinner Inc.) $450

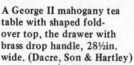

A George II mahogany tea table with shaped fold-over top, the drawer with brass drop handle, 28½in. wide. (Dacre, Son & Hartley) $1,628

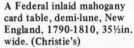

A Federal inlaid mahogany card table, demi-lune, New England, 1790-1810, 35½in. wide. (Christie's) $1,760

A Federal inlaid mahogany card table, 1790/1810, 35¼in. wide. (Christie's) $1,430

A George III satinwood and calamander card table, the top with fan inlay, 35½in. wide. (Christie's) $5,793

A Federal inlaid mahogany card table, Mass., 1800/20, 34¼in. wide. (Christie's) $2,200

CARD & TEA TABLES

A Federal mahogany inlaid card table, circa 1800, 36in. wide. (Robt. W. Skinner Inc.) $1,400

A classical Revival mahogany and mahogany veneered card table with D-shaped top, N.Y., circa 1810, 36in. wide. (Robt. W. Skinner Inc.) $4,500

A George III satinwood and fruitwood card table with baize-lined crossbanded D-shaped top, 36in. wide. (Christie's) $2,913

A Federal mahogany circular card table with demi-lune hinged top, N.Y., 1790-1810, 36in. wide. (Christie's) $1,760

A Federal mahogany card table, the lift top with D-shaped front and sides, Boston, circa 1795, 35in. wide. (Robt. W. Skinner Inc.) $4,100

A Georgian mahogany double fold-over tea/games table fitted with two small drawers. (Worsfolds) $2,448

Federal mahogany and mahogany veneer card table, the lift top with ovolo corners, circa 1795, top 36 x 34½in. (Robt. W. Skinner Inc.) $2,200

An early Georgian calamander wood and walnut card table, the top with candle sconces and guinea wells, 34in. wide. (Christie's) $10,459

A late Federal mahogany card table with hinged D-shaped top, Mass., 1820-30, 36in. wide.(Christie's) $1,870

CARD & TEA TABLES

A George III mahogany
card table with baize lined
serpentine top, 39½in. wide.
(Christie's) $5,637

A Regency rosewood card
table with baize lined top
inlaid with brass lines,
36in. wide. (Christie's)
$10,962

One of a pair of classical
mahogany card tables,
N.Y. or Baltimore, 1810/
70, 35¾in. wide. (Christie's)
$7,150

A Regency rosewood card
table with leather lined
swivelling top inlaid with
brass lines and ivory foliage,
37in. wide. (Christie's)
$12,528

A George II walnut card
table with lobed folding top
and baize lined interior, 34in.
wide. (Christie's)
$15,660

A Regency brass inlaid and
rosewood tea table with
twin-flap swivelling top,
35½in. wide. (Christie's)
$3,067

A late Federal mahogany
card table with serpentine
top, 1810/20, 35¾in. wide.
(Christie's) $825

A Regency ormolu mounted
calamander card table with
baize lined D-shaped folding
top, 38in. wide. (Christie's)
$10,962

A Federal mahogany and
mahogany veneer card table
with lift top, circa 1795,
34½in. wide. (Robt. W.
Skinner Inc.)
$4,400

CARD & TEA TABLES

An early Victorian maho-
gany tea table with swivel
and flap top, 3ft. wide.
(Capes, Dunn & Co.)
$426

A Federal mahogany sofa
card table, the top with
shaped leaves, circa 1810/
30, 51½in. wide, open.
(Christie's) $1,100

A George III kingwood and
satinwood card table, with
baize lined crossbanded top,
36½in. wide. (Christie's)
$1,566

A Regency rosewood card
table, the baize lined top
with boxwood stringing,
36in. wide. (Christie's)
$2,975

A mid Georgian mahogany
combined card and tea table
with candle sconces, possibly
Irish, 35in. wide. (Christie's)
$4,600

A Regency penwork card
table with swivelling top,
36in. wide. (Christie's)
$1,096

A George I walnut tea/games
table with lobed triple-flap
top, 33in. wide. (Christie's)
$7,516

One of a pair of early 19th
century mahogany card
tables, 34¾in. wide.
(Christie's)
$17,226

A mid Georgian mahogany
tea table with D-shaped
hinged top and three frieze
drawers, possibly Irish,
32½in. wide. (Christie's)
$2,624

CENTER TABLES

A William and Mary birch and pine tavern table, New England, circa 1750, 46in. wide. (Robt. W. Skinner Inc.) $2,750

A 17th century Spanish walnut center table with rectangular top and pierced shaped trestle ends, 51in. wide. (Christie's) $2,799

A William and Mary maple and pine tavern table, New England, circa 1700, top 47 x 29½in. (Robt. W. Skinner Inc.) $3,400

An 18th century Queen Anne maple center table, with a single walnut drawer, 42in. wide. (Christie's) $1,650

A rosewood center table, the top inlaid with specimen marbles and semi-precious stones, 23in. wide. (Christie's) $5,011

A Regency parcel gilt and maple center table with circular top, 51½in. diam. (Christie's) $12,268

A 17th century and later Spanish walnut center table, 46½in. wide. (Christie's) $2,488

An 18th century North Italian kingwood center table with leather lined top, 58¼in. wide. (Christie's) $1,788

An Italian walnut center table, the top inset with a panel of specimen marbles, 37½in. wide. (Christie's) $2,177

CENTER TABLES

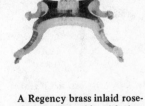

A Regency brass inlaid rose-wood center table with tip-up top, 49½in. wide. (Christie's) $10,962

Late 19th century Renaissance Revival inlaid mahogany center table, America, 45½in. wide. (Robt. W. Skinner Inc.) $850

A mid Victorian ormolu mounted thuya and marquetry center table attributed to Holland & Sons, 51½in. diam. (Christie's) $11,745

An ormolu and mahogany center table of Louis XVI style, on twinned simulated bamboo legs, 27in. diam. (Christie's) $1,710

An early 18th century boulle gilt metal and ebony center table, the top inlaid with a berainesque scene, 37in. wide. (Christie's) $2,488

One of a pair of gilt gesso center tables with later inset honey- colored marble tops, 21in. wide. (Christie's) $7,830

A George III satinwood center table, the tip-up top crossbanded with rose-wood, 41in. diam. (Christie's) $10,179

A grained and parcel gilt center table in the early Georgian style with massive breche violette top, 69in. wide. (Christie's) $3,996

A Regency brass inlaid rose-wood center table with tip-up top, 50in. diam. (Christie's) $7,516

CENTER TABLES

A Regency and parcel gilt
plum-pudding mahogany
center table, 50½in. diam.
(Christie's) $6,696

A Victorian satinwood,
ebony and marquetry center
table with waved frieze, 42in.
wide. (Christie's)
$3,481

A Regency mahogany center
table with tip-up top on a
ring-turned baluster shaft
and quadrapartite base, 50in.
diam. (Christie's)
$2,332

A rosewood center table, the
square top inset with specimen marble, 15½in. square.
(Christie's) $1,768

An oak center table framed
by chequered inlaid lines
executed by Peter Waals
assisted by P. Burchett, 1928,
68.3cm. wide. (Christie's)
$2,207

A Victorian mahogany
center table with marble
and semi-precious stone
top, 27in. diam.
(Christie's) $6,026

An early 19th century Tyro-
lean parquetry center table
on a scrolled tripartite base,
31½in. diam. (Christie's)
$1,283

A Renaissance Revival marble
top parlor table, by T.
Brooks Cabinet & Upholstery
Warehouse, circa 1865, the
white oval top 37in. long.
(Robt. W. Skinner Inc.)
$1,100

A Regency parcel gilt, mahogany and ebony center table,
the circular black fossil marble top with pierced brass
border, 25in. diam.
(Christie's) $12,830

CENTER TABLES

A Regency brass inlaid
rosewood center table with
tip-up top, 50½in. diam.
(Christie's) **$3,645**

A Regency rosewood center
table, the top inlaid with
brass banding, 45in. wide.
(Christie's) **$3,112**

A Regency parcel gilt and
burr-maple center table,
the top inlaid with ebony
banding, 52in. diam.
(Christie's)
　　　　$12,301

A Biedermeier mahogany
center table with circular
marble tray top, 36in. diam.
(Christie's) **$2,851**

A Queen Anne giltwood
center table, the top with
geometric strapwork foliage
and shells, 30in. wide.
(Christie's) **$4,687**

Early 19th century fruit-
wood center table, Austrian
or North Italian, 37in. diam.
(Christie's) **$1,096**

A Regency ormolu moun-
ted mahogany center table
with grey marble top,
32½in. diam. (Christie's)
　　　$4,821

A black and gold lacquer
center table of early
Georgian design, 34in.
wide. (Christie's)
　　　$2,192

A Regency rosewood center
table with inset specimen
marble top, 36in. diam.
(Christie's) **$6,026**

FURNITURE

An Irish giltwood console table, the top with inset serpentine marble slab, 58½in. wide. (Christie's) $3,218

One of a pair of Regency rosewood and parcel gilt console tables with white marble tops, 54in. wide. (Christie's) $9,020

A George II giltwood console table with later, eared serpentine, mottled gray marble top, 46¼in. wide. (Christie's) $6,696

A Louis XVI mahogany console desserte with brass mounts and gray veined marble top, 34in. wide. (Lawrence Fine Art) $2,116

One of a pair of grained pine console tables with marble tops on carved eagle supports, 42¼in. wide. (Christie's) $2,946

A classical brass inlaid mahogany marble top pier table, N.Y., circa 1810/30, 41½in. wide. (Christie's) $2,640

A George II stained pine console table with serpentine marble top, 53in. wide. (Christie's) $11,577

An 18th century Italian parcel gilt and painted corner console, 23in. wide. (Christie's) $1,088

A mid 18th century giltwood console table, sold with another en suite of a later date, 41½in. wide. (Christie's) $6,415

CONSOLE TABLES

A Regency walnut console table with serpentine breccho-litto marble top, 52in. wide. (Christie's) $3,706

An Irish pine console table with shaped rectangular serpentine marble top, 69in. wide. (Christie's) $11,264

A George II white-painted and gilded pier table, after a design by T. Langley, with mottled gray and white marble top, 56¼in. wide. (Christie's) $26,049

A Louis XV Provincial walnut console table with later breccia marble top, 34½in. wide. (Christie's) $1,555

One of a pair of giltwood console tables with serpentine molded white tops, 40in. wide. (Christie's) $3,706

A George II grained pine console table with later onyx marble top, 59½in. wide. (Christie's) $2,896

One of a pair of Italian pine pier tables, the serpentine tops with gadrooned borders, 35½in. high. (Christie's) $4,665

One of a pair of Louis XV giltwood console tables with shaped breccia marble tops, 23½in. wide. (Christie's) $4,043

One of a pair of George II giltwood pier tables, each with D-shaped white marble top, 35in. wide. (Christie's) $159,192

DINING TABLES

A William IV rosewood dining table with circular tilt-top , 55in. diam. (Christie's) $1,350

A Flemish oak dining table with draw leaf top on cup and cover legs, partly late 16th century, 100in. long open. (Christie's) $1,069

A large carved oak dining table. (John Hogbin & Son) $888

A George III satinwood and rosewood breakfast table with tip-up top, 49½in. wide. (Christie's) $13,862

A William IV rosewood veneered circular snap-top breakfast table, 4ft.3½in. diam. (Woolley & Wallis) $994

A George III satinwood and mahogany breakfast table with tip-up top, 53in. wide. (Christie's) $7,516

A William IV twin pedestal mahogany dining table with rounded rectangular top, 69in. long, including one extra leaf. (Christie's) $2,235

A Federal mahogany dining table, circa 1815, 47in. wide. (Robt. W. Skinner Inc.) $800

A Regency mahogany break-fast table with circular tip-up top, 66½in. diam. (Christie's) $10,962

A William and Mary oak
side or refectory table with
a three plank top, 83½in.
wide. (Lawrence Fine Art)
$2,360

An oyster veneered yewwood,
marquetry and parcel gilt
draw-leaf dining table, 97½in.
wide, open. (Christie's)
$1,073

A Regency mahogany patent
dining table, the handles inscribed G. Oakley, Maker,
57 x 147in. (Christie's)
$20,412

A Regency mahogany break-
fast table with molded oval
tip-up top, vase-shaped shaft
and quadripartite base, 64in.
wide. (Christie's)
$3,218

A mid Victorian walnut and
inlaid loo table, 48in. wide.
(Dacre, Son & Hartley)
$529

A George III rosewood and
satinwood breakfast table
with oval crossbanded tip-
up top, 57in. wide.
(Christie's)
$10,854

A late Georgian circular
mahogany breakfast table
centered by an inlaid floral
medallion, 55in. diam.
(Anderson & Garland)
$1,164

An early Regency period, faded
mahogany, circular snap-top
breakfast table, 3ft.10in. diam.
(Woolley & Wallis)
$3,358

An early Victorian mahogany
breakfast table, on heavy gun
barrel turned column, with
curvilinear platform base, 4ft.
9in. x 3ft.7in. (Capes, Dunn
& Co.) $568

DINING TABLES

A William IV mahogany library table with four frieze drawers flanked by dummies, 59 in. diam. (Christie's) $5,103

1920's oak dining table. (British Antique Exporters) $270

A Regency rosewood breakfast table, the top with burr-elm banding on ring-turned ebonized shaft, 59½ in. wide. (Christie's) $2,829

A 19th century circular mahogany tip-top dining table with lion's paw feet, 52 in. diam. (W. H. Lane & Son) $489

Victorian oak draw-leaf table, circa 1900. (British Antique Exporters) $97

Regency rosewood loo table with scroll feet, 1830. (British Antique Exporters) $1,140

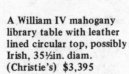

A George III ormolu mounted rosewood library table with leather lined circular top, 44 in. diam. (Christie's) $8,035

A William IV mahogany library table with leather lined circular top, possibly Irish, 35½ in. diam. (Christie's) $3,395

A George III mahogany drum table with revolving octagonal top, 43½ in. wide. (Christie's) $11,577

DINING TABLES

A Restoration mahogany breakfast table with circular top, 45¼in. diam. (Christie's) $2,662

A Victorian mahogany extending dining table with concave-sided plinth bases, 58 x 166in. including four leaves. (Christie's) $13,122

A Regency mahogany library table with circular leather lined top on a tripartite base and claw feet, 47½in. diam. (Christie's) $2,624

A Gustav Stickley round library table, no. 633, circa 1904, 48in. diam. (Robt. W. Skinner Inc.) $1,700

Regency rosewood centre pedestal table, circa 1830. (British Antique Exporters) $1,236

Victorian walnut dining table, 1880. (British Antique Exporters) $103

A George IV oak octagonal library table with leather lined top, 42½in. wide. (Christie's) $2,505

A Federal mahogany and veneer drum table on a tripod cabriole leg base, 31in. diam, circa 1820. (Robt. W. Skinner Inc.) $600

A George III mahogany drum table with leather lined revolving circular top, 38½in. diam. (Christie's) $6,561

DRESSING TABLES

Victorian walnut and ebony dressing table, 1860. (British Antique Exporters) $569

Late Victorian walnut dressing table, 1880. (British Antique Exporters) $334

Victorian oak dressing table, 1880. (British Antique Exporters) $202

A yellow painted pine dressing table with stencil and foliate designs, New England, circa 1825, 34in. wide. (Robt. W. Skinner Inc.) $800

A green and gold lacquer, serpentine top, dressing table with chinoiserie decoration and pull-out writing slide, 31½in. wide. (Christie's) $1,840

A George III mahogany dressing chest, the hinged top enclosing a fitted interior with an easel mirror, 24½in. wide. (Christie's) $4,773

A Country Queen Anne cherry dressing table, central Mass., circa 1800, 24in. wide. (Robt. W. Skinner Inc.) $4,750

An Italian Empire gilt metal mounted walnut and fruitwood dressing table, 49in. wide. (Christie's) $1,555

A Regency mahogany dressing table by Gillows of Lancaster, 41½in. wide. (Christie's) $3,395

DRESSING TABLES

A Chippendale walnut dressing table with scalloped front skirt, circa 1765-80, 35¼in. wide. (Christie's)
$4,400

Victorian mahogany dressing table, 1860. (British Antique Exporters)
$610

A Regency mahogany dressing table, the top with three-quarter gallery, stamped Gillows of Lancaster, 52in. wide. (Christie's)
$2,488

American mahogany dressing table, 1900. (British Antique Exporters)
$112

A Louis XV amaranth, tulipwood and floral marquetry table de toilette by G. Peridiez, 35in. wide. (Christie's)
$5,987

A George III mahogany and satinwood dressing chest, the fitted interior with easel mirror, 28in. wide. (Christie's)
$4,023

A Federal mahogany and mahogany veneered dressing table, circa 1810, 35in. wide. (Robt. W. Skinner Inc.) $750

A small Victorian Duchess dressing table, 1860. (British Antique Exporters)
$1,309

Edwardian mahogany dressing table with cabriole shaped legs, circa 1910. (British Antique Exporters)
$487

A Chippendale walnut drop-leaf table, with two gate legs, 1760-80, 48in. long. (Christie's) $5,280

A Chippendale carved mahogany and cherrywood drop-leaf table, on cabriole legs, 1750-75, 54in. long. (Christie's) $20,900

A Chippendale mahogany drop-leaf table on four stationary and two swing square legs, 47¾in. long, 1770-90. (Christie's) $715

A Chippendale mahogany dining table with two drop-leaves, Phila., 1765-85, 55in. long. (Christie's) $1,320

A Queen Anne maple dining table with circular drop-leaf, circa 1760, 41¾in. wide. (Robt. W. Skinner Inc.) $8,000

A Federal mahogany break-fast table, New York, circa 1815, top 38¾ x 48¾in., open. (Robt. W. Skinner Inc.) $1,500

A Chippendale walnut drop-leaf dining table on Marl-borough legs, 1765-85, 56in. long, extended. (Christie's) $3,190

A late George II mahogany two flap table with oval top, 49 x 59in. extended. (Lawrence Fine Art) $2,930

A Chippendale walnut dining table, circa 1770, 48½in. long. (Robt. W. Skinner Inc.) $6,000

A Chippendale mahogany drop-leaf dining table on six shaped legs with claw and ball feet, New York, 1760-80, 57½in. wide. (Christie's) $1,650

A Federal mahogany drop-leaf table, 1790/1810, 57in. long, open. (Christie's) $3,300

A mid Georgian mahogany gateleg dining table, the adapted oval twin flap top on club legs and pad feet, 60½in. wide open. (Christie's) $1,409

A Queen Anne maple dining table with oval drop-leaf top, New England, circa 1760, 40½in. wide. (Robt. W. Skinner Inc.) $1,200

A Chippendale mahogany card table with scalloped front skirt, Mass., circa 1770, 31½in. wide, open. (Robt. W. Skinner Inc.) $6,100

A late Federal mahogany drop-leaf table, the top clover shaped, N.Y., 1800/20, 37in. wide. (Christie's) $352

A George III mahogany gate-leg dining table with twin flap top, 56in. wide open. (Christie's) $3,680

A classical carved mahogany drop-leaf table, circa 1815, 38in. wide. (Christie's) $935

A Queen Anne walnut drop-leaf table with square top, circa 1750, 34in. wide, open. (Christie's) $2,860

381

GATELEG TABLES

A William and Mary maple gateleg table, the
top flanked by semi-circular drop leaves,
New England, 1710-45, the top 55 x 48in.
(Christie's) $3,300

A Georgian mahogany gateleg dining table,
5ft. wide. (Worsfolds) $5,550

A 17th century oak gateleg dining table with
oval twin-flap top and baluster supports,
67in. wide, open. (Christie's) $7,309

A mid Georgian mahogany gateleg table with
oval twin-flap top on turned legs, 48½in.
wide, open. (Christie's) $4,976

A William and Mary fruitwood gateleg table
on baluster legs, joined by molded stretchers,
and scrolled feet, 29in. wide. (Christie's)
                                $9,646

A George III mahogany gateleg dining table
with oval twin-flap top and two fielded
frieze drawers, 53in. diam., open.
(Christie's) $19,958

An early Georgian mahogany gateleg table
with twin-flap top, on turned tapering legs
and claw and ball feet, 54in. wide, open.
(Christie's) $2,187

A William and Mary mahogany gateleg table,
the drop leaves opening to form an oval,
N.Y., circa 1710/40, top 67 x 53in. open.
(Christie's) $38,500

GATELEG TABLES

An oak gateleg dining table with oval twin-flap top, 17th century, 75in. wide. (Christie's) $2,829

A large oak gateleg dining table with twin-flap rectangular top, 66in. wide, open. (Christie's) $2,546

A William and Mary maple gateleg table, the bowed top with oval drop leaves, New England, 1720-30, 44in. long. (Christie's) $3,960

A George III mahogany gateleg table with oval twin-flap top and a frieze drawer, on cabriole legs, 59in. wide, open. (Christie's) $6,696

An Irish mid Georgian mahogany gateleg table with oval twin-flap top on cabriole legs, 58½in. wide. (Christie's) $8,613

A William and Mary walnut gateleg table with molded twin-flap sixteen-sided top and bobbin-turned frame, 42½in. wide. (Christie's) $9,979

A William and Mary padoukwood and oak gateleg dining table with oval twin-flap top, 56in. wide, open. (Christie's) $4,561

An oak gateleg dining table with oval twin-flap top and bobbin-turned frame, 17th century, 70in. wide, open. (Christie's) $3,678

LARGE TABLES

A George III mahogany serving table, the serpentine top with chamfered corners, 70in. wide. (Christie's) $3,987

A Regency mahogany patent dining table with D-shaped ends, 53 x 123in. (Christie's) $17,409

An Empire carved mahogany three-part dining table, 1825-35, 111½in. long, top extended. (Christie's) $4,400

A Regency mahogany patent dining table with D-shaped end-sections, 45¾ x 113½in. (Christie's) $3,987

A mid 19th century Shaker Community table, possibly New Hampshire, 21ft.3in. long. (Robt. W. Skinner Inc.) $38,000

A mahogany dining table with D-shaped end-sections, 54 x 98in., including two extra leaves. (Christie's) $4,023

A 16th century and later Italian walnut refectory table with solid rectangular top and ring-turned baluster trestle ends, 85½in. wide. (Christie's) $3,110

Late 19th century 'Monarch' marquetry and cast iron pool table, by Brunswick & Balke-Collender Co., Buffalo, 9ft. x 4½ft. (Robt. W. Skinner Inc.) $15,000

LARGE TABLES

A Regency three-pedestal mahogany dining table, on ring turned baluster shafts and splayed tripartite bases, 45½ x 93in. (Christie's) $10,735

A Regency mahogany patent Imperial dining table in the manner of Gillows, 66in. wide, 174½in. extended. (Christie's) $12,722

A George III mahogany serpentine serving table with brass rail at the back, 97in. long. (Lawrence Fine Art) $13,024

A George III mahogany dining table with five pillar supports, 183in., fully extended, the two extra leaves and pillars unillustrated. (Lawrence Fine Art) $56,980

A Regency mahogany three-pedestal dining table with rounded rectangular end-sections on baluster shafts and splayed bases, 53½ x 196in. (Christie's) $11,113

An early 17th century oak refectory table, 18ft.2in. x 3ft.5in. (Woolley & Wallis) $8,700

A Regency padoukwood and mahogany patent dining table, 154in. long, including four leaves. (Christie's) $20,638

A Regency mahogany dining table with ring-turned baluster shafts and quadripartite bases, 52½ x 125in. (Christie's) $11,664

OCCASIONAL TABLES

A William and Mary pine and maple tavern table, New England, circa 1730, 30½in. wide. (Robt. W. Skinner Inc.) $850

A Regency faded rosewood drum table, the frieze with three drawers, 35¾in. diam. (Christie's) $9,082

An early 19th century white marble circular conservatory table, probably Italian, 61in. diam. (Peter Wilson & Co.) $24,480

A revolving mahogany tip-up, tray top table on turned tripod base, 32in. diam. (Butler & Hatch Waterman) $1,704

A Queen Anne maple and pine tea table, New England, circa 1770, 25½in. wide. (Robt. W. Skinner Inc.) $1,700

A Georgian style walnut wine table with two tiers of revolving book racks, 30in. high. (Anderson & Garland) $695

A mid Georgian burr yew tripod table with circular tray tip-up top, 23in. diam. (Christie's) $4,447

A table with glazed, brass framed, hide top supported on elephant feet, 27in. wide. (Christie's) $704

A Federal cherry inlaid tip table, circa 1790, 28½in. high. (Robt. W. Skinner Inc.) $2,300

OCCASIONAL TABLES

Late 19th century Centennial Chippendale Philadelphia mahogany birdcage tea table, 27½in. diam. (Robt. W. Skinner Inc.) $2,200

An early 19th century Chinese Export bamboo low table with later square top, 15¾in. square. (Christie's) $783

A mahogany tripod table, the tip-up top with pierced balustrade gallery, 35½in. wide. (Christie's) $2,021

A transitional parquetry, kingwood and bois-satine table a ecrire, by J. P. Dustantoy, 15½in. diam. (Christie's) $5,443

A Victorian papier mache tray on stand, with deep waved outline, 31½ x 24 x 10½in. high. (Lawrence Fine Art) $683

A 19th century carved Chippendale mahogany tea table with hinged top, 30in. diam. (Robt. W. Skinner Inc.) $575

A Chippendale mahogany tilt-top tea table, on three cabriole legs, Rhode Island, circa 1760, 35in. diam. (Robt. W. Skinner Inc.) $2,700

A rococo Revival laminated rosewood lamp table, by J. B. Belter, New York, circa 1855, 26in. diam. (Robt. W. Skinner Inc.) $23,000

A Regency rosewood pedestal table, the octagonal top with an Italian inlaid marble panel, 24½in. wide. (Christie's) $1,686

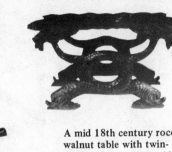

A Regency painted satinwood tripod table with tip-up top, 35½in. wide. (Christie's) $7,128

A George III mahogany tripod table, the tray top on triple-scrolled shaft, 10½in. diam. (Christie's) $1,603

A mid 18th century rococo walnut table with twin-scalloped top, 60in. wide. (Christie's) $16,070

A George III yewwood occasional table, the top inlaid with squares of specimen woods, 20½in. wide. (Christie's) $4,017

A George III mahogany architect's table with double easel top and a frieze drawer, 35½in. wide. (Christie's) $3,961

A boulle jardiniere, the lift-out tin liner with milled edge, on cabriole legs, 17in. wide. (Christie's) $2,851

A mid Georgian mahogany tripod table with tip-up piecrust top, 27½in. diam. (Christie's) $8,019

A set of four satinwood quartetto tables, the tops with ebony stringing, 14in. to 19½in. (Christie's) $4,527

A Regency rosewood tripod table with marble top, 20½in. wide. (Christie's) $4,285

A mahogany tripod table, the tip-up top with a needlework panel worked in gros and petit point, 34in. wide. (Christie's) $1,339

A mahogany and beechwood small table with circular tray top and baluster shaft with leather foot rest on four legs carved as boots, 15in. diam. (Christie's) $583

A mid Georgian walnut architect's table, the frieze drawer with leather lined slide and swivelling ink drawer, 33in. wide. (Christie's) $5,540

An Emile Galle oak and marquetry table a deux plateaux, 60.2cm. wide. (Christie's) $630

Early 19th century Anglo-Indian ebony and specimen wood table with hexagonal top, 23in. diam. (Christie's) $2,041

A mahogany, ebonized and marquetry jardiniere in the style of Charles Bevan, 77.6cm. high. (Christie's) $3,942

A George III mahogany tripod table with webbed claw and ball feet, 16½in. diam. (Christie's) $1,697

A Queen Anne giltwood table on foliate cabriole legs and pad feet, 22in. wide. (Christie's) $3,348

An early George III mahogany tripod table with scrolling scalloped top, birdcage action, 29¾in. wide. (Christie's) $2,041

FURNITURE

A Regency rosewood occasional table, the top inlaid with an Italian octangular panel of specimen marbles, 31in. wide. (Christie's) $4,541

A William and Mary maple tavern table, New England, circa 1730, 34in. diam. (Robt. W. Skinner Inc.) $4,100

Late 18th century Italian fruitwood tripod table with four frieze drawers. (Christie's) $1,866

A George IV ebonized and gilded pedestal table, 24in. wide. (Christie's) $1,174

Early 19th century Chinese Export bamboo tray table, 29in. wide, 26¼in. high. (Christie's) $6,557

A George III satinwood and rosewood tripod table, in the manner of Thos. Chippendale, 26½in. wide. (Christie's) $12,528

A Georgian mahogany tripod table, the circular top with marquetry pattern of birds and flowers, 28in. diam. (Lawrence Fine Art) $638

A George III mahogany architect's table with adjustable top above a pull-out front section fitted with compartments, 37½in. wide. (Lawrence Fine Art) $4,232

A walnut and beechwood tripod table, the tip-up top with a floral gros and petit point needlework panel, 33in. wide. (Christie's) $1,409

OCCASIONAL TABLES

A walnut draw-leaf table, Switzerland, circa 1700, top 43 x 30in. (Robt. W. Skinner Inc.) $4,250

A George IV ormolu mounted parcel gilt and fruitwood library table, 56in. diam. (Christie's) $14,569

A bamboo pattern centre table, the glazed top inset with a panel of 18th century Chinese painting on silk, 37¾in. wide. (Christie's) $4,698

A mahogany urn table, the top with pierced fretwork gallery, 13in. square. (Christie's) $2,349

A set of four Regency rosewood quartetto tables on twinned, shaped and turned supports, 26½in. to 13in. wide. (Christie's) $3,834

A Sheraton design satinwood drum table on a turned, fluted and writhen column, 23in. diam. (Morphets) $1,224

A George III mahogany tripod table on a baluster stem with cabriole shape supports, 34in. diam. (Lawrence Fine Art) $1,790

A Regency circular tripod table with parquetry inlay. (F. H. Fellows & Sons) $1,095

A Victorian circular top table, inset with specimen marbles and hardstones, 34in. diam. (Lawrence Fine Art) $8,294

PEMBROKE TABLES

A George III mahogany Pembroke table, the twin-flap top with one bowed frieze drawer, 42½in. wide. (Christie's) $5,011

A Country Chippendale cherry Pembroke table, with drop leaves and serpentine ends, circa 1780, 33 x 35in. (Robt. W. Skinner Inc.) $1,400

A George III burr walnut and mahogany Pembroke table, the twin-flap top with a wide satinwood band, 43½in. wide. (Christie's) $4,384

A George III satinwood and fruitwood Pembroke table, on square tapering legs, 37½in. wide. (Christie's) $6,508

A Federal cherry, inlaid Pembroke table, circa 1810, 36in. wide. (Robt. W. Skinner Inc.) $900

A George III mahogany Pembroke table with oval twin-flap top crossbanded in faded rosewood, 38in. wide, open. (Christie's) $2,574

A Federal mahogany Pembroke table with two drop leaves, Penn., 1800-10, 49¾in. wide, open. (Christie's) $1,650

A late Regency mahogany Pembroke table with a rosewood crossbanded two-flap top, 20 x 32in. extended. (Lawrence Fine Art) $1,790

A George III satinwood and maplewood Pembroke table, the twin-flap top inlaid with stained and natural fruitwoods, 37½in. wide, open.(Christie's) $4,698

A George III satinwood and fruitwood Pembroke table on square tapering legs, 40in. wide. (Christie's) $15,660

A George III Pembroke table with twin-flap rectangular top, the legs joined by an X-shaped stretcher, 44½in. wide open. (Christie's) $1,749

A Sheraton design mahogany and satinwood Pembroke table with shaped flaps, 36in. wide. (Morphets) $1,633

A Federal mahogany Pembroke table with two drop leaves, 1790-1810, 35in. wide. (Christie's) $2,860

An early Victorian mahogany Pembroke work table with fall leaves, 1ft.7in. wide. (Capes, Dunn & Co.) $460

An Hepplewhite satinwood veneer Pembroke table with drop leaves, circa 1800, top 32 x 37in. (Robt. W. Skinner Inc.) $4,500

A late Federal mahogany Pembroke table with clover shaped top, 1815-25, 40¾in. long, top extended. (Christie's) $1,210

A George III satinwood Pembroke table with harewood, kingwood and other crossbanding and stringing decoration, 32in. wide. (Chancellors Hollingsworths) $2,499

A Federal inlaid mahogany Pembroke table, Mass., 1790/1810, 31in. wide. (Christie's) $1,980

SIDE TABLES

One of a pair of Dutch walnut and marquetry side tables, each with one frieze drawer, 41½in. wide. (Christie's) $5,443

A giltwood side table with sienna marble top, 53in. wide. (Christie's) $2,557

One of a pair of satinwood and marquetry side tables, 36in. wide. (Christie's) $19,575

A Dutch walnut and marquetry side table on cabriole legs and pointed pad feet, 34in. wide. (Christie's) $2,954

A George III parcel gilt and painted side table with distressed D-shaped white marble top, 32in. wide. (Christie's) $2,147

A scarlet and gold lacquer side table, basically late 17th century, 32½in. wide. (Christie's) $2,035

One of a pair of parcel gilt and bronzed side tables with mottled green marble tops, 34½in. wide. (Christie's) $10,179

A Dutch walnut and marquetry side table on cabriole legs and ball and claw feet, 35½in. wide. (Christie's) $3,110

A Louis XVI ormolu mounted side table with inset grey marble, eared rectangular, concave sided top, 41½in. wide. (Christie's) $3,421

SIDE TABLES

An Irish, George III satinwood and fruitwood side table, the D-shaped top crossbanded in faded rosewood, 60in. wide. (Christie's) $8,613

One of a pair of copies of 16th century French walnut hall side tables, 3ft.3in. wide. (Woolley & Wallis) $1,178

19th century carved oak side table, 1860. (British Antique Exporters) $194

A mid 17th century oak side table with brass drop handles, 30in. wide. (Woolley & Wallis) $2,466

A mahogany and satinwood side table with D-shaped top, 39½in. wide. (Christie's) $2,413

An early George III mahogany side table with bowed serpentine top, 30½in. wide. (Christie's) $3,758

One of a pair of Queen Anne gilt gesso side tables, 27½in. wide. (Christie's) $56,376

Victorian carved oak side table, 1860. (British Antique Exporters) $623

An early Georgian walnut side table with carved border, formerly a card table, 33in. wide. (Christie's) $1,456

SIDE TABLES

A George II cream painted parcel gilt side table with gray marble top, 80½in. wide. (Christie's) $32,140

A Charles II walnut side table on bobbin-turned legs joined by conforming stretchers with later oak feet, 35in. wide. (Christie's) $3,353

A Regency mahogany serving table with breakfront top and brass gallery with vase finials, 84in. wide.(Christie's) $10,611

A mid 17th century oak side table with chamfered top, 27½in. wide. (Christie's) $17,107

An early Georgian red walnut side table, the triangular hinged top enclosing a compartment, with later base, 36½in. wide, open. (Christie's) $2,332

One of a pair of George III satinwood pier tables with crossbanded D-shaped tops and ebonized spade feet, 23in. wide. (Christie's) $14,472

A grain painted serving table, New England, circa 1825, 32in. wide. (Robt. W. Skinner Inc.) $4,100

A William and Mary oak side table on slender turned baluster and knopped legs with bun feet, 18½in. wide. (Christie's) $3,991

A Gustav Stickley three-drawer server, no. 818, circa 1910, 48in. wide. (Robt. W. Skinner Inc.) $950

SIDE TABLES

A George II walnut side table with breccia marble top, on hairy claw and ball feet, 56½in. wide.(Christie's) $24,105

A George II giltwood side table with brown jasper veneered top, 52½in. wide. (Christie's) $18,792

A George II mahogany side table with Portor marble top, 43½in. wide. (Christie's) $15,919

A neo-classical giltwood side table with molded D-shaped mottled pink marble top, possibly Scandinavian, 41in. wide. (Christie's) $3,706

One of a pair of gilt gesso side tables with breccia marble tops, on cabriole legs and pad feet, 17½in. wide. (Christie's) $9,266

A 17th century oak side table, the D-shaped top with a flap at the back, 37¼in. wide. (Christie's) $5,702

Late 18th century painted and gilded pier table with Portor marble top, 46¼in. wide. (Christie's) $7,047

A Federal mahogany and mahogany veneer server, New England, circa 1815, 37¾in. wide. (Robt. W. Skinner Inc.)$700

A green and white painted and gilded side table with verde antico top, 53in. wide. (Christie's) $2,818

SOFA TABLES

A Regency yewwood sofa table with twin-flap top, on reeded splayed legs, 64½in. wide, open. (Christie's) $4,071

A George IV painted elm and marquetry sofa table with twin-flap top, 57in. wide, open. (Christie's) $5,556

A Regency rosewood and satinwood sofa table with trestle ends and splayed feet, 58in. wide, open. (Christie's)$8,046

A Regency rosewood sofa table with brass stringing, on reel turned baluster column and quartette supports, 5ft. x 2ft.3in. (Capes, Dunn & Co.) $864

Classical revival mahogany and mahogany veneer sofa table with shaped leaves, circa 1825, 35½in. wide. (Robt. W. Skinner Inc.) $425

Victorian mahogany sofa table on lyre supports with turned stretchers and with two fitted drawers. (Worsfolds) $547

A Scottish George III mahogany sofa table, stamped Bruce EdinH, 63in. wide, open. (Christie's) $8,208

A Regency rosewood sofa table, inlaid with brass in stylized foliate design, 36½ x 59in. extended. (Lawrence Fine Art) $2,711

A George III rosewood sofa table with twin-flap top and two cedar lined frieze drawers, 54in. wide. (Christie's) $5,637

SOFA TABLES

A Regency black and gold lacquer sofa table with brass bordered twin-flap top, 61½in. wide, open. (Christie's) $8,683

A Regency maplewood sofa table with twin-flap top, the tapering feet with claw castors, 63in. wide. (Christie's) $12,025

A Regency calamander sofa table, the twin-flap top crossbanded in satinwood, 59in. long. (Christie's) $7,047

A Regency mahogany sofa table with twin-flap top and one frieze drawer, 53in. wide, open. (Christie's) $3,987

A classical mahogany sofa table, the working drawer with a brass lion head pull, circa 1810/20, Phila., 42in. wide. (Christie's) $3,850

A Regency rosewood sofa table with twin-flap top and frieze drawers, 58in. wide, open. (Christie's) $15,876

A George IV mahogany sofa table with twin-flap top and two frieze drawers, the trade label R. Snowdon, Cabinet Maker and Appraiser, Northallerton., 62in. wide, open. (Christie's) $2,913

A Regency calamander sofa table with twin-flap top, 58in. wide. (Christie's) $15,660

A Regency rosewood sofa table, the solid trestle ends with scrolling bases, 58in. wide, open. (Christie's) $8,731

An early Victorian black and mother-of-pearl japanned papier mache pedestal sewing box with hinged top, 32½in. high. (Christie's) $1,805

Mid 19th century Regency inlaid mahogany and mahogany veneer work table, 36in. wide. (Robt. W. Skinner Inc.) $600

A Federal mahogany and mahogany veneer work table with two drawers and one work bag pull out, Mass., circa 1795, top 21 x 17in. (Robt. W. Skinner Inc.) $6,750

A William IV mahogany pedestal work table, the boxed top enclosed by a hinged canted lid, 19in. wide. (Christie's) $570

A Chippendale mahogany and cherrywood sewing table, New England, 1815-25, 70½in. wide. (Christie's) $660

A mid Victorian black, gilt and mother-of-pearl, japanned papier mache pedestal sewing box, 15in. wide. (Christie's) $2,298

A Federal mahogany work table on water-leaf carved and scrolled sabre legs, 29in. high. (Christie's) $1,430

An Edwardian Sheraton style inlaid and figured mahogany work table on tapering supports, 1ft.4in. wide. (Bridgfords) $616

A Federal mahogany work table with octagonal top, the bottom drawer fitted with bag, New England, circa 1810, 28in. high. (Robt. W. Skinner Inc.) $1,900

WORKBOXES & GAMES TABLES

An early Victorian rosewood work and games table with folding swivel top, 20in. wide. (Dreweatts) $975

A George II mahogany triple folding top games table on cabriole legs, 34in. wide. (Dreweatts) $9,300

A George IV satinwood and fruitwood work table, possibly Scottish, 17¾in. wide. (Christie's) $2,035

A Regency rosewood work table by Gillows of Lancaster, 35½in. wide, open. (Christie's) $1,126

A George II mahogany, triple fold-over, shaped top tea/games table, 2ft.7½in. wide. (Edgar Horn) $7,592

An Edwardian painted maple work table, the top with hinged flap, on square tapering legs, 21in. wide. (Christie's) $1,995

A parcel gilt and calamander games table on twinned simulated bamboo trestles, 28½in. wide. (Christie's) $3,045

A late Regency rosewood, fruitwood and Tunbridgeware games table, 16¾in. square. (Christie's) $3,969

A Victorian rectangular inlaid burr walnut needlework table with hinged top, 24in. wide. (Parsons, Welch & Cowell) $784

A Regency rosewood games/
work table on a U-shape
support, 26in. wide.
(Lawrence Fine Art)
$3,581

A 19th century Netherlands
rococo style mahogany in-
laid games table, top 34 x
31in. (Robt. W. Skinner Inc.)
$700

Victorian maple and rose-
wood workbox, 1840.
(British Antique Exporters)
$603

A late Federal inlaid mahogany work table with a
single drawer, Mass., 1800/
20, 17¼in. wide. (Christie's)
$825

A classical gilt stencilled
rosewood sewing table,
probably N.Y., circa 1815/
30, 24¾in. wide.
(Christie's) $4,400

A Federal inlaid mahogany
and bird's-eye maple sewing
table, attributed to John
and/or Thos. Seymour,
circa 1800/10, 20in. wide.
(Christie's)
$52,800

A Regency period mahogany
work table with two fall
leaves and on lyre shaped
refectory supports. (Mor-
phets) $766

A Country Federal tiger maple
work table, New England, circa
1820, on simulated bamboo
legs, 17½in. wide. (Robt. W.
Skinner Inc.) $2,800

A classical Revival mahogany
work table, possibly Baltimore, circa 1810, 27.3/8in.
wide. (Robt. W. Skinner Inc.)
$2,500

Victorian padoukwood
games table, 1850. (British
Antique Exporters)
$228

A George II mahogany
games table, the hinged top
enclosing a backgammon
well, 36in. wide.(Christie's)
$2,624

Victorian mahogany work
table, circa 1860. (British
Antique Exporters)
$369

A Victorian tole workbox,
the glazed octangular lid
decorated with a winter
scene, 19½in. wide.
(Christie's) $1,331

A Federal carved mahogany
work table, probably New
York, circa 1810, 22in.
wide. (Robt. W. Skinner
Inc.) $15,000

A Regency mahogany com-
bined games and work table,
the sides with candle-slides,
19in. wide. (Christie's)
$5,499

A George III satinwood and
fruitwood work table, the
top crossbanded with maple-
wood and tulipwood, 22in.
wide. (Christie's)
$5,702

Late 19th century lady's
work table in Japanese gold
lacquer, 25 x 17in. (Peter
Wilson & Co.) $748

A Federal maple inlaid work
table, New England, circa
1810, 18¾in. wide. (Robt.
W. Skinner Inc.)
$2,600

403

WRITING TABLES & DESKS

A Chippendale pine standing desk, New England, 1780-1810, 30½in. wide. (Christie's) $1,100

A 19th century George III style inlaid mahogany writing desk, America, 46in. wide. (Robt. W. Skinner Inc.) $900

A Federal carved mahogany lady's writing table, N.Y., 1805-15, 20½in. wide. (Christie's) $3,080

A lady's Federal mahogany tambour front writing desk, 32¾in. wide. (Christie's) $660

A Queen Anne walnut desk with hinged slant lid, 1740-60, 30½in. wide. (Christie's) $3,300

Victorian oak desk with leather top, 1880. (British Antique Exporters) $206

A late Regency mahogany writing table, the top with fluted edge and inset tooled leather panel, 41in. wide. (Lawrence Fine Art) $1,465

Edwardian oak fall front desk cabinet, 1910. (British Antique Exporters) $121

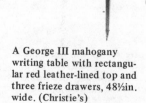

A George III mahogany writing table with rectangular red leather-lined top and three frieze drawers, 48½in. wide. (Christie's) $4,490

WRITING TABLES & DESKS

A Federal cherrywood writing desk, 1800-15, 30½in. wide. (Christie's)
$1,320

A Regency ormolu mounted mahogany writing table, the top with pierced quatrefoil three-quarter gallery, 45in. wide. (Christie's)
$11,907

Victorian oak fall front desk, 1880. (British Antique Exporters)
$125

A Regency mahogany Carlton House desk, in the manner of Gillows, 55½in. wide. (Christie's)$23,155

A mahogany and satinwood crossbanded bonheur du jour by T. Willson, London, 45in. wide. (Reeds Rains)
$1,094

A Regency writing desk in the manner of Gillows, the drawer with Bramah lock. (Christie's) $4,666

A George III mahogany writing table with rectangular faded scarlet leather-lined top, 51in. wide. (Christie's)
$5,322

A George III mahogany writing table with revolving easel top, 25in. wide. (Christie's) $4,071

A Renaissance Revival burled walnut library table, labelled by Alex. Roux, N.Y., circa 1860, 48in. wide.(Christie's)
$2,090

WRITING TABLES & DESKS

A satinwood writing table with leather lined top and two cedar-lined frieze drawers, 39in. wide. (Christie's) $12,117

An Edwardian satinwood, rosewood and marquetry Carlton House desk with leather lined easel, 49in. wide. (Christie's) $8,488

A Regency rosewood writing table with leather lined crossbanded top, 43in. wide. (Christie's) $10,044

An ormolu mounted kingwood bonheur du jour, the superstructure with inset mottled grey marble top, 28¾in. wide. (Christie's) $2,423

A George III burr-yew and satinwood bonheur du jour with a recessed central cupboard door, 35½in. wide. (Christie's) $5,499

An early 18th century walnut and mahogany writing cabinet on stand with folding leather lined top, 19¾in. wide. (Christie's) $3,499

A George III mahogany bonheur du jour, the superstructure with two oval-inlaid doors, 36¼in. wide. (Christie's) $4,687

An early Victorian bird's-eye maple writing table, 36½in. wide. (Christie's) $2,505

A Victorian mahogany writing table with spindle galleried top, 45½in. wide. (Christie's) $1,174

A Regency mahogany writing-table with leather lined top, 55in. wide. (Christie's) $8,704

A late George III mahogany library desk with pierced gallery and Vitruvian scroll frieze, the plinth base 72in. diam. (Christie's) $33,285

A contrepartie boulle bureau mazarin, the top inlaid with a Berainesque scene within strapwork, 53in. wide. (Christie's) $5,417

A mid 18th century German ormolu mounted black lacquer bureau cabinet, 53in. wide. (Christie's) $10,692

A 19th century Dutch walnut and marquetry cylinder top bombe-shaped bureau, 36in. wide. (Dacre, Son & Hartley) $2,088

A William and Mary walnut writing or card table, the top lined with crimson velvet, 30in. wide.(Christie's) $9,979

An ormolu mounted mahogany bureau plat of Louis XVI style with five panelled drawers, 42in. wide. (Christie's) $2,851

One of a pair of Regency ormolu mounted rosewood writing tables, the drawers with leopard mask handles, 35½in. wide. (Christie's) $42,854

An Empire mahogany desk with ten leathered compartments and leather lined easel writing surface, 57in. wide.(Christie's) $4,989

WRITING TABLES & DESKS

A George III mahogany and satinwood bonheur du jour with leather lined writing slide, 26¼in. wide. (Christie's) $2,349

A Regency mahogany writing table with leather lined top and two frieze drawers, 54in. wide. (Christie's) $4,023

A sailor made ship's desk, constructed by a sailor on the Bark Messenger, circa 1850, 23½in. wide. (Robt. W. Skinner Inc.) $2,000

Victorian walnut writing table, 1870. (British Antique Exporters) $329

A Louis XV kingwood and parquetry writing table on cabriole legs, 26in. wide. (Christie's) $8,791

A Regency calamander writing table with ormolu bordered crossbanded top inlaid with brass stars, 48in. wide. (Christie's) $23,490

A George IV ebony inlaid mahogany library table, on trestle ends and bar feet, 57½in. long. (Christie's) $14,094

Late 19th century oak tambour top desk. (British Antique Exporters) $236

A Maurice Dufrene semi-circular wooden desk, 31in. high, and a chair upholstered in red velvet, 32in. high, signed and dated 1935. (Christie's) $3,472

A Chippendale painted pine and poplar blanket chest with lift top, probably Penn., 1750-1800, 50½in. wide. (Christie's) $1,650

Victorian pine trunk with brass carrying handles, 1850. (British Antique Exporters) $180

An 18th century oak six plank chest, 38in. wide. (Peter Wilson & Co.) $506

A red pine painted joined blanket chest, America, circa 1820, 37½in. wide. (Robt. W. Skinner Inc.)$500

An 18th century Chinese black and gold lacquered coffer with hinged lid, 57¼in. wide. (Christie's) $2,741

One of two early 19th century Chinese Export black and gold lacquer coffers on stands, 30¼in. wide. (Christie's) $6,577

A William and Mary painted blanket chest with thumb molded hinged lid, 46in. wide. (Christie's)$286

A basically 16th century Florentine painted walnut cassone, 56in. wide. (Christie's) $3,356

One of a pair of early 18th century Chinese Export black and gold lacquer coffers, 53½in. wide. (Christie's) $8,683

TRUNKS & COFFERS

A grain painted pine blanket chest with turned brass pulls on cut-out base, 36in. wide, circa 1810. (Robt. W. Skinner Inc.) $1,500

A George I oyster veneered walnut and king-wood coffer with a drawer, the sides with brass carrying handles, 47in. wide. (Christie's) $10,962

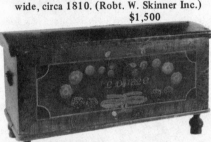

A Scandinavian painted dower chest with slightly domed, hinged top, dated 1828, 51in. wide. (Robt. W. Skinner Inc.) $800

A Queen Anne walnut coffer on spirally turned legs, waved stretchers and bun feet, 38in. wide. (Christie's) $5,832

A 17th century Spanish walnut coffer with plank top, 66½in. wide. (Christie's) $855

A 17th century oak coffer with plain cover, panel sides and front with an arcaded frieze, 55in. wide, with repairs. (Lawrence Fine Art) $3,093

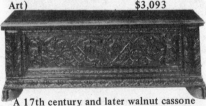

A 17th century and later walnut cassone with panelled front, 67in. wide.(Christie's) $4,043

A 16th century Italian walnut cassone, the spreading panelled lid with foliate and scalloped banding, 73in. long. (Christie's) $9,331

TRUNKS & COFFERS

A Kuwaiti Dowry chest richly decorated with ornate brass overlay. (Butler & Hatch Waterman) $1,917

A 16th century Continental oak coffer, the top formed of three planks and with strap hinges, 5ft.10in. wide. (Woolley & Wallis) $3,045

A partly 17th century walnut coffer on bun feet, 73in. wide. (Christie's) $1,321

A late 17th century Swiss painted pine coffer with panelled rectangular top, 64in. wide. (Christie's) $997

An 18th century oak dower chest with swan neck loop handles, 5ft.1in. wide. (Capes, Dunn & Co.) $460

An 18th century Dutch Colonial padoukwood blanket chest with pierced brass clasps and carrying handles, on bun feet, 67in. wide. (Christie's) $1,425

A 17th century Spanish oak and walnut coffer with rectangular top, on block feet, 61in. wide. (Christie's) $1,010

An 18th century oak dower chest with brass swan neck handles and pierced back plates, 5ft.4in. wide. (Capes, Dunn & Co.) $482

WARDROBES & ARMOIRES

A Federal walnut linen press on French feet, 1800-10, 43¾in. wide.(Christie's) $8,250

A mid Victorian mahogany cylinder wardrobe, the drawers with turned handles, 255cm. wide. (Phillips) $890

A mid 18th century French provincial cherrywood armoire with molded cornice, 56in. wide.(Christie's) $2,138

A French gold and parcel gilt armoire on squat cabriole feet. (Christie's) $2,352

A George III satinwood breakfront wardrobe inlaid with narrow bands and stringing, 104in. wide. (Lawrence Fine Art) $4,884

A Chippendale carved mahogany wardrobe, in two sections, New York, 1760-80, 53in. wide. (Christie's) $4,180

One of a pair of Louis XVI kingwood armoires with two pairs of cupboards filled with gilt wire, 70in. wide. (Christie's) $22,377

A Louis XVI amaranth, tulipwood and parquetry armoire, possibly Dutch, 41in. wide. (Christie's) $4,860

A South African stinkwood armoire on claw and ball feet, with silver handles stamped IB, 64in. wide. (Christie's) $2,280

WARDROBES & ARMOIRES

A Dutch hardwood armoire, possibly Colonial, 64in. wide. (Christie's) $926

A 17th century South German walnut armoire, 79in. wide. (Christie's) $9,642

A classical mahogany armoire, attributed to Chas. H. Lannvier, circa 1800-15, 55in. wide. (Christie's) $24,200

Late 18th/early 19th century oak armoire with molded cornice, 69½in. wide. (Reeds Rains) $1,238

A Regency period mahogany breakfront wardrobe/linen press, 8ft.2in. long. (Woolley & Wallis) $2,740

A Louis XVI oak armoire with molded foliate cornice, 61½in. wide. (Christie's) $2,799

Victorian carved walnut armoire, 1860. (British Antique Exporters) $253

An Empire Gothic mahogany wardrobe, signed by Joseph Stewart Jr., New York, and dated 1831, 69in. wide. (Christie's) $3,850

An 18th century Scandinavian walnut armoire, 57in. wide. (Christie's) $5,443

WASHSTANDS

Late 18th century mahogany bow fronted corner washstand on splay feet, 2ft.3½in. wide. (Bermondsey) $485

Victorian mahogany marble top washstand, 1860. (British Antique Exporters) $247

Federal mahogany corner washstand on splay feet, 21½in. wide, circa 1800. (Robt. W. Skinner Inc.) $1,000

A Federal mahogany carved washstand, probably Mass., circa 1815, 20in. wide. (Robt. W. Skinner Inc.) $2,100

Victorian marble top oak washstand, 1860. (British Antique Exporters) $35

A late Georgian mahogany washstand with gallery back, shelf and single drawer, 18in. wide. (Peter Wilson & Co.) $149

Victorian marble top washstand, 1860. (British Antique Exporters) $249

A George III mahogany pedestal washstand with hinged coffered folding top, 13in. wide. (Christie's) $1,176

Victorian tiled back marble top washstand, 1860. (British Antique Exporters) $279

Victorian walnut four-tier whatnot, 1840. (British Antique Exporters) $521

A mid 19th century parquetry three tier etagere, 19½in. wide. (Christie's) $1,879

Victorian marble top whatnot, 1860. (British Antique Exporters) $396

An early 19th century three-tier mahogany whatnot, 45in. high. (W. H. Lane & Son) $403

An ebonized four tier etagere with galleried top, circa 1830, 29in. wide, 49½in. high. (Christie's) $2,818

Victorian walnut whatnot, 1860. (British Antique Exporters) $249

One of a pair of Regency mahogany whatnots with vase finials, 17¾in. square. (Christie's) $2,818

A late Georgian bird's-eye maple four tier etagere, 24in. wide, 31in. high. (Christie's) $4,228

An early 19th century mahogany whatnot, 1ft.6in. square. (J. R. Bridgford & Sons) $648

WINE COOLERS

A Regency mahogany wine cooler with lead lined interior, 34in. wide. (Christie's) $3,445

A Regency mahogany wine cooler with tin liner, 34in. wide. (Christie's) $3,701

A Regency mahogany wine cooler with detachable liner, carrying handles and hairy paw feet, 27½in. wide. (Christie's) $2,946

A late 18th century Sheraton style mahogany crossbanded and inlaid octagonal cellarette, 19in. wide. (Dacre, Son & Hartley) $3,600

A Regency carved mahogany wine cooler with lion mask brass ring handles, 26½in. wide. (Dacre, Son & Hartley) $1,728

A Federal inlaid cherrywood cellarette and stand, 1790-1810, 36in. high. (Christie's) $7,150

A George III mahogany wine cooler, the tapering brass bound body with carrying handles, 19½in. wide. (Christie's) $2,177

A Federal inlaid mahogany wine cooler with lift top, 22in. wide. (Christie's) $3,080

A mid Georgian brass bound mahogany wine cooler with detachable tin liner, 23½in. wide. (Christie's) $2,770

WINE COOLERS

A Regency mahogany oval wine cooler in the manner of Gillows with lead-lined interior, 27¼in. wide. (Christie's) $5,540

A Regency mahogany wine cooler with lead-lined body, on ebonized claw feet, 28in. wide. (Christie's) $4,631

A Regency mahogany wine cooler in the manner of Gillows, with oval tin liner, 29in. wide. (Christie's) $6,264

A George III brass bound mahogany cellarette with lead lined interior retaining tap beneath, 19in. wide. (Christie's) $3,481

One of a pair of George III brass bound wine coolers with detachable tin liners, 27in. wide. (Christie's) $7,668

A George III mahogany, crossbanded and inlaid cellarette on brass castored feet. (Dacre, Son & Hartley) $864

One of two George III brass bound mahogany wine coolers with detachable liners, 25in. and 24in. wide. (Christie's) $10,713

A Regency ormolu mounted mahogany wine cooler with hinged oval domed fan-shaped top, 29in. wide, 27in. high, 23in. deep. (Christie's) $14,731

A George III mahogany brass bound wine cooler with carrying handles, 25in. wide. (Christie's) $2,971

BEAKERS

An engraved spa glass, the bowl cut with panels, circa 1840, 5½in. high. (Bermondsey) $215

A Bohemian amethyst-overlay, cylindrical beaker, 4½in. high. (Christie's) $195

A Bohemian amber flash, fluted cylindrical beaker cut with oval panels engraved with named buildings, 5¼in. high. (Christie's) $300

A Bohemian lithyalin, flaring cylindrical beaker, 4¾in. high. (Christie's) $330

A German Ochsenkopf flared beaker, the sides enamelled in colors with the usual symbols, 1708, 11.8cm. high. (Christie's) $1,866

A Silesian armorial flared beaker, the ogee bowl with molded and cut flutes to the lower part, circa 1745, 11cm. high. (Christie's) $1,296

A mid 19th century Austrian enamel and clear glass beaker decorated with a scenic band. (Bermondsey) $525

An enamelled milchglas beaker of cylindrical form, circa 1780, 3½in. high. (Bermondsey) $210

A Bohemian transparent-enamelled chinoiserie beaker, circa 1835, 12.5cm. high. (Christie's) $1,480

A late 17th century Nether-
landish blue serving bottle,
17cm. high. (Christie's)
$1,866

A large Roman green glass
bottle with globular bowl,
cylindrical neck and everted
lip, swirling iridescence,
16.5cm. high. (Phillips)
$191

'Figurines Avec Bouchon', a
Lalique frosted glass bottle
and stopper, 11½in. high.
(Christie's) $1,368

A 17th century Facon-De-
Venise bottle in vetro a fili,
30.5cm. high. (Christie's)
$289

A set of four Bristol blue
sauce bottles and stoppers,
the bases incised W. R. & Co.,
and one with a dated 1788?,
11cm. high. (Lawrence Fine
Art) $214

A Dimple Haig clear glass
bottle, decorated with pierced
plated mounts depicting
Chinese dragons, original
stopper, 10½in. high. (Peter
Wilson & Co.) $120

A sealed and dated green glass
wine bottle of mallet shape
with conical neck, the seal
inscribed IOS Dalyzell and
dated 1738, 8¾in. high.
(Christie's) $588

An oak bottle box with
thirteen blown glass bottles,
late 18th/early 19th century,
13½in. wide. (Christie's)
$1,100

A Galle oviform clear and
enamelled glass bottle decanter
with molded flutes, 7¾in.
high. (Christie's) $273

419

A marriage bowl inscribed I. Davyz E. Hannaford Maryd. Oct. 30 1769, 21cm. diam. (Christie's) $891

A Lalique clear and frosted two-handled oval bowl, 'Jardiniere Saint—Hubert', 19in. long, inscribed. (Christie's) $403

A Lalique deep circular bowl, 'Saint-Vincent', the blue opalescent satin finished glass molded with bands of fruit laden vines, circa 1930, 34.5cm. wide. (Christie's) $1,576

One of a set of four cut glass cylindrical bowls, with silver gilt mounts, the glass circa 1820, the handles with maker's mark of John Bridge, 1824, 16cm. wide. (Christie's) $2,268

A Venetian shallow bowl with everted folded rim, enamelled in colors , circa 1500, 22.5cm. diam. (Christie's) $972

A Steuben crystal-footed bowl and cover, 'The Plains', designed by Lloyd Atkins, 33cm. high. (Christie's) $2,365

A Lalique opalescent deep circular bowl, 'Ondine Ouverte', 12in. diam. (Christie's) $864

A Decorchment pate-de-verre bowl, green and brown marbled glass, circa 1940, 25.7cm. wide. (Christie's) $2,349

A Lalique bowl, the opalescent blue satin finished glass molded with budgerigars, 23.7cm. diam. (Christie's) $1,879

An early 20th century Galle glass box and cover, 3in. diam., signed. (Bermondsey) $1,200

A clear and brown stained rectangular box, by Rene Lalique, 4in. wide. (Bermondsey) $450

Mid 19th century Bohemian enamelled and ruby glass casket, 6in. square. (Bermondsey) $600

'Dahlia', a Lalique circular box and cover in clear and satin finished glass, 13.6cm. diam. (Christie's) $626

A Guild of Handicrafts silver and glass box and cover, designed by C. R. Ashbee, with London hallmarks for 1900, 21cm. high, 16oz. 15dwt. gross weight without cover. (Christie's) $6,894

A Bohemian dated, double overlay, gilt metal mounted, rectangular casket for the Persian market, circa 1848, 15cm. wide. (Christie's) $3,240

A Baccarat gilt metal mounted rectangular casket, circa 1830, 13.5cm. wide. (Christie's) $403

'Three Dahlias', a Lalique blue opalescent circular box and cover of clear and satin finished glass, 20.9cm. diam. (Christie's) $469

Mid 19th century Bohemian overlay and enamelled casket, the body in opaque white, 5¼in. wide. (Bermondsey) $600

CANDLESTICKS

GLASS

A baluster stemmed glass candlestick with three graduated knops, circa 1750, 9¼in. high. (Bermondsey) $675

One of a pair of Georgian ormolu mounted, cut and colored glass candlesticks, 13½in. high. (Christie's) $2,138

A Sandwich Clambroth and blue glass dolphin candlestick, circa 1820, 10in. high. (Robt. W. Skinner Inc.) $250

A baluster candlestick the cylindrical nozzle with everted folded rim, circa 1745, 20cm. high. (Christie's) $839

A pair of Charles X ormolu and cut glass candlesticks with faceted, hobnail-cut stems, 16½in. high. (Christie's) $3,136

An airtwist candlestick on a domed and terraced foot, circa 1750, 20cm. high. (Christie's) $807

A baluster candlestick, the stem with true baluster section above a beaded knop and triple annulated basal knop, circa 1745, 19.5cm. high. (Christie's) $901

One of a pair of cut glass five-light wall lights, the nozzles with silver plated liners, 25in. high. (Christie's) $2,349

Mid 18th century pedestal stemmed candlestick, on a domed foot, 20.5cm. high. (Christie's) $648

422

DECANTERS

A green baluster decanter with lozenge stopper, 9½in. high, and a blue decanter, 9in. high. (Christie's) $236

A Victorian electroplate decanter stand, by Elkington & Co., with design registration mark for 2nd October 1868, 29.4cm. high overall. (Lawrence Fine Art) $485

A Lalique glass decanter, the broadly shouldered tapering body with stepped serrated bands to the base, 24.3cm. high. (Lawrence Fine Art) $112

One of a pair of cut glass decanters and stoppers of club shape, circa 1820. (Christie's) $648

A Hukin & Heath 'Crow's foot' decanter, designed by Dr. C. Dresser, electroplate and glass, with registration lozenge for 1879, 24cm. high. (Christie's) $11,275

A Guild of Handicraft hammered silver and green glass decanter, the design attributed to C. R. Ashbee, with London hallmarks for 1903, 22.5cm. high. (Christie's) $1,892

A cylindrical file-cut decanter and stopper, cut with three rings to the neck, 10in. high. (Christie's) $88

A pair of Georgian wine decanters, one with disc stopper, the other with replacement faceted ball stopper, 14½in. high. (Capes, Dunn & Co.) $374

Victorian glass decanter, 1870. (British Antique Exporters) $70

Late 17th century Facon-De-Venise shallow cup with applied pincered scroll handle, 11.5cm. wide. (Christie's) $388

An Almaric Walter pate-de-verre dish of lozenge shape, designed by H. Berge, 24.6cm. wide. (Christie's) $1,879

Mid 17th century Facon-De-Venise filigree tazza, 31cm. diam. (Christie's) $1,056

A sweetmeat glass, the shallow flared bucket bowl with gadrooned underside and folded rim, circa 1730, 9.5cm. high. (Christie's) $528

A Lalique opalescent glass dish, 'Sirene', signed, circa 1925, 14½in. diam. (W. H. Lane & Son) $936

One of a pair of Portland clear overshot glass compotes, late 19th century, 8¾in. high. (Robt. W. Skinner Inc.) $500

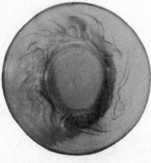

A glass dish attributed to H. P. Glashutte with enamel painted decoration of a purple clematis bloom, circa 1900, 23.5cm. diam. (Christie's) $249

A Baccarat close millefiori wafer dish, the base with a cane inscribed 'B1848', 10cm. high. (Christie's) $1,533

An opalescent 'Ondines' dish, engraved R. Lalique, France, 8in. diam. (Capes, Dunn & Co.) $465

A WMF electroplated liqueur set and tray, the decanters 9in. high, the tray 16in. wide, all with stamped marks. (Christie's) $705

'Coquelicot', a Lalique globular decanter and stopper, 6¾in. high, and five glasses en suite. (Christie's) $187

A Patriz Huber liqueur set, white metal and glass, stamped with 935 German silver mark and PH, circa 1900, decanter 18.4cm. high. (Christie's) $4,099

A Gabriel Argy-Rousseau pate-de-verre eight-piece liqueur service, the tray 40.1cm. wide. (Christie's) $3,132

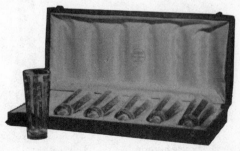

A Lalique oviform clear and frosted glass decanter and stopper, 7in. high, and eight glasses en suite. (Christie's) $288

A set of six Lalique aperitif glasses molded in clear glass with amethyst tinted panels of Grecian maidens, circa 1930, 9.8cm. high. (Christie's) $1,644

FLASKS

A vertically ribbed chestnut flask, golden amber, sheared mouth-pontil scar, 4½in. high, 1820-40. (Robt. W. Skinner Inc.) $160

A Heath & Middleton silver topped glass flask, possibly designed by C. Dresser, Birmingham 1891, 10in. high. (Christie's)$705

A scroll pint flask, GIX-11, golden amber, sheared mouth-pontil scar, 1845-60. (Robt. W. Skinner Inc.) $200

A mid 19th century Nailsea red, white and blue bellows flask, 12½in. high. (Robt. W. Skinner Inc.) $225

One of two half pint Adams-Jefferson portrait flasks, GI-114, olive amber, sheared mouth-pontil scars, 1830-50. (Robt. W. Skinner Inc.) $210

A gimmel flask in ruby glass with a wavy combed design in red and opaque white, 24cm. long. (Lawrence Fine Art) $90

A Masonic eagle historical pint flask, golden amber, White Glass Works, 1820-40. (Robt. W. Skinner Inc.) $275

Late 18th century amethyst flask, the globular body molded with 'nipt diamond waves', 20cm. high. (Christie's) $1,053

A double eagle historical pint flask, GII-40, bright green, sheared mouth-pontil scar, Kensington Glass Works, 1830-38. (Robt. W. Skinner Inc.) $275

426

GOBLETS

An engraved light baluster goblet, the stem with beaded dumb-bell section, circa 1755, 21cm. high. (Christie's) $2,643

A composite stemmed engraved goblet with round funnel bowl with fruiting vinestock, 19cm. high. (Christie's) $403

A Dutch Friendship goblet with funnel bowl, circa 1755, 18cm. high. (Christie's) $372

A baluster goblet, the thistle bowl supported on a cushion above a drop knopped section, circa 1700, 15.5cm. high. (Christie's) $1,088

An armorial light baluster goblet, on a multi-knopped stem and domed foot, circa 1755, 19cm. high. (Christie's) $588

A baluster goblet, the funnel bowl supported on an inverted baluster stem, circa 1720, 20.5cm. high. (Christie's) $372

A baluster goblet with a slender thistle-shaped bowl, circa 1705, 17.5cm. high. (Christie's) $1,166

A composite stemmed goblet by Jacob Sang, on a conical foot, circa 1760, 19.5cm. high. (Christie's) $5,499

A baluster goblet, the funnel bowl supported on an inverted baluster stem above a folded conical foot, circa 1720, 18cm. high. (Christie's) $466

427

A calligraphic baluster goblet, attributed to Bastiaan Boers or Francois Crama, the rim engraved in diamond-point, circa 1700, 17.8cm. high. (Christie's) $7,959

A betrothal goblet by Jacob Sang, supported on a waist-knopped section above a beaded inverted baluster stem, 1755-60, 18.5cm. high. (Christie's) $2,604

An opaque twist shipping goblet attributed to Jacob Sang, circa 1785, 19.5cm. high. (Christie's) $4,631

A pedestal stemmed Alliance goblet in the manner of Robart, 1735-40, 19cm. high. (Christie's) $1,519

A pedestal stemmed armorial goblet engraved by Willem O. Robart, 1735-45, 20cm. high. (Christie's)
$2,098

A facet cut shipping goblet attributed to Simon J. Sang, 1770-80, 23.5cm. high. (Christie's) $3,473

A light baluster betrothal goblet, the funnel bowl decorated in the manner of David Wolff, late 18th century, 19.2cm. high. (Christie's) $4,052

A large armorial goblet, the funnel bowl engraved with the arms of Delfland, circa 1780, 23cm. high.(Christie's) $868

A stipple engraved goblet on a 19th century replacement parcel gilt lower section, by Frans Greenwood, circa 1744, 24.3cm. high overall. (Christie's) $43,416

GLASS

A light baluster goblet by
Jacob Sang, supported on a
waist-knopped section above
a beaded inverted baluster
stem, 1755-65, 19cm. high.
(Christie's) $2,026

An armorial baluster goblet
with bucket bowl, circa
1760, 16cm. high.
(Christie's) $1,736

A light baluster armorial
goblet by Jacob Sang, the
funnel bowl engraved with
the crowned arms of Prussia,
circa 1765, 19.5cm. high.
(Christie's) $1,881

A composite stemmed mar-
riage goblet by Jacob Sang,
on a conical foot, circa 1760,
19.5cm. high. (Christie's)
$2,894

A composite stemmed goblet
by Jacob Sang, supported on
a beaded dumb-bell section
above an inverted baluster
stem, 1759, 18.3cm. high.
(Christie's) $6,946

A mid 18th century hunting
goblet, the engraving perhaps
by a German hand, 22.5cm.
high. (Christie's)
$4,341

A composite stemmed shipping goblet by Jacob Sang,
supported on a knopped section filled with airtwist spirals,
1760-70, 19.5cm. high.
(Christie's) $6,512

A light baluster friendship
goblet by Jacob Sang, on
a conical foot, 1755-60,
19.5cm. high. (Christie's)
$2,894

A light baluster armorial
goblet engraved by the mono-
grammist JB, circa 1750,
22.3cm. high. (Christie's)
$4,341

429

A Galle oviform single-
handled ewer, the silver
mount modelled with styl-
ized flowers, signed, 10¼in.
high. (Christie's) $1,066

A Nailsea jug, pale green,
with strap handle, the neck
with white enamel rim,
19.5cm. high. (Lawrence
Fine Art) $313

A Victorian electroplated
claret jug, by Elkington &
Co., with date letter code
for 1883, 36cm. high.
(Lawrence Fine Art)
$358

A Nailsea jug, dark green
splashed with white, with
flared neck, 23cm. high.
(Lawrence Fine Art)
$115

One of two late 17th century
Venetian small jugs with
applied blue rims, 10cm. high.
(Christie's) $453

A Galle enamelled and green
oviform single-handled glass
jug, 8½in. high, inscribed.
(Christie's) $288

A Hukin & Heath electro-
plated metal mounted glass
claret jug, designed by Dr.
C. Dresser, with registration
lozenge for 12th November
1879, 23.7cm. high.
(Christie's) $9,460

An engraved claret jug with
plated mounts and hinged
cover, circa 1880, 27.5cm.
high. (Christie's) $388

A Hukin & Heath silver
mounted claret jug designed
by Dr. C. Dresser, with
London hallmarks for 1884,
23cm. high. (Christie's)
$1,182

GLASS

A 19th century clear and cranberry glass bell, 13in. high, and a red, white and blue Nailsea float, 5in. long. (Robt. W. Skinner Inc.) $200

A decalcomania rolling pin, profusely decorated with soldiers, sailors, policemen, female figures and animals, 43.5cm. long. (Lawrence Fine Art) $90

A Whitefriar's paperweight inkwell, from the Bacchus period, circa 1840, 7in. high. (Robt. W. Skinner Inc.) $400

A Daum limited edition pate-de-verre and fibre glass surrealist sculpture by Salvador Dali, depicting a soft clock slumped on a coat hanger. (Christie's) $2,975

A 19th century glass drug jar with a lid, 24in. high. (Lots Road Chelsea Auction Galleries) $210

Early 20th century dimpled glass firescreen with an oak frame. (British Antique Exporters) $51

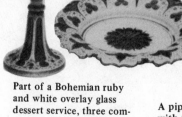

An Etling opalescent figure of a semi naked woman, 11in. high. (Christie's) $691

Part of a Bohemian ruby and white overlay glass dessert service, three compotiers 18cm. high, two 16.5cm. high and ten plates, 25cm. diam. (Lawrence Fine Art) $2,552

A pipe of opaque white glass, with a waved design in red and blue, 46cm. long. (Lawrence Fine Art) $106

431

A St. Louis panelled close millefiori weight, 7.7cm. diam. (Christie's) $5,443

A St. Louis concentric millefiori mushroom weight, on a star-cut base, 7.8cm. diam. (Christie's) $1,321

A French scramble paperweight with blue, green, white and red canes, 3in. diam. (Robt. W. Skinner Inc.) $425

A Clichy pink and white 'barber's pole' chequer weight, 6.5cm. diam. (Christie's) $1,477

A Paul Ysart bouquet weight, the center to one flower with PY initials, 7.6cm. diam. (Christie's) $466

A Baccarat mushroom weight on a star-cut base, 8cm. diam. (Christie's) $2,488

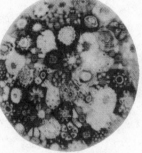

A Clichy moss ground flower weight, 6.5cm. diam. (Christie's) $6,531

A Clichy miniature close millefiori weight, 4.7cm. diam. (Christie's) $777

A St. Louis pink ground pompom weight, 7cm. diam. (Christie's) $1,866

A Paul Ysart double-fish weight on a translucent amethyst base, signed PY on a cane, 7.5cm. diam. (Christie's) $590

A Baccarat dated scattered millefiori weight, 7.8cm. diam. (Christie's) $1,010

A Baccarat garlanded white double clematis weight, on a star-cut base, 7.3cm. diam. (Christie's) $933

A Baccarat dated close mille-fiori weight, a cane inscribed 'B 1848', 6.6cm. diam. (Christie's) $933

A Clichy pansy weight, 6.3cm. diam. (Christie's) $1,399

A Clichy patterned concentric millefiori weight, 5.5cm. diam. (Christie's) $496

A Clichy blue and white dahlia weight, 7.2cm. diam. (Christie's) $9,331

A Clichy garlanded patterned millefiori weight, 7.5cm. diam. (Christie's) $5,443

A Baccarat miniature coloured sulphide pansy weight, 4.7cm. diam. (Christie's) $1,166

GLASS

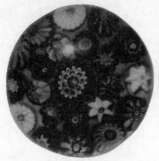

A Clichy turquoise ground
concentric millefiori weight,
6.2cm. diam. (Christie's)
$699

A St. Louis crown weight,
7cm. diam. (Christie's)
$777

A Baccarat cobalt ground
millefiori paperweight, 3in.
diam. (Robt. W. Skinner
Inc.) $1,200

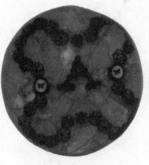

A Clichy patterned concentric millefiori weight, 5.5cm.
diam. (Christie's) $652

A Baccarat millefiori initialled weight, the letter A in
blue canes, 6.2cm. diam.
(Christie's) $1,010

A Clichy rose weight,
6.7cm. diam. (Christie's)
$5,909

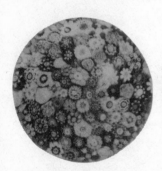

A Clichy close millefiori
weight, 6.5cm. diam.
(Christie's) $1,166

A Baccarat close millefiori
mushroom weight on a
star-cut base, 8cm. diam.
(Christie's) $745

A Clichy blue ground scattered millefiori weight,
6.5cm. diam. (Christie's)
$466

A St. Louis small crown
weight, 5.5cm. diam.
(Christie's) $855

A Clichy green ground patterned millefiori weight, 7.3cm.
diam. (Christie's) $855

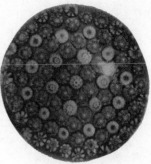

A Clichy blue ground scattered millefiori weight,
8.5cm. diam. (Christie's)
$855

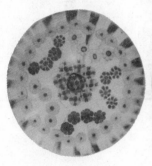

A Baccarat patterned millefiori weight, on a sunray-
cut base, 7.8cm. diam.
(Christie's) $311

A Clichy flat bouquet weight,
7cm. diam. (Christie's)
$13,996

A Clichy faceted patterned
concentric millefiori weight,
6.7cm. diam. (Christie's)
$699

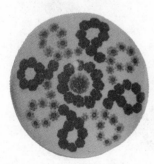

A Baccarat patterned millefiori weight, 7.7cm. diam.
(Christie's) $247

A Clichy swirl weight, with
alternate turquoise and white
staves radiating from a central claret, green and white
cane, 8.2cm. diam. (Christie's) $855

A Baccarat mushroom
weight with star-cut base,
7.3cm. diam. (Christie's)
$933

SCENT BOTTLES

An Apsley Pellatt sulphide and cut glass scent bottle and a stopper, 9.5cm. high. (Christie's) $486

A Franchini silver gilt mounted millefiori scent bottle, the base with a cane dated 1847, 7.2cm. long. (Christie's) $383

One of a pair of Edwardian cut glass cologne bottles, by Wm. Comyns, London, 1905, 5½in. high. (Christie's) $1,036

A Clichy cut glass and patterned millefiori scent bottle and stopper, 18cm. high. (Christie's) $1,533

A glass scent bottle and stopper, inscribed 'Cigalia, Roger et Gallet, Paris', 13cm. high, in original box. (Phillips) $378

A Marinot scent bottle and stopper, with enamel painted decoration, circa 1920, 17cm. high. (Christie's) $1,734

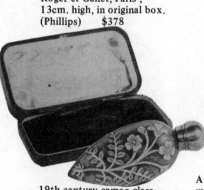

A Baccarat enamelled cut glass scent bottle with gilt metal screw cover, 9.5cm. long. (Christie's) $1,296

19th century cameo glass salts bottle with silver screw top, in case, 4in. long. (Capes, Dunn & Co.) $280

A Franchini gilt metal mounted scent bottle, the hinged cover with ring and bead chain attachment, 7.5cm. long. (Christie's) $367

SCENT BOTTLES

GLASS

'Amphyrite', a Lalique perfume bottle and stopper, the blue tinted frosted glass molded as a snail shell, 9.5cm. high. (Lawrence Fine Art)$626

Late 18th century Spanish opaque opaline scent flask, in the form of a bird, painted in colors and enriched in gilding with flower sprays, 20cm. wide. (Christie's) $1,088

'Worth', a Lalique glass scent bottle, with original Worth paper label, 24.5cm. high. (Christie's) $406

SHADES

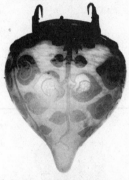

One of a set of four Tiffany Favrile electric light shades, N.Y., circa 1920, 3½in. high, 4¾in. diam. (Robt. W. Skinner Inc.) $525

A pair of 19th century, blown, colorless glass hanging lamps, approx. 15in. high. (Christie's) $1,320

A Le Verre Francais cameo glass hanging lamp shade in the form of a strawberry overlaid in orange and blue, 30.9cm. high. (Christie's) $1,174

TUMBLERS

A Continental blue pressed glass, Royal portrait tumbler, perhaps Bercy, Paris, circa 1840, 11cm. high. (Christie's) $388

A Bohemian ruby overlay engraved tumbler of flared form, circa 1860, 12.5cm. high. (Christie's) $622

A Baccarat molded enamelled cylindrical tumbler, decorated in color on gilt foil, 9cm. high. (Christie's) $372

VASES

A tall vase attributed to Ercole Barovier, with turquoise patchwork decoration, circa 1955, 34.6cm high. (Christie's)
$1,340

A Venini handkerchief vase in blue with a white interior, 9½in. high. (Christie's)
$145

A brass mounted iridescent glass vase attributed to Loetz and the design in the manner of Hans Christiansen, circa 1900, 37cm. high. (Christie's) $788

One of a pair of small Galle enamelled glass vases with bulbous base, 5½in. high. (Christie's) $248

A Lalique opalescent glass vase, 'Bacchantes', 9½in. high. (Christie's)
$3,472

A Richard cameo glass vase overlaid in brown and red, 13½in. high. (Christie's)
$520

A Daum double overlay cameo glass and acid-etched vase, engraved with cross of Lorraine, 50.3cm. high. (Christie's) $3,153

A Lalique conical flower vase with intaglio molded rose design, signed, 9¼in. high. (Capes, Dunn & Co.)
$172

An Aldo Nasson double-neck organic-form glass vase, inscribed Nasson, 14½in. high. (Christie's) $260

438

VASES

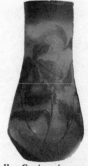

A Delatte cameo glass landscape vase, broad baluster shape with cylindrical neck, 33.1cm. high. (Christie's) $788

A Lalique globular vase, 'Gui', the opalescent glass molded with intertwined fruiting mistletoe, circa 1930, 16.9cm. high. (Christie's) $503

A Muller Croismaire cameo glass vase, the shaded orange and amber ground overlaid with darker orange, circa 1900, 35.3cm. high. (Christie's) $946

A Lalique opalescent tapering cylindrical glass vase, 'Rampillon', 5in. high. (Christie's) $434

A large Galle cameo glass vase, blue glass over a frosted base with stylized floral and foliate decoration, circa 1900, 72.2cm. high. (Christie's) $2,522

A Lalique clear and frosted glass vase, 'Aigrettes', inscribed, 10in. high. (Christie's) $1,122

A large Galle cameo glass vase, pale amber over a ground shading from blue to yellow, circa 1900, 48.6cm. high. (Christie's) $6,307

A Lalique cylindrical glass vase, 'Coqs et Plumes', circa 1930, 15.4cm. high. (Christie's) $503

A glass vase and cover attributed to Fachschule Haida, circa 1910, 32cm. high. (Christie's) $315

A Loetz vase, the body with four dimples and the rim and shoulders with deep blue pulled loop decoration, 13.8cm. high. (Christie's) $2,349

A Daum cameo landscape vase, the tapering cylindrical body with swollen collar, 27cm. high. (Christie's) $783

A free-hand ware vase by the Imperial Glass Co., Ohio, 1920's, 5.7/8in. high. (Robt. W. Skinner Inc.) $300

'Aras', a Lalique opalescent globular vase , engraved France No. 919, 22.7cm. high. (Christie's) $1,096

A Galle cameo glass vase, overlaid in deep mauve with sprays of laburnum, circa 1900, 31.3cm. high. (Lawrence Fine Art) $995

'Formose', a Lalique opalescent vase, molded with a shoal of goldfish, 17cm. high. (Christie's) $626

A Galle double overlay cameo oviform vase with cylindrical neck, overlaid in lilac and green, 18.4cm. high. (Christie's) $783

Victorian red overlay glass vase, 1860. (British Antique Exporters) $59

A Galle cameo vase, the flattened globular body on splayed foot, 23.5cm. high. (Christie's) $1,722

440

VASES

A large Regency ormolu and cut glass vase, the urn-shaped body set with faceted cabochons in latticework frame, 22in. high. (Christie's) $14,968

A Nuutajarvi Notsjo vase, designed by Gunnel Nyman, clear glass over amber with asymmetrical design of air bubbles, 33.8cm. high. (Christie's) $283

A Lalique opalescent glass vase, 'Lievres', 15.8cm. high. (Lawrence Fine Art) $401

'Poivre', a Lalique smoked glass vase modelled with fruiting vine, 10in. high. (Christie's) $835

An iridescent tear vase, attributed to Meyr's Neffe, the pinkish-green glass with silvery blue streak decoration, 22.3cm. high. (Christie's) $1,252

'Vaso a valve', an Italian glass vase, attributed to Seguso and the design to F. Poli, 23.5cm. high. (Christie's) $783

A Ver Centre vase, elongated ovoid shape enamel painted in various colors over a green ground, signature Ver Centre 1927, 29cm. high. (Christie's) $1,576

A glass vase designed by Koloman Moser, the clear glass with gilt loop decoration and iridescent red tears, 17.1cm. high. (Christie's) $2,035

A Galle cameo vase overlaid with brown glass etched with orchid spray against a mottled green, blue and opaque ground, 18.5cm. high. (Christie's) $626

VASES

A Lalique vase, 'Yvelines', gray tinted clear and satin finished glass molded with lug handles, circa 1930, 20cm. high. (Christie's) $661

A Galle fire polished cameo glass vase of squat oviform with flaring stem, 17in. high, inscribed. (Christie's) $845

A Wiener Werkstatte amethyst glass vase and cover designed by Josef Hoffmann, 17cm. high. (Christie's) $1,017

'Perruches', a blue Lalique oviform vase, 25.9cm. high. (Christie's) $4,698

One of a pair of pink-flash narrow tapering two-handled vases, 16½in. high. (Christie's) $1,036

A campana shaped vase, star and stud cut with faceted knop to stem, 10½in. high. (Capes, Dunn & Co.) $57

'Danaides', a Lalique blue opalescent cylindrical vase, the clear and satin finished glass molded with naked maidens, 18cm. high. (Christie's) $1,252

A Venini 'Pezzato' vase designed by F. Bianconi, cigar shaped with patchwork decoration, circa 1960, 27.2cm. high. (Christie's) $6,264

An Argy Rousseau pate-de-verre vase, France, circa 1925, 15.2cm. high. (Christie's) $3,915

VASES

A yellow ground cameo vase of compressed form, circa 1890, 22cm. high. (Christie's) $1,321

A Galle marqueterie de verre vase, bun foot with body shaped like a crocus bloom, circa 1900, 35cm. high. (Christie's) $13,311

A white opaline baluster vase with flaring neck, 12in. high. (Christie's) $266

'Formose', a green Lalique vase, the clear and satin glass molded with goldfish, 17cm. high. (Christie's) $1,722

A blue opaline tapering oviform vase with two gilt metal scrolling foliage handles, 20½in. high. (Christie's) $429

A Stourbridge olive-green opaline vase on four gilt feet detailed in white and black enamel, 12¾in. high. (Christie's) $228

A Venini 'Occhi' vase designed by Carlo Scarpa, the cased red, black and clear glass pressed together to form 'windows', circa 1955, 15.5cm. high. (Christie's) $5,011

A Ferdinand Poschinger Glasshuten vase, the pale green glass with combed deep red 'peacock feather' design, 25cm. high. (Christie's) $1,566

An Arsale overlay glass vase, the flattened slender pear shaped body overlaid with russet- colored glass, 31.6cm. high. (Christie's) $437

443

WINE GLASSES

A 'Lynn' opaque twist glass with horizontally ribbed ogee bowl, circa 1770, 14cm. high. (Christie's) $714

An incised twist wine glass with generous funnel bowl, on a conical foot, circa 1760, 14cm. high. (Christie's) $233

An engraved opaque twist wine glass, the stem with opaque corkscrew core entwined by two spiral threads, circa 1770, 15cm. high. (Christie's) $777

A wine glass by David Wolff, the stem cut with diamond facets, 1790-95, 15cm. high. (Christie's) $5,065

A color twist firing glass with ogee bowl, on a terraced foot, circa 1770, 10.5cm. high. (Christie's) $2,643

A plain stemmed wine glass with ovoid bowl decorated with a nude putto, by D. Wolff, The Hague, circa 1790, 14cm. high. (Christie's) $4,341

A color twist wine glass with waisted bucket bowl, circa 1760, 17cm. high. (Christie's) $2,799

A baluster deceptive wine glass, the thick-walled flared funnel bowl set on a cushion knop above a plain stem, circa 1705, 11.5cm. high. (Christie's) $558

An opaque twist wine glass with octagonally molded ogee bowl, circa 1770, 14.5cm. high. (Christie's) $388

A Beilby opaque twist wine glass, the funnel bowl decorated in white with a border of fruiting vine, circa 1770, 15cm. high. (Christie's) $1,306

A plain stemmed Jacobite wine glass, the funnel bowl with a seven-petalled rose and a bud, circa 1750, 15cm. high. (Christie's) $434

A facet stemmed friendship wine glass by Jacob Sang, 1761, 17.8cm. high. (Christie's) $10,854

A Beilby enamelled opaque twist wine glass, circa 1770, 15.5cm. high. (Christie's) $901

A wine glass with ovoid bowl, by David Wolff, The Hague, 1780-90, 15.3cm. high. (Christie's) $3,473

A Jacobite airtwist wine glass, the stem with swelling waist knop filled with airtwist spirals, 16.5cm. high. (Christie's) $745

A faceted stemmed portrait wine glass, by David Wolff, The Hague, 1780-85, 15.8cm. high. (Christie's) $6,946

A Jacobite airtwist wine glass, the funnel bowl engraved with a rose and bud, circa 1750, 15cm. high. (Christie's) $777

A plain stemmed landscape wine glass by David Wolff, on a plain stem and conical foot, The Hague, 1790, 15cm. high. (Christie's) $7,959

WINE GLASSES

An engraved airtwist wine glass of Jacobite significance, circa 1750, 14.5cm. high. (Christie's) $466

A color twist wine glass with bell bowl, circa 1760, 16.5cm. high. (Christie's) $1,088

A color twist wine glass with bell bowl, circa 1760, 17cm. high. (Christie's) $1,056

An engraved mixed twist ale flute, the flared funnel bowl with a hop-spray and two ears of barley, circa 1760, 18cm. high. (Christie's) $434

An armorial light baluster wine glass, the funnel bowl engraved with the arms of Schieland, circa 1760, 18.2cm. high. (Christie's) $1,399

An incised twist wine glass, the bell bowl with honeycomb-molded lower part, circa 1760, 17.5cm. high. (Christie's) $372

A canary twist wine glass with pan-topped funnel bowl, circa 1760, 14.5cm. high. (Christie's) $3,732

An opaque twist deceptive cordial glass with thick-walled ogee bowl, circa 1770, 14cm. high. (Christie's) $652

A composite stemmed wine glass of drawn trumpet shape, circa 1750, 18cm. high. (Christie's) $185

WINE GLASSES

An engraved color twist
wine glass of Jacobite significance, the rounded bowl
with a rosebud, circa 1765,
13cm. high. (Christie's)
$652

A composite stemmed wine
glass of drawn trumpet shape,
the stem filled with airtwist
spirals set into a beaded inverted baluster section, circa
1750, 17.5cm. high. (Christie's) $247

A 'Lynn' opaque twist wine
glass with horizontally ribbed ogee bowl, circa 1775,
14cm. high. (Christie's)
$496

A Jacobite airtwist wine
glass, the stem with a twis-
ted air core entwined by
spiral threads, circa 1750,
14.5cm. high. (Christie's)
$434

An opaque twist ale or ratafia
glass, the slender funnel bowl
with hammered flutes, circa
1765, 18cm. high. (Christie's)
$434

A baluster wine glass, the
bell bowl with a small tear
to the solid lower part,
circa 1715, 14cm. high.
(Christie's) $403

A Williamite baluster wine
glass with trumpet-shaped
bowl, 18th century, 17.5cm.
high. (Christie's) $2,021

A color twist wine glass
with generous bell bowl,
circa 1760, 17.5cm. high.
(Christie's) $1,866

A light baluster dated betrothal
wine glass by the monogram-
mist ICL, 1753, 19.7cm. high.
(Christie's) $2,894

447

A George II gold and mocha-agate snuff box of cartouche shape, circa 1745, 2¾in. long. (Christie's) $5,114

A Louis XV small gold mounted blonde tortoise-shell snuff box, circa 1750, 2in. diam. (Christie's) $2,077

An early 19th century Scottish octagonal gold mounted presentation snuff box, 2.7/8in. long. (Christie's) $2,643

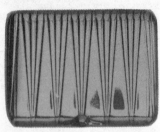

An oblong gold colored cigarette case with cabochon bluestone pushpiece, with Swedish control marks, 3¼in. long. (Christie's) $1,166

A 19th century gold mounted walking stick, the pommel with Japanese ivory okimono of a snake entwined on top of a human skull, 18ct. (Christie's) $544

A George II gold mounted shell-shaped amethystine quartz snuff box, circa 1750, 1¾in. high. (Christie's) $3,265

A shallow gold snuff box of cartouche shape, London, 1824, maker's initials IN probably for John Northam, 2¾in. long. (Christie's) $3,996

A George III oval gold mounted mottled agate snuff box, circa 1760, 2.3/8in. long. (Christie's) $1,358

A French gold presentation snuff box, the interior with gold standard mark for 1798-1809 and warranty mark for 1819-38, 4in. long. (Christie's) $8,553

GOLD

A Swiss oval gold and enamel presentation snuff box, circa 1800, with French prestige marks, 3¼in. long. (Christie's) $4,199

A gold mounted mauve agate sweetmeat dish in the 16th century style, the oval foot en suite to the bowl, 19th century, 5in. high.(Christie's) $7,776

A shallow octagonal gold snuff box, the cover hinged, circa 1725, 2¾in. long. (Christie's) $3,516

Late 18th century circular gold mounted figured white quartz snuff box, with French import marks, 2¼in. diam. (Christie's) $3,356

Charles II cylindrical gold counter-case of upright form, circa 1685, 1.3/8in. high. (Christie's) $12,787

A George III gold and enamel scent bottle of shaped flask form, circa 1755, 2.3/8in. high. (Christie's) $5,287

A vari-colored gold snuff box, Swiss or Austrian, with maker's initial B between two rosettes, the flange with inventory no. 14301, circa 1810, 3.3/8in. long. (Christie's) $2,397

A 19th century Continental oblong gold snuff box with engine-turned body, 3½in. long. (Christie's) $2,021

A 17th century gold and polychrome enamel devotional reliquary of arched form, possibly French, in 18th century red leather case, 1.5/8in. high. (Christie's) $5,909

GOLD

An Irish gold and silver gilt oblong Masonic snuff box, the base inscribed Dublin, 1819, maker's initials E.(?), 3½in. long. (Christie's) $1,772

A 19th century gold mounted striated agate scent bottle of flattened flask form, 1¾in. long.(Christie's) $391

An oblong gold presentation snuff box with slightly bombe sides, by J. Willmore, Birmingham, 1826, 18ct., 3.5/8in. long. (Christie's) $10,886

'Mondain', a Dunhill 9ct. plain gold petrol lighter, Pat. No. 143752, gold marks for 1929, 4.3cm. high. (Christie's) $315

One of a pair of gemset gold lorgnettes in the Russian taste, 5½in. long.(Christie's) $939

A Furstenburg shaped rectangular snuff box and cover with contemporary gold mounts, circa 1770, 8cm. wide.) (Christie's) $12,268

A Dunhill 'Bijou' lady's 18ct. plain gold petrol lighter, Pat. 143752 Fab. Suisse, 3.2cm. high. (Christie's) $473

A gold mounted wooden reliquary crucifix made from the 'Waterloo Tree', the mounts engraved June 18, 1815. (Christie's)$221

A French oblong gold colored cigarette case with cabochon redstone thumbpieces, retailer's name Tonnel, Paris, in case, 3in. long. (Christie's) $1,088

GOLD

A Swiss diamond set, gold and enamel, oval snuff box with scalloped rims, circa 1840, 3in. long. (Christie's) $2,954

A gold desk seal with handle modelled in ivory as a hand clasping a baton with blood-stone or cornelian seal ends, circa 1830, 2¾in. long. (Christie's) $2,557

A Louis XVI oblong gold and enamel toothpick case, by Nicolas Marguerit, Paris, 1778, 3¼in. long. (Christie's) $4,475

A George III gold snuff box formed as a book, by A. J. Strachan, London, 1802, 18ct., 2¾in. long. (Christie's) $1,166

George III gold christening font, by Paul Storr, Figure of Faith 7¼in. high, Figure of Hope 4½in. high, Figure of Charity 4¼in. high, bowl 4½in. high, 220oz.16dwt. gross excluding Hope's foot rest, 22ct. (Christie's)
$1,368,576

A Tiffany & Co. Douglass petrol lighter, patterned yellow metal, stamped 14 Karat Solid gold, 5cm. high. (Christie's)$220

'Mondain', a Dunhill patterned 9ct. gold petrol lighter, gold marks for 1950, 4.7cm. high. (Christie's) $378

A French vari- colored gold and enamel mounted para-sol handle, with Paris restric-ted gold warranty mark in use from 1838, 3¼in. long. (Christie's)$2,877

A French gold, silver and translucent enamel moun-ted photograph frame in the Faberge style, the gold mounts with warranty mark in use from 1838, 7¼in. high. (Christie's) $6,264

A 17th/18th century large rhinoceros horn libation cup, 18.5cm. wide, wood stand. (Christie's) $2,310

A 17th/18th century rhinoceros horn libation cup, 13cm. wide. (Christie's) $1,320

A rhinoceros horn libation cup, 17th/18th century, 14.3cm. wide. (Christie's) $2,138

A Bohemian carved staghorn powder flask decorated with three deer moving through a forest, with silver mounts. (Bermondsey) $1,200

An 18th century stag antler netsuke of a standing bow-legged Dutchman holding a long-tailed cockerel, unsigned. (Christie's) $694

A late 18th century Scottish horn snuff mull carved with the profile of the Old Pretender, 4¼in. high. (Christie's) $466

Victorian horn and brass gong. (British Antique Exporters) $101

17th century flattened cow horn powder flask decorated overall with geometric circles, scallops and foliate patterns, 12in. long. (Bermondsey) $450

Early 18th century rhinoceros horn libation cup, 6½in. wide. (Christie's) $2,250

'Long Hair Dancer', by Bruce
Timeche, tempera, signed,
10 x 13in. (Robt. W. Skinner
Inc.) $275

Southwestern pottery dough
bowl, Cochiti, the interior
painted over a cream slip in
black foliate motifs, 14in.
diam. (Robt. W. Skinner Inc.)
$1,200

'Warrior', by Velino Shije
Herrera, signed 'Ma-Pe-Wi
'45', tempera on white paper,
9½ x 12½in. (Robt. W.
Skinner Inc.) $700

A Southwestern basketry
tray, Apache, woven in
devil's claw on a dark golden
field, 19in. diam. (Robt. W.
Skinner Inc.) $1,400

Two Plains paint decorated
parfleche containers, Crow,
a shoulder bag, 12 x 13in.
and a case 12 x 23½in.
(Robt. W. Skinner Inc.)
$500

A Southwestern polychrome
basketry tray, Yavapai, woven
in red and dark brown designs
on a golden field, 14½in.
diam. (Robt. W. Skinner Inc.)
$950

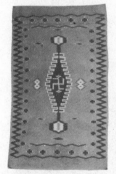

Navajo Germantown
weaving, woven on a red
ground in black and white,
41 x 69in. (Robt. W.
Skinner Inc.)$1,300

'Eagle Dancer', by Raymond
Chavez, signed, 13 x 17¼in.
(Robt. W. Skinner Inc.)
$300

'Rattle for Germination', by
Fred Kabotie, tempera, signed,
15 x 22½in. (Robt. W. Skinner
Inc.) $900

Southwestern pottery jar, Zia, painted over a pinky cream slip in black and red, 12¾in. diam. (Robt. W. Skinner Inc.) $1,000

'Untitled', by Gerda Christofferson, pastel portrait, signed and dated '57, 18½ x 24in. (Robt. W. Skinner Inc.) $260

A Hopi polychrome pottery canteen, painted over a creamy yellow slip in dark brown linear and 'Koshare' figural decoration, 3¼in. high. (Robt. W. Skinner Inc.) $200

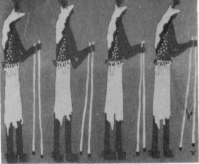

'Owl Kachina', by Peter Shelton, acrylic on paper, signed 'Hoyewva '64', 14 x 21in. (Robt. W. Skinner Inc.) $500

'Deer Dancers', by Harry Fonseca, signed in interlocking initials, dated 1975 on back, acrylic on canvas board, 20 x 23in. (Robt. W. Skinner Inc.) $450

Southern Plains painted buffalo fur robe, 92in. long, 67in. wide. (Robt. W. Skinner Inc.) $500

Large Navajo pictorial weaving, woven on a red field in mustard, white and navy, 61 x 88in. (Robt. W. Skinner Inc.) $2,300

Northwest coast mask, Bella/Bella Coola, of polychrome cedar wood, 12.5/8in. high. (Robt. W. Skinner Inc.) $49,000

'King of the Herd', by Quincy Tahoma, tempera, signed and dated '53, 6½ x 10in. (Robt. W. Skinner Inc.) $650

A Southwestern polychrome canteen, Zia, 19th century, painted over a cream slip in black and red, 10¾in. deep. (Robt. W. Skinner Inc.) $1,200

'Sioux Maiden', by Gerda Christofferson, pastel portrait, signed and dated '57, 19 x 24in. (Robt. W. Skinner Inc.) $375

A Southwestern polychrome jar, Zia, with indented base, flaring sides and tapering rim, 12½in. diam. (Robt. W. Skinner Inc.) $1,000

Yuma polychromed female figure with traditional horsehair coiffure, inscribed 'Yuma, Arizona Indian 1931', 8in. high. (Robt. W. Skinner Inc.) $375

'Apache Mountain Spirit Dance', by Carl Nelson Gorman, signed 'Kin-Ya-Onny-Beyeh', oil on canvas, 19½ x 23½in. (Robt. W. Skinner Inc.) $900

A Hopi wood Kachina doll, 'Mahuu' (locust), with black, mustard and rose decoration over a white painted body, 15¾in. high. (Robt. W. Skinner Inc.) $1,200

Basket Maker, by Patrick Robt. Desjarlait, tempera, signed, 14 x 17in. (Robt. W. Skinner Inc.) $1,300

A Southwestern polychrome storage jar, San Ildefonso, of tall rounded form, 12½in. high. (Robt. W. Skinner Inc.) $700

Navajo Germantown serape, finely woven on a red ground, 47 x 68in. (Robt. W. Skinner Inc.) $2,300

A 19th century three-case Kinji inro, with attached black lacquer bead ojime and red lacquered mokko-gata netsuke. (Christie's) $4,800

A 19th century three-case silver inro, with attached silver filigree bead ojime and lightly stained ivory netsuke. (Christie's) $9,750

Early 19th century three-case inro decorated in gold hiramakie, takamakie, heidatsu and togidashi on a yasuriko ground. (Christie's) $772

A 19th century Tamenuri three-case inro, with cornelian glass bead ojime. (Christie's) $720

A small three-case Ginji inro, decorated in gold hiramakie, with wakasa-nuri bead ojime. (Christie's) $2,100

Late 19th century three-case hirame inro decorated in takamakie and raden, ivory and other inlay, signed Jushuhan Chohei. (Christie's) $1,312

A 19th century three-case Kinji inro, with attached copper and gilt ojime, and a stained ivory netsuke. (Christie's) $5,250

A 19th century three-case Kinji inro, with attached gold and silver lacquer ojime and an ivory netsuke. (Christie's) $3,450

19th century three-case Kinji inro, with attached ojime and stained ivory netsuke. (Christie's) $2,850

INROS

Early 19th century three-case gold sprinkled roironuri inro, with attached pink coral bead ojime. (Christie's) $1,145

A 19th century four-case fundame inro decorated on each side with a hawk on a perch, signed Nikkosai. (Christie's) $1,081

A 19th century three-case ivory inro, with attached ivory bead ojime and ivory manju netsuke. (Christie's) $2,250

Late 18th/early 19th century four-case Kinji inro, decorated in gold, black and red hiramakie, takamakie, hirame and nashiji. (Christie's) $1,275

An 18th century four-case Nashiji inro, decorated in gold hiramakie, takamakie and hirame, unsigned. (Christie's) $1,050

Early 19th century four-case inro, signed Kakosai. (Christie's) $825

A 19th century five-case silver ground, ginji, inro, with attached silver, shakudo and copper ojime. (Christie's) $4,112

A 19th century four-case Kinji inro, signed Hasegawa saku above a red tsubo seal and Shibayama on a shell tablet. (Christie's) $1,321

Early 19th century five-case Kinji inro, signed Shoryusai Kogyoku saku. (Christie's) $1,909

457

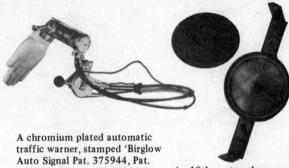

Late 18th century brass 3in. reflecting telescope, on folding tripod base with scroll feet, body tube 46.5cm. long. (Christie's) $770

A chromium plated automatic traffic warner, stamped 'Birglow Auto Signal Pat. 375944, Pat. 376564, Reg. design 767816', 42in. long. (Christie's) $198

An 18th century brass surveyor's compass, signed Gab. Stoak, Dublin fecit, 28.5cm. long. (Christie's) $242

A brass transit on tripod foot with three levelling screws, signed Stanley, London, No. 11013, 42cm. high. (Christie's) $825

An English Withering type botanical microscope and case, circa 1800, with box, 10.5cm. high. (Christie's) $495

A rosewood pedestal stereoscope with turned wood eye pieces with brass lens. (Christie's) $1,147

A small one-day marine chronometer by John Roger Arnold, the dial 64mm. diam. (Christie's) $3,732

A 17th century engraved silver and gilt brass geared astronomical dial, signed Ph. Dagoneau, Grenoble, 13.8cm. diam. (Christie's) $5,500

A brass and mahogany 4in. refracting telescope, signed Steinheil in Munchen, no. 2811, the sighting telescope, no. 2886, 171cm. long. (Christie's) $1,650

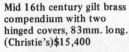

A chromium plated automatic traffic warner, bulb and mounting bracket labelled Rolph's Patents. (Christie's) $62

Mid 16th century gilt brass compendium with two hinged covers, 83mm. long. (Christie's)$15,400

A French 19th century universal dial, signed Bordi, Ing. Cons. Optician, Paris, 18.5cm. high. (Christie's) $660

A gilt brass pedometer, German, possibly Augsburg, circa 1700, 65mm. long. (Christie's) $1,100

A Henry Crouch brass binocular microscope, No. 2092, of Lister limb construction. (Lawrence Fine Art) $814

A brass transit on circular foot with focus levelling screws, signed Troughton & Simms, London, 39cm. high. (Christie's)$715

A two-day marine chronometer, the silvered dial signed James Muirhead, Glasgow, No. 2169, 100mm. diam. of dial. (Christie's) $7,668

A brass astrolabe, signed Georgivs Hartman Norenberge Faciebat Anno MD XXXII, 137mm. diam. (Christie's) $26,400

A watchmaker's wheel-cutting engine, signed Cibert & Cie, no. 53, 24cm. long. (Christie's) $1,045

A chased silver universal equatorial dial with perpetual calendar, signed Jean-David Beyser, Augsburg, circa 1750, 80mm. long. (Christie's) $1,100

A Lambert typewriter No. 2908, by The Lambert Typewriter Co., New York. (Christie's) $259

An early 19th century small brass circumferentor, signed Harris, London, 10.5cm. diam. (Christie's) $495

A London Stereoscopic Co. Brewster-pattern stereoscope with brass mounted eye pieces, in fitted rosewood box, 13in. wide. (Christie's) $513

A French clockwork globe, signed Empire Clock, highlighting in red the British Empire, 16in. high. (Christie's) $2,310

An 18th century brass horizontal dial, signed Butterfield a Paris, 16.5cm. long. (Christie's) $880

A cradle-mounted stereographoscope in black ebonized finish with lens panel, 16in. high. (Christie's) $248

An American brass and plated brass compound monocular microscope, signed E. Gundlach, pat. Sept. 14, 1878, 29cm. high approx. (Christie's) $418

A silver and gilt brass universal dial, signed 'Cadran Universel et a Meridienne. Fait et invenie par Julien le Roy de la Societe des Arts', 80mm. long. (Christie's) $3,300

A Grover & Baker hand-sewing machine, the brass Patent plaque with patents to 1863. (Christie's) $1,584

A 19th century English brass universal equatorial dial with three levelling screws, 11.5cm. diam. (Christie's) $605

A Baird televisor, No. 204, in typical arched brown painted aluminium case with disc, valve and plaque on front. (Christie's) $1,848

Late 16th century gilt and silvered brass astrolabe, probably German, 172mm. diam. (Christie's) $11,000

A brass Martin type orrery with tellurium of American interest, signed T. Blunt, London, 22cm. diam. (Christie's) $15,400

A cast iron sundial by E. T. Hurley, circa 1900, 10¼in. diam. (Robt. W. Skinner Inc.) $425

A mahogany folding Cumino-scope concave mirror photo-graph/print viewer, by The Cuminoscope Patent Brevetes, S.G.D.G. (Christie's) $223

A small Zoetrope optical toy on wood stand with several picture strips, diam. of drum 5¼in. (Christie's) $124

A small brass sextant of T-frame style signed Berge, London, in fitted shaped mahogany case, circa 1800. (Reeds Rains) $1,944

INSTRUMENTS

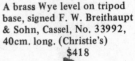

A brass graphometer, signed Canivet a la Sphere a Paris, dated 1765, 13.5cm. radius. (Christie's) $715

A goldsmith's steel scale and set of weights, with the label of Joh. Pet. Poppenberg, dated 1776, 17.5cm. long. (Christie's) $528

A brass Wye level on tripod base, signed F. W. Breithaupt & Sohn, Cassel, No. 33992, 40cm. long. (Christie's) $418

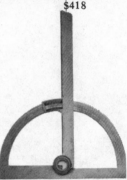

A Regency mahogany library globe, 28in. diam. (Christie's) $23,490

Mid 19th century drum microscope, signed F. Cox, London, within fitted mahogany box, 25.5cm. high. (Christie's) $385

Late 18th century brass protractor, signed Lenoir a Paris, 13cm. radius. (Christie's) $209

A mariner's brass astrolabe, the scale divided from 0° to 90°, with rising loop handle, 23.5cm. diam. (Christie's) $1,430

A German cube dial, the wooden cube with five printed scales, signed D. Beringer, 7in. high. (Lawrence Fine Art) $814

An early 17th century Roman terrestrial table globe, signed by M. Greuter Romae 1630, 27½in. (Christie's) $1,088

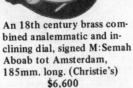

A 19th century brass draining level, signed Newton & Co., London, 35.5cm. long. (Christie's) $550

An 18th century brass combined analemmatic and inclining dial, signed M:Semah Aboab tot Amsterdam, 185mm. long. (Christie's) $6,600

A brass gimbal mounted dumpy level with compass, signed on the body tube Elliot Bros., London, the mount signed Doerings Patent level, No. 16, 39cm. long. (Christie's)$286

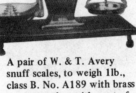

A silver pseudo astrolabe, signature of Abd al-A-imma and the date 1127AH (=1715), 15cm. diam. (Christie's) $3,520

A pair of W. & T. Avery snuff scales, to weigh 1lb., class B. No. A189 with brass pans, together with a set of 5 weights. (Osmond Tricks) $172

Late 18th century brass transit instrument, signed Lenoir (Paris), on circular base with three levelling screws, the telescope 53.5cm. long. (Christie's) $3,080

A 16th century gilt brass miniature armillary sphere, probably German, 55mm. diam. (Christie's) $4,180

A small 2½in. reflecting telescope, signed J. Watson, London, circa 1800, on folding tripod base, 235mm. long. (Christie's) $1,320

A 19th/20th century brass noon cannon on a circular marble base, diam. of base 16cm. (Christie's) $990

An 18th century brass and steel Hahn type geared universal dial, German, 37cm. high. (Christie's) $8,800

A 17th/18th century brass graduated circle, probably French, 13.7cm. diam. (Christie's) $880

An enamel clock globe, signed Redier a Paris, 1873, on octagonal onyx base, 20cm. high. (Christie's) $3,850

A Lahore brass astrolabe, 1666, 25cm. diam. (Christie's) $26,400

A 19th century walnut thunder house, the chimney carrying electrical wire, 19.5cm. long. (Christie's) $770

A large brass mounted lodestone with bail handle, 20.5cm. high. (Christie's) $3,850

An 18th century brass Butterfield type dial, signed LeMaire fils, Paris, 94mm. long. (Christie's) $1,045

Early 19th century brass compound monocular microscope, probably English, length of tube 17.3cm. (Christie's) $605

Late 18th century brass Culpeper type microscope, on circular brass base, with central pivot mirror, 25cm. high. (Christie's) $825

An English 18th century brass universal ring dial, 10.5cm. diam. (Christie's) $605

Late 19th century brass watchmaker's lathe, driven by cranked gear, 38cm. long. (Christie's) $990

One of a pair of Regency Cary's terrestrial and celestial library globes, the terrestrial dated 1815, the celestial adapted to the year 1800, 27in. diam. (Christie's) $32,886

A brass circular protractor with box, signed Blunt, London, circa 1800, 78mm. radius. (Christie's) $418

A 19th century German silver pocket terrestrial globe, engraved with Zodiacal calendar, 60mm. diam. (Christie's) $2,090

An 18th century brass analemmatic and horizontal inclining dial, signed J. Deens, Vienae, 113mm. long. (Christie's) $880

A French 19th century brass orrery on stand depicting the asteroids, 23cm. diam. (Christie's) $1,320

An Ive's Kromskop color stereoscopic viewer, in wood carrying case. (Christie's) $868

A two-day marine chronometer, the dial signed by Dobbie McInnes Ltd., Glasgow, no. 9615, dial 10cm. diam. (Christie's) $880

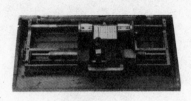

Early 19th century wooden cube dial, signed D. Beringer, 24cm. high. (Christie's) $528

A Hall typewriter with rubber type sheet (defective), in walnut case with instructions in lid. (Christie's) $273

An 18th century brass geared universal ring dial, probably from the workshop of T. Heath, London, 36cm. high. (Christie's) $26,400

Victorian oak cased sewing machine, 1880. (British Antique Exporters) $66

Late 18th century brass drum microscope, possibly from the workshop of G. F. Brander, Augsburg, 28cm. high. (Christie's) $1,980

Late 19th century oak and iron sewing machine. (British Antique Exporters) $40

Late 19th century Turkish turned wood pillar dial, 17cm. high. (Christie's) $2,860

A brass and nickel plated yacht timepiece modelled as a turret with simulated cannons, 4½in. high, and a matching barometer. (Christie's) $107

An 18th century brass sector, signed Briere a Paris, 170mm. long. (Christie's) $209

A Victorian lacquered brass binocular microscope, probably by Smith & Beck, 23in. high, circa 1890. (Reeds Rains) $769

Early 19th century brass refracting telescope, signed Dollond, London, body tube 46cm. long. (Christie's) $715

A brass compound microscope, signed E. Hartnack & A. Prazmowski, Paris, length of body tube 16.5cm. (Christie's) $220

Victorian brass and iron scales, circa 1880. (British Antique Exporters) $58

A Marconiphone V-2 two-valve receiver with BBC transfer, two wavelength plates and regenerator unit. (Christie's) $547

A terrestrial globe on a mahogany stand, globe printed by J. & W. Cary, London, 1818, 24¾in. high. (Christie's) $1,650

A Walmore crystal set in oak case with BBC transfer, glazed cover and two pairs of headphones. (Christie's) $79

An early 19th century American set of brass parallel rules with protractor, signed S. Dod, Newark, 30.5cm. long. (Christie's) $880

Brass ship's barometer, circa 1860. (British Antique Exporters) $71

IRON & STEEL

A late 19th century cast iron Newfoundland figure dog, 65in. long. (Robt. W. Skinner Inc.) $10,500

An early 19th century cast iron ship's bulwark swivel cannon, 22in., bore 1in., with turned reinforces, swollen muzzle and curved iron tiller for aiming. (Wallis & Wallis) $518

A George III polished steel and cast iron basket grate, 35in. wide, and a fender 46in. wide. (Christie's) $3,288

One of a pair of late 19th century russet iron Komai style oviform vases, 20.5cm. high. (Christie's) $1,003

Late 18th century pair of iron and brass 'knifeblade' andirons, 20¼in. high. (Christie's) $1,430

A hollow cast iron 19th century explosive ball for a mortar, 10in. diam., with cast lifting lugs and hole for fuse. (Wallis & Wallis) $93

One of two decorated 19th century steel sipars, Persia, 14in. diam. (Robt. W. Skinner Inc.) $600

A George III paktong and cast iron fire grate with bowed front, 33½in. wide. (Christie's) $27,086

Late 19th century moulded iron and zinc jeweller's trade sign, America. (Robt. W. Skinner Inc.) $600

A Degue wrought-iron mounted circular, mauve to orange glass bowl, the branches forming the central handle, 9½in. high. (Christie's) $175

Late 19th century American cast iron elk figure, 49in. wide. (Robt. W. Skinner Inc.) $2,900

A part 16th century steel composite triptych, 40 x 24cm. (Phillips) $2,250

One of a pair of iron Komai baluster vases decorated in two shades of gilt, signed Moriyama, circa 1890, 13.7cm. high. (Christie's) $1,264

A Regency Gothic wrought iron three-seater garden bench, 57¼in. wide. (Christie's) $1,200

A cast iron pedestal with marble top, 1860. (British Antique Exporters) $230

One of a pair of Regency coal boxes on gilt paw feet, 20½in. wide. (Christie's) $1,770

An early 19th century iron cannon barrel, 32in., with 1¾in. diam. bore, swollen muzzle and cascabel. (Wallis & Wallis) $367

A Regency steel and brass basket grate with detachable later liner, 24in. wide. (Christie's) $1,252

Late 19th century ivory okimono of a girl and a little boy, signed Kogyoku to, 10.8cm. high. (Christie's) $440

Late 19th century sectional ivory okimono of a basket weaver and his wife, signed Eitoku, 10cm. high. (Christie's) $762

A stained ivory censer and fluted cover, signed Tamayuki, Meiji period, 29.8cm. high. (Christie's) $1,321

A two-handled metal gilt mounted ivory cup and cover, the ivory barrel Augsburg, late 17th century, the mounts circa 1800, 17¾in. high. (Christie's) $12,441

A tall ivory group of the Hehe Erxian, the laughing twins, 18th century, 37.5cm. high. (Christie's) $3,706

A large, late 19th century, Continental silver mounted ivory tankard and cover, 16in. high. (Christie's) $10,108

A Ming ivory figure of a bearded scholar, 17th century, 12.5cm. high, with wood stand. (Christie's) $1,568

A wood and ivory carving of a woodcutter, signed Ryukai, Meiji period, 42.5cm. long, 39cm. high. (Christie's) $2,203

A 19th century Tokyo School ivory carving of a lady, signed Koraku, 25.5cm. high. (Christie's) $1,175

IVORY

Large ivory figure of a hunter holding a musket, on natural base with dead hares, 19½in. high. (Reeds Rains) $2,160

One of a set of five ivory groups of musicians, 5¾in. high. (Reeds Rains) $835

Late 19th century ivory carving of a fisherman, signed Shinsai(?), 14.5cm. high. (Christie's) $278

Late 19th century ivory carving of a woodcutter, signed Shunjuken Tadaomi and kao, 28.5cm. high. (Christie's) $881

A 19th century ivory okimono of a human skull, signed Shosai to, 13cm. long. (Christie's) $4,993

Late 19th century wood and ivory carving of a drum seller, signed Kazuyuki, 26cm. high. (Christie's) $1,468

A Tokyo School ivory carving of Fudo Myo-o, signed Shinmei saku, Meiji period, 34cm. high. (Christie's) $2,643

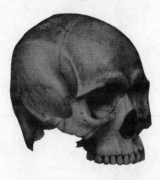

Late 19th century ivory carving of Kannon, signed Shun-yosai Nobuyuki, 13.9cm. high. (Christie's) $734

Carved ivory figure of a fisherman with basket of fish around his waist, 15½in. high. (Reeds Rains) $1,440

An ivory carving of Guanyin standing on a cart among waves, 7½in. high. (Christie's) $942

A sectional ivory group of a kneeling basket maker and his son, signed Toshimasa, Meiji period, 20.5cm. wide. (Christie's) $2,315

Late 19th century ivory carving of a fisherman returning with his catch, signed Gyokudo, 24cm. high. (Christie's) $1,003

One of a pair of ivory bottle shaped vases carved all over with children at play in a garden, 5¼in. high. (Christie's) $870

A late 19th century Chinese ivory carving of a bearded scholar, 20.5cm. high, together with another pair, 23cm. high. (Christie's) $926

One of a pair of ivory tusks carved in relief with figures and animals by a stream, on wood and lacquer stands, 11½in. high. (Christie's) $870

A stained ivory okimono of a standing priest, signed Hozan, late Meiji period, 19.8cm. high. (Christie's) $617

Early 19th century Anglo-Indian ivory sewing box shaped as a cottage, 6in. wide. (Christie's) $4,384

An ivory carving of a girl holding a small boy in her arms, signed Chikayoshi, Meiji period, 21.5cm. high. (Christie's) $1,312

Late 19th century ivory okimono of a girl walking, unsigned, 11.4cm. high. (Christie's) $647

Late 19th century ivory okimono of a kneeling grape seller, signed Gyokuzan, 7.5cm. high. (Christie's) $617

Late 19th century ivory carving of a weaver spinning her yarn, signed Tadaomi to, 20cm. high. (Christie's) $1,467

An oviform vase carved with birds in flight, 3½in. high, together with an ivory group of eight turtles, 4in. high. (Christie's) $551

Late 19th century sectional ivory carving of the Shichifukujin in the Takarabune, 46cm. long. (Christie's) $2,316

Late 19th century oval ivory box and cover, signed on a pearl tablet Tohekido Yoshikazu, 18cm. high. (Christie's) $2,626

Late 19th century ivory carving of one of the Chinese handmaidens, signed Seiso, 21cm. high. (Christie's) $338

Late 19th century ivory carving of a basket seller, signed Jogyoku, 25cm. high. (Christie's) $1,930

Late 19th century ivory carving of Jurojin, signed Nagamitsu, 18.5cm. high. (Christie's) $1,930

IVORY

A 19th century carved ivory figure of a medieval knight, Europe, 10.1/8in. high. (Robt. W. Skinner Inc.) $900

An articulated ivory model of a crab, 13½in. wide. (Christie's) $1,595

Late 19th century ivory carving of Yokhi and the Emperor Meiko, signed Gyoku, 25cm. high. (Christie's) $1,158

A 19th century carved ivory farmer, Japan, signed on base, 7.1/8in. high. (Christie's) $225

A German 17th century ivory plaque carved with half length figures, 11.5 x 9.7cm. (Lawrence Fine Art) $574

An ivory model of a warrior, his hands held to his chest, 9¼in. high. (Lawrence Fine Art) $574

An ivory carving of a monkey trainer, signed Tamahide, Meiji period, 28.8cm. high. (Christie's) $1,835

A pair of ivory figures of Lohands, one carrying a bell, the other a parasol, 9in. high. (Lawrence Fine Art) $638

Late 19th century ivory carving of a fisherman and a small boy, signed Shunpu, 34cm. high. (Christie's) $2,471

Late 19th century ivory tusk vase inlaid in Shibayama style, signed Masamitsu, 89cm. overall. (Christie's) $3,088

An ivory medical figure of a maiden, signed, 7¼in. long. (Lawrence Fine Art) $797

Late 19th century ivory carving of a Rakan, signed Kozan, 29cm. high. (Christie's) $1,235

A 19th century carved ivory fisherman and child, Japan, signed on base, 10¼in. high. (Robt. W. Skinner Inc.) $425

A mid 19th century decorated ivory ink stand, Europe, 3in. high, 5in. diam. (Robt. W. Skinner Inc.) $259

Late 19th century ivory carving of a woodcutter, signature tablet missing, 20cm. high. (Christie's) $1,003

'Nude', an ivory figure carved after a model by F. Preiss, on a green marble base, 43.9cm. high. (Christie's) $12,528

Late 19th century ivory tusk vase inlaid in Shibayama style, signed, overall height 42.7cm. (Christie's) $772

A 19th century carved ivory ewer with nude woman handle, Europe, 17½in. high. (Robt. W. Skinner Inc.) $1,300

JADE

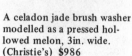

A pale celadon jade figure
of a recumbent horse,
Yuan Dynasty, 4.6cm. long.
(Christie's) $2,143

A jade figure of a recumbent
horse, Tang/Song Dynasty,
6.5cm. long. (Christie's)
$1,140

A celadon jade brush washer
modelled as a pressed hol-
lowed melon, 3in. wide.
(Christie's) $986

An 18th century flecked
celadon and russet jade box
and cover, 8cm. wide, with
fitted box. (Christie's)
$641

A pale celadon and brown
jade vase, 17th/18th century,
12.5cm. high, with wood
stand. (Christie's)
$7,128

An early celadon jade circular
disc, bi, Han Dynasty, 10.7cm.
diam., in fitted box.(Christie's)
$3,564

An archaic jade pierced
circular disc, bi, Zhou
Dynasty, 16cm. diam.
(Christie's) $1,111

A Longquan celadon yanyan
vase, early 14th century,
26.5cm. high. (Christie's)
$3,991

A small Longquan celadon
jarlet and lotus-moulded
cover, 13th/14th century,
7.5cm. high. (Christie's)
$1,568

JADE

An 18th century flecked celadon jade group formed as a slender bodied recumbent deer, 15cm. wide, wood stand. (Christie's) $1,905

An 18th century white jade group of a recumbent horse, 6.5cm. high, with wood stand. (Christie's) $1,140

A large celadon jade peach-shaped brushwasher, late Qing Dynasty, 19.5cm. wide. (Christie's) $2,138

A Mogul dark celadon jade ewer of oval octafoil cross-section, 17th/18th century, 15.5cm. high. (Christie's) $7,840

An early celadon and russet jade burial cicada, Han Dynasty or earlier, 5cm. wide. (Christie's) $570

A celadon lobed hexafoil dish, Northern Song Dynasty, 17.4cm. diam. (Christie's) $8,553

A pale celadon jade model of two mythical birds feeding from a branch of peaches, 6¾in. wide, on wood stand. (Christie's) $3,480

A pale celadon jade tripod libation vessel carved with a single bracket handle, Qianlong seal mark, 13.4cm. high. (Christie's) $6,032

A jade figure of a crouching Buddhistic lion, probably Han/Six Dynasties, 6.8cm. wide. (Christie's) $1,140

477

A diamond pendant roundel brooch set with collets and rose cut stones. (Lawrence Fine Art) $510

A fish brooch designed by Henning Koppel, stamped HK Georg Jensen, 306, circa 1950. (Christie's) $406

A diamond target brooch, the central diamond calculated as weighing 1.24ct. (Lawrence Fine Art) $3,744

A pair of Victorian gold earrings, each of pear shape with raised oval centers. (Lawrence Fine Art) $423

A diamond and pearl brooch of rectangular form. (Lawrence Fine Art) $7,488

An Art Nouveau circular mirror pendant, set with small rose diamonds. (Christie's) $1,096

A tortoiseshell necklace carved with eleven female heads, divided by a graduating ram's mask, with a similar pair of earrings. (Lawrence Fine Art) $1,269

A peridot, diamond and pearl pendant, the central peridot measuring 19.6 x 14.3mm. (Lawrence Fine Art) $1,674

A Victorian diamond Indian star brooch. (Lawrence Fine Art) $748

An emerald and diamond ring, the square cut emerald flanked by three old cut diamonds on an 18ct. gold shank. (Lawrence Fine Art) $1,914

A brooch, pierced and engraved with a fawn among foliage, stamped Georg Jensen 925 S 256. (Christie's) $124

An emerald and diamond cluster ring on a plain shank with bifurcated shoulders. (Lawrence Fine Art) $1,036

A pendant, white metal, designed by P. Wolfers, stamped Wolfers Freres 80, P.W. 1903. (Christie's) $375

A pair of diamond clip brooches, each of open scroll form set with various brilliant and eight-cut stones. (Lawrence Fine Art) $3,828

A Van Cleef & Arpels ruby, diamond and cultured pearl circle and twin rosette and tassel brooch, stamped Paris 34220. (Christie's) $2,049

A Victorian brooch formed of interwoven gold scrolls set with chrysoberyls and amethysts. (Lawrence Fine Art) $733

An emerald and diamond ring, the central emerald within a surround of forty-two diamonds, on a plain shank. (Lawrence Fine Art) $1,116

An emerald, gold and enamel brooch, together with a pair of emerald cluster earrings. (Lawrence Fine Art) $1,244

A diamond three-stone ring, claw set on an 18ct. gold shank. (Lawrence Fine Art) $1,709

A 9ct. gold, diamond and ruby bar brooch, in the form of a diamond set fox mask with ruby eyes. (Lawrence Fine Art) $227

A ruby and diamond ring, the central ruby calculated as weighing 2.37ct. (Lawrence Fine Art) $3,581

A jade pendant carved with three geese amongst lotus and rockwork, with white gold clip and chain attachment, approx. 46 x 17 x 6mm. (Christie's) $3,166

A sapphire and diamond ring, the central sapphire weighing 14.61ct. on a plain shank. (Lawrence Fine Art) $1,754

A jade cylindrical section mounted as a ring in gold, approx. 20 x 12.3 x 2.5mm. (Christie's) $1,333

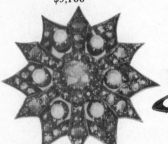

A sapphire and pearl star pendant brooch, one blue stone is a synthetic sapphire replacement. (Lawrence Fine Art) $651

A tree brooch designed by Henning Koppel, stamped HK Georg Jensen, 323, circa 1950. (Christie's) $375

One of a pair of jade bangles, overall diam. approx. 74mm., the thickness 9mm. (Christie's) $2,916

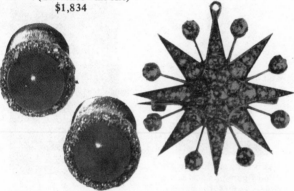

An emerald five-stone ring, the stones graduating from the center, on a plain gold shank. (Lawrence Fine Art) $1,834

An enamel and scarab bracelet, yellow metal, the scarab in oval mount, stamped 585.(Christie's) $1,409

A diamond five-stone ring, the central stone calculated as weighing 1.01ct., on a gold shank. (Lawrence Fine Art) $2,197

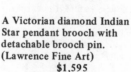

A pair of jade circular cabochons, mounted as earrings in white gold, each with a border of nineteen diamonds. (Christie's) $458

A Victorian diamond Indian Star pendant brooch with detachable brooch pin. (Lawrence Fine Art) $1,595

A pair of earrings, yellow metal, design attributed to H. Koppel, stamped Georg Jensen 1119. (Christie's) $437

A Victorian diamond and turquoise bangle, centered by five old cut diamonds on a Maltese Cross. (Lawrence Fine Art) $1,302

A jade oval cabochon mounted as a ring in white gold, the cabochon approx. 25.2 x 16.2 x 6mm. (Christie's) $4,166

A gold and blue enamel memorial reliquary brooch enclosing a lock of Wellington's hair, engraved on reverse 'Died 14 Sept 1852'. (Christie's) $546

481

A red lacquer circular box and cover, Qianlong, 21.5cm. diam., in fitted box. (Christie's) $997

An 18th century Korean inlaid silver flecked brown lacquer box and cover, 65.5cm. wide. (Christie's) $4,127

A red lacquer peach-shaped box and cover, Qianlong, 37cm. wide. (Christie's) $2,851

A Momoyama period lacquer Christian shrine (seigan), 49.3cm. high. (Christie's) $101,088

A late Ming gilt lacquered wood figure of a seated dignitary, 16th/17th century, 80cm. high, with wood stand. (Christie's) $1,995

A 19th century rectangular lacquer kashibako, unsigned, 15 x 10cm., with hinoki box. (Christie's) $1,698

A carved red lacquer square center table, Qianlong, 87cm. high, 105cm. wide. (Christie's) $4,989

A 19th century lacquer sake ewer with black and gold lacquer handle, 13.5cm. diam. (Christie's) $277

A rectangular black lacquered chest, nagamochi, with carrying handles, late Edo period, 146.3cm. wide. (Christie's) $7,344

LAMPS

Late 19th century boule student lamp with lithophane shades, Germany, 23½in. high. (Robt. W. Skinner Inc.) $1,600

Victorian brass coach lamp, 1880. (British Antique Exporters) $52

A Regency ormolu hall lantern with glazed hexagonal body and foliate corona, 31½in. high. (Christie's) $5,011

A 19th century gilt metal hall lantern with bevelled glazed hexagonal body with scrolled corona, 37in. high. (Christie's) $1,722

A Tiffany Studios favrile glass and bronze ten-light lily lamp, 19½in. high. (Woolley & Wallis) $6,576

Early 20th century Tiffany blue iridescent candle lamp, signed, 1924, New York, 12¼in. high. (Robt. W. Skinner Inc.) $950

A Legras etched and enamelled glass table lamp with mushroom shaped shade, 50.6cm. high. (Christie's) $2,349

'Nymph among the bullrushes', a bronze table lamp cast after a model by Louis Convers, 28.1cm. high. (Christie's) $751

A Tiffany Studios gilt bronze and glass table lamp, stamped Tiffany Studios New York 590, 48cm. high.(Christie's) $2,505

An early 20th century Handel lamp on Hampshire pottery base, with Mosserine shade, 20in. high. (Robt. W. Skinner Inc.) $900

A Victorian iron lamp with green tole shaft, stamped Palmer & Co. Patent, 32in. high. (Christie's) $2,035

An early 20th century pairpoint table lamp with blownout shade, New Bedford, 14in. diam. (Robt. W. Skinner Inc.) $1,400

A George III ormolu hall lantern with arched glazed cylindrical body, 20in. diam. (Christie's) $6,428

A Fulper pottery 'Vase-Kraft' table lamp, circa 1915, 18in. high, 16½in. diam. (Robt. W. Skinner Inc.) $5,600

A plique a jour and metal lantern, each panel depicting a female figure in the manner of Robt. A. Bell, 34.5cm. high. (Christie's)$2,522

An Art Nouveau bronze oil lamp base with jeweled glass shade and glass funnel, cast after a model by G. Leleu, circa 1900, 57cm. without funnel. (Christie's) $867

One of a pair of brass electric headlamps, stamped 'Carl Zeiss Jena', 10½in. diam. (Christie's) $124

One of a pair of mid 19th century French ormolu mounted turquoise glazed baluster vase lamps of Louis XVI design, 25in. high. (Christie's) $4,276

An Empire ormolu lamp bouillotte with tole shade and two adjustable branches, 23½in. high. (Christie's) $2,280

A mid 19th century overlay kerosene lamp, probably Sandwich, 11¾in. high. (Robt. W. Skinner Inc.) $600

A Restoration bronze and ormolu candlestick lamp with tripod base and fringed green silk shade, 21in. high, including shade. (Christie's) $861

One of a pair of black painted and brass carriage lamps, stamped 'Howes & Burley patent No. 2070', 17¼in. high. (Christie's) $86

A Gustav Stickley hammered copper lamp with willow shade, circa 1905, signed, 22in. high, 20in. diam. (Robt. W. Skinner Inc.) $1,500

A carved cameo helmet shell lamp, probably Italy, depicting Homer and nine muses dancing, 11½in. high. (Robt. W. Skinner Inc.) $250

A late Georgian silver plated Corinthian column lamp, 30½in. high, including shade. (Christie's) $1,566

One of a pair of brass Lucas 'King of the Road' paraffin side lamps, inscribed No. 624, 10½in. high. (Christie's) $186

A tole urn decorated in lacquer with flowers and with pleated silk shade, 27½in. high, including shade. (Christie's) $1,800

LAMPS

A Doulton Flambe figure by Noke, modelled as a seated Buddha, mounted as a lamp, circa 1930, 57.5cm. high. (Christie's) $1,252

A lampe bouillotte with green silk shade, fitted for electricity, 26in. high. (Christie's) $2,035

A Daum Art Deco table lamp, frosted glass with wrought iron, engraved with cross of Lorraine, circa 1925, 46cm. high. (Christie's) $4,698

An Art Deco bronzed electric table lamp on oval base with onyx stand, 20in. high. (Anderson & Garland) $397

A Galle blowout lamp, varying shades of red on an amber ground, signed, circa 1900, 44.5cm. high. (Christie's) $59,508

A Galle triple overlay cameo glass lamp, blue and green over a pale amber ground, circa 1900, 61cm. high. (Christie's) $14,094

A Galle double overlay and wheel-carved glass table lamp, the matt-yellow ground overlaid in brown, blue and purple, circa 1900, 52.5cm. high. (Christie's) $9,396

A plated two-branch student's oil lamp with green tinted shades. (Peter Wilson & Co.) $244

Victorian spelter lamp, signed Louis Moreau, 1880. (British Antique Exporters) $399

486

LAMPS

A Victorian three-branch brass light fitting, 1880. (British Antique Exporters) $210

A 1950's French floor lamp, the black painted stand in the form of a stylized praying mantis, 162.4cm. high. (Christie's) $503

A lampe bouillotte with three candlebranches and pleated green silk shade, 20in. high. (Christie's) $2,114

A bronze, marble and glass lamp cast after a model by M. Le Verrier, signed, circa 1925, 86.2cm. high. (Christie's) $2,035

A patinated bronze and ormolu baluster vase, with ivory silk shade, 24½in. high. (Christie's) $2,349

A Galle double overlay cameo glass lamp, circa 1900, 32.4cm. high. (Christie's) $10,962

A Regency gilt metal hanging lantern, fitted for electricity, 19in. wide, 42in. high. (Christie's) $7,356

Victorian brass desk lamp, 1900. (British Antique Exporters) $87

A Louis Comfort Tiffany bronze leaded glass and favrile glass two-light table lamp, 56cm. high. (Christie's) $6,264

Fine French marble bust, 1870. (British Antique Exporters) $441

One of a pair of Verde di Prato models of lions, 21¼in. wide, 16½in. high. (Christie's) $4,071

A white marble bust of a bearded gentleman, with draped shoulders, 30in. high. (Christie's) $330

A white marble relief of a Roman Emperor in white and gold oval frame, 7½in. high. (Christie's) $626

An early 19th century Italian white marble reduction of a sarcophagus, 9½in. wide. (Christie's) $1,174

A Bilbao looking glass with pink marble rectangular frame with gilt beaded borders, 30in. high. (Robt. W. Skinner Inc.) $2,200

Late 17th/early 18th century ·Roman white marble bust of the head of Laocoon, 27in. high. (Christie's) $10,962

A marble relief of a Roman Emperor on a blue ground, in giltwood frame, 8½ x 7in., and another similar. (Christie's) $2,662

A marble statuette of a maiden in classical dress, signed P. Barzanti Florence, 44in. high. (Worsfolds) $2,736

MARBLE

A white marble bust of an elderly man with draped head and shoulders, 28in. high. (Christie's) $225

A white marble sculpture of a standing naked Venus, 26in. high. (Lots Road Chelsea Auction Galleries) $562

A white marble group of a mother and child with a deer, inscribed G. Geefs Premier, Statuaire de S.M. le Roi, 42in. high. (Christie's) $1,200

A white marble classical female torso, Greco-Roman, circa 200 B.C., torso 8½in. (Robt. W. Skinner Inc.) $1,300

A 19th century Indian, Jaipur, white marble bench, the back and sides pierced with trellis and foliage, 60in. wide. (Christie's) $2,250

A white marble figure of Venus seated on a fountain with cupids embracing below, 55in. high, the cylindrical plinth 28in. high.(Christie's) $5,250

A pair of Breccia and black marble obelisks, 15in. high. (Christie's) $643

A marble rectangular relief of a man with a laurel wreath, in giltwood frame, 6¼ x 5½in. (Christie's) $265

Sienna marble column, circa 1860. (British Antique Exporters) $257

A Chippendale mahogany
looking glass, New Eng-
land, circa 1800, 30in.
high. (Robt. W. Skinner
Inc.) $800

Late 18th century George
III dressing mirror with
desk, 19in. wide. (Christie's)
$830

Late 18th century courting
mirror, North Europe, 23in.
high. (Robt. W. Skinner
Inc.) $3,100

A Federal gilt gesso looking
glass, circa 1815. (Robt. W.
Skinner Inc.) $2,700

A walnut and marquetry
mirror with later bevelled
rectangular plate, 32½ x
37in. (Christie's)
$2,035

A walnut and parcel gilt
mirror with waved arched
cresting, 63 x 32in. (Christie's) $3,527

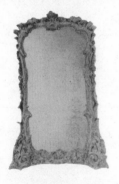

A mid 18th century German
stained oak mirror, 62 x
41in. (Christie's)
$3,110

Victorian inlaid rosewood
overmantel, 1860. (British
Antique Exporters)
$392

A giltwood mirror of Regency
design, the sides with ho-ho
birds, 72 x 48in. (Christie's)
$4,665

Late 18th century Oriental lacquered dressing stand, China, 17in. wide. (Robt. W. Skinner Inc.) $1,100

An 18th century Chippendale carved giltwood oval wall mirror, 122cm. high. (Andrew Grant)$8,352

A Queen Anne scarlet lacquer toilet mirror with fitted interior, 18½in. wide. (Christie's) $2,818

A 17th century Spanish parcel gilt and grained mirror, 40½ x 28½in. (Christie's) $544

A Chippendale curly maple mirror, New Hampshire, circa 1773, 18¼in. long. (Robt. W. Skinner Inc.) $2,900

One of a pair of George II cream painted mirrors, 68 x 33½in. (Christie's) $11,745

An Irish, George III giltwood mirror with oval plate, 32¼ x 20½in. (Christie's) $5,011

A George III giltwood mirror with shaped rectangular plate, 49 x 27in. (Christie's) $4,071

An 18th century giltwood mirror with oval bevelled plate, 49 x 36in.(Christie's) $3,421

A Chippendale mahogany and giltwood mirror, circa 1770, 55in. high. (Robt. W. Skinner Inc.) $3,000

A Regency giltwood convex mirror with two candle-branches, 31½ x 32in. (Christie's) $5,637

A mid 18th century Chippendale rococo style carved and gilded wood wall mirror, 65in. high. (Dacre, Son & Hartley) $7,200

Victorian mahogany marble top toilet mirror, 1860. (British Antique Exporters) $230

An early George II walnut toilet mirror, the box base with three drawers with brass knob handles, 17in. high. (Woolley & Wallis) $648

An ornate Victorian mahogany toilet mirror, 1860. (British Antique Exporters) $210

A gilt gesso mirror with scrolling candle-branches with turned nozzles, 45½in. x 26½in. (Christie's) $7,074

A late 18th century Anglo-Indian vizagapatam toilet service veneered with engraved ivory. (Christie's) $6,026

A giltwood pier glass with arched plate, possibly Scandinavian, 72 x 31in. (Christie's) $2,505

A George I walnut and parcel gilt mirror, 37 x 17in. (Christie's) $4,374

A George III giltwood mirror, the oval plate with rope-twist slip, 48 x 28in. (Christie's) $3,991

A German Art Nouveau bronze domed mirror, 21in. high. (Christie's) $604

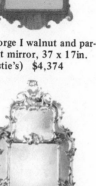

A mid Georgian giltwood mirror with shaped divided plates, 63 x 32in. (Christie's) $8,553

A 19th century birchwood toilet mirror, the oval plate in Gothic arched frame, 29in. wide. (Christie's) $1,096

A giltwood mirror in the mid Georgian style, second quarter 18th century, 95 x 49in. (Christie's) $9,477

An Irish, George III, giltwood architectural pier glass by J. & W. Booker of Dublin, 78 x 45½in. (Christie's) $8,683

A Queen Anne walnut toilet mirror, the sloping flap enclosing a fitted interior, 18in. wide. (Christie's) $2,263

A George II giltwood mirror with rectangular bevelled plate, 46 x 25in. (Christie's) $5,132

A Chippendale mahogany veneer and giltwood looking glass, England or America, circa 1770, 39½in. high. (Robt. W. Skinner Inc.) $2,100

A Regency giltwood and ebonized overmantel in the manner of Thos. Hope, 58½ x 50in. (Christie's) $9,396

A Federal gilt convex mirror, circa 1820, 27½in. high. (Robt. W. Skinner Inc.) $500

An Irish, George III mirror, with later oval plate, 25½ x 17½in. (Christie's) $3,834

A 17th century Flemish ebony and tortoiseshell mirror, 34½ x 28¾in. (Christie's) $1,710

A George III giltwood mirror, the pierced rockwork frame with foliate C-scroll cresting, 44 x 25in. (Christie's) $7,516

An early 18th century William and Mary walnut veneered mirror, 20in. wide. (Robt. W. Skinner Inc.) $1,400

A giltwood overmantel of George III style, 78 x 72in. (Christie's) $10,179

A George III giltwood mirror with later rectangular plate, 64 x 42in. (Christie's) $14,877

One of a pair of George III giltwood mirrors, 45 x 24½in. (Christie's) $8,990

A William and Mary marquetry and oyster-veneered walnut mirror, 48 x 30½in. (Christie's) $11,745

Late 18th century courting mirror, Northern Europe, 21 x 10in. (Robt. W. Skinner Inc.) $1,600

A Queen Anne gilt gesso mirror, fitted with a pair of late Regency gilt brass candlebranches, 47 x 21½in. (Christie's) $5,011

A mirror attributed to Bugatti, various woods decorated with beaten copperwork and copper and pewter inlay, circa 1900, 66 x 61.8cm. (Christie's) $2,035

A Queen Anne giltwood mirror, 47 x 27½in. (Christie's) $3,132

A Chippendale inlaid mahogany mirror, possibly N.Y., 1760/80, 43½in. high. (Christie's) $1,320

A Irish, George III giltwood overmantel with shaped divided plates, the upper panel painted with a Venetian scene. (Christie's) $23,490

A George II gilt gesso mirror with bevelled rectangular plate, 42½ x 23in. (Christie's) $2,662

A Victorian quillwork basket, circa 1880.(British Antique Exporters)$55

A miniature Federal painted and decorated pine blanket chest, Penn., circa 1810/30, 26½in. wide. (Christie's) $24,200

An early 19th century rectangular Roman micromosaic panel, 2¾in. long. (Christie's) $2,975

Two fragments of early George III printed wallpaper, after C. N. Cochin the Younger, 44½ x 22½in. and 47½ x 22¾in. (Christie's) $482

An Empire mahogany miniature sofa, American, circa 1840, 19in. wide. (Christie's) $1,430

One of two sheets of Chinese wallpaper painted in fresh colors , 18th century, 92 x 38in. (Christie's) $1,749

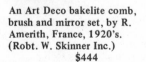

A papier mache model of Nipper with electrically operated wagging tail, 17in. high, in EMI wooden dispatch case. (Christie's) $682

An Art Deco bakelite comb, brush and mirror set, by R. Amerith, France, 1920's. (Robt. W. Skinner Inc.) $444

A 19th century reddish-brown agate bust of a male carved in the antique manner, 3½in. high.(Christie's) $388

Early 19th century micro-
mosaic plaque, depicting the
Temple of Vesta at Tivoli,
2½in. long. (Christie's)
$1,174

A smoked crystal figure of
a hawk, perched on a rocky
outcrop, 9in. high.
(Lawrence Fine Art)
$303

Late 19th century Oriental
carved coral figural group,
8in. long. (Robt. W. Skinner Inc.) $296

Late 18th century George
III mahogany inlaid miniature chest of drawers, 12in.
wide. (Christie's)
$1,540

An ivory staff, the knob
and handle carved with
swarming and entwined
rats, 9¾in. long. (Reeds
Rains) $460

An early 19th century miniature Dutch marquetry and
mahogany bureau. (Woolley
& Wallis) $580

A 19th century Italian mosaic
picture panel, four pigeons
drinking from a bronze bowl,
5½ x 4in. (Peter Wilson & Co.)
$417

A Victorian mahogany min-
iature work table with silk
covered base, 12in. high.
(Christie's) $524

A 19th century large papier
mache tray with raised rim,
30½ x 22in. (Lawrence
Fine Art) $2,472

A Roman rectangular micro-mosaic box top depicting Pliny's Doves of Venus, circa 1840, 3in. long. (Christie's) $1,487

Mid 19th century soapstone group. (British Antique Exporters) $22

An early 19th century American hooked rug, 34in. deep, 53in. wide. (Christie's) $660

A group of yacht 'Gore' sail design books, by the Ratseys and Lapthorn sailmaking firm, New York, 1902-60. (Christie's) $8,250

A group of late 18th century cream-colored wax bust-length profile medallions, each 2¼in. high.(Christie's) $622

A pair of Regency gilt plaster candlesticks, the base inscribed G. Bullock Pub Jan 1804, 24in. high. (Christie's) $3,288

A chromium plated and enamelled Brooklands Aero-Club badge inscribed 21, 3¾in. high. (Christie's) $520

A percussion trap gun with 12in. barrel, combined external spring hammer and rod trigger on swivel pivot mount. (Christie's) $139

One of a pair of glazed waxed octagonal reliefs of Robt. Adam after Tassie, 6 x 4½in. (Christie's) $1,331

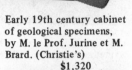

A pair of Victorian wax reliefs of Queen Victoria and Prince Albert, in mahogany frame, 6 x 8½in. (Christie's) $187

Late 19th century American molded zinc mastiff figure, 48in. high, 48in. wide. (Robt. W. Skinner Inc.) $1,400

Early 19th century cabinet of geological specimens, by M. le Prof. Jurine et M. Brard. (Christie's) $1,320

An Eley 'Sporting and Military' cartridge board, including brass rifle and pistol cartridge cases and tins of primers etc., in its oak frame. (Christie's) $205

Pair of Georgian straw-work pictures of the Church at Chilton, Wiltshire, and the Parsonage, 7 x 9½in. (Christie's) $1,331

A silhouette of a young woman in original gold leaf frame, America, circa 1830, image 7¼ x 5in. (Robt. W. Skinner Inc.) $2,600

A Spanish Colonial dress saddle with white leather seat and pommel, also a pair of 'Botas' leggings, 30in. long. (Robt. W. Skinner Inc.) $925

A refrigerator decorated by Piero Fornasetti, on black painted tubular steel framed base, 70cm. wide. (Christie's) $861

One of twenty sheets of Chinese wallpaper painted in fresh colors. (Christie's) $78,408

A 20th century American model of the extreme clippership 'Cutty Sark', on a walnut base, fitted in a glass case. (Christie's) $1,320

A contemporary early 19th century French prisoner of war bone and horn model man of war reputed to be the French ship of the line 'Redoubtable' of 74 guns, 20½ x 26¾in. (Christie's) $11,600

Late 18th century prisoner-of-war carved ivory ship, with rigging and thirty-four gun ports, Europe, 13½in. long. (Robt. W. Skinner Inc.) $800

A planked and rigged model of a Royal Naval Cutter built by I. H. Wilkie, Sleaford, 36 x 42in. (Christie's) $507

A planked and framed fully rigged model of the Royal Naval armed brig H.M.S. 'Grasshopper' of circa 1806, built by R. Cartwright, Plymouth, 32 x 41in. (Christie's) $942

Early 19th century prisoner-of-war bone model of a ship-of-the-line, 7¾in. long. (Christie's) $3,190

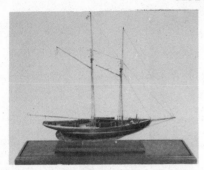

A 20th century American model of a fishing schooner, 'Kearsar', fitted in a glass case, 33½in. long. (Christie's) $935

A 19th century three-masted ship model, sails furled, approx. 36in. long. (Robt. W. Skinner Inc.) $500

A detailed ¼in.:1ft. model of a twelve gun brig of circa 1840 built to the plans of H. A. Underhill by M. J. Gebhard, Tottenham, 36 x 47in. (Christie's) $4,350

A 19th century carved bone model of a frigate, probably French, 16½in. long. (Christie's) $3,080

An early 19th century French prisoner-of-war bone model of a ship-of-the-line, 8½in. long. (Christie's) $2,530

Early 19th century prisoner-of-war bone model of a First Class ship-of-the-line, 21in. long. (Christie's) $9,900

A 7¼in. gauge model of the Great Western Railway 15XX Class 0-6-0 Pannier tank locomotive No. 1500, rebuilt by F. West, Lee Green, 21 x 55in. (Christie's) $7,250

A gauge 0 live steam spirit-fired model of the S.E.C.R. steam railcar, by Carette, circa 1908. (Christie's) $1,450

A collection of the Great Western Railway coaching stock including the twin bogie full brake No. 188, the six wheel full brake No. 95 and the four wheel horsebox No. 88, painted by L. Goddard. (Christie's) $362

A 7¼in. gauge model of the Great Western Railway 4-6-0 locomotive and tender No. 1011 'County of Chester' rebuilt and reboilered by F. West, 21¾ x 10in. (Christie's) $17,400

A 5in. model of the London and North Eastern Railway Class A3 4-6-2 locomotive and tender No. 2568 'Sceptre' built by K. Edge, 1975, 15 x 75in. (Christie's) $4,640

A gauge 0 (3-rail) electric model of a Continental 4-6-2 'Pacific' locomotive and twin bogie tender, Ref. No. HR64/13020, by Marklin, circa 1930. (Christie's) $1,965

A 3½in. gauge model of the 4-4-0 locomotive and tender No. 573 built to the designs of 'Virginia', 11½ x 45in. (Christie's) $1,305

A 7mm. finescale two rail electric model of the London Midland and Scottish Railway Class 7P 4-6-2 locomotive and tender No. 6231 'Duchess of Athol' as built in 1938, the model by D. Jenkinson and painted by L. Goddard, 3¾ x 20½in. (Christie's) $1,087

A gauge 0 (3-rail) electric model of a Continental Doll BLS electric engine, with overhead pantograph, by Bing, circa 1930. (Christie's) $262

An exhibition standard 5in. gauge model of the William Dean diagram 21 Brake Composite twin bogie passenger coach No. 3391 of 1897, 13 x 57in. (Christie's) $2,610

A detailed exhibition standard 5in. gauge model of the British Railways Class 7 4-6-2 locomotive and tender No. 70000 'Britannia', 14 x 76in. (Christie's) $8,700

A 7mm. finescale two rail electric model of the London Brighton and South Coast Railway Stroudley Class D1 0-4-2 side tank locomotive No. 351, built by B. Miller, 3¾ x 8¾in. (Christie's) $609

A 5in. gauge model of the Great Western Railway 4-6-0 locomotive and tender No. 6011 'King James I' built by K. Edge, 15 x 73in. (Christie's) $7,540

A 5in. gauge model of the Great Northern Railway Stirling Single 4-2-2 locomotive and tender No. 9 built by H. Bannister, Burton-on-Trent, 15 x 58in. (Christie's) $4,060

A 3½in. gauge model of the London and North Eastern Railway Class B1 4-6-0 locomotive and tender No. 8301 'Springbok' built by T. Dyche, York, 10¼ x 47in. (Christie's) $2,465

A 5in. gauge model of the London Midland and Scottish Railway re-built Scot Class 4-6-0 locomotive and tender No. 6154 'The Hussar' built by K. Edge, Peterborough, 15½ x 70in. (Christie's) $4,350

A 5in. gauge model of the Great Western Railway 0-6-0 Pannier tank locomotive No. 9716 built to the designs of Pansy, 13½ x 34in. (Christie's) $2,030

A 7mm. finescale two rail electric model of the British Railways (ex L.M.S.) 0-6-0 'Jinty' side tank locomotive No. 47469, built by M. H. C. Models, Bolton, 3½ x 8½in.(Christie's) $609

A gauge 0 clockwork model of the London Midland and Scottish Railway 4-4-0 locomotive and six-wheel tender No. 5320 'George V', by Bing for Bassett-Lowke. (Christie's) $217

An exhibition standard 5in. gauge model of the Great Western Railway Dean Single 4-2-2 locomotive and tender No. 3012 'Great Western', 14 x 61in. (Christie's) $10,150

A 1½in. scale model of a spirit-fired Shand-Mason horsedrawn fire engine of 1894. (Phillips) $1,176

A scale model of a Ferguson TE20 tractor and plough, 15¾in. long overall. (Lawrence Fine Art) $421

An exhibition standard model of the three cylinder compound surface condensing vertical reversing marine engine fitted to the Cunard Liner S.S. 'Servia' and modelled by Thos. Lowe, 1907, 14½ x 12½in. (Christie's) $5,075

A fine contemporary late 19th century small, full size, single cylinder horizontal mill engine, measurements overall 18 x 25in. (Christie's) $968

A well engineered 3in. scale model of a Suffolk Dredging tractor, built by C. E. Thorn, 27 x 30in. (Christie's) $705

A 2in. scale model of a single cylinder three shaft two speed Davey-Paxman general purpose agricultural traction engine built by A. R. Dyer & Sons, Wantage, 23½ x 38in. (Christie's) $2,610

A finely engineered, exhibition standard 1in. scale model of the single cylinder two speed four shaft general purpose agricultural traction engine 'Doreen', built to the designs of 'Minnie', by H. A. Taylor, 1980, 11½ x 18in. (Christie's) $1,617

A 1½in. scale model of a Burrell single crank compound two speed three shaft general purpose agricultural traction engine, built by J. B. Harris, Solihull, 15½ x 25in. (Christie's) $3,190

A finely engineered and well presented model 'M E', center pillar beam engine, built by K. R. F. Kenworthy, measurements overall 13 x 17½in. (Christie's) $1,192

A detailed steam driven model of a Bengali Die Mixing plant, built by A. Sare, Northleach, measurements overall 18½ x 24in. (Christie's) $1,043

An exhibition standard 2in. scale model of the Burrell 5 n.h.p. double crank compound two speed three shaft 'Gold Medal' tractor, engine No. 3846, Registration No. AD7782 'Poussnouk-nouk', built from works drawings by P. Penn-Sayers, Laughton, 19¾ x 27¼in. (Christie's) $10,875

An early 20th century model single cylinder surface condensing 'A' frame beam engine, 19½ x 24in. (Christie's) $2,465

A chromium plated Goddess of Sport, inscribed A.E.L., 5in. high. (Christie's) $176

A brass buckle depicting a copulating couple, incorporating a chassis, 4in. long. (Christie's) $220

A chromium plated and enamelled Brooklands B.A.R.C. badge inscribed 100, 3¾in. high.(Christie's) $210

The Spirit of Triumph, a chromium plated figure, 6½in. high, on mahogany base. (Christie's) $68

Six Brooklands Official Race Cards and Programmes for 1937. (Onslows) $60

A nickel plated brass car mascot, caricature figure of an airman with printed porcelain head and moveable helmet, inscribed Hassall, 4¼in. high. (Christie's) $620

A chromium plated and gilt desk timepiece modelled as an Edwardian tourer, 8½in. high. (Christie's) $661

A chromium plated decanter in the form of a Bugatti radiator, by Classic Stable Ltd., 6¾in. high. (Onslows) $390

The Brooklands Gazette, Vol. 1 no. 3, September 1924. (Onslows) $82

MOTORING ITEMS

A spelter smoker's compendium modelled as a sports roadster, 9in. long. (Christie's) $441

'Cinq Chevaux', a Lalique car mascot molded in clear glass, etched France No. 1122, 11.5cm. high. (Christie's) $3,445

'Levrier', a Lalique car mascot, clear and satin finished glass molded in intaglio with a racing greyhound, 7.5cm. high. (Christie's) $406

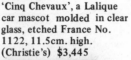

A brass nymph holding a torch in front with leg raised and trailing scarf, 5¾in. high. (Christie's) $74

Official Programme for the 200 Miles Race, October 1927 and the Brooklands Lagonda 2nd Annual Fete Programme, 1928. (Onslows) $84

'Grenouille', a Lalique car mascot in clear and satin finished glass molded as a seated frog, 6.3cm. high. (Christie's) $5,011

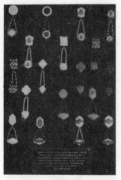

Part of a collection of 62 members' badges and guest brooches, in mahogany display case. (Onslows) $4,800

A chromium plated stylized eagle perched on a globe, inscribed 'C. Brau', 8½in. high. (Christie's) $73

Five Brooklands Official Race Cards and Programmes for 1938 and 1939. (Onslows) $48

MOTORING ITEMS

A nickel plated Milegal 'Meter', 4¼in. diam. (Onslows) $75

A chromium plated Boa-Constrictor horn with mounting brackets and extension, 45in. long. (Christie's) $80

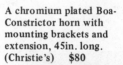

A chromium plated stylized cat, stamped Nikolsky No. 14, 6in. long. (Christie's) $117

A brass bust of Minerva, stamped, 6in. high, on circular plinth.(Christie's) $173

An A. T. Speedometer Co. Ltd. Bentley 6½ or 8 litre speedometer, and a rev counter. (Onslows) $300

A nickel plated speed nymph clutching a scarf, by Lejeune, stamped Reg. AEL, 6in. high. (Christie's) $186

One of two photographs of Leyland-Thomas No. 1 Babs, signed by Parry Thomas. (Onslows) $180

A chromium plated stork, 7in. long. (Christie's) $68

Harrods Ltd. Automobiles, Petrol Steam Electric Cars, Motorcycles Accessories of All Descriptions, catalogue with prices and text, circa 1903. (Onslows)$195

MOTORING ITEMS

Souvenir of the Brooklands Automobile Racing Club, July 6th 1907. (Onslows) $150

A glass mascot in the form of two leaping Borzoi dogs, possibly Red Ashay, 7½in. long. (Christie's) $588

A chromium plated stylized Jaguar Mascot, No. 7100911 WBB, 7½in. long, mounted on circular ashtray. (Christie's) $173

A chromium plated A.A. badge inscribed 'Stenson Cooke, Secretary, No. 12162', 5½in. high. (Christie's) $66

The Austin Magazine, original artwork for the Christmas Number, December 1937, signed, watercolor , 21½ x 17in. (Christie's) $161

A chromium plated charging Red Indian, 6in. long. (Christie's) $74

Six Brooklands Official Race Cards and Programmes for 1936. (Onslows) $69

'Mother', a corning glass female head with flowing hair, 6½in. long. (Christie's) $99

Motor Sport, Vol. 5 no. 1, October-November 1928. (Onslows) $210

A 19th century Swiss musical box, the movement playing twelve airs, striking on six bells and a drum, 25½in. long. (Woolley & Wallis) $1,315

A Gramophone & Typewriter Ltd. New Style No. 3 gramophone, with 7in. turntable and concert soundbox, circa 1904. (Onslows) $834

A Columbia type BS coin-operated graphophone with floating reproducer and glazed oak case. (Christie's) $1,224

A Spanish 32-note miniature barrel piano with castanet and triangle, playing six tunes, 24in. wide, on wood handcart. (Christie's) $554

An Edison Diamond disc phonograph in walnut case of Louis XV design, 50in. high, and 46 Edison discs. (Christie's) $1,188

A Gramophone & Typewriter Ltd. single-spring Monarch, with Kayophone soundbox and original Morning Glory horn. (Onslows) $447

A fairground organ with 58-note paper roll reed-organ action, in covered trolley, 100in. wide, with 63 Angelus/Symphony rolls. (Christie's) $2,376

An Edison Fireside combination type phonograph, Model B No. 89443, with four minute gearing. (Onslows) $700

A buffet style musical box playing eight airs accompanied by drum and six bells with tune indicator, 28in. wide. (Christie's) $2,160

A harp mandolin musical box playing 16 airs (2 per turn), by J. H. Heller, Bern, No. 4534, with zither attachment, 28½in. wide. (Christie's) $1,984

An Edison Standard phonograph, Model C No. 660275, with combination gear and Bettini reproducer. (Onslows) $357

Late 19th century singing bird music box, Switzerland, with bird-shaped key, 4in. wide. (Robt. W. Skinner Inc.) $2,220

An Edison Red Gem phonograph, Model D No. 316478D, with K combination reproducer, maroon fireside octagonal horn and crane. (Onslows) $491

A 19th century square section bird cage of wire and turned wood, the base containing a musical box, 17in. high. (Peter Wilson & Co.) $201

A Decca Dulcephone horn gramophone with fine tin flower horn. (Onslows) $268

A Viel-O-Phone horn gramophone, with light oak case applied with company transfer, and fluted brass horn. (Onslows) $447

A 26-key barrel organ by Willm. Hubt. Van Kamp, Holborn, with two eleven-air barrels and four pipe ranks with stops, 89in. high. (Christie's) $1,860

An HMV horn gramophone, the square oak base with 10in. diam. turntable, with plywood horn, 17½in. diam circa 1920. (Lawrence Fine Art) $503

A changeable cylinder overture box by Nicole Freres, with five cylinders each playing four tunes, 38in. wide. (Christie's) $5,760

An early Kammer & Reinhardt Berliner gramophone with gilt-lined japanned cast iron base. (Christie's) $691

A gilt metal and enamel singing bird box, decorated with Watteauesque scenes. (Christie's) $990

An 11.7/8in. Symphonion disc musical box with twin comb movement in rococo simulated case, with 15 discs. (Christie's) $1,364

An oak HMV Monarch gramophone, 1911 model, with double-spring motor and fluted oak horn. (Christie's) $691

A 15.5/8in. Polyphon in panelled walnut case with double combs and forty-seven discs in circular wood box. (Christie's) $2,304

A portable street reed barrel organ by Chiappa, playing seven tunes, on thirty-one notes, 22in. wide. (Christie's) $4,032

A 15-key chamber barrel organ by H. Bryceson, 38 Long Acre, in mahogany case, 59¾in. high. (Christie's) $1,612

A musical box playing 12 sacredains accompanied by 9 bells with bee strikers, 31in. wide. (Christie's) $2,108

Late 19th century French key-wind singing bird automaton, 4in. wide. (Reeds Rains) $604

A lever wind musical box, by Nicole Freres, No. 51725, playing 4 overtures, with tune sheet and rosewood veneered case, 27½in. wide. (Christie's) $3,300

An HMV Model 29 horn gramophone with single-spring motor in oak case, the horn 18½in. diam., circa 1928. (Christie's) $259

A 14in. Stella disc musical box with twin-comb movement in walnut case with disc storage drawer, and 13 discs. (Christie's) $1,736

A 19.1/8in. upright Symphonion disc musical box with 'Sublime Harmony' combs, and six discs. (Christie's) $2,448

A horn gramophone with mahogany case of HMV Model 7 design, double spring motor and brass flower horn. (Christie's) $547

A horn gramophone with oak case, Big Ben No. 1 sound-box and blue flower horn of early Morning Glory pattern. (Christie's) $259

A 19th century German Symphonion having walnut case inlaid with ivory, 11 x 13in., also a collection of eight discs. (Peter Wilson & Co.) $561

An HMV Junior Monarch oak horn gramophone with panelled oak case, soundbox replaced. (Christie's) $744

An Italian violin,
by Joseph Rocca,
1850, length of
back 13.15/16in.,
in oak case.
(Christie's)
$40,154

A violin by Ernest
L. Holder, dated
1913, length of
back 14in.
(Phillips)
$2,072

An English violin,
by Arthur Richard-
son, 1928, length
of back 13.15/16in.,
with bow. (Chris-
tie's)
$2,007

A French violin by
Jean-Baptiste
Vuillaume, length
of back 14½in., in
case. (Christie's)
$15,876

An English violin, by
Lockey Hill, length
of back 13.7/8in.,
in case. (Christie's)
$5,556

Early 20th century
violoncello, length
of back 30in., with
two bows. (Reeds
Rains) $518

An Italian violin by
Giulio & Eugenio
Degani, the length
of back 14in., in
case with two bows.
(Christie's)
$6,123

An Italian violin by
Eugenio Degani,
1896, the length of
back 14.1/8in.
(Christie's)
$6,123

MUSICAL INSTRUMENTS

A violin by Vincenzo
Carcassi, Florence,
dated 1763, length
of back 13.7/8in.
(Phillips)
$13,320

An Italian violin by
Ferdinando Gagliano,
length of back
13.7/8in. (Christie's)
$23,133

A French violin,
by Joseph Hel,
1878, length of
back 14.3/16in.,
in case. (Christie's)
$4,533

An Italian violin by
Joseph Rocca,
length of back 14in.,
in case with bow.
(Christie's)
$38,102

An Italian violin by
Nicola Gagliano, 1761,
the length of back 14in.,
in case. (Christie's)
$13,122

A French violin by
Jean-Baptiste
Vuillaume, length
of back 14.1/16in.
(Christie's)
$28,576

A violin by Richard
Duke, London, circa
1770, length of back
14in., with a bow in
shaped case. (Phillips)
$3,700

A French violin by
Caressa & Francais,
1903, the length of
back 14.1/16in.,
in case with two
bows. (Christie's)
$3,645

An Italian violin by
R. Antoniazzi, 1910,
the length of back
13.14/16in., in
double violin case
with two silver moun-
ted bows. (Christie's)
$4,374

An Italian violin,
by H. Fagnola,
1893, length of
back 14.3/16in.,
in case. (Christie's)
$13,899

An Italian violon-
cello by Romeo
Antoniazzi, 1910,
length of back 29.
13/16in., in case
with bow.
(Christie's)
$14,580

An Italian viola
labelled Antoniazzi
Romeo Cremonese/
fece a Cremona
l'anno 1910, length
of back 15.11/16in.
(Christie's)
$6,998

An Italian violin,
by G. Gagliano,
1765, length of
back 13.15/16in.,
in case. (Christie's)
$30,888

An Italian violin by
A. Orlandini, 1976,
the length of back
14.1/16in., in case
with bow.(Christie's)
$1,458

A French viola,
labelled Bennettini
Milano 1881, length
of back 15¾in.
(Christie's)
$2,625

A violin ascribed to
Bernard Calcanus,
1749, the length of
back 14in., in case.
(Christie's)
$6,561

A violin, possibly
Neapolitan School,
length of back 14.
3/16in., in case.
(Christie's)
$2,625

A French violin by
Jean-Baptiste Vuil-
laume, the length
of back 14in., in
case. (Christie's)
$18,954

A French viola by
Justin Derazey,
the length of back 16.
1/16in., in case.
(Christie's)
$3,790

An Italian violin by
R. Antoniazzi, 1910,
the length of back
14in. (Christie's)
$4,665

An Italian violin,
labelled Leandro
Bisiach, Milano
1895, length of
back 14.1/16in.,
in case. (Christie's)
$9,266

A violin ascribed
to Giovanni Gaida,
length of back
13.15/16in., in
case. (Christie's)
$4,015

An English violin,
by John Lott,
length of back
14in., in case.
(Christie's)
$23,166

An English violin,
by Wm. Atkinson,
1905, length of
back 14in. (Chris-
tie's)
$1,158

NETSUKE

Late 18th century ivory netsuke of a dragon coiled around a wave-beaten rock, unsigned. (Christie's) $881

A 19th century ivory netsuke of a Temple horse being groomed, signed Kigyoku, Edo School. (Christie's) $660

Early 19th century ivory netsuke of a green frog sitting on an awabi shell, unsigned. (Christie's) $499

Early 19th century well-carved boxwood netsuke of a snail, signed Shigemasa. (Christie's) $1,909

A 19th century boxwood netsuke of a monkey, unsigned. (Christie's) $395

Early 19th century ivory netsuke of Hotei holding an uchiwa, inscribed Okakoto. (Christie's) $233

Early 19th century ivory netsuke of Kanzan and Jittoku reading a makimono, unsigned. (Christie's) $514

Early 20th century stained ivory netsuke of a partly open chestnut, signed Yazan. (Christie's) $660

An 18th century ivory netsuke of a Chinese sage, signed Yoshitomo (Boku-saisai), Kyoto School. (Christie's) $1,762

NETSUKE

Late 18th century wood netsuke carved as a group of five clam shells, signed Sari, Iwashiro School. (Christie's) $734

A 19th century wood netsuke of a cicada on half a walnut, unsigned. (Christie's) $527

A 19th century ivory netsuke of a dove on a group of three lotus leaves, the eyes inset in dark horn. (Christie's) $674

A 19th century ivory netsuke of a large rat gnawing at a sheaf of millet, inscribed Okatomo. (Christie's) $1,028

A 19th century ivory netsuke of a cicada, signed Masatsugu. (Christie's) $5,875

Late 19th century ivory netsuke of a monkey and her two young, signed Masatami (Shomin), Yamada School. (Christie's) $1,395

Late 19th century boxwood okimono-style netsuke of the Sennin Shiyei, signed Kogyoku (Anrakusai). (Christie's) $660

A 19th century wood and ivory manju-type netsuke in the form of a gourd, signed Yamahiko. (Christie's) $514

An ivory netsuke of Nitta No Shiro Tadatsune about to stab the boar, inscribed Masakazu. (Christie's) $1,028

A wood and ivory netsuke of a kneeling fox priest, signed Kaigyokusai. (Christie's) $4,324

An ivory netsuke of a catfish, inscribed Masanao, probably Meiji-Taisho period. (Christie's) $1,111

Early 19th century carved kurogaki netsuke of a squatting toad, signed Yoshitada(?), Echigo School. (Christie's) $617

A 19th century marine ivory netsuke of a seated puppy playing with an awabi shell, unsigned. (Christie's) $261

Late 19th century ebony and ivory netsuke of a standing karako, unsigned. (Christie's) $849

Late 19th century ivory okimono style netsuke of two seated Manzai dancers, signed Fujiyuki. (Christie's) $308

Late 19th century lacquered netsuke of a monkey dressed as a Sambaso dancer, unsigned. (Christie's) $540

A 19th century boxwood netsuke of a dragon coiled inside a pumpkin, style of Toyomasa, Tamba School. (Christie's) $400

Late 19th century ivory netsuke of Daikoku, signed Masatamo. (Christie's) $308

A 19th century ivory net-
suke of a shrimp, unsigned.
(Christie's) $1,698

Mid 19th century ivory netsuke of a tigress seated with
her cubs, signed Hakuryu,
Kyoto School. (Christie's)
$2,625

A 19th century pale boxwood
netsuke of a cicada, signed
Issai. (Christie's) $1,028

A late 18th century wood
netsuke of a seated tigress
licking her cub, signed Kokei,
Tsu School. (Christie's)
$1,248

A marine ivory netsuke of a
faceless female ghost rising
from her grave, unsigned,
circa 1800, 10cm. high.
(Christie's) $4,406

Mid 19th century circular
ivory manju netsuke carved
in shishiaibori, signed Ono
Ryomin. (Christie's)
$849

Late 19th century ivory
okimono-style netsuke of a
monkey, signed Masatami
(Shomin), Yamada School.
(Christie's) $734

A 19th century okimono
style ivory netsuke of the
Annamese tribute elephant,
signed Shibayama. (Chris-
tie's) $1,389

Late 19th century ivory
netsuke of Ebisu, signed
Eishin. (Christie's)
$386

Mid 19th century ivory netsuke of a karako stooping to lift Hotei's tasselled bag, signed Komin, and kao. (Christie's) $308

An ivory netsuke modelled as a flatfish, signed Hodo, probably Neiji-Taisho period. (Christie's) $647

Late 18th century ivory netsuke of a karashishi lying down, unsigned. (Christie's) $694

An ivory netsuke of a maddened bull about to charge, unsigned, probably Taisho-Showa period. (Christie's) $617

An early/mid 19th century well-carved ivory netsuke of a Chinese festival boat, signed Ryukosai. (Christie's) $386

An ivory netsuke of a seated ape munching a persimmon (kaki), signed Kaiguoku. (Christie's) $15,444

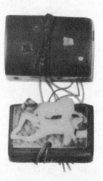

A 19th century well carved boxwood netsuke of a group of vegetables and fruits, signed Shuji. (Christie's) $849

Late 19th century ivory manju netsuke decorated in Shibayama style, signed Nobuyuki. (Christie's) $463

Late 19th century pale box-wood netsuke of a chest tied with a tasselled rope, signed Tomoyuki. (Christie's) $1,028

A 20th century boxwood netsuke of the 'Miraculous Tea Kettle' Legend, unsigned. (Christie's) $734

Late 18th/early 19th century wood netsuke of The Great Wanderer Saigyo Hoshi contemplating Mount Fuji. (Christie's) $514

Early 19th century ivory netsuke of a quail on a sheaf of millet, inscribed Okatomo, Kyoto School. (Christie's) $1,028

An early/mid 19th century ivory netsuke of a professional sneezer, signed Ryuko, and kao. (Christie's) $679

Early 19th century ivory netsuke of a sumo wrestler, unsigned. (Christie's) $2,162

A 19th century stained boxwood netsuke of the Bodhidharma, signed Minko, (probably Juntoku). (Christie's) $1,544

Late 19th century ivory okimono style netsuke of a group of five terrapins, signed Chuichi. (Christie's) $617

A 19th century dark wood manju netsuke decorated in Shibayama style, unsigned. (Christie's) $431

Early 19th century ivory netsuke of a monkey cradling one of its young, unsigned. (Christie's) $540

Bahamas: 1937 4/-, plus Bermuda 1937 5/-
and 1957 5/-. (Phillips) $75

Cyprus: 1955-57 Queen Elizabeth II set of
250 mils—£5. (Phillips) $255

Lincoln & Lindsey Banking Co: £5 proof on
card, plus a letter dated 1839, instructing
Perkins, Bacon & Petch to print and deliver
4,000 £5 notes. (Phillips) $56

C. P. Mahon: Bank of England £5, 10 October
1925 issued at Leeds. (Phillips) $138

South Africa: 1864 Durban Bank £25.
(Phillips) $184

1927 50 tomans Pick Plate Note, some pieces
missing top edge. (Phillips) $568

Ireland, Northern Bank: £5 proof on paper
1850, plus Ulster Bank £5 1942 and 1943.
(Phillips) $93

Provincial Bank: £1 and £3 1881 plus £1 1882,
all proofs on paper with signature area cut out.
(Phillips) $191

Costa Rica: 1928 Banco Internacional 2 colones plus 1925 10 colones. (Phillips) $150

Bolivia: 1911 El Banco Mercantil 10 bolivares. (Phillips) $90

New Zealand: 1916 Bank of Australasia £1 issued at Wellington. (Phillips) $300

Newmarket Bank: £5 1899, overstamped 'Cancelled' twice. (Phillips) $56

Russia: 1819 10 roubles State Assignat. (Phillips) $71

National Bank: £1 Specimen 1870. (Phillips) $149

Argentina: 1880 Banco Otero & Ca. 20 pesos proof, engraved by Bradbury Wilkinson. (Phillips) $130

Bury & Suffolk Bank: (Oakes, Bevan & Co.), £5 un-issued. (Phillips) $67

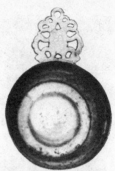

Mid 19th century pewter flagon, the cast handle with heart-shaped end drop, base marked James Dixon, 13in. high. (Robt. W. Skinner Inc.) $350

A pyriform teapot, by Thos. Danforth, Conn., 1805-50, marked on bottom, 7in. high. (Christie's) $935

A pewter porringer, by Samuel or Samuel E. Harbeson, Providence R.I., circa 1780-1820, marked on handle with Laughlin touch 337, 4in. diam. (Christie's) $605

One of two pewter beakers, by James Weekes, New York City, 1820-35, 3.1/8in. high. (Christie's) $308

A Kayersinn pewter jardiniere, stamped Kayersinn 4093, 29.8cm. high. (Christie's) $375

A Liberty pewter and enamel clock, designed by A. Knox, stamped 0608 Rd, 426015, 14cm. high. (Christie's) $1,446

A pewter porringer, by Wm. Billings, Providence R.I., circa 1791-1806, marked on handle with Laughlin touch 346, 4.1/8in. diam. (Christie's) $330

A WMF rectangular shaped pewter mirror, 14in. high, stamped marks. (Christie's) $691

A pewter covered flagon, the flat lid with ball finial and cast C-scroll handle, 9½in. high. (Robt. W. Skinner Inc.) $300

Early 19th century unmarked pewter porringer, with Rhode Ialand flowered handle. (Robt. W. Skinner Inc.) $200

A teapot, the domed lid with finial, by Morey & Ober, Boston, 1852-55, 7½in. high. (Christie's) $275

One of a pair of late 18th/ early 19th century, German, pewter flagons, 17¼in. high. (Christie's) $440

A water pitcher, by Roswell Gleason, circa 1830, 11½in. high, together with a coffee pot and a water cooler. (Christie's) $418

A WMF silvered pewter jardiniere cast as a conch shell with a salamander, 32cm. high. (Christie's) $702

A lighthouse shaped flagon, by Thos. D. Boardman, marked with eagle touch, name touch and Hartford touch on base, 13¼in. high. (Christie's) $1,870

A Liberty pewter and Clutha glass bowl on stand, designed by Archibald Knox, stamped Tudric 0276, circa 1900, 16.3cm. high. (Christie's) $656

A 17th century pewter charger with reeded rim, 22in. diam. (Woolley & Wallis) $1,957

A pewter tankard, by Henry Will, New York, marked on inside with Laughlin touch 491, 7.1/8in. high. (Christie's) $3,300

An apple-shaped teapot, by Roswell Gleason, Mass., 1821-71, 7½in. high. (Christie's) $176

A Liberty pewter and green glass bowl, designed by A. Knox, stamped Tudric 0320 Rd, 426933, 20.3cm. diam. (Christie's) $532

A pewter bedpan, by Thos. D. and S. Boardman, Hartford, 1810-50, initial touch struck once on base, 17½in. long, overall. (Christie's)$385

A 19th century pewter leech jar, the pierced lid with carrying handle, 7in. high. (Christie's) $382

A Jugendstil polished pewter triptych mirror in the style of P. Huber, 32.2 x 53.4cm. (Christie's) $626

A covered pitcher, by Boardman, Boardman & Hart, 1828-53, marked on bottom, 7¾in. high. (Christie's) $660

One of two similar Italian, late 18th/early 19th century, pewter flagons, 14¼in. high. (Christie's) $528

A pair of pewter fluid lamps, by James H. Puttnam, Mass., 1830-55, 7¾in. high. (Christie's) $660

A tankard with a domed lid and scrolling thumbpiece, late 18th/early 19th century, unmarked, 6¼in. high. (Christie's) $1,540

A pewter covered Church tankard of lighthouse shape with C-scroll handle, circa 1766. (Robt. W. Skinner Inc.) $550

A pyriform teapot, by Wm. Calder, Providence R.I., 1817-56, marked on base, 7in. high. (Christie's) $2,640

A pewter porringer, by J. Danforth, Jnr., Virginia, circa 1807-1812, 5in. diam. (Christie's) $1,760

A lighthouse coffee pot, by Israel Trask, Mass., circa 1813-56, marked on base, 10½in. high. (Christie's) $605

A WMF electroplated pewter drinking set with shaped rect-angular tray, circa 1900, tray 48 x 34cm. (Christie's) $946

One of a pair of mid 19th century pewter lanterns. (Robt. W. Skinner Inc.) $500

An electroplated pewter mirror frame attributed to WMF, circa 1900, 50cm. high. (Christie) $630

A pair of early 19th century English pewter candlesticks, 9in. high. (Christie's) $75

A tapering, cylindrical cann, by Robt. Palethorp, Phila., 1817-22, marked inside, 4.1/8in. high. (Christie's) $1,980

Eight mammoth albumen prints of the classical architecture of Rome, 16 x 12½in. to 21in., early 1860's, photographer unknown. (Christie's) $691

Royal Engineers album of 84 photographs , comprising ten salt prints, the remainder albumen, 1862-64. (Christie's) $1,584

A whole plate cased daguerreotype of a riverside mansion, the oval mat stamped 'Electrotypo', 'Fredricks e Weeks', 1850's. (Phillips) $4,116

Still-life with game, stereoscopic daguerreotype, paper label in image reading 'Mr T. R. Williams, 35 West Square, Lambeth', paper cased, 1850's. (Christie's) $547

Ten waxed paper negatives, five 10¼ x 12in., five 7 x 9in., by William Robert Baker, early 1850's. (Christie's) $1,152

'Princess Alice, 1854', by Roger Fenton, albumen print, 5 x 6¾in. (Christie's) $562

A half plate cased daguerreotype of riverside houses, the oval mat stamped 'Electrotypo', 'Fredricks e Weeks', 1850's. (Phillips) $4,410

A leather bound album, embossed 'Jerusalem, 1865' and titled on flyleaf 'Ordnance Survey of Jerusalem . . . by Capt. Charles W. Wilson, R.E. . . . 1865'. (Phillips) $2,499

'Camera Work', Nos. XXIV and XL, original wrappers, 4to., New York: Alfred Stieglitz, October 1908 and October 1912. (Christie's) $1,170

A half plate part cased daguerreotype of a riverside mansion, 1850's. (Phillips) $1,323

A gelatin silver print of 'Mary, Santa Marta', by D. Lyon, ref. no. '11/78/2' on reverse, 8½ x 12½in. (Christie's) $80

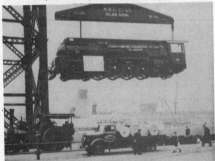

Standing female nude, stereoscopic daguerreotype, gilt painted passe-partout, paper cased, re-bound, 1850's. (Christie's) $864

Album of 79 albumen prints and one two-print panorama, of Ceylon, Burma and Singapore, by W. L. H. Skeen & Co., Scowen and others. (Christie's) $936

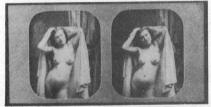

Northern British Locomotive Co. Ltd., approx. 120 gelatin silver prints, from 4½ x 6in. to 10 x 15in., majority 1900-20, all captioned and documented on the reverse. (Christie's) $234

A whole plate cased daguerreotype of a harbor, the oval mat stamped 'Electrotype', 'Fredricks e Weeks', 1850's. (Phillips) $6,615

An 1850's scrap album, including twelve salt prints from paper negatives, various sizes up to 23 x 19cm. (Phillips) $235

An albumen print of a man and woman, mounted on paper, 1870's or early '80's, 5¾ x 4¼in. (Christie's) $33

An albumen print of two men, mounted on paper, 1870's or early '80's, 5¾ x 4¼in. (Christie's) $113

Profile portrait of a young woman, albumen print, by O. G. Rejlander, circa 1860, 7¼ x 5¾in. (Christie's) $134

An albumen print of a young woman in studio setting, 5¾ x 4¼in., 1870's or early '80's. (Christie's) $87

A gelatin silver print of 'Peruvian Women', by Robt. Frank, 13½ x 11in. (Christie's) $241

A gelatin silver print of Cecil Beaton, by E. Blumenfeld, 1940's, 13 x 10in. (Christie's) $643

'Cathedral de Mollins', albumen print, by Chas. Marville, 1860's, 14 x 9¾in. (Christie's) $536

'Princess Royal & Prince Arthur as Summer', by Roger Fenton, albumen print, 1854, 6 x 6¼in. (Christie's) $348

Cathedrale de Mayence, facade sud-est', Blanquart-Evrard salt print, by Chas. Marville, early 1850's, 13½ x 10in. (Christie's) $938

A gelatin silver print of 'London, Two Gentlemen', by Robert Frank, 9½ x 6¼in. (Christie's) $402

Palais du Louvre and Palais des Tuileries, four albumen prints, approx. 10¼ x 13¼in., 1850's or early 1860's. (Christie's) $214

An autotype print of Chas. Hay Cameron, by Julia Margt. Cameron, 1869, 12½ x 9¾in. (Christie's) $402

An album of 168 albumen prints of India and Ceylon, by Bourne, Shepherd and Bourne & Shepherd, 1890's, 9 x 11in. (Christie's) $1,072

A gelatin silver print of 'NYC 1949', by Robert F. Frank, signed in ink in margin, 1949, 10½ x 14in. (Christie's) $737

An albumen print of Nguni-speaking women, 5¾ x 4¼in., mounted on paper, 1870's or early '80's. (Christie's) $201

A collection of 53 waxed paper negatives, 29 approx. 13 x 9in., the others 7½ x 9in., by G. Shepherd, 1853 and 1854. (Christie's) $1,340

A gelatin silver print of 'Mohandas Gandhi', by Margt. Bourke-White, 13½ x 10¼in. (Christie's) $562

A glossy gelatin silver print of 'Carnival Girls', by Robt. Doisneau, 12 x 9½in. (Christie's) $134

Portfolio, 'Idylls of the Norfolk Broads', by Peter Henry Emerson, cover design by T. F. Goodall, oblong folio, London, 1886. (Christie's) $1,820

A glossy gelatin silver print of Backstage Ballet Girls by Gotthard Schuh, 1950's, 11½ x 9½in. (Christie's) $67

Spring Morning, Busbridge, by Henry Taylor, salt print, 8¼ x 6½in. (Christie's) $241

An albumen print of Julia Jackson, by Julia Margt. Cameron, 1860's, 10¼ x 8¾in. (Christie's)$402

Prince Albert, albumen print, mounted on card, 6¾ x 6in., 1854, by Roger Fenton. (Christie's) $804

A gelatin silver print of 'A New Way to Look at the Statue of Liberty', by Margt. Bourke-White, 13½ x 10½in. (Christie's) $402

'Illustrations to Tennyson's Idylls of the King, and other poems', by Julia Margaret Cameron, publ. Henry S. King & Co., London, 1875.(Phillips) $3,234

A Scottish Pictorial album of 69 photographs and six loose prints, platinum and gelatin silver prints, early 1900's to 1920's. (Christie's) $172

'The Hairy Family of Mandalay', albumen print, 8½ x 7.1/8in., mounted on card, 1860/70, photographer unknown. (Christie's) $338

PHOTOGRAPHS

Three cased quarter plate daguerreotype of two brothers, with a cased plate ambrotype of one brother alone. (Phillips) $352

A gelatin silver print of Marilyn Monroe, by Cecil Beaton, 1940's, image size 7¼ x 7¼in. (Christie's) $174

An albumen print of Chas. Darwin, by Julia Margt. Cameron, 1868, 12½ x 10½in. (Christie's)$113

A half calf gilt album, 'Photographs from Abyssinia', with printed list of contents. (Phillips) $882

A gelatin silver print of 'Cyril Ray in Islington', titled in ink on the reverse, by Bill Brandt, 9 x 7.5/8in. (Christie's) $294

A 4¼ x 5¾in. daguerreotype with rounded top, of three little sisters in matching dresses, the front of the case embossed 'Prof. Highschool Daguerreotype Institution, 433 West Strand'. (Phillips) $191

A gelatin silver print of Ava Gardner, by Man Ray, 13¾ x 10¾in., signed and dated in pencil on image, 1950. (Christie's) $720

A gelatin silver print of an 'East End Girl, Dancing The Lambeth Walk', dated in ink on the reverse 1939, by Bill Brandt. (Christie's) $670

Portrait album of 48 albumen prints, approx. 7½ x 6in. to 13½ x 10½in., by R. T. Crawshay, 1870's. (Christie's) $1,728

A Federal mahogany pianoforte, label G. Gilfert, N.Y., circa 1805, 63in. long. (Robt. W. Skinner Inc.) $3,400

An English spinet by Baker Harris, 1766, in a mahogany case, on a stand of Virginia walnut, 74in. wide. (Christie's) $19,828

A 4ft. overstrung baby grand piano with steel frame and mahogany case, by A. Ramsden, Leeds. (Peter Wilson & Co.) $1,656

An upright grand pianoforte, iron framed, overstrung and underdamped movement, by R. Gors & Kallmann. (Capes, Dunn & Co.) $1,008

An English spinet by Thos. Hitchcock, in a case of Virginia walnut, on a later oak stand, circa 1725, 74in. wide. (Christie's) $8,019

A marquetry boudoir grand piano by Steinway & Sons, the case by C. Mellier & Co., 57 x 86in. (Christie's) $11,502

A classical mahogany pianoforte, labelled by P. & W. Geib, 68in. wide. (Christie's) $2,200

An Eavestaff Art Deco mahogany and satinwood baby grand piano, inlaid metal inscription Healy, circa 1930, 151.2cm. wide. (Christie's) $3,468

A concert grand pianoforte, by C. Bechstein, the rosewood case with square section trestle type supports, 8ft. x 5ft.2in. (Parsons, Welch & Cowell) $2,625

A pianoforte by Wm. Southwell of Dublin, in the form of a semi-elliptical side table, 32½in. high, circa 1785. (Christie's) $34,992

A classical carved mahogany pianoforte, by James L. Hewitt & Co., Boston, 1820-30, 67in. wide. (Christie's) $1,650

An overstrung grand pianoforte, seven and a quarter octaves, by T. H. Steinway, no. 10625, in a painted satinwood case, 65in. wide. (Christie's) $13,500

A gentleman facing right in black coat and waistcoat, by Alexander Gallaway, oval, 3in. high. (Christie's) $652

A gentleman facing right in powder-blue coat, by Gervase Spencer, enamel, signed with initials and dated 1753, oval, 1½in. high. (Christie's) $1,010

Edward Salmond in blue coat, by William Bone, signed on the reverse and dated 1821, oval, 3.1/8in. high. (Christie's) $466

A gentleman full face in green coat, by Charles A. Claude Berny d'Ouville, signed, oval, 3in. high. (Christie's) $466

A gentleman full face in black coat and waistcoat, by T. or J. Wheeler, locks of hair reverse, oval, 1½in. high. (Christie's) $201

The Revolutionary Chaumette full face in gray coat, by Claude Alexandre Belin, oval, 2½in. high. (Christie's) $544

A gentleman full face in blue coat, by Christian F. Zincke, enamel, oval 1.5/8in. high. (Christie's) $1,010

A fine portrait of Mrs. Charles Edward Smith, by Richard Crosse, oval, 6.1/8in. high. (Christie's) $185

The Hon. Francis Bowes Lyon as a child, by Miss Annie Dixon, oval, 4in. high. (Christie's) $1,166

PORTRAIT MINIATURES

Abdul Mejid, Sultan of Turkey during the Crimean War, by Jean Portet, oval 1.3/8in. high. (Christie's) $434

Miss Sharp facing left in blue dress, by Samuel Shelley, oval, 1¾in. high. (Christie's) $933

A gentleman facing left in blue coat, by Charles Shirreff, oval, 1¾in. high. (Christie's) $1,010

Captain Sir J. Wheate, R.N., by John Ramage, plaited hair reverse, oval, 1½in. high. (Christie's) $1,244

A gentleman facing left in blue coat, by Thos. Hazlehurst, oval 1.3/8in. high. (Christie's) $434

Lieutenant Charles Howard, by Sir Wm. John Newton, oval, 2½in. high.(Christie's) $247

One of two children in white shifts, by Henry Burch, oval, 1½in. high.(Christie's) $777

Mrs. Siddons in brown dress with white edges, by Samuel Shelley, signed with initials and dated 1783, oval, 3.3/8in. high. (Christie's) $1,710

The Countess of Rochester, by D.M., circa 1660, oval, 2½in. high. (Christie's) $372

William Pitt (the Younger), plaited hair on reverse, by Michael Keene, oval, 1½in. high. (Christie's)$652

A gentleman in red coat, by Horace Hone, signed and dated 1783, oval, 2¾in. high. (Christie's) $1,866

A gentleman facing right, by Wm. Marshall Craig, the reverse with gold monogram HW on plaited hair, oval 2.5/8in. high. (Christie's) $699

A boy full face in blue coat, by Aimee Thibault, signed, oval, 2½in. high. (Christie's) $544

A child full face in white shift, English School, circa 1830, oval, 2½in. high. (Christie's) $777

A gentleman in brown coat, by Gervase Spencer, enamel, signed with initials and dated 1755, oval, 1.5/8in. high. (Christie's) $777

Captain Salmond in blue coat with black collar, by George Engleheart, oval, 3¼in. high. (Christie's) $1,166

A gentleman facing right in black coat, by Simon J. Rochard, oval, 1¼in. high. (Christie's) $699

A gentleman facing right in black coat, by Thos. Day, signed with initials and dated 178(1), oval, 1½in. high. (Christie's) $544

Napoleon III, by Jean Baptiste Fortune de Fournier, signed and dated 1857, oval, 1.5/8in. high. (Christie's) $745

A miniature of a young man by Francois Ferriere, signed and dated 1800, oval, 3½in. high. (Christie's) $1,088

Francois Courtier, later Madame Navarre, by Jean Marie Voille, signed and dated l'an 1e (1793), oval, 2.5/8in. high. (Christie's) $4,043

The Hon. Mrs. Stewart facing left in white dress, by John Bogle, signed with initials and dated 1801, oval, 2½in. high. (Christie's) $1,710

Lady Emily Hervey, by Nathaniel Hone, signed with initials and dated 1760, oval, 1½in. high. (Christie's) $1,244

A gentleman facing left in blue coat, by Sampson T. Roche, signed and dated 1811, oval, 3in. high. (Christie's) $313

A gentleman facing left in blue coat, by Richard Conway, oval, 3¼in. high. (Christie's) $1,944

A fine portrait of a gentleman called George Frederick Handel (1685-1759), by Christian F. Zincke, enamel, oval, 1.5/8in. high. (Christie's) $1,710

A girl facing left in a white dress, the reverse with locks of hair, by Andrew Plimer, oval, 3in. high. (Christie's) $1,866

Edward Maria Lichnowsky
in gray coat, by Christian
Tangermann, signed and
dated 1812, 3¼in. high.
(Christie's) $5,594

A lady called Princess Amelia,
by Richard Cosway, dated
1801, 3¼in. high.(Christie's)
$2,237

A nobleman in crimson
coat and lace jabot, by
Christian F. Zincke, 1.5/8in.
high. (Christie's)
$1,118

A lady facing right in decol-
lete white dress, Circle of
Engleheart, signed with
monogram, 3in. high.
(Christie's) $719

A gentleman full face in blue
coat, School of Daubigny,
3in. diam. (Christie's)
$434

Maria Pavlovna, by Alois G.
Rockstuhl, after Lampi,
signed and dated 1864, 4in.
high. (Christie's)
$3,036

Frederick V, Elector Palatine,
King of Bohemia, enamel,
by Henry Pierce Bone, 3.5/8in.
high. (Christie's) $670

A lady holding a rose, by
Castor, Gonzalex Velazquez,
signed, 2¼in. diam.
(Christie's) $544

Alexander, 6th Earl of Gallo-
way, by James Reily, signed
with initials and dated 1773,
oval, 1¾in. high. (Christie's)
$341

Charles II facing right in lace jabot, by David des Granges, oval, 1in. high. (Christie's) $622

Christiane Lichnowsky in white dress and pink stole, by Heinrich F. Fuger, 3in. high. (Christie's) $14,385

General Ernest Frederick Gascoigne, as a child, by Andrew Plimer, signed with initials and dated 1787, gold frame, 2.1/8in. high. (Christie's) $2,397

A Don facing right in black gown and white bands, by Samuel Collins, oval, 1.3/8in. high. (Christie's) $155

The Stolen Kiss, Circle of Claude Jean Baptiste Hoin, oval, 2¾in. high.(Christie's) $933

Master James Parke, by Andrew Plimer, gold frame with split pearl border, 3in. high. (Christie's) $6,713

A portrait miniature of a gentleman in armor, by John Hoskins, signed with initials and dated 1657, 2½in. high. (Christie's) $6,713

Charles James Fox and Lord North, enamel, oval, 1.7/8in. high. (Christie's) $622

A Lady called Elizabeth, Lady Willoughby D'Eresby, by Isaac Oliver, 2.1/8in. high. (Christie's) $6,393

Camp Romain, Vin Rouge, Rose, Blanc, by L. Gadoud, lithograph in colors , on wove paper, 1600 x 1200mm. (Christie's) $240

Laren, Tentoonstelling 1916, Hotel Hamdorff, Zunki Joska, by Willy Sluiter, lithograph in colors , printed by Senefelder, Amsterdam, 1086 x 778mm. (Christie's) $420

For Real Comfort, New Statendam, Holland-America Line, by Adolphe Mouron Cassandre, lithograph in colors , 1928, 1050 x 806mm. (Christie's) $1,500

Rhum Charleston, by Leon D'Ylem, lithograph in colors , published by Vercassou, Paris, 1982 x 1275mm. (Christie's) $112

Steinhardt, Unter Den Linden, by Hans Lindenstaedt, lithograph in colors , 1912, on wove paper, 710 x 945mm. (Christie's) $450

Bruxelles, Exposition Universelle, 1935, by Marfurt, lithograph in colors , printed by Les Creations, Publicitaires, Bruxelles, 1000 x 620mm. (Christie's) $105

Etoile Du Nord, by Adolphe Mouron Cassandre, lithograph in colors , on wove paper, 1048 x 752mm. (Christie's) $1,275

Alcazar Royal, by Adolphe Crespin and Edouard Duych, lithograph in colors , 1894, 1010 x 775mm. (Christie's) $420

David Hockney at the Tate Gallery, lithograph in color , 1980, on wove paper, signed in pencil, 760 x 505mm. (Christie's) $67

Pousset Spatenbrau, by Jean Carlu, lithograph in colors , on wove paper, printed by J. E. Goosens, Lille, 795 x 508mm. (Christie's) $330

S. V. U. Manes, 150 Vystava, Clenska, lithograph in colors , 1929, printed by Melantrich Praha, Smichov, 1250 x 950mm. (Christie's) $180

'Lenin's Push Into The Business Generation', by K. Poliarkova and R. Mozchaeva, lithograph in colors , 965 x 650mm. (Christie's) $142

L'Oiseau Bleu, by Adolphe Mouron Cassandre, lithograph in colors , 1929, on wove paper, 996 x 616mm. (Christie's) $1,170

Peugeot, by Rene Vincent, lithograph in colors , printed by Draeger, 1170 x 1540mm. (Christie's) $1,200

Poster, 'P & O Cruises'. (Onslows) $139

Opera, Bal Des Petits Lits Blancs, L'Intran, by Marie Laurencin, lithograph in colors , 1931, 1600 x 1196mm. (Christie's) $1,500

G. Marconi, Le Maitre De La Radio, by Paul Colin, lithograph in colors , printed by Bedos & Cie, Paris, 1578 x 1130mm. (Christie's) $330

Soiree De Paris, Spectacles, Choregraphiques et Drama- tiques, by Marie Laurencin, lithograph in colors , signed in pencil and dated 1924, 796 x 578mm. (Christie's) $255

Jane Renouardt, by Pierre
Stephen, lithograph in colors ,
printed by M. Picard, Paris,
1538 x 1175mm. (Christie's)
$150

F. S. N. Van Hauteghem Freres,
Liege, by Milo Martinet, lith-
graph in colors , printed by
Benard, Liege, 1190 x 800mm.
(Christie's) $480

Job, by Alphonse Mucha,
lithograph in colors , 1898,
on wove paper, printed by F.
Champenoise, Paris, 1500 x
1010mm. (Christie's)
$5,250

Wilhelm Mozer Munchen-Nord
Adalbertstr, by Ludwig
Hohlwein, lithograph in
colors , 1909, on wove paper,
1250 x 911mm. (Christie's)
$270

XXVI Ausstellung Secession,
by Ferdinand Andri, lithograph in colors , circa 1904,
on wove paper, 920 x 602mm.
(Christie's) $13,050

Raphael Tuck, Celebrated
Posters No. 1501, Ogden's
Guinea Gold Cigarettes and
another. (Christie's)
$47

Exposition Des Peintres Litho-
graphes, by Fernand Louis
Gottlob, lithograph in colors ,
1899, printed by Lemercier,
Paris, 1195 x 790mm.
(Christie's) $450

G. B. Borsalino Fu Lazzaro &
C, by Marcello Dudovich,
lithograph in colors , 1932,
printed by R. Questura,
Milano, 1390 x 1000mm.
(Christie's) $375

Nord Express, by Adolphe
Mouron Cassandre, lithograph
in colors , 1927, on wove
paper, 1048 x 752mm.
(Christie's) $1,950

Raden Van Arbeid, by R. N.
Roland Holst, lithograph in
colors , on wove paper,
1084 x 794mm. (Christie's)
$600

Pierre Stephen, lithograph in
colors , on wove paper, printed by Bauduin, Paris, 1538
x 1175mm. (Christie's) $630

La Revue Des Folies Bergere,
by Jules Alexandre Grun,
lithograph in colors , 1905,
printed by Ch. Verneau, Paris,
1246 x 880mm. (Christie's)
$225

Raphael Tuck, Celebrated
Posters No. 1501, Rown-
tree's Elect Cocoa, and
two others. (Christie's)
$60

Summer; Spring; Autumn;
Winter, by Alphonse Mucha,
lithograph in colors , 1896,
on wove paper, 1040 x 530mm.
(Christie's) $10,200

Chemin De Fer, Martigny-
Orsieres, by Albert Muret,
lithograph in colors , 1913,
on wove paper, printed by
Sonor, 1000 x 700mm.
(Christie's) $525

Ein Rausch In Rot, Maskenball
Wilder Mann, by C.M.I., lithograph in colors , 1928, on
wove paper, 920 x 612mm.
(Christie's) $225

Absinthe Robette, by Privat
Livemont, lithograph in colors ,
1896, on wove paper, printed
by J. L. Goffart, Bruxelles,
1105 x 806mm. (Christie's)
$1,125

Poster, 'Dolomiten Ski-Schule
Val Gardena (Grodental)
m.1300-2200'. (Onslows)
$110

'The Champion in Luck', published by Currier & Ives, 1882, small folio. (Robt. W. Skinner Inc.) $95

'The Trotting Mare Goldsmith Maid, Driven By Budd Doble', published by Currier & Ives, 1870, large folio. (Robt. W. Skinner Inc.) $1,200

'The Great Fire at Boston', published by Currier & Ives, 1872, small folio. (Robt. W. Skinner Inc.) $425

'The Accommodation Train', published by Currier & Ives, 1876, small folio. (Robt. W. Skinner Inc.) $300

'The Celebrated Horse Dexter, 'The King Of The World' Driven By Budd Doble'', published by Currier & Ives, 1867, large folio. (Robt. W. Skinner Inc.) $2,100

'Rysdyk's Hambletonian', published by Currier & Ives, 1876, large folio. (Robt. W. Skinner Inc.) $1,700

'The Darktown Yacht Club — On The Winning Tack', published by Currier & Ives, 1885, small folio. (Robt. W. Skinner Inc.) $250

'The Four Seasons Of Life: Middle Age', published by Currier & Ives, 1868, large folio. (Robt. W. Skinner Inc.)
$1,200

'Pigeon Shooting, 'Playing The Decoy'', published by Currier & Ives, 1862, large folio. (Robt. W. Skinner Inc.)$1,500

'Camping in the Woods, 'Laying Off'', published by Currier & Ives, 1863, large folio (Robt. W. Skinner Inc.) $3,200

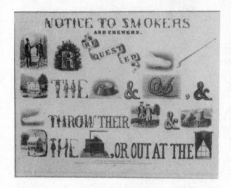

'Notice To Smokers And Chewers', published by N. Currier, 1854, small folio. (Robt. W. Skinner Inc.) $800

'Maple Sugaring', published by Currier & Ives, 1872, small folio. (Robt. W. Skinner Inc.) $650

Kupplerin, by Otto Dix, lithograph printed in red, yellow and blue, 1923, 597 x 465mm. (Christie's) $13,678

Tiger, by Franz Marc, woodcut, 1912, on Japan, early proof before the edition, 249 x 332mm. (Christie's) $1,367

Zinnie in un Vaso, by Giorgio Morandi, etching, 1932, on wove paper, first state (of two), 204 x 195mm. (Christie's) $4,023

A nude seated on a red stool, entitled 'Asa', Morning, from the series Rajo Jusshu, 48.8 x 37.7cm. (Christie's) $493

Plakat Muim Institut, by Ernst Ludwig Kirchner, woodcut printed in blue and black, 1911, on rose laid paper, 728 x 492mm. (Christie's) $7,241

Saint Jerome in his Study, by Albrecht Durer, engraving 244 x 186mm. (Christie's) $5,909

Okubi-e of the actor Ganjiro Nakamura in the role of Kamiya Jihei, signed Kamp, 42 x 27.3cm. (Christie's) $463

Der Kuss, by Edvard Munch, etching with drypoint, 1895, on firm wove paper, signed in pencil, 346 x 277mm. (Christie's) $16,092

Oban tate-e, a partly disrobed woman leaning against a pillar, signed Utamaro hitsu. (Christie's) $4,633

L'Artisan Moderne, by Henri de Toulouse-Lautrec, lithograph printed in colors, 1894, on cream wove paper, 923 x 648mm. (Christie's) $10,459

Selbstbildnis mit Frau, by Conrad Felixmuller, woodcut printed in colors, 1921, on soft Japan, 582 x 451mm. (Christie's) $9,655

Campbell's Soup, by Andy Warhol, screenprints in colors, 1969, on wove paper, 907 x 657mm., and album. (Christie's) $5,443

Melancholisches Madchen, by Ernst Ludwig Kirchner, woodcut printed in three colors from one block, 1922, on soft Japan, 752 x 445mm. (Christie's)$64,368

Yvette Guilbert, by Henri de Toulouse-Lautrec, lithographs printed in olive green, 1894, on Arches, album, 410 x 393mm. (Christie's) $11,264

From the Meisho Edo Hakkei series, Sudden Shower at Atake, signed Hiroshige ga. (Christie's) $6,949

A nude woman seated, entitled 'Dokusho', from the series Rajo Jusshu, 48.6 x 37.5cm. (Christie's) $493

Sun, from the Weather Series, by David Hockney, lithograph printed in colors, 1973, on Arjomari mold made wove paper, 750 x 645mm. (Christie's) $9,331

The actor Nakamura Kichiemon in the role of Mitsuhide, signed and sealed Shunsen. (Christie's) $386

Jahresgabe fur die Kandinsky-Gesellschaft, by Wassily Kandinsky, lithograph with extensive handcoloring , 1925, on Japan Imperial, 355 x 255mm. (Christie's) $27,356

'The Celebrated Horse Lexington (5 years old), by 'Boston' out of 'Alice Carneal'', published by N. Currier, 1855, large folio. (Robt. W. Skinner Inc.) $600

Le gros Pigeon, by Pablo Picasso, lithograph 1947, on Arches, signed and no. 29/50, 400 x 510mm. (Christie's) $5,632

Le Repos du Modele, by Henri Matisse, lithograph, 1922, on Chine volant, signed in pencil, 223 x 304mm. (Christie's) $2,735

'Ethan Allen and Mate and Dexter', published by Currier & Ives, 1867, large folio. (Robt. W. Skinner Inc.) $1,200

The Battle of the Sea Gods, the left half, by Andrea Mantegna, engraving, a clear but later impression, 296 x 413mm. (Christie's) $2,954

'Autumn Fruits', published by Currier & Ives, 1861, medium folio. (Robt. W. Skinner Inc.) $225

'The Celebrated Trotting Stallion George Wilkes, Formerly 'Robert Fillingham'', published by Currier & Ives, 1866, large folio. (Robt. W. Skinner Inc.) $1,600

Femme nue an Repos avec un Chat, by Tsuguji Foujita, etching on laid paper, signed in pencil, 355 x 455mm. (Christie's) $2,413

Adonis in Y fronts, by Richard Hamilton, screenprint in colors , 1963, signed and dated in pencil, from the edition of 40, printed by Kelpra Studio, 604 x 815mm. (Christie's) $5,909

The Portico with the Lantern, by Antonio Canal, II Canaletto, etching, third (final) state, 302 x 431mm. (Christie's) $1,710

Nature Morte, by Gino Severini, lithograph printed in colors , 1958, on BFK Rives, signed in pencil, 391 x 564mm. (Christie's) $1,609

Late 19th century crazy quilt with The Lord's Prayer, America, consisting of velvets, brocades and cottons of varying shapes, 69in. wide. (Robt. W. Skinner Inc.) $375

An appliqued coverlet with pineapple pattern, America, circa 1840, 82 x 98in. (Robt. W. Skinner Inc.) $2,000

A patchwork cover worked with hexagonal pieces of mid/late 19th century printed and plain colored cotton, 2.50 x 2.34m., lined. (Phillips) $367

Early 19th century red and blue patchwork Calamanco coverlet, America, 108 x 100in. (Robt. W. Skinner Inc.) $1,200

An appliqued quilt with attached label 'Made by Mrs. J. Walter Marshall of Old Frankport Rd., Lexington, Kentucky', circa 1860. (Robt. W. Skinner Inc.) $2,000

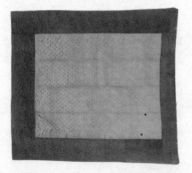

Late 18th century American Linsey-Woolsey coverlet with red center area enclosed by a green border, 85 x 93in. (Christie's) $1,210

QUILTS

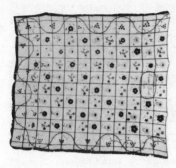

An embroidered blanket, probably New York, 'Lucretia Brush(?) Busti, 1831', large blue and white check, 6ft.4in. x 7ft.4in. (Robt. W. Skinner Inc.) $5,800

A patchwork quilt, Penn., signed and dated in ink on the back, 'Phebeann H. Salem's(?) Presented by her Mother 1848', 8ft.11in. x 9ft. (Robt. W. Skinner Inc.) $1,900

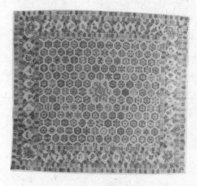

A wool bed rug, worked with a darning stitch in a tree-of-life pattern on a natural wool foundation, dated 1773, 84 x 85in. (Christie's) $11,000

An early 19th century patchwork coverlet in plain and colored printed glazed cotton, circa 1830, 2.70 x 2.24m. (Christie's) $911

A 19th century American appliqued quilt, 7ft.1in. x 6ft.2in. (Robt. W. Skinner Inc.) $1,200

A pieced and quilted cotton coverlet, lily pattern, American, circa 1900, approx. 84in. long, 80in. wide. (Christie's) $715

Early 20th century Heriz Area carpet, 9ft.8in. x 13ft. (Robt. W. Skinner Inc.) $4,250

Late 19th/early 20th century S.W. Persian Qashqai bag face, 1ft.1in. x 1ft.3in. (Robt. W. Skinner Inc.) $325

Late 19th/early 20th century Kazak rug, the red field with concentric hooked medallions, 4ft.6in. x 7ft. (Robt. W. Skinner Inc.) $2,200

Early 20th century Kurdish Kelim rug, the ivory field with red and blue forked medallions, 6ft.1in. x 8ft.4in. (Robt. W. Skinner Inc.) $275

Late 19th/early 20th century N.W. Persia, Soumak bag face, the dark blue field with medallions of various colors , 2ft.1in. x 2ft. (Robt. W. Skinner Inc.) $1,500

A Kashan embossed part silk pictorial rug, 35½ x 24½in. (Capes, Dunn & Co.) $864

A J. J. Adnet wool pile carpet in tones of russet, black, brown and beige, circa 1930, 156.5 x 144.4cm. (Christie's) $1,340

Late 19th century Caucasian Kelim, red, blue, green, yellow, black and ivory rows of stepped medallions, 5ft.5in. x 10ft.5in. (Robt. W. Skinner Inc.) $1,100

Late 19th century Kuba mat, E. Caucasus, the blue field with flowerheads of blue and red, 2ft.8in. x 2ft.9in. (Robt. W. Skinner Inc.) $800

Late18th/early 19th century Tekke main carpet, Turkestan, with five rows of ten guls. (Robt. W. Skinner Inc.) $2,300

Early 20th century Khamseh rug, S.W. Persian, with ivory, red, gold, blue, green and aubergine all over pattern, 4ft. x 6ft.3in. (Robt. W. Skinner Inc.) $550

Late 19th/early 20th century Tekke Ensi, with maroon center panel with dark blue 'candelabra' motif, 4ft. x 5ft.1in. (Robt. W. Skinner Inc.) $900

Late 19th century Eastern Caucasian/Kuba rug, woven in the afshan or 'crab-kuba' design, 3ft.5in. x 4ft.10in. (Robt. W. Skinner Inc.) $500

Late 19th/early 20th century Chi-Chi prayer rug with dark blue field, 4ft.3in. x 4ft.7in. (Robt. W. Skinner Inc.) $950

Late 19th/early 20th century Kazak rug with madder red field, 4ft.5in. x 6ft.9in. (Robt. W. Skinner Inc.) $400

Late 19th century Bergama Village rug, 3ft. x 3ft.9in. (Robt. W. Skinner Inc.) $750

A silk Kashan rug, the ivory field with a column of palmettes, 6ft.8in. x 4ft.3in. (Christie's) $5,065

Early 20th century N.W. Persia, Soumak bag face with white field, 1ft.8in. x 1ft.8in. (Robt. W. Skinner Inc.) $175

Mid to late 19th century
Kazak rug, S.W. Caucasus,
4ft.10in. x 7ft.2in. (Robt.
W. Skinner Inc.)
$2,800

An early 19th century English pile
carpet, rebacked, 27ft. x 17ft.
(Christie's) $42,854

Late 19th/early 20th cen-
tury Karabagh, S.W. Cauc-
asus, 5ft.2in. x 9ft. (Robt.
W. Skinner Inc.)
$1,100

A Kirman Laver prayer rug
with burgundy field, 6ft.
10in. x 4ft.2in. (Christie's)
$1,447

A Persian carpet sampler,
3ft.2in. x 3ft.10in. (Robt.
W. Skinner Inc.)
$1,300

Late 19th/early 20th cen-
tury Kuba rug, with a brown-
black 'wine-cup' border, 4ft.
x 6ft.1in. (Robt. W. Skinner
Inc.) $1,000

An Isfahan rug, the ivory
field with three flower vases
and flowering trees, 6ft.11in.
x 4ft.10in. (Christie's)
$4,052

Late 19th century Soumak
bag, 1ft.8in. x 1ft.9in. (Robt.
W. Skinner Inc.)
$2,000

A silk Kashan rug with yellow
gold field, 7ft.2in. x 4ft.5in.
(Christie's) $5,788

Late 19th century Yomud main carpet, W. Turkestan, featuring Dynak and 'spread eagle' guls, 5ft.4in. x 10ft.1in. (Robt. W. Skinner Inc.) $10,500

Late 19th/early 20th century Tabriz carpet, 25ft.9in. x 13ft.10in. (Robt. W. Skinner Inc.) $8,500

Late 19th/early 20th century Marasali prayer rug, E. Caucasian, with light yellow field, 3ft.7in. x 4ft.9in. (Robt. W. Skinner Inc.) $600

An early 20th century Mahal carpet with blue field of green, red, pink and light blue flowering vines, within a red floral border. (Robt. W. Skinner Inc.) $350

Late 19th/early 20th century Soumak rug, E. Caucasus, with rust-red field, 4ft.8in. 6ft.9in. (Robt. W. Skinner Inc.) $600

Early 20th century Hamadan Area rug, 4ft.10in. x 7ft.6in. (Robt. W. Skinner Inc.) $1,250

Early to mid 19th century Konya Kelim, Central Anatolia, 5ft.4in. x 10ft. (Robt. W. Skinner Inc.) $550

One of a pair of silk Kashan rugs, the ivory field with palmettes and floral sprays, 7ft. x 4ft.1in. (Christie's) $10,130

A silk Kashan rug with pistachio-green field, 6ft.8in. x 4ft.3in. (Christie's) $7,959

Late 19th century Persian Serapi carpet, 10ft. x 11ft. 9in. (Robt. W. Skinner Inc.) $13,000

Late 19th/early 20th century Kurdish Soumak salt bag, 1ft.1½in. x 1ft.6in. (Robt. W. Skinner Inc.) $350

Late 19th century Ziegler Mahal carpet, 10ft.9in. x 14ft.1in. (Robt. W. Skinner Inc.) $5,250

A Heriz carpet, the dark red field with dark blue center medallion, circa 1930's, 6ft. 10in. x 9ft.1in. (Robt. W. Skinner Inc.) $800

A silk Kashan prayer rug, the ivory field with central flower vase, 6ft.8in. x 4ft. 3in. (Christie's) $4,920

A Qum silk carpet, the ivory field with palmettes and floral sprays around a blood-red cusped panel, 12ft.11in. x 9ft.7in. (Christie's) $20,260

A Shirvan rug the center with six star medallions on a blue field and dated 1894, 6ft.5in. x 4ft.1in. (Woolley & Wallis) $1,450

Early 20th century Heriz carpet with rust-red field, 8ft. x 11ft.2in. (Robt. W. Skinner Inc.) $3,750

A Senneh rug, the indigo field divided into panels of flowering plants, wreaths and prayer arches, 6ft.8in. x 4ft. 4in. (Christie's) $4,052

Early 20th century Kashan carpet, 13ft.4in. x 9ft.9in. (Robt. W. Skinner Inc.) $3,300

An early 20th century reverse Soumak animal trapping, one bag, 1ft.3in. x 1ft. 4in., flanked by two small bags, 7 x 8in. (Robt. W. Skinner Inc.) $850

Early 20th century Tekke Main carpet, W. Turkestan, 7ft. x 9ft.10in. (Robt. W. Skinner Inc.) $2,100

A Mashad carpet with maroon field, circa 1930, 8ft.4in. x 12ft. (Robt. W. Skinner Inc.) $625

Late 19th century Bergama Village rug, W. Anatolian, 3ft.2in. x 3ft.8in. (Robt. W. Skinner Inc.) $375

A Souf silk and metal thread Kashan prayer rug, 6ft.9in. x 4ft.3in. (Christie's) $4,631

Early 20th century Afshar rug, the dark blue field with rows of large boteh, 4ft. x 6ft. (Robt. W. Skinner Inc.) $750

Late 19th/early 20th century Qashqai bag face with dark blue field. (Robt. W. Skinner Inc.) $350

Early 20th century Kazak prayer rug, S.W. Caucasus, a red field with ivory medallion, 4ft.2in. x 6ft.11in. (Robt. W. Skinner Inc.) $1,600

A Fetjiye rug in the Bessarabian style with a central medallion of roses and the date 1915, 86 x 55¾in. (Christie's) $1,566

Late 19th century Mahal carpet, 13ft.9in. x 20ft. (Robt. W. Skinner Inc.) $10,000

Late 19th century Karabagh long rug, S.W. Caucasus, 3ft.8in. x 11in. (Robt. W. Skinner Inc.) $1,300

Late 19th century Northwest Persia, Heriz-Area carpet, 11ft. x 8ft.6in. (Robt. W. Skinner Inc.) $13,000

Late 19th century Central Persian, Sultanabad carpet, the ivory field woven in all over flower filled trellis, 8ft.4in. x 10ft.5in. (Robt. W. Skinner Inc.) $2,900

Late 19th/early 20th century 'Eagle' Kazak rug, Southwest Caucasus, 5ft. 11in. x 7ft.7in. (Robt. W. Skinner Inc.) $2,100

A Kashan rug, the blue field woven with floral arabesques and centered by a brick red medallion, 6ft.10in. x 4ft. 10in. (Lawrence Fine Art) $1,530

An antique Shirvan rug with indigo field, 8ft.1in. x 3ft. 8in. (Christie's) $2,192

A Shirvan rug with multiple floral decoration on indigo field, 80 x 51½in. (Reeds Rains) $720

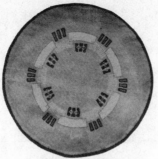

Late 19th century South
Caucasian Karabagh rug, 4ft.
4in. x 7ft.11in. (Robt. W.
Skinner Inc.)
$3,300

A Jules Leleu circular
woollen rug, 188cm. diam.
(Christie's) $1,252

A Ziegler carpet, 17ft.10in.
x 12ft. (Christie's)
$10,962

Late 19th century North-
west Persian carpet, the
yellow field woven in all
over Mina Khani floral
trellis, 10ft.5in. x 14ft.
7in. (Robt. W. Skinner
Inc.) $4,100

Late 19th century Karachoph
rug, 5ft.2in. x 6ft.4in. (Robt.
W. Skinner Inc.) $425

Late 19th century North-
west Persia, Serapi carpet,
with a 'turtle' border, 9ft.
6in. x 13ft.4in. (Robt. W.
Skinner Inc.)
$4,200

A Navajo pictorial rug,
9ft.11½in. x 5ft.5½in.
(Robt. W. Skinner Inc.)
$2,500

A 19th century Serapi carpet,
the red field with large ivory
and pale blue green medallion,
10ft.10in. x 13ft.11in. (Robt.
W. Skinner Inc.)$6,500

A Kashan carpet, the light
blue field with palmettes,
trees and floral sprays, 11ft.
3in. x 6ft.4in. (Christie's)
$5,637

A sampler by Mary-Ann Hayter, aged 8 years, 1823, worked in colored silks, 15 x 13in. (Christie's) $482

Early 19th century woolwork sampler, worked by Elizabeth Shufflebottoms 1841, 23½ x 23¾in. (Reeds Rains) $432

An early 19th century American needlework sampler, 19½ x 21in. (Robt. W. Skinner Inc.) $2,750

A sampler by Julia Matild Paisey, 1845, worked in dark silks, 16 x 12½in. (Christie's) $738

A George IV needlework sampler, by E.H., 1826, 17 x 12½in. (Graves, Son & Pilcher) $465

A needlework sampler by Mary Anne Hunter aged 14 years 1844, 26 x 16½in. (Anderson & Garland) $454

Needlework sampler, marked 'Elizabeth C. Engle's work done in the 12th year of her age, August 23th, 1837', 17½ x 17½in. (Robt. W. Skinner Inc.) $600

An American needlework sampler, signed Jane Littlefield, circa 1810, worked in silk threads on a dark green canvas, 24in. high, 15½in. wide. (Christie's) $3,740

An early 19th century needlework sampler, 'Hannah L. Slessor aged 13 years', New England, 16½ x 15½in. (Robt. W. Skinner Inc.) $850

A needlework sampler, 'Emily Furber her sampler aged 10, wrought March 16, 1827', 23 x 26in. (Robt. W. Skinner Inc.) $2,400

An early 19th century needlework sampler, 'Jane Slessors work aged 13 years January 16', New England, 17 x 17½in. (Robt. W. Skinner Inc.) $500

Needlework sampler marked 'Wrought by Sally Alden June 14 1811', Mass., 16 x 21in. (Robt. W. Skinner Inc.) $3,750

A needlework family register worked by Lucia A. Daniels in 1832, 16 x 18in. (Robt. W. Skinner Inc.) $1,000

An 18th century needlework sampler well decorated in colored silks, 17 x 12½in. (Graves, Son & Pilcher) $712

A sampler by Charlotte Way, Portland, 1841, worked in pale brown silk, 14 x 11½in. (Christie's) $198

A needlework sampler, 'Anna Fowler born March 2, 1739, this sampler I did the year 1754', 13 x 19½in. (Robt. W. Skinner Inc.) $2,300

Early 19th century needle-work sampler, 'Phebe L. Slessor work aged 11 years', New England, 16 x 16in. (Robt. W. Skinner Inc.) $900

Late 18th century needle-work sampler family record, 10½ x 16in. (Robt. W. Skinner Inc.) $3,100

BASKETS

A George II shaped oval cake basket, by Edward Aldridge, probably 1746, 14½in. long, 56oz. (Christie's) $2,397

One of a pair of George III oval dessert baskets, by Wm. Pitts & J. Preedy, 1799, 11in. long, 119oz. (Christie's) $5,594

A George II shaped oval cake basket, by Edward Wakelin, 1749, 14½in. long, 59oz. (Christie's) $4,475

A George II shaped oval bread basket, by Paul Crespin, 1753, with later Russian marks, 14½in. long, 62oz. (Christie's) $21,772

A George III sugar basket, by Abraham Peterson, 1795, 17cm. across. (Lawrence Fine Art) $510

A George III Irish cake basket, by J. Graham, Dublin, circa 1765, 35.2cm. long, 38oz. (Lawrence Fine Art) $3,581

A George II cake basket, by Eliz. Godfrey, 1743, 35.3cm. across, 64.2oz. (Lawrence Fine Art) $8,140

One of a set of seven Victorian two-handled baskets, by Carrington & Co., 1899 and 1900, one 17¾in. long, two 14in. long and two 12in. long, 212oz. (Christie's) $16,416

A George IV shaped oval cake basket, by Rebecca Emes and E. Barnard, 1827, 33.5cm. wide, 34oz. (Lawrence Fine Art) $846

BEAKERS

A Continental beaker, possibly 17th century, punched only with an Augsburg pineapple and an assay scrape, 17cm. high, 10oz. (Phillips) $1,198

A Latvian parcel gilt beaker, by J. D. Rehwald, Riga, circa 1740, 7in. high, 10oz. (Christie's) $1,395

A Dutch tapering cylindrical beaker, by Agge Jelles Reinalda, Franeker, 1669, 6¾in. high, 9oz.17dwt. (Christie's) $6,073

A 17th century Friesland beaker, by Paulus Sakes, Dokkum, 1649, 16.2cm. high, 10.25oz. (Phillips) $4,512

One of a set of six George III small silver gilt cylindrical beakers, by Wm. Burwash & R. Sibley, 1809, 2.1/8in. high, 8oz.13dwt. (Christie's) $2,717

A German parcel gilt beaker, late 17th/early 18th century, maker's mark only DL struck twice, 3¾in. high, 4oz.17dwt. (Christie's) $1,231

A Commonwealth tapering cylindrical beaker, 1658, maker's mark RF between pellets, 4in. high, 5oz. (Christie's) $3,888

A German silver gilt beaker, Strasbourg, circa 1700, maker's mark perhaps EB, 3¾in. high, 4oz.18dwt. (Christie's) $2,332

A German silver gilt beaker, by J. P. Hofler, Nuremberg, circa 1690, 3¾in. high, 4oz. 17dwt. (Christie's) $1,313

A Victorian two-handled circular punch bowl, by F. B. Thomas, 1878, 10½in. high, 86oz. (Christie's) $2,626

A 19th century Indian bowl, heavily chased in the usual manner, 24cm. diam., 37oz. (Lawrence Fine Art) $472

A Dutch two-handled octagonal brandy bowl, Bolsward, circa 1685, maker's mark indistinct, 8oz.12dwt. (Christie's) $4,698

A 19th century Indian silver deep bowl, 8½in. diam., 33 troy oz. approx. (Robt. W. Skinner Inc.)$400

Late 19th century Viennese circular jewelled and silver gilt mounted striated agate bowl, 5½in. high. (Christie's) $3,132

A George III Irish bowl, maker's mark script IL for John Laughlin Jnr., J. Lloyd Snr., or J. Locker, Dublin, 1784, 23.5cm. diam., 19.8oz. (Lawrence Fine Art) $814

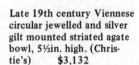

A punch bowl, the hemispherical body divided into arched panels, maker's mark probably that of Chas. S. Harris & Sons, 1929, 28.2cm. diam., 37.5oz. (Lawrence Fine Art) $748

A Victorian fluted shell design bowl on reeded supports, by George Unite, Birmingham, 1870, 6¼in. high, 11oz. (Christie's) $444

A footed bowl designed by J. Rohde, stamped Dessin J.R. 925 S Georg Jensen 242, circa 1920, 12.6cm. high, 16oz. (Christie's) $1,722

A Victorian partly fluted two-handled circular punch bowl, by Elkington & Co., Birmingham, 1889, 12½in. high, 109oz. (Christie's) $2,557

An Edwardian Arts & Crafts circular hammered bowl, by A. E. Jones, Birmingham, 1908, 10in. across handles, 9oz. (Woolley & Wallis) $281

A 17th century two-handled silver gilt circular bowl and cover, probably Flemish, maker's mark only CD, diam. of bowl 7½in., 39oz. (Christie's) $6,264

A footed bowl, stamped Georg Jensen 925 S 197B, 11.1cm. high, 8oz.19dwt. (Christie's) $861

A Queen Anne two-handled circular Monteith, by R. Syng, 1705, 11in. diam., 69oz. (Christie's) $15,984

An Indian circular sugar bowl and cover on four fluted lion's paw supports, by Davd. Hare, Calcutta, circa 1820, 6½in. high, 21oz. (Christie's) $3,758

A silver mounted wood mazer, by Omar Ramsden, 1921, 8¾in. diam. (Christie's) $4,043

A George II plain circular punch bowl, by Edward Vincent, 1730, 9½in. diam. 38oz. (Christie's) $14,774

A George II Irish circular bowl on a rim foot, by Alexander Brown, Dublin, 1735, 6in. wide, 13oz.7dwt. (Christie's) $8,311

A shaped oblong silver casket by Omar Ramsden, 1921, 8¾in. long, gross 53oz. (Christie's) $4,354

Early 19th century silver mounted coquilla nut with bird finial, 6in. high. (Christie's) $783

A German oblong dressing table box with hinged cover, 7¼in. long. (Christie's) $562

A Danish white metal and ivory box and cover, stamped marks W/G and CF Heise assay mark, circa 1925, 13.5cm. high. (Christie's) $600

Victorian silver tobacco box, Birmingham, 1900, 3½in. high, 10oz. (Hobbs & Chambers) $446

A Victorian lozenge shaped plated biscuit box, with formal engraving and panel feet. (Parsons, Welch & Cowell) $125

A 17th century Dutch silver oblong marriage casket, maker's mark only PH conjoined, 2.7/8in. long. (Christie's) $2,877

A Queen Anne oval tobacco box, Britannia Standard 1708, maker's mark rubbed, possibly AS, 10cm. long. (Lawrence Fine Art) $574

A Victorian silver mounted octagonal oak jewel casket, by John S. Hunt, 1856, 10in. high. (Christie's) $1,566

A circular silver cosmetic box and cover, Tang Dynasty, 5.2cm. diam. (Christie's) $3,175

A silver and silver gilt Freedom casket, 'The City of Bristol', by Walker & Hall, Sheffield, 1921, 116oz. approx. (Edgar Horn) $1,153

A Charles II circular silver gilt spice box, circa 1680, maker's mark FS/S, 3¾in. wide, 4oz.13dwt. (Christie's) $11,188

A shaped square silver casket, by Omar Ramsden, 1929, 4½in. high, 18oz.4dwt. (Christie's) $1,555

A 17th century Dutch silver marriage casket on four ball feet, 3in. long. (Christie's) $2,877

A George I spherical soap box, by William Fawdery, 1720, Britannia Standard, 3½in. high, 8oz.19dwt. (Christie's) $5,594

A 17th century Dutch silver oblong marriage casket on four ball feet, 3.1/8in. long. (Christie's) $3,836

A Liberty & Co. silver biscuit box with Birmingham hallmarks for 1902, 20oz.14dwt., 14cm. high. (Christie's) $630

A silver sugar box and scoop of scuttle form, maker's mark S.D.L.D., London, 1911, 17½oz. (Parsons, Welch & Cowell) $577

CANDELABRA

One of a pair of late 19th century four-light candelabra, maker MAU, Dresden, 800 standard, 154oz. (Christie's) $3,256

One of a pair of George III style reeded two-light candelabra with inverted bell-shaped sockets, 14in. high, weight of branches 31oz. (Christie's) $666

One of a pair of Empire ormolu and bronze five-light candelabra on turned engraved pedestals, 27in. high. (Christie's) $1,710

One of a pair of late Victorian table candlesticks, maker's mark J. and T., Sheffield, 1894, 46cm. overall height, loaded. (Lawrence Fine Art) $861

One of a pair of Georg Jensen candelabra with five cup-shaped candle nozzles and circular drip pans supported on U-shaped branches, 27cm. high. (Christie's) $32,400

One of a pair of three light candelabra, by Thos. Bradbury & Sons, Sheffield, 1933, 45.3cm. high, loaded. (Lawrence Fine Art) $2,197

A George III silver gilt four-light candelabrum, by Paul Storr, 1815, 20½in. high, 143oz. (Christie's) $27,172

A Victorian candelabrum centerpiece by Paul Storr, 1837, 24½in. high, 297oz. (Christie's) $11,988

One of a pair of George III three-light candelabra, by Paul Storr, 1816, 16¾in. high, 262oz. (Christie's) $135,864

SILVER

CANDELABRA

One of a pair of Victorian five-light corinthian column candelabra, dated 1886, 26½in. high, weight of branches 116oz. (Christie's) $7,516

One of a pair of mid 18th century style three-branch candelabra, with scrolling branches, 10¾in. high, 75oz. (Christie's) $1,323

A silver three-branch candelabrum, no. 159 of a limited edition of 250, London, 1977, 11in. high, 25oz. (Peter Wilson & Co.) $187

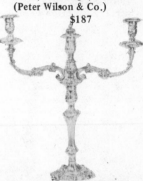

One of a pair of silver gilt three-light candelabra, by The Goldsmiths & Silversmiths Co. Ltd., 1911, 33.2cm. high, 71oz. (Lawrence Fine Art) $2,392

A Victorian six-light candelabrum centerpiece by S. Smith and Wm. Nicholson, 1860, 26¾in. high, 201oz. (Christie's) $5,594

One of two George IV three-light candelabra, by John Watson, Sheffield, 1823, one branch 1820, 25¼in. high, weight of branches 99oz. (Christie's) $4,698

One of four Louis XV four-light candelabra, Paris, 1732, femier-general Hubert Louvet, 217oz. (Christie's) $71,928

A pair of late Empire bronze and ormolu three-light candelabra, 25in. high. (Christie's) $2,138

A George III three-light candelabra, by Digby Scott and Benjamin Smith, 1804, 17in. high, 83oz. (Christie's) $6,566 :4,320

CANDLESTICKS

Pair of table candlesticks, maker's mark of S. Dawson Ltd. overstriking another, Sheffield 1912, 30.2cm. high. (Lawrence Fine Art) $651

One of a set of six candlesticks designed by H. Nielsen, stamped Dessin H.N. Georg Jensen 747B, 2cm. high, 7oz. 3dwt. (Christie's)$939

A pair of George III candlesticks, by John Scofield, 1792, 11¼in. high, 41oz. (Christie's) $4,384

Two of a set of four William IV square base candlesticks, by T. J. & N. Creswick, Sheffield, 1832, 11in. high., (loaded). (Woolley & Wallis) $1,460

One of a set of four William III candlesticks, by Joseph Bird, 1699, 6in. high, 50oz. (Christie's) $41,469

Pair of early George III cast table candlesticks, by Wm. Cafe, 1760, 22.6cm. high, 30oz. (Lawrence Fine Art) $1,465

A pair of silver Louis XVI candlesticks by Saint-Omer, 1784, 9.3/8in. high, 31oz. (Christie's) $2,799

One of a pair of Queen Anne candlesticks, by John Elston, Exeter, 1706, 8¾in. high, 20oz. (Christie's) $5,443

Pair of George III table candlesticks, London marks of 1776 overstriking the original Sheffield marks, 27.9cm. high. (Lawrence Fine Art) $781

574

Pair of Victorian table candlesticks embossed, on square bases, Sheffield, 1844, 9½in. high. (Hobbs & Chambers) $1,036

One of a pair of Liberty & Co. three-branch silver wall sconces, with Birmingham hallmarks for 1901, 29oz., 20cm. high. (Christie's) $1,734

Pair of George III coffee house candlesticks, by E. Coker, 1765, 28.6cm. high, 29oz. (Lawrence Fine Art) $1,628

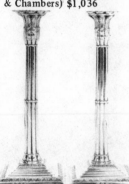

Two of a set of four George III cluster-column candlesticks, by Ebenezer Coker, 1766, 11¾in. high. (Christie's) $4,541

One of a pair of George I candlesticks, Dublin, 1726, maker's mark presumably that of Thos. Bolton, 6in. high, 22oz. (Christie's) $4,665

One of a pair of George II cast table candlesticks, by John Priest, 1754, 20.4cm. high, 27.3oz. (Lawrence Fine Art) $1,834

One of a set of four George II candlesticks, by E. Wakelin, 1757, 12½in. high, 187oz. (Christie's) $80,870

A pair of silver candlesticks with rococo and floral embossing, Edinburgh, 1893, 4½in. high. (Edgar Horn) $350

One of a pair of George III silver gilt candlesticks, by John Scofield, 1796, the gilding later, 12¾in. high. (Christie's) $5,434

CANDLESTICKS

One of a pair of Victorian candlesticks, by Elkington & Co., Birmingham, 1896 and 1899, 10½in. high. (Christie's) $1,438

A pair of early George III cast table candlesticks, 1762, maker's mark DM over a star and 1763, by E. Coker, 26.1cm. high, 42oz. (Lawrence Fine Art) $1,914

One of a pair of mid 18th century style cast baluster candlesticks, 7¼in. high, 28oz. (Christie's) $454

A matched pair of George II cast table candlesticks, by Wm. Gould 1758, and 1760 maker's mark perhaps that of J. Cafe, 22.7cm. high, 34oz. (Lawrence Fine Art) $1,435

One of a pair of George II candlesticks, by Thos. Heming, London, 1759, 28cm. high, 55oz. (Christie's) $2,886

Two of four silver candlesticks, by Omar Ramsden, two 1919, two 1922, loaded, 22.5cm. high. (Phillips) $4,410

A George II taperstick, by James Gould, London, 1737, 10.5cm. high. (Christie's) $1,140

A pair of George III telescopic candlesticks, by John Roberts & Co., Sheffield, 1805, 26cm. extended, loaded. (Lawrence Fine Art) $1,148

One of a pair of George II cast baluster candlesticks, with detachable nozzles, by John Priest, London, 1748, 7¾in. high, 28.75oz. (Christie's) $2,272

One of a pair of candlesticks designed by J. Rohde, stamped Dessin JR Georg Jensen GI925S 453, circa 1920, 15cm. high. (Christie's) $1,331

A pair of George III bedroom candlesticks, by Thos. & James Creswick, Sheffield, 1814, 10.8cm. high. (Lawrence Fine Art) $905

One of a pair of George I table candlesticks, by Matthew Cooper I, London, 1726, 16cm. high, 22oz. (Christie's) $3,108

A pair of George I table candlesticks, by David Green, London, 1723, 16.1cm. high, 23oz. (Christie's) $3,404

One of a pair of 18th century Sheffield candlesticks, each with a square removable nozzle, 12.3/8in. high. (Christie's) $462

A pair of modern table candlesticks with detachable nozzles, by Leslie Donn Ltd., 1964, 29.5cm. high. (Lawrence Fine Art) $436

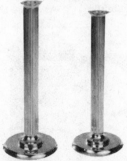

One of a pair of William II candlesticks, by William Denny, 1701, 23cm. high, 23oz. (Phillips) $3,666

Pair of candlesticks designed by S. Bernadotte, stamped Georg Jensen 355B Sigvard and London import marks, 25.9cm. high, 25oz.11dwt. (Christie's) $1,331

One of a set of four George III table candlesticks, with detachable nozzles, by John Scofield, London, 1784, one nozzle 1792, 29cm. high. (Christie's) $7,200

CASTERS

A sugar caster designed by Harald Nielsen, stamped Dessin H.N. 925S Georg Jensen S Wendel A/S 645, circa 1949, 11.4cm. high, 7oz.14dwt. (Christie's) $626

A Continental caster modelled as a kingfisher, import hall-marks for Glasgow, 1908, 16cm. from beak to tail. (Christie's) $262

A plain cylindrical sugar caster with domed cover, by Goldsmiths & Silversmiths Co., London, 1911, 7¼in. high, 11.50oz. (Christie's) $222

A George I, West Country, muffineer, with the mark of Joseph Collier, circa 1725, 11cm. high. (Phillips) $630

A George II vase-shaped caster, 6¼in. high, with a pair of matching smaller casters, 5¼in. high, by Samuel Wood, London, 1747 and 1750, 11oz. (Christie's) $1,278

One of a pair of Charles II cylindrical casters, by F. Garthorne, 1683, 5in. high, 11oz.7dwt. (Christie's) $12,441

One of a pair of Dutch spirally fluted pear-shaped casters, by J. Siotteling, Amsterdam, 1765, 8¾in. high, 27oz. gross.(Christie's) $7,992

One of a pair of pounce pots, by John McKay, Edinburgh, 1798, 3oz. (Worsfolds) $331

An Edwardian inverted pear-shaped sugar caster, W.F. and A.F. Sheffield, 1901, 8½in. high, 8.50oz. (Christie's) $133

A George II epergne on four foliage, scroll and shell feet, and with four detachable scroll branches with openwork dish frames, maker's mark CM, 1759, 63oz. (Christie's) $4,795

A George II epergne on four shell and scroll feet, by E. Wakelin, 1751, length of basket 12in., 153oz. (Christie's) $14,385

George III silver table centerpiece, by Wm. Pitts, London, 1764, 10½in. high, 81oz. (Hobbs & Chambers) $6,048

A Victorian table centerpiece candelabrum, by S. Hayne and D. Cater, 1845, 57.5cm. high, 66oz. (Lawrence Fine Art) $1,237

A George III oval epergne, 1802, maker's mark IP, probably for Joseph Preedy, with cut glass bowl, 10in. high, 38oz. (Christie's) $2,192

A Victorian parcel gilt centerpiece and mirror plateau, by F. Elkington, Birmingham, 1893, 27in. high, 207oz. (Christie's) $7,047

A George III epergne and mirror plateau, by M. Boulton, Birmingham, 1810, length of plateau 26in., height of epergne 10½in. (Christie's) $14,774

One of a pair of late 19th century repousse sterling silver compotes, by Tiffany & Co., 9.3/8in. diam., 40 troy oz. (Robt. W. Skinner Inc.) $1,258

A gilt Old Sheffield plate epergne with large central glass dish and four smaller dishes on mirror plateau, by Roberts, Cadman & Co., circa 1822, 13½in. high, 24in. wide. (Christie's) $2,975

Late 19th century silver
chamberstick by Mappin &
Webb, London, 5in. high,
5oz. (Bermondsey)
    $150

A Hukin & Heath electro-
plated chamberstick with
snuffer designed by Dr.
C. Dresser, stamped H & H
9658 Rd No. 228142,
12.5cm. high. (Christie's)
    $1,340

A George IV circular chamber
candlestick with leaf-capped
handle and conical snuffer,
by R. Garrard, London, 1828,
5½in. diam., 14oz. (Christie's)
    $444

A Victorian shaped circular
chamber candlestick, by
Henry Wilkinson, Sheffield,
1863, 6in. diam., 11oz.
(Christie's) $473

A Perry Son & Co. maroon
painted metal chamber
candlestick, designed by Dr.
C. Dresser, registration
lozenge for 1883, 14.5cm.
high. (Christie's)$425

A George III circular chamberstick, with detachable nozzle
and snuffer, by Thos. Law,
Sheffield, perhaps 1806, 15cm.
high, 11oz., and a pair of plated
snuffers. (Christie's)$444

George III shaped circular
chamberstick, by William
Stroud, 1805, 13½oz.
(Bermondsey)
    $1,500

George III chamber candlestick, by John Crouch and
Thos. Hannam, London,
9oz. (Bermondsey)
    $600

George III chamber candlestick with removable drip tray,
maker Thos. Robins, London,
1798, 4in. high, 8oz. (Capes,
Dunn & Co.) $411

CHOCOLATE POTS

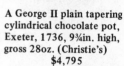

A Queen Anne plain tapering cylindrical chocolate pot, by Nathaniel Lock, 1708, 8¾in. high, 18oz.18dwt. gross. (Christie's) $4,315

A cylindrical chocolate pot, by S. C. S. Groth, Copenhagen, 1884, 17.5cm. high, 17oz. (Christie's) $421

A George II plain tapering cylindrical chocolate pot, Exeter, 1736, 9¾in. high, gross 28oz. (Christie's) $4,795

A George III chocolate pot, by Milne & Campbell, Glasgow, circa 1770. 36oz. (Christie's) $1,776

Mid 18th century Flemish silver chocolate pot of baluster form, Ghent, 1200gr. (Bermondsey) $4,200

An early 18th century silver chocolate pot, by Wm. Fawdery, London, 12oz. (Robt. W. Skinner Inc.) $450

CIGARETTE BOXES

Silver cigarette box and cover, in the Art Nouveau style, by Ramsden & Carr, circa 1903, 7½in. wide. (Bermondsey) $1,125

An Alfred Dunhill silver gilt and enamel cigarette box and lighter, London hallmarks for 1929. (Christie's) $1,149

A Chinese wood lined oblong cigarette box ornately molded with carp, 8¼in. long. (Christie's) $284

CIGARETTE CASES

An Austrian cigarette case applied with two-color gold and gem set monograms and facsimile signatures, circa 1895. (Phillips) $774

A Victorian cigarette case, the cover enamelled with a nude girl lying beside a stream, Birmingham, 1887. (Phillips) $588

An Austrian white metal and enamel eight-sided cigarette case, the enamel by F. Zwichl, depicting a Samson car in black, red and cream. (Christie's) $783

A Continental plated cigarette case enamelled with a collie dog on a sky background, circa 1910. (Phillips) $223

An Edwardian gilt lined cigarette case, polychrome-enamelled with a picture of a lady, R.C., Birmingham, 1905. (Christie's) $284

A German cigarette case enamelled on cover with a spaniel carrying a dead duck in its mouth, circa 1900. (Phillips) $367

An Austrian enamel cigarette case, signed 'Schleiertanz', circa 1895. (Phillips) $735

A white metal and enamel cigarette case, the enamel by F. Zwichl, circa 1920. (Christie's) $2,818

A late Victorian gilt lined cigarette case, enamelled with a scene from R. Kipling's poem 'Absent minded beggar', C.S. & F.S., Birmingham, 1899. (Christie's) $372

CLARET JUGS

A Victorian large vase-shaped claret jug with an applied cast putto handle, by Houles & Co., London, 1841, 14½in. high, 38oz. (Christie's) $1,837

A George IV claret jug, maker's mark probably that of Joseph Angell, 1829, 29cm. high, 31oz. (Lawrence Fine Art) $2,392

A Victorian pear-shaped cut glass claret jug, hob cut, 13½in. high. (Parsons, Welch & Cowell) $214

A William IV fluted, inverted pear-shaped claret jug, with presentation inscription, Messrs. Barnard, London, 1836, 12¼in. high, 29.25oz. (Christie's) $962

A pair of French silver gilt mounted clear glass claret jugs, by Risler & Carre, Paris, circa 1870, 11¾in. high. (Christie's) $4,924

A 19th century Indian silver claret jug, snake coiled around body forming handle and lid stop, 14¾in. high, 32 troy oz. (Robt. W. Skinner Inc.) $375

A Victorian claret jug, by Marshall & Sons, Edinburgh, 1865, 35cm. high, 30oz. (Christie's) $1,110

A late Victorian mounted glass claret jug in the form of a cockatoo, by Alex. Crichton, 1882, 27cm. high. (Phillips) $3,450

A George III claret or hot water jug, by Henry Chawner, 1791, 31cm. high, 23oz. all in. (Lawrence Fine Art) $1,914

COASTERS

Pair of George III silver wine coasters in the Adam style, 5in. diam., London hallmark. (Bermondsey) $450

A pair of George III circular decanter stands, by Thomas Robinson I, London, 1809. (Christie's) $1,391

A pair of George III pierced silver wine coasters, by I. R. & Co., Sheffield, 1774, 5½in. diam. (Bermondsey) $900

One of a pair of silver mounted Regency papier mache coasters, each with twin ring handles. (Phillips) $1,275

A Sheffield plated trolley coaster, 44cm. long. (Lawrence Fine Art) $582

George III circular coaster, by Jabez & Thos. Daniel, London, circa 1773. (Bermondsey) $750

A pair of Old Sheffield plate 5¾in. circular wine coasters, with turned wood bases, (Parsons, Welch & Cowell) $217

A superb pair of George IV brass bound mahogany wine coasters, 12½in. high. (Christie's) $3,400

A pair of George III plain, circular wine coasters, by Solomon Hougham, London, 1802, 14.5cm. diam. (Christie's) $525

COFFEE POTS

A Queen Anne plain tapering cylindrical coffee pot, by Simon Pantin, 1705, 10.3/8in. high, gross 29oz. (Christie's) $3,836

A George IV small coffee pot, by Wm. Bateman, 1827, 19.4cm. high, 34oz. (Lawrence Fine Art) $797

A George II Irish plain tapering cylindrical coffee pot, Dublin, 1734, 9in. high, gross 32oz. (Christie's) $7,672

A George II plain tapering cylindrical coffee pot, 1727, maker's mark probably IE for John Eckfourd Jnr., 8.5/8in. high, gross 20oz. (Christie's) $2,877

A George II pear-shaped coffee pot, by Isaac Cookson, Newcastle, 1748, 9¼in. high, gross 26oz. (Christie's) $2,035

A George II plain tapering cylindrical coffee pot, by Thos. Farren, 1717, 9½in. high, gross 21oz. (Christie's) $2,505

A Queen Anne plain tapering cylindrical coffee pot, by Edward Yorke, 1711, 9¼in. high, gross 20oz. (Christie's) $3,601

A George I plain tapering octagonal coffee pot and stand, by John East, 1714, 9¾in. high, gross 33oz. (Christie's) $38,361

A Queen Anne plain tapering cylindrical coffee pot, by A. Courtauld, 1710, 10in. high, gross 27oz. (Christie's) $5,950

COFFEE POTS

A double pyriform coffee pot, by C. Wiltberger, Phila., circa 1785-90, 14¼in. high, gross wt. 51oz. (Christie's) $16,500

A Continental fluted baluster coffee pot on scroll feet, with a grotesque mask spout, 9½in. high. (Christie's) $325

A George III vase-shaped coffee pot, by Henry Chawner, London, 1789, 11.5in. high, 26oz. all in. (Woolley & Wallis) $1,200

A Queen Anne plain tapering cylindrical coffee pot, by Robt. Timbrell, 1707, 10in. high, 23oz. gross. (Christie's) $4,315

A George III pear-shaped coffee pot, by Francis Butty and Nicholas Dumee, London, 1765, 11½in. high, 31.75oz. gross. (Christie's)$1,136

A George III gadrooned, pear-shaped coffee pot, probably by John Scofield, London, 1776, 10¾in. high, 26.25oz. (Christie's) $1,562

A George II plain tapering cylindrical coffee pot, by John Cafe, circa 1750, 9¾in. high, gross 25oz. (Christie's) $2,349

George III silver coffee pot, by Henry Chawner, 20oz., 11¼in. high. (Robt. W. Skinner Inc.) $1,200

A George III vase-shaped coffee pot, in the Neo-Classical manner, by John Carter II, London, 1774, 29.5cm. high, 27oz. (Christie's) $1,539

COFFEE POTS

An early George III coffee pot, by Wm. Shaw II and Wm. Priest, 1757, 29.5cm. high, 31oz. all in. (Lawrence Fine Art) $1,139

Epping Forest Centenary flagon of tapering cylinder shape, London 1978, 41oz. (Peter Wilson & Co.) $331

An early George III baluster coffee pot, by Wm. Cripps, the cover with standard mark, 27.5cm. high, 31oz. all in. (Lawrence Fine Art) $3,719

A George II plain baluster coffee pot, by Wm. Shaw and Wm. Priest, London, 1753, 9in. high, 21.25oz. (Christie's) $1,349

An 18th century French Provincial cafetiere, by Henry Louis Le Gaigneur, Saint-Omer, circa 1730, 29cm. high, 35oz. (Phillips) $4,512

A George II baluster coffee pot with scalloped spout, by Whipham & Wright, 1757, 31oz. (Phillips) $1,500

A George II baluster silver coffee pot, London, 1746, 10¼in. high, 27oz. all in. (Parsons, Welch & Cowell) $1,221

A Liberty silver coffee pot, designed by Archibald Knox, with Birmingham hallmarks for 1906, 21.5cm. high. (Christie's) $3,040

A George II plain, tapering coffee pot, George Hindmarsh, London, 1755, 10in. high, 27.75oz. gross. (Christie's) $1,215

587

CREAM JUGS

A silver oval covered cream jug, by Omar Ramsden, 1925, 11cm. high, 8.5oz. (Phillips) $1,176

A Continental cream jug formed as a pug dog, wearing a link collar and with curled tail, 5in. long. (Christie's) $444

A George II silver gilt cast cream jug, unmarked but in the manner of Paul de Lamerie, 4¾in. high, 11oz. (Christie's)
$14,385

A double pyriform cream pitcher, by Cary Dunn, Newark, circa 1780-90, 5¾in. high, 7oz. 10dwt. (Christie's)
$3,080

A George III silver gilt vase-shaped cream jug, maker's mark only IS, pellet between, 4½in. high, 11oz.2dwt. (Christie's) $3,516

A silver cream jug of inverted pyriform with a scroll handle, by Wm. Hollingshead, Phila., circa 1760/80, 5in. high, 4oz. (Christie's) $3,300

A covered cream pitcher, by Chas. Moore and J. Ferguson, Phila., circa 1801-05, 8¼in. high, 8oz. (Christie's)
$1,870

Late 18th century silver creamer, maker's mark INR, Phila., 4½in. high, 4 troy oz. (Robt. W. Skinner Inc.) $400

A George III plain, inverted, pear shaped cream jug, London, 1774, 11cm. high. (Christie's) $111

CRUETS

A George III oval boat shaped condiment cruet, by Wm. Simmons, London, 1788, and a later mustard spoon, London, 1809, 29oz. (Woolley & Wallis) $1,725

Victorian plated egg cruet, circa 1880. (British Antique Exporters) $41

A boat-shaped cruet stand by Omar Ramsden, 1925, 10in. long, gross 42oz. (Christie's) $5,598

A George III egg cruet stand with spoons, five by J. Emes, London 1804, and one by E. J. & W. Barnard, London 1837, (Christie's) $621

A Victorian circular egg cruet, with a pair of casters, by John S. Hunt, 1853, 10½in. high, 76oz. (Christie's) $3,356

A Hukin & Heath electro-plated six-sided cruet frame, designed by Dr. C. Dresser, with lozenge for 11th April 1878, 9cm. high.(Christie's) $867

A plated cruet stand with eight bottles. (Worsfolds) $144

A George IV egg cruet stand with revolving frame, by Robt. Hennell II, fully marked 1823, 19.5cm. high, 29oz. (Lawrence Fine Art) $732

A Regency egg cruet with six matching egg cups, London, 1820, together with six George IV eggspoons, by Eley & Fearn, London, 1824, 32oz. (Woolley & Wallis) $1,197

A Queen Anne two-handled cup and cover on circular fluted foot, by Lewis Mettayer, 1712, 9½in. high, 45oz. (Christie's) $6,998

One of a pair of George III silver two-handled cups, by Thos. Whipham and Chas. Wright, 1760, 5½in. high, 35oz. (Christie's) $1,788

A George II silver gilt two-handled cup and cover, by B. Godfrey, 1738, 12¼in. high, 81oz. (Christie's) $10,179

A George III silver gilt two-handled cup and cover, by Henry Chawner, 1789, 19¼in. high, 92oz. (Christie's) $5,909

A George IV silver gilt racing trophy cup, by Benjamin Smith, 1824, 34cm. high, 116.5oz. (Phillips) $3,525

An Elizabeth I plain wine cup, engraved 'The Towne of Wollterton, 1568', by Peter Peterson, Norwich, 5¼in. high, 6oz. (Christie's) $5,253

A George III cup and cover, by Wm. Holmes, 1789, 32cm. high, 32oz. (Lawrence Fine Art) $669

A George IV silver gilt two-handled campana-shaped cup and cover, by Wm. Burwash, 1821, 15¼in. high, 136oz. (Christie's) $7,464

A George III vase-shaped two-handled cup and cover, by Wm. Pitts and J. Preedy, 1794, 18½in. high, 128oz. (Christie's) $6,393

DISHES

One of a pair of oval entree dishes, covers and detachable handles, by Walker & Hall, Sheffield, 1911, 27.7cm., 108oz. (Lawrence Fine Art) $877

A silver chafing dish with a flaring brim, by Jacob Hurd, Boston, 1745, 12½in. long, gross weight 19oz.10dwt. (Christie's)$55,000

One of a pair of George IV shaped oblong silver entree dishes and covers, by B. Smith II, 1825, 12½in. long, 146oz. (Christie's) $4,976

One of a set of four early Victorian shell butter dishes, by Thomas James & Nathaniel Creswick, Sheffield, 1837, 23oz. (Phillips) $1,911

One of a set of four George III meat dishes, by J. Parker and E. Wakelin, 1761, 13½in. long, 108oz. (Christie's) $8,553

A fruit dish modelled as a shell with a seated merman, by the Goldsmiths & Silversmiths Co., 1910, 37cm. high. (Phillips) $2,425

A George III Irish oval butter dish with green glass liner, by Joseph Jadison, Dublin, 1779, 17.1cm. long, 14oz. (Phillips) $1,269

A German parcel gilt circular dish, by Jeremias Ritter, Nuremberg, circa 1630, 7¾in. wide, 5oz.12dwt. (Christie's) $3,836

One of a pair of George III octagonal entree dishes and covers, by Paul Storr, 1800, 12¼in. long, 104oz. (Christie's) $7,192

DISHES

A William III large silver gilt
charger, by Ralph Leeke,
circa 1695, 22in. diam.,
134oz. (Christie's)
$10,108

One of a set of four silver
George III shaped oblong
entree dishes and covers, by
Paul Storr, 1810, 11.3/8in.
long, 309oz. (Christie's)
$27,993

One of twelve George III
shaped circular dinner
plates, by J. Young and O.
Jackson, 1774, 9.5/8in.
diam., 237oz. (Christie's)
$9,270

A silver chafing dish, by A.
Hartwell, Mass., bowl 6in.
diam., 27oz.10dwt.
(Christie's) $1,210

One of a pair of George II
butter shells on three shell
and rocaille feet, by Paul de
Lamerie, 1746, 4¾in. wide,
10oz.6dwt. (Christie's)
$52,876

One of a pair of silver George
III entree dishes and covers,
by Paul Storr, 1810, 12¾in.
long, 153oz. (Christie's)
$13,996

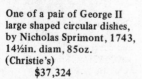

One of a pair of George II
large shaped circular dishes,
by Nicholas Sprimont, 1743,
14½in. diam, 85oz.
(Christie's)
$37,324

One of twelve George III
silver gilt shaped circular
dinner plates, by Wm.
Stroud, 1804, the gilding
later, 9¾in. wide, 231oz.
(Christie's) $8,791

A George I Irish strawberry
dish with scalloped rim,
by David King, Dublin, 1714
(Christie's) $6,713

DISHES

One of twelve George II shaped circular dinner plates, by Paul De Lamerie, 1741, 9½in. diam., 233oz. (Christie's) $44,755

A C. R. Ashbee silver muffin dish and cover with London hallmarks for 1900, 180z. gross weight, 22cm. high. (Christie's) $2,207

One of four George II circular strawberry dishes, three by Chas. F. Kandler, 1747, one by S. Herbert & Co., 1753, 9.3/8in. diam., 81oz. (Christie's) $22,377

A Regency Sheffield plate oval meat dish and matching cover, 18in. diam. (Woolley & Wallis) $473

A silver compote on a spreading cylindrical foot, by Whiting Mfg. Co., circa 1850, 8½in. diam., 15oz. 10dwt. (Christie's) $440

One of four George III silver gilt shell-shaped butter dishes, by J. Foskett & J. Stewart, 1810, 24oz. (Christie's) $2,818

A George II silver gilt circular alms dish, by R. Beale or R. Bayley, 21.8cm. diam., 18.9oz. (Lawrence Fine Art) $3,093

A William IV silver gilt vine leaf fruit dish, by John Watson, Sheffield 1834, 12in. wide, 29oz. (Christie's) $3,110

One of twelve George II shaped circular dinner plates, by Wm. Grundy, 1753, 9¾in. diam, 215oz. (Christie's) $10,886

An American ovoid wine ewer, the body chased over-all in the Chinese style, by S. Kirk, Baltimore, circa 1830, 16¼in. high, 48oz. (Christie's) $2,349

A Queen Anne style ewer with caryatid handle, London, 1926, 8¾in. high, 20.25oz. (Christie's) $894

A William IV Irish wine ewer, maker's mark R.S., Dublin, 1833, 12in. high, 30oz. (Christie's) $2,368

One of a pair of inverted, pyriform ewers, by F. Marquand, New York, 1826-39, 14½in. high, 38oz. 10dwt. (Christie's) $2,750

A silver vase shaped ewer, by Jones, Ball & Poor, Boston, circa 1846, 16¼in. high, 41oz. (Christie's) $1,100

Silver presentation ewer, maker's mark Shreve, Brown & Co., coin on base, 10½in. high, approx. 29 troy oz., circa 1857. (Robt. W. Skinner Inc.) $700

A Victorian silver mounted claret jug, by Messrs. Barnard, 1873, 34cm. high. (Lawrence Fine Art) $1,628

A vase shaped ewer, by B. C. Frobisher, circa 1816-25, 11.1/8in. high, 25oz. (Christie's) $935

A Victorian Scottish wine jug, by Wm. Marshall, Edinburgh, 1866, 15in. high, the handle altered for hot water and reassayed H.W.C., London, 1866, 27oz. (Woolley & Wallis) $1,125

FLATWARE

A George II Irish soup ladle with deep pear-shaped bowl, Dublin, circa 1745, date letter and maker's mark lacking, 15in. long, 12oz. 19dwt. on fitted wood stand. (Christie's) $1,252

One of a pair of jam spoons designed by Georg Jensen, the hammered and cut bowls in the form of a leaf with curving handles. (Christie's) $313

A silver fish slice with a faceted handle, by Hayden & Gregg, South Carolina, 1846/52, 12in. long, 6oz.10dwt. (Christie's) $715

A Guild of Handicraft Ltd. silver preserve spoon, stamped G. of H. Ltd. and London hallmarks for 1902. (Christie's) $406

Part of a set of George IV double shell and laurel pattern table service, by Eley & Fearn, 1824, in fitted wood canteen, 235oz. (Christie's) $7,192

Part of a silver gilt composite Kings pattern table service, 1815, 1819, etc. and modern, in fitted canteen with nine drawers, 377oz. (Christie's) $19,180

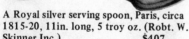

A Royal silver serving spoon, Paris, circa 1815-20, 11in. long, 5 troy oz. (Robt. W. Skinner Inc.) $407

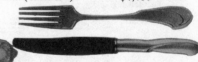

A silver double-ended marrow scoop, by Thos. Colgan, N.Y., circa 1775, 8in. long, 1oz. (Christie's) $4,400

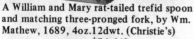

A William and Mary rat-tailed trefid spoon and matching three-pronged fork, by Wm. Mathew, 1689, 4oz.12dwt. (Christie's) $74,649

A knife and fork designed by Henry van de Velde, the handles with curvilinear art nouveau design, circa 1900. (Christie's) $1,252

A Georg Jensen 64-piece 'chess pattern' table service stamped Georg Jensen, Sterling, Denmark, 50oz.12dwt. weight not including knives. (Christie's) $2,680

A Georg Jensen 180-piece 'acorn' pattern table service, first designed in 1915 by Johan Rohde, 181oz. weight not including knives. (Christie's) $29,959

FLATWARE

A 106-piece 'Cypress' pattern table service designed by Tias Eckhoff, 112oz.2dwt., weight not including items that are part steel. (Christie's) $3,601

An 89-piece 'Cactus' pattern table service, designed by Gundorph Albertus, stamped marks, 102oz., weight not including items that are part steel. (Christie's) $3,915

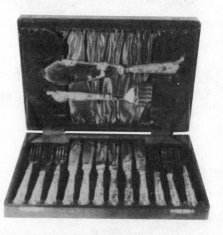

A 134-piece 'Pyramid' pattern table service designed by Harald Nielson, stamped marks, 181oz.5dwt., weight not including items that are part steel. (Christie's) $9,396

A set of King's pattern fish knives and forks having plated blades and embossed handles, also a matching pair of fish servers, Sheffield, 1928. (Peter Wilson & Co.) $108

FLATWARE

A large part service of George III Old English and thread pattern cutlery, by various silversmiths, circa 1780, 139oz. (Lawrence Fine Art) $3,987

A George IV service of fiddle, thread and shell pattern cutlery for twelve place settings, by Wm. Chawner, 1827, 140oz. (Lawrence Fine Art) $8,140

A 193-piece 'Acorn' pattern table service, designed by Johan Rohde, stamped marks, 245oz., weight not including items that are part steel. (Christie's) $7,516

A service of Hanoverian pattern cutlery for .twelve place settings, maker's mark G. & H., Sheffield 1960/63, 169oz., excluding steel mounted items. (Lawrence Fine Art) $4,884

FRAMES

A Ramsden & Carr silver picture frame, with London hallmarks for 1900, 15.5cm. high. (Christie's) $1,425

A Victorian embossed silver photograph frame, Birmingham, 1899, 8in. high. (Dacre, Son & Hartley) $187

An Art Nouveau stand photograph frame, repousse with fruiting vines and panels, Birmingham 1910, 8½ x 6½in. (Capes, Dunn & Co.) $176

An embossed and pierced shaped silver photograph frame, London, 1900, 8in. high. (Dacre, Son & Hartley) $270

A WMF plated figural easel-backed mirror, stamped maker's marks, 37cm. high. (Phillips) $870

An Art Nouveau silver mounted photograph frame, by A. & J. Zimmerman, Birmingham, 1906, 28.8cm. high. (Lawrence Fine Art) $305

A Liberty silver and enamel picture frame, designed by Archibald Knox, with Birmingham hallmarks for 1904, 21.2cm. high. (Christie's) $5,909

An Art Nouveau silver photograph frame, stamped maker's marks W.N. and Chester hallmarks for 1903, 22.3cm. high. (Christie's) $450

A William III large silver gilt dressing table mirror, by Wm. Lukin, circa 1700, 32¾in. high. (Christie's) $20,217

GOBLETS

SILVER

A 20th century enamelled and jeweled sterling silver chalice, approx. 4 troy oz. (Robt. W. Skinner Inc.)
$550 £376

One of six George IV partly fluted thistle-shaped goblets, maker's mark WE for Wm. Eaton or Wm. Elliot, 1822, 5.5/8in. high, 65oz. (Christie's) $6,713

A Channel Islands plain wine cup, by Guillaume Henry, circa 1740, 5½in. high, 6oz. (Christie's) $1,722

A Charles I plain wine cup on circular foot, 1640, maker's mark RW over a cinquefoil, within a dotted heart, 7in. high, 10oz. (Christie's) $7,776

A Commonwealth wine cup on trumpet-shaped foot, 1655, maker's mark ET a crescent below, 3½in. high, 2oz.18dwt. (Christie's) $3,421

A 19th century Indian Colonial goblet, by Hamilton & Co., Calcutta, circa 1860, 19.6cm. high, 8.5oz. (Phillips) $451

An Arts & Crafts Movement chalice in medieval style, by Omar Ramsden & Alwin Carr, London, 1912, 5.2in. high, 10oz. all in. (Christie's) $1,124

A large goblet designed by H. Nielsen, stamped Dessin H.N. G.J. 535, circa 1928, 19.9cm. high, 25oz.15dwt. (Christie's) $2,505

A wine cup, Guernsey, circa 1695, maker's mark RB a fleur-de-lys and coronet above, 5.5/8in. high, 7oz. 3dwt. (Christie's) $2,114

599

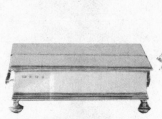

A Victorian treasury inkstand on four bun feet, by Elkington & Co., Birmingham, 1900, 10¾in. long, 90oz. (Christie's) $3,036

An Edwardian rectangular inkstand, fitted with two glass inkwells, Mappin & Webb, London, 1908, 12¼in. long, 46oz. (Christie's) $888

Indian chased white metal inkstand with two glass bottles, ivory inlaid border to stand, 10½in. wide. (Hobbs & Chambers) $144

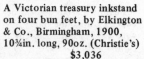

A late Victorian double inkstand, by W. J. Barnard, London, 1894, 11in. long. 25oz. (Woolley & Wallis) $769

A silver oblong inkstand with flat hinged lid, the interior with two glass inkwells and silver dip pen, 9in. wide, Birmingham 1918, 32oz. (Capes, Dunn & Co.) $395

A George III rectangular inkstand, by Wm. Allen III, 1798, 30.3cm. long, 41oz. (Lawrence Fine Art) $1,953

A Russian metal and marble desk set with three-quarter pierced gallery, 18½in. wide. (Christie's) $4,976

A Guild of Handicraft white metal and enamel inkwell, attributed to C. R. Ashbee, seven sided on ball feet, 10.5cm. high. (Christie's) $2,522

A George IV oblong inkstand, by Rebecca Emes and Edward Barnard, 1824, 25.7cm. long, 23oz. of weighable silver. (Lawrence Fine Art) $1,697

A silver baluster ale jug, in the 18th century taste, 8in. high, 23.25oz. (Christie's) $134

An English silver mounted malling-type turquoise blue tin glazed earthenware jug and cover, circa 1590, 7½in. high. (Christie's) $5,434

A 19th century American cordial or water jug of baluster form, maker's mark of Jones, Ball & Poor, Boston, circa 1845, 28cm. high, 30oz. (Phillips) $999

A George II plain silver pear-shaped beer jug, by Philip Elston, Exeter, the date letter probably for 1742, 7¾in. high, 22oz. (Christie's) $4,354

A silver hot water jug, of oval section, by Omar Ramsden, 1930, 27cm. high, 36.5oz. (Phillips) $3,969

A jug with ebony handle, stamped Georg Jensen 407A, 23.2cm. high, 35oz. 5dwt. gross weight. (Christie's) $2,662

A Victorian claret jug, the oval body engraved at a later date, by Messrs. Barnard, 1867, 31.2cm. high, 21oz. (Lawrence Fine Art) $553

A Victorian 'ascos' jug, by Hunt & Roskell, 1844, 33.25oz. (Phillips) $1,984

A 17th century Rhenish stoneware baluster jug with contemporary English silver mount, 19.5cm. high. (Christie's) $766

MISCELLANEOUS

A curved shaped oblong silver spirit flask with detachable gilt lined cup and cover, by Omar Ramsden, 1924, 6½in. high, 18oz. (Christie's) $1,710

A Christofle white metal saucepan designed by Lino Sabattini, the almond shaped pan with curving sides, 18.9cm. wide. (Christie's) $391

A Hukin & Heath plated spoon-warmer with ebony handle, the design attributed to Dr. C. Dresser, stamped H & H 2857, 14.4cm. high. (Christie's) $378

A French Christening set, post 1838 guarantee, with maker's mark of Veyrant, 8.8oz. of weighable silver. (Lawrence Fine Art) $510

A Victorian composite silver gilt dressing table set, by various silversmiths, 1885/89, 21-pieces including Dutch silver gilt colored metal box. (Lawrence Fine Art) $1,355

A Boucheron powder compact and two lipstick holders, Made in France. (Christie's) $315

A rock crystal and sterling silver crucifix, 14½in. high. (Robt. W. Skinner Inc.) $2,100

A set of six early Victorian cast swag shape wine labels, by E. J. & W. Barnard, London, 1851, 4oz. (Woolley & Wallis) $562

Victorian silver scent phial, Birmingham, 1892, 8in. long, 5oz., in case. (Hobbs & Chambers) $374

A silver kojiri formed as a growling karashishi, signed Yasuyoshi (Nukagawa), early 19th century. (Christie's) $293

A shallow saucepan designed by H. Nielsen, stamped Dessin H.N. Georg Jensen G.J. 925S 644, circa 1920, 5.3 cm. high, 11oz.12dwt. gross weight. (Christie's) $548

A Hukin & Heath electroplated letter rack designed by Dr. C. Dresser, stamped H & H 2555 and registration lozenge for May 1881, 12.3cm. high. (Christie's) $408

A Victorian electroplated meat press, by Elkington & Co., 44cm. high, excluding wood base. (Lawrence Fine Art) $2,073

A George II triangular kettle stand, by John le Sage, 1734, 11½in. wide, 36oz. (Christie's) $4,475

One of three George III silver gilt wine labels for Port, Claret and Champagne, by Benjamin Smith, 1808, 3in. high, 7oz.5dwt. (Christie's) $3,676

Victorian oak hanging brush set with plated mounts, 1880. (British Antique Exporters) $40

Three pieces from a dressing table set, die stamped with foliage in the Art Nouveau style, Chester 1903/04/05, by W. Neale. (Lawrence Fine Art) $112

A Lacloche Freres patterned silver and red gold minaudiere set with five sapphires, stamped with import marks for 1935, 13oz.14dwt., 13 x 8.6cm. (Christie's) $1,576

MODELS

A Continental silver model of a magpie, import marks for 1899, 19½in. overall, 29oz. (Christie's) $2,177

A late Victorian novelty port bottle carrier in the form of a donkey and cart, 13in. long, by H. T., London, 1890. (Woolley & Wallis) $1,372

A 19th century Continental silver gilt model of a seated bear, 8in. high, 22oz. (Christie's) $1,805

A Victorian model of an equestrian knight in armor, by Stephen Smith, 1870, 9in. high, 28oz. (Christie's) $1,518

A late 19th century English silvered bronze group of a jockey on horseback, signed and dated J. Willis Good, 1875, 32.5cm. high. (Christie's) $3,000

'Nude Girl with Shawl', a silvered bronze figure cast from a model by Lorenzl, decorated by Crejo, 37.5cm. high. (Christie's) $1,879

'Vestal' a silvered bronze figure by Le Faguays, on stepped square shaped marble base, 14½in. high. (Christie's) $1,617

A late 19th century English silvered bronze group of a jockey on horseback, signed and dated J. Willis Good, 1875, 27cm. high.(Christie's) $3,750

A Victorian cigar lighter, formed as a deer-hound, by J. S. Hunt, 1851, 5¼in. high, 18oz.17dwt. (Christie's) $1,879

MODELS

A silver cast model of a
Clydesdale horse, the sculp-
tor G. Halliday, made by
Elkington & Co., Birming-
ham, 1911, 21in. high,
309oz. (Christie's)
$14,385

A sectional silvered model
of a crayfish, unsigned,
Meiji period, 43cm. long.
(Christie's) $1,158

A Continental silver model
of a grouse, by B. Muller,
import marks for 1902,
10½in. high, 26oz. (Christie's)
$1,632

MUGS

A George II plain baluster
mug, by Robert Albin Cox,
London, 1758, 15cm. high,
17oz. (Christie's) $651

A George II beer mug, of
good gauge, by John Gorham,
1759, 12cm. high, 11oz.
(Phillips) $450

An early George II mug, by
Francis Spilsbury I, 1735,
11cm. high. (Lawrence
Fine Art) $733

A George II Provincial mug
with leaf-capped scroll handle,
by Langlands & Goodrick,
Newcastle, 1756, 9cm. high,
7.25oz. (Phillips) $570

A George II plain baluster
mug, London, 1733, 13cm.
high, 11oz. (Christie's)
$407

A William IV panelled campana-shaped child's mug, by
Chas. Fox, London, 1831,
4oz. (Woolley & Wallis)
$335

MUSTARDS

George III silver mustard pot of plain cylindrical form with scroll handle, 3½oz. (Bermondsey) $150

A Charles Boyton hammered silver four-piece condiments set, London hallmarks for 1947, 11oz. (Christie's) $882

A Guild of Handicrafts silver mustard pot, designed by C. R. Ashbee, with London hallmarks for 1902, 8.5cm. high, 4oz.11dwt. gross weight. (Christie's) $1,395

One of a pair of George III vase-shaped mustard pots, by R. Emes and E. Barnard, 1811, 5¼in. high, 42oz. (Christie's) $3,996

A George III pierced and bright cut reeded oval mustard pot, with two matching salt cellars and spoons, by Peter and Anne Bateman, London, 1798. (Christie's) $497

A C. R. Ashbee silver mustard pot, set with six turquoise cabochons, London hallmarks for 1900, 8cm. high. (Christie's) $1,313

George III silver mustard pot, by Edward Capper, London, 1797, 3¾in. high. (Bermondsey) $325

A Charles Boyton hammered silver four-piece condiments set, the mustard pots with spoons and glass liners, 1947, 10oz. (Christie's) $913

George III oval mustard pot, by Hester Bateman, London, 1787, 3in. high.(Bermondsey) $325

NUTMEGS

An English silver nutmeg grater, maker's marks for T. Phipps and E. Robinson, circa 1791/2, 2in. long. (Robt. W. Skinner Inc.) $400

A 19th century Continental silver nutmeg grater, with two hinged ends, 2.7/8in. long. (Robt. W. Skinner Inc.) $250

An English silver nutmeg grater, maker's marks for T. Phipps and E. Robinson, circa 1800/1, 2.3/8in. long. (Robt. W. Skinner Inc.) $350

A George III kitchen nutmeg grater of semi-circular section, with arched handle, by Phipps & Robinson, 1805. (Phillips) $323

A 20th century sterling silver nutmeg grater, Gorham Mfg. Co., in the form of a melon, 2in. long. (Robt. W. Skinner Inc.) $375

A George IV kitchen nutmeg grater with tongue and dart borders, by Charles Rawlings, 1824. (Phillips) $617

PORRINGERS

A Victorian two-handled porringer with leaf capped scroll handles, 19cm. high, Britannia Standard 1884, 67oz. (Phillips) $1,386

A Charles II two-handled porringer and cover, 1674, maker's mark CM, 7in. high. (Christie's) $28,771

A Charles II silver gilt two-handled porringer and cover, 1676, maker's mark TC, a fish above, a trefoil below, 5¾in. high, 21oz. (Christie's) $5,594

SALTS

Two of a set of four Hukin & Heath silver salts with salt spoons, Birmingham hallmarks for 1879, 6oz. 4dwt, each 3.4cm. high. (Christie's)$1,261

One of a pair of silver octagonal salts, by Wm. Forbes for Ball, Tomkins & Black, N.Y., 1839-51, 2½in. high, 7oz. (Christie's)$605

A pair of George III silver circular salts, maker possibly S. C. Young & Co., Sheffield, 1813, 3½in. diam., and a pair of salt spoons. (Edgar Horn) $452

One of a pair of George IV silver gilt shell-shaped salt cellars, by Edward Farrell, 1824, 8¾in. high, 70oz. (Christie's) $16,783

A three-piece condiment set in the Art Nouveau style, by Wm. Hutton & Sons Ltd., Birmingham, 1905. (Lawrence Fine Art) $224

One of a set of six silver gilt Victorian swing handled salts, 9cm. long, 1872, by George Fox, also one of six cast gilt salt spoons, by G. Adams, 1880, 16oz. (Phillips) $2,058

One of a set of six George III fluted circular salt cellars, by Paul Storr, four 1815, two 1818, 49oz. (Christie's) $7,992

Four Victorian silver salt cellars, each formed as a standing figure, by E. & J. Barnard, 7¾in. high, 70oz. (Christie's) $26,438

One of a set of four George III plain circular salt cellars, by Paul Storr, 1798, 15oz. 5dwt. (Christie's) $1,879

SAUCEBOATS

One of a set of four George II plain shaped oval sauceboats, by John Pollock, 1752, 8½in. 60oz. (Christie's) $4,315

One of a pair of George IV oval ogee sided sauceboats, by I. H. and G. Lias, London 1824, 28oz. (Woolley & Wallis) $1,850

One of four George II plain sauceboats, by Edward Wakelin, 1757, 74oz. (Christie's) $6,713

One of a pair of George II plain sauceboats with serpent scroll handle, by Robt. Brown, 1743, 24oz. (Christie's) $3,132

One of a pair of Georgian oval sauceboats, London, 1759, 22oz. (Worsfolds) $792

A George III sauceboat, makers probably WF for Wm. Fountain, 1809, 15oz. 13dwt. (Christie's) $2,488

·One of a pair of George II plain sauceboats with rising dolphin handles, by Francis Crump, 1742, 29oz. (Christie's) $6,531

One of a pair of George III sauceboats, by Abraham Portal, 1763, 42oz. (Christie's) $5,594

One of a pair of George II sauceboats on three rococo scroll and shell feet, by J. Kirkup, Newcastle, 1754, 46oz. (Christie's) $3,132

SNUFF BOXES

A mid 19th century Russian niello snuff box with foliate scroll decoration, maker's mark EE, Moscow, circa 1850. (Phillips) $447

A Continental silver and tortoiseshell snuff box, unmarked probably French, circa 1820. (Christie's) $170

An Austro-Hungarian rectangular snuff box, Vienna, 1852, 9cm. long. (Christie's) $125

An early Victorian gilt lined, engine-turned box with applied cast floral thumbpiece, possibly by E. Edwards, London, 1839, 4¾in. long. (Christie's) $666

A George IV rectangular snuff box, maker I.W.G., London, 1828, 3¼in. long. (Woolley & Wallis) $432

A Victorian silver snuff box engraved on the cover with a view of Wricklemarsh, Blackheath, Kent, by Yapp & Woodward, Birmingham, 1845, 4¾in. long.(Christie's) $1,957

A George III double section silver snuff box, maker's mark I.A., London, 1814, 3½ x 2½in. (Parsons, Welch & Cowell) $301

A silver mounted stag's horn snuff mull with chained pricker and perforated stopper, circa 1700, 4¾in. wide. (Christie's) $466

An early 18th century oval mounted tortoiseshell snuff box, impressed with a portrait of Queen Anne and signed 'OB' for Obrisset, circa 1710. (Phillips) $294

A Scottish silver mounted cowrie shell snuff box, circa 1810. (Christie's)$162

A Victorian rectangular silver snuff box, maker's mark F.M., Birmingham, 1854, 3½ x 2½in., 4½oz. (Parsons, Welch & Cowell) $287

A French 19th century oblong snuff box, the base and sides nielloed with a chequered effect, 3½in. long. (Christie's) $518

A George IV hunting scene snuff box, by John Jones III, 1824, 8.8cm. long. (Lawrence Fine Art) $814

A late 17th/early 18th century oval tortoiseshell snuff box, the cover inlaid with chinoiserie scene. (Phillips) $176

A French 19th century oblong gilt lined snuff box, the lid finely nielloed with 18th century hunting scene, with house and trees beyond, 3½in. long. (Christie's) $473

An early Victorian castle top snuff box, by N. Mills, Birmingham, 1838, 7.2cm. long. (Lawrence Fine Art) $574

A Victorian table snuff box, by F. Clark, Birmingham, 1843, 3¾in. wide, 4½oz. (Woolley & Wallis) $414

A Swiss rectangular gold musical snuff box, circa 1830, 2¾in. long. (Christie's) $9,590

A late 17th/early 18th century tortoiseshell snuff box inlaid in silver with a seascape, circa 1700. (Phillips) $323

A George II silver gilt fox mask snuff box, by T. Phipps & E. Robinson, 1807, 3¼in., 3oz. 10dwt. (Christie's) $3,110

An Italian rectangular silver gilt mounted hardstone snuff box, by Giacomo Sirletti, Rome, 1811-36, 3½in. long. (Christie's) $4,510

George IV silver snuff box, London, 1825, 3¼in. wide, 5oz. (Hobbs & Chambers) $403

A late 18th century Italian silver gilt circular snuff box, Venice, circa 1770, 5.6cm. diam. (Phillips) $372

A Birmingham rectangular silver gilt snuff box, by Joseph Willmore, 1841, 3¾in. long. (Christie's) $1,278

A William and Mary plain, slightly tapering cylindrical tankard, 1690, maker's mark FS, 6in. high, 18oz. 14dwt.(Christie's) $3,732

A Charles II tankard and cover engraved with scenes of the Plague and Fire of London, 1675, maker's mark IN mullet below, 7¾in. high, 38oz. (Christie's) $87,912

A Charles II plain cylindrical tankard and cover, 1671, maker's mark EG, 6½in. high, 21oz. (Christie's) $5,114

A George I tankard, fully marked Britannia Standard 1719, by C. Canner II, 17.2cm. high, 22oz. (Lawrence Fine Art) $2,073

A George III silver baluster tankard, London, 1760, 4¼in. high, 8oz.4dwt. (Dacre, Son & Hartley) $374

A George III baluster tankard, by John Payne, 1768, the handle with maker's mark, 20cm. high, 26oz. (Lawrence Fine Art) $1,609

A Sir Edmund Berry Godfrey flagon, maker's mark IN mullet below, 1675, with short molded lip added, circa 1720, 12.3/8in. high, 66oz. (Christie's) $63,936

A George IV cylindrical lidded quart tankard, by R. Emes and E. Barnard, London, 1826, 7.75in. high, 38oz. (Woolley & Wallis) $1,650

A George III plain tapering cylindrical tankard, by Peter, Anne and William Bateman, 1800, 8in. high, 26oz. (Christie's) $1,758

A Charles II silver gilt tankard and cover, maker's mark MK in a lozenge, mullet above and below, 1683, 7½in. high, 34oz. (Christie's) $3,676

A German silver tankard and cover, Augsburg, circa 1690, maker's mark PS, 4½in. high, 8oz.11dwt. (Christie's) $3,732

A William III Irish plain tapering cylindrical tankard, by Joseph Walker, Dublin, 1699, 7½in. high, 28oz. (Christie's) $3,356

A 19th century Continental parcel gilt peg tankard and cover, 8½in. high, 38oz. (Christie's) $2,177

A George II silver lidded tankard by James Manners, London, 1734, 7in. high, 20oz. (Chancellors Hollingsworths) $1,102

A James II plain cylindrical tankard and cover, York, 1686, maker's mark IO, perhaps for John Oliver, 6¾in. high, 21oz. (Christie's) $4,795

A Charles II plain slightly tapering cylindrical tankard, 1681, maker's mark IC, mullet below, 6¾in. high, 24oz. (Christie's) $3,996

A George II silver baluster tankard with leaf and scroll decorated handle, London, 1759, 4¾in. high, 10oz.12dwt. (Dacre, Son & Hartley) $374

An Indian tapering cylindrical tankard, by Robert Hamilton, Calcutta, circa 1812, 6in. high, 19oz.8dwt. (Christie's) $3,445

Part of a suite of Queen Anne tazze, comprising one large, 26cm. diam., and a smaller pair, 18cm. diam., by Jacob Margas, 1709, 37oz. (Phillips) $4,410

Sterling silver covered chalice, by Georg Jensen, Denmark, circa 1923, 5¾in. high. (Robt. W. Skinner Inc.) $703

A small tazza designed by G. Albertus, stamped GI 925 S 468, circa 1928, 8.9cm. high, 9oz.5dwt. (Christie's) $1,096

A tazza designed by Georg Jensen, stamped G J 025S 265, circa 1940, 12.7cm. high, 7oz.5dwt.(Christie's) $939

A covered tazza designed by J. Rohde, stamped Dessin J.R. Georg Jensen 43, circa 1920, 15.5cm. high, 14oz. 9dwt. (Christie's) $1,466

A large tazza, designed by Georg Jensen, assay mark with London import mark for 1924. 26.5cm. high, 36oz. 6dwt. (Christie's) $6,000

A tazza designed by Georg Jensen, stamped 1921, G J 830 S 263, 18.8cm. high, 16oz.5dwt. (Christie's) $1,409

A Georg Jensen silver tazza, stamped with maker's marks, Georg Jensen, Denmark, Sterling, 263B and London import marks for 1928, 18.5cm. high, 18oz. (Christie's) $1,576

A large tazza designed by G. Jensen, stamped marks Georg Jensen GI925, 264, 26.7cm. high, 35oz.12dwt.(Christie's) $6,264

TEA & COFFEE SETS

SILVER

Three-piece silver partial teaset, America, 1870's, coffee pot 12in. high, approx. 78 troy oz. (Robt. W. Skinner Inc.) $550

An early Victorian four-piece tea and coffee service, 1838 and 1839, by Wm. Eaton, the coffee pot 21.5cm. high, 75oz. (Lawrence Fine Art) $1,914

A Victorian four-piece tea and coffee service, by John Edward Terrey, 1844, the coffee pot 26.5cm. high, 73oz. (Lawrence Fine Art)
$1,850

A Victorian four-piece tea and coffee service, by Thos. Smiley, 1865, the coffee pot 21.5cm. high, 68oz. (Lawrence Fine Art) $1,515

Part of a William IV tea and coffee service, by Henry Wilkinson & Co., Sheffield, 1832, coffee pot 24cm. high, 62oz. (Lawrence Fine Art)
$1,084

A five-piece tea service, by Joseph Lownes, Phila., circa 1815, teapot
7in. high, gross weight 115oz. (Christie's) $4,400

Late 19th century Portuguese tea and coffee service, comprising a teapot,
coffee pot, a two-handled sugar basin and cream jug with bracket handles
and rope twist rims, coffee pot 9in. high, 175oz. (Christie's)
     $2,975

A six-piece part tea and coffee service, by various makers for Ball, Black
& Co., N.Y., circa 1851, coffee pot 11¼in. high, gross weight 162oz.
(Christie's) $2,640

A three-piece tea service with a pair of teacups and saucers, by Gorham
Mfg. Co., Providence, 1880, teapot 4½in. high, gross weight 24oz.
(Christie's) $1,870

An eight-piece tea and coffee service and tray, by Tiffany & Co., N.Y.,
circa 1860/70, Etruscan pattern, coffee pot 11¾in. high, tray 34in. long,
gross weight 397oz.10dwt. (Christie's) $20,350

A six-piece tea and coffee service, the wooden handles squared and
reeded, by Fletcher & Gardiner, Phila., 1813/14, coffee pot 10in. high,
gross weight 194oz. (Christie's) $12,100

One of a set of three George II tea caddies and sugar boxes, by Isabel Pero, 1741, the caddies each with a pewter liner, and a George III Old English pattern caddy spoon, 68oz. (Christie's) $21,772

A George I plain, shaped oblong tea caddy with slide top, London, 1722, Britannia Standard, 4½in. high. (Christie's) $681

A George III plain, oval tea caddy, by Hester Bateman, London, 1785, 12.5cm. wide, 10oz. (Christie's) $1,924

One of a set of three George III oblong tea caddies and sugar box, by Peze Pilleau, 1743, 38oz. (Christie's) $4,071

One of a set of three George II silver gilt, vase-shaped tea caddies, by Samuel Taylor, 1752, 31oz. (Christie's) $7,992

A George III oval tea caddy, by Thos. Phipps and Edward Robinson II, 1784, 12.4cm. high, 12.4oz. (Lawrence Fine Art) $1,455

A George III rectangular tea caddy on rim foot, with blue glass liner, unmarked, circa 1775. (Christie's) $4,795

A George II plain, shaped rectangular tea caddy, by Edward Gibbon, London, 1721, 4¾in. high. (Christie's) $1,136

A George III cylindrical tea caddy, by J. Parker and E. Wakelin, circa 1765, 5¼in. high, 19oz. (Christie's) $4,155

Part of a silver five-piece tea and coffee service, the tea kettle on scroll pierced stand with burner, 13¾in. high. (Christie's) $681

An electroplated kettle, the design attributed to Dr. Christopher Dresser, 15cm. high. (Christie's) $181

A beaded and foliate chased, part fluted tea kettle with mother-of-pearl finial, on a naturalistic crossed branch stand fitted with a burner, 13¼in. high. (Christie's) $127

A George II tea kettle stand and lamp, by Ayme Videau, London, 1733, 35cm. high, 70oz. (Christie's) $2,190

An Austro-Hungarian, mid 19th century, compressed swing handled tea kettle, on a trefoil stand, fitted with a burner, 14½in. high, 55oz. free. (Christie's) $1,013

George III embossed spirit kettle, London 1760, 12½in. high, 47oz. (Hobbs & Chambers) $2,400

A Hukin & Heath electroplated picnic kettle with folding tripod stand and spirit burner, designed by Dr. C. Dresser, 14.5cm. high. (Christie's) $242

A George III plain circular tea kettle, stand and burner, the kettle by H. Bateman, 1783, the stand and burner by Chas. S. Harris, 1881, 63oz. (Christie's) $1,598

A Georgian design plated spirit kettle, the stand complete with burner, circa 1900, 12in. high. (Peter Wilson & Co.) $132

TEAPOTS

A silver teapot of compressed globular shape, by Jones, Lows & Ball, Boston, 1839/40, 5¾in. high, gross weight 50oz. (Christie's) $880

A George II plain bullet-shaped teapot with hinged cover, by Thos. Farren, 1727, gros 14oz.7dwt. (Christie's) $5,287

An English silver teapot, Sheffield, maker's mark of Thos. Law, 1804/5, 4¾in. high, 15oz. (Robt. W. Skinner Inc.) $275

A George III teapot with beech scroll handle and finial, by J. Emes, 1801, 27cm. across, 16.7oz. all in. (Lawrence Fine Art) $239

A silver teapot, oval, with a domed hinged lid, by F. Marquand, Georgia, 1820/26, 9½in. high, gross weight 33oz. (Christie's) $660

An Indian oval teapot on rim foot, by Hamilton & Co., Calcutta, circa 1822, 6¾in. high, gross 29oz. (Christie's) $2,505

A William IV naturalistic melon-shaped teapot, by E. J. & W. Barnard, 6in. high, Port Cullus crest, London, 1835, 17oz. all in. (Christie's) $562

One of a pair of early Victorian flared cylindrical teapots, by Robert Garrard, London, 1844, 46oz. all in. (Woolley & Wallis) $1,533

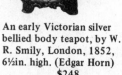

An early Victorian silver bellied body teapot, by W. R. Smily, London, 1852, 6½in. high. (Edgar Horn) $248

A George III oval teapot on stand, 1796, the stand 1795, by Henry Chawner, 26cm. across, 19.2oz. all in. (Lawrence Fine Art) $1,116

A silver teapot with an S-shaped spout, by Samuel Williamson, Phila., 1794/1813, 7¾in. high, gross weight 28oz. (Christie's) $1,210

A George II bullet shaped teapot with straight tapering hexagonal spout, by Gabriel Sleath, 1728, gross 15oz. 3dwt. (Christie's) $5,287

TRAYS & SALVERS

A two-handled tea tray, by Walker & Hall, Sheffield, 1910, 74cm. across handles, 131oz. (Lawrence Fine Art) $1,467

An oval tea tray with plain center, by Walker & Hall, Sheffield, 1914, 62.3cm. wide, 92oz. (Lawrence Fine Art) $1,052

One of a pair of George III oblong salvers, by Wm. Bateman, 1817, 30.5cm. wide, 52oz. (Lawrence Fine Art) $3,588

A shaped rectangular two-handled tea tray, maker's mark JS, Sheffield, 1927, 66.2cm. across handles, 104oz. (Lawrence Fine Art) $1,212

One of a pair of George III Irish circular salvers, by John Laughlin Jnr., Dublin, 1782, 21.6cm. diam., 26oz. (Lawrence Fine Art) $1,052

An early George III shaped circular salver, by John Crouch, 1772, 30.5cm. diam., 30oz. (Lawrence Fine Art) $957

A rectangular two-handled tea tray with plain center, maker's mark rubbed, 1906, 70.5cm. wide, 145oz. (Lawrence Fine Art) $1,674

One of a pair of two-handled oval trays each on four feet, by J. Crouch and T. Hannam, 1791, 22¾in. long, 158oz. (Christie's) $19,699

A George II plain octafoil
salver, by John Robinson
II, 1738, 13½in. diam.,
30oz. (Christie's)
$3,196

A George I silver gilt fifteen
sided salver, by A. Courtauld,
1723, 11¼in. wide, 35oz.
(Christie's) $44,755

A George III two-handled
plain oval tray, by John
Crouch, 1807, 25¾in. long,
102oz. (Christie's)
$5,754

One of twelve George III
plain shaped circular dinner
plates, by Robt. Calderwood,
Dublin, circa 1760, 9½in.
diam., 210oz. (Christie's)
$5,909

A George II shaped circular
salver, by Elizabeth Buteux,
1732, 12.3/8in. diam., 33oz.
(Christie's) $4,665

A Regency two-handled oval
tray on four shell, foliage and
lion's paw feet, by R. Sibley,
28¼in. long, 152oz.
(Christie's) $7,992

A silver salver on four cast
foliate lion's paw feet, by
Obadiah Rich, Boston,
circa 1835, 14in. diam.,
47oz. (Christie's)
$550

A Victorian large Irish silver
circular salver, by R. Sawyer,
Dublin, 1842, 25in. diam.,
215oz. (Christie's)
$5,909

A George III shaped circular
salver, by Richard Rugg,
1775, 14in. diam., 42oz.
(Christie's) $2,349

TRAYS & SALVERS

A silver tazza on circular foot, by Gorham Mfg. Co., bearing the mark of Kennard & Jenks, Boston, circa 1880, 10½in. diam., 19oz. (Christie's) $13,200

A George III circular salver, by Wm. Fountain and D. Pontifax, London 1793, 13in. diam., 30oz. (Woolley & Wallis) $947

A George II shaped circular salver, by Sarah Holaday, 1740, 16.3/8in. diam., 70oz. (Christie's) $4,635

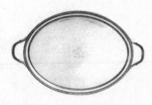

An English silver oval serving tray, maker's mark for J. Edward, circa 1798/9, 30¼in. long, 108oz. (Robt. W. Skinner Inc.) $3,200

An oval silver salver, by Wm. Forbes for Ball, Tompkins & Black, N.Y., 1839/51, 13in. long, 24oz.10dwt. (Christie's) $528

A George III oval two-handled tray, by Thos. Hannam & J. Crouch, 1800, 20¾in. 53oz. (Christie's) $2,818

One of a pair of George I plain circular salvers, by R. Timbrell & J. Bell I, 1714, 9¾in. diam., 33oz. (Christie's) $8,791

A George I shaped square waiter, probably by E. Cornock, 1725, 5.7/8in. square, 6oz.4dwt. (Christie's) $1,399

A George III shaped circular salver, by James Ellis & Co., Sheffield, 1818, 25.8cm. diam., 23.5oz. (Lawrence Fine Art) $455

SILVER

One of a pair of George III shaped oval two-handled sauce tureens and covers, by D. Smith and R. Sharp, 1767, 9in. long, 41oz. (Christie's)$6,073

One of a pair of Sheffield plated boat shape sauce tureens and covers, 23.7cm. across handles. (Lawrence Fine Art) $701

A George II two-handled shaped oval soup tureen and cover, by George Methuen, 1752, with plated liner, 14in. overall, 88oz. (Christie's) $7,992

A George II two-handled oval bombe soup tureen and cover, by Wm. Cripps, 1751, 14½in. long, gross 117oz. (Christie's) $11,162

A George III circular soup tureen, stand and cover, by Paul Storr, 1805, 11¾in. high, 267oz. (Christie's) $68,947

A Victorian two-handled shaped oval silver soup tureen and cover, by S. Hayne and D. Cater, 1845, 14½in. long, 111oz. (Christie's) $6,531

A two-handled shaped oval soup tureen and cover, by Elkington & Co., Birmingham, 1909, 126oz. (Christie's) $4,698

A Regency two-handled oval soup tureen, cover and stand, by Thos. Robins, 1811, the liner 1812, 20¾in., 387oz. (Christie's) $28,771

A Sheffield plated oval soup tureen and cover, 41cm. across handles. (Lawrence Fine Art) $1,180

SILVER

A George III soup tureen, probably by Charles Hougham, 1763, together with a spare cover and plated liner, 130oz. (Phillips) $6,750

A George II two-handled shaped oval soup tureen and cover, by F. Kandler, 1753, 11¼in. long, 132oz. (Christie's)
$13,996

One of a pair of George III Regency two-handled oval sauce tureens and covers, by Thos. Robins, 1810, 9in. long, 74oz. (Christie's)
$4,698

One of a pair of Regency ormolu mounted Pontypool chestnut urns, 10½in. wide. (Christie's) $6,696

A Victorian soup tureen and cover, by T. W. H. & H. Dobson, 1880, 30cm. across handles, 46.5oz. (Lawrence Fine Art) $1,515

A Victorian silver two-handled shaped oval soup tureen and cover, by B. Smith II, 1838, 17½in. long, 179oz.(Christie's)
$6,220

A Hukin & Heath electro-plated soup tureen and cover, designed by Dr. C. Dresser, 31cm. diam. (Christie's)
$4,099

One of four George III boat-shaped two-handled sauce tureens and covers, by John Emes, 1798, 9¾in. long, 72oz. (Christie's) $6,264

A tureen and cover designed by Georg Jensen, stamped Georg Jensen 337B, 132.5cm. wide, 63oz.16dwt. (Christie's) $26,622

A silver plated Art Nouveau covered urn, circa 1900, 16¼in. high. (Robt. W. Skinner Inc.) $200

A sugar urn with a pierced gallery and a tapering conical lid with an urn finial, circa 1785-1810, 9½in. high, 15oz. (Christie's) $880

A Belgian fluted, pear-shaped tea urn, on an ebonized trefoil base fitted with a burner, hallmarked in London, 1899, 14¼in. high, 53.25oz. gross. (Christie's) $2,235

A large Victorian two-handled vase shaped tea urn in the style of Robert Adam, 22¾in. high. (Christie's) $616

A Russian silver two-handled samovar, by Adolf Sper, 1847, 15¼in. high, gross 129oz. (Christie's) $5,909

A Victorian electroplated tea urn with domed cover, 58cm. high. (Lawrence Fine Art) $1,034

An early 19th century Sheffield plate hot water urn, complete with burner, 14in. high. (Robt. W. Skinner Inc.) $600

An early 19th century silver plated samovar with campana shaped body and scroll handles, 16in. high. (Bermondsey) $270

A silver George III tea urn, by J. Wakelin and R. Garrard, 1792, 18½in. high, gross 99oz. (Christie's) $4,976

A William IV vase, by Charles Fox II, 1830, 11.7cm. high, 14.7oz. (Lawrence Fine Art) $371

A William Hutton & Son silver and glass vase, stamped maker's marks, and London hallmarks for 1902, 11.2cm. high. (Phillips) $150

One of a pair of reproduction Warwick vases, by the Goldsmiths & Silversmiths Co. Ltd., 1910, 29cm. diam., 245.5oz. (Phillips) $5,640

A silver double vase on stand, by The Sweetser Co., New York, circa 1900-15, the stand of copper, 11½in. high, gross wt. of vase 20oz.10dwt. (Christie's) $1,540

A pair of crocus-shaped embossed silver vases with leaf decoration, 6¼in. high. (Dacre, Son & Hartley) $150

A Liberty silver vase, the design attributed to A. Knox, stamped Cymric. L & Co within three lozenges and with Birmingham hallmarks for 1907, 17cm. high. (Christie's) $391

A silver enamelled bud base, by Tiffany & Co., N.Y., circa 1893, 5.3/8in. high, 5oz.10dwt. (Christie's) $1,210

A George IV replica of the Warwick vase and cover, by The Boulton Plate Co., Birmingham, 1827, 13in. high, 163oz. (Christie's) $12,787

A George III sugar vase with swing handle, by Robt. Hennell, 1782, 8oz. (Phillips) $661

An oblong silver 'Castletop' vinaigrette chased on the cover with a view of Westminster Abbey, by N. Mills, Birmingham 1842, 1¾in. long. (Christie's) $959

A 19th century Chinese Export oblong vinaigrette with engine-turned base, by Khecheong of Canton, circa 1850. (Phillips) $178

An oblong gold vinaigrette with perforated grille, London 1818, maker's initials GL, 18ct. (Christie's) $959

A George IV vinaigrette in the form of a purse, by Lawrence & Co., Birmingham, 1821, 3cm. long. (Lawrence Fine Art) $287

An early Victorian castle top vinaigrette, the cover case with a view of Windsor Castle, by John Tongue, Birmingham, 1845, 4cm. long. (Lawrence Fine Art) $614

A George IV rectangular vinaigrette, by Thos. Newbold, Birmingham, 1821, 3.2cm. long. (Lawrence Fine Art) $223

A Victorian gilt lined, bright cut, shaped oblong vinaigrette with vacant scroll cartouche, by F. Clarke, Birmingham, 1846. (Christie's) $111

A William IV silver gilt vinaigrette, by Taylor & Perry, Birmingham, 1833, 2.1cm. long. (Lawrence Fine Art) $63

A George IV engine-turned and gilded vinaigrette, L. & Co., Birmingham, 1822. (Christie's) $205

A George III 'goldstone' mounted vinaigrette, by J. Shaw, Birmingham, 1809, 2.9cm. long. (Lawrence Fine Art) $127

A William IV silver gilt engine-turned vinaigrette with reeded sides, by Thos. Shaw, Birmingham, 1830. (Christie's) $133

A George III vinaigrette, by Samuel Pemberton, Birmingham, 1809. (Phillips) $205

An Old Sheffield plate wine cooler of campana shape, by Matthew Boulton & Co., 9in. high. (Capes, Dunn & Co.) $331

One of a pair of wine coolers, stamped Georg Jensen GI 925S 289, 9.8cm. high, 29oz. 9dwt. (Christie's) $5,481

One of four silver William IV two-handled vase-shaped wine coolers of krater form, by Paul Storr, 1834, 12¾in. high, 384oz. (Christie's) $116,640

One of a pair of George III silver gilt two-handled wine coolers, by Paul Storr, 1810, the collars and liners 1809, 11¾in. high, 369oz. (Christie's) $47,952

One of a pair of Russian silver campana-shaped two-handled wine coolers, by C. J. Tegelsten, 1849, 16in. high, 406oz. (Christie's) $23,328

One of a pair of Old Sheffield plate two-handled campana-shaped wine coolers, by T. & J. Creswick, circa 1830, 10¼in. high. (Christie's) $3,516

One of a pair of Sheffield plated wine coolers, by T. & J. Creswick, 23cm. high. (Lawrence Fine Art) $2,197

One of a pair of electro-plated Victorian wine coolers, by Elkington & Co., 1873, 22cm. high. (Phillips) $1,833

A George IV silver gilt two-handled campana-shaped wine cooler, by Paul Storr, 1825, 11¼in. high, 102oz. (Christie's)$15,552

A plain amber flattened
disc-shaped snuff bottle,
with a dragon around the
neck, with stopper.
(Christie's) $227

An agate flattened disc-
shaped snuff bottle, banded
with an irregular concentric
panel, with stopper.
(Christie's) $199

A mottled apple and celadon
jadeite disc-shaped snuff
bottle and stopper.
(Christie's) $570

A red lacquer spade-shaped
snuff bottle, relief carved
with two pairs of figures
on fenced terraces.
(Christie's) $1,069

An agate rounded square snuff
bottled carved in intaglio from
a brown inclusion on one side,
with stopper. (Christie's)
$683

An inside painted glass disc-
shaped snuff bottle, dated
1981. (Christie's)
$270

An inside painted rock crystal
rounded rectangular snuff
bottle with figures on a
snowy terrace, inscribed, with
stopper. (Christie's)
$199

An agate flattened disc-
shaped snuff bottle, carved
from an area of darker inclusion as a sage sitting on rockwork. (Christie's)
$2,138

An agate rounded square
snuff bottle of translucent
grayish tone with gilt metal
collared coral stopper.
(Christie's) $2,138

An inside painted glass rectangular bottle with two equestrian archers pursuing a deer, signed Chen Zhongsan. (Christie's)$369

A Beijing four-colour overlay white-ground spade-shaped snuff bottle carved with dense flowering peony sprays. (Christie's) $369

An agate rounded rectangular snuff bottle carved on one side from a caramel shadow with three birds around a tree. (Christie's) $683

A red lacquer spade-shaped snuff bottle, relief carved with two groups of children playing, with stopper. (Christie's) $427

An inside painted glass rounded square snuff bottle painted with a leopard beneath bamboo, signed Wang Bai-chuan, dated 1982. (Christie's) $327

A white jade rounded square snuff bottle and matching stopper, carved overall with bands of wicker work. (Christie's) $1,568

An agate rounded square bottle with animal mask ring handles. (Christie's) $398

A green overlay caramel-ground disc-shaped bottle carved with figures on terraces, with stopper. (Christie's) $570

An agate rounded square snuff bottle carved on one side from the caramel skin with two grazing horses and a monkey. (Christie's) $512

Late 17th century Buddhist stone stela of typical form, dated Genroku 5 (1692), with a later inscription and date Meiji 34 (1901), 77.5cm. high. (Christie's) $1,389

Contemporary Eskimo carving of a moustached walrus, in mottled greenish-dark gray stone, 21in. long. (Robt. W. Skinner Inc.) $450

One of a pair of carved granite Foo dogs and stands, China, 19th century, 28½in. high. (Robt. W. Skinner Inc.) $4,200

Contemporary Eskimo carving of a wrestling man and bear in mottled greenish-gray stone, 18in. high. (Robt. W. Skinner Inc.) $700

A 19th century Italian alabaster model of the Warwick Vase, after the Antique, 64cm. high. (Christie's) $2,700

A carved limestone sculpture of Mother and Child, by W. Edmondson, circa 1934/39, 15in. high. (Christie's) $9,900

Contemporary Eskimo carving of a weeping woman holding a child, in greenish-gray marblized stone, 17½in. high. (Robt. W. Skinner Inc.) $850

A stone horse's head, Han Dynasty, 12.9cm. high. (Christie's) $13,500

An Egyptian alabaster ointment jar, pear shaped with short flat rimmed neck, nub handles, 5½in. high, in brocade covered box. (Robt. W. Skinner Inc.) $300

A group of stone fruit in a wooden bowl, comprising fourteen pieces of various fruit, bowl 11.5/8in. diam. (Christie's) $605

Contemporary Eskimo carving, Abraham, Port Harrison, of marbled green-graystone, 23in. high. (Robt. W. Skinner Inc.) $1,600

Contemporary Eskimo carving of three men skinning a seal, in polished medium gray soapstone, 19in. long. (Robt. W. Skinner Inc.) $1,300

A James Woolford plaster figure modelled as a diving mermaid with a dolphin, circa 1930, 59cm. high. (Christie's) $315

A pair of carved stone putti, the plump figures standing, one holding a bird, the other a basket of fruit, 38in. high. (Christie's) $3,300

A greenish-gray and black stone figure of a seated roaring lion, Tang Dynasty, 13cm. high. (Christie's) $1,746

A Northern Qi stele with two figures of Buddha seated side by side, dated Tianbao 6th year, tenth month, tenth day, corresponding to AD555, 29cm. high. (Christie's) $15,000

A pink granite column with turned shaft and spreading base, 9¼in. diam., 46in. high. (Christie's) $1,566

Late 17th century English stone figure of 'Prometheus Bound', in the manner of Cibber, 175cm. high. (Phillips) $15,750

A 17th century Brussels tapestry woven in silks and wools, 10ft.11in. x 10ft.6in. (Christie's) $8,553

A 17th century Brussels tapestry woven in well preserved wools and silks, 8ft. x 11ft.2in. (Christie's) $14,256

A late 17th century Brussels tapestry in well preserved silks and wools, 9ft.8in. x 7ft.10in. (Christie's) $19,245

Mid 18th century Brussels tapestry woven in silk and wool with Jupiter and his eagle receiving thunderbolts from Vulcan, 13ft.1in. x 8ft. 4in. (Christie's)$5,909

A 17th century Spanish or Italian tapestry woven in muted colors , 94 x 99in. (Christie's) $6,577

An Aubusson tapestry woven with lovers and sheep in a rustic landscape, 7ft.6in. x 4ft.8in. (Christie's) $3,576

A 17th century Flemish Verdure tapestry woven with a dog beneath a tree in a pond by a forest clearing with a palace beyond, 8ft.5in. x 9ft.7in. (Christie's) $3,421

An 18th century Louis XV Beauvais tapestry from the Tenture des Verdures Fines, woven in silk and wool, 8ft. 7in. x 6ft.1in. (Christie's) $5,702

A late 17th century Flemish Verdure tapestry with a shepherd and shepherdess in a forest with their flock, 9ft. 3in. x 8ft.7in. (Christie's) $4,561

TAPESTRIES

A 17th century Flemish Verdure tapestry woven with a man with a billowing cloak and a lady in a forest clearing, 8ft.9in. x 6ft.4in. (Christie's) $2,566

A 17th century Brussels Verdure tapestry with dancing peasants in a forest clearing, 6ft.10in. x 11ft.9in. (Christie's) $7,840

A 16th century Flemish tapestry woven in wools and silks with a hunting scene, 7ft.8in. x 9ft.7in. (Christie's) $7,413

An 18th century Gobelins tapestry woven in wools and silks with two Chinamen in a landscape, 9ft.6in. x 5ft. 4½in. (Christie's) $9,979

Early 18th century Brussels tapestry woven in silk and wool with the family of Darius prostrate before Alexander the Great, 13ft.9in. x 22ft.7in. (Christie's) $6,998

Early 18th century Brussels tapestry woven in wool and silk depicting Neptune, 13ft. 10in. x 10ft.4in.(Christie's) $4,665

A 16th century Dutch tapestry woven in silks and wools with Christ and the woman caught in adultery, 7ft.10in. x 6ft.7in. (Christie's) $18,662

A 17th century Brussels tapestry depicting a boar hunt, 9ft. x 6ft.1in. (Christie's) $5,702

Late 16th century Flemish Verdure tapestry woven with various scenes in a forest, 8ft. 5in. x 21ft.11in. (Christie's) $24,883

A Flemish tapestry woven with a pair of partridges in a landscape, 8ft.2in. x 13ft. 8in. (Christie's) $3,421

Late 16th century Brussels tapestry woven with the story of Tobias and the Angel in a landscape, 6ft.9in. x 14ft.4in. (Christie's)
$7,776

Mid 18th century Brussels tapestry woven in silk and wool with the triumph of Mars, 16ft. 2in. x 12ft.11in. (Christie's) $8,553

A Flemish tapestry, depicting Athena in three feathered helmet beside a warrior, late 17th/ early 18th century, 9ft. high x 4ft.7in. (Woolley & Wallis) $1,260

A 17th century Brussels tapestry woven in silks and wools with Hercules holding the severed head of the Nemean Lion, 6ft.11½in. x 12ft.3in. (Christie's) $3,564

Mid 18th century Brussels tapestry woven in silk and wool, with the god Apollo playing his lyre, 12ft.11in. x 9ft.6in. (Christie's)
$5,909

TEXTILES

'A faithful representation of Her Most Gracious Majesty, Caroline Queen of England in the House of Lords, 1820', a handkerchief on linen, 22in. wide. (Christie's) $576

'A representation of the Manchester Reform Meeting dispersed by the Civil and Military Powers, August 16, 1819', handkerchief on linen, 20 x 22in. (Christie's) $504

'The Reformers attack on the Old Rotten Tree — of the Foul Nests of our Morants in Danger', handkerchief printed in color on silk, circa 1830. (Christie's) $316

An early 19th century embroidered picture worked in silks and wools, 16 x 22in. (Christie's) $264

A Nazca textile, comprising three bands divided into rectangular sections of motifs in pink, yellow, white and brown on a red ground, 44 x 49cm. (Phillips) $147

Late 19th century embroidered picture worked in coloured silks, probably Mexican or South American, 19 x 24in. (Christie's) $382

TEXTILES

Mid 19th century needlework picture, wool, silk and metallic yarns, 8¼ x 9¼in. (Robt. W. Skinner Inc.) $20,500

A raised work picture of an ornamental pheasant against a Berlin woolwork ground, mid 19th century, 22 x 17½in. (Christie's) $78

Mid 18th century embroidered bed valance fragments, Mass., 4ft.2in. x 9½in. and 2ft.2in. x 9¼in. (Robt. W. Skinner Inc.) $3,400

Early 19th century appliqued table mat, America. (Robt. W. Skinner Inc.) $425

A circular Berlin woolwork picture of an Indian Nabob, in black glass mount framed and glazed, circa 1840, 16in. high. (Christie's) $249

A needlework carpet embroidered in colored wools, circa 1850, 43 x 82in. (Christie's) $1,146

A Navajo child's blanket, woven on a white saxony ply ground, 32 x 48in. (Robt. W. Skinner Inc.) $1,550

Probably early 19th century wide needlework border embroidered in pale colored wools in 17th century style, 17 x 90in. (Christie's) $297

TEXTILES

One of a set of five cushions worked in colored wools with sprays of flowers and edged with pink and yellow wool fringe, one 14 x 22in. the others smaller. (Christie's) $3,132

Mid 18th century framed needlework panel, worked in silk and metallic thread on silk faille ground, England, 7¾in. long, 32¾in. wide. (Robt. W. Skinner Inc.) $350

One of a set of four gros point borders worked in colored wools and silks, 11in. deep, 126in. long. (Christie's) $594

Plains paint decorated parfleche case, Yakima, 15 x 30in. (Robt. W. Skinner Inc.) $275

A Berlin woolwork cushion, the central medallion worked with raised plush roses, circa 1860, 18in. square. (Christie's) $2,035

Mid 19th century Berlin woolwork picture of a Turk, 29 x 25½in. (Christie's) $548

A raised work applique picture of a poodle against an orange velvet ground, in gilt frame worked with cornucopiae, circa 1800. (Christie's) $594

A Berlin woolwork cushion with a large central medallion and sprays of flowers, 18in. square. (Christie's) $1,409 £97

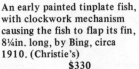

Dinky 28M green delivery van advertising "Atco Motor Mowers'. (Christie's) $420

An early painted tinplate fish, with clockwork mechanism causing the fish to flap its fin, 8¼in. long, by Bing, circa 1910. (Christie's) $330

A Gunthermann painted and lithographed four-door limousine with clockwork mechanism, German, circa 1910, 11½in. long. (Christie's) $1,200

An early printed and painted tinplate automobile, 'Tut Tut', EPL No. 490, by Lehmann, circa 1910, 6¾in. long. (Christie's) $1,350

A large dappled rocking horse, on metal hinged rockers, 51½in. high. (Lawrence Fine Art) $162

'Mickey Mouse Organ Grinder', tinplate toy with clockwork and musical mechanisms, by Distler, circa 1930, 6in. long. (Christie's) $975

A Triang Minic pre-war Learner's car, boxed, with key (M). (Phillips) $441

An Edwardian plush model bear on wheels, 1ft.4in. high, one ear and one eye missing. (Hobbs & Chambers) $148

A Triang Minic pre-war Rolls Tourer, boxed, with key. (Phillips) $323

A Jep painted tinplate 'Panhard Levassor', finished in tan with red lining, French, circa 1925, 30½in. long. (Christie's) $975

An early painted metal gunboat with clockwork mechanism, by Bing, circa 1904, 10½in. long. (Christie's) $330

Dinky 917, Guy van advertising 'Spratts'. (Christie's) $150

A dark plush teddy bear with straw stuffed body and elongated arms, back hump and felt pads, probably by Steiff, 40cm. high. (Phillips) $625

A carved and painted rocking horse with hair mane and tail, America, circa 1880, 52in. long. (Robt. W. Skinner Inc.) $1,200

One of three Britains' model Lifeguards and Officer, unboxed, damaged. (Hobbs & Chambers) $32

A Triang Minic pre-war 59 ME Searchlight lorry, boxed (M). (Phillips) $264

A dark plush teddy bear with wide apart rounded ears, black button eyes and pointed snout, probably by Steiff, 34cm. high. (Phillips) $596

A Triang Minic pre-war taxi (M), boxed, with key. (Phillips) $514

'Mac 700', a printed tinplate motorbike with rider, by Arnold, W. Germany, circa 1955, 7½in. long. (Christie's) $330

A Louis Marx tinplate 'Main St.' Tramway, the loop track with overhead power pylons with trams and trucks moving between station and terminal, 24in. long. (Lawrence Fine Art) $148

Gunthermann, Gordon Bennett clockwork racing car, finished in yellow with gold detail, 28cm. long. (Phillips) $5,880

A golden plush covered teddy bear, the front unhooking to reveal a metal hot water bottle, by Steiff, 17in. high.(Christie's) $1,584

Meccano, No. 2 Constructor Car constructed as a tourer, boxed. (Phillips) $1,764

A Steiff pale plush teddy bear with black thread stitched nose and straw stuffed body, with button in left ear, 33cm. high. (Phillips) $745

A printed and painted tinplate beetle, EPL No. 431, by Lehmann, circa 1906, 3¾in. long. (Christie's) $150

A wood and metal electric powered model of a Watson Type self-righting lifeboat, circa 1925, 24in. long, by Bassett-Lowke. (Christie's) $473

'New Century Cycle', EPL 345, with clockwork mechanism, by Lehmann, circa 1910, 5in. long. (Christie's) $1,275

A mechanical cast iron money box, as a football player with articulated right leg, causing the player to shoot a coin into a goal and ring a bell, circa 1890, 10½in. long. (Christie's) $825

A painted tinplate cat, 'Nina', EPL No. 790, by Lehmann, circa 1907, 11in. long. (Christie's) $1,500

A hand enamelled 'New Orleans Paddle Wheeler', probably by Dent, U.S.A., circa 1903, 10½in. long. (Christie's) $600

Part of a collection of five tinplate toys, comprising two prancing horses, a steam engine, a circular saw bench and another item. (Lawrence Fine Art) $14

A boxed set of diecast Build-Yourself vehicles, by Solido. (Phillips) $66

A Steiff blonde plush teddy bear, with metal disc in left ear, 17in. high. (Lawrence Fine Art) $1,465

'Baker and Sweep', E.P.L. No. 450, by Lehmann, circa 1905, in original box. (Christie's) $2,368

A painted wood dapple grey 'pony size' rocking horse, with horse hair mane and tail, 56in. long, British. (Christie's) $518

An early Carette carpet toy tinplate sailboat, with fly-wheel mechanism, German, circa 1905, 11¾in. long. (Christie's) $270

A teddy bear of gray plush with brown button eyes, embroidered nose, hump back and long paws, 13in. high. (Christie's)$419

A Magic Disc phenakisticope optical toy with 8 discs, each 7in. diam., a viewing disc, 9in. diam., and a Fantascope disc, 5in. diam. (Christie's) $595

A plush-covered teddy bear with round ears, button eyes, pronounced hump and long paws, probably by Steiff, 21in. high. (Christie's) $393

A miniature violin in original case with mother-of-pearl inlay, the case 5in. long. (Christie's) $340

'Bulky Mule, The Stubborn Donkey', EPL No. 425, by Lehmann, circa 1910, 7½in. long.(Christie's) $217

A doll's Jacobean style chair upholstered in dark red velvet, 21in. high. (Christie's) $917

A Crown illuminated Panorama optical toy theatre, illuminated by a candle mounted behind, 9½in. wide. (Christie's) $223

A gauge 1 signals gantry, with four signals, oil fired lamps and ladders on both sides, by Bing, circa 1910, 21in. high. (Christie's) $576

A clockwork automaton toy of a bisque headed doll pulling a wooden two-wheeled cart with driver, 13in. long. (Christie's) $1,703

A cast iron mechanical bank, 'Trick Pony', by Shepard Hardware Co., American, circa 1890, 7in. long. (Christie's) $393

A tinplate model of a fairground traction engine, with a four-wheeled car containing a carousel, by Bing, circa 1906. (Christie's) $628

A golden plush-covered musical teddy bear, playing Sonny Boy by Al Jolson, 20in. high, circa 1930. (Christie's) $720

A 17th century wooden skittle doll carved as a puritan woman, 6in. high. (Christie's) $262

A Carette lithograph limousine, with clockwork mechanism, German, circa 1911, 8½in. long. (Christie's) $1,044

Mid 19th century papier mache two-faced clockwork musical automaton figure, 18in. high. (Christie's) $550

A long plush-covered teddy bear with black button eyes, with Steiff button in the ear, 25in. high. (Christie's) $1,703

A model of a hall with marquetry floor dividing at the landing into stairs on either side going up to a galleried landing, 26in. wide. (Christie's) $393

A painted tinplate toy of a monkey on a four-wheel musical carriage, German, circa 1903, 7½in. long. (Christie's) $366

A printed and painted tinplate model of a four-door limousine with clockwork mechanism, by Tipp & Co., circa 1928, 8¼in. long. (Christie's) $628

A Bing hand-enamelled early two-seater Benz racing car, with steerable front wheels, German, circa 1904, 11¼in. long. (Christie's) $12,052

Britains' set No. 315, 10th Royal Hussars, Prince of Wales' Own, at the halt with swords, and bugler, in original box. (Christie's) $370

'Popeye the Sailor', No. 268, a printed and painted tinplate toy of the cartoon sailor in a rowing boat, 14in. long, by the Hoge Mfg. Co., Inc., U.S.A., circa 1935. (Christie's) $1,924

Various model road signs, nine Dinky petrol pumps, three street lamps and seven figures, unboxed. (Hobbs & Chambers) $44

An early Lines Bros. pedal car, the wooden body painted suede gray with sprung chassis, 39in. long. (Lawrence Fine Art) $814

A Hess printed and painted tinplate toy of Dreadnought, with clockwork mechanism, circa 1911, 8½in. long. (Christie's)$87

A Dinky model Guy van with upright radiator grill, unboxed. (Hobbs & Chambers) $62

Lesney Yesteryear model No. 9 Fowler show-man's engine, unboxed. (Hobbs & Chambers) $32

A painted tinplate model of a P2 Alfa Romeo racing car, with clockwork mechanism, by C.I. G., France, circa 1926, 21½in. long. (Christie's) $1,048

A Britains' farmer's gig, No. F28 with horse, together with Fordson tractor, unboxed. (Hobbs & Chambers) $44

Britains' set No. 1634, The Governor-General's Foot Guards, marching at the slope arms, with officer, in original box. (Christie's) $133

Part of an eighteen piece set of Britains' model hunt, unboxed. (Hobbs & Chambers) $74

A tinplate toy gramophone, printed 'Made in Germany', 1930's, 8¼in. long. (Lawrence Fine Art) $88

A painted metal model of an Austin J40 Roadster pedal car, 64in. long, British, circa 1950. (Christie's) $1,110

A Dinky Series 28 first pattern delivery van, painted in black and red with gilt decals, 'The Manchester Guardian', circa 1935. (Lawrence Fine Art) $355

1923 Rolls Royce 40/50 H.P. Silver Ghost limousine, coachwork by Maythorn, Reg. No. AA 46, Chassis No. 16NK. (Christie's) $31,680

1933 Rolls Royce 20/25 H.P. Sports saloon, coachwork by Park Ward, Reg. No. ALD 333, Chassis No. GSY 92, Engine No. N4A. (Christie's) $12,495

1963/4 Ferrari 250 GT Berlinetta Lusso, coachwork by Scaglietti, Reg. No. NJ KHI 791 (U.S.A.), Chassis No. 250GT/L 5851. (Christie's) $41,160

1954 Jaguar XK 120 Drophead Coupe, Reg. No. 664 BHX, Chassis No. 667183, Engine No. F-1935-8. (Christie's) $14,400

C. 1904 Jackson Open two-seater, Reg. No. BM 657, Chassis No. not recorded, Engine No. 19850, De Dion Bouton two-cylinder 1141 c.c. (Christie's) $10,290

1935 British Salmson S4C four-door saloon, coachwork by Ranalah, Reg. No. DPC 769, Chassis No. CZ 305, Engine No. CZ 305. (Christie's) $3,675

1952 Bentley MK VI four-door 'Lightweight' Sports saloon, coachwork by H. J. Mulliner, Reg. No. CVV 62, Chassis No. B142NZ, Engine No. B307L. (Christie's) $14,700

1935 MG NA Magnette two-seat Sports Racer, Reg. No. NJ 6218, Chassis No. NA0726, Engine No. 799A 134N. (Christie's) $11,520

1958 BMW 507 two-seat Roadster with detachable hardtop, coachwork by Vignale, Reg. No. PPR 615W, Chassis No. 70184, Engine No. 40204. (Christie's) $69,090

1930 Alfa Romeo 6C-1750 Fourth Series Gran Turismo four-seat Drophead Coupe, coachwork by James Young, Reg. No. GH 4124, Chassis No. 8613252, Engine No. 8613252. (Christie's) $50,400

1969 Aston Martin DB6 Superleggera four-seat Grand Touring saloon, Reg. No. ALU 39H, Chassis No. DB64060RE, Engine No. 4004232. (Christie's) $10,080

1935 Alva Speed Twenty four-door Sports saloon, coachwork by Charlesworth, Reg. No. WS 7223, Chassis No. 17811. (Christie's) $10,290

1921 B.S.A. 986 c.c. Solo motorcycle, Frame No. 1296, Engine No. 1268, twin cylinder. (Christie's) $1,550

A Morris Cowley 6 saloon, first registered 19.1.34, colour — midnight blue and black. (Reeds Rains) $2,304

1930 MG M-Type Midget Sports two-seater, Reg. No. VR 9230, Chassis No. 2M/723, Engine No. A2685. (Christie's) $8,640

1939 Packard One Twenty Drophead coupe, Reg. No. ERO 54, Chassis No. 312550, Engine No. 312550. (Christie's) $29,400

1955 Bentley R-type Continental two-door
Sports saloon, Reg. No. AHJ 448A, Chassis No.
BC2E, Engine No. BC2E. (Christie's)
$32,340

1933 Lagonda M45 4½-litre four-seat
tourer, Reg. No. AMT 77, Chassis No. Z
10605, Engine No. Z 2354. (Christie's)
$26,640

1933 Norton Racing International 500 c.c.
Solo motorcycle, Reg. No. AFC 310, Frame
No. 40-50946, Engine No. 2433. (Christie's)
$5,145

1929 Riley 9 H.P. San Remo Fabric saloon,
Reg. No. YC 7391, Chassis No. 606616,
Engine No. 16588. (Christie's)$4,320

1925 Lanchester Twenty-One limousine,
coachwork by Penman of Dumfries, Reg. No.
OSV 764, Chassis No. LVL 039 9W1 377.
(Christie's) $6,468

A sturdily constructed small full size steam
timber tractor, Reg. No. 889 FUF, built by
E. Bauchen, Steyning, 46 x 90in. (Christie's)
$2,940

1938 Alvis Speed 25 four-door Sports saloon,
coachwork by Charlesworth, Reg. No. EYR 219,
Chassis No. 14599, Engine No. 15083.
(Christie's) $8,820

Red MGA Coupe 1960 with MOT and taxed
until October. (Butler & Hatch Waterman)
$4,464

1924 Brough Superior SS80 Solo motorcycle, Reg. No. RK3250, Frame No. 205, Engine No. KTC YM 19706/5. (Christie's) $7,791

1956 Ferrari 250 GT two-seat coupe, coachwork by Boano, Reg. No. XRX 507, Chassis No. 061 3GT, Engine No. 061 3GT. (Christie's) $44,100

1903 Miniature Velox 3½ H.P. Open two-seater, Reg. No. AY 66. (Christie's) $13,230

1984 Lynx Replica of Jaguar D-type with Weslake 3-litre Grand Prix engine, Reg. No. — not registered. (Christie's) $36,750

1908 Buick Model 10 three-seat Roadster, not registered, Chassis No. 14392, right-hand drive. (Christie's) $8,085

1925 Fiat 501B four-seat tourer, Reg. No. TD 5457, Chassis No. 1253283, Engine No. 1153883. (Christie's) $6,912

1969 Daimler V8 250 four-door Sports saloon, Reg. No. KUR 80G, Chassis No. PIK5278BW, Engine No. 7K5553. (Christie's) $3,168

1964 Rolls Royce Phantom V limousine, coachwork by H. J. Mulliner, Park Ward, Reg. No. EUC 100C, Chassis No. 5VD63, Engine No. D 31 PV. (Christie's) $294,000

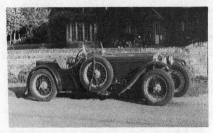

1934 Frazer-Nash TT Replica Sports two-seater, Reg. No. BMC 446, Chassis No. 2118, Engine No. 11743. (Christie's)
$20,160

1973 Porsche 911 Carrera RS 2.7 2 + 2 Sports Coupe, Reg. No. RLX 5L, Chassis No. 9113601363, Engine No. 6631325.(Christie's)
$20,160

1952 Bristol 401 Sports saloon, Reg. No. UMG 999, Chassis No. 1214, Engine No. 1991. (Christie's) $5,760

1934 British Salmson S4C four-door saloon, Reg. No. BKK 80, Chassis No. CZ 317, Engine No. CZ 317. (Christie's) $6,912

1922 Rolls Royce 40/50 H.P. Silver Ghost replica Open Tourer, Chassis No. 19RG, Engine No. P271H. (Christie's)
$28,800

1970 Ferrari 365 GTB4 Daytona two-seat Berlinetta, Reg. No. PUV 100, Chassis No. 12853, Engine No. 251. (Christie's)
$46,080

1954 Healey Tickford four-seat fixed head Coupe, Reg. No. OXU 489, Chassis No. F3094. Engine No. F8227. (Christie's) $2,736

1952 Bentley MK VI four-door saloon, coachwork by Freestone & Webb, Reg. No. PKK 275, Chassis No. B291NY, Engine No. B395N. (Christie's) $10,800

1948 Lea-Francis 14 H.P. Sports open 2/4-seater, Reg. No. GJB 82, Chassis No. 7072, Engine No. S3331. (Christie's)
$8,640

1938 Morris Ten-Four Series III four-door saloon, Reg. No. EWE 119, Chassis No. 53/7N/115599, Engine No. 7273. (Christie's)
$1,296

1960 MGA 1600 Sports two-seater, Reg. No. 370 YMP, Chassis No. GHN/82765, Engine No. 14057. (Christie's) $4,896

1921 Ford Model T four-seat Tourer, Reg. No. R 1878, Chassis No. 209225, Engine No. 209225. (Christie's) $9,360

1926 Rolls Royce Twenty-Three-Position Drophead Coupe, coachwork by Jack Compton, Reg. No. DXR 888, Chassis No. GYK 30. (Christie's) $27,360

1933 Rolls Royce 20/25 four-door saloon, coachwork by Park Ward, Reg. No. AKN 658, Chassis No. GYZ 20, Engine No. Y70. (Christie's) $10,800

Replica 1958 Maserati 450S Sports racing two-seater, Reg. No. OCN 766, Chassis No. 115140, Engine No. OA 03074. (Christie's)
$36,000

1926 Rolls Royce Twenty Foursome Drop-head Coupe, coachwork by Salmons, Reg. No. OX 20, Chassis No. GOK 64, Engine No. G 1606. (Christie's) $20,160

A sulkie and rider with horse weathervane figure, attributed to T. W. Fiske, America, circa 1880, 36in. long. (Robt. W. Skinner Inc.) $2,500

Late 19th century running horse with jockey weathervane figure, possibly J. L. Mott & Co., circa 1880, America, 16in. long. (Robt. W. Skinner Inc.) $2,000

A 19th century running horse and hoop weathervane, America, 30in. long. (Robt. W. Skinner Inc.) $3,900

Ethan Allen running horse weathervane figure, America, circa 1880, 26½in. long. (Robt. W. Skinner Inc.) $600

A cast metal and copper rooster weathervane figure, American, circa 1890, 27in. high. (Robt. W. Skinner Inc.) $1,900

A molded copper stag weathervane, attributed to J. Harris & Co., Boston, circa 1879, 30½in. high. (Robt. W. Skinner Inc.) $28,000

Mid 19th century American copper cow weathervane, possibly from the Howard Co., 15½in. high. (Robt. W. Skinner Inc.) $800

A 19th century sheet iron silhouette weathervane, a prancing horse with military rider, 27in. long. (Robt. W. Skinner Inc.) $2,000

An iron prospector's weathervane, Penn., circa 1900, 27½in. high. (Robt. W. Skinner Inc.) $750

Late 19th/early 20th century American gilt copper weathervane depicting a peacock, 29in. long overall. (Christie's) $3,520

A late 19th century American carved wooden weathervane in the form of Gabriel blowing his horn, 47in. long. (Christie's) $1,650

A 20th century grasshopper weathervane figure, the molded copper figure with verdigris mounted on vertical shaft, 19in. high, America. (Robt. W. Skinner Inc.) $925

A cast metal and molded copper horse weathervane figure, attributed to J. Howard, circa 1880, 21in. high, 29in. long. (Robt. W. Skinner Inc.) $3,300

Mid 19th century American copper horse and groom weathervane, 20½in. high. (Robt. W. Skinner Inc.) $650

Late 19th century American copper weathervane depicting a cow, 14½in. high, 24in. long. (Christie's) $440

Late 19th century American copper weathervane in the form of a pig, 35in. long. (Christie's) $11,000

A carved and painted counter top cigar store Punch figure, by Chas. Henkel, Vermont, 1870, 26in. high. (Christie's) $19,800

A stained wood smoker's compendium in the form of a motor car, 6½ x 11½in. (Christie's) $322

Early 19th century carved and gilded eagle, America, 14in. high. (Robt. W. Skinner Inc.) $525

One of a pair of giltwood wall brackets, one supported on a dragon, the other on a displayed eagle, 20½in. high. (Christie's) $2,041

A 19th century painted wood No mask of Kumasaka, signed Deme Eiman, 20.6cm. high. (Christie's) $762

A 19th century American carved wooden rooster, 12½in. high. (Robt. W. Skinner Inc.) $1,500

An engraved and painted wood pantry box, New England, circa 1800/20, 10½in. diam. (Christie's) $3,410

A painted wooden hollow standing horse, American, circa 1850/90, 49in. long, possibly used as a harness-maker's sign. (Christie's) $3,520

One of a pair of early George III white painted and gilded picture frames attributed to Wm. Vile and John Cobb, 75 x 59in. (Christie's) $40,176

WOOD

A 19th century wooden model of a seated camel, 50in. wide, 27½in. high. (Christie's) $20,358

An African carved wood fertility god, 26in. high. (Dacre, Son & Hartley) $6,912

A 20th century carved and stained pine ox cart with driver and two donkeys, by Peviri, blind carver of Cape Cod, 21½in. long, together with a pitcher and six mugs. (Christie's) $88

A mahogany waste paper basket with slightly tapering octagonal body with paper lining, 13½in. diam.(Christie's) $3,395

Northwest coast hawk mask of polychromed alder wood, 9½in. high, 8in. wide. (Robt. W. Skinner Inc.) $41,000

A Gustav Stickley slat-sided wastebasket, circa 1907, no. 94, unsigned, 14in. high. (Robt. W. Skinner Inc.) $1,000

A 19th century carved head of Bodhisattva, Japan, 13½in. high overall. (Robt. W. Skinner Inc.) $675

A carved wood relief picture of a tropical port in a Georgian ebonized frame, 14 x 18½in. (Christie's) $704

A wooden bust of a negress by Forrest, 18½in. high. (Christie's) $201

Late 19th/early 20th century carved wooden rooster, 31in. long overall. (Christie's) $1,650

An 18th century Italian creche blackamoor, painted carved wood and molded clay body, 8in. high. (Robt. W. Skinner Inc.) $300

One of a pair of Rohlfs oak and copper chambersticks, dated 1902, 5¼in. high. (Robt. W. Skinner Inc.) $1,000

An 18th century carved pine figure of Francis of Assisi, Italy, 8½in. high. (Robt. W. Skinner Inc.) $200

A Momoyama period Christian folding lectern (shokendai), decorated in aogai and hira-makie, circa 1600, 50.5cm. high. (Christie's) $38,880

Late 19th century Oriental gong with carved teakwood stand, and wrapped leather knocker, 43in. high. (Robt. W. Skinner Inc.) $650

Victorian oak biscuit barrel with plated mounts, 1870. (British Antique Exporters) $29

Ornate carved mahogany wall bracket, 1845. (British Antique Exporters) $194

A carved gessoed and painted pine soldier, polychrome decorated, circa 1780/1815, 14in. high. (Christie's) $6,380

WOOD

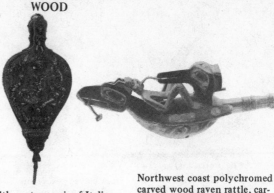

A Tapio Wirkkala laminated
wood dish shaped like an
oyster shell, circa 1950,
28cm. long. (Christie's)
$4,099

A 17th century pair of Italian
walnut bellows, 27in. wide.
(Christie's) $2,488

Northwest coast polychromed
carved wood raven rattle, carved in two sections, 12¼in.
long. (Robt. W. Skinner Inc.)
$4,000

One of a pair of George III
painted and gilded urns,
28in. high, 18in. wide.
(Christie's)
$31,320

A carved and painted wooden
zebra carousel figure, attributed to H. Speilman, circa 1880,
33in. high. (Robt. W. Skinner
Inc.) $3,400

One of a pair of giltwood
wall brackets supported
on scallops held by a mermaid and a merman, 20in.
high. (Christie's)
$1,312

A carved and painted band-
wagon figure of Victory,
American, circa 1880, 69½in.
high. (Robt. W. Skinner Inc.)
$4,000

A Biedermeier walnut cradle,
the oval body with detachable tin liner, 52in. wide.
(Christie's) $6,073

An 18th century American
cherry pipe box, 20½in.
high. (Robt. W. Skinner
Inc.) $1,500

WOOD

A gilt bronze and carved wood figure of a Spanish flamenco dancer cast and carved from a model by Hagenauer, 23.9cm. high. (Christie's) $939

A carved and painted wood figure in the form of a French Cantiniere, 39¼in. high. (Lawrence Fine Art) $703

An early 18th century red lacquer and giltwood folding bible stand, 53.5cm. high.(Christie's) $1,428

Eastern Plains/Wester Woodlands wood and stone pipe, 23¾in. long. (Robt. W. Skinner Inc.) $750

Pair of 19th century carved and painted parcel gilt panels, one depicting St. Jerome and the other St. Catherine, 32¼in. high, 17in. wide. (Robt. W. Skinner Inc.) $1,300

A carved gessoed and painted pine soldier, polychrome decorated, circa 1780/1815, 14.1/8in. high. (Christie's) $4,950

A life size carved and painted black duck, Birchler, circa 1925, full length 18in., 19in. high. (Robt. W. Skinner Inc.) $2,700

A George III mahogany cistern, the vase shaped body with lead lining, 17in. diam. (Christie's) $2,770

Early 20th century American carved and painted trade sign, 39¼in. high. (Christie's) $550

660

One of a pair of Italian parcel gilt and painted brackets with molded D-shaped tops, 20in. wide. (Christie's) $933

Early 19th century painted and carved pine hanging wall box, America, 12.5/8in. long. (Robt. W. Skinner Inc.) $1,500

Northwest coast portrait mask of polychrome carved and incised cedar, collected pre 1884, 10½in. high. (Robt. W. Skinner Inc.) $25,000

Late 18th century carved and painted tavern figure, 43in. high. (Robt. W. Skinner Inc.) $3,400

Two carved and painted wooden figures, modelled as a rooster and chicken, American, circa 1893, 11in. and 13in. high. (Christie's) $660

Late 19th century signed heavily carved folk art scoop, West Indies, 22in. long. (Robt. W. Skinner Inc.) $300

A carved wood polychrome head of Kuan Yin, 21½in. high. (Lawrence Fine Art) $414

A George III pine chimney piece with molded foliate cornice, 59½in. high, 69in. wide. (Christie's) $3,862

A stained wood portrait figure of a man, 11¾in. high. (Lawrence Fine Art) $478

A 16th/17th century Provincial wood sculpture of Amida, 71cm. high. (Christie's) $1,650

A Shinto wood sculpture of a seated deity wearing Heian/ Kamakura style robes and hat, Edo period, 58.8cm. high. (Christie's) $2,400

An early wood sculpture of Buddha, late Heian period, 36.8cm. high. (Christie's) $1,275

A 19th century large wood sculpture of a recumbent deer, the antlers formed from natural stag-antler, 66cm. long. (Christie's) $1,575

A giltwood medical shop sign carved as a carp with black lacquered eyes, Meiji period, 126cm. long. (Christie's) $3,300

A large red lacquered wood sculpture of a seated emaciated priest, early/mid Edo period, the figure 49cm. high. (Christie's) $4,500

A 17th century Zen buddhist wood carving of a guardian figure in the style of the monk Enku, 52cm. high. (Christie's) $1,050

A carved oak panel depicting the martyrdom of St. Lawrence, 1764, 96cm. high. (Phillips) $2,100

One of a pair of gilded and green lacquered wood standing frogs, 15in. high. (Lots Road Chelsea Auction Galleries) $414

INDEX

ABD AL-A-Imma 463
Absolon 212
Abuja 106, 181
Acorn 597
Acteon 75
Adam 42
Adam, Robt. 498
Adams 187
Adams, George 68
Adams-Jefferson 426
Adnet, J. J. 556
Advertising Signs 16-19
Aeronautical 20-23
Aeronautical Paintings 23
Aircraft 22
Albertus, Gundorph 596
Alcora 123
Alcyon 22
Alden, Sally 565
Aldis 90
Aldridge, Edward 566
Alfa Romeo 647, 649
Allam, Robert 223
Allen, Ethan 654
Allen & Wheelock 39, 41
Allen, Wm. 600
Allison, M. 338
Almaric Walter 424
Alpa 91
Alva 649
Alvis 650
American China 94, 95
American Forecast 65
Amerith, R. 496
Amours Pastorale, Les 256
Amphyrite 437
Anagke 74
Analemmatic Dial 463
Andri, Ferdinand 546
Anfibio 346
Angell, Joseph 583
Antoniazzi, R. 516, 517
Apache 453, 455
Aprey 127
Apsley Pellatt 436
Aras 440
Architect's Table 388-390
Argyll & Sutherland
    Highlanders 29
Argy-Rousseau 425, 442
Arita 96
Armand 224
Armillary Sphere 463
Armoires & Wardrobes 412,
    413
Arms & Armor 24-62
Army Veterinary Dept. 37
Arnold 642
Arnold & Dent 199, 213
Arnold & Son, John 229
Arsale 443
Art Union of London 114
Arts & Crafts 239, 333, 341,
    569
Ashbee, C. R. 421, 423, 593,
    600, 606
Ashworths 102
Asselin 196, 209

Aston Martin 649
Astrolabe 459, 461, 462, 463,
    464
Astronomical Dial 458
Atco Motor Mowers 640
Atkins, Lloyd 420
Atkinson, Wm. 517
Aubert & Klaftenberger 222
Audu Mugu Sokoto 181
Aug Luneburg Kile 48
Auster 22
Austin 509
Austin Roadster 647
Automatons 63
Avery, W. & T. 463

B.A. Swallow 22
Babs 508
Baccarat 421, 424, 432-435,
    436, 437, 438
Bacchus 431
Backstage Ballet Girls 534
Baden Infantry 36
Bailey, I. 313
Bailey, Lebbeus 210
Baird 461
Baker Harris 536
Baker & Sweep 643
Baker, William Robert 530
Baker's Cocoa 98
Ball, Black & Co. 616
Ball, Tomkins & Black 608,
    623
Balthazar 198
Bambocci 278
Banco Internacional 525
Banco Mercantil, El 525
Banco Otero & Ca 525
Bank of Australasia 525
Bark Messenger 408
Barlow, Florence E. 181
Barlow, Hannah 120
Barlow's Patent 243
Barnard, E. 566, 606, 608,
    612
Barnard, E. J. & W. 589, 602,
    620
Barnard, Messrs. 583, 594, 601
Barnard, W. J. 600
Barometers 64-67, 467
Barovier, Ercole 438
Barry, Madame Du 169
Bartram & Co. 44
Bartram, James 308
Barye 68, 77
Barzanti, P. 488
Basket Maker 455
Baskets, Silver 566
Bassett-Lowke 503
Bat Dancer 81
Bate 47
Bateman 213

Bateman, Hester 606, 618,
    619
Bateman, Peter & Anne 606,
    612
Bateman, Wm. 585, 621
Battle Abbey 87
Bauchen, E. 650
Bauduin 547
Bavarian Infantry 34
Bavarian Jager Regt. 36
Bayes, Gilbert 74, 119
Bayley, Ed. 196
Bayley, R. 593
Bayreuth 128
Bazu-Band 24
Bazzi 356
Beakers, Glass 418
Beakers, Silver 567
Beale, R. 593
Beardmore, H. 189
Beaton, Cecil 532, 535
Beaumont Adams 40, 43
Beauvais 336
Bebe Francais 255
Becchi, Alessandro 346
Bechstein, C. 537
Bedos & Cie 545
Beds 262, 263
Beilby 445
Bell, J. 623
Bella Coola 454
Belter, J. H. 295, 349
Belter, J. B. 387
Belin, Claude Alexandre 538
Bell, Glass 431
Bell, Robt. A. 484
Belleek 97
Belet 126
Benckendorff, Count A. 26
Bengal Regt. 25
Benham & Froud 240, 241
Benner, Johannes 212
Bennettini 516
Bentley 648, 650, 652
Bercy 437
Berge 461
Beringer, D. 462, 466
Berlin 98
Berliner 512
Bernadotte, S. 577
Berry, John 208
Bettini 511
Bevan, Charles 387
Beyser, Jean-David 460
Bhuj 62
Bianconi, F. 442
Bichwa 31
Big Ben 513
Bigelow, Kennard & Co. 215
Bijou 450
Billings, Wm. 526
Bing 502, 503, 640, 641, 644,
    645, 646
Birchler 660
Bird, J. 67
Bird, Joseph 574
Bisiach, Leandro 516
Bisson De Recy, B. 260

Bizarre 113
Blanch & Son, J. 48
Bland & James 52
Blandford Yeomanry Cavalry 36
Blanket Chests 409-411
Blanquart-Evrard 532
Blondeau 168
Blue Band Margarine 18
Blumenfeld, E. 532
Blunderbuss 48-51
Blunt 461, 465
BMW 649
Boa-Constrictor 508
Boardman, Thos. D. 527, 528
Boardman, Boardman & Hart 528
Boche 44
Boers, Bastiaan 428
Bogle, John 541
Bohm, Hermann 257, 258
Bolton, Thos. 575
Bolviller 200
Bombay Horse Artillery 32
Bone, William 538
Bone, Henry Pierce 542
Bonheur, I. 76
Bookcases 264-266
Booker, J. & W. 493
Book Rack 386
Bordi 459
Borrell 212
Borsani, O. 288
Botas 499
Bottger 180
Bottles, Glass 419
Boucher 256, 257
Boucheron 602
Boulard, J. B. 291
Boullemier, H. 155
Boulton, M. 579
Boulton & Co., Matthew 629
Boulton Plate Co., The 627
Bourke-White, Margt. 533, 534
Bourne Shepherd & Bourne & Shepherd 539
Bow 99
Bowie Knife 28, 29
Bowle, Lt. Col. C. W. 27
Bowls, Glass 420
Bowls, Silver 568, 569
Box, Glass 421
Boxes, Silver 570, 571
Boyd, George 249
Boyer 75
Boyton, Charles 606
Bracket Clocks 196-198
Bradbury & Sons, Thos. 572
Bradford Academy 248
Bramah 355, 405
Bramah Lock 87
Brander, G. F. 466
Brandt, Bill 535
Brass & Copper 238-243
Brasso Metal Polish 18
Brau, C. 507
Breguet 213, 219, 225, 227
Breithaupt, F. W. 462
Brenneiser, S. 211
Briere A Paris 466
Bridge, John 420
Bristol 99, 652
Britains 641, 647
Britannia 49, 503
British China 100-104
British Grenadiers 33
British Salmson 648
Brocot 214
Brodon, Nicolas 215
Brodt, Johan Georg 229
Bronze 68-82
Brooke, B. 50
Brookbank 21
Brooklands 506, 507, 509
Brooklands Aero Club 498
Brooks, T. 370
Brough 651
Brown, Alexander 569
Brown Bess 47, 48

Brown, Nathaniel 208
Brown, Robt. 609
Brownfield 102, 103
Bru 250, 251, 253
Bruce 398
Bruhl, Count 149, 153
Brush(?) Busti, Lucretia 555
Brush Set 603
Brunswick 46
Brunswick & Balke-Collender Co. 384
Brunswick Hussars 32
Brunswick Infantry Regt. 34
Bryceson, H. 512
Brysons 206
BSA 649
Bubble Dance 80
Buckets 83
Buckle, Eliz. 104
Bugatti 495, 506
Buick 651
Build Yourself 643
Bulidon 169
Bulky Mule 644
Bull & Co., F. 245
Bullock, G. 498
Bulow-Hube, Torun 232
Burch, Henry 539
Burchett, P. 275, 370
Bureau Bookcases 267-269
Bureaux 270-273
Burgonet 32
Burmantofts 102
Burrell 505
Bursley Ware 103
Burwash, Wm. 567, 590
Bury & Suffolk Bank 525
Busby 32, 33
Busch Rapid Aplanat 92
Bushu 59, 60
Buteux 170
Buteux, Elizabeth 622
Butter Maker 358
Butterfield 460, 464
Butty, Francis 586

Cabinets 274-278
Cactus 596
Caddies & Boxes 84-89
Cadran Universal 460
Cafe, J. 576, 586
Cafe, Wm. 574
Caiger-Smith 405
Calamanco 554
Calcanus, Bernard 516
Calder, Horatio H. 97
Calder, Wm. 529
Calderwood, Robt. 622
Caldwell & Co., E. 201
Callowhill 194
Camera Work 531
Cameras 90-92
Cameron, Chas. Hay 533
Cameron, Julia Margt. 533-535
Caminada, P. 65
Canada Goose 249
Canal, Antonio 553
Candelabra, Silver 572, 573
Candlesticks, Glass 422
Candlesticks, Silver 574-577
Canivet 462
Canner, C. 612
Canterburys 279
Canton 105
Capper, Edward 606
Caps 33-35, 37
Carcassi, Vincenzo 515
Card & Tea Tables 364-367
Cardew, Michael 106, 107
Caressa & Francais 515
Carette 643, 645
Carlton House 264, 405, 406
Carltonware 107
Carlu, Jean 545
Carnival Girls 533
Carpenier, Wm. 209
Carr, Alwin 599
Carr Bros. 51
Carrette, G. 510

Carriage Clocks 199-201
Carrier De Belleuse, Albert 157, 158
Carrington & Co. 566
Carter II, John 586
Cartier 230, 231
Cartwright 207
Cartwright, R. 500
Cary 465, 467
Cassandre, Adolphe Mouron 544-546
Cassone 409, 410
Castel 167
Casters, Silver 578
Castletop 628
Cater, D. 579, 624
Cathedral De Mayence 532
Cathedral De Mollins 532
Caughley 102
Cayette, J. 274
Cellarette 416, 417
Centerpieces, Silver 579
Center Tables 368-371
Cetta, J. 66
Chaffer 145
Chairs 280-303
Chamberlain 194, 195
Chambersticks, Silver 580
Champenoise, F. 546
Champion, Richard 99
Chandeliers 93
Chapka 32
Chavez, Raymond 453
Chawner, Henry 583, 586, 590, 620
Chawner, Wm. 597
Chelsea 108
Chelsea Keramic Art 94
Chen Zhongsan 531
Chesne, Claude Du 207
Chests of Drawers 304-307
Chests on Chests 308, 309
Chests on Stands 310, 311
Chevalier et Comp 226
Chiappa 512
Chi-Chi 557
Chiffoniers 312
Chikayoshi 472
China 94-195
Chinese China 109-112
Chiparus 73, 80, 82
Chipmunk 22
Chivers' Carpet Soap 17
Chocolate Pots, Silver 581
Chohei, Jushuhan 456
Choshu 58
Choshu-Noju-Sakushinao Tomohisa 60
Christening Set 602
Christian, Philip 145
Christiansen, Hans 438
Christofferson, Gerda 454, 455, 465
Chronometer 458, 459
Chuichi 523
Churchman's 'Tortoiseshell' 18
Cibber 633
Cibert & Cie 459
Cigalia 436
Cigarette Boxes, Silver 581
Cigarette Cases, Silver 582
Cigarette Lighter/Watch 228
Cinq Chevaux 507
Circumferentor 460
City of London Yeomanry 27
Civil War 24
Claret Jugs, Silver 583
Clarke, F. 628
Classic Stable Ltd. 506
Clichy 432-435, 436
Cliff, Clarice 113
Clock Sets 202, 203
Clocks & Watches 196-233
Cloisonne 234-237
Clothes Presses 313
Clutha 527
C.M.I. 547
Coal Box 85-87
Coalport 114

664

Coasters, Silver 584
Cobb, John 656
Cochin, C. N. 496
Cochiti 453
Coffee Pots, Silver 584-587
Coffers & Trunks 409-411
Cogswell & Harrison 50
Coker, E. 575, 576
Coldstream Guards 53
Cole, T. 214, 216
Colgan, Thos. 595
Colin, Paul 545
Collas, A. 75
Collet, Edward-Louis 71
Collier, D. 210
Collier, Joseph 578
Collins, Samuel 543
Collis, Chas. 118
Colt 45, 47
Columbia 510
Combat, The 120
Comfort, E. 106
Commode Chests 315-317
Commodes & Pot Cupboards 314
Compass 463
Compass/Sundial 224
Compendium 459
Compulsion 74
Compur 90
Comyns, Wm. 436
Concorde Watch Co. 231
Connaught Rangers 27
Console Tables 372, 373
Constabulary 56
Constantinidis, Joanna 179, 180
Convers, Louis 483
Conway, Richard 541
Cooke, Stenson 509
Cookson, Isaac 585
Coombe Richards 23
Cooper 227
Cooper I, Matthew 577
Copeland 114
Copeland & Garrett 114
Coper, Hans 115
Copper & Brass 238-243
Coqs et Plumes 439
Coquelicot 425
Corner Cupboards 318, 319
Cornock, E. 623
Cossack's Adieu, The 78
Costume 244-248
Cosway, Richard 542
Cotton, Jn. 197
Couches & Settees 344-349
Coultre Co., Le 233
County of Chester 502
Courtauld, A. 585, 622
Courvoisier Freres 228
Cox, E. 46
Cox, F. 462
Cox, Robert Albin 605
Crama, Francois 428
Crane, Walter 162
Craven & Co. 52
Crawshay, R. T. 535
Cream Jugs, Silver 588
Crejo 81
Crespin, Adolphe 544
Crespin, Paul 566
Creswick, Nathaniel 591
Creswick, Thos. & James 577, 629
Creswick, T. J. & N. 574
Criaerd, A. M. 273
Crichton, Alex. 583
Cripps, Wm. 587, 624
Crofts, Thos. 204
Crossbow 62
Crosse, Richard 538
Crot 223
Crouch, Henry 459
Crouch, John 580, 621, 622, 623
Crow Bar Tobacco 19
Cruets, Silver 589
Crump, Francis 609

Crystal Set 467
Cube Dial 462, 466
Culpeper 464
Cuminoscope 461
Cumming, Alexdr. 197
Cunard 504
Cupboards 320, 321
Cups, Silver 590
Currier, N. 549, 552
Currier & Ives 548, 549, 552, 553
Curtis, Lemuel 221
Cutty Sark 500
Cymric 627
Cypress 596
Cyril Ray in Islington 535

Dagenite 19
Daggers 28-31
Dagoneau, Ph. 458
Dahlia 421
Dai Nihon 143
Daihei 235
Daimler 651
Daisho 54, 60
Daisy 132
Dali, Salvador 348, 431
Dallmeyer, J. H. 91
Dalou, Aime Jules 74, 76, 77
Dalyzell 419
Danaides 442
Dance of the Harlequinade 79
Dancing Girl 81
Danforth, Jnr., J. 529
Danforth, Thos. 526
Daniel, H. & R. 102
Daniel, Jabez & Thos. 584
Daniels, Lucia A. 565
Daoguang 72
Darwin, Chas. 535
Daum 431, 438, 440
Davenport China 104
Davenports 322, 323
Davey-Paxman 504
Davis 23
Davyz, I. 420
Dawson, S. 574
Day, Thos. 540
De Havilland 22
De Morgan 118
Dean Single 503
Deane Harding 42
Decanters 423
Decca Dulcephone 511
Decorchment 420
Decoys 249
Dedham 94, 95
Deens, J. 465
Deer Dancers 454
Degani, Eugenio 514
Degani, Giulio & Eugenio 514
Degue 469
Delander, Daniel 226
Delatte 439
Delft 116, 117
Della Robbia 118, 189
Delynne, F. 226
Deme Eiman 656
Denecheau 82
Denny, William 577
Dent 199-201, 643
Deptford, Thomas A. 211
Derazey, Justin 517
Derby 118
Derby & Co. 360
Desjarlait, Patrick 455
Desk Cabinet 404
Desks & Writing Tables 404-408
Dessin 599
Devisme 42
Diana 79, 82
Diato, Albert 179
Dimple Haig 419
Dining Chairs 280-287
Dining Tables 374-377
Dinky 640, 641, 646, 647
Dinky Doo 119
Dirk Set 29
Dishes, Glass 424

Dishes, Silver 591-593
Display Cabinets 324-327
Distagon 91
Distler 640
Dixon & Sons, James 44, 45
Dixon, James 526
Dixon, Miss Annie 538
Djinn Series 347
Dobson, T. W. H. & H. 625
Dod, S. 467
Dodd & Son, P. G. 211
Doisneau, Robt. 533
Dollond 64, 467
Dolls 250-255
Donald, W. 205
Donatello, F. 131
Donn Ltd., Leslie 577
Donzan Seizo 140
Doppel 90
Doreen 505
D'Orsay, Comte 70
Doulton 119, 120
Dower Chest 410, 411
Dr. Samuel Johnson's House 132
Draeger 545
Dragoon Guards 32
Draining Level 463
Drake, The Hatless 120
Dreadnought 646
Dresden 98, 121
Dresser, C. 158, 426
Dresser, Dr. C. 103, 104, 240, 241, 423, 430 580, 589, 619, 625
Dressers 328, 329
Dressing Chest 378, 379
Dressing Tables 378, 379
Drinking Sets 425
Drocourt 199, 201
Drop-Leaf Tables 380, 381
Duc D'Orleans 184
Duchess of Athol 502
Dudovich, Marcello 546
Duesbury & Co. Wm. 118
Dufrene, Maurice 408
Duke of Cambridge's Own Lancers 32, 35
Duke, Richard 515
Dumbwaiters 330
Dumee, Nicholas 586
Dunand, Jean 238
Dunant, Wm. 198
Dunhill 228, 450, 451
Dunhill, Alfred 581
Dunn & Co. F. 71
Dunn, Cary 588
Durer, Albrecht 152
Durban Bank 524
Durham, J. 114
Dustantoy, J. P. 387
Dutton, Mattw. & Willm. 223
Duych, Edouard 544
Dyche, T. 503
Dyer & Sons, A. R. 504
D'Ylem, Leon 544
Dyson & Sons, John 229

Eagle Dancer 453
Earl of Chester's Rifles 33
Earthenware 121
Easel 357
East End Girl 535
East India Company 25
East, John 585
Easy Chairs 288-295
Eaton, Wm. 599, 615
Eavestaff 537
Eberlein, J. F. 149
Ebisu 72
Eckfourd, Jnr., John 585
Echigo School 520
Echizen 58
Eckhoff, Tias 596
Eckmann, O. 78
Ecole Horlogerie De Paris 213
Edge, K. 502, 503
Edison 510, 511
Edmondson, W. 632

Edo School 518
Edward, J. 623
Edwards, A. 208
Edwards, E. 610
Edwards, W. H. 39
E.H. 564
Eickhorn 29
Eiroku Ninen 54
Eisentrager, J. H. 130
Eishin 521
Eitoku 470
Elbow Chairs 296-304
Eley 499
Eley & Fearn 589, 595
Elkington & Co. 423, 430, 569,
    576, 600, 605, 624, 629
Elkington, F. 579
Elkington Mason & Co. 71
Elliot Bros. 463
Elliot, Wm. 599
Elliott, John 208
Ellis, James 623
Elmar 92
Elston, John 574
Elston, Philip 601
Embree, E. 205, 209
Emerson, Peter Henry 534
Emes, J. 589, 620, 625
Emes, R. 606, 612
Emes, Rebecca 566, 600
Empire Clock 460
Enamel 256-259
Engle, Elizabeth C. 564
Engleheart, George 540, 542
English School 540
Enku 662
Epping Forest Centenary 587
Equatorial Dial 461
Erfurt 129
Ernemann 90, 92
Ernoflex 90
Ernon 90
Etagere 415
Etling 431
European China 122, 123
European Watch & Clock Co.
    Inc. 230
Evans 168
Ewers, Silver 594
Exotic Dancer 78

Faberge 451
Facon De Venise 419, 424
Fagnola, H. 516
Fairy III, D. 23
Fairy Firefly 23
Fairyland Lustre 186-188
Famille Rose 124, 125
Famille Verte 125
Fan Dancer, The 80
Fang 31
Fans 260, 261
Fantasque 113
Farmer 39
Farrell, Edward 608
Farren, Thos. 585, 620
Faucard 228
Faux 81
Favrile 437
Fawdery, William 571, 581
F. C. Franc JME 339
Feathers Hotel, The 132
Feibleman, D. 103
Felixmuller, Conrad 551
Fencing 336
Fenton, Roger 530, 532, 534
Ferguson 504
Ferguson, J. 588
Ferrari 648, 651, 652
Ferriere, Francois 541
Ferro Email 19
Feure, Georges De 122
Fez 35
Fiat 651
Field 223
Field Service Commando
    Knife 28
Figurines Avec Bouchon 419
Fireside 510

First Cardigan Vol. Artillery 26
Fish, Henry 196
Fish Slice 595
Fisher 66
Fisherman 69
Fiske, T. W. 654
Fladgate, John 198
Flashman, George 197
Flasks, Glass 426
Flatware, Silver 595-597
Fleming & Co., Andw. 279
Fletcher & Gardiner 617
Fleury 228
Flight & Barr 194
Flower Seller 80
Fokker III 21
Foley 100, 101, 104, 214
Fonseca, Harry 454
Fontaine, J. 167
Foo Dog 81
Forbes, Wm. 608, 623
Forcker, Cristoph 216
Ford 653
Forgeron, Le 71
Formose 440, 443
Fornasetti, Piero 499
Forster, G. 204
Fortune Teller, The 120
Foskett, J. 593
Fountain, Wm. 609, 623
Fournier, Jean Baptiste 541
Fowler, Anna 565
Fox, Chas 605
Fox II, Charles 627
Fox, George 608
Foyne, W. 65
Frames, Silver 598
Franchini 436
Frank, Robt. 532, 533
Frazer-Nash 652
Fremiet, E. 76
French Carabiniers 32
French Cavalry 57
French China 126, 127
French Dragoons 33
Fritsch, Elizabeth 179
Frobisher, B. C. 594
Fromery, Pierre 98
Fudo Myo-o 471
Fuger, Heinrich F. 543
Fujiyuki 520
Fulda 128
Fulper 484
Funcke 98
Furber, Emily 565
Furniture 262-417
Furstenberg 130, 450

Gadoud, L. 544
Gage, Miss C. 248
Gagliano, Ferdinando 515
Gagliano, G. 516
Gagliano, Nicola 515
Gagnant, Rougier Le 23
Gaida, Giovanni 517
Gaigneur, Henry Louis Le 587
Gallard 41
Gallaway, Alexander 538
Galle 389, 419, 421, 430,
    438-443, 486, 487
Galner, Sara 94
Games Tables & Workboxes
    400-403
Gandhi, Mohandas 533
Gandolfi 90
Gardner, Ava 535
Gargory 66
Garnier, Paul 199
Garrard, R. 580, 620, 626
Garthorne, F. 578
Gateleg Tables 382, 383
Gebhard, M. J. 501
Gebruder-Heubach 98
Geefs, G. 489
Geib, P. & W. 537
Geill, Matthias 219
Gentso 349
George V 503
German China 128-130

Gibbon, Edward 618
Giles, Fayette S. 226
Giles, James 192, 193, 195
Gilfert, G. 536
Gillibaud 126
Gillman, Emily 119
Gillows 265, 266, 292, 332,
    378, 379, 385, 401, 405,
    417
Ginji 456
Gipsy Fortune Teller, The 256
Gipsy Major 22
Gipsy Minor 22
Gladstone, Margaret 244
Glashutte, H. P. 424
Glass 418-447
Globe 462, 464, 465, 467
Globe Wernicke 266
Gloucestershire Engineer Vols.
    57
Go To Sleep 114
Goblets, Glass 427-429
Goblets, Silver 599
Godard 80
Goddard, L. 502
Goddess of Sport 506
Godfrey, B. 590
Godfrey, Eliz. 566
Godfrey, Sir Edmund 612
Godwin, E. W. 275
Goffart, J. L. 547
Gold 448-451
Gold Medal 505
Golden Eye 249
Goldscheider 131
Goldsmiths & Silversmiths Co.
    Ltd. 573, 578, 591, 627
Gonic 162
Goodall, T. F. 534
Goosens, J. E. 545
Gordon Highlanders 24, 27
Gore 498
Gorham, John 605
Gorham Mfg. Co. 607, 617,
    623
Gori, A. 78, 80
Gorman, Carl Nelson 455
Gornik, Friedrich 79
Gors & Kallmann, R. 536
Goshu Ju Soheishi Sei 61
Goss 132
Goto 52, 54
Gotthard Schuh 534
Gottlob, Fernand Louis 546
Gough & Bowen 47
Gould, James 576
Gould, Wm. 576
Graceful Parachute Descent 21
Graham, Geo. 207
Graham, J. 566
Gramophone & Typewriter
    Ltd. 510
Granges, David Des 543
Graphometer 462
Grasshopper 500
Gray & Reynolds 221
Great Western 503
Greek Fire 122, 123
Green, David 577
Green, J. 206
Greenwood, Frans 428
Grendey 287
Grenouille 507
Greuter, M. 462
Greuze 127
Gricci, J. 66
Griffen, Smith & Hill 95
Grimalde 206
Grimshaw, A. 66
Grodenthal 252, 253
Groth, S. C. S. 581
Grover & Baker 461
Grubbe 195
Grueby 133
Grun, Jules Alexandre 547
Grundy, Wm. 593
Guandi 79
Guanyin 472
Gui 439

Guild of Handicraft 421, 595, 600, 606
Gundlach, E. 460
Gunthermann 640, 642
Gurschner, G. 69, 81
Guy 641, 646
Gyokud0 472
Gyokuzan 473
Gypsy Moth 23

Hackwood 186, 187, 189
Hadley 191, 193
Hagenauer 660
Hahn 464
Haida, Fachschule 439
Hairy Family of Mandalay, The 534
Hakuryu 521
Halberd 62
Halbig, S. & H. 254
Hall 466
Hall, R. 174
Halliday, T. 605
Hamburger & Co. 38
Hamburger Rogers 52, 57
Hamilton, Richard 553
Hamilton, Robert 613
Hamilton & Co. 225, 599, 620
Han 133, 134
Handel 484
Handschar Division 35
Hannaford 420
Hannam, T. 621, 623
Hannam, Thos. 580
Hanoverian Hussars 25
Harbeson 526
Hardy 213
Hare, David 569
Harper, Sally 176
Harradine, L. 119
Harris 460
Harris, J. B. 505
Harris & Co., J. 654
Harris & Co., W. 64
Harris & Sons, Chas. S. 568
Harrods Ltd. 508
Hart, Chas. H. 249
Hart, John 204
Hartnack, E. 467
Hartwell, A. 592
Hasegawa 457
Hassell 506
Hastings Kettle 132
Hauer, B. G. 152
Hauer, Bonaventura G. 149
Hausmalerei 130, 154
Hawkes & Co. 33
Hawksley, G. & J. W. 45
Hayden & Gregg 595
Hayter, Mary-Ann 564
Hayne, S. 579, 624
Hazlehurst, Thos. 539
Healy 537
Healey 652
Hearnshaw Bros. 240
Heath, T. 466
Heath & Middleton 426
Hehe Erxian 470
Hel, Joseph 515
Heller, J. H. 511
Helmets 32-37
Heming, Thos. 576
Henkel, Chas. 656
Henko 17
Hennell, Robt. 627
Hennell II, Robt. 589
Henry, Guillaume 599
Herbert & Co., S. 593
Herder, F. 31
Hereford Kettle 132
Herefordshire Militia 49
Hernantis, Sebastian 57
Herold, C. F. 152
Hess 646
Hesse Infantry 37
Hewitt & Co., James L. 537
Higgs, Robt. & Peter 198
Higo 58-60

Hilliard, J. 67
Hindmarsh, George 587
Hirato 55
Hirochika 61
Hiroshige Ga 551
His Master's Choice 16
Hisatoshi 73
Hitchcock, Thos. 536
HMV 511, 513
Hocker, J. 229
Hockney, David 544
Hodo 522
Hoffmann, J. 442
Hofler, J. P. 567
Hohlwein, Ludwig 546
Hoin, Claude Jean Baptiste 543
Holaday, Sarah 623
Holder, Ernest L. 514
Holland & Sons 369
Hollingshead, Joseph & John 205
Hollingshead, Wm. 588
Holmes, Wm. 590
Holmes, L. T. 249
Holst, R. N. Roland 547
Holzl 17
Homer 485
Hone, Horace 540
Hone, Nathaniel 541
Hope, Thos. 494
Hopi 454, 455
Hopi Placca 95
Hopkins, O. 204
Horn 452
Horoldt 150, 153
Hoskins, John 543
Hosteter, Jacob 207
Hosono Sozaemon Masamori 59
Hotchkiss & Benedict 216
Hougham, Chas. 625
Hougham, Solomon 584
Houghton 92
Houles & Co. 584
Howard, J. 655
Howard Co., The 654
Howes & Burley 485
Hozan 472
Hsuan-Te 78
Huber, P. 528
Huber, Patriz 425
Hughes, Thos. 196
Hukin & Heath 423, 430, 580, 589, 602, 608, 625
Humidor 85
Hunt, J. S. 604
Hunt, John S. 570, 589
Hunt & Roskell 601
Hunter, Mary Anne 564
Huntingdonshire Light Horse Volunteers 37
Hurd, Jacob 591
Hurley, F. T. 461
Hush, He's Busy 18
Hussars 503
Hussar, The 24
Hutchins, A. 204
Hutton, Wm. 608
Hutton & Son, William 627

Idylls of the Norfolk Broads 534
Illinois Watch Co. 225
Illustrations to Tennyson 534
Imari 135-137
Immelmann 21
Imperial German Army 56
Imperial German Cavalry 25
Imperial German Hussars 32
Imperial Glass Co. 440
Indian Art 453-455
Indian Craftsman Series 191
Inkstands, Silver 600
Inniskilling Dragoons 36
Inros 456, 457
Inspiration 113
Instruments 458-467
Intarsio 214

I. R. & Co. 584
Iron & Steel 468, 469
Isis 113
Issai 521
Italian China 138, 139
Ivory 470-475
Iwashiro School 519
Iye Mushi 33

Jackson 648
Jackson, Julia 534
Jackson, O. 592
Jacot, Henri 199, 201
Jade 476, 477
Jadison, Joseph 591
Jaeger 71
Jager, Lorenz 57
Jaguar 509, 648
Jambiya 28
James, Thos. 591
Japanese China 140, 141
Jaquemart 229
Jardiniere 388, 389
Jefferys 223
Jelliff, J. 294
Jenkinson, D. 502
Jenson, Georg 232, 478, 479, 568, 569, 572, 574, 577, 578, 595, 601, 603, 614, 625, 629
Jep 641
J.E.R. 84
Jewelry 478-481
Jinty 503
Jobbagy 71
Jogyoku 473
Johns & Pegg 53
Joi 60
Jones, A. E. 569
Jones, Ball & Poor 594, 601
Jones, George 142
Jones, Hen. 196
Jones, John 611
Jones, Lows & Ball 620
Jones, Norman 23
Jones Sewing Machines 16
Joyce, Richard 162
Jugendstil 528
Jugs, Glass 430
Jugs, Silver 601
Jumeau 254, 255
Jumelle 90
Juntoku 523
Jurgensen, J. 228
Jurine 499
Jurojin 473
J.V. 87

Kabotie, Fred 453
Kabuto 33
Kachina 455
Kaiguoku 522
Kaigyokusai 520
Kakosai 457
Kammer & Reinhardt 512
Kamp 550
Kamp, Willm. Hubt. Van 511
Kandinksy, Wassily 552
Kandler, Chas. F. 593
Kandler, F. 625
Kandler, J. J. 127, 149-153
Kanesada 54
Kangxi 142
Kanjiro Kawai 179
Kannon 471
Kao 522, 523
Katana 54, 55
Kauba, C. 72
Kayersinn 526
Kayophone 510
Kazuyoshi 53
Kazuyuki 471
Kearsar 501
Keene, Michael 540
Keiko Hasegawa 141
Kelly Boy 253
Kelpra Studio 553
Kenworthy, K. R. F. 505
Kennard & Jenks 623

Kensington Glass Works 426
Kenya Beer 16
Kern Switar 91
Kesslier 74
Kestner 252
Kettle Stand 603
Khanjarli 31
Khecheong 628
Kigyoku 518
Kindjal 30
King & Co., Henry S. 534
King, David 592
King George III & Queen
   Caroline 70
King James I 503
King of the Herd 454
King of the Road 485
King's Own Regt. of Norfolk
   Imperial Yeomanry 26, 34
Kinji 456, 457
Kinkozan Zo 143
Kinsburger, S. 75
Kintozan 165
Kinzan 143
Kipling, R. 582
Kirchner, Ernst Ludwig 550,
   551
Kirk, S. 594
Kirkup, J. 609
Kirschenbach, J. J. 339
Kitamura 24
Kitosai Terumitsu 55
Kiyomitsu 54
Kloster Veilsdorf 128-130
Kneehole Desks 331-333
Knibb, Joseph 197
Knox, Archibald 218, 526,
   528, 587, 598, 627
Kodak 93
Kogo 88
Kogyoku 470
Kogyoku (Anrakusai) 519
Kogyoku, Shoryusai 457
Kokei 521
Komai 87
Komin 522
Konig & Wernicke 250
Koppel, Henning 478, 480,
   481
Koraku 470
Koshare 454
Kozan 475
Kris 28, 30
Kromskop 465
Kruse, Kathe 254
Kutani 143
Kyoto 143
Kyoto Namikawa 236
Kyoto School 518, 521, 523
Kyo-Sukashi 59
Kyusekirin 143

L. & Co. 628
L. G. of Le Guay 170
La Verite Meconnue 76
Lacloche Freres 603
Lacquer 482
Lacroix, Ld. 217
Lacy & Co. 39
Lagonda 507, 650
Lahore 464
Lalique 420, 421, 423, 424,
   425, 438-442, 507
Lamerie, Paul De 588, 592,
   593
Lampi 542
Lamps 483-487
Lancaster 47
Lancaster & Sons, J. 91
Lancaster International 92
Lancere, Eugene 78
Lanchester 650
Langlands & Goodrick 605
Langley, T. 373
Lannvier, Chas. H. 364, 413
Laocoon 488
Laporte, Emile Henri 75
Large Tables 384, 385
Laughlin, Jnr., John 568

Laughlin, John 621
Laurencin, Marie 545
Lautier, B. 217
Law, Thos. 580, 620
Lawrence 46
Lawrence & Co. 628
Le Faguays 604
Le Forgeron 71
Le Maire 464
Le Verrier 487
Lea-Francis 652
Leach, Bernard 144
Leach, Janet 144
Leach, John 144
Lead Cutter 57
Learner's Car 640
Lederer, Hugo 75
Leeke, Ralph 592
Legras 483
Lehmann 640, 642
Leib Regt. 36
Leica 92
Lejeune 508
Leleu 484
Leleu, Jules 563
Lemercier 546
Lenci 139, 145, 252
Lenoir 202
Lenoir A Paris 462, 463
Lenzkirch 219
Lepine 227
Leroy 201, 209, 224, 227
Leroy, Desire 155
Les Creations 544
Lesney 647
Letter Rack 603
Levrier 507
Levy, Lucien 126
Leyland-Thomas 508
Lias, I. H. & G. 609
Liberty & Co. 159, 218, 219,
   326, 526, 528, 571, 575,
   587, 627
Lieberich Fabre. C. F. Woerffel
   79
Liege, B. 546
Lievres 441
Lifeguards & Officer 641
Light Company 24, 25
Lily Maid, The 119
Limbach 67
Lincoln & Lindsey Banking Co.
   524
Lindenstaedt, Hans 544
Linderman, Clara C. 164
Linen Press 412, 413
Linnell, J. 290, 347
Linsey-Woolsey 554
Linthorpe 103, 104
Lip Sofa 348
Littlefield, Jane 564
Livemont, Privat 547
Liverpool 145
Lloyd George 18
Lloyd, Snr., J. 568
Lock, Nathaniel 581
Locker, J. 568
Lockey Hill 514
Lodestone 464
Loetz 438, 440
Logan, G. 100
Lohands 474
Lomax, J. 210
London Aerodrome 20
London Sporting Park Ltd. 49
London Stereoscopic Co. 90, 92
London, Two Gentlemen 533
Long Hair Dancer 453
Longcase Clocks 204-211
Longton Hall 146
Lorenzl 76, 81, 604
Loring, J. 208
Losanti 95
Lott, John 517
Louvet, Hubert 573
Lowboys 334
Lowe, Thos. 504
Lowestoft 104, 146
Lowne's, Joseph 616

Lucas 485
Lucy Anne 120
Lukin, Wm. 598
Lund & Blockley 202
Lustre 146
Lynn 444, 447
Lynx 651
Lyon, D. 531

MacDonald, Barbara 77
McLaughlin, L. 95
McInnes, Dobbie 465
McKay, John 578
M.G. 648-650, 653
Ma-Pe-Wi 453
Macallan Swan, J. 77
Maggiolini 315
Magic Disc 644
Magnette 648
Magnum Ruger Super Black-
   hawk 40
Mahon, C. P. 524
Maine Flying Scoter 249
Maltese Cross 481
Mameluke 52, 53, 56, 57
Man Ray 535
Manchester Guardian 647
Manners, James 613
Mantegna, Andrea 552
Mantel Clocks 212-219
Manticha, P. 65
Manton, Joseph 49
Mappin & Webb 580, 600
Marble 488, 489
Marblehead 94, 95
Marc, Franz 550
Marconiphone 467
Marfurt 544
Margaine, F. A. 199
Margas, Jacob 614
Marguerit, Nicolas 451
Marinot 436
Markham, J. 225
Marklin 502
Markwick 208
Marples, Robt. 240
Marquand, F. 594, 620
Marseille, Armand 63, 253-255
Marsh & Tatham 264
Marshall & Sons 583
Marshall Craig, Wm. 540
Marshall, Mrs. J. Walter 554
Marshall, Wm. 181, 594
Marti & Cie 202, 203
Martin 461
Martineau 224
Martinet, Milo 546
Martinware 147, 148
Marx, Louis 642
Marville, Chas. 532
Mary, Santa Marta 531
Masakazu 519
Masamitsu 475
Masanao 520
Masatami (Shomin) 519, 521
Masatamo 520
Masatsugu 519
Masayuki 336
Maserati 653
Masileau & Co. 23
Masonic 300, 341, 426, 450
Mason's China 148
Master Mariner 233
Mathew, Wm. 595
Matisse, Henri 552
Matthsson, Bruno 346
Mauser 'Broom Handle' 41
Maws 146
Mayer, T. J. & J. 17, 18
Maythorn 648
Mazarin 333
Meat Press 603
Meccano 642
Medcat 71
Mees 222
Meiko, Emperor 474
Meir & Son, J. 101
Meissen 149-153
Mellier & Co., C. 536

Melling, Jno. 208
Mendicant, The 119
Mene, P. J. 70
Mentor 90
Merganser 249
Merkelbach, Reinhold 129
Methuen, George 624
Mettayer, Lewis 590
Meyer 150
Meyer, F. E. 98, 151
Mickey Mouse Organ Grinder
    640
Microscope 458, 459, 460, 462,
    466, 467
Mignon & Diana 82
Milegal Meter 507
Mills, N. 611, 628
Miller, B. 503
Miller, Junr., & Co., H. 21
Milne & Campbell 581
Minaudiere 603
Minerva 508
Ming 154, 155
Miniature Furniture 496, 497
Minko 523
Minnie 505
Mino Kanetsune 52
Minton 155-158
Miochi 59
Mirrors 490-495
Miscellaneous Antiques 496-499
Miscellaneous Glass 431
Miscellaneous Silver 602, 603
Mitchells & Butlers' Ales 19
Mito Kinko 61
Miyao 72
Mode 171
Model Ships 500, 501
Model Trains 502, 503
Models 504, 505
Models, M. H. C. 503
Models, Silver 604, 605
Mohandas Gandhi 533
Moigniez, J. 77
Mole 57
Momoyama 89, 482
Monarch 384, 510, 512, 513
Mondain 450, 451
Money Box 643
Monroe, Marilyn 535
Montgolfier 21
Moore, Bernard 146
Moore, Chas. 588
Moorcroft 159
Moorcroft Macintyre 159
Morane Saulnier 22
Moreau, Louis 486
Morel & Hughes 293
Morel & Seddon 286
Morey & Ober 527
Morgan & Saunders 300, 302
Morgan, Willm. 198
Morning Glory 510, 513
Morris 649, 653
Morris Service 16
Morrisware 103
Mortlock 132
Moser, Koloman 441
Mosserine 484
Moth Minor 22
Mother 509
Motley, Jn. 206
Motor Sport 509
Motoring Items 506-509
Mott & Co., J. L. 653
Mourgue, Olivier 347
Movado 230
Mozchaeva, R. 545
Mucha, Alphonse 546, 547
Mugs, Silver 605
Muirhead, James 459
Muller 439
Muller, B. 605
Murdoch of Doune 43
Murray, Keith 188, 189
Muret, Albert 547
Muroe 72
Musical Boxes & Polyphones
    510-513

Musical Instruments 514-517
Musket 49, 50
Musketoon 48, 51
Mustards, Silver 606
Mycock, Wm. S. 162
Myochin Munenaga 32

Nagamitsu 473
Nailsea 426, 430, 431
Nakamura Haruhiro 55
Nantgarw 160
Nashiji 457
Nasson, Aldo 438
Nast 161
National Bank 525
Navajo 453, 454, 455
Nazi 24, 29, 31-37, 56
Neale, W. 603
Neapolitan School 517
Neffe, Meyr's 441
Nepveu, Le 217
Netsuke 518-523
Neu, Wenzel 128, 129
New Bedford 484
New Century Cycle 642
New Land 49
Newbold, Thos. 628
Newbury, Bessie 180
Newman Cartwright 209
Newmarket Bank 525
Newton & Co. 463
Newton, John 224
Newton, Sir William John 539
Nicholson, Wm. 573
Nicole Freres 512, 513
Nicquet 167, 168
Nielsen, H. 574, 578, 599, 603
Nielson, Harald 596
Nihon Yozan 143
Nikkormat 90
Nikkosai 457
Nikolsky 508
Nilson 130
Nina 643
Nipper 496
Njers, Ljerka 121, 180
Nobuyuki 522
Nock, H. 47
Nocturne 71
Noke 486
Noke, Chas. J. 120
Noon Cannon 463
Norfolk Champion Boots 17
Norge 21
Norman 104
Northam, John 448
Northern Bank 524
Northern British Locomotive
    Co. Ltd. 531
Norton 650
Norton, Eardley 197
Noshu Seki 55
Notron, Yeldrae 197
Notsjo, Nuutajarvi 441
Nottinghamshire Volunteers 47
N.P. 50, 51
Nude Girl With Shawl 604
Nutmegs 607
Nutting, Wallace 299
NYC 1949 533

O-Wakizashi 54
Oakley, G. 375
Oates, Captain L. E. G. 36
Oboshi-Hoshibachi 32
Obrisset 610
Occasional Tables 386-391
Occhi 443
Ochsenkopf 418
Odartchenko 167
Odundo, Magdalene A. N. 121
Ofner, J. 69
Ohr, G. E. 95
Okatomo 519, 523
Okatoto 518
Old Balloon Seller, The 119
Oliver, Isaac 543
Oliver, John 613

Ondines 424
Onin 60
Ono Ryomin 521
Ontoflex 90
Orchies 123
Ordnance Survey of Jerusalem
    530
Oriental China 160
Orlandini, A. 516
Orrery 215, 461
Ortelli & Co., N. 67
Orton Bradshaw, Stanley 23
Ota Tameshiro 234
Oudry 168
Ouville, Charles A. C. d' 538
Ovaltine 16
Owari 60
Owen, George 194, 195
Owl Kachina 454
Ozier 184

Pace, Thomas 198
Pacific 502
Packard 649
Paisey, Julia Matild 564
Pajou, A. 167, 170
Palais Du Louvre 533
Palais Du Tuilleries 533
Palais Royale 84-86, 88
Palethorp, Robt. 529
Palethorpes 19
Paliand A Besancon 198
Palmer 64
Palmer & Co. 484
Panhard Levassor 641
Pankok, Bernhard 242
Pannier 502, 503
Pansy 503
Pantin, Simon 585
Paper Money 524, 525
Paperweight Inkwell 431
Paperweights 432-435
Parallel Rule 467
Parang 29
Parian 160
Paris 161
Park Ward 648
Parker Field & Sons 56
Parker, J. 591, 618
Partizan 62
Passenger, Chas. 118
Pastorelli 64
Patent Steam Carpet Beating
    Co. 16
Patrick, J. 66, 67
Pattison 48
Pauly 51
Payne, John 612
Payne, W. 155
Peaslee, Judith N. 248
Pedometer 459
Peekhaus, E. & H. 56
Pemberton, Samuel 628
Pembroke Tables 392, 393
Penn-Sayers, P. 505
Pennell 43
Pepys 264
Peridiez, G. 379
Perkins, Bacon & Petch 524
Perl, Karl 82
Pero, Isabel 618
Perruches 442
Perry, A. 114
Perry Son & Co. 580
Persil 19
Peruvian Women 532
Pesh-Kabz 30
Pet, Joh 462
Peterson, Abraham 566
Peterson, Peter 590
Petitot, L. 218
Peviri 657
Pewter 526-529
Peynot, E. 82
Pezzato 442
Pfranger Snr. 129
Philippe & Co., P. 224, 227,
    229, 233
Philippe, R. 104

Phipps, T. 607, 611, 618
Photographs 530-535
Photographs from Abyssinia
    535
Pianos 536, 537
Picard, M. 546
Picasso, Pablo 552
Pick Plate Note 524
Pickelhaube 35-37
Pier Table 396, 397
Pierre Le Doux, Jean 169
Piguet, Audemars 233
Pike & Son 67
Pilgrim Century 298
Pilkington 162
Pillar Dial 466
Pilleau, Peze 618
Piranesi, G. B. 70
Pistols 38-43
Pith Helmet 32
Pitts, Wm. 566, 579, 590
Planche, Andrew 118
Player's Please 17, 18
Pleydell-Bouverie, Katharine 181
Plimer, Andrew 541, 543
Pliny's Doves 498
Plummer, John F. 20
Pobjoy Cataract 22
Pogliani 275
Poivre 441
Polarkova, K. 545
Polito 174
Pollock, John 609
Polyphones & Musical Boxes
    510-513
Poncelet, Jacqueline 179
Pontifax, D. 623
Pool Table 384
Pope, Francis C. 120
Popeye 646
Porringers 607
Porsche 652
Portal, Abraham 609
Portet, Jean 539
Portland 424
Portrait Miniatures 538-543
Poschinger, Ferdinand 443
Posters 544-547
Potez 22
Potschappel 129
Pouss-Nouk-Nouk 505
Powder Flasks 44, 45
Power, Tho. 209
Praha, M. 545
Pratt & Whitney 22
Prattware 162
Preedy, J. 566, 590
Preedy, Joseph 579
Preiss, F. 81, 215, 475
Priest, John 575, 576
Priest, Wm. 587
Priestess 82
Primitive Brant 451
Prince Albert 534
Prince of Wales's Own Royal
    Wiltshire Yeomanry 26
Princess Alice 530
Princess Royal & Prince Arthur
    as Summer 532
Prints 548-553
Prof. Highschool Daguerreo-
    type Institution 535
Protractor 462, 465
Provender for the Monastery
    128
Provincial Bank 524
Prussian Artillery 36, 37
Prussian Infantry 35, 37
Prussian Line Cuirassier Regt.
    34, 36
Prussian Regt. of Garde Du
    Corps 25, 32, 33
Punch Magazine 21
Puritan Soap 18
Puttnam, James H. 528
Pyramid 596

Quare, Daniel 207

Queen's Lancers 25
Questura, R. 546
Quilts 554, 555

Radford 225
Raingo Fres. 216, 217
Rakan 475
Raleigh 16
Ramage, John 539
Ramsden, A. 536
Ramsden & Carr 581, 598
Ramsden, Omar 569-571, 576,
    588, 589, 599, 601, 602
Ramsey, Robt. 196
Ratseys & Lapthorn 498
Rattle for Germination 453
Ravenet 256, 259
Rawlings, Chas. 150
Ray, Man 535
Reckitt's Blue 17
Red Ashay 509
Red Gem 511
Redding's Luzo 91, 92
Redier A Paris 464
Redoubtable 500
Redware 162
Reed, Olga G. 164
Refrigerator 499
Rehwald, J. D. 567
Reily, James 542
Reinhalda, Agge Jelles 567
Reinicke, P. 153
Rejlander, O. G. 532
Revenue, Police 56
Rey, Margaret 180
Rhodes, David 187
Rich, Mary 104
Rich, Obadiah 622
Richard 438
Richards, T. 38
Richardson, Arthur 514
Richthofen, Manfred Von 20
Rie, Lucy 163
Riemerschmid, R. 129
Riessner, Stretmacher & Kessel
    122
Rifles 46-51
Rikouku Nokami Fujiwara
    Kanenobu 55
Riley 650
Risler & Carre 583
Ritter, Jeremias 591
Riviere, G. 123
Riviere, M. Giraud 73
Robart 428
Robert, L. V. E. 77
Roberte, Jane 175
Roberts 290
Roberts & Co., John 576
Roberts, Cadman & Co. 579
Robin Starch 19
Robins, Thos. 580, 624, 625
Robinson I, Thomas 584
Robinson & Leadbetter 160
Robinson, E. 607, 611, 618
Robinson, John 622
Rocca, Joseph 514, 515
Rochard 73
Rochard, Simon J. 540
Roche, Sampson T. 541
Rockstuhl, Alois G. 542
Rodgers, Joseph 29
Roe, N. 21
Roger et Gallet 436
Rohde, J. 568, 577
Rohde, Johan 595, 597
Rohlfs 658
Rolleiflex 91
Rolex 230, 233
Rolls Royce 648, 651-653
Rolls Tourer 640
Rookwood 164
Rose, John 114
Rosenthal 129, 130
Roseville Pottery 118
Ross 92
Rossay, J. A. 226
Rossetti 139
Roswell Gleason 527, 528

Rotali, Frateli 290
Rothenbush, F. D. H. 164
Rouff 247
Roux, Alex. 405
Rowland's Aqua D'Oro 19
Rowland's Macassar Oil 17
Rowntree 16, 18
Roy, Charles Le 221
Royal Army Medical Corps 27
Royal Artillery 34, 56
Royal Dockyard Bn. 36
Royal Dux 164
Royal East India Vol. 25
Royal Horse Guards (The Blues)
    35, 37
Royal Irish Dragoon Guards 35
Royal Lancashire Militia 34
Royal Mail Stereolette 92
Royal Military Academy 34
Royal Polytechnic 65
Royal Scots 24
Rozane Ware 118
Rozenburg 122
Rubberoid Roofing 18
Rubicon Twist 19
Rugg, Richard 622
Rugs 556-563
Rushton, J. 191
Ruskin 165
Russell, G. 118
Ryozan 141
Ryukai 470
Ryuko 523
Ryukosai 522

S.F.B.J. 253, 255
Sabattini, Lino 602
Sado 58
Safavid 160
Sage, John Le 603
Saint-Omer 574, 587
Saint Vincent 420
Sakes, Paulus 567
Salazar, Fiona 100
Salem's(?), Phebeann H. 555
Salmone, M. 65
Salmson 648, 652
Salome & Herodias 82
Salts, Silver 608
Samplers 564, 565
Samson 126, 127
San Ildefonso 455
Sandoz 127
Sandwich 485
Sandwich Clambroth 422
Sang, Jacob 427, 428, 429, 445
Sang, Simon J. 428
Sancai 182, 183
Santa Ana 94
Santa Clare 94
Santa Clause 119
Sare, A. 505
Sari 519
Sashu No Ju Toshioki 58
Satsuma 165, 166
Saturday Evening Girls 94
Sauceboats 609
Saviouress 78
Savoye Freres & Cie 228
Savy 127
Sawyer, R. 622
Scent Bottles 436, 437
Scepter 502
Schieland 446
Schleiertanz 582
Schliepstein 129, 130
Schmidt, Franz 253
Schneider 91
School of Daubigny 542
School of Koloman Moser 122
Schott, N. 349
Schubert, Carl G. 130
Schwarzlot 165
Scofield, John 574, 575, 577,
    586
Scott, Digby 573
Scowen 531
Screens 335-337
Sea Coast 66

Secretaire Bookcases 340-343
Secretaires 338, 339
Sector 466
Seguso 441
Seidel 153
Seignior, R. 207
Seiso 473
Seiya 74
Selchow, J. H. C. v. 130
Sellers, J. Henry 301
Semah, M. 463
Senefelder 544
Senzan 143
Serrurier-Bovy 287
Servia 504
Settees & Couches 344-349
Settles 344-346, 348
Severini, Gino 553
Sevres 167-170
Sewill 221
Sewing Machine 461, 466
Sextant 461
Seymour, Thos. 402
Shades 437
Shakespeare's Cottage 132
Shako 34, 36
Shand-Mason 504
Sharp 46
Sharp, R. 624
Shaw II, Wm. 587
Shaw, J. 628
Shaw, Thos. 628
Shelley 171
Shelley, Samuel 539
Shelton, Peter 454
Shepherd, G. 533
Sherratt, Obadiah 174, 178
Shibayama 521
Shichifukujin 473
Shields, Micha 209
Shigemasa 518
Shije Velino 453
Shinko 336
Shinmei 471
Shinsai 471
Shirreff, Charles 539
Shizan 336
Shoji 141
Short Solent 23
Shosai 73, 471
Shourd's, Samuel 205
Showato 55
Shreve, Brown & Co. 594
Shrewsbury Service 102
Shufflebottoms, Elizabeth 564
Shuji 522
Shunjuken Tadaomi 471
Shunpu 474
Shunyosai Nobuyuki 471
Sibley, R. 567, 622
Side Tables 394-397
Sideboards 350-353
Siebe, Gorman & Co. 241
Sika, Jutta 122
Silex 287
Silhouette 499
Silver 566-629
Silver Ghost 648
Simon & Halbig 63
Simmons 48
Simmons, Wm. 589
Simpoles 266
Sinclair, John 19
Singer Sewing Machines 16
Siotteling, J. 578
Sioux Maiden 455
Sirene 424
Sirletti, Giacomo 611
Skates 245
Skean Dhu 30
Skeen & Co., W. L. H. 531
Skeleton Clocks 220
Skinner's Horse 53
Slater, Eric 171
Sleath, Gabriel 620
Slessor, Hannah L. 564
Slessor, Jane 565
Slessor, Phebe L. 565
Sloane, Hans 108

Slodtz 77
Sluiter, Willy 544
Smiley, Thos. 615
Smily, W. & R. 620
Smith II, B. 591, 625
Smith & Beck 467
Smith, Benjamin 573, 590, 603
Smith, D. 624
Smith, S. 573
Smith, Stephen 604
Smith, Steven 331
Snake Tree 113
Snowdon, R. 399
Snuff Bottles 630, 631
Snuff Boxes 448-450, 610, 611
Sofa Tables 398, 399
Sohlingen, J. J. R. 52
Soiron 259
Somalvico & Son, J. 67
Song 172
Sonnar 91
Sonor 547
Soten 61
Sousy Ricketts, Charles De 82
South Australia Militia Lancers
   27
Southwell, Wm. 537
Spavento, Capitano 128
Speedometer Co. Ltd., A. T.
   508
Speilman, H. 659
Spencer, Gervase 538, 540
Sper, Adolf 626
Spilsbury, Francis 605
Spirit Flask 602
Spirit of Triumph, The 506
Spitfire 23
Spode 173
Spoon Warmer 602
Spratt's 19, 641
Sprimont, Nicholas 592
Spring Morning, Busbridge 534
Springbok 503
St. Andrew 30
St. George 120
St. Louis 432, 434
St. Michael 76
Staffordshire China 174-178
Stands 354-358
Stanley 92, 458
Starr Arms Co. 40
Stauffer 229
Steel 158
Steiff 641-645
Steiner 250, 251, 253
Steinheil 458
Steinway, T. H. 537
Steinway & Sons 536
Stella 513
Stephen, Pierre 546
Stephens Inks 19
Stephens, Wm. 211
Steps 354, 355
Stereographoscope 460
Stereoscope 458, 460
Steuben 420
Stevengraph 20
Stevens, Samuel 204
Stevens, T. 20
Stewart, J. 593
Stewart, Jr., Joseph 413
Stickley, Gustav 210, 272, 277,
   295, 325, 377, 396, 485, 657
Stickley, L. & J. G. 348
Stieglitz, Alfred 531
Stinton 191, 192
Stirling Single 503
Stirn's Waistcoat Detective
   Camera 91
Stoak, Gab 458
Stone 632, 633
Stoneware 179-181
Stools 359-361
Storr, Paul 451, 572, 591, 592,
   608, 624, 629
Stourbridge 443
Strachan, A. J. 451
Straeton, Van Der 68
Stralsund 129

Strasbourg 123, 126
Stratford, W. 312
Street, R. 205
Streeter, E. W. 213
Stroud, William 580, 592
Stroudley 503
Stubborn Donkey 644
Stubbs, J. 177
Sturm, F. 98
Sublime Harmony 513
Sucher 91
Sue et Mare 275
Suffolk Dredging Tractor 504
Suites 362, 363
Sundial 461
Sunshade Girl 81
Suzuribako 88
Swan Ink 18
Swedish Livregementel 33
Sweetser Co., The 627
Swords 52-57
Sykes 44, 45
Sylvester 226
Symphonion 210, 211, 512, 513
Syng, R. 569
Systeme Campiche de Metz 222

Tabako-Bon 89
Table A Ecrire 387
Table Bureau 89
Tables 364-408
Tachi 54, 55
Tadamitsu 54
Tadaomi 473
Tahoma, Quincy 454
Takarabune 473
Tamahide 474
Tamayuki 470
Tamba School 520
Tamenuri 456
Tang 182, 183
Tangermann, Christian 542
Tankards 612, 613
Tantallon Castle 114
Tanto 52, 54, 55
Tapestries 634-636
Tapio Wirkkala 181
Tassie 498
Taylor & Perry 628
Taylor, E. A. 327
Taylor, H. A. 505
Taylor, Henry 534
Taylor, John 197, 205
Taylor, Samuel 618
Tazzas 614
Tea & Coffee Sets 615-617
Tea Caddies 618
Tea Kettles 619
Tea Tables 364-367
Teapots, Silver 620
Tecno 'P45' 288
Tegelsten, C. J. 629
Telescope 458, 463, 467
Televisor 461
Temple of Vesta 497
Temple, Shirley 255
Terracotta 184
Terrey, John, Edward 615
Tessar 90, 91
Tetes-De-Boule 85
Textiles 637-639
Thibault, Aimee 540
Thomas, F. B. 568
Thomas, Parry 508
Thorn, C. E. 504
Thornhill & Co, W. 200
Thornton-Pickard 92
Thoughts 73
Three Dahlias 421
Thuillier 213
Thunder House 464
Tiffany 437, 451, 483, 487,
   617, 627
Tiffany & Co. 225, 227, 579
Tiger Moth 22
Timbrell, R. 623
Timbrell, Robt 586
Timeche, Bruce 453
Tinworth, G. 120

Tipp & Co. 646
Tohekido 473
Toilette Pastorale, La 257
Tolly, Jean 198
Tom 68
Tomoyuki 522
Tompion, Thos. 217
Tongue, John 628
Tonnel 450
Tools 240
Toshimasa 472
Touchon & Co. 224
Toullet & Co. 224
Toullet Decamps 254
Tourni 184
Tower, James 181
Toyomasa 520
Toys 640-647
Traffic Warner 458, 459
Transport 648-653
Tranter 41, 42
Trask, Israel 529
Trays & Salvers 621-623
Triang Minic 640, 641
Trick Pony 645
Trigg 65
Trivulzio, Count 185
Tropical Goertz Tenax 90
Tropical Model Improved
    Artist 90
Troughton & Simms 459
Trunks & Coffers 409-411
Tsu School 521
Tsubas 58-61
Tsuguji Foujita 553
Tsunemitsu 68
Tuck, Raphael 546, 547
Tudric 218, 219, 527, 528
Tumblers, Glass 437
Tureens,'Silver 624, 625
Turn Teplitz, R. St. K. 123
Tut Tut 640
Tutt Hannah 95
Typewriter 460, 466

U.S. Army 24
Ullmann, Th. 79
Ulster Bank 524
Underhill, H. A. 501
Union 114
Union Castle Line 18
Unite, George 568
United Kingdom Tea
    Company 17
Universal Dial 460, 464, 465,
    466
Urns, Silver 626
Utamaro Hitsu 514

V. P. 91
Vacheron & Constantin 230
Vajradhara 72
Van Cleef & Arpels 479
Vase-Kraft 484
Vases, Glass 438-443
Vases, Silver 627
Vaso 441
Velazquez 542
Velde, Henry Van De 595
Velox 651
Venini 438, 442, 443
Ver Center 441
Vercassou 544
Verde Di Prato 488
Verga 230
Verneau, CH. 547
Verre Francais, Le 437
Vestal 604
Veyrant 602
Vichy, G. 63
Videau, Ayme 619
Viel-O-Phone 511
Vienna 185
Vile, Wm. 656
Villanis, E. 82
Vinaigrettes, Silver 628
Vincent, Edward 569
Vincent, Rene 545
Virginia 502

Voille, Jean Marie 541
Volkstedt 128
Vuillaume, Jean-Baptiste
    514, 515, 517
Vulliamy 227
Vyse, Charles 185

Waals, 275, 370
Wackerle, Prof. J. 128
Waffen S.S. 35
Wagner 98
Wain, Louis 103
Wakelin, E. 575, 579, 609,
    618
Wakelin, Edward 566, 591
Wakelin, J. 626
Wakizashi 53
Walker & Hall 571, 591, 621
Walker, Joseph 613
Wall Clocks 221-223
Walley 94
Wallis, R. 50
Wallpaper 496, 499
Walmore 467
Walrath 94
Ward, Benj. 197
Ward Bros., L. T. 249
Ward, John 179
Ward, Richd. 196
Wardrobes & Armoires 412, 413
Warren 223
Warrior 453
Wartenberg, S. 203
Washstands 414
Wasp 22
Watches 224-229
Watchmakers Lathe 465
Waterloo Tree 450
Watkins, J. 64
Watson Type 642
Watt, Wm. 275
Watts Gun, The 49
Watts, Jas 214
Watson, J. 463
Watson, John 573, 593
Way, Charlotte 565
Weapons 62
Weathervanes 654,655
Webster 198, 218, 224
Wedgwood 186-189
Wedgwood & Bentley 186,
    188, 189
Weeks 71
Weeks, Fredricks 530, 531
Weekes, James 526
Weeks Museum 216
Weigall, H. 71
Weisweiler 354, 358
Weller Dickensware 95
Wellington 70, 71, 75
Wendel, S. 578
Wenford Bridge 106, 107
Werkstatte Wiener 442
Wesson's & Leavitt's 43
West, F. 502
West Norfolk Regt. 24
Westerwald 100, 180
Westward Ho Smoking
    Mixture 16
Weston of Brighton 43
Weyersberg, Paul 30, 56
Whatnots 415
Wheeler 538
Whieldon 187, 189, 190
Whipman & Wright 587
Whipman, Thos 590
White Glass Works 426
Whitefriars 431
Whitelaw, David 225
Whiting MFG., Co. 593
Whiting, Riley 218
Wilkes John 118
Wilkie, I. H. 500
Wilkinson, Bradbury 525
Wilkinson, Henry 580, 615
Wilkinson Sword 28
Will, Henry 527
Willard, Aaron 206, 207, 221
    221

Willard, Alex. J. 205
William Dean, The 502
Williams 46
Williams, T. R. 530
Williamson, Samuel 620
Willings & Co. 18
Willis Good, J. 604
Willmore, J. 450
Willmore, Joseph 611
Wills's Star Cigarettes 17
Wills, W. D. & H. O. 16, 17
Wilson, Capt, Charles W. 530
Wilson, 'Gus' Aaron 249
Wilson, Margaret 226
Willson, T. 405
Wiltberger, C. 586
Winchester 46
Winchcombe Pottery 106
Windmills 208
Wine Coolers, Silver 629
Wine Coolers 416, 417
Wine Glasses 444-447
Wine Label 602, 603
Winter, James 344
Winters, Christian 204
Wisker 67
Wittelsbach 167
Wittingham, R. 239
Wolfers Freres 479
Wolff, David 428, 444
Worcester 191-195
Workboxes & Games Tables
    400-403
Worth 437
Wood 656-662
Wood, David 212
Wood, Enoch 190
Wood, H. J. 103
Wood, Ralph 190
Wood, Samuel 578
Woodhead, G. 29
Wricklemarsh 610
Wright 21
Wright, Chas. 590
Wristwatches 230-233
Writing Tables & Desks
    404-408
Wucai 155
Wye   Level 462
Wyland, N. 210
Wylie & Lochhead 327
Wyon, E. W. 103

Xenar 90
Xpres 92

Yamada School 519, 521
Yamahiko 519
Yamashiro 55
Yapp & Woodward 610
Yasuyoshi 603
Yavapai 453
Yazan 518
Yokhi 474
Yorke, Edward 585
Young, Grace 164
Young, J. 592
Young, S. C. 608
Yoshitada(?) 520
Yoshitomo 518
Ysart, Paul 432, 433
Yukimune 55
Yuma 455
Yun, Wenming 239
Yvelines 442

Zappler 222
Zeiss 91
Zeiss, Carl 484
Zeshin 89
Zettel, J. 164
Zia 455
Zimmerman, A. & J. 598
Zinke, Christian F. 538, 541,
    542
Zeotrope 461
Zoffany, Johann 261
Zuccani 65
Zwichl, F. 582